THE FIGHT FOR
IMMORTALITY

A Science Fiction Novel

Peter Arthur

Copyright © 2014 by Peter Arthur

Cover design and illustration by:
Brad Fraunfelter
www.bradfraunfelterillustration.com

The text of this book was set in 11-point Adobe Garamond Pro by:
Rigney Graphics, Pasadena, Calif.
www.rigneygraphics.com

ISBN-13: 978-1-482645-35-4
ISBN-10: 1-482645-35-1

This book is dedicated to those who enjoy it. Thank you.

There are many who hold the firm belief
That man lives just once and, oh, so brief
In too short a span to make his mark
Before the body, aged, falls into dark.

With hopes and dreams left unachieved
When motionless form is now bereaved.
And like so-much-useless-refuse tossed,
All hard-earned knowledge gained – now lost.

But there is another school of thought
Oft suppressed and seldom taught
That when body's breath and heartbeat ends
The life within goes on – transcends.

Rachael Adams

PRAISE FOR
FIGHT FOR IMMORTALITY

"I thoroughly recommend this science fiction masterpiece and look forward to reading the next book in the series." – W.

"To say I loved this book is the understatement of the year. I have read it three times.

"Peter Arthur gives us the wisdom and ethics of the ages in this well-paced page turner. I am a SciFi nut and I have read none better." – G.J.

"I loved *The Fight for Immortality* as much as I loved *Hitchhiker's Guide to the Galaxy.*" – S.

"*The Fight for Immortality* is a great book. It's engaging from the very beginning and the interesting twists and turns in the story will keep you glued to the book." – A.C.

"I was really impressed with this book. I was hooked by the great story very quickly. I enjoyed every minute of reading it and am hoping for a sequel soon." – J.P.

"The characters are wonderful. You really get to know them. This is something I value in a good book. It is very original in the concept of immortality, a refreshing look at what could be." – J.W.

"Could not put the book down. Great story line. Not just for sci-fi lovers but for anyone… So happy I got this book, I would most definitely recommend it!" – E.B.

"This was a great book. I usually do not read space stories but a friend told me this one I would love... and I did." – R.D.

"I was locked into the story right at the start and couldn't put it down. I must say I deprived myself of sleep due to this. If you're looking for a great read, I would highly recommend this story." – K.

"This was an exciting book! The lead character is so appealing – I spent many a late night reading as I had to find out what happened next and what amazing thing he would do next. He inspired me." – C.

"I say! This book is a real page-turner deluxe and this comes from a reader who is not easily impressed!" – M.M.

"This book was fantastic. The story is brilliant, very unique, and intriguing. I couldn't put it down. The characters were engaging, and the story well written; however, the story itself is what gripped me. It also had some great comic relief. I can't wait for the next book." – C.V.

"With every passing moment as I read this book I felt myself getting more and more immersed into the fantastic story that they tell." – E.B.

"I've read a lot of Sci-Fi, all the greats. This story is full of danger and mystery, but emphasizes personal responsibility in a way no other comes close to." – W.E.N.

"*The Fight for Immortality* is one of those rarities: great science fiction, that fits together well in a gripping tale! I found it hard to put down…. It has my highest recommendation. I am waiting impatiently for a sequel!" – G.S.

"A thought-provoking, driving storyline with lots of action. It had me from the first few pages and kept me engaged throughout. A very satisfying read." – B.R.

"What makes this book so great is the story winds itself into many fantastic situations but never goes too far to make it unrealistic. This is science fiction at its best." – H.K.

"I loved this book! I found myself pleasantly surprised when I started this book. The story was original and gripping. I also really enjoyed the relationships between the characters." – P.A.

PROLOGUE

Escape!

The instinct shot through him as though it were the primordial urge of life itself.

Enemy spacecraft were again closing in; he had to get away soon or it would end right here.

His 3D locator display showed the two closest ships surging forward on an attack run. Minutes seemed like seconds as they swiftly approached effective weapons range.

"Acquire target... fire!" Despite the pilot's barked command, his ship's computer failed to lock on.

Another system failure.

He grasped the weapons controller and blazed at the attackers with his guns, then rapidly maneuvered to avoid the debris field as the ships disintegrated in a spectacular display.

His ship, though ravaged, remained superior in these close encounters.

With the last two attackers gone, he finally reached the outer edge of the encircling net. Their formation began to collapse as he broke away. The horde of rag-tag pirate vessels fell in behind and raced to prevent his escape.

More enemy ships streaked toward him.

Approaching weapons range his locator display lost perspective and dissolved: his targets disappeared from sight.

He looked at the flat exterior-visio screens and got a fix on the approaching spacecraft.

In the fraction of time remaining, he failed to properly target the attacking ships – his M-Star class interstellar spy vessel shuddered as she took another direct hit.

The shielding held.

Intense pain shot through him. It was a good sign, any quantity of pain short of death was a pleasure.

I'm still in the game, he thought.

He fired his guns. Half way through his second burst they quit. More damage. But the enemy was out of commission and falling away.

What he had battled for all day was now directly ahead: freedom lane.

With his main weapons offline his only options were shielding or speed – he chose speed.

Pushing pain and exhaustion aside he executed a series of repairs; power surged through rerouted circuitry and his M-Star accelerated sharply away from the killer pack.

With unobstructed stars before him he hit a pre-set destination on his interstellar drive, but it would not kick-in till he reached a certain speed.

His burden was not the threat of personal extinction, but what would happen to others if he died in this desolate sector of space.

He must complete this mission.

If not, the civilized portions of the galaxy would plunge into turmoil.

I must alert Crown authority.

Without warning, he was pounded violently as a particle beam penetrated his defenses, vaporized protective coatings and chewed into who-knows-what vital equipment.

His acceleration should have taken him far out of weapons range.

Something was very wrong.

There was no space ship in the enemy's arsenal with the speed to catch him.

Obviously this was wrong.

The enemy must possess restricted technology. They had a ship with the speed of his M-Star.

Staggering.

Seconds remained before his foe's energy weapons recharged and launched the final attack.

External screens flashed and faded as the latest damage paralyzed more electronics. His ship was mute and going blind but raced onward.

With a jolt her interstellar drive engaged and she exited the universe.

He entered Other Space.

Away!

For the duration he and his ship were untouchable.

The enemy base left behind was a remote planet with many moons, thrown out on the galactic edge; Frascette Galactic Arm, Tail Section, Intergalactic Rim, Planet Seven of Star System 11917. No intelligent life. A no-name system in an unoccupied, poorly surveyed sector.

Perfect camouflage.

With both hands free he raced to make repairs.

A small plaque on a manual control console read: "To Tac-U-One, terror of the deep, oppressor of the wicked. Please accept this ship with our compliments and may our efforts contribute to your success. And please, please, please, bring it back in one piece!" The pilot laughed. Those guys loved their toys – so did he.

Seeing his name, "Tac-U-One" (or Crown's Tactical Unit One), he felt the importance of his mission. He was Crown's chief problem-solver.

I am Tac-U-One.

He scanned his ship systematically.

On the M-Stars brutalized exterior the weapons array looked like twisted skeletal claws.

Despite his repairs, many of the auto-systems were still off-line. Sparks shot out and smoke seeped from between gaps in adjoining consoles. He waited for the fire retardant to deploy, then laughed; he grabbed the chemical cylinder.

"I need you, girl," he coaxed his ship. "We don't want to be stuck out here, do we?"

A lengthy crackle was the only response to his plea. He felt warmed; the garbled static was an attempt by his ship to communicate. Like him, she was giving her all.

Black smoke billowed forward, slowly filling the cockpit. The air scrubbers were quickly overwhelmed; he inserted new filters, but knew they would soon be saturated. His M-Star would never again boost herself to interstellar speed, nor, he knew, could she maintain it for long.

If the enemy base was left unchecked to fulfill its purpose, it could undermine the entire interstellar culture.

With his escape a fact, his report to Crown authority would soon be made. Within days battle cruisers would surround that world and the crisis averted.

He smiled.

Tac-U-One returned focus to his ship and with speed continued repairs, battling against the advancing disintegration. Despite his efforts, the atmosphere in the cockpit continued to thicken. The din of buzzers and hazy flash of warning lights escalated. Soon there was an evil chorus with each demanding his immediate attention until an overwhelming number of the M-Star's hastily completed repairs sputtered, flared briefly to life, and failed.

He pressed on, holding it together.

A deafening klaxon shrieked a second's warning before the Interstellar Drive failed. A blast of pure terror filled him before the M-Star dumped him with crushing violence back into Normal Space.

Interstellar drive failure.

Oh no, not this, no....

He felt the universe simultaneously expand and contract within him. This wasn't a physical sensation, but a violation of the spirit. Those who lived through it only lasted long enough to wish they hadn't – if they could think at all through their own raving screams.

Oddly, he didn't immediately succumb to the "Screaming End," as it was called in seedy starport bars by derelict Spacers who, with morbid fascination, told of shredded vocal cords and the contorted features of the few corpses ever recovered.

He lost all control as the ship went into a tumbling spin, shattering his senses and destroying his equilibrium. He was paralyzed, nauseated and sliding into shock. A sound in his head rose in volume till it shrieked at a terrible pitch, consuming him with its all-encompassing power.

It went on and on....

Finally the scream began to fade, he vaguely noted – it wasn't so much a lessening of intensity as an increase of distance from its source. Swirling blackness gathered and pressed in, cushioning him in its dark embrace.

The comfort of death.

This grim knowledge ignited a blinding surge of relentless endeavor deep within him and he chanted to himself: "No, no, no, no, no, NO, NO, NO, NOOOOOO!"

The impulse grew until it thundered through him. It would not end this way; he would not succumb. Such was the imperative of his mission, his duty, that the gut-sickening nausea and disorientation began to fade. By an exertion of pure will, he began to function again.

Tac-U-One came back from the brink with determination and wrestled his ship into a semblance of control. All other distractions were blocked; his concentration again absolute.

A death's head grin split his taut face and laid bare his clenched teeth. He let out a growl that was pure triumphant animal. He had made it! He really had made it.

But... during one of the ship's wild gyrations, Tac-U-One glimpsed and then confirmed that he was still being followed.

I'm still being followed.

How could that other pilot be there? Irrational frustration blossomed and he slammed his fist into a blackened console, buckling it.

He couldn't make his report.

How could he have been so careless? His enemy must have been so close that Tac-U-One's Other-Space field had enveloped him too – pulled him through. This guy was really good. Even OS drive failure had not shaken him – but then, *his* drive hadn't failed.

Tac-U-One finally got his ship under control by using a planet, near ahead, for orientation and alignment. Entering a planetary system instead of the dead vastness of space in a crippled ship was fantastic, if short-lived luck. Automatic thrust reversal kicked in and waves of heavy pressure passed over him, twisting his guts and compressing and flattening his head and chest. The gravity coils jerked and shuddered against their mounts beneath his feet and whined piercingly as they struggled to maintain standard gravity. Again, hours felt like minutes.

Why wasn't the other pilot firing upon him? Both ships were in Normal Space. Did the other ship have weapons trouble? It must be obvious to his enemy that his rear shields could not deflect even one good shot.

He focused his stinging eyes through the curls of smoke on the last functioning screen; looming before him was the planet. With the rush of a rampaging bull it filled his screen. Coughing and choking on smoke, he frantically attacked the failing controls, diverting all available power to increase thrust reversal and forward shielding, trying to drop speed before he hit the atmosphere and disintegrated.

The M-Star howled like a banshee as it struck the planet's atmosphere. The murderous shriek, totally absent in interstellar reaches, battered him with concussive force. Its sudden occurrence was yet another shock to his senses which were fraying under this new onslaught.

Would this day never end?

The ship flared incandescent yellow. The inside temperature took a forty-degree jump and continued to climb. With lungs searing, eyes burning, and sweat pouring from his entire body, the pilot rode the bucking and pitching M-Star as it hammered deeper into the atmosphere. He fought the disabled controls like a wild man and still there was no final blast from his enemy's weapons.

He left a trail of debris as the atmosphere wrenched away molten chunks from the ship's lightly shielded skin. How he achieved controlled atmospheric flight he'd never know; but it only prolonged the swing of the Reaper's scythe.

Twin low energy blasts from the enemy ship clipped his right side, inflicting further damage. He got the message: his pursuer preferred capture to kill.

With frantic speed and consummate skill, he bypassed dead electronics and corrected the headlong tumble. He finally recognized it had come down to how he would go out.

He suppressed this morbid conclusion as he descended into a mountainous area. In a last desperate attempt to escape, he threaded his ship like a needle through passes and canyons, over ridges and around jutting mountains. It tortured his equilibrium as the landscape flashed by. He barely missed one peak or cliff before pulling his ship away from another.

The enemy pilot, in his functioning ship, stayed with him easily.

Knowing the end was truly at hand, Tac-U-One felt no irrational grasping at life, no pleading to a deity for another fate. He had lived life to the fullest and finally, faced with dissolution, set himself to relinquish it.

"Screw it," he growled as he deactivated the artificial gravity and impact safety devices. As they phased out, raw G-forces clutched and thrashed him. Deactivation spelled the end; there would be no messy search and destroy. He would not eject, because capture was worse than death.

"*Elon dorea larr gere*," he rasped through shredded vocal cords. In the old tongue it meant, "Until we laugh together again." Defiance, farewell and a promise.

Ahead a cliff face came at him with maniacal speed. He made no attempt to evade it.

CHAPTER 1

"Aw, hell!" Coach Williams muttered, "We're never gonna beat those boys." He was an athlete gone to seed, his own youthful dreams now a series of suppressed regrets. With his belt length inching out year after year, his sandy blonde hair thinning and turning gray and any chance of coaching at the college level long gone, he was not a happy man.

The ball game was going poorly. His team, the Granite High Farmers, was losing by two runs and not one of his boys had made a base hit today. On the bright side, it was normally a lot worse when the Farmers played the Cougars.

Coach Williams looked at his boys sitting on the bench waiting their turn to strike out. They were slump-shouldered and miserable, and he couldn't blame them, he felt the same way.

His eyes were drawn to one of the lads. His name was Jack – Jack Something-or-other. His back was straight and his shoulders were square. His expressionless face wasn't masking dejection and for a fleeting moment Coach's curiosity and ire were roused. Then he muttered to himself, "Aw, hell. It don't matter."

In the bleachers, one of the girls turned to her friends and said with forced optimism, "We could still win, you know." Her friends, sitting on either side, were astonished.

"Wendy, your team spirit has made you delusional; it's not going to happen."

"There is no way our Farmer boys are going to successfully plow this field today."

Sitting together the three girls caught the roving eye of every boy there. Natalie Wilk, with her mass of auburn hair and perfect complexion, was a visual aphrodisiac. Wendy White, sitting in the center, had long silky black hair, pale skin and warm green eyes. Deidre French was blonde, with vivid blue eyes. The four years of high school had made them close friends.

Wendy kept her eyes on Jack. She found herself doing that a lot recently, and realized *again* that she was anxious about the future. Jack himself was restless and the changes in the world around them had gone into overdrive. Even the simple act of watching this baseball game made Wendy think such things may all be gone soon. She wondered how it was all going to work out, for them and for the world.

•

"Uppfhh." The air rushed from Coach Williams' lungs as he was shoved sharply in the back; only the fence saved him from falling on his face. Recovering quickly, he turned with fist cocked ready to strike. Then he saw who it was, who had pushed him. His arm went limp.

His abuser was Donald Harvest, Sr.

Coach looked at the people nearby to see if anyone had noticed, but Harvest had shielded the shove with his large body. Harvest Sr. glared at the coach and stepped close.

"You're not thinking of pulling my boy from the lineup, are you Williams?"

Coach gave an obsequious half smile and said, "No... I'm not." Coach flushed red. "Wouldn't think of it!" Damn the man.

"With the game this close I thought your "team spirit" might get the best of you. I won't allow my boy to be humiliated like that. I mean, the Farmers are going to get their asses kicked anyway. You know it and I know it. So leave it alone. Don't pull the kid out, all right?"

"No... No, he won't be." Inside he felt belligerent and combative, but his voice betrayed him and made him seem weak before this man who could get him fired with merely a phone call.

Harvest gave him a penetrating "don't mess with me" stare, a hard finger to the chest along with a final "Good," and went back to the bleachers thinking it funny that Williams took such humiliation without protest.

"Shit, shit, SHIT!" Heads turned as Coach's mutter gained volume. He took in the frowns from those nearby. *Bad example*, they piously communicated in censorious silence. A few of the boys smiled, liking their coach's less-than-restrained ways.

He'd been about to bench the Harvest kid. Couldn't now. He let out a last defiant, "Shit!"

The incident with Harvest Sr. had played like a scene in a corny "B" movie. He wondered why crap like that always happened to him. *Why do people push me around?* he wondered.

•

Jack Something-or-other was sitting on the bench behind the chain link fencing that protected the unwary from foul balls and wild pitches. He was waiting his turn at bat, but it was obvious he wouldn't have a chance this inning. Tom Johnson, the Cougars' top pitcher, was doing a workmanlike job of putting the Farmers' best batters away.

It was depressing.

Jack looked around, his young face hiding the revolution of emotion that had overcome him as the game progressed. Being defeated in game after game earlier this season and even the previous years had not affected him much.

But something was different with his own attitude now and he didn't know why. But it was. As he sat on the hard wooden bench watching the game progress, the idea of losing to the Cougars had become – intolerable.

The thinning home crowd was quiet on the bleachers behind him. Jack felt the cumulative effect of their emotion as they watched Farmer batters strike out. He looked at his teammates as they walked slowly back to the bench and drop onto it. The shutout was crushing.

Then, feeling someone's attention on him, he turned and looked up into the bleachers. Wendy, his girlfriend, met his gaze and smiled. He felt her warmth and pleasure at their eye contact but winced from his own inner turmoil. He couldn't return her affinity right now, so he waved and quickly turned his head, hoping she wouldn't take the abrupt response personally.

It amazed him that baseball, something he was not passionate about, could cause him to react so strongly. The absurdity of being this upset about something so unimportant amused him. He let out a short laugh. The others looked at him, offended.

Coach zeroed in on Jack, "Something funny about this game we don't know about, boy? Care to tell the rest of us what the joke is?"

Jack sputtered out, "No, n-no, sir. There's no joke, I was thinking about something else."

"Keep your mind on the game, boy. If you'd been paying attention you would know we need it!" Coach slowly turned away.

Coach Williams despised himself for venting his impotent frustration on a boy who had done nothing wrong, but then he consoled himself: that was life. Shit rolled down hill and struck without respect to victim. It was this kid's turn.

●

Jack looked at the mussed-up chalk lines of the baseball diamond. The feet of his teammates had not done that. No Farmer had even made it safely to first base. Once again he rebelled at the thought of losing, intensely rejecting it. What was happening to him?

The inning was over. It had been quick: three up, three down.

The Cougars were running from the field. Excitement and a sort of casual contemptuous acceptance of victory came off them and it struck Jack like a physical blow. He felt sandwiched between the dejection of the Farmer fans behind him and the confidence of the Cougars in front of him.

He wanted to do something to restore his team's confidence. But of course he couldn't. He looked at his teammates. They were already defeated. They needed help – *his* help. But he shouldn't do anything.

What? What had he just thought? He examined the train of thought closely. It occurred to him that whenever he considered doing something noticeable, the same impulse kicked in – he couldn't, he shouldn't do it.

Perplexed, he wondered when it would be all right to win a game of baseball. The weight of the world, certainly, was not hanging on it.

This was wacky. It was okay to win, wasn't it? Sure, sure it was. But he really shouldn't: it felt wrong.

There it was again. He hadn't actively thought that thought, impulse, desire – whatever. It sort of popped into his head by itself. It happened every time he thought of doing something that would draw attention to him.

Then he embarrassed himself by realizing: *I'm hiding.*

This was an unpleasant view of himself… but true.

He looked at his thoughts and emotions more closely. It was more than that. He always felt he should be unnoticed, ordinary. He should stay away from the spotlight. He had been doing this for as long as he could remember.

Underneath the hiding… was… *fear.*

A hot surge of raw emotion seared him.

Someone was after him. Someone was looking for him, searching for him. He shook his head, confused.

No… How could that be? He wasn't in trouble at school. The police weren't after him. The FBI – no, that was absurd. No one was after him.

The whole thing was crazy.

It didn't matter, crazy or not, he had a strong feeling of being pursued, chased, and even hunted. He shivered.

The next question, the obvious question, was the dangerous one. If he *was* being hunted, *who* was after him?

Who were they? Where were they?

Dizziness enveloped him. He felt hot and sick. He shook his head to clear it.

There was no rational explanation for any of this: wanting to hide, feeling as if someone was after him.

All this was nonsense – brought into view by wanting to help his friends win the game, an action that would cause people to notice him. Immediately he felt the compulsion: *Hide.*

Forget it, he fumed to himself. *Just drop it* (as he always had).

No!

Today he wouldn't let it go, he would not drop this train of thought no matter how uncomfortable it made him – he would understand it.

Jack stood up. He looked all around: at the building that housed the pool, the running track, the stadium and behind it, the old red brick buildings and classrooms. In the parking lot little kids were running among the parked cars. He turned and looked at the crowd, the baseball diamond, and then across the green field to the homes past the chain link fence. The backdrop to all this was Mt. Olympus –a sheer-faced cliff rearing thousands of feet above the valley floor.

He looked, and looked....

He couldn't see a single person hunting him. There were no lurkers, no one peering around the corner, no one waiting for him to make a false move, no large black vehicles with tinted windows. No helicopters in the sky. If there truly were a threat, here and now, he would see it. He trusted his perceptions.

He saw only what was there – parents, students, teachers, a school, and a baseball field in a quiet residential area, backdropped by a magnificent mountain.

No one was after him. The observable facts were in conflict with his emotions. There was nothing counterfeit about his emotions on this subject – they were real and they were strong and so must have a valid source, if for no other reason than the fact that he knew he wasn't easily rattled and wouldn't feel this way without a valid reason. He could and always had been able to keep his cool.

He conducted an experiment. He alternately thought of winning the game and standing out, then he thought of coasting along unseen.

Back and forth he alternated these two ideas. With the idea of standing out, there was hot fear and as he changed his mind it slowly subsided. As he ran these two ideas through his head, first one and then the other, the intensity of the fear began to diminish and the speed with which he recovered his equilibrium increased. Over and over he alternated the thoughts. He got bored with it. There must have been some powerful event that caused those feelings, but the event certainly wasn't in the "here and now" and it certainly was not in the future (he almost laughed again). That left the past... the past – but there was nothing he could remember. Still, he felt a growing certainty that there was some past event causing the need to hide and fear.

Someone *had* been after him.

In the past.

And it had been vital at that earlier time to avoid discovery. Of that conclusion he was now completely certain. *It won't worry me again,* he knew.

He stifled a laugh, a real one this time. He had overcome an emotional imbalance that had powerfully affected his life. He had come through something, was over it, had reached a safe shore.

His friends were running onto the field. He grabbed his glove and followed, amazed no one had noticed anything wrong with him.

The home crowd gave little encouragement.

One Farmers "fan" said to another, "We should hoot and holler and get these boys revved up, but beating a dead horse just gives you a beaten dead horse." They both chuckled.

Jack shivered as waves of excitement coursed through him. He took his place in the outfield and, for the first time since he began playing the game, was ready to make the most of any opportunity.

●

In the bleachers Wendy caught her breath; her slim hands went to her throat as she watched Jack take the field. He moved with such certainty. That he was "someone" was more apparent to her now than it had ever been. Just look at him. He was tall and blonde and handsome and kind and, and... she frowned slightly... and *mysterious.* There was something about him that was different, there always had been. She admitted to herself that this was part of his attractiveness. A flush of pride warmed her neck: he was her boyfriend.

Wendy, along with everyone in the stands, knew the Farmers were going to lose. It wasn't losing the game that bothered her, she realized, but the thought of losing him. She looked at him again and the thought came to her that she could never keep him. He was too grand, meant for extraordinary things, things that would leave her behind. She winced and let the feeling go. She wasn't going to fight it. *If it comes, it comes*, she thought. It wasn't that she wanted to lose him, or wouldn't fight to keep him. But she refused to indulge in pointless emotional battles with herself over the possibility. She shrugged her shoulders; her composure mostly restored, she put her attention back on the game.

She watched as Cougars' batters safely hit balls and moved over the bases. The boys on first and second were edging away, arms outstretched, ready to run or steal a base. The Cougars were pushing to increase the score and end any chance of a Farmers comeback.

●

Crack! Another base hit.

The Cougars' fans stood and cheered, then abruptly stopped. The noise switched to the opposing bleachers where the Farmers' crowd surged up and let out a startled roar. An outfielder, Jack Something-or-other, had leaped high into the air and made a catch. Ball in hand he threw to the second baseman. The ball went right into his glove, so unexpectedly, he almost dropped it. Grasping the situation, the second baseman quickly tagged the base and the runner returning from his dash to third was out. He then threw to first base and that boy was out, too.

Triple play. As if by magic, it was the top of the ninth inning and the Cougars, with two men on base, were out.

The Farmers were stunned. The Cougars' batter was dazed and resentful – that ball had been safely hit, no question. His teammates were lined up behind the chain link fence with their fingers laced through it looking back and forth trying to grasp this terrible turn of fortune. Something weird had happened.

Everyone – players, school kids and parents – looked at Jack.

What he had just done was not great, it was... strange, disturbing. Like seeing someone swallow an ostrich egg – whole. You know it can't be done, but then you see it with your own eyes.

As the seconds slipped by, their minds minimized what they had seen, reducing it to the believable. The ball had not been hit so high; it had been fielded further out; the fielder hadn't really thrown to second base while he was still in the air. Normality, blessed normality, returned. Someone started to clap, and everyone joined in.

Jack stood where he had landed with no attitude at all. Then he smiled broadly and jogged with his teammates to the Farmers bench.

●

Wendy watched the Farmers pounding Jack on the back. She was pleased and disturbed. He had just done something extraordinary: the same boy who shunned any kind of spotlight.

He even avoided a math competition.

He explained very seriously that he did not want to draw *any* attention to himself for any reason – yes, he knew he could win, but no, he wasn't going to compete.

In total contrast he made an extraordinary play – in front of everyone. Jack's attitude had changed or he wouldn't have done it. She wondered if that catch was a fluke, but no, it wasn't. This was an intentional act.

Wendy concluded his desire to avoid public exposure had changed. She wondered what had caused it.

He looked the same.

Natalie and Deidre looked at their preoccupied friend, their eyes met and they shrugged. She should be happy, shouldn't she?

Deidre nudged Wendy and said ironically, "Jack, the glory hound." Wendy had told them about Jack, how he never showed his talent. "Stranger things have happened." *As if,* thought Wendy, *that explained it.*

"Couldn't he have become a star a little earlier in the season?" Natalie quipped, and two of the three friends laughed.

"Great play, wasn't it!" Wendy said, ignoring the bait.

Her attention drifted to other conversations around them. All were centered on Jack's catch and throw. People, after loudly voicing their praise, were still looking at him strangely, shaking their heads then breaking into grins: trying to integrate what they had seen with the doable, while happily accepting the result.

●

Coach and the Farmers team were excited; they had come to life even though the scoreboard still read Visitors – 2, Farmers – 0.

A teasing little voice chuckled in the back of Coach Williams' mind. It whispered: "Maybe, Coach, maybe!"

Hell, thought Coach, *what was two or three runs now? A miracle had happened, why not another?*

Coach hawked and spat. The team was huddled around him. He looked at the young faces, flushed with excitement.

"So this is the lineup. Sean, you're up first, then Donald, Dean, Jack and Jones. Sean, you're our best hitter and I need you on base for sure. Don't go for the big hit. Just get there, okay, son?"

"Sure, Coach," Sean said casually. *No problem – sure thing.* He wanted to scream. *All you want from me is the first base hit of the entire game against the best pitcher in the league. No sweat.*

Coach turned to Donald and felt a stab of fear. Donald Harvest, Jr. was on the team against his wishes. The Principal demanded that he win games and then they pull something like this. He hated it, but there it was; money talks and bullshit walks. And the kid's father had the brass to threaten him not ten minutes ago, creating a nasty scene in front of everyone. Rude bastard.

If this kid screws up the game he'd use it against Harvest Sr. and those S.O.B.s who forced Jr. onto the team. He'd give them so much grief that they'd drill holes in the bottom of their boats before they messed with his lineup again. Still, he would prefer not to have to justify anything. It would be good to win. Really good.

"Don, you just belt that ball and run like hell!" What else could he tell a kid with no game experience? It would have to do.

"Y-Yes, sir." Don replied in a tremulous voice.

Oh, great, thought Coach, and turned to the next boy.

"Dean, it depends on where we are when you're up to bat. Sean could easily be on third so I'm looking for an RBI from you. And from you too, Jack, when you're up." Coach gave him a long blank look that hid his awe, along with a heartfelt hope he could perform another miracle.

●

Wendy was fascinated to hear the fathers in the stands chatter.

"Holy shit! I still can't believe the play that kid made."

"It's just the thing this game needed." Heads nodded.

"How high was it, do you think, that the kid jumped? I mean I keep trying to guesstimate it, but when I get a figure I just can't believe it."

"Know what you mean." More heads nodded.

"Doesn't matter. Winning the damn game is all that matters."

"Yeah!"

"Oh, yeah. Right."

"He did it. Now we can win. That's all there is to it."

"Yeah."

Wendy could see the die-hard teache'rs, parents and students in the Farmers' bleachers were excited – chattering and joking. Could this turn of fortune mean they could win, could beat the Cougars? Other Farmers' fans began drifting back from the parking lot, having heard the uproar and wanting to find out what had happened.

The Farmers were in a position to score without the Cougars coming to bat again. That was the beauty of the bottom of the ninth – if you could make good.

Wendy was amused by the shouts, whistles and general commotion coming from the Cougars' fans. It was a very noisy scene.

•

Tom Johnson was filling in as the Cougars' relief pitcher for the last few innings today. He was still fresh. Tom liked to think he pitched like a big leaguer and the Farmers hit the ball like they were in middle school. He smirked. Many of these kids were afraid of him. He loved it. He was a large part of the Cougars' success. He gazed around the field and felt confident, trying not to be bored.

Tom knew he had to take the next three batters out. The Cougars coach casually signaled, three up three down. Tom nodded. He sneered at the kid waiting outside the batter's box, thinking, *these guys are assholes to get excited. Some kid makes a lucky play; so what. They still have to get by me and that's not going to happen. What can a Granite High Farmer do but use a pitch fork?* The dumb jerk even held the bat like he was throwing hay. *And what kind of a school name is "Farmers" anyhow: the school is in the middle of town? Dumb.* He smiled to himself, and shook his arm out. His pitcher routine always made them nervous. *Let 'em sweat a little.*

"Play ball!"

Sean stepped up to the plate, touched the far side with his bat, then drew it behind his head and nervously took a few practice swings. He tried to swallow away the metallic taste in his mouth – no saliva. He watched Tom Johnson nod and smile at some unseen signal from the catcher and imagined they had just agreed on a plan that would make him look stupid.

He was shaken out of a daze when the ump called, "Stee-rike!"

Sean heard Coach say, "Oh shit, oh shit, oh shit!"

In his pressured state, Sean was more aware of the crowd and Coach than he was of the pitcher, the baseball or the bat itself. He couldn't feel his body properly and was bathed in a hot, disconnected sensation.

He was scared.

Sean managed to swipe at the second pitch. The swing was too high, as the sinker dropped.

"Strike two!"

He sweat so much his eyes stung from salt perspiration. The next thing he heard was a crack as the bat hit the ball. With a comical look of surprise he took off down the first base line.

The crowd surged to their feet and cheered.

Touching his foot to first base was an incredible relief. *The team won't lose the game because of me!*

•

Donald Harvest, Jr. stepped up to the plate. He kept repeating to himself, "Belt the ball and run like hell, belt the ball and run like hell."

In the stands his father, Donald Harvest, Sr., was in pre-humiliation agony. His kid was going to screw up the whole team! And everyone was going to blame him and talk about him behind his back and give him sly, snide smiles. *If that asshole kid hadn't caught that ball the Farmers would have lost and it wouldn't matter what my kid did.* His shirt was damp with foul-smelling fear sweat. *Why did I force my son on the lineup today? Why did I ram it down Coach's throat just now? Why didn't I just let it be? Why?*

His gaze wandered upward, beseeching the heavens for relief. Briefly he considered yanking his kid out of the game by faking a family emergency – no, can't do that, he would look mean and foolish. The mousy kid might even kick up a fuss. No, he was going to grin and bear it – do it for the kid.

He looked down and his eyes locked onto Coach's. Disaster, they both thought. He saw a malicious glint in the coach's eyes. A "now you'll get yours" look.

Don, to everyone's surprise belted the ball and ran like hell. Harvest Sr. bounded from the pits of despair with joyous bellows and jabbed the man next to him with his elbow.

"Damn it, John, did you see that. That's why I've been pushing all season to get my kid on the team!" He didn't wait for an answer but kept cheering and pumping his fist into the air.

Farmer runners were on first and second base.

•

Jack waited quietly for his turn at bat. His sense of well-being from the great play was fading fast. Then, hearing a high-pitched happy shriek from behind him, he looked into the parking lot and saw a little kid with a remote control car having a great time with his toy. He was running the car all over the place, really making it hop. Jack looked away, but the kid was a distraction; he looked back. The grubby little kid had a rapt expression on his face. He was really ecstatic. *Must be some toy,* Jack thought.

As Jack turned back to the game, a sharp pain flashed through his head and settled into a dull throb behind his eyes.

●

Tom Johnson was losing it. His coach had just walked off the field. All he said was, "Don't lose this one, Tommy. That would be humiliating. No base hits all day and now two in a row." Shit.

Dean stepped up to bat and swung three times at thin air.

"Yer out!"

The crowd became one solid roar. There was no mistaking it; this was a real game. The stakes were high: pride.

The pitcher Tom Johnson smiled at his coach. *Screw you!* he thought. *I'm not going to lose this game.* Victory was often his but any loss was always the coach's fault. He could almost hear his dad giving it to the coach, "Damn it, Hugh. Why did you go out there and throw Tommy off his game? It must have been something you said to him." Tom smiled. *No, I won't lose this game, no matter what happens.*

●

Jack had a nasty prickling tension inside his head and he looked at the kid in the parking lot again. *What?* he thought. *That kid has a new remote control car, the ones they say can be operated by a thought-controlled circuit in the helmet.* Sure enough, the kid was wearing a helmet and he wasn't holding a control box. Wow, he was really doing it – controlling the car with the helmet. In the same moment, the car swerved toward the fence, directly at Jack.

The kid looked startled and irritated. His face was scrunched up in concentration – or frustration. After a few moments he ran after his car. It had run into the fence that separated the parking lot from the baseball field.

The kid with the helmet picked his car up and took it back to where he was playing a minute ago. As he walked he shook the car violently. He turned it over and inspected the undercarriage and apparently finding nothing amiss, carefully placed the car back on the ground. Immediately the car took off toward the fence – toward Jack. A look of intense concentration came over the kid's face, his eyes flashed with ferocity, he shook his head, he rapped his knuckles against the helmet, but whatever he tried to do didn't work. He repeatedly stomped his foot on the ground, really mad. He jumped up and down in frustration. The car was bucking at the fence, unable to get past it.

Then Jack felt someone grabbing him. It was Coach and he looked mad, too.

"Can't you hear me, kid?" Jack couldn't respond. "It's your turn at bat." He gave Jack a shove in the right direction. Jack stumbled and went down on one knee. He felt dizzy, couldn't stop thinking about the angry kid, that car. His head was swirling.

The mini-drama of Jack's stumble attracted instant notice. Heads turned.

●

A frantic scream was unleashed. It was so frenzied and intense it interrupted the game. Without consultation, the home plate umpire threw off his headgear and ran toward the sound. Others, after a moment's hesitation, charged out of the bleachers over to the wildly screaming child who was standing alone in the parking lot, beating the side of his helmeted head with his clenched fists. The umpire looked about for the cause of the trouble – a molester running away?

"What's wrong?" the umpire shouted, but got no answer. The scream went on and on. Little fists punching the side of his helmeted head.

Parents, teachers and some students gathered around and looked on helplessly. What was the kid screaming about?

No one wanted to lay their hands on someone else's kid, but the sight of him beating his own head was so disturbing a man reluctantly grabbed the kid's arms and held them at his side. There was blood on his knuckles.

The kid stopped screaming to yell, "Let me go! Let me go!" Over and over. "You're hurting me…."

"Is there a doctor here?" the umpire asked when the kid paused to take another deep breath. Others took up the call for a doctor but none emerged. "This isn't a tantrum. Something is wrong with this child, will someone call 911? We need the paramedics to check him out!" the umpire yelled. "Does anyone know his name? Are the parents here?" Heads shook in the negative.

"He lives near the school, I think."

"Well, you better go knock on some doors and get his parents located." People talked for a few seconds then ran toward the nearby homes.

The umpire looked at the frantic kid and waited till he drew another breath. "What's the matter, little buddy?" The tirade continued.

"Someone put a clamp over that kid's mouth!" Though many wanted to, no one did.

"Are you hurt?" someone bellowed.

"Damn, that kid can really scream."

"Where are your parents?" The surrounding crowd obscured the kid, but the screaming kept going.

●

Jack was on one knee. He looked back at the kid's car; its wheels were spinning as it tried to negotiate the fence. It ran up the chain link fence about a foot then flipped over, only to go at the fence again with tiger-like ferocity. *Is the car trying to reach me?* Jack wondered. It seemed to be; *how weird.* Again it climbed a short way and overturned.

Jack remembered seeing a TV ad for this new gadget. It was improbable: "You simply put on the control helmet and away you go. Control the car directly with your mind. Nothing could be easier or more exciting! Buy yours today." While watching the ad, Jack had become sick – nauseated. Minutes later he had been okay.

Here it was again. The toy, the same toy. His stomach turned and another flash of pain stabbed through his fuzzy head.

●

"Hey kid, kid, hey kid." The umpire was now desperate to find out what was wrong. "Are you sick? Are you hurt?" Then he had a bright idea, "Do you miss your mommy?"

The kid abruptly shut up. "No, I don't miss my mother!" And he glared at the umpire. "My car won't work!" he screamed. "It won't do what I tell it to anymore."

The kid gave a sharp shove and broke loose from the surprised umpire and pushed the adult bodies aside. He bolted to his car, picked it up and smashed it on the ground, again and again, scattering wreckage far and wide. He stomped his heel on the larger pieces. Once it was completely ruined he gave an evil little smile and quieted right down. His smug look said, "I'm in control of you now."

●

The crowd lost its interest in the nasty little kid, who, after all that drama, was just having a tantrum. The umpire returned, and the game resumed.

Coach Williams returned from the edge of the crowd and saw Jack still on one knee. He pulled the distracted boy to his feet and said, "Hit a homer Jack, bring those boys in," sending him off with a push in the right direction. "God, I hope that kid can do it twice!"

Jack didn't answer. The kid hadn't hit a homer all season and was walking a little stiffly. *Must be nerves,* thought the coach.

In the batter's box, Jack's head was swirling. The first pitch went by. *Can't you give me a chance to feel all right?* he wondered. In a moment he would feel okay, he was sure of it.

"Strike!" the umpire yelled.

Coach Williams was nervous and uncertain. He couldn't stand how casual Jack looked – nerveless, vague and… distracted. Hell, the other boys had just about pissed themselves. And apart from the phenomenal catch today, this kid had been a nothing player all season. Maybe he just didn't care: hadn't he laughed at the team earlier? Who knew? The kid looked pale, what a time to get sick. *Get your mind on the game, boy,* he silently willed.

Coach's mind skipped tracks and he thought, *Can you beat that Harvest kid, a base hit at a time like this? God!* And smiled foolishly.

●

Wendy realized Jack was in serious trouble. He had a faraway look and he felt all wrong. Some slight awareness of Jack was always with her and if he was disturbed or upset she often sensed it. Something was wrong with him *right now.*

Startling her friends, Wendy flew down the steps and rushed to the fence behind the batter's box.

●

In that same instant, Tom Johnson threw the ball to second base and almost nailed Sean, whose lead off second base had been reckless. Sean ran and dove for the base. There was a scuffle but he was called safe. The call provoked cheers and protests. All the coaches converged on second base. One of the Farmers' parents claimed to have captured the moment on his hand held camera and a loud argument about its admissibility began.

"Good call!" someone yelled from the Farmers' bleachers.

"Are you blind?" was the retort.

The argument escalated; parents and teachers rushed onto the field yelling at the umpire who made the call, at the coaches and at each other.

●

"Jack!" Wendy called with piercing urgency.

He didn't hear.

"Jack!" She fired the word like a bolt from a crossbow. He turned and for a moment didn't recognize her, then, fascinated, she saw awareness of her presence come into his eyes.

She smiled at him with all the warmth and love she possessed; it was a dam-burst of affinity, enveloping him. With awe and elation she saw him settle and come back to himself. He stood more erect and moved his grip on the bat and rotated it a few times. He shook his head slightly and gave her a smile.

"Thank you," he said quietly. He turned back to the pitcher.

Oh, wow! Wendy had never experienced anything like that before. Never done anything like it. She went back into the stands.

"What did you say to him?" asked Deidre.

"Just hello." It was too intimate a moment to share with anyone else, anyway they wouldn't understand. She wasn't sure what happened either. "And he said hello back."

●

The original ruling stood and Sean was safe on second. Everyone but the players cleared off the diamond. Now, if the Farmers won, the Cougars could blame the loss on a bad call from the umpire. Not ideal – but something – anything was better than losing to the Farmers.

The second pitch was coming fast; Jack took a swipe and clipped a foul. He wasn't fully into the game yet, but at least he was functioning.

"Strike two!"

There was a note of hysteria in the air; it swept through the home crowd. Jack saw fear in the eyes of the Farmers' fans as they seemed to understand for the first time that he was in trouble.

The Cougars' fans were jeering him. "Couldn't catch that one!" they laughed.

Anticipation and fear of defeat were fighting a war on the faces of every Farmers fan.

Most of the Cougars and their fans continued to be confident and very loud. The game was close, but they still expected to win. *Only* win.

All emotions and attention were centered on Tom and Jack.

The pitcher, the batter.

Tom had the experience and skill to put this nobody kid and the whole Farmers team away. He had done it before and he would do it now. The pitcher pressed the ball between his hands and then rotated it, imbuing it with his strength and will. Tom leaned forward looking for signals from his catcher. He hawked and spit. Not chew, but as close as he could get.

Jack felt more oriented. Wendy's affinity for him immersed him in such warmth that his connection to the outside world, his sense of reality, improved and the disruption that had gripped him began to dissipate. He had come back to himself a little at first, then more – all in a rush. She had really helped him.

Tom Johnson felt nervous. To this point he had not doubted victory. Even two base hits hadn't touched his confidence. That was sheer luck.

But he couldn't register this batter. Tom couldn't feel anything coming from him at all. No fear, no tension. It was strange because there was no confidence either. The guy was just looking at him. It was weird, the guy wasn't even waiting.

The batter was ready.

Tom felt a pulse of hatred for this batter. He didn't know who the no-name dumb jerk was, but he hated him.

Tom wanted to humiliate this guy. Put him in his place. Ignoring the coach and the catcher's signals, Tom threw a curve ball that was low and outside, hoping the batter would chase it and look stupid.

"Ball!"

Jack didn't move a muscle, this time by choice. He felt better, aware of the game and its progress and more like himself again.

*

Coach Williams eased himself as the ball was called. "Kid's got nerve," he said to no one in particular, wisely nodding his head. In less than a minute he would either be a King or a Horse's Ass. With each pitch and swing of the bat, Coach gave a slight swing himself in an unconscious effort to assist the action.

*

Tom Johnson really had it in for this guy now. That last pitch made *him* look bad. *Ignore me, will you?* he thought. *This asshole didn't even twitch.* He wanted to rattle the batter so much he could taste it – *I'll hit him,* he decided. A fastball to the body would scare the crap out of him and would look unintentional.

Johnson faked a misstep on the pitcher's mound and the pitch came hard and fast. Jack danced out of its path as it slipped past his chest. The whole crowd let out a loud "OOOOhh" of real concern. A small smile was teasing around the edges of Tom Johnson's mouth. *Let's see him face the next pitch now.*

Tom's euphoria was short-lived. One glance at Jack and he deflated. Jack calmly stepped back into the batter's box and smoothly swung the bat a few times, then set himself for the next pitch.

Damn him to hell! He wanted to be rid of this guy now – walking him would load the bases but he could strike out whoever came next. *Who in the hell is this guy?!*

I should walk this guy. Sure enough, there was the coach's signal. But pride wouldn't let him.

●

"Can you believe how good he looks?" said Wendy to her friends, and they hated her a little. The game was Jack and Tom. There was a heightened expectation; the push and pull of the crowd's tension. They all felt it.

"I can't believe this!" Wendy said. "Look at him, look at him. He's going to do it. I know he is!"

●

The count was two balls, two strikes. *Why didn't I hit him?* Tom angrily wondered. *How did I miss?* His coach was signaling "walk" over and over. The catcher could see the look in Tom's eye and knew there was not going to be a walk.

His wind-up was slow and easy, so deceptive of the power he could deliver. And then he smiled, his confidence returning in a rush. *I'm going to nail you with this one,* he decided. Tom unleashed all his strength, speed and accuracy, sending the ball in a blur toward the intended target.

Jack knew that the last pitch was meant to hit him. Ironically, instead of intimidating him it had only served to sharpen his senses, to fully return his attention to the here and now. He looked at the pitcher.

The ball was on its way. It was fast, straight and hard.

There is a satisfying sound a wooden bat makes when the ball is hit just right. Like a throaty pistol shot. And that sound was music to the home crowd's ears.

It was gone!

All heads in the bleachers seemed connected to the ball by invisible threads, so closely did they follow its path. The crowd felt a sense of timelessness as the ball, cushioned by wonder, ignored gravity. It came down, finally, over the center field fence and onto the roof of a passing car. In their excitement, no one commented that the ball had gone further than it had any right to go.

Even some the Cougars' fans joined in the roar of approval for the young man who could hit a baseball like that.

Wendy felt a stab of heat pass through her body. *God,* she thought, *he is fantastic!*

Jack took his victory lap.

The school, Wendy later read in the local paper, took great pride in paying for the auto repairs, but they refused to increase the height of the eight-foot fence located in center field, claiming (and rightly so) that no ball could ever go over it again.

CHAPTER 2

THE FARMERS' BASEBALL WIN WAS CELEBRATED that night with a party at Wendy's home. She was surprised by the way Jack handled their school friends and others who came by to enjoy the fun and see the guy who could jump too high and hit too far. They crowded around congratulating him, saying he had won the game and how great he was. With a performance like that, he was certain to attract attention from many good universities offering scholarships. Wendy had seen the adulation given to successful athletes, but it was a complete surprise to see Jack receive it.

He said "Okay" and "Thank you" and "Thanks, I really appreciate it" and "Wow, it's great of you to say that!" many times over. Wendy knew baseball wasn't that big a deal to him and saw his frustration mounting with all the attention he was receiving. When one person too many told him how good he was, he shook his head decisively, grabbed a pair of drumsticks and rapped out a beat on the coffee table.

Having gotten the attention of everyone in the room, he stood on a low stool so he could see all the kids clearly.

"I want to thank you all for coming to this celebration of the Farmers' unlikely win over the Cougars. It's really good to have this reason to get together." The kids clapped and whistled.

"I also want to thank you for the personal compliments. I appreciate it." After some more clapping they quieted to hear what else he wanted to say. "But baseball is a team sport. When I caught that ball in the top of the ninth inning, it took two other Granite High Farmers playing their positions to get that triple play." Jack swept his eyes over them. "When I hit the home run, there were two others on base before me. Sean James over there," Jack pointed to him, "made the first Farmers base hit of the entire game against the best pitcher in our league! But that's not all. Donald Harvest, over there, made the first base hit of his entire life!" The kids laughed and hooted and clapped. Don blushed.

"What I did today was unusual for me, too!" More laughter, clapping and whistling. "But without the whole team, we wouldn't have defeated you Cougars," Jack said, looking at the Cougars cheerleaders who smiled at him. A couple of the boys in the room wore very jaded expressions and knew a "modesty speech" when they heard one. Its purpose, they were certain, was to give him more girls to choose from.

As if Jack could read their thoughts, he said, "My part in the game was the most noticeable. But the whole thing would have been nothing if we hadn't beaten the Cougars. And that took the team working as a team."

One Cougars cheerleader said, "You can beat us any time you like, Jack." She slapped herself suggestively on her hip. They really laughed.

Jack laughed too and his color heightened. Then he continued, "There was another significant event at the game that only one person noticed." He stopped; they waited for him to continue, looking puzzled. "About the time Sean tried to steal third base, I had a pounding headache and was really dizzy – unable to play." He saw skeptical looks. "No, really! Remember, as I was going out to bat I tripped, and then that little kid threw a fit so no one really noticed I was having trouble. I didn't even see the first pitch, I was so out of it. But Wendy knew I was in trouble. She came down behind the batter's box and called my name. I turned and saw the most wonderful sight a guy has any right to hope for." The boys turned to Wendy.

"Oh yeah, she's a babe!"

"She's *hot*!" They hooted and whistled. When it quieted, Jack continued, "That set me straight. I wasn't dizzy anymore, and I played on." He looked at Wendy. "Thanks Dee, I would have embarrassed us all out there today, if it weren't for you."

"You're welcome, Jack, but we all agree, you did it out there, not me." After a smattering of clapping and laughter, conversations broke out in smaller groups.

Wendy wasn't certain until that moment what she experienced earlier with Jack had been real.

●

Amanda White, Wendy's mother, was in the kitchen when Jack was talking. She moved to the doorway to listen and to see him. She saw the interplay between her daughter and this young man and knew for the first time with complete certainty that Wendy would never willingly leave him. That made her sad. She forced aside her reservations and apprehensions about the match. She knew if she attempted to separate them or disrupt their relationship, Wendy would hate her and go with Jack, regardless.

Jack was not of their religion and no discussions about this had moved his opinion in the slightest. To make it worse, he was always so frustratingly polite about it. She could never get him into a passionate debate. "I don't want to fight about religion, Mrs. White. Everyone has a right to their own beliefs without it being stomped on by others."

Trying to convert him had been a waste of time and emotional energy. That boy, no matter how nice, was never going to go to Heaven.

Time and again she had felt she had achieved victory, a conversion, when he expressed interest in some of the religious ideas she loved to talk about. He had willingly read their religious books when she asked him to. Disconcertingly he had a better grasp of the material than she did, and could even recite extensive passages without reference to the quoted verses. He knew her religion but did not believe. He was not one of them and would never be. It was a source of great pain to her. How could she allow her beautiful, intelligent daughter to marry outside their religion; for the children – her grandchildren – to have no religious community as she had, and to suffer even a worse fate than that? Worse than anything?

But in spite of all this, of his polite rejection of her religion, there was something about them. Looking at them now, at their interaction, it came to her.

They were partners. How extraordinary.

What teenage boy proclaimed he was not the hero everyone thought him to be, that it was his unnoticed girlfriend who helped win the game, save the day. He was proud of her, thankful and sincere. He would give to her emotionally as much as she would give to him. That was how it was supposed to be – but never was; not in her own observation of others nor in her own life.

Looking at the girls in the room, Amanda White could see how powerfully they had been stirred by this boy. Jack Cousins. All the females understood what had happened between this girl and this boy and craved such a relationship for themselves. They felt the connection between Jack and Wendy emotionally, if not intellectually. In contrast, as she looked at the boys crowded in her living room she could see that the significance of what had passed between those two had passed them by. She knew she couldn't even tell her husband so that he would understand as she did. He would say, "He's a nice boy, dear, I've always said so," and give it no more thought. She felt a pang of jealousy for her daughter.

Wendy came into the kitchen.

"Mom, can you believe how many girls are here now? Look, those four over there, the blonde heads, are Cougars cheerleaders!"

"Mmmm," said Amanda.

"Those over there are from Highland High and there are girls from other schools too. What I can't figure out is who told them. I mean, we never had one of these parties before." Wendy laughed at the idea. "They make me nervous. Can you believe the way they're looking at Jack? Even Deidre and Natalie, my best friends for crying out loud, can't take their eyes off him."

"Yes, he does seem to be the center of it all, doesn't he?" Amanda White smiled. "But he deserves it. You were the one who told me that."

"But, Mom, this is just a bit too much!"

"Well, I think you best get used to it." Just as she now had to get used to the idea that this nice young man was going to take Wendy away from them, from her, from the Church. Oh, Wendy, she thought, I don't want to lose you, but I'm afraid we will.

"Don't complain about it. You wanted Jack performing up to his ability. If you don't like what these girls are doing, then do something about it instead of complaining to me."

●

Wendy stood indecisively in the kitchen doorway looking at the crowd. This was new territory for her and she needed to adapt and respond properly to Jack's higher profile.

When the girls were not talking to Jack, or listening in on those who were, they were keeping track of him as if this gave them possession. So much high profile female competition was unnerving, and even though Jack was down-to-earth, she was anxious.

Wendy decided. She needed a higher profile too. Taking her mother's advice she shouldered her way through the crowd.

"Excuse me, please," she said sweetly and took Jack by the arm, drawing him away from the pack of girls.

She led him to the piano alcove and cornered him alone. She took his face between her hands, drew him to her and placed her lips over his. She let the kiss linger. Her performance was the center of attention: she wouldn't be ignored.

"Jack," she said quietly, "what really happened out there today? What made you change your mind about avoiding the spotlight?"

Jack hesitated, unable to give a sensible answer. What could he say when he didn't know the truth himself? He shrugged.

Thinking he was withholding the answer, she whispered in his ear, "You can tell me, I won't tell anyone else." She pressed the full length of her body into his and kissed his ear and then his lips, taking her time. It was intense and charged the whole atmosphere in the White home. Wendy smiled, aware of the female hackles that had risen across the whole room. Good. They needed to know.

"Something changed today, Jack. I have no way of knowing what it is, except by asking you." She looked imploringly into his eyes. As she waited for an answer she had to suppress a smile. Poor Jack was floundering a bit.

He was thrown back into himself to search for he knew not what. He couldn't ignore her appeal and didn't want to, but even he couldn't explain what had happened. Telling her wild speculation would only disturb and frighten her. So he told her a partial truth.

"My whole attitude changed today." Wendy nodded, feeling strangely relieved by this confirmation. "Some internal pressure was stopping me from doing things in public, but somehow, today, it went away." He shrugged. "I refused to let it get the best of me."

"Thanks, Jack. All this," she waved an arm indicating all the kids and why they were there, "is so... different. I was worried, especially when you sort of 'checked out' there in the batter's box."

"Dee, I can't tell you how much... I was in trouble there. You brought me through and I still don't know how you did it." He shook his head as if some of the experience still clung to him.

"That's okay, it's one of those *girl* things." *And love,* she added silently.

"Thank you." His tone was quiet, eloquent and just for her.

She felt it deep inside and shivered. Excitement? Apprehension? Some of each she suspected.

"You're welcome." She looked around. "You better get back to your fans before we have a riot."

He smiled.

Ah, Jack, you move me. She walked through the crowd to the kitchen.

●

Later Wendy scanned the room, pleased with the results of her long kiss. Feeling at ease for the first time since the game, she sat in a vacant recliner, closed her eyes and let herself pleasantly drift... her and Jack. Jack.

She couldn't remember when they started dating. It was never a thing that had been formally declared. They had known each other from the time they were seven years old and had walked to school together nearly every day of their lives. There was a blurry period when their relationship went from childhood friendship to something more.

The "more" her mother constantly warned her to guard against. "I know Jack is a good boy, but he *is* a boy," she cautioned Wendy with infallible logic.

One night, coming home from a movie, Jack had driven to a place overlooking the lights of the city and parked the car. Instead of just talking, which was their usual thing to do, he slowly took her in his arms and kissed her: her first real "leave the world behind" kiss – and his. She had been stunned, never totally certain he felt that way about her. His apparent lack of physical interest had begun to worry her, but after that kiss there was no doubt.

If her mother knew it was Jack who had stopped them from going all the way she would have been shocked. Wendy laughed, remembering her last attempt to scale the walls of his moral fiber.

Jack was the one she talked to when something was important or when it was funny or when it meant nothing at all. Sometimes he was very intense and would talk of how he had a great purpose to achieve. "I feel like I'm stalled in the middle of something. I feel stuck. But soon, soon it will end. And then... well, I don't know what, then." He looked perplexed and embarrassed by his passion. "But watch out!" He smiled widely, taking the seriousness away. She shivered, excited and fearful. There were depths to Jack. Sometimes mystery was all about him.

When she would talk about making a family and raising children, the kind of architecture she liked in a family home, what part of the Salt Lake Valley was the nicest, and wouldn't it be great to have a home on such and such lane or so and so street, Jack would become withdrawn to the point of being remote. "Jack, I feel like I'm talking to myself. Please answer me; I want to know what you think!" He would just look at her. "Should we start our family right after we're married or should we wait until we have money of our own, finish college? What do you think?"

"I don't know, Dee. It sounds nice though." This was totally vague, and definitely not the agreement and necessary planning in advance of these major life-changing events she was seeking. The third time Jack replied in a similar manner was the last. Wendy was laying out the plans for her life, their lives, and his answers were vague. A year ago it had come to a head; she became angry and refused to listen to how "nice" her plans were.

"That's no answer and you know it, Jack! Every time we talk about family, a house, even something as simple as what your college major is going to be, you say this, you say that and it adds up to a lot of nothing."

Jack shrugged.

"It makes me think you don't want to have a family with me, or care about our future together." She had been afraid to push him, frightened that his answer might be, "You're right, Dee. I don't want to start a family with you, goodbye." She felt certain that she and this boy, this man, were destined to be together. *And life needed a plan.* The right college, the proper timing for engagement, then marriage, the number of children and the size and location of their first home were early and important goals and events in any couple's life.

Without thorough preparation life was easily thrown into disarray. Without proper organization she and Jack wouldn't amount to anything. Wendy wanted to leave her mark on the community, the city and state. Who knows, with Jack, they may walk on the national stage and do some good for the nation? She had major aspirations. But when she discussed the future with him, the only thing that lit Jack's eyes was talk of a strange and mysterious and undefined future. But he never said what the first step on that path would be, or if it included her. *Her* plans were real, about how life was really lived.

Finally she had enough.

"I want a real answer Jack, and I want it from you now."

He looked at her.

Wendy continued, "I'm upset, I'm lost, I don't know what to do, what to think. You won't commit. You won't commit to our future, you won't commit to us!" She had served up her deepest fears and desires for him to do with as he would. A brave act. Win or lose, at least she would have a real answer. If they were to part, best it happen sooner than later.

Jack was cornered and upset. If he were to remain true to himself she would be crushed. He loved her; he didn't want to shatter her. The simple truth was his vague idea of the future and her well-structured plans did not align. Their eyes met and held. "I've been evasive." The words felt like they were backing up in his throat. "The reason is, Dee, I don't think it's going to happen. The house, the kids and all."

It came crashing down around her. *All my worst fears are true.*

He said he loved her but didn't want a commitment, didn't want a family, he doesn't want our children. The rejection was total. She felt herself beginning to dissolve into tears, but instead she got angry, very angry. "Before I say something I'll regret all my life, you better explain yourself, Jack! Because right now I feel like leaving here and never talking to you again!" She punched him on the chest and despite herself, tears cascaded from her eyes.

"I know I've upset you, and I'm sorry." He had to stay in control of his emotions or he would lose her. "Dee, whenever I think about the future, I don't see a house filled with kids. It's not that I don't want it, I just don't see it." This was the clear truth to him.

With an enormous effort she forced herself to stay where she was and respond. "Jack, what you've said is just a more elaborate evasion than the one you've been giving me this whole time!" She put the heels of her palms to her forehead. "What do you want me to believe, that you can see the future? Come on, Jack, it's a question of what you want. Please be honest with me. When you say 'I can't see it,' what you really mean is, 'I don't want it.' Please be man enough to give it to me straight." She was defiant through her grief.

Staring at the sky, Jack felt completely misunderstood, and he knew if he couldn't get his point of view across to her that they would part, probably not even remain friends. But how to say it? "I've never thought about our future the way you do, Wendy. I look around this city, this whole world and what passes for a 'normal' life seems strange and unnatural to me. It is nothing I could or would ever… do." He paused for a moment, and then continued. "When you speak of a house and kids, I don't see it. I know it's very important to you – I didn't want to upset you, so I never said clearly and plainly how I felt. I haven't intentionally been leading you on. My indecisiveness comes mainly from the fact that I don't know what the future holds. You're right, I can't clearly see the future. But I know enough to know what is not there. If you want to interpret this as 'me not wanting it,' in a sense you're right."

Wendy was numb – past being hurt. She didn't hate him, she just didn't understand him. It was so simple. Why couldn't he get it? You don't *see* the future, you *make* it.

"You want something definite." She felt despair as his words ripped through her. "The house and kids thing, it won't happen, not with me."

He couldn't reach out to console her; she would reject his touch and go, never to return. So he waited, and was very still. It was some time before her breathing lost its ragged edge. The best thing was – she was still there.

Jack quietly said, "I think we can be together Dee. I have wanted that for a long time. I still do." There was something about this girl, something familiar, and something unique.

They walked home in silence, descending into tree-lined streets, walking back among well-kept houses and lawns. Past children playing, their excited voices a harsh reminder of her lost dream, a future that would never be. Not with him, he had said.

Jack took her unresisting hand and gently squeezed it; there was no return pressure, but neither did she pull free. They had finally reached Wendy's house. "I can't leave you without saying something more." He looked at her until she raised her beautiful liquid eyes. "I love you, Wendy." She went rigid, rejecting what he said.

He pressed on. "I think we are alike. We have a similar attitude toward life even if our plans have been very different. I know it doesn't seem that way to you right now, but I feel it's true. Without ever really thinking about it, I realize now, I've always thought this.

"I don't know the specific details of my future. Or, potentially, our future." He looked away, and for a moment the look in his eyes conveyed a sense of longing that hardened into implacable determination. "We've talked about this before; you know I feel I have a duty to perform. I want to invite you to come with me wherever it is I go.

"I can go alone, but I want you with me. I would like your help, your companionship, and your touch. Without you my life will be barren. Not that I won't achieve great things – because I will," he asserted, "but because *we* could achieve even more. And you would be there. We would be together."

She looked into his eyes and knew this was no idle invitation. Not a spur of the moment statement said to ease the impact of his earlier refusal. She felt herself courted by a prince who had a kingdom to consider before making any proposal.

"Happily ever after" was not on the menu, but when she thought about it, his offer was something far more substantial. A deep chord had been touched by his heartfelt sincerity; this was a defining moment.

"Without you," he said, "there will be no personal love. What substitute for that is ever enough?" She gave him the briefest of hugs. It was short, but to Jack, incredibly gratifying. He hadn't lost her.

Over the following days and weeks, Jack's "proposal" had caused her to examine her own motivation. The real turning point came when she realized that she had been forwarding her mother's hopes and wishes that had been drilled into her from the moment she could hold a doll. It was an enormous relief to realize her conflict with Jack was a result of blind acceptance of her mother's expectations. And not just her mother, but the whole structure of society seemed to have a very tailored niche carved out for everyone to fill. Neither her mother's plans nor society's socket-like space, ready and waiting for her to plug into, were something she had decided was best for her own life. It freed her to make up her own mind or to simply wait and decide later.

At that point she began to see things from an entirely different perspective. She felt a greater measure of independence, of space. She changed her mind. Jack wasn't offering anything specific. She guessed it could be termed "adventure."

With her new outlook she could just as easily reject Jack's plans for their future as well – if they weren't what she wanted.

She had not exchanged one rigid future for another.

She could make her own decisions.

•

That was a year ago and nothing had noticeably altered their lives. So today was something. Jack publicly displaying ability. *Is this the start of something new, is the adventure about to begin?* she wondered. She opened her eyes.

The celebration was over. All friends and visitors were gone.

"I'm sorry Jack. I should have seen everyone off."

"We saw you sleeping so your mom and I took care of it." Jack hugged and kissed Wendy, then left for home.

As he slowly paced the sidewalk his thoughts wandered over the day. He'd conquered a generalized fear, but there were other fears and personal obstacles he could see more clearly now that the first barrier was out of his face. At the game he'd felt a surge of confidence, then immediately after that, the kid and his car had derailed that personal achievement.

Before the party tonight he'd seen another ad on TV for the toy car. They claimed it was remotely controlled by the TAC, or Thought Activated Circuit. The TAC was electronics and programming that allowed the helmet wearers mind to control the motion of the car directly.

Astonishing!

The circuitry for the toy was made by Directory Electronics, a Las Vegas-based company.

Seeing the toy in action had disturbed him profoundly. Today had the feeling of a "major life incident" – something pivotal, a day that changed the direction of his life.

There was something personally distressing about this toy car and its unbelievable new technology. And he had no idea what that was.

There was a disturbing mystery to uncover here.

More importantly were the implications of this technology for Earth. The impact would be significant. *The Thought Activated Circuit is the first trickle of advanced technology, there will be a lot more.* Why did he think that?

And then, *this technology has something to do with me.* He shook with an unrecognized premonition. Something massive was moving beneath deep waters.

The wind took his hair, his pulse quickened and his step lengthened. A new direction. And a feeling… the *right* direction. The *inevitable* direction, and danger.

But danger was only dangerous when you ignored it and allowed it to come upon you unprepared.

There was something important to discover about this electronics company.

He remembered a saying his uncle had once used: "Fools rush in where angels fear to tread." Well, he may act quickly, but he was no fool. And he had no concern about the fears of angels.

This meant an immediate trip to Las Vegas.

●

Wendy went up to her room and tried to envision what the future could possibly hold after such a day. No vistas formed in her mind, and tomorrow remained a blank page. She had no idea of what was to come. Finally she grew tired, then lay down to sleep. She dreamed of chaotic things she could not recall.

The world continued to turn.

Had it known its own future, the planet might have skipped a beat in anticipation… or foreboding?

CHAPTER 3

COLIN CRAIG, DIRECTOR OF THE CENTRAL Intelligence Agency (D/CIA), had the remote control car that was operated by the TAC, the Thought Activated Circuit, sitting motionless on the table in front of him. His senior officers were ranged about the conference table waiting for him to begin the meeting.

He was in trouble because the CIA, and he personally, had failed to be aware of or see the significance of the new technology that made the toy function.

Many influential people were bombarding the Agency with demands for information, information the agency did not immediately have and could not promptly produce. These powerful people hurled accusations of incompetence.

He and his entire organization had missed the emergence and importance of this new technology. It was unpardonable.

Last night his tech department had checked the toy out. The report on the table beside the toy outlined their findings. Bottom line: it worked. Second bottom line: they couldn't figure out how. It was a "quantum leap forward" and it was unlikely they could back-engineer the TAC in the next ten years. He had nothing to report; no, it was worse than that: he had to report "it works but we don't know how and are unlikely to discover its secret any time soon."

Another report asked the question, "Why would a company introduce a world-shattering new technology and sell it in toy stores?" The speculation was... disturbing. Hiding the new technology in plain sight had fooled the CIA. He felt a flash of pure rage. He'd been made to look like a rank amateur.

His tech report on the toy stated there was "a wide variation, person to person, of demonstrated skill." Some could use it, some couldn't. But it worked.

A field report had been hastily thrown together by a team rushed out to Las Vegas to investigate the people who manufactured the toy. The production facility owned by Directory Electronics was located in an industrial park on the west side of Las Vegas. The building had no windows; the exterior walls were painted a shade of off-white with a sand-colored stripe around the middle and there were loading docks to the rear along with a row of dumpsters. There were large smoky glass doors with chromium handles at the business entrance. It looked plain. Ordinary.

Colin Craig was with his senior officers to conduct a personal test of the toy. They would then formulate and execute plans to bring them up to speed on the TAC technology.

He found it difficult to believe that the TAC worked as described. Mind over matter in a kid's toy – absurd. How could that be?

Craig read the printed instructions that came with the toy, then without a word to the other men in the room put the helmet on his head and stared at the car. When there was no immediate response he shook his head, then realized how absurd that must look. He took the helmet off and checked the instruction sheet again and looked at the power switch; it was in the "on" position. The batteries were inserted correctly. He picked up the car and turned it over; the power switch was on there too. He checked the car's battery compartment; all was as it should be.

Craig settled the helmet over his head once again. The instructions said, "Direct the car to move in the same manner you command your arm to change position." He did this, with no result. His forehead creased and he felt a tickle of sweat. Still nothing happened. He stared harder, trying to will the thing to move. Imagine it? Picture the wanted motions? It just sat there. Long seconds edged by, then more, until the silence in the room and the car's motionlessness were uncomfortably long. He let out a small moan – part concentrated effort, part despair. His face flushed bright red. He was earning his humiliation the hard way. Why couldn't he do this? Why?

He looked up and his confusion deepened. These men were openly enjoying themselves at his expense. They weren't usually so obvious. Why would they do this when any one of them could just as easily find himself in the same predicament in minutes? All of them were going to try the toy out.

Smirks hidden behind raised hands and shared looks became open laughter. Real uproarious prankster laughter – knee-slapping, tear-streaming laughter. Looks of comic glee were exchanged.

Colin Craig, the Director of Central Intelligence, had gone white. Had his face remained in a red flush, the boys would have continued laughing, but for some reason this episode struck to the core of Craig's confidence as a man. His face drained of all color. He wondered if it were true – that he had little or no control over his mind and thoughts?

The Directory Electronics people were clear. You could evaluate a person's state of mind (or lack of it) by their ability to use the toy. Maybe he was stupid. In an organization where intelligence was at a premium, to be seen as stupid was the ultimate criticism.

The merriment died. For most there is no joy in seeing a man stripped of a thing that secures him personally. Like a sexual failure with a woman, made public. They knew they had gone too far. Much too far; career-damagingly far.

A heavy silence settled. Some seconds passed.

"Sir, it was a joke. Look." One of the men displayed another helmet. "This is the correct helmet, the one that controls the car in front of you." The D/CIA looked at him and then the others. He wanted to kill them.

"You sons of bitches!" The venom made them flinch. Immediately grasping the situation, Craig's self-possession rushed back and he snatched the offered helmet and exchanged it with the one on his head. Instantly, the car leaped off the table and started describing figure eights over the maroon carpet. Then circles and reverses. The D/CIA even held the toy car on two wheels as he took corners very fast. Clearly, he was in excellent control of the little vehicle and, by extension, his mind. A look of violent satisfaction suffused his features.

"Now, everyone in the room is going to have his turn," he said with utter finality. His Deputy Director for Operations reached for the helmet, but the D/CIA said, "You last, Ralph." They all took their turns with varying degrees of success but no one matched Craig. No one came close.

"Your turn, Ralph. I'm sure you arranged this little farce. I'm gonna watch you humiliate yourself – you won't control the car. That'll show us all that you've no control over your mind." The D/CIA said it with certainty, and the others in the room wondered what he knew that they didn't. They looked back and forth between the two men. The tension between them hummed like the string of a drawn bow.

Ralph Perrywhite had indeed engineered this event; he'd had his satisfaction – however short-lived – and now Craig wanted *his*. Craig felt certain that Perrywhite would fail, for as surely as Craig was straightforward, Perrywhite was devious; Craig dynamic, Perrywhite evading. So it stood to reason that if he could exert good control over the car, then Perrywhite would fail.

Perrywhite had Ph.D.s in a number of fields, including Psychology. He was very intelligent and quite insufferable. His self-proclaimed understanding of human nature led him to undermine others with snide comments about their supposed mental condition. When challenged, he invariably responded, "Just kidding. Don't be so touchy. You might convince me there *is* something to it."

"Come on, Perrywhite, the enjoyable portion of your little game is over. Now it's your turn to entertain this audience, to entertain me." Perrywhite hesitated, intimidated by the D/CIA's tone. "Pick up the helmet." Perrywhite reached for the helmet and again hesitated. "Pick it up." Craig felt like beating the crap out of this worm.

Ralph Perrywhite panicked; he hadn't tried the toy himself, he hadn't needed to. His self-assessed brilliance extended to all areas of life and easily encompassed something as minor as this toy.

Now he wasn't so sure. But he could think of no way out of the corner he was in. If he blew out of the room now he would be finished at the Agency. No one would respect him; he would be a laughingstock, an eternal butt of jokes. He'd felt *so good* just minutes ago. Where had that gone?

Perrywhite snatched the helmet – his motions confident, assertive and disdainful. He had the training and the brain power and the will. He settled the helmet on his head.

Some in the room were wondering how such a professional group of men could be reduced to this level; others knew exactly why. The Director had ignored Perrywhite's continual undermining sarcasm and obstructive plotting. His tolerance of this had reached an end. That much was obvious.

Ralph Perrywhite, Deputy Director for Operations of the CIA, adjusted the helmet on his head and immediately the car went into reverse and banged into a wall. It then shot across to the far wall and banged into it. The car wheels kept spinning on the rug for so long that any impression of controlled action was lost. Eyes were moving between the car and the Deputy, his forehead dotted with emerging droplets of sweat. The beads fattened and ran down his face and the smell of fear arose.

Finally, the car did some jerky movements, and then went into a manic reverse circle. Some had thought Perrywhite would get the best of the Director. Looking at him now, this was clearly not the case. He was sweating profusely and had an intense crazed look twisting his features. The toy's movements degenerated until it would only move an inch forward, then an inch backward, then a slight rocking movement, then stillness.

Ralph Perrywhite ripped the helmet from his head, threw it violently at the car and rushed from the room.

•

Colin Craig gave orders directing an immediate and thorough investigation.

"The TAC technology must quickly come under our control. This emerging technology in the hands of the wrong people, will cause catastrophic consequences. The power structure of the world will be reordered in an unforeseeable image.

"We must prevent this."

"Sir, the TAC has thousands of other applications far more profitable, more obvious, and more dangerous. This toy car is almost inexplicable."

Craig replied. "You're right. It feels like we're being deliberately provoked, or baited, by Directory Electronics. The toy car is an absurd 'vehicle' for the release of this extraordinary technology."

"What I can't figure," said one of his men, "is how Directory Electronics felt they could release the TAC technology and expect to survive inevitable backlash? They're in the United States and they need our protection. What will the Russians or Chinese do to get control?"

"Just about anything," someone murmured.

"This whole thing with this toy is insane," said Craig. "I've never seen a situation like this before."

"Maybe DE are tech geeks and have no idea of the firestorm they've started," an officer commented.

"I don't think so," Craig replied. "The release of the toy is an act of supreme confidence – and that is unique. How can a startup company in Las Vegas Nevada expect to survive the onslaught of every covert agency in the world?"

"One thing, sir, explains it all." He paused for dramatic effect. "They have other technology. They don't act afraid because they aren't."

That observation kept everyone at the table quiet for some time.

"We must assume," said Craig, "this company is not irrational – they have goals we are unaware of. We must be very careful.

"There is an undefined threat here – knowing its extent is crucial. From a business or economic, or technological or political perspective nothing DE is doing makes sense.

"From all your desks I need proposals for immediate, medium, and long range action.

"Have the short term proposals to me in one hour." Craig would ensure the CIA takeover of Directory Electronics, or its destruction.

The tentacles went out.

●

Ralph Perrywhite was in hell. The confidence his education had bestowed, his personal superiority, was crumbling. The hick farm boy who was the D/CIA, a Business major no less, had defeated him in a public showdown.

What Perrywhite would never tell another living soul was this: when he willed the car forward it went backwards. He willed it backward, it went forward. He tried to stop it and the wheels just about burned themselves out. Then it wouldn't move at all, no matter what he did, no matter what he tried. His head pounded and throbbed.

He put a hand to his forehead. It was hot.

Sick. That was the reason. "I'm sick!"

"I would have beaten the D/CIA in that silly test if I wasn't ill!" he said to himself.

He was sure the illness had started before he went to the D/CIA's office. When he awoke that morning he had coughed. He had begun the day physically sick and it got worse.

Only supreme dedication to his job enabled him, heroically, to hold out to the end of that terrible meeting.

Illness was the cause of his failure.

I don't lack for brain power, he thought.

Perrywhite went to the medical station on the ground floor and saw the resident physician.

"Mr. Perrywhite, you have a temperature of 101.7 degrees. You should go home and make an appointment to see your personal physician immediately."

"Please inform the Director of my medical condition."

"Right away, sir."

He left the building and headed home. He would never use that toy car again. What a piece of crap.

The fever raged for days. He came to one conclusion during those days: he would seek out the head of Directory Electronics.

● ● ●

Jack was in his jeep headed south on Interstate 15, his loaded backpack in the rear. But he wasn't going camping. The destination was Las Vegas, where else? He didn't know what he could learn about Directory Electronics, or what he could do, but the frustration of inactivity and doing nothing to find out more about them had been too much. Increasingly he felt the need to take control of events, but had no real goal – only that he must do something.

The incident at the baseball game with the kid and his TAC car still bothered him. It was an abnormal reaction.

Up ahead was an exit, Cedar City; he took it and was soon in the drive-thru at a burger joint. He pulled into a large empty parking lot to eat his lunch and not surprisingly, there were a bunch of kids playing with their TAC cars. They were having a great time doing drag races, smashing the cars head on, performing agility tricks and jumping ramps as they whooped with laughter.

These kids look liberated in a way he had never seen before. They loved those toys.

Not so for him. As had happened at the baseball game, just by looking at them playing with the toys Jack felt a growing pain in his head. He let the pain come in at him. He didn't try to stop it, push it aside, compress it, wish it away or take an aspirin, as one might do with a normal headache.

He let the sensation take its course and observed himself. After a while of simply watching the kids and cars the sharpness of the pain diminished. Finally the kids sat under a tree, pulled out sandwiches from lunch bags and chattered, laughed and told jokes. Jack reached out mentally and tried to make a car move. Nothing happened. Then he realized the TAC was in the helmet. He reached out again, placing his attention on one helmet, then the next, until he found one with the power still on.

"Hey, that's my car!" The kid jumped up and ran after it. He skidded to a halt and came back for the helmet and turned the power off. The car stopped and he walked over to it and picked it up. Back with his friends Jack heard the kid say, "That was weird."

The pain in Jack's head had peaked and died, then peaked again and settled into a nasty throb at the back of his head. It was as he suspected, he could use the TAC, but didn't want to. It made him sick, made his head hurt.

Jack drove south through St. George and then across the tip of Arizona, dropping into the Virgin River Gorge. His head cleared as he looked at the red cliff faces and panoramic landscape. The scenery was stark, lonely and captivating. He began to breathe freely and enjoy the trip. Then he was through the gorge and running south.

Less than two hours later, with his head feeling better, he arrived in Las Vegas. Over the last hundred miles he had clarified his plans about what to do in this city. He located the coffee shops closest to the Directory Electronics facility and did drive-bys. He was not looking for the DE workers, but for those who were looking for them. He was in no position to take any action. Drawing attention from DE intelligence agents was something he did not want.

He parked some distance away and walked to the coffee shop. He had suspicions. The first of them was soon confirmed.

Jack was sipping his latte when an older guy who had that military look took a seat near him. Jack tipped the cup back and swallowed. Good coffee. He smiled.

This guy is an agent of the U.S. government investigating Directory Electronics, Jack thought. To confirm this he looked over at the older man and said, "How 'bout those kids' cars and their thought-activated circuit!" Jack smiled as the guy sputtered out some of his beverage.

Got ya. Jack smiled.

If Directory Electronics was a known entity, there would be no investigation. This told Jack almost all he needed to know about DE and fulfilled the purpose of his trip.

Jack looked at the guy.

"That coffee too hot?" Jack asked politely. He chatted with the military guy for some time about sports, cars, the weather and other trivial things. And then he made up a story about a science fiction book he had read, describing the subtle differences between the earth natives and the others.

The drive home was long and lonely. The dark of night descended and the spray of the Milky Way was bright where the lights of man were absent. His thoughts were dark, without any illumination. His suspicions were dredging up emotions he was not prepared to face. But his conclusions had solidified. He knew what he needed to know; that gave him a vastly bigger problem.

The Salt Lake valley was home, but for some reason there was no comfort in that thought. Comfort, he realized, would be in short supply for some time to come.

● ● ●

Sharon Cousins, Jack's aunt, was following the controversy over the Thought Activated Circuit as it played out through the media. There were elements of absurd comedy and serious undertones. She wondered if the Directory Electronics compound in Las Vegas would end up being surrounded by the military and taken over by force. But it was too soon for that yet.

After a short time on the market their toy car was the talk of the town. No, that didn't do it credit; it was the talk of the planet.

Directory Electronics PR did not have all public opinion going their way. There were some very vicious and determined critics of DE and their Thought Activated Circuit (TAC).

Sharon sat down to watch a popular but trashy daytime TV talk show. Four pairs of people had been selected to demonstrate their skill using the TAC car.

The first two "competitors" who would contrast their skill level were escorted to the stage.

Show host: "Please introduce yourselves to the studio audience."

"My name is Dr. Andrew Collison. I'm a college professor," declared a man from the hallowed halls of academia. "I have Ph.D.s in physics, chemistry and electronics. I have serious concerns about the so-called 'thought activated circuit.' I consider it defective and non-functional."

The audience jeered him; they had heard it before – some snooty educated person who couldn't pass the TAC test.

Show host: "And who are you?"

"My name is Billy Stubbs and I'm a kid in third grade. I love my car and it works just fine."

The audience cheered the spunky kid.

Show host: "Each of you have had ten minutes back stage to practice with your cars. Now the competition begins. The professor versus the third grader!"

The audience let loose with cheering, cat calls and whistling.

Show host: "Gentlemen, start your engines."

The studio trolls loved it.

Show host: "Set your cars on the track in front of you." Black for the professor and red for the kid. "Now place the helmet on your head." The professor and the kid did it.

The show host raised a checkered flag and then swooped it down.

"Go!!" yelled the audience.

The red car shot across the start line and began to run the elaborate track with some skill.

The black car moved in fits and starts and the professor cheated by using his foot to get his car going.

Thirty seconds later accompanied by applause the kid's red car flashed across the finish line. The show host really got the checkered flag going.

Show host: "We have a winner!!"

The black car had hardly made it to the first turn.

Show host: "Professor Collison, can you explain your humiliating loss to an eight year old?"

"Yes, I can. Obviously the helmet is defective." He set it on a chair.

The kid made a face, to the crowd's delight. He took off his own helmet and snatched up the adult-sized one which covered half his face. Soon the black car was racing around the track.

"Oh yeah, see that car go. Oh yeah, I'm good. I-am-so-good!" The kid stuck his tongue out right at the professor and did a great sloppy raspberry.

"You little shit!" The professor lunged for the kid, but was held back by the stage bouncers.

"You're an idiot – that's why you can't make the car work!" Then he put his hands on his small hips and ran the car right at the professor. "Even my little sister can make it work, you dork." The professor threw something and the kid danced aside, the smirk never leaving his face.

He stuck his tongue out again, then took off running as the infuriated professor broke away from his guards and gave chase.

The studio audience loved it.

Sharon had tears in her eyes. Billy Stubbs had a career in show business.

Sharon could tell the humiliation of those who failed to make the TAC work was visceral. Watching a program that played people's lower emotions against each other was not something she often did.

But the TAC was important. Strangely, Jack had not purchased a TAC car to investigate its technology – as he had done with numerous other new gadgets the first moment they were released.

It seemed, from all she had learned about the TAC, some people could guide their cars from blocks away, while others could barely get them to operate at all. And all skill levels in between. Newsprint, TV and radio talk shows, internet bloggers and the nightly news were all demanding an explanation.

People who couldn't control the cars attacked the invention savagely. They returned the toys to their point of purchase as defective. Eventually so many "defective" units had been refunded that Directory

Electronics was forced to consider holding a press conference to clarify the matter.

Then another incident changed the nature of the debate about the toy, Directory Electronics, and the TAC.

Sharon was intrigued when Directory Electronics and the Thought Activated Circuit infringed upon another power base embedded in Earth's culture – the Psychiatrists. And she was fascinated when they came out swinging.

●

Jack and Wendy, finished with school for the day, walked into the Cousins' house a week after the big baseball game.

"Jack, is that you?" called Sharon Cousins, his aunt, the woman who had taken on the role of *mother* in his life. When she and Norman adopted Jack, it was for her a fulfillment that had come in the wake of the definite knowledge that she could not have a child of her own. She knew her brother-in-law and his wife, Jack's birth parents, were not affectionate and resented Jack's presence in their home. She had seen this for herself on the few occasions they had been invited to visit. Little Jack was completely lost and unloved in that home and it had broken her heart to see him alternately resented or ignored. She, on the other hand, was a naturally affectionate woman.

"It's Wendy and me, Aunt Sharon."

Sharon looked at them as they came into the living room where she had been watching the outrageous TV shows. For years she had devoted her time to Jack and had taken him and Wendy to many of their after-school activities, a duty she shared with Amanda White, Wendy's mother.

A few years ago, as Jack grew older and she had more time to herself, she decided to put her training as a CPA to good use. First she went to the local community college and became expert in the latest software programs being used and specifically those used in her husband Norman's many businesses. She began side-checking the figures the lead accountants were giving him. This led to a quiet investigation she personally conducted, a number of dismissals and the eventual prosecution of three very guilty conspirators for taking a lot of money they had not earned. Her role never became public knowledge. She saved and recovered millions for Norman.

Instead of continuing to work for her husband as she had planned, Sharon was quietly approached by another company to check their books. Now she called herself a Forensic Accountant. She consulted only the largest corporations around the world and did this from seven in the morning to one in the afternoon four days a week, and kept to this schedule strictly so it didn't take over her life. She charged hourly or a percentage of the recovery, whichever was greater. It was amazing the amount of money some people thought they could steal without detection. Often the plans to defraud were brilliant and went undetected for years. She liked the challenge and the satisfaction of a job well done, but life at home was still where her real concern and attention were directed. When Jack was gone from their home she would then more fully reorganize her life. But that was still to come.

Sharon enjoyed seeing Jack and Wendy together and the casual affection they had for each other. They came into the room hand in hand and she smiled. When Jack had first arrived in their home years ago, it had taken him more than a month to begin to put his slender boy's arms around her when she hugged him. The wariness finally went out of his eyes when he realized she loved him and what that really meant. His mother, it turned out, had said she loved him but avoided all human contact. Sharon was looking right at him when he finally *knew* her affection was real and would remain constant. They had exchanged the look of love. With the moment over, young Jack happily took off running and she walked to her room, closed the door and cried her heart out.

Jack touched Sharon's arm and gave her cheek a kiss.

"Hello, Mrs. Cousins," Wendy said.

"Hi, Wendy." It was time, Sharon decided, for a transition. "Wendy, I'd like you to call me Sharon."

Wendy looked at the older woman and realized that when she called her "Mrs. Cousins" she felt a little uncomfortable. It dawned on her that Sharon was aware of her discomfort. She really was a good detective, and not just with figures and balance sheets.

"Thanks Sharon, that feels more natural."

"You're not a kid anymore, and we are friends."

They smiled. Then Sharon turned to Jack. "Got a great story for you two."

Jack had watched the two women closest to him and decided it was time for another transition. "Tell us, Mom."

Sharon, who was excited to tell them the story, checked what she was going to say and blinked and blinked again, and was quiet.

"You are my mom, Aunt Sharon. I hope you don't mind me calling you that."

Sharon shook her head. "No, I don't mind at all!" Jack glanced at Wendy and she gave him a slight nod. And Jack, who had thought about doing this from time to time, seeing her reaction, wondered why he had waited.

"You were going to tell us a story, Sharon," said Wendy quietly, happy for her and wanting her to recover gracefully.

"Yes. It's amazing. You know I have a reputation now for tracking down…"

Jack and Wendy laughed. Sharon was good at understatement.

"Norman and I were talking a couple weeks ago and we hit upon a plan to increase the number of clients I handle, but at the same time reduce the amount of work."

"That sounds like a great plan, Mom."

"Yes, well, it worked." Sharon laughed. "Last week a UK company contacted me. Norman, four of his attorneys and I stayed up all night and drafted an agreement. The company liked the idea so much they signed three days ago.

"What we did was to announce to all the employees that if they came clean on their malfeasance and made restitution, they would be exempted from civil and criminal prosecution. I informed them my audit had begun and gave them two days to decide. Three of their senior executives left the country that night."

She sat at her laptop and tapped a few keys. "Eleven employees have taken advantage of the program and are giving details of their embezzlement as we speak. We've reduced the time of the investigation to about five percent, given some of the lesser offenders a break, and we'll still catch and prosecute the three big fish who took off!

"So this is quick and thorough, and the UK company will get back on track much sooner. *My* fee will be bigger because the attorney fees are less, and sometimes after we start an investigation the offenders rip a company apart before we can track them down. That whole scenario is avoided.

"We've also been contracted to find and install replacement executives. So we eliminate the bad guys and patch the holes; a full service operation. How do you like that?"

Jack looked dumbstruck. "Wow, Mom, I'm impressed." Wendy nodded her agreement.

"What will your fee be, Sharon?"

Sharon tapped a few keys on a calculator. "It's in excess of two million dollars as of this moment. It's a large multinational corp. based in London. Whatever my final fee is, it will only be a small fraction of their yearly legal budget!"

Wendy goggled at the amount. "You could buy a really nice house with that!"

Sharon didn't mistake Wendy's intent. "Norman and I could have lived in the very best part of town or anywhere in the world for that matter. But we never wanted to."

Wendy had gone a little pink. Sharon continued, "Do you remember, Jack, why that is?"

Jack looked at her and for the life of him couldn't remember a conversation about the subject. They had never talked about moving; he had never wanted to move, and the subject had never come up. He shook his head.

"We were all at the dinner table, you, Norman and me. This was just after your first day at school. You were really excited. You were talking about this girl you met. And among other things, you said, 'I'm really glad we live near Wendy,' and that was it."

"That's why you never moved?" Wendy asked.

"Yep. And after you two are out on your own, we may move. It just hasn't been important. And as you know, we don't lack for anything."

This woman, Jack's mother, was really something. Wendy wondered at how you could be around someone, be very familiar with them, like them, love them even, but not fully know them. For the first time she saw Sharon was a strikingly capable woman: independent, married, taking care of family responsibilities, an integrated person. And she's happy. You could see it.

Sharon could see Wendy taking her measure, probably for the first time in any meaningful way. That's why Sharon never worked in the afternoon, never allowed work to impinge on family, ever. Norman could and probably should, but not her: she did not want it to.

But today was a transition in more than how she and Wendy addressed each other. In Sharon's own childhood there had been many friendships with boys and no matter how intense those relationships felt at the time, they had never developed into anything more. She and Norman met in college and got married after they graduated. Wendy was a casual visitor who in time became a smitten young girl. When Wendy entered her mid-teens, Sharon could tell that she felt Jack was rejecting her because he made no sexual advances. Sharon and Jack had discussed it thoroughly on a number of occasions and she had advised him to be affectionate but not sexually active. That advice, she was happy to observe, had corresponded to Jack's native inclination.

"I think, Aunt Sharon, that I should figure out if Wendy and I are likely to survive in a marriage before we have sex. And you can't find that out in a month or a year. Not at my age." His opinion had surprised her – shocked her, really. "There is no dignity in having sex with anyone and everyone you can, even if you want to at that moment. I always want to be able to respect myself."

"That's very mature, Jack."

Jack frowned, "You know, I never felt like a kid, even when I was little."

Sharon marveled that in this sex-driven culture Jack remained unaffected by it. More than this, he had strong opinions and strong morals and she loved him more for it. And he was right: although he was happy, excitable and imaginative like other children, his attitudes had always been mature.

So today she fully realized something else. Her expectation that Wendy and Jack's relationship would be short-lived, as her own early encounters had been, was wrong: Wendy was here to stay and from all she could tell, for the right reasons.

●

"I watched some television today. You know the remote control cars with the Thought Activated Circuit, the control helmet?"

Jack and Wendy exchanged a look and laughed. "Mom, there is *nothing else* being talked about at school – and when I say *nothing* I mean n-o-t-h-i-n-g."

"Sharon, after the boys had their TAC drag races – and this was done during every free minute – they began to wonder what other uses this technology could be used for."

"Oh yeah, what'd they come up with?"

Embarrassed, Wendy said. "These are high school boys – mostly sex toys."

"Yes, they would think like that." Sharon said dryly.

The whole subject of the TAC continued to make Jack nauseated, literally. While his friends yammered on and on, he tried to ignore it all. They wanted his opinion, he felt increasingly sick.

He was not about to admit this weakness to anyone, so he avoided the conversation where he could. Now Wendy and his mother were shoving it at him again. The more he tried to avoid it, the more it followed him.

"There were so many cars at school today the Principal banned them from the campus," Wendy explained. "After the boys' obvious sex toy jokes, kids argued about whether the technology worked. And 'mental control.' Like everyone else – some can work it, some can't." Wendy shook her head. "The kids who can't get their cars to work are sometimes those with the best GPAs. The arguments were intense."

"I imagine the future holds employment for those who can control a TAC." Sharon said.

"You're right. I hadn't thought about that." Wendy continued, "Then the kids talked about who had developed this technology. That's the big mystery. No one, and I mean *not one single person,* thinks some rinky-dink company in Las Vegas invented this technology. How could they?"

Sharon frowned. "Is that right, Jack?" He shrugged and nodded.

"It's everywhere, and to tell the truth, I've had more than enough of it." Jack looked away.

Sharon frowned. *Maybe he couldn't use the TAC. That would make anyone touchy.* She would know soon enough.

She pushed a little, to engage him, so he could understand his resistance and get past it. *This is an important human and technological issue. It appears to be the crossover point – man meets machine.* What she had seen on TV today was an interesting quirk. After the show she'd gone out to purchase five of the toys (with different helmet sizes). She noticed a long line at the return counter, most with the helmet and toy car in hand and angry looks on their faces.

"There was a panel of mental health experts on TV today and they were discussing their findings about the Natell car and the TAC." She picked up the TV remote and replayed the segment. "Watch this." Jack was about to protest and then shrugged. He wasn't going to escape it. The warmth he felt on their arrival home evaporated as the pain in his head returned, dull and thumping, in rhythm with his pulse beat.

Absurdly dramatic intro music played before the talking head introduced a panel of eminent psychiatrists and psychologists to discuss the Natell toy car and the TAC. The panel's credentials were given to prove that this group of men and women were experts on the brain, human behavior and human potential.

Jack got up to go the bathroom and told them not to pause it. He ran the cold tap for a few seconds and splashed water on his face again and again. He felt a bit better. As he approached the living room he heard Sharon and Wendy talking, but didn't hear what they said. He sat and looked at the TV.

Talking Head: "You have some startling results from the intensive research your panel conducted over the last few weeks. Can you tell us about that?"

Psych #1: "Yes, we have concluded, after serious study of the Natell car and the TAC, that it is a hoax being perpetrated on the unsuspecting American people and the people of the world."

Talking Head: "That's quite an accusation. Especially in light of the kids who claim it works as advertised by Natell Toys and Directory Electronics."

Psych #2: "Children are easily deceived."

Psych #1: "Everyone has been deceived. After intensive study and practical trials we have concluded that there is no such thing as a thought activated circuit and we advise that all parents return the toy before irreparable harm is done to their children's mental health."

Talking Head: "Those are strong words."

Psych #1: "All the children in our trials displayed a disturbing and deepened state of mental anxiety while using this toy."

"Actually that's not true at all," said Jack. "Any of the kids I've seen using the toy were either very intent or very excited or both. To call it 'anxiety' is stupid and intentionally misleading. It's a dishonest interpretation of results." Wendy and Sharon frowned but did not reply.

Psych #2: "Proof of extreme mental harm these kids suffered was demonstrated conclusively. Once we administered the standard dosage of the appropriate medication, the usual prescription for ADHD, the children returned to normal and our research was complete."

Talking Head: "What do you mean by 'normal'?"

Psych #2: "The children's minds were then unaffected by the TAC helmet. In fact the children, when properly medicated, uniformly rejected the headgear and sought other forms of entertainment."

Talking Head: "That does seem conclusive."

Psych #1: "We are recommending to the appropriate governmental bodies that immediate action be taken to suspend sales of this toy. We're also advising a Congressional panel be formed immediately to review our findings with the ultimate goal of banning the toy, and protecting young minds from unnecessary turmoil and irreparable damage. Would any caring parent knowingly place their child in harm's way for a dangerous and misleading thrill which can place the child's mental stability in jeopardy? This toy has the potential of adversely affecting the child's entire developmental future. We recommend psychiatrists prescribe appropriate medication for any child who has come into contact with this dangerous toy."

Talking Head: "A public service has been done today…"

Jack reached for the remote and silenced the TV. "I wonder what that was all about."

Sharon nodded. "I thought that too. There's plenty of evidence that the toy works. So why…" Sharon had used one of the helmets with the red toy sports car this afternoon and it worked very well for her.

"Probably money," Wendy said.

"No, no…" Jack had their attention. "Well, yes, money, Dee; but not just money. It's power, too."

"What 'power,' Jack?" Wendy asked.

"Well, for the psychiatrists, it's the power that comes from being the acknowledged leader in the mysteries of the mind. When something goes wrong with someone's head, when they go batty, who is called in to treat it, to comment on it, to determine what is wrong? To fix it? It's the psychiatrist, or in some cases psychologists. They control what is done to a person. They control the state of that person's mind by the administration of drugs and other procedures. They can deprive a person of their freedom. The *power* of their position is very strong and scattered through the society, even in the law. Who's guilty, who's innocent. That's strong stuff and big money. Something to protect."

Wendy and Sharon looked at him. "You see, don't you? If the Thought Activated Circuit really works, then someone knows much more about the workings of the mind than all the psychiatrists you can bake into a rhubarb pie. And the toy will actually help a child's or anyone's state of mind. If they had done a real study then this would have been obvious."

"But why attack Directory Electronics with false accusations if the toy works and it helps someone's mind? Why attack if DE is more knowledgeable, can bring greater understanding?" Sharon asked.

"The person who set this psychiatric panel up must be looking into the future and seeing he no longer exists." Jack paused. "You were in the toy store today, Mom?"

"Yes, I was there." She smiled. Jack was good at connecting the dots too.

"How many people were returning the toy?"

She thought for a minute. "Maybe fifty people."

"That's a lot. Multiply that across the country and around the world and that's big. Very big. Enough for DE to take notice, enough for a strong reaction."

"You think this psychiatric panel was just a ploy to extort money from Directory Electronics?" Wendy asked.

"Yes! The toy does work, even if some people can't make it function well. Its technology is based on actual mind function or else it *couldn't* work. A month from now, without the interference from the psychiatric panel, there will be no one seriously arguing the toy isn't a legitimate phenomenon. The world will be divided into three categories – can use it, can't use it, and too scared to find out. It's timing. They have to undermine confidence now or miss their opportunity to squeeze out any money at all."

"So psychiatrists eventually *will* be discredited on this issue and eventually lose whatever power they retain," Sharon mused. "Why didn't whoever is behind today's show just quietly approach DE and become their ally, learn what they know?"

"Too many easy dollars to pass up," Wendy concluded. "Also no guarantee DE would share any real information; the TAC must be a trade secret, and even if it isn't, DE would lose all their leverage if the technology got out into the open. They aren't going to risk that." She thought it through. "Can you imagine any leader of the mental health profession going cap in hand to a startup company in Las Vegas, for post-graduate studies about the mind? I can't – too humiliating."

Jack nodded. "Yes, big bucks for one or two people and demise for the rest of the profession. But this issue will settle, soon. The psychiatric panel will repudiate today's conclusions, probably tomorrow or the day after. But it's not just the psychiatrists who are in for a shakeup. Many long-treasured sacred cows will fall in the face of this technology, and many groups will find the power they once held, erode and vanish." He smiled through the pain in his head.

"That's very broad, Jack," Sharon said.

"Maybe so. Who can see at this point what other technology DE has, or the changes it will cause? This toy, alone, is like an atomic bomb of truth. You can be sure it's only the beginning."

"Do you know something about Directory Electronics that we don't, Jack?" Wendy asked. Jack gave a grim smile.

"No, I'm extrapolating; trying to logically extend from known data and guess its effects on the future. But don't underestimate the impact the TAC alone will have, is having. One whole profession is already scrambling."

"I think he's right," Sharon said. "The TAC is big. I used one of the cars today. I can work it. It's a little miracle, really, quite profound in its own way. But it won't end here." They were quiet for a minute. Sharon continued. "Can you imagine what this is doing to the governments of the world? To our government? What they must be doing to try to find out what is really going on?"

Jack said, "Anyone in power on earth who has a little imagination or foresight must be scared to death. There must be a lot of confusion. And I wouldn't like to be a psychiatrist on the day it comes to pay the bill for what that panel said today. I think they stood in front of a freight train."

No one commented on that grim prediction.

"Wendy, I got the toy for you and Jack as well as myself and Norman."

"You did? Thanks, Sharon. I tried one of my friend's TAC car for a few seconds but haven't had the chance to become familiar with one yet."

"You're welcome, Wendy. Want to try yours, Jack? It's really a lot of fun once you get the hang of it."

"I've tried it already." Wendy and Sharon hadn't seen him try the toy car and Jack was not about to explain about his controlling other kids' toys from a distance; his head was a ball of pain.

"Let's go outside and race our cars around." Sharon and Wendy went outside and were soon laughing and having a great time.

● ● ●

Later that night, after a long run to clear his head, Jack lay in bed pondering. As he looked at his own immediate future he saw darkness; it both scared and exhilarated him. How does one communicate such a nebulous disturbing thing to another; to the two women who love him? To his uncle? He would not scare them with his dark premonition. He'd had disturbing visions of the future before which had not come to pass.

Who could tell if this was one of those?

He didn't think it was.

CHAPTER 4

FOLLOWING HIS USUAL MORNING ROUTINE, THE Chief of Directory Electronics sat in his office in Las Vegas viewing a summary of press and assorted media generated about his high tech "toy" over the last twenty-four hours. He had acquired a taste for hot coffee, bagels and strawberry cream cheese with a sugary donut thrown in.

A minute into his reading he let out a howl of rage.

The Chief quickly scanned through thousands of column inches of negative press. He looked at video clips of the psychiatric panel and its discussion. Then clips of the press reporting the panel's conclusions.

How dare they, he seethed.

He switched from the summary and looked at the unedited versions. A bellow of rage stopped production throughout the facility.

The story would not end. All over the world it was repeated and regurgitated and analyzed by the press.

Over and over and over and over.

The endless reverberation of the most damaging and inaccurate data was *still* coming in from news services all around the world. *Across this planet people are waking up to lies about my car*, he thought.

Psychiatrists must be a deeply entrenched influential group. Had to be, to create this much trouble, get this much press coverage this quickly.

"Research!" he bellowed.

They came running.

"I need to know what a psychiatrist is. I need *full* profiles on every person on that panel and their families and business associates."

"Yes, sir."

"I want to know everything about the study they conducted with our TAC cars. I want to know who the children were, their ages, their parents. I want to know where and when this study was conducted, how long it took. I want the drugs they were given analyzed. I want everything on the psychiatric researchers – and reasons they would lie. I want to know everything about it."

"Yes, sir.

"Start now!" The researchers ran back to their office.

The lies spread by the media were cutting across the execution of vital program targets. He had to take immediate action or risk derailing his entire mission.

The situation could go critical.

It must not.

Standard planning could still go forward after this hiccup – if it could be made into a hiccup. Or the operation could go to hell. A worse time couldn't have been chosen and he felt a stab of paranoia, wondering how the enemy knew just when to strike.

No. No one is aware of our plans, he thought, *most of my people have no idea of what we are doing or why. To succeed, our goals for the planet and its people must remain secret.*

At this stage he was juggling many separate actions, each one must follow the other in proper sequence. Take one out…

Damn these people.

The Chief was thinking fast, *the language used by the psychiatric panel could be used by US politicians to justify a public move against our facility here in Vegas with their military.* The clandestine crap was easy to thwart. But a public move? *If that happens,* he thought, *I'll lose my job.* A job he had mortgaged his soul to obtain.

This crisis response required delicacy. Fury welled up, choking him. *No. No.* He forced his emotion down. *I must finesse this. I must consolidate my position, then all else will follow.*

The Chief looked in on the researchers – hard at work. Good.

"Action and PR, you're on alert. As soon as Research has data we'll evaluate and you'll get your orders."

"Yes, sir."

The professional teams (PR, Research and Action) now at his disposal would only be staying on station through Recognition. They were here to help with unpredictable problems. As now. Every culture was different. No matter how well planned each operation was, unseen variables always came up.

Recognition was the stable point he needed to achieve; all his efforts were driving toward this goal. This quickly led to Acceptance, Expansion and Full Control.

Research, PR and Action teams plus the many construction staff would be reassigned after Recognition. He had to take advantage of their expertise, because once they were gone he would be forced to make do with the inferior permanent personnel allotted to the station.

All problems must be settled before Recognition.

The research team quickly infiltrated all relevant information networks. In minutes he had full preliminary data and ordered immediate electronic surveillance on the leader of the psychiatric panel, a Doctor Melliander, who was isolated and confirmed as the driving force behind yesterday's fiasco and as the originator of the content. No one on the panel had surveilled the Las Vegas facility; they were not government agents.

He picked up a long neglected donut and slowly chewed on it as he read the final report. The report contained a startling word: "DuChu."

"Research!" They arrived.

"Sir?"

"DuChu, are you sure?"

"Quite sure. Psychiatrists are equivalent to the long extinct DuChu." *It's good to know whom we are dealing with*, the Chief thought, *especially when they don't know you.*

The Chief read further into the report. "So there was no study?"

"Correct, sir. The study location, time, personnel and subjects do not coincide. It's a false report, sir."

"Purpose?"

"Extortion," the researcher said.

"Why?"

"Melliander is not stupid – well not completely. He sees our TAC car as a threat to his profession. The psychiatric power base on this planet is very extensive. We come along with our thought activated circuit. Melliander must know that if our toy works then we know a hell of a lot more about the mind than he does."

"So he thinks we'll put him out of work?"

"Essentially that's it."

"What was the drug Melliander said he gave the kids?" The researcher handed over the chemical breakdown.

"There were no kids, because there was no study. But we looked into it for you." The Chief loved how thorough these guys were.

"They give this chemical compound to children?" asked the Chief.

"All the time." The researcher grimaced.

Within minutes the PR and Action teams gave the Chief their proposals.

"We recommend massive bribery of Melliander. He reverses his study findings and gives full support of the TAC and Directory Electronics. Elimination teams should be ready to remove other opportunistic psychiatrists who may try to copycat Melliander's successful operation."

"Good, do it."

The Chief of Directory Electronics referred to the basic Mission Reference Manual (MRM). Prior to Recognition, resistance fell into a few main categories. The government of the host country usually had an Intelligence agency. The United States of America had many. Research was still classifying them and analyzing which were engaging in the investigation of DE. Opposition could come from the military and its Intelligence arm. Lawmakers could use economics to stifle growth. Public Relations and news outlets could impose major barriers to Recognition. And there it was in the manual: if the DuChu ("Psychiatrists") were powerful and smart, they could cause trouble in a wide variety of ways. Bribery and suppression were listed as the only solutions. His team had taken their solution straight from the manual. Good.

Foreign countries were sometimes a factor. This was minimized by locating the first site in the most dominant country.

One noisy psychiatrist and a few of his buddies and a willing media were the cause of the trouble. He would handle them today and continue on and achieve full success of the entire mission.

Media outlets were not listed as a *high level* potential threat in the MRM. Earth had its own cultural idiosyncrasy though. These media idiots could have done what he did: investigate. Instead they had simply parroted lies. If the media could help create a war between Directory Electronics and the Psychiatric establishment of Earth, then the *story* would go on and on. The media would get what *they* wanted: conflict. A story to tell – manufactured by the media themselves.

Bottom line. He could understand why the psychiatrists were feeling threatened by his new technology, why they would attack his operations. Also he could appreciate why the Intelligence agents were resorting to dirty tricks to get information about Directory Electronics for demanding bosses who rightfully felt threatened by their presence.

But he had no sympathy for a media institution that would broadcast unsubstantiated claims, when a single day of investigation would have made for a completely different story. The media made it possible for lies to spread unchecked around the world. They aided in spreading lies. They didn't care about facts.

He went back into the research room and looked at the figures as the tech put them on screen. The number of returned toys was huge. In the United States they were being returned to stores faster than they were being sold.

He savagely suppressed his rage.

Handle the problem.

Get even.

* * *

"Good morning, Doctor." Melliander's secretary greeted him.

Melliander grunted a reply.

"You have a guest waiting to see you."

"I have no appointments till noon! I won't see anyone! Tell them to go away!"

"But Doctor, the gentleman is a representative of Directory Electronics."

The tall, stooped, dour faced Dr. Melliander smiled. "Is that so?"

"Yes, sir."

"Give me five minutes and show him in."

"Yes, Doctor."

Melliander walked into his paneled office. It was located in a large university in the Chicago area.

Five minutes later there was a polite knock. The secretary opened the door. "Dr. Melliander, may I introduce Mr. Spock of Directory Electronics."

"Please enter."

Certain financial arrangements were concluded that were both startling and satisfying to the doctor. Very satisfying. Transfers of funds occurred immediately.

Right from the beginning he had felt the tug of a big fish on the hook – and he had just reeled it in. Far more satisfying than dealing with drug company reps.

For many generations to come both he and his progeny were going to be very wealthy.

This was his last chance to make a killing.

On the drive into work he had seen a pack of kids in the park playing with their TAC cars. It was the first time he had seen them in use. He had stopped and looked. The kids were having the time of their lives. He was there for half an hour. He got the fright of his life.

They worked.

The kids loved them.

It confirmed his first instinct: the moment he heard of the TAC a chill had gone through him.

He suppressed a new awareness.

Something he couldn't confront.

Then it slipped past his defenses, and before he could stop himself he was thinking.

Someone knows how the mind works! Total shock. He sat in his BMW, head spinning like a top. His whole world was turned upside down. It was the last thing he ever expected. *They are going to find out about us.* Melliander felt exposed. *I was right to attack.*

Now, sitting in his office, money in the bank, he felt safe.

I've got my money so what does it matter? If I need to, I'll just disappear. He smiled and made a call.

● ● ●

The Chief of Directory Electronics received immediate gratification. The action team leader, completing the pay off, programmed the mobile audio-visual bug to follow Melliander. It was set to record and transmit in real time his every word and action.

The Directory Chief listened to the good Doctor's phone conversation.

"I told you it would work," said the Doctor. "There are millions in the initial payment and an agreement for further secret negotiations."

The Directory Chief selectively dialed up the sound output, but not in time to catch the response from the speaker in the phone's ear piece.

Melliander continued, "Yes, it's obvious they're running scared or else why the huge immediate payoff? We're the powerhouse in the U.S. when it comes to the brain and what we say has an impact on people's attitudes and their sales."

"The big question is: does the toy really work?"

"I don't know if the toy works." Melliander lied. "On television I implied it didn't and then implied it did. I'm sure it doesn't. How can it? Nobody knows what goes on inside someone's head.

"The key is this: Directory Electronics needs our approval to sell any product we can condemn, and we can charge them whatever we want for our endorsement."

"It seems like you were right about the study."

"Of course I was right. Why spend all the time and money on an actual study when my report was all we needed – if we had done a study our condemnation would have been too late to hurt them…"

The Chief had listened to enough. All the details of the extortion were going into the data banks. He had what he needed.

Publicizing this conversation would destroy Melliander's reputation. It was additional insurance. The payoff had cost many dollars, but produced the needed result. Floating on the euphoric bubble of cash, the Doctor had been incautious and spoken freely.

The psychiatrists' threat was all but gone and their full day of reckoning would come as sure as sunset, if not as soon. He turned his attention to the other enemy, the media.

Now he would have some fun.

● ● ●

The sign on the door read, "Directory Electronics Public Relations Office."

"Okay, tape the short announcement as written and then send it by electronic mail," the Directory Chief ordered.

They had made a "set." It was a back drop complete with logo and a podium in front. The PR guy read the message.

"Responding to increasing desires by the public to know more about the Thought Activated Circuit, our CEO John Smith will host a press conference. It will be held at our Las Vegas facility. The primary points being covered will be as follows: 1, the supposed threat to the mental health of children. 2, the supposed threat to the mental capability of children. We shall provide additional information necessary to the successful safe use of our product. Our CEO will also take questions for a brief period."

The announcement was received at media outlets across the U.S. and around the world.

● ● ●

"Breaking news from Las Vegas, Nevada. My name is Johnathon Quick of ABD News and as you can see we are outside the production facilities of Directory Electronics, the controversial manufacturer of the thought activated circuit that powers Natell Toys newest remote controlled race car.

"We are being told Directory Electronics' Chief Executive Officer John Smith will host a press conference on this very spot tomorrow morning.

"Recently DE has been mired in controversy when a psychiatric panel denounced their toy as a 'hoax' that could cause 'mental anxiety' leading to 'irreparable harm' to the nation's children.

"Fueling the controversy has been DE's earlier refusal to grant access to the media. Many of the biggest names in news and information have been denied contact, causing some to speculate that the company was funded by the CIA and the toy is a form of mind control.

"What prevented an immediate government crackdown is the magic of the Thought Activated Circuit itself and its many supporters. It seems the mere possibility the technology is real has sheltered it from further criticism.

"The eyes of the world will be focused here tomorrow and you can expect sparks to fly as long denied top media personalities come face to face with DE executives and put the hard questions to those accused of causing irreparable harm to the mental health of the nation's most vulnerable citizens: our children.

"This is Johnathon Quick reporting."

Quick gave his camera man the kill signal.

"It's going to be a blood bath here tomorrow. I almost feel sorry for this company."

"I couldn't care less," the cameraman said.

●　●　●

Wednesday morning arrived desert shimmer hot; a scorching day was well on its way. Seven a.m. saw 100 Las Vegas degrees. Conveniently a huge digital time and temperature display was placed on the lush green grass at the entrance to the DE facility.

From early in the morning city workers and police had placed barriers restricting traffic and pedestrian flow into the area.

As reporters and crews began to arrive at six a.m., police directed their vehicles to a remote location blocks from the DE main entrance, forcing them to schlep their equipment to the site by hand or on dollies. This required many trips by the support staff who were pushed hard to make the deadline. They all noticed how hot it was around the DE building itself.

On this day, they vowed: all sins, imagined or real, would be paid for. The press was the firing squad and DE the condemned man.

Eight a.m. sharp was the scheduled beginning of the event and the producers of all news outlets had been severely admonished – don't be late.

At five minutes to eight the press corps had themselves properly arrayed – ready to strike.

Eight a.m. came and went, unremarked by DE personnel. The frosted glass doors of the DE facility remained closed. The reporters became restive. No one explained the delay.

The temperature on the ground had risen to one hundred and three clearly visible degrees. Luckily a water vendor showed up. He set up on the lush grass that fronted the DE property and began selling small bottles of water for ten dollars each. This was steep, but the gofers were refusing to go-fer in the heat and the water was ice cold, so trade was brisk even at his inflated prices. His demand for "cash only" ended when the last available greenback was gone; then he took credit electronically.

At a quarter past the hour the DE spokesman approached the agitated mob.

"I ask your indulgence. There has been an unavoidable delay."

"Where is John Smith?" interrupted a rude person.

"Of course," continued the Directory rep, "anyone who feels this imposition is too serious a breach of etiquette should feel free to leave."

Ten a.m. was now in the past and the polite DE spokesman was not in sight. A group of "star" reporters had decided to walk the distance to their air-conditioned coaches for relief from the oppressive heat. They had almost reached this sanctuary when they were recalled by breathless sweat-streaked gofers, sent to announce the imminent start of the conference.

They hurried back and took their places.

The spokesman came to the podium.

"Please accept profuse apologies from our CEO John Smith. He would be here to explain the delay himself were it not for the time consuming nature of the emergency."

●

Inside the building on the production floor the Directory Chief "John Smith" smiled. "We're going to have some fun today! Put the viewing field against the wall. Set it to thirty feet high and fifty feet across." The huge "screen" would provide great detail. "Put those recliners in rows. Come on, pack 'em in and watch the show."

The Chief had been promising his production people some extra time off and this was it.

The viewing field showed the exterior with great clarity. In the heat some reporters were discussing if they were being baited. The DE personnel were betting on which "star" reporter was going to throw the first fully fledged fit.

Cameras were tracking every word and image. The details were shown on split screen.

Finally at 10:45 a.m. one woman, taking a mirror from an assistant and looking at her reflection, heard an off-color remark about her looks and threw the mirror at the offending network anchor. The mirror hit an innocent cameraman on the head. The wounded man started toward her and the mirror thrower let the four-letter words fly. There was a mixture of groans and applause from the DE spectators in their comfy chairs as money changed hands.

New bets were placed and the laughter continued.

●

Outside there was serious resentment about the water vendor as he implemented a new pricing structure.

"As the temperature goes up degree by terrible degree my job becomes more and more intolerable! My umbrella does very little to protect me. To compensate for my increasing discomfort I raise my prices."

"You can't do that!" shouted one crew member.

"It is too hot! I am leaving!" The water seller stood up.

"No, no. I'll pay. Please take your seat. Please, please?"

The severe look left the water seller's face.

Trade continued. Those in line groaned as the temperature continued to climb.

At eleven thirty, with the mercury at one hundred and twelve scorching degrees, there was mutiny in the ranks. The sound and camera people and other crew were less interested in revenge against DE than they were in getting out of the sun.

Earlier speculation that the delays were deliberate was now considered fact.

"These DE assholes are keeping us out here to fry!"

Calls were placed to producers back in the various studios with requests to pull out and boycott the conference. There were tears of frustration as they were told to stay.

●

Inside the climate-controlled DE building two huge faces were side by side on the screen. One anchorette's eyes were brimming with tears as she was instructed to stay put. Another reporter was yelling into her phone. Without warning a flood of tears spilled. Directory workers cheered and groaned as they won or lost bets.

They started to argue over what "crying" actually was.

"Okay, okay, that was close. Run a slow motion replay and we'll see what's what," instructed a DE supervisor. The tears were closely tracked. The anchorette's eyes were definitely full of tears but had not let go.

"So what if the tears haven't left her eyes. That is crying – she is definitely crying! That reporter's tears came out of nowhere. She is dry eyes to floodgates in a split second."

"We'll ask the Chief for a decision."

John Smith was told of the photo finish and made his ruling. "The tears have to leave the eye before it can be counted as crying." There were cheers and whistles as the initial verdict was upheld.

●

Johnathon Quick saw a reporter openly crying as she yelled at someone on her phone. *This is getting out of control*, he thought. Quick looked into the distance where a line of packed school buses were crossing a bridge. *There it goes! A bus full of kiddies has smashed through the guard rail and plunged onto the roadway below! They are all dead!* Too bad his imagination wouldn't rescue him from this humiliating scene outside DE.

Even if the bus had gone over, he thought, *all these vultures with their microphones would ruin my exclusive.* He shook his head. He dug a sweaty hand into his pocket and pulled out a container, struggled with the child-proof cap and finally washed his prescription down with some very expensive ice cold water. Everyone turned to the glass doors as they opened.

●

"Imagine my distress," said the DE spokesman who emerged from Directory Electronics and stepped up to the podium, "Being forced into this blistering heat and made to deliver a sad message to an unhappy group of people. There is another delay." He quickly retreated.

●

Fifty plus people were drenched with sweat and reeked as their deodorant was taken past human limits and antiperspirant no longer restrained moisture.

"I actually believed this guy when he said his boss was running late. The chance of that is now deader than week-old road kill," a blogger said.

He got a few laughs.

Anger surged and died in waves as did the scathing dialogue that washed from sweaty shore to shore of the mob.

"I'm really going to bury these bastards! Nobody, and I mean n-o-b-o-d-y, does this to me and lives," a reporter chimed in as she mopped the running sweat from her eyes.

"Nixon had a hit list, I have a shit list and DE is item numero uno."

"To be or not to be – these guys won't exist after I file my report."

The big media "stars" gathered to discuss the disrespect being unloaded on them. "We all agree? Death to Directory Electronics?" The group cheered. "These people are going to get chopped."

Another said, "I stood in the water line and that asshole charged me thirty dollars for this tiny water bottle! Can you believe the shit we're taking to get this story?" He tipped his head back and drained the water. "Ah, that tastes good! Gofer, get me another bottle!"

●

The Directory Chief looked at the huge screen, enjoying the bedlam he had created.

"Send the e-mail."

The PR guy hit a key. "It's gone."

"Good, very good." The Chief looked back to the screen, feeling a little anticipation. Then for fun he said, "Fifty thousand U.S. dollars to the person who picks the first reporter to throw a fit when they get the word."

His staff cheered and quickly logged their picks.

Minutes before the Directory Chief's appearance, news services and television stations everywhere received electronic mail from Directory Electronics.

Urgent. Highest priority.

To: CEO....

Please be advised:

At Directory Electronics we have under consideration which industries and which specific companies we intend to license our TAC technology to.

All companies and industries that DE considers to be her friends and supporters will find themselves first in line.

Additionally, an extensive lineup of new technical releases will soon be made available – to those friends.

John Smith, CEO.

The phone lines burned as the network executives were informed of this development. Newspaper owners were notified. They considered it for a millisecond and came to independent but unanimous decisions.

Instructions went down the phone lines to the reporters in Las Vegas standing in the blazing hot sun outside Directory Electronics, gushing sweat, spewing venom, and oozing hate.

Instructions to this elite cast arrived just before the press conference began. The whole group began to buzz and burn, flapping around in confusion and seething with impotent rage. There was a lot of shouting and cursing.

⬤

It was two p.m.

"Please prepare yourselves," announced the DE spokesman with great formality. "Our Chief Executive Officer will be at the podium in less than a minute."

"You're kidding!" someone yelled.

They all looked disheveled and absurd as makeup had been applied over and over until nothing could be done and was abandoned. They were tired, (not thirsty) and angry. And worse – powerless.

The few reporters who had not been contacted by their stations demanded to know what was going on. They found out. They rushed to confirm. It was a seething, jostling mob. The word from above was simple: "attack DE, lose your career." Not job, but career. Those who attacked DE would be blackballed by the entire industry.

The DE spokesman walked to the entrance and pulled open the frosted glass door, and out stepped John Smith. He spoke a few words to the spokesman and returned inside the building.

The spokesman came to the podium.

"Attention! Attention here!" The noise continued.

"Shut up!" The volume had been boosted to an ear-splitting level.

"I have just been given instructions by my CEO John Smith.

"Only those reporters who represent national and international media will be allowed to remain. Be prepared with your identification and press credentials, as each one of you will be checked." Violent shoving broke out in pockets. Others cursed as their equipment was knocked to the ground by the furious passage of the rejected.

"It's a hundred and twenty degrees out here! I came half way across the country only to be told two minutes ago that I have to be nice to you or else. And now you won't let me stay!" The man was thrashing about with his equipment, knocking others over, creating a chain reaction of falling bodies and cries of pain, frustration and rage. There were screams as some were trampled. More cameras and equipment were dropped. It was mean, sweaty mayhem.

●

The Directory Chief looked at the screen, "This scene is a news event in itself," he laughed, "an irony which I'm sure is under-appreciated by these irony-loving people."

The DE staff laughed and cheered as a group of reporters took a tumble.

The guards carefully checked those reporters who sought to remain. They were all rumpled and dirt-streaked. Clothes were torn and blood smeared in places.

They were humiliated, and humbled.

●

At two-thirty p.m., the glass doors swung open again and he strode forward.

"I am the Chief of Directory Electronics. My name is John Smith." He beamed at the chosen.

"I am, of course, sorry to have kept you waiting," he said insincerely. When no one contradicted, he continued. "And in such heat!" Waving vaguely at the heavens he waited again. Silence was heard. John Smith was entertained by the lack of response and his smile broadened.

"Before we get started I want to demonstrate a new technological advance you will fully appreciate." Over the next few seconds the ambient temperature of the air dropped swiftly. "I have lowered the temperature to a comfortable thirty-five degrees. Now I ask you, isn't that better?"

"Oh God!" choked out one network anchor. "It's gone from the Sahara to Siberia." Her teeth were chattering violently.

It took all his skill not to laugh in their faces. "It takes prolonged exposure to high temperatures to fully appreciate temperature conditioning like this, doesn't it?" They were all shaking at the shocking chill temperature but also amazed that such an effect could be achieved in the open air. Of course Las Vegas in the summer was the perfect place and time to promote sales of this new technology.

"Anyway, we will terminate this technology demonstration as it has interrupted the press conference." And with that the heat returned in full force. The temperature gauge by the water seller read a remarkable 126 degrees. The quicker minds of the group realized that they had been sweltering at John Smith's pleasure….

John Smith had watched these media people closely over the last few months. He looked at this disheveled, ill-treated mob in front of him with satisfaction. Established Directory policy dictated that he remain uncommunicative with the native population till a certain point was reached. They were not quite there – but the press had forced his hand by spreading Dr. Melliander's lies far and wide. *How dare these people think they can come here and dictate anything to me!*

Smith was an imposing figure with an impressive and deeply penetrating voice. The women present seemed to feel his machismo as a personal invitation. The men were simply dominated, and accepted that they were overmatched without really being aware of it.

"I have a prepared statement to give you and then I'll open things up for a few questions." It never occurred to anyone to interrupt. Amazing.

He smiled.

"Firstly, the returned Natell cars: there is no electronic or programming problem. We at Directory Electronics have checked over five hundred refunded units, and apart from four that had our marvelous Thought Activated Circuit incorrectly installed by Natell Toys, Inc., all functioned properly."

"What about the thousands of other returned cars?" asked someone.

"We have not reached the Q and A portion of the news conference." John Smith continued.

"Some children have inferior thought processes. This is the reason they cannot operate our product. They have little or no direct control over their own thoughts, and so fail to operate our cars successfully."

They all shouted questions.

Smith ignored them. "I know this statement is not politically correct, but it's rescued from that dilemma by being factual."

Many of the reporters present were incapable of controlling a car – his claim did not sit well. Comments and questions were shouted at him. Some were jabbing their microphones forward like stubby spears trying to intimidate. He stood there without responding and let their ranting wash past him.

How truly rude these people are, he thought.

It was obvious he didn't have an accurate measure of this culture as yet, but this didn't worry him. He smiled as he activated a small device. He had saved it for just such discourtesy as he was now experiencing. All their electronics malfunctioned – but DE technology seamlessly continued the broadcast without their knowledge.

Uproar.

The technicians scrambled as their equipment failed.

"Hold on, hold on!" yelled a tech. "We'll be back up in seconds."

John Smith said, "We must continue immediately, I cannot be delayed by your incompetence."

They searched for pencil and paper.

"What about the psychiatric panel and their conclusions that your toys are mentally unbalancing the children who use them?"

"I have spoken to the eminent Dr. Melliander and he has assured me that his findings were skewed by a high percentage of children who have a pre-existing mental defect and that the ongoing study shows no harm to any child. In the future we will work hand in hand with the good Doctor."

●

Dr. Melliander sat furiously impotent in his office as he watched the live feed from the Directory press conference.

"You lying sack of shit! I never said any such thing!" he screamed at the TV.

This man Smith was directly challenging him. Smith had the upper hand now because of the money, but Melliander vowed, *I'll stick it to you the first chance I get.* He had to admit that watching the news people get humiliated was an unexpected treat.

●

"Does the same apply to adults?" someone finally got out.

"No. Adults who already have an adverse condition of the mind will find an improvement through the use of our toy. And I would not be surprised to find that this is true for children, too, once all the facts are in."

"So if I practice… if people practice with the TAC they can improve?"

"Yes, absolutely. Having a workable technology that allows a direct interface between the thoughts a person has and the material universe helps anyone's state of mind.

"Through our research we've come into possession of factual mechanics that are common to the minds of all people. We have developed technology that is undisputable in its proofs and beneficial in its application.

"It cannot be overstated: the TAC is a giant step forward in understanding the mind of man. In fact, more than working closely with Dr. Melliander, we invite all mental health experts to consult with us for any necessary clarification before releasing information that is found to be contrary to these established facts."

"Will there be any refunds?"

"There are no defective Thought Activated Circuit units. Failure comes directly from mental incompetence or, rarely, from improperly installed Natell units. Our policy is strict. 'Let the buyer beware!' Our products are superior and we are in no way responsible for the state of mind of the user." He paused, "Or the lack of it." There was furious scribbling on tiny notepads. It put a pause between one question and the next.

"Also we expect the returns of the toys to stop almost completely."

"Why is that?"

"Returning the toy is a public admission of being a mental defective."

That caused a few seconds' pause in the questioning.

"How did Directory Electronics invent such radically new electronics?"

"We have an R&D department like many other companies."

"Some experts say that your invention is an unprecedented leap forward in electronics. Can you comment on that?"

"Thank your experts. We appreciate the praise."

"What other applications will the TAC be used for?"

"We have no definite plans in that regard."

They looked skeptical. Clearly they did not believe him, but no one asked anything further about it.

"Are you going to tell us anything?" said one frustrated reporter.

"As I said, continued use of the TAC will improve the mental condition of anyone who perseveres."

John Smith smiled and waited.

One of the female reporters was looking at the Directory Chief and could think of nothing but the crazy theories going around about these DE people. She assumed that because all their equipment was malfunctioning no recording was being made. This gave her courage to ask questions she normally wouldn't. And truly this guy just did not register properly – with all the powerful forces gathered around this company and this facility he was just too confident. It was as if he thought he couldn't fail, couldn't be taken down and that would make sense only if one outrageous thing were true. The DE technology certainly was a leap into an unearthly stratosphere. Maybe he was too, she thought.

"Are you an alien?"

"That is correct. I was not born in the USA."

"We all know that. My question is, were you born on this planet?"

"Sleep with me tonight and then you tell me."

"Touché," she said, and laughed, embarrassed.

With this, the "press conference" was over and though she did sleep with him, and his performance was "stellar," she was none the wiser.

John Smith was happy with the press conference. After this episode it was unlikely the media could be used as a tool to slow or halt his plans, and if unfavorable material did arise, there was a good chance it could be suppressed. That had been the point of this entire exercise (with a little revenge thrown in for fun). Consolidation of power by demonstrating he could not be pushed around had been partially achieved, and putting these people firmly in their places had not been unpleasant.

● ● ●

Dr. Melliander shaded his eyes as he was hit by the press lights outside his office. Minutes ago his secretary called to let him know the media were there demanding a statement about the DE matter. "Don't let them in." He scribbled on a sheet of paper.

The press, thought Melliander, *are like a virus. I'm not certain how I first came in contact, but they make me sick and I hope they'll be gone soon.* He chuckled at his own wit.

How had they arrived so quickly? *I was watching John Smith on television only minutes ago.* There was no escape from the pressure of unseen influences at work, he felt threatened by the speed of events, and he'd taken all that money.

"Get that light out of my eyes," he demanded.

They ignored him.

"Dr. Melliander, John Smith, CEO of Directory Electronics, claims you have reversed your earlier position regarding the Thought Activated Circuit. Can you comment on that?"

"Why have you corrupted the results of your study?" shouted someone else.

Melliander held up a hand. "I have a statement for you. If you will be quiet long enough, I'll read it." He pulled out his scribble and read. "We have been in close contact with Mr. John Smith and his representatives at Directory Electronics.

"Since the release of our findings about the effects of the Thought Activated Circuit on the delicate minds of children we conducted an additional review of our study participants and discovered flaws in our conclusions. Ongoing tests are still underway as we speak and tend to confirm that the TAC is harmless and quite possibly a valuable tool in the training of a child's mind."

"That's a major shift in your position in very little time, Doctor. Has the force of Big Corporations swayed independent psychiatric research?"

"Not at all. We in the psychiatric community have never claimed anything more than an incomplete understanding of the mind. If a flaw has occurred and invalid conclusions have been drawn, then it is incumbent upon any researcher to be humble and re-evaluate. That is what happened here."

"And if we 'evaluated' your bank account, Doctor, what would we find?"

"Your implication is absurd. I have nothing more for you." He retreated to his office.

● ● ●

Alone in his office at the Las Vegas facility John Smith smiled.

I'm right again, he gloated. *Toy sales have recovered and sharply increased. And no one is returning the toys.* He laughed out loud. *None of these primitives want to admit they are mental defectives. And worrying about it will spur them on to increase their ability.* "Good. Practice, practice, practice makes you perfect." he said to the air.

Smith knew the primitives were trying back-engineer the TAC or connect it to other devices. They would fail. The patents he had filed were a hoax. *Work very hard Earth people, work as cleverly as you can: you will never discover anything I don't want you to know.*

The Chief of Directory Electronics watched as millions of dollars on deposit became billions. Partial payment on advance orders for the Temperature Control Technology flooded in. Anyone in the world who needed an exterior/interior space heated or cooled paid and paid. This technology, too, would change the world. Earth's economic problems were energy related. TCT would give him and every person on the planet more money to spend. Except the HVAC technicians. But he would solve that by only allowing the existing HVAC personnel to train on TCT. Good.

DE needed the goodwill of the people.

Earlier that night John Smith guided his PR department as they worked on the high definition digital recordings with crystal clear sound of embarrassing moments of each major media personality. These hilarious works of art were provided to their competing networks.

Minutes after receiving these bomb shells the networks went live with "breaking news."

Smith had watched these "media personality giants" cutting themselves to shreds as they attacked each other and the opposing networks. But not him or DE. Then he got bored. *Those piss-ants will think twice before attacking me again.*

The Temperature Control Technology (TCT) had been accurately reported. That was more like it.

A lesson learned. He smiled.

But the night was still young. Outside the building the nightlife was stirring. John Smith went to the facilities control room. "Any action yet?"

"No, sir," his operations man said. "They're all scuttling into position."

"Should be a fun show."

"Oh yeah. Can't wait."

● ● ●

The new TCT had taken the CIA, and everyone, by surprise. This new technology, so frivolously exposed to the world by Directory Electronics, would shift the global balance of power.

Oil Money could see the writing on the wall. Their industry could be shot down next if something wasn't done about DE. Done now. DE must be controlled or destroyed before they too became yesterday's news.

The CIA took it on the chin. They were supposed to know. Know beforehand. This current failure to inform after the TAC fiasco was bad. The world was changing without warning. How was anyone supposed to hold on to power?

Extreme pressure came down.

Federal agents masquerading as trash removal workers, drove up to Directory Electronics in a dump truck to empty the dumpsters at the rear of the building. It was so easy to place a satchel of explosives by the rear entrance across from the loading dock.

It was a timed device.

Time quickly ran out.

No detonation occurred.

The agents attempted to remotely detonate the explosives. And failed.

The agents sitting in the cab of the dump truck a block from DE were chattering over the radio, trying to figure what to do next or to abort.

"Ah! Ahhh. Ahhhhhhhh!" screamed one agent. The bomb's remote control device on his lap was red hot. Already burning his skin. He jumped from the cab and fell to the pavement screaming in agony.

The remote burst into flames.

Something was weirdly wrong.

Two DE employees came out the rear door with a load of trash and stepped over to the dumpster enclosure.

The DE workers heard the agent screaming. They ran into the street.

"Are you alright? Do you need help?"

The second agent was helping his comrade. "He broke his leg. The paramedics are on the way."

"That sounds like more than a broken leg."

"We have it under control, thanks."

"Okay, hope your friend is okay."

"Yeah, me too, good night."

The DE employees walked to the rear entrance.

"Hey, look at this."

It was a canvas sack wedged against the wall. He took a swing at it with his foot. It shot toward his friend, who booted it off the loading dock.

They chased after it and played soccer with it for ten minutes, joking and laughing, and finally sent it sailing into the dumpster with the rest of their load.

The paramedics arrived, they'd all been on call two blocks away, ready to respond to the bomb.

The plan to enter the facility as emergency firefighters and in the confusion take what they could was moot.

● ● ●

DE began licensing their TAC electronics to other industries. Within month's electronics containing a TAC component were available to the general public. It was used in an incredible number of ways, the only condition being that the manufacturing had to occur on the United States mainland. DE, for all its mystery, was at once very acceptable to the current administration.

TV remotes were revolutionized. Now the couch potato didn't even have to lift a finger, if he could think. "A contradiction?" joked one reporter.

Those who could use the TAC with skill were a minority, possibly one in a hundred. Most could make the TAC devices do something and they discovered, as DE claimed, the more they used the devices the better they got.

It quickly became a status symbol. "Oh yes, Mrs. Jones, I use my thought-controlled garage door opener all the time. I'm just one of the lucky ones who has no problem operating them!" It was a wonderful put-down.

The new devices began to pour into the world market through the US manufacturers, causing a dramatic upturn in the national and international economy. The US, in a very short time, was once again a real competitor in the production of manufactured goods.

Each new DE venture riveted the world's attention.

"We have David Weston reporting live from Directory Electronics' new construction site just outside Los Angeles. What's the latest there, Dave?"

"Well, John, there's growing excitement and some very wild speculation. The question on everyone's tongue is, 'What new wonders will this bring?' DE has become such a source of prosperity – fortunes are literally being made overnight. A signed contract with DE means unlimited funding from any financial institution in the world at very low rates. Naturally, industrialists from across the planet are interested in this new venture as it may be *their* golden egg being laid here."

"Dave, is there any word what the new facility will house or is it all speculation?"

"That's just it, John, there's been no official word. But the people seen entering the main DE offices tend to indicate that this may be a computer development facility. And we all know how fast DE can put useful technology to work."

"Do we have any names at this point? Names of the people and companies seen at DE?"

"Yes, John, we have, but at DE's request, we're not at liberty to release that information. I can tell you they are the industry giants in both hardware and software. Even without official word, it's still very exciting out here. Just think, in mere weeks or months we can expect to see the DE revolution sweep the computer industry and you can be sure that this means prosperity for all those companies, and fantastic new products for us to use at very reasonable prices."

"Some have said that it's a DE world. How does it seem to you on the ground?"

"John, I have to agree, but with a proviso. It may not be a DE world as we speak, but in a year from now with their fantastic growth rate, it can't be anything else."

"That was David Weston, reporting live from the newest Directory Electronics construction site, just outside Los Angeles. I'm John Thomas. And you are watching 'Another Hour,' setting the standard of journalism for the new millennium by providing you with the information you need to live your life. Please stay with us as we delve into DE and its growing impact on the world around us."

●　●　●

Two hundred and fifty FBI agents were assigned to Las Vegas to investigate DE.

The fiasco at the DE facility had humiliated them. They were determined to succeed.

The CIA ran their own illegal operation in the shadows.

The FBI agents tailed DE employees to apartment buildings, casinos and the local 7-Eleven and concluded these were normal people going about normal lives.

Exhaustive background checks were run on all DE personnel. The information compiled checked and cross-checked. One for one they were foreign nationals whose backgrounds were impossible to trace, but had legally entered the US.

A number of abductions were attempted but botched. The failures were due to seemingly casual circumstances, resulting in an inability to detain, question, arrest, drug or use other coercive techniques on DE personnel.

A spy satellite was tasked to cover the Vegas facility. A day later the satellite began sending impossible imagery which fractured and became pornographic live feed from various web sites. The satellite became totally unresponsive and soon reentered the atmosphere, plunging into the Pacific Ocean. No one said that DE had knocked out the eye in the sky. But they all thought it. And that was scary.

Drones crashed into the FBI offices.

The NSA bugging of phone lines was dropped after several attempts resulted in the same recorded message, "You have reached Directory Electronics, please hold," a short musical interlude, then "Phone taps are illegal. This warrantless intrusion into our constitutional right to privacy has been reported to the local authorities." Apparently DE had a sense of humor, even if it was not appreciated.

A signal intercept vehicle assigned to tap personal communication devices melted down. Its electronics fused.

They looked like Keystone Kops.

● ● ●

Behind the walls of the U.S. government was fear. There was fear in the FBI, the Joint Chiefs, CIA, and all the alphabet agencies including Homeland Security. There was fear in the Executive branch. Congress did not know what to do as they met secretly to discuss the growing threat to US sovereignty.

Could a company take over a country, the world?

There was confusion too.

FBI reports showed Directory Electronics – the organization itself – was not threatening. Just the opposite. Its personnel were law-abiding. Some of them raised hell in Las Vegas, but it was very tame.

Their technology had exploded across the world. There was hardly a city, town or household on the planet that did not utilize the new TCT. It was inexpensive and functional. It had even revolutionized research at the South Pole.

The Gross Domestic Product graph went straight up. And that was fabulous, but: the technology within US borders – good, technology outside of US control – bad.

Directory Electronics was the focus of attention of whole departments of CIA employees. They were concentrated on producing an Intelligence estimate. A prediction of future activity.

Initially there was only one real need – more data. Good estimates feed on accurate data and wither in its absence.

Finding the source of DE technology was impossible. DE inventions had no past. "Where were the scientific papers?" asked the white coats.

Where are the inventors of these scientific advances, howling for recognition?

The analysts, without data, did the only thing possible: speculate. One observation was made: the real story is our failure to get any information. It always appears coincidental. No one is that lucky.

That's the intel.

The analysts produced a negative. They were able to determine where the technology had not come from: China, Japan, Europe, or Russia. It was not from Israel, the Baltic States, nor the English. The South Africans had nothing to do with it; no secret conclave of the world's greatest scientists hiding on a Pacific island had produced it.

DE had no ties to corporations other than toy makers and, more recently, legitimate industrialists legally operating in the USA. Finally one brave soul suggested what many had been thinking – it hadn't occurred on Earth.

The tabloids had won that race.

CHAPTER 5

"WHY IS IT," SAID THE PRESIDENT of the United States, "that all I can get from the CIA is a series of alarming reports with each one more distressing than the last? I mean, if I were to actually believe this," he picked up a sheaf of paper and dropped it, "I would be a confused idiot. To top it all off, we have the best analysis of them all!" His voice dripped with sarcasm, "Listen to this – we are dealing with ALIENS! I've heard it all!" He slammed his fist on the table. He shook his head at the imbeciles in front of him. "This really explains things very neatly. I'll read the last lines of this report."

The President theatrically cleared his throat and stated in a sarcastic tone, "And I quote, 'As earlier stated, combining ALL the factors related to Directory Electronics and the data uncovered by subsequent investigations into their personnel, technology and operating strategies there is only one conclusion that leaves no further speculation, namely they are offworld in origin.'"

Sweeping his gaze over the faces of those present and locking onto the Director of the Central Intelligence Agency (D/CIA), he continued, "This is a cute way of saying 'aliens.' Not those coming across the southern border, but the ones in space ships. The ones Captain fucking Kirk dealt with. But I thought he handled them all and left nothing for me to do."

The Director of Central Intelligence was about to interrupt, but the President plowed on.

"Now look, I want to point out that any mystery can be explained by aliens! Things in the sky that zoom past and scare people – aliens. Large footprints in the forest – aliens! Why, even an unexpected crash in the stock market!" He was fuming. "This is the ultimate answer to any unknown event.

"But, mister, I'm a simple man and I'd like some real live answers, something we can do something with. You know, someone we can buy, legal usurpation of DE patents, secret legislation declaring a national emergency requiring the seizure of all DE research, something of that nature!"

There was silence in the room. The word "alien" had been mentioned. People had been speculating about it – but this was not the forum to present this explosive theory without evidence.

There was a silent consensus that Spook Central had gone too far with this report and the D/CIA was going down. They were looking at him; he was pale and drawn. He was not going to get any support, lest they, too, bite it by association.

This was politics in the meeting of the Combined Agencies Task Force, newly formed to investigate and resolve the security threat that Directory Electronics had become. It was one thing to have a company that generated prosperity like never before and another to find that same company might be able to take over your entire economy, and possibly much more. So they sat with blank faces and would not support the D/CIA, even though some secretly thought he was right – that DE were aliens.

This close to power, it was every man for himself.

The President stood up and began walking slowly down the length of the table behind the other seated men. This obliged those on the same side as him to swivel in their chairs so they would be facing him. It was inevitable that if one didn't turn when the President was walking the room, the next question or comment would be directed to the individual who had not turned his head. It sometimes got ugly.

"DE technology and policies have led us to unmatched economic prosperity. We must examine the source for our own protection. This report proves we have been unable to find out *who* and *what* we are dealing with.

"I'm astonished that we are out-gunned, out-maneuvered, out-spooked by some company in Las Vegas, Nevada? It just doesn't add up. Gentlemen, it's your job to advise me, and provide me with sufficient data and a variety of solutions. We are nowhere near that point."

He reached the rear of the room.

"The CIA wants me to believe we are dealing with Klingons. This is baloney. I want some guidance based in the here and now and not with Lewis Carroll and Alice in her wonder land!"

That was it. The D/CIA, Colin Craig, knew he was done for. There had been dressing-downs done in this room that had been a lot less severe, but each had spelled the end of another's career. Well, thought Craig, he hadn't been much liked at the Agency anyhow.

The D/CIA distractedly straightened the papers in front of him. There was one small point, he thought, *The DE people are not from this planet*. The data gathered by his people had convinced him, but there was no smoking gun.

No one said a word.

After completing his route around the conference table, the President stood once again at its head and glared at the only man present whose eyes hadn't followed him. This man had been looking at the ceiling. His features were blank.

The man's name was Augustus McMillan, an admiral in the naval service of the United States of America.

"Well, McMillan, what is it?" The President asked sharply. The rest of the men in the room let out small sighs of relief. They were glad not to give an opinion on this particular issue. "You had better have something intelligent to say!"

McMillan turned his gaze to the President, who sat down.

"Sir, I believe we should acknowledge these people as a visiting alien race and open formal negotiations with them on that basis."

"Bullshit!" POTUS said, enraged.

The gall of this man. He had never liked McMillan, and his statement was a slap in his face.

The others gaped at him.

McMillan stood and raised a hand in a dominating gesture. With a sharp slashing motion there was silence in the room. The generals and admirals and suits settled and looked with curious perplexity at McMillan. He hadn't *seemed* suicidal, but then one never can tell. The President was so livid at being cut off he was mute, and Augie took instant advantage.

"Look, gentlemen, there is no room for politics in this. We are confronting the single biggest change our planet has ever seen. It will make the industrial revolution, the American Revolution, or any upheaval look small.

"I'll lay out what I have discovered point by point, so please take notes, and after I'm done we can discuss any observations, questions or comments you have."

The President nodded his head, satisfied to let McMillan hang himself.

Augie McMillan was apolitical. He could always be counted on to express his opinion on important matters and his reasoning was always sound. He was obviously competent at political maneuvering, but he wasn't here to defend and support his career.

McMillan spent the next half hour laying out the reasons for the conclusions he had arrived at. He made no attempt to convince the President. After a glance he was sure that the President wasn't really listening.

Augie was establishing his conclusion point by logical point, talking directly to the men and women around the table. He was preparing them for action; it would come soon.

Augie concluded his remarks.

Everyone was waiting for the President's comment and he was finally forced to lamely say, "Continue your discussion."

McMillan pulled a sheaf of paper from his briefcase and handed out copies of reports and said to the D/CIA, "Sorry, Colin, but I ran my own operation, and this is a report of the results."

The D/CIA gave him a wry smile. McMillan was supporting his hypothesis, but it was clear Augie had arrived at the same understanding of the facts some time ago and had gone much further in his conclusions.

"A number of girls from the local Nevada dude ranches were employed to sexually engage any DE employee they could get their hands on. This report is a summary with conclusions, and a few suggestions on what we can do."

The President was shocked. "What do you mean, mister? Do you have proof that we are dealing with aliens?"

McMillan had enough.

"Mr. President, if you had listened to my briefing, something vital to the nation's future, you wouldn't have to ask that question!"

There was a shocked silence around the table. The President's face was beet red. He was actually making small involuntary grunting sounds. This made a strange counterpoint to the tension in the room with the rest trying desperately to hold everything still. This type of rebuke, up the chain of command, had never happened. Not in a world where sucking up to those in power was, if not a noble act, at least an intelligent one.

McMillan continued into the strangled silence. "We recovered semen. Ten separate samples. There was only prostate ejaculate and no sperm and, very surprisingly according to our science boys, no DNA; all those tested are sterile and their bodily fluids devoid of the building blocks of life. Some of the girls were instructed to obtain a blood sample in any manner they could and to retain it under a fingernail. There were over twenty attempts and each one failed. Some of these women honed their fingernails to razor sharpness, but they couldn't penetrate or puncture the skin or even get a real skin scraping. What we did get were some samples of body oil, sweat and a few hairs.

"The hair samples were obtained when one of the girls complained about the hair style her partner had and took him to a salon. Not one single hair had fallen out during any of the sexual engagements, some of which were exceptionally vigorous!

"There wasn't a single report of any physical 'alienness' from any of the women. These boys were well hung and could go all night if they wanted. This may not have been unusual except that it was uniform, night after night."

One crusty old general said, "Sounds inhuman to me!" There were chuckles and grins around the table that helped to loosen the tension.

"The hair, after microscopic examination and laboratory analysis, was found to be superficially normal, but one of the women at the lab noticed that not one hair had a split end. We couldn't find any other DE person who had one. This may sound frivolous or insignificant, but to the contrary, it is so unusual that not one non-DE person we checked had hair that healthy. Their body oil and sweat had components that could be found in a human body. The important thing was that the concentrations were quite uniform from one night to the next. These boys had very well regulated bodies and uniformity to one another. They look different externally but they test similarly.

"DNA testing is null; their basic bodily structure has no DNA signature as we know it. When encouraged, they casually displayed feats of enormous strength. We had a professional wrestler start an altercation. He said, and I quote, 'No one is that strong.' This guy was no pansy and we really quizzed him in depth. He wasn't trying to excuse himself. The man was huge, almost seven feet and three hundred pounds. He said when the DE employee manhandled him, it felt like he was two years old and in the hands of his coal miner father.

"We conducted an 'on the ground' investigation, just meat and potatoes stuff, no high tech."

McMillan turned formally to the President and said in a calm, dignified tone of voice, "I suggest we open formal negotiations with the aliens... Sir."

The President just glared.

Admiral Stone said, "How long have you been studying the DE people, Augie?"

"A week after they came out with the remote control car, Ed."

Craig was surprised. The CIA began its investigation at about the same time.

McMillan continued, "I've never believed in aliens, but I've never disbelieved either. I suspected it from the start and designed tests to prove/disprove my theory. I continued this until I had proof. These DE people will probably keep pouring out the technology until we contact them or seriously attack them; at least that's my guess. This is the neatest planetary takeover plan there is. Saves them a lot of useless waste in personnel and property and generates no ill will among the general population. All they have to do is dump their trinkets on us until they are in total financial control. The good part is that if we don't try to nuke them, I don't think we will ever see a bomb or whatever weapons they have, used on us.

"I assume they could snuff us without much effort. They haven't objected to any of the CIA tactics, conventional explosives fail to detonate around their buildings, and by this I surmise they would prefer dialogue to violence since they remove even the pretext for direct opposition. Heck, they're just waiting for us to wake up and smell the coffee. We're probably the cause of quite some amusement to these folks. But hell, they even look like us, so I say let's say hello!"

The President jumped right in. "McMillan, obviously you've put some very extensive study into this matter. I was never made aware of your operation and was never asked to approve it. My earlier position was based on inadequate information, this is now obvious. In future, you will obtain my approval for anything this critical in nature!" Well, there it was; the solution. Obviously McMillan was a prick for not informing him of the results of his unapproved intelligence gathering.

What the President could not know was that instead of saving face with this remark, he had reached a new low on the esteem meter with these men whose job it was to protect and defend the United States of America.

McMillan, having already gone all the way, was in no mood to give quarter. He said, "I attempted to get through your Chief of Staff on a number of occasions, including last night, when I was hoping to brief you before this meeting."

The President knew this, because he'd turned him down through his Chief of Staff, and hated McMillan for saying so.

Everyone at the table knew what the score was. The President was trying to slither out, but McMillan wasn't having any of it. The President thought maliciously, *You prick McMillan, you'll get yours, I can wait.*

The President smiled his thin-lipped smile, and then continued as if he had not heard McMillan's last comment, "However, it appears your presentation of this new data requires our attention. Is there any other information you have that bears on this matter?"

There was a scuffle in the hallway outside and all heads turned toward the door. A breathless major was admitted and gave McMillan a sheet of paper. He read it quickly and passed it to the President, saying, "Yes, sir, this is directly related, I believe."

The President's face went pale as he silently read the sheet. After the official headings and language he got to the meat of the text:

EIGHT SPACECRAFT (?) OF UNKNOWN ORIGIN ARE POSITIONED IN SPACE DIRECTLY OVER WASHINGTON DC. THEY WERE DISCOVERED IN THIS LOCATION AT 11:06 A.M. NO APPROACH TO THEIR POSITION WAS DETECTED.

The President read the contents aloud.

Pandemonium!

Men were shouting at each other, at the President, at the walls. It was total turmoil, where nothing but noise and wild emotions reigned. It went on and on. Augie, like the eye of a storm, remained calm. He was the only one who had truly accepted the nature of the new elements at work on their planet. So, for him, there was no surprise. The shock the others were experiencing was a measure of how little they had believed what he had told them. It never ceased to amaze him that men could be presented with clear, unequivocal data and still fail to see its significance or draw obvious conclusions.

The commotion began to lessen and as each person got a grip on himself their attention gravitated to Augie McMillan, until everyone was looking at him.

"I want you to understand clearly what has happened here."

They waited.

"This is the first time anyone in a position of power in this country has acknowledged the possibility of an alien presence on our planet." He let them absorb the obvious. Some of the eyes flickered with a startled realization.

"Within seconds of our recognizing them for who and what they truly are, they announce themselves to us in a way we can't ignore or misinterpret." In the dullest faces there was still incomprehension.

"It appears they were successful in bugging us."

Some of the less than quick looked fearfully at the walls as if they might detect a listening device. Augie had a tough time not laughing in the faces of these dimwits. *These people are responsible for our safety? Heaven help us,* he thought.

His own disparaging assessment of them lessened, for truly recognizing that aliens are among us was a difficult adjustment. To be able to move in one irrevocable heart beat from the old world to the new was an impossible standard to judge someone by.

Because of this radical change, the future of Earth and its people might be broad and bright and encompass the limitless stars. In fact, if this group of men could see it, unknown vistas yawned, and that was very exciting. But for these military/political creatures the confines of the USA and Earth was their domain and to move beyond it was to lose all power, lose all they had worked their entire lives to obtain. And so knowingly or unconsciously they became, in this one irretrievable pulse, minnows in a tea cup.

"Our era of isolation has passed." McMillian murmured.

As was so often the case in politics, Augie knew, their own personal interests were in conflict with the welfare of those they were elected to serve. Unable to adjust to the new role required of them, many would abandon their posts in the coming months. They would feel cheated. They could not destroy, maneuver or vote the aliens out of power or existence.

No meetings of tribal elders in the teepee stopped the US Army from mowing the American Indians down and seizing their lands. Facing the technology gap from the losing end is never fun. One positive thing it does do is isolate the sensible people – and this could be judged by how well the indigenous population integrated. Resentment and the outcomes of resentment are never part of a workable solution. Earth would have to become a brave new world. Brave enough to describe new goals and be industrious in achieving them.

Augie smiled.

CHAPTER 6

"ALIENS ARE AMONG US." ANNOUNCED THE President of the United States to the world. "And they are friendly."

The day following the President's announcement the Directory of Stars and Planets website was launched to great success. Many images and videos of far distant worlds, exotic cities, sublime landscapes, remarkable people, unusual wildlife, thriving businesses and massive star ships were available for all to see.

The Directory PR office slowly expanded the site, releasing information on one planet after another, causing public interest to remain at fever pitch about the universe out there.

Planet Earth was enthralled.

Where were you when you discovered we are not alone in the universe? Every person had an answer.

The holdings of Directory Electronics continued to expand. Another burst of construction was commenced and this held the nation and the world in thrall.

Despite predictions of calamity, the knowledge that aliens were already among the populations of Earth caused only the slightest ripple. The Directory people had insinuated themselves into the culture of Earth favorably and very smoothly.

Speculation that DE were aliens had started in the tabloids and on the Internet as outlandish commentary. It was picked up by the mainstream press and talk radio long before the President said a word. Some wondered if the aliens had planted these rumors.

The off-worlder's, and who could call them aliens anyhow because they looked just like humans, were here and spreading their bounty. What was there to be afraid of?

● ● ●

"What are you girls up to?" Asked Gloria French, standing in the door to the TV room at her home in Salt Lake City.

Natalie Wilk was sitting on a sofa with Deidre French.

"Mom, there's going to be an announcement from Directory Electronics on TV any minute now."

"What do you think it'll be this time?"

"I don't know, Mom." Deidre said.

"It's so exciting, isn't it Mrs. French? All these new things from the aliens." asked Natalie.

"Yes. Yes, it really is." She smiled. "Where's Wendy? I haven't seen her around lately."

"She's with Jack. I think she forgot we exist." Natalie said. "Ever since the baseball game she's been stuck to him like glue."

Deidre laughed. "You can't see any light between them at all!"

"Well, she must really love him."

The girls looked at each other. "Yes, she does." they said in unison.

Deidre grabbed the remote and raised the volume.

"It's just been announced," said the network anchor, "with the beginning of the coming school year, Directory Electronics will be offering courses in the theory, manufacture, assembly and maintenance of high tech offworld devices."

He stopped to let the wonderful significance work its way through the viewing public.

"Oh-my-god!" Natalie said.

As he continued, the broadcaster's voice went up an octave. "After successful completion, the graduates will have the option of going *offworld* to seek jobs in other sectors of the Directory." The words came fast and tumbled off his tongue.

"I can tell you I'm signing up right now!" He stared at the camera fixedly, trying to imagine his future. He looked to his right and it was obvious from his comic expression that someone was frantically trying to get him to continue reading from the prompter.

He returned to the moment, looked resolved, and abruptly stood. The cameraman lost his head from the frame.

"Can you believe it? We can go to another star, another world! I quit! I quit!" He ran off the set.

Gloria French said, "That's the funniest thing I've ever seen." They were all laughing.

"The truth is, Mrs. French, I feel exactly like that broadcaster. I want to go work on another world. I really do."

"Yes," said Natalie, "I'm with you Deidre, anything else has just become passé."

"You two have been spending altogether too much time on the DE website. I know it's interesting but you're obsessed, both of you."

The girls smiled; they were.

The commercial break ended and a flustered woman was seated at the news desk.

"My name is Annie Breck and I will be continuing the news." Job placement to successful graduates was guaranteed, a minor Directory official was interviewed. He explained there was a shortage of individuals within the Directory to do the jobs Earth students would be trained for.

"The training will be high tech for Earth, but it is low tech for the Directory and that is why we're seeking applicants here," the DE spokesman said.

"I understand you have some clips of worlds and businesses seeking foreign trained workers?"

"Yes, we have a small selection." The spokesman said and narrated as the clips and images were displayed.

There were inhabited planets containing startling vistas and cityscapes including odd but sophisticated looking humanoid and a few non-humanoid races.

The news cast continued. "You said the Directory Chief has invited a special group to participate in an offworld program, can you tell us more about this preferred treatment?" asked Annie Breck.

"Yes," said the DE spokesman. "The Chief has made an in-depth study of your planet and discovered a group that has been carrying a great burden. The Psychiatrists of Earth. These people have shouldered an incredible load uncomplainingly for many years."

There was a break for an applause track.

"We're offering training to these professionals at no cost, including an obligatory offworld apprenticeship where other peoples will be studied. Earth psychiatrists will have the chance to educate professionals of other worlds about the exact conditions on their planet and indulge themselves in paid speaking engagements across the Directory of Stars and Planets. Through this interaction a broader understanding of the human condition on Earth and throughout the Directory will result."

"That is very generous and I'm sure it's well deserved," Annie said.

"Yes, it will certainly be an adventure for all involved."

"Thank you for joining our broadcast."

"You're welcome," the Directory rep said.

"Well, that's it for this evening, we'll see you all tomorrow." Annie Breck signed off.

As the closing credits rolled the station showed Directory building sites around the world. The rate of construction was staggering.

"Amazing! The psychiatrists are really lucky. I'm sure their pay scale will be incredible – and traveling all over the Directory – that's a dream job!" Gloria French said.

"Careful, Mom; you might sign up for the training yourself," Deidre teased.

"No chance of that," she said with just a tinge of sadness as she left the TV room.

"I'm seriously thinking of signing up for the training on my birthday," said Deidre.

"Really?" Natalie asked.

"Yes, really. When I'm eighteen mom can't stop me."

"In that case, I'll wait till your birthday and we'll sign up together." They smiled.

"Let's go see the boys and get them to come with us." They hit the lights and were out the door.

● ● ●

The Directory Chief's offer to the psychiatric community caused an avalanche. Fully eight thousand psychiatrists took advantage of the program. It was a time of great excitement all around the world.

A few days later The Chief of Directory Electronics made another announcement. "We've been asked by the media to allow camera crews and journalists to tour with the psychiatrists as they travel to the far-flung reaches of the Directory of Stars and Planets to document with words and images the experiences they have and the knowledge they spread and acquire.

"It is my pleasure to inform you that we will accept four-person crews for each psychiatrist. This means a total of eight thousand documentary reporters and twenty-four thousand camera/support crew. Only the highly trained may apply. As you can imagine these will be some of the first missions to leave Earth and will supply the home planet with some interesting, entertaining and educational viewing in the coming years."

Each psychiatrist had a media crew assigned and they were trained as a team. They would spend the next five plus years together.

● ● ●

The rush to fill the available technical training positions was immediate. From all over the world the brightest and most adventurous people applied for the training. The first semester saw over one hundred and thirty thousand people on various courses of study. Everything about the Directory and its operations ran at a speed that far outstripped the most efficient earthly enterprise.

Payment for the training was handled in three major ways. First, the trainees who were willing to sign a five-year offworld contract were immediately given priority and the best in accommodations at a DE training facility. The second method was government-sponsored payment, where the various nations of the world wished to have certain advanced technology under their control. This included weapons technology that, through agreement, only went to sponsored candidates of certain governments.

This was secretly laughed at by Directory officials. Did these people think that they would be allowed military independence or that they would get anything like state-of-the-art technology? Stupid.

Thirdly, private enterprise had its own major group of students who were being trained in energy, transport, communications and gadgetry. These graduates would stay here on Earth to benefit the home planet.

The courses were quite short and involved the introduction of the basic principles into the students' minds through what was called an Imprinter Field. The remainder of the time was used in familiarizing each student with the application of the principles, so they could be readily used in the appropriate situations. There was a correlation between how well a student could operate the TAC and how well the Imprinter Field "took." The astute observed that this was a very good reason to have introduced the TAC, as it allowed the aliens to more effectively grade their applicants.

The culture of Earth was undergoing major upheavals. Increasingly, on the streets of Copenhagen, Paris and Los Angeles there were seen truly divergent applications of the new technology. What had taken thousands of years to develop in a stable Directory culture was being thrust on an already turbulent Earth in months. Doomsayers were almost as prolific as the rabid adherents to this new and wonderfully expanded universe.

Directory medical facilities sprang up overnight. They provided, for those who could afford it, the most startling physical recovery from virtually any ailment. This included the replacement of almost any defective body part, including the brain. To the distress of certain segments of the population, this did not change the personality. There were no long waiting lists for the medical treatment, as it was expensive and very rapid. The Directory folks were not philanthropists. It was pay as you go. The rich hypochondriacs became frantic as they ran out of diseases to complain about.

Before the end of its first year, Directory Enterprises, as it was now called, had become the single most dominant economic force on the planet; there was no formal assumption of sovereignty or taking control of any government, but whatever DE wanted, DE got, and so became the de facto ruler of Earth.

At the beginning of the second year a major press conference was announced by the Directory Chief.

His PR people stated: "This is the most significant scientific advancement to be made available on the Earth. In fact," the PR man continued, "all other technological releases to the Peoples of Earth will shrink by comparison. This new information with its accompanying knowledge and equipment will change the face of Earth."

The proclamation exploded.

The speculation was immense.

Anyone who was anyone now owned an Ether Vision (EV, not TV) set. The field technology that drove it could be expanded to almost any size, depending on your credit. The three dimensional pictures were flawless and could be manipulated with a TAC controller that clamped lightly on the temple. And so, in beautiful color, exact resolution and real depth, Earth plunged into a new level of visual perfection.

What better way to enter the brave new world than to watch the announcement of it on EV?

The impending release caused an orgy of speculation in the novice press (as most of the anchors were doing their DE training), within the walls of academia, among the clergy, at the pulpit and around the world in homes where families wondered if this new technology might have a favorable impact on their lives.

Governments and corporations scrambled to gain any inkling of what it might be and how it would impact them. Could they prepare for this and gain some advantage over a neighbor? Those things that DE had infused into the planetary culture were like an adrenaline shot to the heart – they had invigorated dying cultures and revolutionized life on Earth.

People who had been struggling through life now wanted to be alive and rejoiced in their luck to be alive at the time of the Alien Invasion.

The Directory had produced a new level of understanding for man. The TAC for control by and of the mind, and the Imprinter Field which produced people who could actually do what they learned.

Now, with the new release impending, many wondered if the *big* questions were about to be answered.

Was "The Veil" about to be parted? Was "Truth" to be revealed? On Earth there was apprehension, fear and excitement. There was more communication between friends and family, between strangers, than ever before. Everyone was talking, and people were listening.

Or, if you were the Chief of Directory Enterprises, it was just turning another page of the instruction manual and following the steps one by one. And remembering the insults and slights he had endured, enjoying what he had already done to some of the offenders and what he would do to the others.

CHAPTER 7

NATALIE WILK STOOD ON THE PORCH of Wendy's home. She pressed the doorbell and waited with her friend Deidre French for someone to come to the door. The two young women were nervous, excited and very determined. They wanted the opportunity Earth had been offered – they wanted the stars.

In one stroke, adventurous souls had become inmates serving time; the only release from this was in the hands of the aliens. Balancing an earthbound future against offworld travel was an unequal equation.

The girls looked at each other, affirming their purpose. Wendy was the third friend and made their group whole. They wanted her to come with them.

No one came to the door.

Natalie pressed the doorbell again. A faint breeze lifted their tresses; one auburn-colored, one blonde; the raven-haired one was inside. With time running out, Deidre stepped forward and rapped her knuckles against the inset wooden panel, then knocked again. The door opened.

"Deidre, Natalie, I guess you want to see Wendy. She's in her room." Amanda White opened the door wide and the girls trotted up the stairs. They knocked on the bedroom door.

"C'mon in." The friends sat around and chatted for a few minutes, but the guests were too keyed-up to delay the reason of the visit.

"We have something to tell you." Natalie said.

"Yeah," Deidre said, "we do!" She was nearly bursting.

"Well, go ahead and tell me." Wendy laughed.

"We're signing up for offworld training." Wendy looked from one friend to the other. Their faces solemn. She laughed again.

"You can't be serious." They continued to look at her. "You're not serious!"

They exchanged another look, their synchronicity clear. Natalie began, "We're totally serious about checking out the Directory Schools program. We haven't decided to actually sign the papers yet. Not without first hearing the pitch, seeing the facilities and talking to the other students.

Deidre continued, "The Directory people have a guy from another planet who completed his contract and now tours the new worlds – the ones like ours that are being opened up – speaking to kids about doing the training. Going offworld." There was a hush in the room. "And he's in Salt Lake tonight." For a moment great possibility loomed.

Wendy ended it. "I'm going to call Jack."

Deidre and Natalie nodded. "We knew you'd say that."

"And your point is?" Wendy was curious.

"We talked to the boys, our boys, about this last night and they don't want to go, they want to wait till the first wave of Earth's students return home before they'll consider it."

"That's at least five years." Natalie said.

Wendy heard the frustration in her friend's voice.

What does their decision have to do with Jack? They didn't talk to him last night; he was with me the whole time, she thought.

"We want you to make up your own mind. If Jack is against it… " That was left to hang.

That was insulting. They were implying she couldn't decide for herself.

"You realize your attitude toward your boyfriends has nothing to do with me wanting to talk to Jack?" Wendy looked at them in turn. "And I hope, for the sake of our friendships, that you weren't hinting that Jack's opinion would overwhelm my ability to make up my mind?"

"We want you to come with us. If it checks out we can sign contracts tonight." Wendy frowned; this was wild talk.

"If our boyfriends love us they'll join us." Natalie said. Wendy could not believe what she was hearing. Her two best friends intended to blackmail their boyfriends into making a life-defining decision against their wills. This was crazy. More than crazy.

Deidre said, "You hear about it all the time, a husband signs his contract and the wife gives in and joins him at the Directory School and the next thing you know is they are off on the greatest adventure there is."

Wendy shook her head.

"I'd never do this without talking to Jack. No way will I sign a contract that would separate us for five years." She looked at her friends. "I don't want to leave the planet. Everything I want is here. And the truth is the boys are right to be concerned, no one knows if anyone will come back."

"Will they return?" Was the question that concerned the relatives of those who chose to leave – could the aliens be trusted? Without independent confirmation, no one knew. So the cautious said, "Let's wait," and the incautious took the leap. There were many arguments for both viewpoints. But the smart money was on letting the reckless go first and see if they returned.

"That's why we go listen to this guy; his name is Tyfon Arolia, the guy who completed his contract. There's a picture show with it, all the places he went, people he met, the jobs he did, living conditions, friends he made – everything!"

There was something disturbing here, something frantic; her two friends were out of control. It was happening a lot. People were abandoning relationships, jobs, money, status, family and friends to attend the Directory School. They wanted to leave ASAP.

Her friends had the fever.

"Wendy, millions are signing up."

Wendy shrugged.

"We heard the Directory will be imposing quotas on the people allowed to train and go. So we have to check this out. We won't be left on Earth, with no way out." That was extreme – truly disturbing. They weren't thinking clearly. A bad time to make a decision.

Wendy had to go with her friends and try to protect them. If she didn't, they would be lost.

"I'll come with you," she said.

● ● ●

The Chief of Directory Enterprises looked at the man in charge of the Advance Team.

"Transport numbers are low." The A Team leader said. "We're ten thousand units a month behind the next slowest planet. There'll be hell to pay if we don't fix this – soon.

"And the wrath will come down on you, not me." the team leader said.

The Chief replied, "There must be some other method to boost the numbers than what you suggest. The units volunteering for our training and the units shipped to Mars for processing are increasing."

"But not fast enough. We're behind. Way behind. Our low numbers are being watched."

The Directory chief tried to suppress a shudder. Seen from afar this job had looked easy.

"Earth is more advanced than other planets you've been to. You told me that. Earth chemical analysis is sophisticated enough to cause us trouble. If your shortcut is discovered by their scientists, there will be trouble. The peaceful mission on Earth will become war.

"I don't want to expose the whole program to failure just because you want to get out of here faster."

"My method works." The team leader said, "and I have another planet to open." He shook his head. "You're off timetable. Don't you get it? Command doesn't care why! Your problems with the media, the psychiatrists – you handled both situations perfectly. But they don't c-a-r-e. They want numbers, and you aren't delivering.

"Command is to the point of approving a war footing, almost. They'll be rid of you and give the job to someone who will get it done." the team leader said.

"Don't threaten me." snarled the Chief.

"My people and I were scheduled to leave at Recognition! Instead we're trapped on this shit hole. Because of your delays my leave has been canceled and we have to go directly to the next primitive shit hole!

"If you had agreed to do it my way from the beginning, we'd have been out of here." he grated.

"So that's it. You blame me for losing vacation time." The Chief glared. "I had nothing to do with you being held over. Your method is dangerous here. Each planet is different – you know that better than anyone."

The Advance Team leader calmed down. "Yes. I know it." He smiled thinly. "My overdue departure has nothing to do with you.

"But you don't have the big picture. Other occupied planets are losing stability and falling behind quota too. Command decided that my advance team stay past Recognition because of the potential harvest we can pull off this planet.

"My instructions are to remain on Earth until minimum transport quota is met.

"Now you know.

"You're a small cog in a team working toward a large goal."

This prick has been threatening me with war and my removal when all he cares about is his lost vacation time. He's rushing me so he can leave. The rest is PR BS, the chief thought.

"If anyone on this planet detects the chemicals you use, there won't be any more willing sheep filling the quota.

"There will be war.

"But you and your team will be gone and I'll take the fall." the Chief shouted.

"I've noted your concerns, but it's my choice. The order went out today. The quota will be met. I will leave. You will remain here and complete the mission and enjoy yourself abusing the locals just as your sleazy counterparts do." The team leader smiled. "For the record, I would never take action that would place the overall mission on this planet in jeopardy."

• • •

The day was hot and the wind dry and brisk. The sky was clear blue; the surrounding mountains sharply cut the horizon. The three friends were headed to the local Directory School recruitment office. Conversation in the car lagged, each girl lost in thought, and, for a time, intimidated by the potential future, so different from what anyone could have considered a short time ago.

"I called the Directory office and Tyfon Arolia will be speaking here today," Natalie said.

"This should be interesting," Wendy said.

"Yes, it should," Natalie said.

Deidre explained, "We've been planning this for quite some time. Ideally Jeremy and Fern were supposed to be with us today, and you would bring Jack. Now it's just us girls, the adventurous ones. I can't believe our men are not really men."

"What you're saying; it's not true of Jack – or of me, either." Now she had their attention.

Does Wendy really want to come with us? Deidre thought.

Wendy didn't elaborate, so Deidre said, "You can't leave a provocative statement hanging like that without telling us what you mean! What about Jack and you?"

"I shouldn't have said anything." She looked away. Now she was stuck. "Jack and I have a… pact. I guess you could say. But it's private, between him and me. And I would have to ask him first if it was okay to say anything about it."

"So ask," Natalie said, "call him now."

Wendy realized she hadn't been completely honest. *She* was not willing to tell her friends about her private business, about her and Jack's plans. Even if they were vague. Her bond with Jack and how it came to be would sound silly if put into words. Her friends could never feel the actual emotions that led up to… the pact. Wendy had no intention of inviting ridicule for something so close to her heart.

But as she watched the buildings drift past the car window, it occurred to her that Natalie and Deidre needed to hear what she and Jack had agreed to, and that their pact may be just the thing to bring this intense desire to attend the Directory School into perspective. If they heard that she and Jack were intending to live a life of adventure and had made the agreement long before the Directory people had made their presence known, they may realize that timidity was not the reason she nor Jack refused to sign up for training.

"I'll call him." After a brief conversation with Jack, Wendy explained what had happened between them. The girls were amazed that conservative Wendy was really out on the edge and they hadn't known it.

"That Jack is a bit of a dark horse," said Deidre. "He told you flat out that he didn't want the family, nice home and kids thing and sold you on a life of adventure?" Wendy nodded, a little startled to hear it put in those terms, but realized it was essentially true.

"Yes, he did. And I've been much happier since then."

That shocked them both.

They had to re-order all they thought they knew about their friend.

"If this is all true, then why aren't you both done with your Directory training and headed for other planets right now?"

"Jack doesn't like the aliens."

"Jack doesn't like the aliens?" Deidre repeated it as a question.

"Can you please explain that?" Natalie asked.

"I can't explain it because he doesn't know why himself. He doesn't trust the Chief of the Directory. He says that they shouldn't be here on Earth – but doesn't know why."

"How can Jack be the authority on how much trust we place in the Directory people? Can't you make a decision on your own without being influenced by Jack's feelings?"

Wendy looked hard at Deidre. "You tried this at the house. Don't you dare say I'm Jack's pawn!" Deidre thought Wendy's stare might take her head off.

"Okay, okay, I was out of line. I shouldn't have said that."

"You implied Jack has unsound judgment and I'm his dupe. I respect Jack. He is not subject to whimsical or cowardly emotions about this or anything.

"And I make my own decisions. I agree with, or disagree with, whomever I choose, for my own reasons, based on my own evaluation. That's why I'm with you."

There was no more conversation until they reached their destination.

● ● ●

The Directory had rented the huge hall #5 in the Salt Palace. The whole place was ablaze with color. More "otherworldly" but spectacular alien technology on display. The crowds were packing in. Jack parked blocks away.

Disguised, Jack looked very different.

His boots made him two inches taller and he walked with a glide. His face was unrecognizable and he was wearing one of the ball caps they were handing out in the lobby. The cap had "Tyfon Arolia, Earth's favorite Alien," printed on it.

This supposedly was an alien who had completed his five-year contract.

Jack hadn't intended to go to the Directory School recruitment pitch, but changed his mind last minute.

He was walking down the rows of seats deciding where best to sit when he saw Wendy, Natalie and Deidre.

What? She just called, why didn't she say she was coming? Jack wondered.

His whole plan underwent a rapid change. Instead of positioning himself strategically close to the speaker so as to gauge the audience reaction, he slipped in behind the girls as they passed.

Why is she here? Jack wondered. *We talked about the Directory programs. We agreed not to do the training.* Something was going on and he was glad he came so he could monitor it.

Jack looked at Deidre and Natalie. Their expressions were ecstatic. Wendy looked serious. *The girls dragged her here,* Jack knew.

He took the row behind the girls, but the seat directly in back of Wendy was already taken. Jack bent and whispered in the ear of the man seated behind Wendy; he looked horrified, got up and quickly moved away.

Jack opened the program and leaned forward so he could hear the girls' conversation. Wendy, as usual, was seated in the middle. He soon realized that Wendy was here to discourage her friends from signing up for the training. Good.

Satisfied about her intentions and safety, Jack let his attention wander over the crowd. The location was less than ideal, but it would serve.

The hall was now packed, with many standing along the walls. The MC stepped to the podium.

"Hello everyone! My name is Jessup Monroe and tonight is the night you've all been waiting for!"

The crowd surged to its feet clapping and yelling.

"Just back stage is Earth's Favorite Alien!" The roar of the crowd drowned him out. "He's here to tell a simple story. Tuam-Tek, a planet in our Pleiades constellation, was contacted by the Directory. Tyfon was trained and went to another world for five years, then returned home a wealthy man. He's here to tell you his experiences.

"Please give a warm Utah welcome to Tyfon Arolia." Monroe backed away and clapped. The crowd was on its feet again. The admiration was intense.

A man dressed in odd clothing passed between the curtains and slowly walked toward the lectern. A hush fell over the crowd.

Jack took his seat and evaluated him. Tyfon Arolia was five eleven. His complexion olive-skinned but with a subtle sheen. His posture was erect but tilted slightly backward. His form of dress was colorful and patterned. His features were "normal," if slightly elongated. He looked like a non-threatening alien.

Tyfon gave a great smile and began speaking.

No one could understand a word he said.

Jessup Monroe stepped forward and threw a metallic silver ball into the air. Translations began immediately.

"Hello, hello." Tyfon waved enthusiastically to the crowd. It was clear he was genuinely happy to be here. He was an appealing fellow. "I am happy to talk to you! As you know my name is Tyfon and I am from a non-Directory world."

Jack skipped ahead in the pamphlet and read, "Tyfon spends only a short time on any given planet and so has no chance to learn the dominant language. You will hear his voice with accent and nuance accurately translated into English." Jack felt a series of slight bumps at the bottom right of the pamphlet. Over each ridge was a symbol. He pressed the first one and the text changed to an unrecognizable language. He pressed it again and then held it down. Languages scrolled rapidly by. He tried a few combinations and finally got English back. He continued to read. "So what you hear will be as close and natural as if he spoke English as well as a native." Jack looked up at Tyfon.

"About ten Earth years ago the Directory announced their presence on my planet. My home is in your constellation of Pleiades, my world is called Tuam-Tek, and means 'sacred ground' or 'home of the faithful.' Long before the arrival of the Directory we'd been watching reruns of *I Love Lucy* and were baffled about your culture and language." There was stunned silence in the hall and Tyfon laughed. "It is my little joke. I saw *Lucy* only yesterday." There was scattered laughter and then the entire audience caught on that this guy was playful, like a young boy, and they laughed and clapped and whistled. Tyfon bowed to the audience. The effect was strange as he bowed backward.

"When I first had the opportunity of doing Directory training my planet did not believe the Directory aliens' promise and I did not really believe them either. I was in difficult circumstances. I had left the armed forces without permission and was being hunted. With a signed Directory contract I was protected from imprisonment and financial attack. I left Tuam-Tek with the first wave of workers and went to the Directory world called Loaems End where I was assigned many factory positions requiring me to use the knowledge I had acquired in my training. I was there for four and a half of your years. I was contacted and asked if I was willing to extend my tour and travel the galaxy doing speeches like this one here, telling of my experiences on Loaems End and of the Directory culture.

"First I wanted to go home. I returned to my planet to great acclaim. I purchased a home. I did many things but I became bored.

"Now I stand before you."

He talked for thirty minutes, then the question and answer period went on for more than an hour. There were many visuals and funny stories that made the entire presentation disarming and believable.

Jack felt there was no reason to disbelieve Tyfon, and thought Tyfon's experiences were real and not contrived. But nonetheless, Jack considered the whole presentation a set piece with the sole purpose of enticing the population of Earth to leave the planet.

It was very effective.

Jack could almost read their thoughts, "If he can do it, so can I."

They felt safe.

Though tempted, Jack asked no questions and drew no attention to himself. From time to time he strained to follow Wendy's conversation. He was pleased she remained skeptical throughout the entire presentation and clearly told her friends she had no intention of signing a Directory contract and advised Natalie and Deidre to pass as well.

A major advantage of Tyfon not knowing the native tongue, Jack knew, was that he could be electronically edited by Directory security personnel. So he was the perfect front man: completely honest – he would never know if he was lying or being lied to.

As Jack headed for his jeep, a large cargo van pulled up to the side entrance of the hall and large boxes were hurriedly offloaded.

● ● ●

"We're not leaving yet." Natalie said.

"Of course not." Deidre agreed.

"Alright, I can stay for a few more minutes." Wendy said, attracted by the lights ahead.

They were walking from the hall caught in the slow crush of people.

They emerged into the foyer.

Large signs scattered around the vast lobby were flashing, "Sign your contract now," "Go to the Stars," "Vital Work Force," "Adventure Starts Now," "Your Starship Awaits," "Sign and Go." The signs were stroboscope bright. Wendy closed her eyes and could see the afterimage – start your adventure now.

The recruitment desks were scattered everywhere and hundreds of people were talking to the Directory people.

People huddled in groups, discussing the presentation or Tyfon or signing up immediately. It was all very exciting; the atmosphere was electric with possibility.

Attendants began handing out free gifts to the entire crowd. The three girls opened their sample packets of skin cream and inhaled the delicious bouquet. Deidre squeezed the slim packet and the cream spread across her palm. She smiled, "This is so smooth, my skin feels like silk." Her two friends followed suit. Wendy's eyes widened as the cream absorbed into her skin. Natalie said, "Wow."

The men got a container of "silly putty." This green blob of stuff could be molded into any shape and then rapped on with a fingernail which made it go rigid and slightly cold. To unfreeze it all they had to do was warm it in their palms for a few seconds and the putty was back. It was great fun to play with and another example of offworld technology that was part of the perks to be routinely expected once the contract was signed.

There was a rush to the sign-up desks. The recruiters were left without anyone to talk to as signature after signature was placed on contract after contract. Surprisingly no one was interested or careful enough to read the details of the legal obligation to which they had committed themselves for the next five years.

Wendy felt dazed as she stood in line anxiously awaiting her turn to sign. *What is taking these people so long to sign a simple contract*, she thought.

"Please hurry." She urged those in front. The golden glow she felt continued to grow.

The three girls held hands as they waited. "Deidre, Natalie, I finally know how you feel. I'm so excited." Wendy was shaking.

She was consumed with an urgent desire to be part of the most vital work force the universe had ever seen.

She signed her contract.

"I'm going to the stars." she cried out.

● ● ●

Within a week of implementing the new recruitment tactics, the trainees were flooding in – the shiny-faced youth of Earth pledging themselves to an unknown future with manic intensity.

The advance teams, Research, PR, Action and Construction, who handled the installment of the Directory presence on virgin planets and did the majority of building facilities, had finally exceeded their quotas and were able to leave Earth.

"John Smith," the Chief of Directory Enterprises, was glad to see them go. He was now in control of all operations. He ruled an entire planet. The drawback was that if things began to blow up he only had the less than expert permanent staff to quash any trouble.

It was his vast skills and abilities that would save the day and secure a personal victory here on Earth.

When the mission on Earth was successfully completed, a limitless future would unfold. He would move to a civilized world inside the Directory.

That was his goal – to become legitimized. To be accepted by the Directory mainstream. To come out of the shadows, to put this whole murky business behind him and live at the very top of Directory society.

● ● ●

Ralph Perrywhite had taken enormous heat from Colin Craig, the Director of the CIA.

In a private meeting Craig dressed him down: "The embarrassment this agency has suffered is due to your incompetence. Your investigation of DE and its personnel was inadequate and inconclusive. An Admiral named McMillan ran a side operation. He netted the crucial data that changed the world.

"A squid with one thousandth the budget did your job."

Craig placed Perrywhite under review. "One more screw-up and you're gone. Now get out of my sight."

No such administrative procedure actually existed. When Perrywhite pointed this out, Craig asked if he wanted to be fired immediately.

Perrywhite bit down on any response. He got out of the Director's office.

They were now living in a different world with a different set of rules, and if Perrywhite were to survive with any power, he had to hold on to his job until he could transition to other circumstances.

The command structure of the planet was shifting rapidly: the halcyon days of U.S. government power were in decline and fall. This was obvious to everyone, but how do you tell a President, Congress and Judiciary they were passé, yesterday's news? You don't. You milk the situation till the udder was dry.

Perrywhite got to work. He interviewed Dr. Melliander about his curious change of heart on his TAC study.

"Dr. Melliander, you're stone-walling. Your lies are creative but farfetched."

Perrywhite pulled out a thick file from his briefcase and thumped it on the good doctor's desk.

"Your financial situation is a curious one. In fact, the CIA's forensic accountants spent day's dissecting your fiscal life and came to some curious conclusions.

"Would you like to hear what they said, Doctor?"

The man broke down. He was terrified. Perrywhite marveled that Melliander was still breathing after he heard the whole extortion story.

Melliander said, "I wanted to leave Earth with my colleagues and tour the other Directory planets. The Chief of Directory Enterprises called me personally and said the cost for me to leave was the exact amount he had paid me plus interest." The doctor was hyperventilating.

"But I had spent millions already. The DE Chief then said, 'I realize your situation is fragile.' It was a threat. I've never been so scared in my life.

"I begged him to take a lesser amount. He finally agreed – it was the exact amount remaining in my accounts. He knew exact totals, banks and account numbers.

"I was too afraid to hold on to anything."

Perrywhite nodded. "Go on."

"He let me do the training. On the day I was to leave there was a huge ceremony. The first hundred psychiatrists and our media teams going to new worlds. So much excitement." His smile faded. "We were about to board the beautiful space ship. I was stopped. I was arrested. They put handcuffs on me and leg shackles." The doctor started crying.

Perrywhite remembered seeing this on television.

"The local police held me for forty-eight hours and then let me go.

"The police said nothing. They didn't even tell me to leave; an officer just opened the cell door. Finally I walked out. No one stopped me.

"It was a frightening experience.

"As I walked out a janitor gave me an envelope. It was marked 'read immediately' and I did. My life and that of my whole family was dependent upon the 'worldwide goodwill and continuing support from the psychiatric profession.'

"I'm scared to death and have been run ragged preventing any dissent from my few remaining co-workers."

He looked around his paneled office nervously. His head ducked between his shoulders and whispered, "I think someone is spying on me and following me everywhere I go."

Melliander is paranoid, Perrywhite thought. *But extorting incredibly powerful aliens was probably a mistake.* He chuckled. *But at the time he did it who knew? Just one very unlucky guy.*

"Is there anything else you can tell me Doctor?"

Melliander frowned.

"What is it?"

"I have these dreams. Strange dreams."

Perrywhite raised his eyebrows.

"They started when I was doing the DE training…." Melliander drifted off.

"Yes, Doctor, the dreams. What about them?"

"I see a large slug like body about the size of a killer whale. It's grey-green and slimy, just like a slug. It swims in polluted waters."

"So?"

"Well, I know everything about it. Down to the most minute detail. It has three mouths. One is to ingest fecal matter. The second mouth is for urine intake. The third mouth is for eating. It can live for a thousand years."

"So what, Doctor? I have strange dreams too."

"It's a biological sewer processing plant."

"Yeah?" Perrywhite was becoming impatient.

"Every psychiatrist I talked to had the same dream."

"Now that," agreed Perrywhite, "is strange."

"Can you protect me?" asked Melliander.

Perrywhite smirked. "You're joking? Consider yourself lucky I don't have you thrown in jail myself."

"What for?" Melliander was stricken with fear again. "I gave the money back!"

"For jeopardizing alien relations."

• • •

Perrywhite was fascinated by the contact between the psychiatrist and the Directory Chief. He needed to learn all he could about the Chief. Clearly he was a vengeful man.

The next person on Perrywhite's private interview list was Augustus McMillan. Without this man's private investigation of the aliens, Perrywhite's position at Langley would still be secure. Therefore the admiral already had the feel of an enemy. Granted, McMillan had to be good at intelligence operations to plan and successfully carry out his investigation. So the guy was no dummy.

To shift to the new source of power Perrywhite had to get closer to the DE Chief, had to make himself known, make himself valuable. In short Perrywhite had to align himself with Directory goals.

Finding out what McMillan knew and what he was doing now was the logical next step in his upward spiral toward ultimate power and dominion over Earth.

● ● ●

The Chief of Directory Electronics was alerted to the meeting between Melliander and Perrywhite.

He had kept Melliander on Earth to toy with him. He wanted him running scared.

So when the Deputy Director for Operations of the CIA showed up at Melliander's office, his Investigator identified him almost immediately and called in the Chief to see and hear the meeting in real time.

The Chief replayed a short section of the meeting, "I think someone is spying on me and following me everywhere I go." Dr. Melliander was terrified. Good. The Chief played it again.

"Put a bug on the CIA guy," he instructed the Investigator.

The Chief was impressed. The Investigator acted with speed and contacted him with a potentially important development. And knew who Melliander's visitor was. It promised good things for ongoing operations on Earth. Anyone who came against him would be immediately discovered and eliminated at leisure.

CHAPTER 8

So many things had changed in such a short period of time. Jack and Wendy were caught in the middle of a whirlwind. Earth was no longer the sole lonely outpost of humanity in the universe.

The promise of star travel was just weeks away for another massive group of Directory School graduates. Prosperity and technology were all around and people had more stuff, they smiled more and there was the potential of a very broad future.

Internal affairs on planet Earth had changed radically over the past months.

It seemed that the simple awareness that there were other friendly humans in the universe had, after the initial confusion dissipated, a very calming effect.

The wars and turmoil on Earth had begun to subside as everyone realized that tomorrow was going to be different for everyone.

No matter your background, if you could read and write, you could sign up, get a fast Directory School education and leave Earth. So who really cared if a racial or tribal enemy across a national border was not to one's liking?

There were bigger and better games to play. There was something new and different to look forward to. There was so much more *space*, that the planet-wide pressure found release….

• • •

One thing around the White and Cousins' households had an immediate personal impact, and it was tearing Jack apart.

Wendy had made a decision, signed a contract, gone to the Directory School and graduated. She was going away. And, so far, nothing Jack said had changed her mind. Wendy had just completed her training in an elite section of the Directory School, the Accelerated Learning Section for Very Bright People, and there was no restraining her enthusiasm.

The final exams had been earlier that day and she had scored a 99.7 out of 100. She then completed a short review of the materials where her understanding was imperfect, raising her score upon retest to 100. She was energized and motivated and couldn't wait to get on a space ship, strap in and start an unbelievable new adventure with her friends.

Wendy, Deidre and Natalie over the past months, had spent more time together than ever before and had endless debates over where to go. They each had the DE recruitment computer, which was a flat touch screen. This device had an EV mode where recruits could look at 3D vistas and city centers on worlds across the Directory.

Job availability was updated on a weekly basis as a star ship from the Directory arrived in the solar system and uploaded the latest data. Because their training was different, the girls hunted to find openings in the same city on the same world. Deidre had stayed with marketing and because this was more a function of art and communication skills, she had spent most of her time learning languages. Wendy and Natalie had their positions set to semi-lock pending a petition that Deidre win her application to a company in the city they had chosen. If she was accepted, their computers were set to secure the positions of all three automatically. It then would print tickets containing their full itinerary, including an irrevocable departure date.

Many recruits received welcome notices from the company managers if their departure date was more than six weeks from their lock-in date. Star routes and availability of seats on star lines varied greatly.

Recruits with lock-in dates and tickets showed these around. Wendy had seen a ticket where the recruit would be traveling for four months. It made her shiver. There were to be so many new sights and new people. Her imagination ran wild with the vastness of her prospects.

Wendy couldn't explain to Jack or her parents why she hadn't consulted them before signing her contract. But each time she thought of it she felt that warm glow again, and that potent feeling reassured her she had made the right decision.

It was especially strange to Jack because he knew that fifteen minutes before signing her contract, Wendy had no intention of doing so – at least that was how it had appeared at the time. He felt responsible for it happening. He had left the recruitment center too early. If there were ever a worse time to be wrong, for his judgment to fail so abysmally, where the consequences could be worse, he didn't know what it was.

Being wrong on the small things was tolerable, but here, where all he had needed to do was wait for Wendy to leave, to ensure nothing bad happened… and instead he had walked away.

And Wendy would not talk about the point where she had changed her mind. Even when he reminded her of their earlier conversations, about their agreement to not do the Directory School program, she was vague, nonspecific, but would brighten up only when talking about her schooling and the future – out there.

Even stranger was Wendy's expectation that Jack applaud her bold initiative and follow her lead and sign up for the training himself. She had anticipated, she said, they would adventure together somewhere in the Directory.

This about-face was confusing, inconsistent and made no sense. If he stretched his mind it was vaguely plausible that she had changed her mind. But expecting him to do the same after their exhaustive conversations and her knowing his strong opposition made no sense at all.

It made no sense. *Something is rotten in the state of Denmark,* Jack thought, and it was frustrating to "know it, but know not what," as Shakespeare had phrased it.

Jack pointed out that because he wasn't yet eighteen, he couldn't legally do it. Then he had refused to consider doing the training under any circumstances. When he again tried to get a straight answer about why she had changed her mind, she accused him of trying to undermine her independence.

Wendy could see that Jack was devastated by her taking such an irrevocable course of action. In fact, she couldn't even remember thinking about him at all as she waited in line at the recruitment table waiting to sign her name – even she felt this was strange, and it *was* strange, but the glow, the inner sense of well-being, could not be denied….

●

Jack felt the future accelerating and the inevitable clash of powerful forces rushing at him. His sense of imminent danger shifted into high gear, *because I have to do something about it*, he thought.

I can't just wonder why and watch Wendy go to her… death? He wasn't sure what would happen when she left Earth, but he knew it was bad. Worse than death. He shook his head. The depth of his dread for her safety engulfed him. It took a conscious effort to shake it off.

But it never really went away.

During her training it had become more painful to spend time with her. His emotions would overwhelm him and he would shout at her. Then he would be very apologetic. But it happened over and over. So he had seen far less of her recently.

Jack suppressed his upset and called her.

"Hey, Wendy."

"Hello, Jack," she replied.

"I've spent a lot of time arguing with you about your training."

"Yeah, you have. And it's been very unpleasant."

"I know. And we never get anywhere when we argue."

"You finally noticed?"

Jack deserved the sarcasm. "Yes, you're correct. I've made it impossible for you to talk to me – even to spend any time with me. I'm sorry for that."

"I'm glad you realize that."

"You're welcome. So I wanted to change that. Would you be willing to explain your training to me?"

Wendy didn't answer immediately. She had cut herself off from Jack more and more over the last few months. She was leaving. He was staying. Their relationship would not survive the five year absence. To protect herself she put more and more emotional distance between them.

But this offer was different. His tone of voice soft.

"Okay, Jack, I'll tell you anything you want to know."

"Great. Can you come over now?"

Never one to let the moss grow was her Jack. "Okay. See you in a minute."

●

Jack wanted to understand as much as he could about Wendy's situation. *I can't help her if I'm upset all the time*, Jack thought.

The doorbell rang.

There she was.

He opened the door. She was the most beautiful girl he had ever seen.

"You got me here. Are you going to ask me in?"

He smiled. "C'mon in."

Jack asked questions for hours. On the sofa Wendy told Jack about the technical stuff she had learned. How it had changed her understanding of the world and how it worked.

Wendy mentioned a section of training on biology. Jack's attention had stuck on this, it seemed out of place in her training line-up.

"Tell me more about the biological stuff, Dee," he asked.

Wendy frowned. She thought his attention had wandered. Not so. "It was interesting, but some of it was really strange."

"Strange?" He asked.

"Yes, I have the idea that if I secrete a certain hormone, the bones in my arms and hands will soften and lengthen." She had a puzzled expression on her face. "It's really weird. There's another hormone to restore the proper bone structure. My body has neither hormone. *Human* bodies don't have those hormones."

She paused and rubbed her arms as if assuring herself they were still rigid. "There was other stuff like that – un-hinging a knee joint and coupling it together again." She shook her head. "It made no sense. But it was easy to learn." She shook her head. "What I mean, I guess, is that if I saw a creature whose body worked that way, I could identify it. Could understand how it worked and grasp its potential for specialized activity." Her confused expression remained.

Jack went cold as stone. His heart beat with heavy sluggish thumps. Not noticing his reaction, Wendy thought of something else and brightened.

"Other things were really helpful. I can now partially control my pineal gland hormone release. When I do it I'm more aware of the things around me, colors are bright and my vision clear and I almost don't even know I have a body at all. That's a good thing, right Jack?"

"Yes, that's a good thing."

"I mean I *feel* good and there seems to be no aftereffect. It's not like a drug you come down from and feel terrible."

Alarm bells were going off in his head.

"Jack, can you believe…" said Wendy, but he failed to hear the rest. There was something truly sinister about Directory Electronics. They shouldn't be on Earth. He knew the truth of this as he knew the Earth was round. He could prove what he knew about the Earth but had no facts about the Directory people.

Listening to Dee telling of her bio-training had turned a strong suspicion into an irrevocable certainty. There was a terrible darkness connected to all this.

His trouble was that he had no facts, no hard information to refute all the legitimate educational benefits Wendy had received. She'd had a uniformly positive experience. Opposing that were his dark emotions and ominous but vague sense of dread premonition. But even without corroborating information and hard facts, he trusted what he felt.

He knew DE was crooked; all he had to do was find concrete evidence. Infiltrating this high tech organization was not going to be easy, but had to be done.

"Jack! You haven't been listening!"

"Sorry, Dee."

"And you were doing so well, Mr. Cousins. Listening and not arguing." She looked off for a few seconds. "Do you hate me Jack? Do you hate me for signing the contract?"

"I hate that you signed the contract. But I will never…" Words left him as his throat felt tight. "I love you. Just you Dee. We are the three musketeers, the two of us. All for one and one for all…"

She laughed. "You clown." She reached out and took his hand. Walls were coming down. She sobbed once and was in his arms. "Oh Jack. Oh Jack."

●

They talked and talked, and along the way came close together again. But this made the future more difficult for Wendy. For, once again, the coming loss of Jack was too terrible to contemplate.

Then, with ill-fated timing, her DE computer on the coffee table gave a melodious chime.

Wendy picked it up. There it was: her job confirmation and transport date lock-in. Irrevocable. She and Jack watched as the ticket printed and dropped into her hand.

"Jack, oh Jack. I leave in fifteen days! Deidre, Natalie and I are going to Regulus. You have to look at the travel brochure. It is sooo beautiful!" Wendy continued to gush.

Then she felt horrible. Being so excited about leaving. Leaving Jack. Then she felt exultant again.

She was fully done. Departure on a space shuttle in two weeks. Short trip to Mars base for processing. Then off. To a star that couldn't be seen in the night sky.

Jack looked at her.

No, No, No, Nooooooo! he thought. His felt like a train wreck that never ended. Every emotion inside him kept smashing and howling in torment, seeking brutal expression. He was holding it all in desperate check. If he let go, he had no idea what he would say or do.

It was frightening.

He felt kind of crazy. He wanted to reach for her, but didn't want to touch her. He wanted to run far away, but couldn't leave.

Her future was not exciting tourist destinations as she expected – it was death or worse.

He knew it.

He couldn't prove it.

He had to delay or stop Wendy's departure. And he had to get her enough real information that would cause her to change her mind. *She* had to decide this. How to change her mind? How to disrupt the Directory programs on Earth?

I'm going to do this, he decided. *No more complaints, no more "why did she sign up?" Just action.*

This was no futile howling into the void.

●

While Wendy was away at the Directory School getting her training, Jack had been searching for something he could use to prevent, or delay, her departure.

First, he needed more information. Tyfon Arolia had been a puff piece. Nothing of value there – except to understand the lengths to which DE would go to make their plan work. They were determined intelligent, persistent and had resources he was unable to assess.

They were doing something.

It didn't include helping the people of Earth.

I know it, he thought, *I don't know why I know it but I do.*

Jack studied the problem from many angles, absorbed all the available data about the Directory: its personnel, their commercial activities, locations and movement. He had talked to those who completed Directory training. Were the aliens superhuman in strength or mental capacity? Did they talk about personal hopes or dreams – if so, what? He was collecting real data, speculation and rumor. He read print media, watched the EV and scanned web sites and postings.

He had not come up with The Plan.

This failure helped fuel his upset.

●

Jack and Wendy's conversation had dwindled. Jack was reminded that the only plan he had was not very strong. Tomorrow was the day of the Directory Chief's world-shattering announcement.

This announcement would provide the first step.

He had been seeding the last days and weeks with, "I know what his proclamation is going to be," to his mother, to Norman and even a few times to Wendy.

The fateful day of her departure was set. If they were to have a life together, he had to act.

She sat quietly at his side.

He had to change the whole equation. It never occurred to him that he couldn't do it. The problem was to find the correct entry point. He couldn't just attack DE and be captured; he had to be effective and remain free to push forward.

With her itinerary ticket in hand, Wendy moved very close to Jack, trying to compensate now with forced intimacy for the five years of separation that would begin in two weeks. Jack seemed not to notice her attempts to gain his attention. The EV absorbed him, or so she thought.

Her excitement about receiving her ship date, about leaving Earth, had upset him again.

Jack recalled their first conversation after she signed up for Directory training.

●

Jack answered his phone. "Hey, Dee."

She must have just gotten back from protecting Natalie and Deidre from Tyfon Arolia and Directory Electronics.

"Jack, I'm outside. Come talk to me." He stepped outside.

"Let's sit in your jeep."

"Alright."

She dropped the bombshell. "I signed a Directory Contract. I'm going to the stars!" She was radiant.

Jack sat stunned for a few minutes, then he spoke.

"Look, my love," said Jack, "we have no information from an independent source. All we know about Directory operations on Earth and out there in the galaxy is what they choose to tell us. They've taken control of this planet with a bloodless coup; they're more firmly in control of Earth than any of history's conquerors have ever been. That they are here fills me with, with, I don't know… I feel nervous, anxious and threatened."

"Jack, you said this all before I signed up. You said it many times."

"I can't explain it! I know it sounds crazy! I don't know why I feel this way, but I do. I'm convinced that DE should not be here. They, they…" he stumbled over his words unable to continue – upset that he was not convincingly communicating something that was vitally important. If a hunch could be cast in bronze, well, that was how certain he was.

"We have no way to determine their true intentions. What they really want. I just don't buy that they are a do-gooder race here to benefit us backward Earth folk."

"Jack, we know what they want; we know what they're doing. They've told us. Tyfon Arolia described his experience in great detail – I believe him. Wow, the things I've already learned," the glow in her eyes was radiant and unquenchable, "and will learn... and the adventure of it all is," she hesitated, searching for appropriate adjectives, "incredible, fantastic. It's beyond belief!"

Her excitement dimmed as she saw his eyes because in them there was... suffering. *My God,* she thought, *this is really tearing him apart!*

"Jack, five years is not very long. With Directory meds we won't lose any time...."

"Dee, you sound like a Directory infomercial." And he couldn't help but add, "It used to be you who was afraid of losing me and wanted us to be together always. Was that a lie? Were those just words? I guess so, because look at what you're doing." It wasn't what he had planned to say. It had come out – the abandonment.

She turned to him, eyes flashing. "Jack, that's not fair! I asked you to come to the stars with me. I thought that adventure was what you wanted. That was our pact. But you wouldn't. It was you, you who wouldn't come with me."

"I'm not eighteen! I can't legally go!"

"Don't give me that, Jack! If for one minute I thought you would go, I would have waited for us to go together. You know that's true!

She was upset now, "When I agreed to go with you on *your* adventure, it was okay. But when I wanted *you* to come with *me*, you wouldn't. Here's how it looks to me: I can agree with you and that's okay, I can follow your lead and that's okay too, but as soon as I have an independent idea of my own, you dump me." She knew how untrue that was, but couldn't stop herself. He deserved it. He had been cruel. "I want you with me, Jack. It would be so good, such a journey, both of us on a new world, together..." Her voice trailed away. She sighed for what was lost – forever?

He turned his head away and lonely tears tracked down his cheeks. He had found her, only to lose her?

●

"You were drifting, Jack."

"I recalled our chat after you signed the contract."

"Chat?" Wendy winced. "That didn't go well, did it?"

"Not our finest hour," Jack said.

She laughed. "It wasn't, was it?"

"Hmmmmm," he said.

Wendy moved Jack's arm over her shoulder and leaned her head against his. Ironically, after all the arguments and all her assertiveness, she had begun to have doubts about the wisdom of her choice to leave on a Directory ship.

Jack had gotten under her skin. But she felt a deep glow of hope, promise and an unreasoning happiness about her voyage. She wanted to go, she really wanted to. No matter the disruption it caused, in fifteen days she was going to leave this planet and she promised herself she would do so without regret.

"The big announcement is tomorrow," Jack said. "Will you watch it with us?"

She said she would, then went home.

CHAPTER 9

Jack and Wendy were on the sofa watching the sycophantic build-up to the *big announcement* from DE. The EV commentary was a series of wild speculations about the nature of the upcoming revelation.

The EV personality said, "Here we are and it's not even noon. It's like the Directory Chief has given the entire world a day off! Can you imagine one single person who is not glued to their EV or old fashioned TV? I can't." And they chattered on using many exclamations.

"Jack?" He did not hear her and continued to stare at the 3D display. Wendy moved in front of him and Jack's eyes focused on her after a second or two. "Jack?"

"Yes, Dee?" He tried to smile.

"You told us you knew what the Directory announcement is going to be. Are you ready to tell me now?"

"I'll tell you just before the announcement, okay?" Jack wouldn't normally bait her like this, but he had a point to make.

"All right, Jack." She didn't want to start another ugly confrontation. There had been too much of that already.

Norman Cousins came rushing down the stairs, not wanting to miss the broadcast. He was a tall man with regular features. He owned a diverse array of businesses and consulted on the side. He had a knack for turning failing companies into profitable ones. He was well liked and respected in the local community.

"Has his 'high and mightiness' made his entrance yet?"

"Mr. Cousins, he's called the Directory Chief," Wendy said. She felt compelled to support the top Directory executive because she was in his program.

"Yes, but he looks down on all the little people and doesn't try to hide it anymore. Compare him now to the bland, inoffensive guy he was when he first arrived; it's a change."

"Are you giving our guest a hard time *again*, Norman? That's not very kind." Wendy looked at Sharon Cousins as she entered the room and felt a wave of gratitude.

"You're right, my love. Sorry, Wendy." Norman was slightly chastened.

"Thank you. I know you and Jack don't think I should go, but I'm locked in and have a ship date in two weeks."

"You're going to the same planet as Natalie and Deidre?" asked Sharon.

"Yes, Sharon, we're all going to the same city. We'll be able to share the same apartment."

"You're lucky, and I'm glad you three will be together. That's comforting." Sharon thought it was a hoax too, but with a ship date locked in there was no changing it now. So she played along.

Norman said, "I want to hear what the Directory Chief has to say, but I don't have to like him."

"He'll be on in a few minutes, it's probably a good time to get settled," Jack said. "Did Aunt Sharon tell you I call her 'Mom' now?"

"Yes, she did," Norman replied. "She likes it." Sharon smiled.

"Well how 'bout 'Dad,' Dad?"

Norman smiled. "How 'bout Norman instead of Uncle Norman?"

"How 'bout 'Norm'?"

"How 'bout I kick…."

"Will you two stop! I want to listen to the EV," Sharon said.

"Did we resolve something there, Norman?"

"Please!" Wendy said. "It's gonna start any second now."

Jack was glad of a little humor. He and Wendy scooted over and they all piled onto the sofa.

"Okay," Norman said. "We'll shut it."

"That's a British expression."

"I picked up a few expressions while I was in 'Old Blighty' on business. It's what the Brits call their island paradise, you know." Jack smiled at his uncle. Norman loved the quirky stuff.

The cameras began to pan across the stage where the Directory Chief was to make his appearance. The network announcers were wrapping up their commentary.

"This is going to be big; it's going to be the biggest thing this planet has ever seen!"

They showed scenes from around the world where some communities had set a huge EV in a sports stadium or an auditorium. Many of the people in these mass audiences were holding hands. It was clear they wanted a closer connection to their friends and neighbors. They wanted to share the moment together. Times Square was a teeming mass of excited and happy people. The expressions of anticipation and awe had a powerful impact on Jack. Everything petty in their lives had been put aside in the hopes that the revelation of a greater truth would be given to them and their lives would be changed forever. He hated his cynical feelings, but there was a betrayal of magnitude here, and the combined populations of Earth were going to be very upset when they found out. He knew it. He still had no facts, but *he knew*.

"Have you noticed," Sharon asked, "that Earth is no longer 'Earth' but referred to as 'this planet' now? We are one of many, no longer the only one."

"It's wonderful to see all the new planets and cities and people on the recruit computer," said Wendy.

Poor girl, Sharon thought, *she has to defend them at every opportunity.*

The EV commentator said, "Some speculate that the new technology will be the 'transporter' device made popular on *Star Trek*. Wouldn't that be something?" On the screen flashed an old episode with Captain Kirk saying "Beam us up, Mr. Scott."

"My personal theory about the new technology," continued one of the announcers, "is the 'happy drug.' What more could mankind need than a substance that allows us to enjoy life and doesn't make you want to commit suicide? When hasn't life on this planet been a sorry thing? It's been war, war, war." The guy looked ready to cry. "We sure could use a break."

"It's a bit weird to hear these guys saying what they actually think. You could see the anchorman ignoring the teleprompter and speaking his mind," Sharon said.

"You know the world is really changing when something like that happens!" Norman observed.

"They have it all wrong," Jack said. "They've all been guessing along technological or biological lines, and that's not it." Wendy looked at him, wanting to ask, but waiting.

"That's right. You have to tell us what the big announcement is before *he* does. Right, Jack?"

"Right, Mom."

"And you're baiting us for what reason, Jack?" Norman asked.

"For effect, Norman."

Slowly, then, above the stage an area began to darken, and a swirling began to merge and solidify. The fanfare of music was heightening and with a splitting of rainbow color and sound, the Directory Chief was before the cameras. He was three feet off the stage but appeared to be standing on solid ground. That is, his feet were not dangling as if his body were merely suspended. He looked like a rock star in a concert gone high tech.

"People of Earth, it has been more than a year since the formal declaration of our arrival on your planet. We are pleased that you chose to accept us without demonstrations of a military nature. Such an occurrence would have delayed acceptance of each other and made complete trust impossible. As you have seen in these past busy months, we have the technology to build, but it can also be used to destroy. So let me formally commend the planet Earth for the combined wisdom of both you and your leaders.

"Much has been accomplished in the intervening year. The technical and educational standards of the planet have been raised markedly. This is all as it should be, and the benefits will continue to expand as other ventures are embarked upon." He gestured grandly.

"We of the Directory have been aware of your existence for many thousands of years. The time was recently deemed right for you to be made aware of *our* existence. We of the Directory of Stars and Planets have the greatest concern for your welfare and wish to promote it so that you can become eligible for formal entry into the principal interstellar culture that exists within this galaxy. It is entirely possible that at some future point this can occur – if you so wish.

"As you now know, I am the representative of a community of hundreds of stars, planets and various comets, asteroids and so on. We have explained much of this to you in the past, but please bear with me. There is a basic component of our culture that we've not yet disclosed." Caught in a convergence of light he looked like Apollo: he radiated. "That is the specific topic of illumination in today's address.

"This thing, to those of us of the Directory, is an aspiration, the attainment of which is the heart's fondest desire. This goal is the single dominating factor in the lives of many trillions of Directory citizens. In our culture the attempt to attain this particular state is the cause of excellence in the vast array of life's endeavors. Our citizens live and breathe for the realization of this goal. They form strong family units which advance a selected candidate for attainment of this goal. Once the goal is reached, a person is presented with a galactic panorama of possibilities that were not possible before its accomplishment."

The mystery was thick and inviting. Wendy shivered.

"This is a thing we hold within our grasp!" he shouted and theatrically thrust his clenched fist into the air.

Wendy had been staring at Jack while listening to the speech. It would not be long till the alien told his secret, the build-up was almost over. She looked at the EV and could see the grand, melodramatic and faintly comic figure pause for effect. Then Jack, without taking his attention from the alien, said clearly, "Immortality."

The music and light reached an otherworldly crescendo.

"And this thing is… IMMORTALITY!" A fanfare cascaded from the EV. Goose flesh broke out over Wendy's body and her teeth chattered slightly till she forced her jaw closed. How? How did he know this? How?

"Jack!" Norman said. "You know too damn much about these people for my comfort." His voice was unsteady.

"I'm sure there's an explanation," Sharon said.

"You ever get so certain about something, you just know it's true?" Jack asked.

"Yes, but it's more like I know the meal I'm cooking will be fine – not what alien races are thinking," Sharon said.

Wendy was frightened because Norman and Sharon were right. Jack's knowing about the Directory intentions made it far more real that she could be in danger. She felt a desolate foreboding wash over and quash the golden glow she always felt whenever she thought about leaving Earth. She could no longer picture the beautiful world she and her friends had selected. Instead it would be some dark and loathsome planet no one in their right mind would ever go to.

She felt isolated and alone. Her fate was sealed; there was no Earthly force that could vacate the validity of the Interstellar pledge.

Norman was worried about Wendy. She was in serious trouble. "You wanted to create this upset." He looked at Jack. "Take a look at her, Jack. You got what you wanted. She's really disturbed."

"Yes, I am! Why wouldn't you tell us what you knew sooner?" Wendy accused.

Jack looked at her, at them.

"Dee, I did it this way because I love you."

She shook her head. "You're not answering the question."

"I love you," he persisted, "so I waited to tell you when it would have the greatest impact. I may not know everything about these Directory people, but I've shown I know something – and it's real. My opinion about the Directory people and their intentions deserves respect, respect from you." His look softened. "Don't go."

She choked up and couldn't answer. She was now doubtful it was safe to go; the whole program may be a fraud. But Directory law made certain she had to. She was locked in, had an unchangeable ship date. She could say to her man, 'I don't want to go, Jack' and he would risk his life to help her, and probably lose it trying to save her because he wouldn't give up.

The Directory was in control of Earth. No one could do anything to them and win. If she asked him to help she would become the reason he died, so she said nothing. And then there was her pride. It was hard to abandon something one had fought hard for, even if it proved wrong.

Jack watched her. If she hadn't been so caught up in the problem, she would have realized she had no need to ask for his help. He had achieved the first goal: if she wasn't forced to, she wouldn't go.

Sharon watched the kids. Adult problems were now theirs and she had no power to help.

As the Directory Chief continued his speech, it was clear that he was offering immortality to only a small portion of Earth's population.

"As has recently been instituted on those planets newly contacted by the Directory, we will likewise commence the Gladiator Immortality Games here in the coming months. These Games are intended to provide a means whereby those beings with superb martial ability can swell the ranks of the finest, most powerful military organization in this or any other galaxy. It's an open invitation to become part of the military structure of the Directory and gain citizenship *and* immortality!"

"That's horrible." Jack said.

They looked at him but he said no more.

Jack felt deep revulsion at this announcement. He was not disturbed that immortality was available to the population of Earth; that was okay. But making soldiers immortal so they could be more effective killers as a primary purpose was revolting.

This violation was visceral; it betrayed a principle he could not articulate but nevertheless knew existed. The reward and ultra-glorification of violence. It was wrong. It was bad policy. Short-term gain for some, long-term disaster for any culture.

The Directory Chief continued on about the new era that the people of Earth were witness to, were lucky enough to be living in. The visual impression was god-like and the message was elemental, touching the very core of a desire that has been present on Earth from the beginning of history.

Immortality.

There for the taking, to be fought for – literally. It would far outstrip *any given Sunday*.

"The details of how the contest is to be administered will be released shortly. The means as to how immortality is achieved and the practical application will be detailed at that time."

The Directory Chief bade them good evening. "Dream of the future, people of Earth, because it is bright and you will be living it, soon."

The producers scrambled to find a fire and brimstone preacher to comment on this latest development. They had many experts lined up to comment, but had failed to foresee the need for religious commentary. After a commercial break they asked the opinion of a televangelist preacher the producers had found on short notice.

"This is a damnation, an abomination in the sight of God. Immortality and the Resurrection is God's and God's alone to withhold or dispense as he sees fit and can only be done with his knowledge and divine power. No agency of man, or any alien race for that matter, can enter the divine realm."

"But Reverend, the claims and promises made by Directory officials have been true. And one wonders, if this can be easily proved or disproved, why make your claim?" But the Reverend's answer was not broadcast.

Norman turned to his wife. "I remember when I was a kid, a South African, Doctor Christiaan Barnard, performed the first human to human heart transplant and many preachers condemned him for invading God's province." Norman shook his head in a dismissive way. "Who, today, wouldn't have a heart transplant if they needed one and could afford it? If this preacher was personally being offered immortality by the Directory people I doubt he would complain. He would find a way to see how his immediate immortality fit into God's plan.

"If this is true, about immortality I mean, then a major piece of artillery in the religious arsenal has just been blown away. If this is true," he repeated, "then the principles that many were certain controlled the universe will be shaken to the core. Who knows what belief system will take its place?"

"Something closer to the facts, I suspect," Jack said offhandedly, and got a long stare from Norman.

"Why the look, Norman? I knew he was going to say 'immortality.' This will transform Earth." He pointed to the EV. "People will talk of nothing else for a long time."

The commentary and speculation were continued by the network hosts. Immortality was a fine thing, they supposed, but what form would it take? Was it eternal youth? Did you grow old and then become young? Was immortality a disembodied state that could hardly be conceived? Immortality, all well and good, but how was it to be done? How? And was it only the best fighters who would become immortal or could you buy it? How much would it cost? There was endless speculation. And, truly, wasn't happiness more important? Who would want to live forever in a sad, unhappy or depressed state? Wasn't death a release from this Vale of Tears?

"It is clear that the populations across the planet will be as agitated by this revelation as we are, and many a head will get no rest tonight as it struggles with the simple primal question it can no longer ignore.

"If this alien race has achieved immortality living in this world, this galaxy, this universe, then we are about to learn more about man's true nature, and the rest will be seen for what it may always have been: unfounded speculation."

"That was a little more profound than I ever expected to hear from an EV commentator," Sharon said to no one in particular.

The living room was quiet. Norman was staring at the floor. Sharon felt her family coming apart. Wendy was dazed. Jack shivered.

●

Jack knew what specific action he had to take. Right now. Immediately.

Inwardly he cursed his cowardice for putting off the inevitable for so long. He had delayed and delayed. He had many justifications as to why he hadn't done the single most obvious and necessary thing. It all came down to fear. He was afraid of what would happen.

Then it struck him. The solution. He would take Wendy with him. That would handle many things, or it would all go to hell.

With her leaving it was all going to hell anyway. *Good*, he thought, *I'll take her with me.*

What was to have been his private solo journey, the reckoning, the pilgrimage, the resolution – or the death of him – was the perfect solution to his conflict with Wendy.

Jack turned to Wendy and asked, "Dee, would you like to go camping before you ship out?"

"Jack," she said quietly, "I'd love to."

"Is your Mother going to be okay with this?"

Wendy laughed. "You're kidding?"

Jack looked a little confused.

"There was hell to pay when I told my parents that I had signed a Directory contract. And what that meant. Mother accused you. I told her you weren't coming with me." She laughed. "She was sure you, Jack

Cousins, were the 'bad influence' in my life and was shocked to find it wasn't true."

"I never...."

"Jack, I'm due to ship off planet soon, with or without her permission. I don't think she'll complain about a trip to the mountains – especially since they're located on Earth."

CHAPTER 10

"Great, let's go." Jack smiled.

Wendy gave him a long stare. "You want to leave right now?"

"There's nothing to stop us. Let's go."

What followed was a flurry of activity. Jack raced around collecting the needed supplies and stuffed his backpack with clothing, equipment and rations. He threw the scuba gear into the back of the four wheel drive jeep, then he and Wendy jumped in. Norman was at the door and waved Jack over.

Jack looked at Wendy, "I'll be right back."

●

"Who is your dive partner?" Norman asked. It was standard practice to never dive alone.

"This is a solo dive."

"You can't do that. I'll get my gear." He turned to go inside.

"Uncle!" Norman stopped. "I must do this alone." Jack could have given many reasons, but Norman deserved the unvarnished truth. "I want it this way. I have something to confront, something intensely personal. It will be dangerous." Jack shrugged. "Some things in life you have to face alone… this is one of them."

"But, but…" The look on Jack's face made it impossible for Norman to continue.

"This dive? Solo?" Jack said. He looked at Norman for a long moment. "How stupid, how dangerous is it for me to dive alone?" Jack shrugged. "Very."

"Then, why do it? Your whole life is ahead of you."

"The help another diver could give me won't keep me alive if I get in trouble."

"If you die trying to do what you need to do up there, it will destroy Wendy. You know that," Norman said.

"If I don't succeed, she's dead anyway." Jack had said it with no particular emphasis, but Norman was pierced to the core. Jack had shed something tonight. There was a new feeling of determination about him. Solo diving was dangerous by itself. He acknowledged the dive itself was hazardous. Norman's head began to spin. He couldn't allow his boy to go into such peril without his help.

Jack reached out and took his uncle's arm in a viselike grip. "Norman!" Jack said. Norman looked into the boy's eyes. His son's eyes were so full of warmth.

"Father," Jack said. "Of all the men on this planet, I am pleased to call *you* that. There comes a time in life where a father must let the son make his own way, or the son does not become a man, does not take responsibility for himself. For you and me this is that time. Any son who goes to war faces extinction. I don't deny that that possibility exists now. This is my rite of manhood." He looked at Norman with a clear gaze.

"Father, do I have your blessing to do this?"

Norman pulled him into a hug and said, "I'll see you when you get back." And he hid from his son the tears that filled his eyes.

●

They drove to Wendy's, where she jumped out and ran inside her home. She was gone for twenty minutes. Finally she ran back out, threw her gear in back and jumped in.

Jack asked his question with raised eyebrows.

"Mom gave me the third degree. But I'm over 18 and I'm leaving Earth, so I prevailed."

"You had a pretty strong hand. But it's nice to know she cares so much." Jack said.

"Yeah, it is. My parents love me and all this is very hard on them."

They were on the freeway five minutes later.

●

The cool air streaming past the vehicle cleared Wendy's head. This was just the change she needed to dispel, at least for a short time, the dread she felt. At first she had no idea where they were headed and felt no reason to ask. Then, as they sped on, she realized their destination was the camping site in the high mountains Jack often felt compelled to visit.

No, she thought with an intuitive leap, *fate is our destination. The road is blacktop, our path is destiny*. She looked over at the speedometer and at ninety miles an hour Jack was wasting no time in reaching it. *The future must be powerful for me to feel it coming before it get here. Now that*, she thought, *is an interesting idea*.

Hours later they reached the exit and within a few miles began a steep climb up through rugged mountain passes. The sun was setting, clouds were scattered in and about the majestic peaks. Mauve and purple splashed across the scattered pattern, colored by the orange and red beams that streaked the sky like the flowing mane of Pegasus. Wendy was lost in the splendor of it. A timeless forever that soon vanished. Dread and beauty.

She longed for her life to escape its terrible predicament. She wanted the freedom to be with Jack, to have a future worth living.

The nearness of her departure from Earth added extra clarity to her perceptions, and normal things now appeared vibrant and striking: a cactus, the jumble of a rocky outcrop, the sweep of the road as they climbed toward their destination. Beauty was everywhere. How strange that it took desperate circumstances to really see it. Like a condemned person from a scaffold, she looked around her, gathering in a lifetime of wonder.

Jack moved in his seat to a more comfortable position and her thoughts were drawn to him. She knew now, with finality, she would lose him, and the hollowness filled her with grief. The tears cascaded over her cheeks and were stolen by the wind. Then grief, the companion of lost love, ran dry and left her numb. Shadowed mountains moved.

Her thoughts returned to her predicament and how it began. She could not, even to herself, say precisely why she had originally decided to go off-planet, to sign a contract, without talking to Jack or her parents first.

Even now, looking at the decision that had changed her life, she couldn't remember the logical progression of thought that led her to change her mind.

That was strange.

She looked at that time again and remembered the speech by Tyfon, then her conversation with Natalie and Deidre while walking out after the show was over. Now, in a moment of clarity, she recalled thinking she had to prevent her friends from signing the contract.

The next thing she felt was a golden glow. Then the bright lights, the signs. Oh my God! In her memory she looked at her hands, felt the beautiful soft skin as she rubbed in the lotion. Oh my God! Now in the jeep she felt it again. The initial tingling sensation of her hands and arms, the spreading warmth, the disconnected sensation and how true the message the flashing lights communicated – it was so right, she had to sign the contract. Wendy sat for some minutes and replayed her memories until her suspicion became more real.

Finally she was certain.

She had *not* changed her mind. She felt a rush of nausea and quickly turned her head and vomited out the open window. She retched again and was disgusted as some of it blew back into the vehicle.

"Are you okay?" Jack pulled over. He jumped out and got a shirt from his pack and a bottle of water and gave it to her. She stepped out of the vehicle and cleaned herself, as he cleaned the mess inside. She took the bottle and washed as much of the taste away as possible. She grabbed his arm.

"Jack, I was drugged!" He looked at her. "I was drugged. They gave me hand cream." He looked concerned and puzzled, but didn't understand her. "At the Salt Palace where Tyfon spoke, where I signed my contract. I never intended to sign a contract, I was trying to stop Deidre and Natalie from signing. Then they passed out samples of a wonderful hand cream." She described the sensations and the bright flashing signs, repeating their message over and over and the rush by *everyone* to sign the contract. She remembered more. "They gave the guys a type of silly putty to fool with. The drug must absorb through the skin.

"I was drugged. I never intended to go." She grabbed him and hugged him to her, feeling their bond restored. Jack got back behind the wheel.

"That explains so much." The resentment he had built up towards her blew away. He looked down and told her about seeing her there and listening in on their conversation and thinking she was okay and not about to sign up. How he felt responsible for leaving her.

"It's okay, Jack. You protected me. You waited till you thought I was okay before you left. No one could have imagined they would drug us."

"It's a really dark operation the Directory people are running on Earth. They must be desperate to fill a quota or why else take the obvious risk of using a drug? How do you know, no, how did you discover it was a drug – that you had been drugged?"

She described how she remembered more and more of her exact thoughts that night. "I never really knew why I did it. Why I chose to go. Why I signed the contract. I was just happy I did. Every time I thought of that night I felt a sense of euphoria and never looked any further. If you're happy with a decision, then that's all you need to know, right? But after this afternoon and your prediction, I kept pushing. I broke through the bubble of euphoria and remembered what actually happened. The warmth came through the hands and arms as I rubbed the cream in and the sensation spread all over. And the flashing lights, it was like a command. I was happy. Really happy to go."

"And so has everyone else since that time. The Directory people are desperate to get high numbers through their programs and shipped off-planet. This is a weakness we may be able to exploit." Jack looked at her.

"Well done, Dee, it's not easy to see through the effects of drugs, especially the way it was done to you."

"You know the drugs they used, too?" Wendy asked, incredulous.

"Yes," Jack answered casually. Then he frowned. "No. No, I guess I don't." His forehead cleared. "But your discovery still means we have another piece of the puzzle. And each piece leads us closer to the answer."

Wendy smiled at him. Jack was being Jack. *But how do you accuse an all-powerful force of such a crime, even if true, and expect to live? How do you use it against them when they control everything? I'll leave that till tomorrow,* she thought, *we're together now and that's enough.*

As the sun crested, then dropped behind a curtain of silhouetted peaks, the shadowed river of air winding its way through the canyon cooled and touched her skin. She was glad for the woolen sweater she wore, and hugged it to herself. One by one the stars appeared, until the sky was a shimmering cascade of light.

A shudder passed through her; she was irrevocably committed to enter the unthinkable depths of space. Looking at the twinkling points of light, the distant stars took on a different feel. No longer were they mysterious markers, but real suns with planets populated by real people. They were inhabited by civilized humanoid races and her next scheduled flight was not to the West Coast, New York or D.C., but to some unnamed planet circling a star she could not even see.

She now believed the schedules printed on her tickets were there to fool the unwary. And she was one of the dupes. Who would drug a person without their knowledge?

Evil people with something to hide.

They continued on their winding course, with headlights piercing the black of moon shadow, unveiling night's domain with tunnel vision. Rodents with staring eyes momentarily caught in the glare would pause in fright, then disappear in search of a meal or a mate, tiny hearts beating fast.

The swift but safe swaying motions of the four wheel drive finally lulled her fears and she slipped back through memories of good times. She settled on the time they first met, her and Jack, and smiled.

● ● ●

It was early in the second grade and she was walking to school, just out of sight of her home. Her older brother Michael, with whom she normally walked to school, had run off in the opposite direction. He was determined to play hooky with his friends no matter the consequences. When he left they were only two blocks from home, but she had not called after him. Wendy knew she was not allowed to walk to school alone, but was unwilling to return home and rat on Michael. She stood rooted with indecision, a frown on her soft, dignified little girl's face. It was a serious problem for a seven-year-old; loyalty was strong to both parents and brother. Finally she got herself moving, realizing that if she waited any longer she would be late for school. That would have its own unpleasant consequences.

She was walking slowly along with her head down trying to solve the puzzle. She couldn't go to school alone and she couldn't tell on Michael. It was a problem.

"Hello, are you going to school?"

She looked up... and there he was standing behind a white two-rail fence. After a short interval, with her not having answered, he said, "I'm Jack Cousins, what's your name?" When she still didn't respond, he continued, "I'm new here, and I don't know anyone yet. Can I walk to school with you?"

She studied him. This was a boy talking to her and he certainly wasn't shy. This was not to be taken lightly. She had been hammered with "Don't talk to strangers" so often she was reluctant to be her normal chatty self. She looked at him. He had on blue cotton shorts, a Spider-Man T-shirt with white socks and white sneakers. He looked neat and clean. His teeth were white, eyes a clear blue, and his hair a sandy blonde color. He just stood waiting for an answer.

There was none of the nastiness of other seven-year-old boys about him, but you often couldn't tell. Boys could be okay by themselves but get them near another boy or boys and there could be nasty pranks or pulled hair, which sometimes really hurt. And they often said things that didn't make any sense at all.

Her only response to these prankish peculiarities was to ignore them or tell her big brother, who would fix things for her. This usually worked. She had noticed that the girls who really complained and got upset got more of the yanks on the hair, shoves, trips or skullduggery involving spiders or frogs or worms that only the mind of a seven-year-old boy could invent.

So this boy was not what she had come to expect from the species and she was waiting for him to poke out his tongue or pick his nose right in front of her.

"Hello, Wendy," an adult said.

"Oh, hello, Mr. Cousins." She smiled up at the big man in front of the two-story brick house – Norman Cousins. Jack and Norman walked to the gate. Norman had said hello to her on many mornings but she was always with her brother Michael.

"Have you met my nephew, Jack? He's living with us now, and starting school today." Norman looked at her closely and continued, "He's in the second grade, just like you." Norman paused again. "That *is* the grade you're in, isn't it?" She nodded solemnly. They had been introduced, so he wasn't a stranger any more.

"Hello, Jack." She did a little curtsy to the young man and he, not to be outdone, performed a small bow. It was a picture-perfect response, and gave the moment formality. Jack's poise, Norman could see, made Wendy nervous and she didn't know what to say to his nephew.

Jack, in the face of all odds and personal experience to the contrary, seemed to be nice. "I would like to walk to school with you, but my mother wants someone *older,* like my brother, to take me so the school bullies can't take my backpack." She held it up for him to see. This would put this too-sure boy in his place. Someone bigger and stronger was needed to protect her.

Norman smiled, amused at how early in life these games started.

"I think Jack will prove to be a very capable escort for you, young lady. I'm sure you and your possessions will be safe with him." Jack smiled a happy, grateful smile up at Norman, then put his hand on the railing and swung over the fence in a graceful, fluid movement. No stumbles or trips there.

Jack put out his hand and hers seemed to slide into his of its own accord. Though startled by her own response, she did not pull her hand free till they were almost all the way to school, and withdrawing it, she felt the loss. But it couldn't be helped; being seen hand in hand with a BOY was completely out of the question, no matter how nice he was.

By the time they reached the schoolyard she had extracted a promise from Jack that he would walk the two extra blocks to her house to pick her up and take her to school each day. She heavily stressed how unreliable her brother was (which he was not) and how dangerous the bullies were (which they were not), establishing the primary need for his presence. Not, of course, her own desire for it. But it was there in her eyes, budding love and innocence, from the very first.

Later she was troubled by the thought that Jack had seemed to know she liked him but didn't even try to tease her about it. He had waited while she had explained about the bullies and things. Then she realized that this didn't bother her at all. She smiled. In fact she smiled all the way till lunch time. He liked her too.

"Mom?" she said. "Yes, dear." Her mother waited for her daughter to say what she wanted while continuing to prepare dinner.

"Mom-m." This time said in a slightly querulous tone.

Without turning, her mother answered, "Yes, dear, what is it?"

"*Mo-um.*" This said with definite impatience.

Smiling, Mrs. White turned to her daughter, understanding now that this was to be an important conversation. She walked over to Wendy and said, "Yes, dear. I'm all yours, but only for a few minutes or dinner will be late for your father."

Wendy opened her mouth to speak, but nothing came out. Her mother suppressed a smile, amused that Wendy considered her topic very important, important enough to distract her from her work, then had be coaxed to get started.

"Yes, dear, I'm listening." Seeing Wendy still hesitating, she added, "But not for very long."

"Mom, I want a boy to take me to school." This was nothing Mrs. White had expected, and she found it a bit confusing.

"Your brother Michael is a boy," she said with infallible logic.

"Oh Mom, that's not what I mean. I mean another boy, a nice boy." Her mother looked at her curiously and wondered where this had originated. Wendy had never before said anything but general comments about boys. It was boys this, and boys that, if at all. Now this was, if she were not mistaken, an individual boy.

Thinking her mother's delay meant she was going to say "No," Wendy hastily said, "He is really nice, Mom, his name is Jack Cousins, and he can protect me, he lives close, and I, and I... I already asked him to!" she said with a note of defiance that dissolved into a look of pleading.

Mrs. White was a little taken aback. She didn't mind, of course. But to have her daughter so adamant about it was a surprise. Later that night she called the Cousins' household, people she vaguely knew from somewhere, and satisfied herself that all was okay.

For all her forthrightness with her mother, it is not to say that young ladies do not undergo some horrible moments of uncertainty. The next morning she brushed her teeth three times, and her long dark hair fairly shone from repeated brushings. It was an agonizing eternity till Jack showed up at her front door, right on time. But it seemed late, very late. So late, in fact, she had thought over and over that he wasn't coming. It took all of her not inconsiderable resources to appear unconcerned when she came face to face with him at last.

Amanda White, who had her curiosity roused by her daughter's peculiar behavior, was looking through the curtains when Jack came to her door. At the sight of him, her breath caught and her hand went to her breast. *Oh my God,* she thought, having unknowingly caught a glimpse of the future.

They had gone about a block before Wendy had looked at Jack, unable to keep the joy of seeing him from her face. They both broke into peals of delighted laughter and went skipping hand in hand down the street.

● ● ●

A wave of very cold air carried her back to the present just as Jack pulled the jeep to the side of the road.

"You're shivering. I'll get my jacket for you." Wendy said nothing, just smiled. Jack rummaged around in his gear and came out with the item. She pulled it close about her, feeling warmed. A minute later they were back on the road, the path.

It was two hours more before Jack pulled onto a dirt road that was not used much. Its beginning was marked by a large distinctive rock formation and a cluster of trees. The rough road was covered in places by fallen branches and at one point she had to get out and guide Jack past part of the track that had eroded away. It had at one time been used as an access road to a mining site, but regular maintenance was a thing of the distant past.

An hour later, at the end of the winding switchback track, Jack pulled up to a ramshackle log cabin. It was set to the side of a small canyon that Jack knew went several miles back through the woods before running into a lake which lapped against the base of a shattered cliff face.

In the glare of his headlights, a thin wisp of dark curling smoke was visible escaping from the stone chimney of the cabin and twisting its way up through the branches of trees the cabin was nestled between.

Jack parked the jeep and walked up a short trail. He approached the door and it was yanked open. The light from behind framed a tall man, bent with age. The old-timer stuck out his palm, and Jack clapped his own hand into this paw and shook it vigorously.

"How long 'is time, Jack?"

"I'm not sure Jeb, maybe as much as week, possibly just a couple of days. Wendy and I are going to the lake to do a bit of swimming, diving and relaxing. Is anyone else up there now?"

Jeb shook his shaggy head. "No siree. Ain't seen a body up here for over a month. And to tell ya rightly I was kind a hoping yud show up as I bin gitten low on grub and could use your vee-hicle to resupply." Jack gave him the keys. Jeb tossed them into the air and caught them neatly.

"Glad we timed it right then. Hey, I got something for you." And Jack went to the jeep and pulled out a box.

"Whazzat?" Jeb said suspiciously.

"It's the spark arrester I said I'd get for your chimney. You know the one you told me not to get?" Jeb shook his head. "I'm sorry," Jack said, "I just don't want you to burn up."

"Aw, Jack!" Jeb moaned. "I'm an old man. You want me ta live fo ever?"

"Don't mind if you do, Jeb. That'd be fine by me." Jeb just shook his head.

"There is something you could do for us if you want." Jeb brightened at the request. "The road needs a bit of shoring up. Can't miss it when you go to town."

"I'll see t' it."

"See you soon then."

"Okay Jack, I'll come lookin' for ya if you two ain't back five days frum now." Though there had never been any need for this, the old-timer assured them each time they came to camp that he would come searching if they were not back on time. Jack was sure he would.

"Thank you kindly, Jeb. You know how much safer that makes us feel. We appreciate it." Wendy stepped up and gave Jeb a hug which embarrassed the old-timer greatly.

"Well, young lady, 'bout time you quit doing that. Purdy as you are, old man like me mebe git the wrong idea." To answer him she gave him another hug. He smiled so hugely she stretched up and gave him a quick peck on the cheek. He shook his head in wonder.

"That sure is one lovin' gal you got there, Jack. You hang on to her, ya hear," he said emphatically.

"I'd like to Jeb. I surely would." That was a bit of a strange answer, thought Jeb, but he caught their mood and said nothing. And they did not want to give Jeb their troubles.

Jeb could use the jeep as he wanted during the time they were camping, an arrangement beginning from the time Jack and Norman first explored the area. He appreciated these kids and their folks more than most he'd ever met.

Wendy and Jack got out their backpacks, with Jack also lugging along his scuba gear in a metal and wire frame cart with two large all-terrain wheels.

"I love that boy more'n me own 'f I ever had one," Jeb mumbled to himself as he watched them go up the trail.

CHAPTER 11

WENDY AND JACK HIT THE TRAIL that led up to the lake. They had miles to go in the moonlight. Jack was drawn to the mountain lake but Wendy had never been able to find out why. It was possible that he did not know the reason for his attraction. Jack was mysterious and the lake was another example of it.

Walking beside him she could feel his growing tension. Admittedly the area was beautiful, with its thousand-foot cliff plunging vertically into the lake on one side and the open-ended valley on the other. The lake was more than one hundred and fifty feet deep in places and fed by the spring run-off of melted snow. The water was chilly even in the height of summer and colder the deeper you went.

By eleven p.m., they reached the high valley floor and saw the moon reflected below in the tranquil waters. They wearily trudged over the disintegrating granite and around huge rock piles with moon shadow stuck like a black cape to the same side of each. Their usual camp site was slightly to the north of the lake and consisted of a flat bare patch of ground surrounded on three sides with rocks that formed a natural windbreak.

Jack had their tent up in twenty minutes. He pulled a fire starter from his pocket and had a small blaze going while Wendy gathered more wood. Soon he had hot coals and bright flame and a boiling pot of water. The crackle of the burning wood and the occasional spray of sparks in the dancing flames accompanied the lonely calls of distant animals.

Jack brewed some cinnamon tea and they lay back and watched the stars. Wendy felt herself tugged toward them irresistibly, and by some strange metamorphosis the stars became brighter, more colorful and felt closer. Jack stirred slightly and she turned to look at him. He smiled slowly and there was no pain or worry in the world. They melted into each other's arms and held on tight. Sometime later they moved into their tent.

After Wendy had fallen asleep, Jack lay awake for a long time. He drifted over a patchwork of memories from his life. He no longer tried to bring his attitudes and emotions into alignment with family, friends or culture. Even the philosophers and great thinkers he had read could not reconcile him to his disagreements with life as it was lived. As he felt forced over the years of childhood to live it.

Jack slipped out of the tent and walked the shoreline. He was, even to himself, quite inexplicable. Long ago he had stopped any prolonged self-investigation; it only led to more questions without answers.

Recently, with the baseball game and the arrival of the aliens and their technology, he'd become agitated and confused. His disorientation worsened when Wendy signed her contract. Now he and the Directory establishment were on a direct collision course.

The lake, its dark waters slapping gently at his side, represented a personal hurdle he must overcome. Logically this carried no weight, but instinctively it was everything.

At about age seven, after almost drowning in the local pool, he started seeing the images. Something had triggered in his mind and he often saw imaginary scenes, pictures, and memories.

Jack saw things he had not experienced in seven years of life. One time he mentioned a particularly upsetting image to Norman. His uncle was startled and gave him an "are you crazy" look. "It was a nightmare, Uncle!" Jack said and laughed it off. He never spoke of his "inner life" to another person. If it wasn't safe to tell Norman, it wasn't safe to tell anyone.

Jack had no point of reference to understand the contents of his own mind.

He looked out across the lake and remembered the frustration. Sometimes he *knew* the images weren't fantasy but memories: experiences, places, people and important events of the past – other times he was sure the pictures were imaginary. So he stopped trying to figure it out. If an image appeared in his mind he looked at it – and let it go.

Living with Norman and Sharon, Jack got to go camping. His uncle enjoyed the outdoors; hiking, climbing and the personal discovery of wild new country not often traveled by other feet.

After their first camping trip, Jack spent hours viewing mountain lakes on the 'net, proposing new trips. Slowly he and Norman combed the high mountain trails till they found *the* lake with *the* cliff face.

Jack bent down and passed his fingers through the cool water and splashed some on his face. This is the lake. *I knew it then*, he thought, *and I know it now.*

I cried my eyes out when I saw this, Jack remembered. He chuckled, *Norman was worried.* He hadn't stubbed a toe or broken his arm, *I felt so much loss I thought I would die.* But after a few days of strenuous hiking and exploring he got over the initial reaction.

The addiction was born.

The lake became their base camp on the journey to the mountains.

At night in this place with a vagrant moon or blazing stars he would have the most intensely vivid waking dreams. Visions both exciting and deeply unsettling. There was something to be understood about his attraction/repulsion to the lake. He was determined to get to the bottom of it. And afraid to....

This had led to investigating the cave.

That was then.

He kicked a rock and it skittered away beneath the indigo waters. He was here now and this was it: *I won't let the fear stop me again.*

With that decision made, a fatalistic comfort cloaked him.

The presence of the Directory people had ultimately forced the issue and for this he was perversely grateful. He felt guilty for not uncovering the mystery before this, before Wendy contracted to go offworld, but he just… couldn't.

The lake drew him like a moth to flame.

Will I burn too? he wondered. *No turning back, tomorrow is my personal day of judgment.*

A fish broke the lake surface and concentric rings expanded away. Stars blazed. Space was infinite.

The morbid spell broke.

With a swipe of his hand he gathered in the celestial gossamer, compressed it, wound up and threw a strike. He smiled, shrugged, turned and strolled back to the tent.

Jack took off his boots, loosened his belt and ducked inside. He yawned, lay down, and dreamed of dice flying high, tumbling, floating, but never landing.

● ● ●

At six a.m. Jack was laying out his scuba gear in the company of the local wildlife and to the tune of a bird's song. Was he being mocked? He chuckled.

The morning was fresh with a clean invigorating breeze which sent a few vacationing leaves into a lazy dance. The sun had not yet risen over the peak of the easterly elevation, rearing fifteen hundred feet above the lake.

Life was going on all around, impatient for him to begin the business of breakfast so his scraps could become their first meal also – didn't he know they were hungry? In the tent behind him he could hear Wendy stirring, but not yet awake.

By the time she emerged from the warmth of her sleeping bag, Jack had the cook fire going and breakfast ready. It was not often they had a country breakfast, and the aroma of the bacon and eggs drew her rapidly to her place by the fire, laying an arm over his shoulder in a casual affectionate greeting.

Jack slipped into his English butler mode and became polite, formal and foolish.

"Your breakfast is served, Miss Priss."

Wendy primped her sleep-mussed hair and looked at him coolly. He handed her the plate, utensils, napkin and orange juice with a conservative flourish and said in a superior nasal upper crust English accent, "Is there anything else I can get your ladyship on this fine morning?" He looked absurd and, conversely, somehow appropriate doing this role in his swimming trunks.

She replied in the same high-bred English inflection. "Yes, James, there is," she said with a flicker of irritation. "I have nowhere to rest my elbow." She waved the offending wing. "Would you be a good fellow and crouch down so I can rest it on your head?"

They both started laughing. It was a letup from the tension of the previous days and months, however brief. Jack sat and devoured his food. "This breakfast was a surprise, Dee. It'll be camp rations for the rest of the time or whatever fish or varmints we catch."

"Varmints" caused Wendy's nose to wrinkle. "Gross. Thanks for the surprise, though!" she said through a stuffed mouth. Jack smiled around another mouthful.

After breakfast Jack retreated to a rock overlooking the lake, shrouded in silence.

Wendy doused the fire, cleaned the plates and utensils, straightened up the tent. She bustled around till everything was ship shape. She then noticed Jack sitting on the rock, quiet and tense.

She sat near him feeling subdued.

Finally he began to speak.

"What I do today will change things." Jack said, then fell silent.

His words were abrupt and odd – it was more like hearing his thoughts verbalized than being spoken to.

"Okay, Jack," she quietly replied, then frowned, realizing this trip was no "couple's getaway" before leaving the planet. It was something else entirely.

Her intuition and Jack's demeanor told her that today was a rite of passage. *Of all the paths our lives could take, avoiding what must come today will defeat us.*

How can I think this, know this? Bewildered, she waited for Jack to continue.

The sun cleared the eastern elevation and shone directly on the westerly cliff face.

Jack looked up at the large cave, about two-thirds of the way up the cliff top.

"Do you see that cave, Dee?" Jack asked. She nodded. "Well, it wasn't there eighteen years ago." Jack handed over a pair of binoculars she hadn't known he had. "Take a look at it and tell me if you notice anything out of the ordinary."

She did as he asked.

Wendy looked over the whole cliff face, then scanned with the binoculars. The sun was at the correct angle to see into the cave. The back and sides of the cave were smooth, fused and glass-like in places. It looked unnatural.

"I've been up there twice with Norman. We dropped ropes and rappelled down to it from the cliff top. We photographed it and showed shots and rock samples to the geology professors at the University; they couldn't explain its origin.

"I dove in this lake and there is something scattered on the bottom. But I could never bring myself to check closely." He shrugged. "To be honest, it scares me."

"What are you saying, Jack? You're not diving for pleasure? There's some other reason?" She stepped close to his perch. "And why, if the cave and what's in the lake are so important to you, have I never heard about them before?" she asked.

He paused, shaken from his self-absorption by her tone and look.

"There *is* something down there, a wreck of some sort, and it has something to do with me. I've known and feared this for a long time, Dee, but..." He'd been about to say, "I haven't felt like dying to find out what it is." Not wanting to scare her, he said, "The time was never right, but with you leaving Earth, this is the time."

Wendy's face drained of color. "I forced you to do this?"

"No! I'm sorry Dee, I said that badly. Signing your contract has nothing to do with why we're here today."

"Okay, then why are we here?"

"I've delayed this dive for years. From fear and for other reasons… But now is the time. Don't you feel it?"

That stopped her.

"Yes! Just a few minutes ago." She frowned, felt melodramatic and then said it anyway, "I had an instinct, a feeling. Today feels like – dire destiny."

"That sounds about right. Somehow it's all connected – me, you, the Directory people and this lake."

"Okay, I think you're right. It's creepy," she looked off, "but important. That still doesn't explain why you've kept this from me, Jack, especially if it's so important to you, to us?" Wendy felt betrayed. "I thought we talked about everything."

Jack shrugged helplessly.

She looked wounded.

"Sorry. I'm not trying to brush you off. But talking about this is… very difficult."

She waited.

"I don't know what it's all about. I have fears and worries and wild ideas. If I told you any of it you'd think I was crazy."

"Look, Jack Cousins, you don't have to protect me from *anything*. You can tell me – I'm not seven years old anymore!"

"Okay, I hear you. But I'm not trying to protect you. I'm trying to protect me."

That took her by surprise.

"What? What do you mean?"

"What would you think of someone, Dee, who kept saying wild unproven….. no, that doesn't describe it properly. Someone talking out and out crazy stuff – all the time? How would you feel about a person who described stuff like that to you?"

"I don't really know, Jack. It would depend who it was and what they said." Even to herself that answer was less than honest. We reject the people who make us too uncomfortable.

"Well, Dee, you're gonna get a chance to find out. Because that person with all the crazy ideas in his head? It's me!"

She had no idea what to say.

"The good thing is this: when I resurface there will be something to say that isn't wild speculation or fear."

She looked frightened.

"I'm sorry, Dee. I didn't mean to scare you." He gave a wry smile and jumped down from his rock and hugged her. *I'm right, she would have listened to one or two of my wild stories and then – as Norman had – thought me crazy. And when I told her another crazy thing, left me forever.*

Jack walked back to camp, *no more talk, I have to do this now.* He methodically donned his wetsuit and dive apparatus, one piece at a time. Wendy watched for a minute, then went to help.

Jack smiled, "Thanks."

He moved out into the lake and set his tanks on a shallow rock, made a final check, then slipped them on and fastened the buckles. Jack picked up his weight belt and secured it around his waist.

"See you soon, Dee."

On went his flippers and face mask. He adjusted the position of the tanks. They were full, so there should be ample compressed air for this dive at the depth he planned.

Then, as Norman had, Wendy asked, "If today is so dangerous, and diving alone is too, then why are you doing it?

What could he say to her? That if he died, it would be from something another diver would be unable to prevent? To unnecessarily involve an additional person was contrary to his ethical code? That what he faced here was so personal, he wanted no spectators? Any of these reasons was enough for him.

But impossible to say to her. Not in a way she would understand.

This was his truth.

"I have two hours of air, but shouldn't be under for more than one. If there's trouble, Jeb is at the cabin or you can call for help from the sat phone in my backpack."

"Okay, Jack." If there was a problem, Wendy knew, there would be no rescue.

"See you." He went into the cold abyss.

CHAPTER 12

THE WATER WAS CLEAR EMERALD GREEN and chilly. The visibility near the surface was excellent. As he went deeper the visual envelope began to close in and the outlines of things blurred as the ambient light dimmed. The darker depths had impeded an easy inspection on his previous dive. That, and fear.

Jack went down about twenty feet and leveled off. The lake bottom toward the cliff was a murky patchwork of projecting rocks, sandy patches, varied clumps of decomposing tree limbs and other organic stuff moved there and deposited over the years by the seasonal currents.

The lake bottom in the area of his search was another sixty to eighty feet down and the material on the floor appeared as fuzzy blotches of muted hue. It was a dark indistinct world down there.

This darkness cloaked a mystery; a shudder resonated through his body in sympathy with the thought. As he continued to descend, he felt the pressure increase in his ears, and equalized it.

From the shoreline it was perhaps seventy yards to the cliff face. Jack moved steadily out of the shallows until the bottom of the lake dropped away in a deep trench.

Fifteen minutes after submerging, Jack had his first look at the out-of-place objects. What appeared to be metallic panels were scattered over a large area. Most of the panels were covered by mounds of sludge, rock and algae. He moved in close enough to touch one. He took out his knife and scraped a section. It gleamed brightly in the beam of his underwater flashlight. This was no junk car rotting away on the bottom. This was, this was... and though he stretched his mind, he couldn't even compose the thought. Couldn't name it. It would mean too much, be too much, to accept as hard fact.

He scanned the area as best he could and was shocked to realize that an enormous section of the cliff must have separated on... impact? Yes, that seemed right. Wow, it wasn't fire crackers that had exploded, or even a bundle of dynamite. Jack started a methodical search pattern, looking for something easily identifiable, something intact. Failing that, the largest section of, of... wreckage.

There. He'd finally said it to himself. He felt relief and an even deeper dread. Yes, wreckage. Impact, explosion, wreckage. Surely there must have been incredible pain, if only for an instant. Whose pain? He shook his head to clear it of an electronic buzzing sound that had started up. He shook his head again. The noise inside his skull would not go away. He thought he could smell smoke. But that was impossible.

Outside the debris-littered area the lake bottom tended to have rocky outcroppings, but these were minor in size compared to the cliff slippage and what he thought was wreck debris.

The explosion. The *explosion*. It was almost as if he could see it. His head was buzzing furiously now and he spun around trying to clear it. It wouldn't go. Damn it! Smoke? His lungs felt full of it. Impossible. His breathing became labored.

On a previous dive he'd reached a point where he felt stone cold – not from water temperature, but on the inside. A sensation he'd come to think of as death. For death to have a sensation seemed a contradiction. Last time, feeling this, he retreated to the surface. If he fled now he would lose all self-respect. On that last dive he had been a kid; today he was a man.

Jack was now in the midst of the wreckage, but there was no way to survey it from one point in the murky green water. He had to get close to see anything clearly. Moving from one rock pile and algae-coated metal panel to another, he felt a heavy sadness. He advanced slowly and touched another twisted and torn panel. Touching it seemed to give it power over him, and his thoughts. *What happened on that day*, Jack wondered, *what had it been like: that explosion.*

Light flared brilliant before his eyes. The steady buzzing in his head abruptly stopped and began zoning in and out, cycling up to head-splitting intensity and fading to barely perceptible. And smoke, smoke, smoke. It was clogging his nostrils and chocking his lungs.

I have to escape, his mind screamed. *It's so hot.* He was immersed in confusion.

Through it all he continued to search.

In a pass of his dive light the silent tomb revealed a large pile of metal and rock.

He let himself drift, the mild current carried him toward it. He felt more oriented with something definite to focus on. He touched it. *Wow, it looks...*

Vicious muscle cramps twisted his body and he writhed in nameless agony, thrust into the lake bottom muck.

Jack was a soul in torment. *It's come down to the way I go out*, he thought, as the energy bled from his cooling torso into the frigid water.

Blackness was everywhere, the muck embraced him, *the comfort of death.*

No, No, Nooooooo… He fought the inevitable.

Contortions wracked him again. Numbness settled into his muscles as the icy temperature seeped through his wetsuit until he was barely moving.

Cold, desolate, dying. *It cannot end here,* he thought vaguely. *It must not end here, not again?* But the outcome was foreordained.

This place was death.

I knew it.

Had always known it.

I don't want to die again. What did I see? I looked at something.

It slowly replayed: an egg shaped structure partially covered by an enormous slab of rock. *I passed my dive light over the metal object…* the muscle in his lower back cramped in a spasmodic jerking death grip. *Goodbye my friends, until we laugh together again. What?*

● ● ●

On her perch, Wendy followed Jack. Steady rhythmic bursts of bubbles were breaking the surface to mark his progress. By looking at them she could almost feel him breathing; the slow regularity of it was calming.

Jack made it to the cliff face. Fifteen minutes gone. He moved in an arc. Thirty minutes gone. He swung back inside its radius and toward the center. Forty minutes.

She turned and put the binoculars up to the cliff face. Yes, there was something very odd about that feature. It was seductive and she wondered just what had caused it.

She turned back to the lake and searched for his trail. Her chest constricted. She saw the patch of water boil for too long. Then go still. Long boil and still. It was the pattern of a panicked diver – taking deep ragged breaths.

Oh, my God. Jack's in trouble. What she saw wasn't conclusive proof. But, just like at the baseball game, she knew he was in danger.

She felt crazy frantic.

She decided.

She stripped and dived into the lake. As she stroked through the cold water she pleaded – let me save him. Let me help him. Please, don't let him die. In three minutes of hard swimming she was near to the bubbles. A large burst of bubbles broke the surface ten feet away.

She hyperventilated. Took a final deep breath.

As her head went under the cold hit. Her hands and feet were already numb and the rest would soon follow.

She kicked hard for the depths.

● ● ●

It's a wrecked space ship, Jack thought. The terrible agony of spirit had subsided. His jaw was aching from his clenched teeth which kept the mouthpiece in place.

That egg shaped structure must be the ship's cockpit, he supposed, *where the pilot sat, where he died.*

The contorted muscles in his lower back released and the pulsing spasms diminished. He drifted, exhausted. Slowly his breathing evened out, the smell of smoke no more than a stale aftertaste.

He checked himself over; he had bruises from banging into rocks but no serious injury. All the frantic breathing had choked his blood with nitrogen under considerable pressure. Safe diving procedure dictated he make a slow ascent. Breathe it out on the way up.

He examined his gauges. He was okay.

Jack pushed clenched fists into the small of his back under the tanks to relieve the residual pain.

I have no time for this, he knew. *Got to finish it.* Some visibility had returned. He watched the bubble path and followed it up. In seconds he was out of the muck. The slight current had moved the cloud away from the starship cockpit. He swam toward it.

Ten feet away he saw his dive light nestled between two rocks, and retrieved it. The nylon retaining cord had been slashed through. He re-tied it.

Jack breathed deep and with determination swam directly toward the wreck. He felt a blast of terror, the lake rippled, expanding and contracting within him, a horrible sensation.

He kept going. As he got closer a distant noise started up. He stroked closer to the ship. The noise escalated. He took two more strokes and his head started to scream. The pitch was excruciating. The intensity all-encompassing.

His head exploded in a chaotic shower of light and thrashing agony, his jaw jerked open in a gargled scream. The mouth piece dislodged and Jack sucked water into his lungs.

He surged and writhed in agony, losing all presence of mind. His head was blinding pain and his lungs were stabbing fire. He would be dead in seconds.

● ● ●

Wendy was twenty-five feet deep when the air bubbles began to come up in regular pockets again. She stared down but could see nothing distinctly. A large murky cloud enveloped the down current side.

She stroked ten feet further, but the scene did not clarify. More even pockets of bubbles rose.

With a sense of relief she knew Jack must be all right. Something had gone wrong, but he was okay now. With that worry gone, all her attention transferred to herself.

She was cold, so very, very cold. Where Jack had a wetsuit, she was in panties and bra, the water biting and unmerciful. She turned to ascend. What had been powerful strokes to get her to this depth were now ineffectual swipes at the water. Finally her head broke the surface and she quenched the burning in her chest with long, deep breaths.

She looked at the shore; it was sixty yards away. Her heart sank. She no longer felt her hands and feet at all and her arms and legs were going numb.

This terrified her.

With the frantic purpose of rescuing Jack gone, so was her strength. Her face felt like rubber. She broke into a dog paddle. She tried to maintain the strength of her purpose, but her paddling didn't seem to bring the shore closer.

Body sensations were receding. What if she drowned trying to rescue Jack, who ended up not needing any help? Her eyes dipped in and out of the water, and in her distress she lost her bearing and was paddling parallel to the shore, not closer to safety. Oh, no.

Her head went under for a long period. She struggled to the surface and sucked more air. Her brain was frozen. She was fighting for her life.

Just staying afloat was becoming impossible. She went under again. The lower part of her body was now completely unresponsive and dragging her deeper. She tried to wobble her hips to get some kind of forward motion but this only pulled her under again. Unable to coordinate her upper body with her hips and legs, she swallowed more water.

Pain seared the arch of her foot. How can that be? Her feet were numb.

She looked down and saw a submerged log directly beneath her. Her foot had been stabbed by the nub of a broken branch. Blood was in the water.

Hope surged.

She let herself drop lower and once again jammed her foot onto the trunk of the tree. Her toes were ripped but the pain felt better than the numbness.

With a few strokes she centered herself above the trunk and exerted enough control to thrust to the surface. She paddled a few strokes ahead before going under again. She dropped directly down, expecting to come into contact with the tree – if she hadn't gone astray? Finally she did. As she made her way along the trunk, skeletal branches thrust at her. She inched and pulled her way forward. The trunk made a diagonal approach to the shore; to her it was a royal road.

She finally pulled herself onto dry land, exhausted and bleeding. She lay for minutes on a warm rock, on her back, soaking in the heat and being replenished by the hot morning sun. Soon she got up and staggered over the sharp pebbles to their camp, rubbed herself down with a towel and felt the last effects of diminished circulation dissipate.

Feeling a bit better she threw on her clothes.

She walked back to her perch overlooking the lake. What a weird story she would have to tell. "Jack, while you were in trouble down there, I almost drowned!" After he got over the shock of it they would laugh. How ironic. Romeo and Juliet – no thank you. Even now the utter desperation she felt only minutes ago had begun to fade and she chuckled a little nervously. Death was closer than it had ever been.

Wendy lifted her head and looked out over the lake. She picked up the binoculars. She swept over the area where Jack's bubble trail had been and found nothing. Nervous fingers dialed the focus knob in one direction and then another. Finally she had the bubbles in focus. She stared. She looked away and then brought the glasses back into focus on the lake surface. The wind was gusting and falling, so it was difficult to be sure. Then she felt sheer horror.

"Oh no! No, Jack, not again!" she shouted. The water was placid. There was no intermittent burst, burst, burst of regular breath: just the absence of bubbles, indicative of a dislodged mouthpiece.

Jack was in trouble again. It was too much. She felt helpless. What was she to do, wait till his body floated to the surface? Run for help?

That was absurd; by the time she made it halfway down the trail to Jeb's cabin Jack would either be safe or drifting lifeless and beyond any help her frantic dash could secure. And Jeb had no phone. No scuba gear. Then she remembered the sat phone and ran to Jack's pack. She called Norman. "Jack is in trouble!"

"You're at the lake?"

"Yes."

"We'll be in a chopper in twenty minutes. And then it will be an hour flight time." Too late.

"Send the rescue chopper now and then you come later."

"Of course, yes. It'll leave in thirty seconds. Arrival time is fifty-five minutes from now."

"Tell them to hurry, Jack could be drowning right now!" However long it took, it would be much too late.

"Noooooooooooo!" she screamed out over the lake. She must help, but couldn't help. The only response was fading echoes of her agony.

Finally the nausea and disorientation engulfed her and she sank to the ground.

● ● ●

His body screamed for air, he jammed his jaw closed till his teeth creaked, and did not breathe. One more mouthful of frigid water and his lungs would be so full it would be impossible to breathe and it would be over.

His body was jerking rhythmically with the need for air. His arms and legs were numb with cold, his fingers and toes ice, spasms continued to wrack his body as it cried out its need for air. And when the need went unfulfilled the body spasmed again, air, air, air.

How strange, he thought, he could see his body drifting there some feet away. As he looked, the body was getting smaller and its outline was a dim shadow in the murky water. Further and further. It was, he idly noticed, motionless. He was losing interest. The whole scene was becoming the past. He could still feel pain, but it was "over there," less and less to do with him.

Then from some dim corner the automatic response of a diver's safety training kicked in and caused body motion. Slowly, in a dreamlike absence of urgency, he saw his right arm curve back and hook the air line in the crook of his elbow. His hand followed the line till the regulator was in his nerveless grasp. Then with a snap of viewpoint he was looking right at the regulator. He was seeing through his eyes again. Pain. Agony. Air, AIR.

He tried again and again to properly grip the regulator in his numb hands, to force his fingers to respond to his commands. To grip. To hold. If only for a few seconds. He used his hands as pincers and held the regulator trapped between the flippers and forced the mouthpiece through his frigid unfeeling lips and sucked air. Breathe. Breathe. Breathe.

Water spewed from his mouth. Breathe. Yes, breathe. He was breathing. He hung inverted in the water so the liquid in his lungs could drain and be spluttered out.

Soon the air was flowing in and out, in and out. He spent a minute just breathing. He looked at the gauges. Air. Air was running out. He had floated this time and not disturbed the lake bottom.

He illuminated that ferocious sunken object. No wonder he couldn't bring himself to dive this lake. There *was* death down here. His.

He looked at the object again. There was a twinge of fear and then, not. The stored violence was discharged. He was through the death trap that had lain dormant in his own mind and in the deep waters of the lake.

He played the beam over the distorted form and imagined how it looked before the crash. Rebuilding it in his mind's eye. It had been a beautiful ship flashing across space.

Escaping the enemy.

He saw the past. Being chased. To a…. planet. Chased through… mountain ranges. A cliff face rushing at him. Then impact-force-pain. Blankness.

But he did not back off, he looked at it again. He ran it through his head again and again. As its emotional power and force diminished, his understanding rose.

He had been drawn to this lake. Its waters had cloaked terror, pain and death. The closer he came to the wreck, the closer he had come to death.

But now he knew.

He had been the pilot – his life had ended here, ended badly. Knowledge of his past – his true self – had been buried beneath the sheer horror of this event. It had lain here like a cursed treasure chest for seventeen years.

He felt a surge of relief – no wonder life on Earth was so strange to him.

The details and circumstances of *why* this crash and his death had happened, and how it was he had come to be near Earth, came rushing at him.

He felt a sense of vast expansion and was overtaken by a surge of pleasure, exhilaration, euphoria, an acute intensity of well-being.

He had always felt there was something very urgent and important to know, to do.

"What am I neglecting?" was the personal question he had tormented himself with, the question he had driven himself half-crazy with. The vital question that had no answer.

Now he had the answer.

The anxiety caused by the sense of his own neglected but unknown responsibility would at times overwhelm him. So he suppressed it and suppressed it until he almost convinced himself it was gone.

But not really.

Now, finally, he felt restored. He understood the mission, the *interrupted* mission. The relief was vast and intense. He was right. Is there anything as sweet, he wondered, as being vindicated? Being right? Where all the pieces of the puzzle fall into place and you see the *big picture* for the first time.

The secrets of the lake were key to unlocking the door into the galaxy beyond.

But only if he lived.

*

He was dangerously low on air. The job down here was not done.

Jack examined the ovoid-shaped structure under the wedge of rock. The entire bottom quarter was torn away. Over the years the sand and silt had built up and partially buried this section. He swam closer, sending the beam through the liquid ink. There should be an entrance. The cavity was merely a blacker black, but as he approached, the angle changed and the beam played across the opposite wall inside the capsule. His breath caught. He hesitated: to enter was to find "himself."

He grabbed the jagged edge and pulled himself completely through. He was standing on sand and above him was the back of what he supposed was the remains of the pilot's chair. Jack touched the edge of the seat, a metal framework. The seat must have been a foot thick and quite complex when intact, but now, strangely, the upholstery on the forward section of the seat was all that remained.

Jack maneuvered around a thin metal rod protruding from the rear of the seat at about waist level. He took hold of the rod and shoved hard against it. As the chair came swiveling around with surprising ease, into Jack's arms was propelled a golden tangle of bones.

Startled by the macabre embrace, Jack back-swam and shoved it off with nervous slow-motion speed. He felt embarrassed to be so easily rattled. He had expected that remains would be in the seat, still... He looked at the thing sprawled on the sand, then picked it up and noticed something. The lower spine was almost severed where the metal rod had driven through the seat.

That must have been an agonizing injury if the pilot was still alive at that point. His back gave another twinge of sympathy. Then he felt amused. So that was it.

Jack looked over the cockpit. The section protecting the pilot was the only intact wreckage. Made sense. Safety systems or some such devices.

He held the skeleton up and was surprised to find it stood quite a bit taller than himself and was very broad in the shoulders, with a rib-cage that had housed a deep chest. This was once a mighty figure of a man. Somehow he had thought it would be exactly his own size.

It was time to go, past time: he would still have to decompress on the way to the surface. With the skeleton in tow, he adjusted his buoyancy compensator and slowly ascended. With each ten vertical feet he stopped and breathed normally. His body was expelling nitrogen from his bloodstream.

The lake is a womb, he thought, *for surely I am reborn.* It had been a baptism of old fire, frigid water and fantastic realization.

He had plunged into the lake a confused but determined boy with half-formed ideas.

Jack was amused to find that the problems from his former life that had been bothering him at the time of his death, were again foremost in his mind. He chuckled.

He continued to decompress.

His problems now had a different priority. Amazingly his mind was clear. Good.

His first problem to solve was making it to the surface alive.

Breathe slowly, move up ten feet, and breathe slowly.

He looked at his air gauge.

Deadly compressed nitrogen was leaving his bloodstream, passing the membrane in his lungs and being expelled from his system with each inhale and exhale. Because the nitrogen must be purged, he couldn't slow his breathing, but the air was running out; one necessity in conflict with another, his life in the balance. He rose another ten feet. How much further was it?

CHAPTER 13

"I'M HERE FOR MY APPOINTMENT WITH Admiral Augustus McMillan."

"Who are you?" asked the lieutenant seated at the Pentagon information counter.

"I am DD/CIA Ops." Before the Directory arrived, for security reasons he would never have given his post title. Now nobody cared.

The infighting between nations had slowed to a trickle. His job had little relevance and no respect. To most citizens he was a loser hanging on to a pay check.

"Oh, yes sir, the Admiral himself briefed me on how important he considered this use of his time."

Perrywhite looked at the thinly veiled smirk on the kid's face. "Please take a seat over there while I make the Admiral aware you've arrived."

Perrywhite had a new goal: immortality. He had redoubled his efforts to contact the Directory Chief.

His thoughts shifted.

I hate being a redundant person in a redundant agency. I get no respect. He had begun a list of people who disrespected him, but it had grown into the hundreds and then so long that he knew he could never kill them all.

To get power, he needed more information – data he might get from McMillan.

The ultimate goal was a face-to-face meeting with the chief alien. First he must become indispensable to DE.

Then immortality.

Then death to anyone who crosses me. Oh yeah.

An hour later the Admiral strode out to greet his guest. McMillan was usually above this type of petty rudeness, but when the DD/CIA Ops had called for a face-to-face meeting, he immediately called Colin Craig and had listened to a long tirade about Perrywhite. *This rat-fink is not going to take up any of my time,* Augie assured himself.

"What do you want?" Ralph dropped his hand to his side when he realized it was not going to be shaken. Obviously the Admiral intended to talk to him in the reception area. Craig must have gotten to him.

He was going to kill Craig if it was the last thing he ever did. And he would drown this Admiral in Craig's blood. *Yeah, that'll make me feel a bit better.* He smiled.

"I don't believe we should be discussing matters in the Pentagon lobby, Sir."

"Your superior at the CIA assured me you're not here on Agency business. So there can be no reason for privacy or secrecy."

You smug bastard. "That's basically correct. But as it is now lunch time, I wonder if you would like to accompany me." Perrywhite named the Admiral's favorite restaurant and mentioned his preferred vintage of wine. The Admiral's taste buds assaulted his senses and he had to swallow the output of his salivary glands.

Augie looked at his wristwatch and nodded his assent, reassuring himself that this jerk would get nothing from him. But why deny himself his favorite lunch? *Free lunch.* He had planned to eat immediately after getting rid of this useless spook anyway.

McMillan turned to the lieutenant at the reception desk. "I'm going to lunch with Ralph Perrywhite of the CIA." And he named the restaurant and the time he expected to return. He didn't trust this jackal.

Perrywhite smiled. At least this old squid feared him. That was something.

●

The waiter poured, Augie enjoyed the rich bouquet, then sipped the wine. Fine. With the meal over he felt replete and entirely mellow.

Augie looked at the dark alcoves, the silent waiters and the subdued lunch guests. Because he had accepted this free lunch there was a bill to pay. He had given Perrywhite very little information. He had used "old guy rambling" to confuse and change the subject.

But strangely, what the spook wanted to know seemed inconsequential. He had written a full accounting of his DE investigation. Perrywhite had obviously read it.

"I need the names of all the people involved." Perrywhite asked.

"I don't trust you. I would never give you the name of a person you might contact and question. That, in my opinion, would jeopardize their safety." The sublime flavor of medium rare filet mignon and the subtle tickle of the wine added a feeling of satisfaction to the comment.

"I'm just looking for small details that may have slipped by, or unimportant particulars that went unreported. I don't wish to interrogate anyone in any fashion that exceeds the bounds of normal coffee shop conversation."

"You are who you are. I don't believe you," said Augie. Perrywhite had to exert full control; to expose any of the fury he felt would bring the conversation to a close.

"The nature and importance of my position has changed radically since the advent of DE. I no longer have a pressing or relevant mission in this altered world." A little self-deprecation added to the appearance of Perrywhite's sincerity.

"I know. That's why I'm wondering what these questions are really about."

Perrywhite was not going to tell this about-to-be-retiree his true purpose. Ignoring the last probe, he continued, "Is there anything that happened during your investigation you can't explain or that seemed strange?" Perrywhite saw the Admiral's inward look. "Yes?"

Augie had just the thing. Something so meaningless, he could tell this spook without really saying anything, something he had forgotten in the crush of later events. So he told him about the kid at the coffee shop and the questions he asked and the science fiction story he talked about, and what he looked like. Both men were satisfied. Augie gave him an unexplained curiosity and Perrywhite felt a rush; even if McMillan saw this as a trivial contact with a teenager, this kid had prompted a successful investigation. In the mix of defining events related to the aliens' arrival on Earth, this kid could merely be a plant sent in by the Directory people to hurry events along, or Perrywhite could be on the trail of an anomaly. An "X" factor.

CHAPTER 14

JACK WAS OUT OF AIR. As he held his breath, he looked at his dive watch and ran the equations in his head. They did not lie. He was still twenty feet below the surface, and in trouble. Most of the compressed gases inhaled at one hundred feet should be out of his bloodstream.

"Most" wasn't good enough; just a little nitrogen fizzing in the blood could kill him, or seriously harm his body – and now that he had his memory back, his plans couldn't go forward if this body was incapacitated.

There was a mystery.

The Jack Cousins body should be so cold it wouldn't function. He tracked it back and discovered the freezing sensation had gone after finding the skeleton. Ahhh. *Could that be?* Jack wondered. *It must.*

At any rate, his tanks were out of air: he surged to the surface.

Breaking the surface of the lake, he breathed in the mountain air and detected something out of place. There was a distinct aroma carried on the breeze. *I know it*, he thought. *It's the scent of an alien world.*

"I am Tac-U-One," he said out loud.

This is the first day of the rest of my life. It was enjoyable to have a cliché describe reality.

Jack gently made his way toward shore.

In fits and starts his memory rushed at him as he drifted on the lake surface.

Jack experimented. He thought of his home. His house on Crown Planet came immediately to mind. Then all the details he cared to have.

He thought of his boss. There he was. Once again everything he needed to know was a thought away.

I'm functional, excellent. He may not have the vast store of knowledge in his present awareness as he used to have. *But I can access memory as needed.*

He would re-learn his own past a section at a time as life or his own interest demanded.

He recalled his decision to allow his M-star to impact the cliff. Jack turned to see the cave. He compared his memory of the event to the actual site. There was a jarring sensation. Once again he felt an echo of that long gone violence resonate through him, and dissipate.

With that death he had escaped immediate capture by Bio-One's minions. But he failed to escape another trap. The trap laid in over eons of the life-death cycle.

Amnesia.

Trapped on Earth not knowing who he was. Desperate to find out what was wrong. Sometimes just desperate.

Jack had lost personal functionality. He had lived in a world of confusion.

No more.

Light, unfettered and free, skittered across the wavelets, as he was free, free to be himself.

The lake shore was close. He touched bottom and stood. He leaned on a rock, took off the flippers and threw them onto dry ground. He pushed off the face mask.

Tac-U-One needed to come to terms with his presence on Earth.

I'm here because I failed to complete my last mission. A brutal but necessary assessment of his life. *The "Directory" people wouldn't be here if I'd done my job.*

No wonder he "knew they shouldn't be here" with such violence.

He unstrapped his tanks and set them on the rock.

I have personal responsibilities on Earth, he knew, *I have to straighten out the mess my failure helped create.*

His first action must be to slow the damage being done by the Directory programs on Earth. Then bring the planet directly under his control, stopping the damage. After that begin the repair and replace the leadership.

Then, in good conscience, he could leave. A simple plan. He laughed.

Wendy?

"Dee... Dee," he called, wondering where she was, blithely expecting to see her waiting for him, to rush into his arms, or at least hug him, but she wasn't there.

The dive boots came off and the pebbles dug into his bare feet.

"Hey, Wendy, I'm here." He started to worry. "Dee, Dee, where are you?"

●

Wendy, coming from a place much like hell, was slow to make out the sound of his voice.

"Wendy!" Jack yelled as he hobbled to the camp site, still shedding dive gear. "Wendy!" The sound of his voice pierced her mental fog. She felt dizzy.

"Wendy?" *Jack*. She was up in an instant. She ran to him, oblivious of the pain in her foot.

"Jack!" To his amazement she threw herself into his arms crying. "Oh Jack, Jack." With her grief, the horror of the last two hours came pouring from her in disjointed fragments. "Jack, Jack, Jack." He held her, a little bewildered, and wondered what was wrong. Slowly in the gentle pressure of his arms she became quiet.

He felt her recover.

She drew away and looked at him. Accusing him. Then she pounded his chest with her fists. It hurt; fire was pouring from her eyes.

"Jack Cousins, if you ever...." She could not go on. The fire died. "I thought I'd killed you..." She slumped into him. He held her. How could she think that? Then it came to him. Of course.

"You knew I was in trouble."

"Yes." That one word said much.

She thought she'd killed him – in her mind he was diving because he had to rescue her. He'd said as much.

"I really put you through it, didn't I?" They held each other for some time. "We're good now."

"You're right," she said. "And I need to make a call." She walked over and grabbed the satellite phone. She called Norman and told him to turn his chopper and the emergency chopper back. "Yes, yes. He's okay. I'm afraid I panicked. Everything is fine. Yes, please return home. That would be best. Okay, I will. Thank you."

"Your parents are glad you're fine, and send their love."

"You had the cavalry coming?"

"Wouldn't have mattered, would it?" Her eyebrow arched. "By the time the paramedics arrived you would've been beyond help, if it had gone that way."

"As they say – all's well that ends well?" Jack grinned.

Apart from the torture you put me through, she thought. *But I wouldn't have been anywhere else.*

"A cliché wouldn't have saved you, Jack." Now she smiled a little, and added. "But truthfully you don't look worse for wear."

"Touché!" Jack laughed and she joined in.

She is a wonder, he thought, *I now have a different viewpoint on everything, but not her.* She hadn't become a "native," a "normal," or someone he rejected as being from an uncivilized planet.

It surprised him. *Everything else is changed, but our love is independent of this time on Earth.*

He smiled at her. "You are amazing."

Her mood surged. She looked at him quizzically. "Oh, yeah? Don't sound so surprised." She paused. "It took you all this time to figure it out?" She shook her head and muttered, "I thought he was smart."

She helped him to remove the sheath knife. She took off his dive watch. She unzipped his wetsuit and peeled it off. She took his hands and rubbed them, but they were only cool to her touch, not frozen as she had expected – as hers had been. The hot sun did its restorative work and soon he was walking with freedom. *Half an hour ago*, he thought. *Just the half part of an hour…* he shook his head.

They strolled back to the lake shore.

The time had come.

●

"When I left you earlier this morning I was confused and upset."

"Yes, you were. You said I was going to find out what it was like to have someone tell me crazy things – all the time." She arched her brow.

"Yes, I said that – and yes, you are."

"Okay, tell me – I'm up for it," she said. "Maybe I'll surprise you."

"Okay, good," he acknowledged. "I've made progress already, I'm not confused anymore."

"That's great Jack. So the dive helped you?"

He smiled. "It did."

"You're still upset?"

He frowned. "Well, yes, but about different things." He turned to look at the lake and she saw his profile.

Ah Jack, you're so handsome, but you've never known it, have you? Then it struck her. His features were the same, but at the same time undeniably different. His face looked squared and firmer. It was him, her Jack, but then not.

A transformation has taken place. For a moment she was scared.

"Okay. I'm ready to listen to whatever it is you want to say." Confident that no stories from the lake bottom could disturb her.

He smiled wistfully. "I don't want to disturb you, but I'm going to." The murmur was taken by the breeze.

Jack could think of no easy way to tell Wendy any of what he had to say. The pace of life was going into high gear and beyond. *If she believes me she'll have decisions to make.*

"Let's sit down 'cos I'm gonna tell you what happened."

"Alright." She took a couple of energy bars from her pocket and tossed him one.

"Thanks, Dee."

"You're welcome."

He took a bite, then started. "There's a wreckage at the bottom of the lake."

"Okay. Is that what you were looking for?" she asked.

"Yep. Five years ago I couldn't bring myself to look closely. Today I explored the whole site."

"Find anything interesting?"

"I did."

"Well, show me."

"I will." He paused. "There was a skeleton in the wreck."

Wendy shuddered. "You invaded someone's tomb?"

He hadn't for a second thought of it that way. You can't rob your own grave. Can you?

"I did."

"Oh, Jack."

"It's not normal skeletal remains."

"What does that mean?"

"For starters it's golden – bright and glittery. It's not made of human bone."

"Why would someone put a Halloween skeleton at the bottom of the lake?"

"I'll show you."

She shrugged.

Jack waded into the lake to retrieve the skeleton and took it to shore. It shone in the sun, the golden color seeming to absorb the light and reflect it back with greater intensity. He laid it out on the ground.

"If this was a real skeleton the bones wouldn't be held together." Wendy said.

"You're right. A human skeleton would have fallen apart." Jack took a deep breath. "This is an alien's skeleton."

"What do you mean, alien skeleton?"

"On the bottom of this lake there's a single seat interstellar star ship. It crashed here eighteen years ago. These are the remains of the pilot."

She looked at him.

"How can you possibly know that? I believe you when you say there's wreckage down there. But you have no way of knowing it's a space ship. Or that the skeleton is an alien!"

Her disagreement didn't faze him.

He looked so calm.

Jack had changed – not just his features. There was an aura about him, nothing visible, nothing religious, but he "felt" quite different.

"But I do know."

"How?"

He was somehow gone beyond the range of their shared experience. Jack not only felt different but had become, to her, alien. *How can this have happened?*

"The reason is simple. I am that alien."

"W-what?" she stuttered.

"Dee, I know all about the wreck and the alien, because I was him. He is me."

What is he saying? Her head was spinning. *Nothing he says makes sense.*

"You thought I'd become an alien. I said you were right. I said I was that alien." He pointed to the skeleton. "That's how I know what happened to him."

He can't read my mind. He wasn't that skeleton. How can anyone be a skeleton?

"Yes, I can. Yes, I was."

"Yes, you *can* what? Jack! I don't understand you." *He's answering my thoughts, as if we're having a conversation. He's waiting for me to ask about it*, she could see it in his eyes.

"You see me waiting. The question is, 'Can I read your mind?' The answer is yes, if I want to."

I'm confusing and overwhelming her. Slow down, he thought.

He looked but she didn't believe he was telepathic. *Take it one step at a time.*

"Dee, see that skeleton?"

"Yeah. I see it."

"Good. Notice anything?"

"Oh! It's sort of, well, beautiful. Not scary at all, really." She gave a tentative smile.

"Dee, I was that alien." She shook her head, not knowing she was doing it. *It's not real, what was he saying? What?*

Jack took her hand. "I warned you, my love." Jack smiled at her. "I said you'd find out what it was like to hear crazy ideas. Didn't I?"

He did warn me. Twice. I've got to calm down and listen.

"Yes, you did Jack." She looked a bit better.

"We've started this, can't stop now."

"Okay, Jack. I'm trying to understand."

"I know you are and I know it's difficult."

Jack took her hands in his.

"Wendy, before I was born into this body I have now – *I was alive in that one.*" He pointed to the skeleton. "On the bottom of the lake is the wreck of a space ship. That skeleton is all that remains of the pilot's body. I was that pilot. That body died when the space ship collided with the cliff face. I did not. I was born into this body, the Jack Cousins body. Here I am." Jack's voice shook. "There's no helping it, Dee, I am no Earthman."

She stared at him blankly.

Time passed.

Abruptly she placed her hand on his forehead, checking for a temperature. She took his wrist and felt his pulse. His eyes were equal and reactive when she blocked the sunlight from one eye at a time. His head had no bruises or lumps. Could this talk be a symptom of the bends? Jack was not scratching himself, his breathing was even, and there were no visible red patches on his skin.

"Are your joints sore?" she asked.

"I don't have the bends, Dee," he replied.

"Well, Jack, what am I supposed to think when you just come from a life-threatening dive and start talking like this? Symptoms of the bends don't start right away, you know."

"I don't have the bends, Wendy. My head is clear."

"Okay, so it's not the bends. You say you're an alien. I say you're Jack Cousins! I've known you since you were seven years old. We've gone to school together for years. I know who you are."

Jack looked at her steadily.

"What are you saying, Jack?" She shook her head, trying to clear the confusion. Trying to think. To talk. "You aren't one of the Directory people. You were born long before they arrived. Years and years before."

He looked sane but he was talking crazy. He lived a few blocks from her home, ate the same food she did. He'd been to the doctor. They would have been able to tell if he was an alien. He wasn't.

The truth was obvious – he was Jack Cousins. Born and raised on Earth.

"Jack, Jack, Jack! You're scaring me. You're saying crazy things!"

She dropped to her knees in front of him and looked imploringly into his eyes. He pulled her close. *He's gone, he's gone. I've lost him.* She thought, and cried. It was a day of turbulent events and meteoric emotions, for both of them.

"Don't worry, Dee, I'll be yours as long as you want me."

Wendy melted against him. "You will? You will? You're not going away?" Jack smiled and did not comment on the fact that it was she who was going away, not he.

She pulled back and looked into his eyes. "I guess that was a silly thing to say." Though she didn't really know it, she'd just picked up on what he was thinking. It wasn't important to point that out.

They held each other until the tight hold finally relaxed and they slept.

Jack moved gently and Wendy smiled faintly. He looked into her dream and saw them together running across a lush green field; he smiled. Her dream was a real dream. He inserted a space ship and it landed near them. Wendy frowned. The landing ramp extended and they walked hand in hand into the ship. The frown smoothed and the smile returned. The ship rose and disappeared beyond the blue. He cast the dream in black and gently shook her awake. Her eyes came open and he reveled in the pleasure she felt at seeing him close.

CHAPTER 15

JACK'S PROBLEM WAS TO CONVEY A different reality to Wendy without blowing her off.

"Hey, Dee, you're back."

She stepped over to him. *I need to check him for bends symptoms.*

"No bends, Dee."

"Oh. Okay, then." She ignored what happened.

"You're okay to talk some more?" Jack asked.

"Sure, Jack."

"Good." He paused, "Do you think aliens are real?" He smiled. "Not me – but other aliens?" Jack asked.

"Yes, Jack, I do."

"You're certain, no doubts?"

She looked away. "At first I didn't know what to think. And then, with everyone talking about it, accepting it," she shrugged, "I got closer to believing. Then came Tyfon Arolia, my contract and the DE training. They are real."

"Good. Have you ever seen a space ship?"

"Yes, Jack, you know I have."

"You saw it fly like no Earth craft could?"

"Yep. I did."

"Do aliens have advanced technology and have you personally used it and observed it work?"

"Yes, Jack, I have."

"Realize, Dee, that one month before the Directory people came to Earth, anyone answering these questions with a 'yes' was a crackpot." He let that sink in.

"Now it's common knowledge. Everybody knows it's true. The crackpots, now, are people who refuse to accept that aliens are among us!

"Have you seen how the 'non-believers' are treated by the media?" Jack asked.

"Yes, I have." Those who refused to believe aliens were on Earth were ridiculed. Lampooned. Satirized. "And I don't like it."

"The Directory has caused a complete reversal."

She nodded slowly.

Point by point he was driving home the foundations of a new reality. This would take them forward together or sever their relationship permanently. *She'll know me as I am and want me, or not.* She looked ready to hear more.

"In the early years up here, Norman and I got to know Jeb pretty well. We spent some time at his cabin. When I was a kid I told Jeb about an argument between Norman and me. 'Remember our first trip to the lake?' I asked Jeb, he nodded, 'Well,' I said, 'There was an explosion at the cliff.' Jeb looked at me strangely. 'Uncle Norman thought I was hallucinating. It means using my imagination to make up something that isn't really there. I wasn't "hallucinating" Jeb! I saw and heard that explosion. My uncle can't use big words to make me say I didn't see it.'

"'You stick to your guns, Jack.' Jeb said. But he had gone pale. Norman got him a glass of water. He gulped it down.

"Jeb looked at me.

"'You're talking about the strangest day of my life.' Jeb said. 'There *was* an explosion up in the mountains, Jack, but not when you first visited. It was years ago.'

"He went to a desk and hunted out an old calendar and flipped the pages until he got to the correct month. There was a big red asterisk on one of the days. He passed it to me.

"'That's two days before my birthday.' I said. Jeb and Norman looked at each other, then at me. It gave me goose bumps.

"'I thought the Thunder God himself had struck his hammer!' Jeb said. 'The earth shook. Outside was clear and warm so I hiked up there. Took two hours maybe. The cliff face had sheared off and there was a deep cave. The rock was glowing red hot and still smoking. I could see where a large wave had come up on shore and receded. And something else I never told no one. I saw a space ship.'

"You can see his sketch of that ship drawn on the back side of the calendar page. I'm sure Jeb still has it.

"There *was* an explosion, Dee. I had it misplaced in time."

Wendy was quiet for some time.

"Why didn't you ever tell me?" she asked quietly.

"Finding out about the space ship, seeing the sketch was… disorienting. I was only eight at the time. And remember, back then, people who claimed to see space ships were crazies.

"Each part of this – Jeb's story, my 'imagination,' the arrival of the DE people, were random and disconnected. None of it fit together until today."

Ah, Jack, I thought you were crazy. Not fruit loop bonkers, but overwhelmed by life. Now she had to re-evaluate.

"Can you please repeat everything you told me?"

"Sure I can, but why?"

"Well, half the time you were talking I was rejecting what you said, so I didn't really listen."

"Okay, Dee." He went over it again.

●

To move forward together he had to give her a great deal of information. But knowing and understanding the situation meant doing something about it.

And that will be dangerous, Jack knew.

He would do it for many reasons. But once she understood what was happening, she would insist on helping. He couldn't leave her out of it, take care of the danger, then say, "I was protecting you."

She wouldn't go for it. Ironically, to continue their relationship he had to put her in danger instead of shielding her from it. He knew without asking that's what she would want…. And there it was – why he would tell her: she was willing to confront the danger, too.

"Dee, I know how hard it is to take this in. I've had to live with not knowing who and what I am for years. And it got worse when the aliens arrived.

"Today. Today has cracked it wide open, and I feel better."

She looked at him for a long time.

"I don't think I can believe it yet, but I'll listen to you without the hysterics."

"That's all I want."

"Jack, I've been thinking. Everything's been tense since I signed the Directory contract. Being drugged and duped doesn't change the facts.

"Two weeks is all we've got." She waved at the lake. "So what does any of this matter?" She smiled sadly. "I love you, you love me. Forget the rest. Let's do things we can remember for the rest of our lives – wherever you or I go."

She kissed him. And kissed him again.

Jack finally understood. *I've convinced her she has no future.* He put his head between his hands. *I didn't mean we couldn't fight and set things right.*

"Okay, Dee. The Directory people have you locked in, don't they?"

"That's what I said. Can we just do something I enjoy? I don't want to worry about things we can't change."

"That makes perfect sense." Jack looked at her.

"I detect a 'but'."

"You're right, Dee. The 'but' is that if we work smart and hard over the next ten days, you won't have to leave Earth."

Tears streamed down Wendy's face. *I know he means well, but he casually dangles the impossible in front of me – it's cruel....*

"It's not impossible. If we fight we can win."

He guessed my thoughts.

"I'm not that good a guesser."

"Jack! Stop it!"

"Dee, I'm telepathic. I recovered that skill down there." He pointed to the lake. "I need you to know that – to acknowledge the truth of it. I'll use this skill to help get you out of trouble."

Wendy looked at the clouds, the trees, the mountains. She felt the breeze on her skin, saw a squirrel dash. She was comforted by all the "real" things around her.

She knew Jack could see her thoughts.

But to admit it. To say, "I know, Jack!" was to cross a barrier into the unknown. It was to leave solid ground. To drown in the nameless.

"Can you take my hand?" he asked quietly.

She gave it. "You've crossed the barrier, my love. I'm still me. You know me. I'm Jack Cousins – feet planted on terra firma."

Oh my god. He can do it. He really can.

"Thanks, Dee. Believing me – that means a lot."

She stared at the skeleton.

"You really were that, that thing?"

"Yep. That was me."

It was difficult, but she tried to see it from his point of view. "It must be strange to look at the bones of your last body."

A light went on.

"You had a whole different life, a different name and other responsibilities." Her voice trailed away. "Something bad was happening before your space ship wrecked and that body, your body, died." She shook her head, realizing something about him. "You've been trapped on Earth!"

He nodded. "Yes."

"That's why..... Oh, Jack. It must have been horrible for you."

Jack shrugged. "The confusion is gone. And I have you."

"Jack!"

"I mean it. I love my parents, but you made my life on Earth livable. Only you, Dee."

She took him in her arms and cried again, but for other reasons.

●

"So tell me who you are, where you come from and what you do."

Jack laughed. "That's all?"

She nodded.

"I'm Tac-U-One. That's short for Tactical Unit One Crown."

"That's not a real name."

Jack frowned. "I guess you're right. It's what everyone calls me. The guys in the office call me "One" sometimes. It's my job title. I am Crown's problem solver."

"Who's Crown?"

"He's the ruler of the Directory of Stars and Planets."

"You work for the ruler of the Directory?" She was stunned. "He's your boss?"

"Yep."

"That makes me feel a bit better."

"Why's that, Dee?" He laughed.

"According to my pamphlets the Directory has trillions of citizens."

"Yes, it does."

"I can't imagine Crown, with that many people to choose from, would employ a useless person."

"No, I guess he wouldn't." He smiled.

Maybe I can get out of this mess, she thought.

Jack's smile deepened.

Wendy continued. "So what do you do?"

"In the Directory problems are divided into three categories – short term (zero to two years), medium term (two to twenty years) and long term (above twenty years). You would call the short term problem solvers, police. My department is the Tactical Unit and we deal with problems of medium duration. Long term is the Strategic Unit."

"Is the Tactical Unit civil or criminal?"

"We don't make that distinction."

"Oh."

"On my last mission Crown gave me a confidential assignment. Bio-One, the head of the Biological Department, was being investigated for treason.

"I discovered a planet where he was mass producing biological weapons and other illegal biological products.

"I was detected, but still lifted off the planet in my star ship. The battle went on for a long time. I finally got away, but my damaged ship malfunctioned and it dumped me near Earth. An enemy ship chased me and I crashed into that cliff."

"So it's an accident you're here?"

"As much as anything is ever an accident. Sure."

Wendy had nothing to say.

"Two days later I was born in Salt Lake City." She looked to be coming to terms with it.

"I'd like to see Jeb's calendar," she said. He understood. Some things need solid evidence to make them believable.

"Of course."

"These last seventeen years have been…." He shook his head and turned his attention outward.

He had other pressing concerns.

One look and the truth exploded in his head.

"There's only one explanation for the presence of Directory personnel on Earth." He looked at her, his face a terrible mask. "Crown has been overthrown! He would never have allowed this planet to be officially contacted!"

With infallible logic, Jack convinced himself of this truth. After his own death, the Directory power structure must have crumbled. How could it? He was only a small cog in a huge empire.

But it must have.

He thought it through, letting each domino of logic fall. Each piece thundered into place with conviction.

"I was lured to that planet for elimination. The only reason they got me was because they knew I was coming. They must have moved against Crown immediately after. Even so, I can't believe… can't imagine how Bio-One did it.

"But it's true.

"Directory people are here on Earth. That means Crown's government has fallen!"

Tears rolled down Jack's cheeks, and as he continued to speak his tone went from grief to hard biting anger.

"This planet, Dee, or any planet in this same category, is not due for contact until the technology for interstellar travel has been independently developed. Earth, left in isolation as it should have been, might have reached that plateau in another hundred years. But probably not. We have seen it over and over. Planets such as this one, post-nuke but pre-interstellar, are very volatile and often as not, destroy their technology base before making it to the stars. Such self-destructive societies are not allowed to integrate with or in any way disrupt the stable Directory worlds."

Wendy remained silent.

She was aghast. And very angry.

In his despair over the loss of Crown, he had badmouthed planet Earth horribly.

"That's a real policy?" she asked. Not able to accept that Crown (whoever he was) would let her planet go to hell.

He just looked at her.

"Do you support the 'trash Earth' policy, Jack? Do you?" She was furious.

"You want to know why that policy exists?"

"Yes."

"Membership into the Directory of Stars and Planets is barred unless that make/break point is reached without outside interference. Every current member planet has this qualification. History proves that interstellar travel guarantees expansion of a culture for many thousands of years, and reaching this level indicates a true survival/ sanity instinct of a race and culture."

He couldn't keep his mind on point. As he tried to continue with the explanation, his voice gave out. He needed Wendy to understand why Directory policy excluded Earth from any help....

Grief filled him. Holding the awareness of Crown's overthrow away became impossible. He could no longer deny that the man he loved most in the universe was dethroned, imprisoned, dead or worse.

He measured the loss of Crown and his government against his own difficulty on earth. *I should never have lost my memory. I should have finished the dive years ago.*

He had indulged personal weakness while the galaxy rotted.

Crown is gone, Tac-U-One thought.

It was too much. His body convulsed with wracking sobs. His mind choked with remorse.

Jack crumbled before her. Wendy put aside her upset and embraced him tightly, rocking him slowly back and forth.

So much was changing for her in so little time it was hard to keep up. She felt better holding him; at least she was doing something other than feeling uncertain, disbelieving or angry. She was helping him and wanted to.

Holding his body she realized she only halfway believed him. It came back to the same point.

How can he know any of this? She wondered again – then her viewpoint shifted. *How could anyone make this stuff up? If it was lies he wouldn't be so upset, and he isn't faking it – I'd know it.*

His story is rational because it's too crazy to be crazy. A twisted logic – but a compelling one.

She felt relieved.

She rocked him, soothed him, murmured assurances softly in his ear, and kissed his cheek. The driving emotion lessened until he lay quietly. Then she felt a distinct change and could almost see him gathering his thoughts, lining them up, pulling himself together. He sat up and they disengaged.

"You're always here when I need you. Thanks for your kindness."

"You're welcome." The speed of his emotional recovery took away from the validity of the upset.

He leaned against a rock and resumed speaking.

"My mission has been interrupted by my death/birth here on Earth. I now know what I have to do. The "life of adventure" we agreed on earlier?"

Wendy nodded.

"This is where it starts."

She was staring at him.

"What?" he asked. "What's that look for?"

"You were just crying your eyes out."

"Yeah," he shrugged. "I was upset."

"You stopped."

"I'm over it. A little bit of self-pity goes a long way." He gave a theatric shudder.

"It's time to get the show on the road. Get the ball rolling. The first step is talking to you about things." He paused.

"Is that okay?" he asked.

She smiled, but wondered, *how am I the first step in anything?* His priorities were jumbled. She wasn't going to forget the Directory policy that would have let Earth self-destruct.

"It's okay, Jack. Thanks for asking." They both smiled.

Jack gave an involuntary sigh.

"What?" she asked.

"Today I discovered I wasn't crazy. My past attitudes and experience made it impossible for me to see life on Earth as anything but strange."

She realized that Jack must have been questioning his own sanity for a long time. She was glad to see him free of self-doubt.

"Remember the baseball game?"

Jack was jumping from one thing to another.

"Yeah."

"The little kid screaming in the parking lot?" She nodded. He laughed. "I took control of his car with my mind, so he *lost* control and went berserk. I was doing it automatically without any real conscious direction. It really upset me. That piece of Directory technology was pushing me back into my former life and I couldn't handle it." On an echo of that earlier time he felt her warmth suffuse him once again. "When I needed it most, you were there. Without a plan or knowledge of how to help, you pulled me out a spin.

"You restored me."

His love filled her. Doubts faded. *Whatever else you might be, you are my Jack.*

He touched her hand, stroked her fingers. Then she startled him by getting back to business.

"Were you controlling that kid's car directly or through the kid's helmet?" she asked. Now that was a question. He looked at the incident to see what he had done.

"Actually I could exert more control over the TAC in the helmet than the boy could."

"But he had the helmet on his head."

"Call it a survival skill." He laughed as a memory popped into his head. "Back in the day, twenty or thirty of us would get together and battle each other for control over multiple TACs from various distances in a mock war room. We used many types of gadgets; funnily enough, some of them were ground vehicles like the kid's toy. Back then it was high sport, with stuff flying through the air, mini-explosions, and great fun, but with the purpose of honing a skill that would keep us alive on a mission to some far-flung world when our lives were on the line." He got back on track.

"Close proximity to the wreck caused me to relive the time when my spacecraft impacted the cliff face. I almost drowned." He laughed a little. "By going through the whole incident I recovered my memory." Some of the experience showed through. "Now I can fulfill my duty."

"Okay, Jack." Her voice trembled.

He was on a mission. It didn't take her long to realize the consequences. Her emotions crashed. If what he said was true, he would soon be gone, would leave Earth to continue his very important mission. *I bet this plan doesn't include an Earth girl.* She had helped him in the past but that wouldn't allow him to carry her along as extra baggage. *One space ship, one ray gun, one interstellar GPS, one Earth girl. No, I'm not on that list.*

"So let's get this clear, Jack. It's a mistake we ever met? You would never have chosen to come here, to this backwater, primitive, uncivilized, uncultured, third-rate, 'voted most likely to destroy itself' planet if you hadn't been stranded here?" This question took him completely by surprise.

"I'm astonished you would even talk to a native like me – who knows what I might say or do that would contaminate you.

"I think I like the new ruler, who is it – Bio-One? better than the old one. At least he doesn't think Earth requires quarantine and should be left to its self-destructive fate!" As she finished she pushed Jack away. "Leaving us to kill ourselves off is the best thing for you, isn't it, Jack?" She was very upset.

Wendy was not going to let Jack dump her and her planet and hit the road – bye, bye baby.

Earth was all she knew. For an accurate evaluation she needed something to compare it to.

"I'm sorry I offended you. Let me give some background that might explain the policy a little better." Her look was still all thundercloud, so he added, "But please feel free to completely reject what I say." Still the dark look. "I mean just verbally stomp on my ideas, logically dismember them and throw them so far away that…." She cracked a tiny smile.

"All right, Jack. Get on with explaining why my home planet is so backwards et cetera, et cetera, and so on."

"Look, Dee, the history of Earth is what it is. Within the Directory a thousand years can go by without war."

"You're kidding?"

"No."

This made an impression.

"We do have something to protect."

Jack spoke about politics and leaders and freedom, and then…

"What's happened on Earth isn't unique – there are parallels in Directory history. Our founder Jolo Patwaal faced and defeated opposition from many entrenched and self-interested power factions that opposed his movement based on practical immortality.

"When he empowered others to discover their own immortality, to realize forgetfulness from life to life was just a shadow, he was attacked from all sides. To this day, Immortals within the Directory are called 'Jolos'."

"You're talking about the 'immortality' that the Directory Chief announced yesterday?"

"Yes, Dee, there's an exact method."

"I'd like to see that!"

"And I'd show you, if I had the equipment."

"There's a machine that makes you immortal?" She couldn't believe it.

Jack laughed. "A machine can't make you immortal – but you can discover immortality for yourself by using it. A piece of equipment, no larger than a clothes closet, is used to transfer 'you' from one body to the next."

"You said 'you' in quotes, right?"

Jack smiled. "The 'you' who controls your body. The 'you' who thinks and feels and makes decisions. The 'you' who does not die when the body is gone."

"Okay, so you mean 'me.'" Wendy smiled.

"It's an important distinction, Dee. Some folks think when you 'die' you cease to exist except as ashes or a moldy body. Others think 'you' enter into the presence of 'God,' or are denied this and suffer.

"People who think existence is – one life then death only, are convinced truth is found after passing. For many life has 'gone on too long' and see death as a release from pain. They long to be free.

"For my part I find that truth is found in living and not death. Transferring from one body to another allows you to see life as it is. Without transfer it's just a theory and you can be misled."

Wendy was staggered.

"I'm sure transferring from one body to another would remove all doubt." She felt a great longing. *I want the truth. Finally and forever I want it.*

"Religion would become fact." She nodded. She was impressed by Jack's personal philosophy, and liked the idea of "truth is in living and not death."

"Who is Jolo…?" she asked.

"Jolo Patwaal, our founder, gave us freedom and power through practical immortality. Jolo Patwaal's fledgling movement grew and, as I said, the new technology threatened the power brokers who claimed dominion over men."

"You talk about it like it was yesterday."

Jack smiled, instantly recalling all the intent faces of the little kids. "That's because every child in the Directory of Stars and Planets listens to Jolo Patwaal's original lectures that describe the initial Fight for Immortality.

"Sometimes when I'm not on a mission I go to schools and talk to the kids about this time in our history. Our children learn the early sacrifices that were made to give them their chance at practical immortality. I tell them of the current situations we handle to protect their opportunity in the life they now have."

She was listening closely.

"Jolo Patwaal made certain promises to his people. Some of us dedicate our lives to keep the potential for a *greater future* alive in every generation. For our culture to succeed we need these kids to strive, to make it, to do well, go all the way."

"I can see you doing that." She yawned.

"Stop me if I'm boring you. Long, long ago I was a college professor – I love to tell stories, ahem, lecture."

"For a moment there I felt exhausted. Please tell me more, Jack."

"You asked for it."

She nodded.

"It's said if you don't know your history you're doomed to repeat earlier mistakes. I believe that's accurate.

"And true on a personal level. If you don't know you've lived before, you make the same blunders.

"If you lose your history, national or personal, Dee, you can be easily manipulated."

"You make it sound so real."

"I'm not without personal experience."

"Okay, Jack."

"Jolo Patwaal's revolution was the practical emancipation of the soul, which is the most basic freedom. It's the true freedom on which all others depend.

"If all the oppressors can do is kill the body, but you know you will live to fight another day, what control do they have?"

"Not much." she admitted.

"Very little. It infuriates them and makes you strong. But immortality must come from personal knowledge and not a belief system.

"We citizens of the Directory are a profoundly spiritual people, Dee, also intensely practical. Our religion would be worthless if it didn't result in a better life.

How would I feel if I had that much certainty about life? Wendy tried to imagine it and failed.

"We've had practical immortality for," Jack paused a second to do the conversion, "more than nine thousand Earth years within the Directory."

"That's a long time." And that made her wonder about him.

He responded to her thought. "When the Egyptians were helped with the construction of pyramids, I was already in the Tactical Unit."

She did her own calculation. "More than five thousand years?"

"Yes."

"You're asking me to believe that?"

"Don't. I rarely 'believe' anything." He smiled. "I make it my business to find out."

Once again Wendy felt a longing.

Jack said. "My prediction is you'll find out for yourself if any of what I've said is true."

"That's what I want."

●

"Jack, I don't think the people of Earth are a threat to the Directory people or their occupation.

"Directory technology is rapidly changing old ideas. And that means Earth, even as she was, never represented a serious 'cultural infection' problem to the Directory.

"All that's needed before Earth could be accepted into the Directory is a probationary period where the wrinkles were sorted out. And that leaves one question: does anyone in the Directory want to help Earth or other planets like it?"

He met her gaze and held it. The policy of ignoring planets like Earth could be faulty. At least it deserved another look.

The conversation flowed back and forth for some time. Even in his recovered state, with all the data in his memory, she took him to task about Directory isolationism.

"Dee, you're right. I think the policy should be revised."

"Thank you." She reached out and gently stroked his arm. It was good to know she could challenge Jack on his ground and win. It went some way in restoring her confidence.

"Are you hungry?" she asked. And though he had had a few bites earlier, he was now ravenous.

●

The meal was cold and taken from cans and placed between dry crackers and hard squares of cheese. They ate quickly and put the morning behind them.

"Let's take a walk." Jack suggested.

They went for a stroll along the lake shore and up a serpentine mountain trail. Jack saw her limping along and asked her about it. When she told him how she injured her foot he was astonished. Wendy's determination to help him almost cost her life. It was sobering. He took her hands in his. There was no eloquence sufficient for this moment, no poetry expressive enough.

"Thank you, Dee."

"You're welcome."

The dark vortex at the lake bottom and in Jack's mind had found release. This place had become a significant landmark for him; a nexus of importance. He looked around and judged the area from a different perspective: yes, there was room enough. Its limited accessibility and remoteness were also attractive. Other events, he decided, would take place here.

●

"We need to talk about our relationship," Jack said. He'd picked up she was disturbed about their bond.

"Okay, Jack." She looked forlorn.

She thought, *He's just waiting to tell me I can't come, that it's too dangerous, it's against regulations, that I'm untrained – have no skills, that, that...*

All adding up to one fact: she couldn't go. *He must remember women far more sophisticated, more skilled, and more desirable. We haven't even....*

"I'm just an *Earth* girl. I'm not...." She couldn't properly express her own feeling of inadequacy.

Jack looked at her. "What is it, what's wrong?"

"Jack, it's all different. You know who you are. You know about your important mission. You know your past. I couldn't, I won't hold you to an agreement we made when you didn't know who you really were." The wind tossed her hair. *Now he can dump me without feeling bad.*

"Thank you, Wendy." Jack said with some formality. "The future now has a definite direction," he said with a smile. "The first step is to tell you what I think will happen so you can decide if you want to be involved. You see, Dee, it's going to get rough quite soon, and that is my life."

"You're not trying to scare me off, are you, Jack?" She felt enormous relief.

"No, Dee. I want you with me if you're willing. But you need to know what you're getting into."

"Years ago when you said a 'life of adventure' you meant 'dangerous adventure.'"

"I guess I did." He got a distant look, then smiled. "Not all adventure is dangerous, just the best of it." His grin was infectious and she smiled too.

He sobered.

In the past, he had sought action, overmuch. He must be ready to use force, but willing to seek the intelligent option more often, or combine the two with greater skill.

"I'm sorry if I gave you reason to think you are inadequate in any way. You need to know more about the Directory, but that won't take long.

"There is nothing inadequate about you. You won't cause me or you embarrassment anywhere in the Directory. No matter whom we meet. You lack for nothing in intelligence, manners, charm or beauty."

Wendy sat blank-faced. And Jack intuited her thoughts.

"Look, I'm not saying these things to make you feel better, well no, that's not true, I am saying this to make you feel better. What I'm not doing is *lying* to make you feel better."

Her look softened, but she was still apprehensive.

"You may think that because we haven't made love I don't desire you." Wendy's color deepened. "Nothing could be further from the truth. I have imagined us many times…" He let the image fade.

"Because of my position within the Directory I've had a greater opportunity than most to seek out and engage in casual relationships. And, so, personally, I've had to guard against needlessly causing emotional distress in the women I meet. I do not believe in casual sex. Life holds many pleasures, but without responsibility those become vices."

Wendy looked skeptical.

"This is not a long-winded excuse said prior to breaking up with you. Please listen to me Dee, this is important to me and always will be.

Even though I previously had no memory of the events I now recollect, my *attitude* toward sex is exactly the same. The way I feel about sex required no specific memories – I knew it was right for me.

"I haven't and won't treat a sexual relationship with you casually. No matter what you see in the movies or how our friends or others live their lives, nothing will ever change the respect I give you. I think when the moment comes we'll both know it."

"Oh Jack, oh Jack! I knew it, I knew it! It was the girls and all their talk. They went on and on until I became insecure. I know you want me just as I want you. And you're right; it makes it special to wait." She snuggled up to her man and felt love, a love that knew sex would follow but had become less important.

In his arms Wendy said, "I want to go with you Jack, or Tac-U-One. I want to go with you – not because of a schoolgirl crush, or even from the real love I have for you." She paused to gather her thoughts. "I want to go with you because I know I will have more of everything life has to offer if I do. I want to know about your mission and I want to help you complete it."

Jack's was speechless.

"I know, I know, it's a bit of a turnaround from my argumentative self of a little while ago. Let's just say today is a day like no other, the fear of death, the alien strangeness, the uncertainty, the wild information, emotions exploding from one extreme to another. It's been a day. An undeniable day. But there has been a constant through this day and all the others, and that is from the moment I saw you I've wanted to spend my life with you."

Jack bowed his head and wiped his eyes. "Ahh, Wendy my love. I always wondered if that was true for you."

"You did?"

"When I first saw you…I felt my future change. You were in my life and I never wanted you to leave." They came together.

●

They discussed many things late into the night. He told her about telepathy and the wide variety of skill level there was from one person to another. There were many questions that Wendy had, and she asked them freely. The answers were alternately startling, disconcerting, interesting and unbelievable.

Later Jack returned from gathering more firewood. He chopped the old branches with a hatchet and threw the dry wood onto the fire.

They watched the flames lick and catch hold, sparks shooting high into the night sky.

●

The following morning dawned fine and fair, they had a quick cold breakfast. Jack was excited. Plans of how to keep Wendy on Earth ran through his head. This was going to be fun!

"I don't think it will be a problem, Dee, to get a delay on your contract. It should be easy to get a six month extension at least."

"How can you do that, Jack? I've heard just the opposite; everyone who signed a Directory contract goes on schedule, no exceptions."

"I know a lot of Directory law, Dee." Jack paused; he'd said it without thinking. He took a moment and thought about the law. His jaw dropped and pupils dilated – so fast did the data come at him – and then he smiled. "Yeah, we can do it."

"No, you can't, Jack, even if you do remember something that applies to what? Student contracts? How are you supposed to be able to know about it? Let's say you know the right statute, you can't just walk up to a Directory recruitment office and quote Directory law without them becoming very suspicious of you. They would hold you, take you away, the law you quoted would be suppressed and I'd still be off to wherever. I don't think it's a good idea."

"This is really great fun, Dee. When fighting an enemy, you deceive him. The first law of warfare is deception; the second is to deceive the enemy about the deception, so when he uncovers the first set of lies all he finds are more lies. This makes him think the second set of lies is truth.

"We just say that you pleaded with an unnamed Directory staff member and he told you how to defer the contract, blah, blah, blah."

"But what if the Directory person is telepathic, or if they claim the law you cite is false and ignore it?"

"I can make sure the person you talk to can't read your mind." He waved his hand vaguely. "Things have changed out there, but not so much, I think, that if presented with their own law they'll ignore it." He smiled maliciously.

"But you say they're here illegally. Why would an illegal operation follow any real Directory law you or I give them, especially when it will harm them? They won't do it. They can simply deny it or ignore it or suppress any evidence it happened at all. Or we could just run into someone from the Directory who doesn't know Directory law, tells me I'm crazy, and off I go."

"Hmmm, you're right, Dee." He looked into the distance. "There has to be a central computer on the planet – Directory Data Archives on Crown Planet has cookie cutter databases and time-tested business and management programs that are preloaded and regularly updated for many situations and 'How to take over an illegal planet' isn't on the list. So they'll have some form of standard programming – probably the one they use to open planets newly accepted into the Directory. I doubt they'll have gone to the trouble of editing out Directory law from the database. They won't expect anyone on the remote planets to have knowledge of Directory law or operations – and they would be right, except for my unlikely presence.

"Those databases and their programming are impossible to crack without destroying their ability to function. There are many obvious threats the operation here on Earth must handle. Some external person messing with computers or knowing Directory law isn't even on their list."

"So what use is the central computer to us?"

"We approach the dumbest Directory employee we can find and get him to query the computer about a point of law. The computer will spit out the Directory statute. After the first successful deferment, we swamp the Directory recruitment sites with the same inquiry, get it reported over the media and flood the world with the information. All this, done before the Directory Chief even knows it's happening."

"Then I blend anonymously into the mix. Oh, Jack, it could work. So, if they're doing something bad, other people having second thoughts can defer too. We can save a lot of people."

"With you safe we can find out what's really going on. And stop them completely." Jack said.

Wendy smiled. Who was being naïve now? Just a deferment was a long shot. She couldn't see her and Jack toppling the Directory power structure on Earth. But doing nothing was pathetic. *Who knows what we can do, or where this will end?* she wondered.

"As we talked about earlier," Jack said, "Directory presence on Earth violates long-established policy. All DE personnel know they are committing a serious breach of the Law; resulting in loss of citizenship.

"We gotta be careful."

"Let's plan this carefully, then." she said.

"Yes. They know it's all illegal. Even those high tech courses you liked so much?" Wendy nodded. "They're useless in the Directory."

"You're kidding."

"Nope, the whole thing is a scam."

She shook her head.

"The question is: do the staff know what these courses are covering up."

"That's important?"

"If they know, it's bad for us. It means they are bad people and will do anything to hide their crimes. Any attempt to free Earth will be far more difficult."

Wendy felt fear. "What *is* happening to Earth?"

"I don't have any facts now, but I will."

"Okay, Jack."

He was relieved when she didn't ask more. Nothing Wendy could imagine would be that bad.

"Can we do it, Jack, can we?" Her smile was so unsure that his heart went out to her.

"Yes, Dee," he said. "We make a plan. We do it. Simple." *In complete secrecy. Or I'll be without a body and you'll be gone,* he thought. He casually shrugged the possibility aside. *Gather data, evaluate, plan, execute.*

"The Directory person we fool will be crushed by the Directory Chief." She looked concerned. Jack was impressed with Wendy's empathy.

"Dee, don't fear harming someone in a just cause."

She looked skeptical. "That idea could easily be abused."

"That's true. It's only for use by honorable people. A destructive person will hurt or kill whomever they want regardless. But an honest and honorable person needs to know that harming another is not always wrong." She was still frowning. "Dee, you've gotta evaluate the situation, make up your own mind."

"Okay, Jack."

Soon he would enter the fray. He felt a rush of excitement. Oh yeah, he loved it. He was the right man for the job. The triumphs of a thousand yesterdays flitted across his vision, boosting him higher and higher.

●

On the way down the mountain Wendy went into Jeb's cabin and spoke to him alone.

CHAPTER 16

"You scared us to death, Jack," his aunt said. "What you did was a disgrace."

Norman nodded. "Jack, we've always given you a long leash and you've never abused it. Until now. We won't even discuss the thousands of dollars those emergency choppers cost. I could say other things. But before I do, please tell us why."

No one had much fun yesterday. Jack thought with a tinge of resentment.

"I'm sorry." Jack took a deep breath and let it out slowly. "Without knowing what happened and why it happened – it's easy to think I was thoughtless, reckless and irresponsible.

"Mother, that's not true. At all. Yesterday wasn't a prank gone bad."

They were seeking to preserve the family unit and exert parental control. The family was fine, control was not. But her expression changed as his words penetrated.

"What happened out there?" Sharon asked.

He had to tell them something. The question was how much and when.

As he moved forward their lives would change irrevocably. The priorities were different already. The family unit would be split – long before they expected.

He had the same security concerns about them as he had with Wendy. They were so closely connected that if he were discovered and captured by the Directory, they would be pulled into his troubles and their lives lost.

He *must* go forward. To succeed he needed help. Their help.

"What happened, Jack?" Sharon repeated.

Okay, move ahead.

"If the Directory finds out what I am about to tell you our lives will be forfeit." It was hard not to sound formal. He was now Tac-U-One and "Jack" would soon be a memory.

His parents looked at him. Clearly a turning point had been reached.

"What have you done?" Norman asked.

"I've committed no crime. What I've discovered and plan to do will cause them to hunt me down. If I'm found too soon we'll be lost."

Husband and wife exchanged a glance, their agreement immediate. "Tell us." they said.

For the next hour Jack went over what had happened at the lake and the personal revelations it led to. Now that he had settled down, the whole thing was relatively easy to explain.

They had expected many things from their son – but not this.

"It's true about the space ship." Norman said. "Jeb described it in detail. He got there two hours after the explosion and there it was. He watched it for hours. It submerged four times. Inspected the cliff cave. It came right up to him for a few minutes, then swept away.

"Jeb had the idea the pilot was scared."

"I'm sure he's right. There's more to that old man than I knew." Jack said.

He continued to answer their questions. Soon he could see they believed him – or at least they thought he believed what he was telling them.

Through all this, Sharon waited. She was very angry with her son, but as he told his story she couldn't help but be amazed. The situation was extraordinary. After he was done and Norman had asked many questions, she still had a bone to pick with Jack.

"Jack, I spoke to Wendy. I had to drag the story out of her. While you were diving and almost dying, Wendy was scared to death; she was all alone at the lake shore. You were in deadly danger and no help in sight."

Jack told them the details of Wendy's dive to save him.

"She didn't mention that." Sharon said. It made her doubt her son's good intentions.

She took a deep breath and exhaled slowly. "Norman and I questioned your judgment, about how you treated Wendy, and still do. We'd flown half way to the lake in the chopper. It was torture to turn back, not knowing, but we did it out of respect to you and Wendy. It was a very hard thing to do, Jack." He hadn't known she had been with Norman on that aborted flight. "How could you allow that situation to develop? That frantic call from her was horrible." She shook her head and looked hollow-eyed at Jack. "What you put that girl through. And us for that matter."

"Mom, I took the sat phone so Wendy would feel more secure. I never thought she'd need it." He stopped to look at her. "Well, that's not exactly true. I knew I might die. I was worried it could happen.

But more fundamentally, when I looked at my immediate future I felt I would survive. I never expected any call she might make would bring help in time to save me if I got in trouble."

"Damn, Jack!" Norman said.

Jack shrugged. "Sometimes I decide things and then fill in the details as I go. This was one of those times."

Sharon went pale. "That is reckless, Jack. You've explained to us some of your responsibilities to the people of the Directory and yet you risked it all in an unsupported dive, knowing and planning for no help being available? From a man such as you claim to be, that is more than irresponsible; it sounds like self-destructive behavior."

To hear that from his mother was very difficult to take and caused Jack some minutes of introspection. They waited for his response without interruption, eyes upon him.

"First off, I love the family we've created and no matter what comes in the future you will always be my family." Jack felt Sharon's intensity ebb. He should have addressed her concern about this first. Now they would listen to him without thinking he was going to sever the bonds of love.

"I delayed for *years* going to the lake and making that dive, I put it off many times. I even tried it once but never reached the bottom. Not one of my finer moments."

"I was there with you, Jack. For heaven's sake, you were just a kid." Norman said.

"Please don't make excuses for me."

Jack continued, "That dive was never going to be anything but a solo attempt. *Never.*" His voice shook. "I am here on Earth due to a very real personal flaw that led to bad decisions and my death.

"The threat to Wendy made me determined. Even without any real knowledge of what was ahead, or who I really was, I retained a complete awareness of what I find acceptable to myself.

"I created the situation. I resolved it. I've demonstrated competence to myself. In handling situations you have resolve, confidence, competence, drive and an overriding certainty that you're going to make it go right.

"Wendy and I have decided to stay together. What happened at the lake, while very upsetting to her, is simply the beginning. Other dangerous situations will have to be faced. If she couldn't handle what happened there," Jack shrugged, "then it's unlikely that she or I would think it a good thing to continue our relationship."

Now it was Sharon's turn to contemplate what had been said. It was a surreal situation. There was nothing in her experience to compare it to. Therefore she went with her feelings. Despite her doubts, did she trust Jack? Yes. But there was something very wrong here.

"Why would the Directory send an invasion force to a planet where a rival such as yourself had been eliminated? When they know you must have been reborn into the population?" Jack looked at her. It was an incredibly perceptive question for someone who'd just been introduced to an entirely new set of factors.

"It's strange, no doubt about it. But even in the Directory, among the Jolos, it's not common for a Jolo who dies accidentally to wake up next life and say, 'I was Joe Blow and I want my status back.'"

Norman said, "But Jack, that doesn't explain…."

"It's reckless, isn't it? I know. That's one of the reasons I have a hard time believing the architect of this entire scheme is Bio-One. That Earth has been chosen for contact is the type of mistake I expect from him. And a man who can make this type of fundamental misjudgment couldn't have succeeded for this long without being exposed. There's too much that is too well organized. What they're doing is massive…." He shook his head; once again speculation without sufficient data was counterproductive.

"Jack, I was so mad at you for what you did to Wendy and the scare you gave us." Sharon was still caught up in the flux of her emotions.

"Times have changed. There are going to be other unexpected changes. I need you to bear with me if sometimes I don't have time to keep you completely informed, or if I do something you don't approve of. I won't do anything without thinking it through.

"The lake dive uncovered the knowledge necessary to know to make progress. To push our cause ahead we need to form a team and right the wrongs that are being done to Earth and its people by the Directory operation. Everything needed we have or can get. We can do it!

"We force a change of management. To get this done we need the support of a few key people." Norman's jaw dropped. What Jack said was of course hypothetically true. But accomplishing the overthrow of the Directory, that subtle and powerful entity that had subdued all the governments of the world through advanced technology and economics was… a pipe dream. And a real war required things they did not have; most of all time, weapons, manpower….

"Yes, Father, there's a lot to do, a lot to risk, a lot to gain. If we want to reclaim and salvage the world for those who remain, we'll have to fight for it." Norman marveled at Jack's casual confidence, and was even more surprised that he felt swept along with it. Rigid barriers seemed to dissolve from Norman's mind.

It could be done, somehow.

Jack's stance became unyielding and formal, "Norman, Sharon, I ask for your aid in accomplishing the recovery of Earth. Will you help me?"

"Yes," they said.

Norman looked at his wife and they were of an accord. Parental rights were obviously a thing of the past. Their son was now calling the shots. Jack's story couldn't be a fabrication. And what if it were? They were now irrevocably committed to a purpose that would dictate they follow his lead and directions.

They knew Jack had an exceptional future and had discussed this topic deep into the night on many occasions. The future was here. Even if his plans were sci-fi on steroids. Sharon clasped Norman's hand in hers. While she had lost her anger over the situation at the lake, she still had reservations about Jack's conduct; but who can criticize a man in full possession of his faculties about decisions so personal? One had a right to live one's life, adhere to a code of honorable conduct and handle the consequences, come what may.

"Thank you, Mother." Jack nodded and smiled at her. Ah, Sharon thought, the telepathy. He's letting me know…. Norman frowned and Jack said, "She'll tell you later." Norman's brow cleared, he shrugged and said, "Okay."

Norman took one final grasp at parental control. "We will help you, of course. But understand that your welfare is still our first concern."

"Thank you for that, but I assume full responsibility for my actions from this point. And complete liberty."

"Jack…" Sharon couldn't continue.

"I know, I know, Mother. But the action of my life has moved far beyond these four walls."

"You're just *seventeen*," Norman said, the last flicker.

"How curious, do you really think so?" He said it as himself, as Tac-U-One. There was an unmistakable shift in the tone of his voice.

And that was that.

●

"Norman, I need access to a quarter-million dollars from a blind off-shore account."

Norman smiled to cover his shock. "And you need this pocket change for what purpose?"

Jack smiled too, able to tell he had stunned his father. "The money is to fund my plan to keep Wendy from being forcefully shipped off-world."

"But two hundred and fifty thousand dollars?"

"We need a lot of high tech gear and we'll travel extensively. It's more than we need, but it includes a necessary contingency cushion. It cannot be traceable to you or me. I need this by close of business today. We've got very little time to get this done."

Norman looked at Jack and was about to voice another objection. He looked at Sharon who had been sitting quietly, listening to this exchange. She said, "If you don't give it to him, I will."

Jack smiled again, "Thanks, Mom." Sharon was happy to hear Jack's old tone of voice. Then, divining her thoughts from her expression, said, "I'm still me, Mom. It's just there's more of me."

Norman said, "Okay, Jack, I'll get it done."

"Thank you. These next few weeks and months are going to be hard on you. Please stay with me on this." Norman had no idea what Jack was talking about.

"Okay, Jack," he said.

Jack then told them what else he needed them to do.

"He always prized his independence; now we know why." Norman later said. Sharon agreed. But if Jack felt it necessary to warn Norman of difficulties to come, then she knew his plans were well advanced and knew, also, she and her husband would be severely tested.

CHAPTER 17

JACK SAID GOODBYE TO HIS PARENTS and locked himself in with Wendy. Subtracting their two days in the mountains, they had twelve days till her scheduled departure.

"Can I look at your ticket, Dee?" She passed it over.

Wendy constantly put off Natalie and Deidre who wanted to talk about their future. She turned off her personal phone and told her Mother to tell callers or visitors she was still in the mountains with Jack.

Her mother knocked and came in with a tray holding two plates stacked with food.

"Thanks, Mom. That's so thoughtful." Wendy's speech to her mother was unaccountably formal. There was so much she could not say. All they had told her parents was that Jack would be spending a lot of time at their house over the next two weeks. With Wendy's pending departure from the planet, they had not objected.

She and Jack were going over plans. Rejecting, refining, writing out the necessary steps, figuring out all the equipment they would need and then rushing out to buy it or having it shipped overnight.

To her surprise it was all coming together. She felt some hope that her life would continue here.

The television was muted, but the screen showed fascinating hectic activity. In Los Angeles the Directory was building its new headquarters and stadium for what had been dubbed "the Fight for Immortality." Three space ships hovered above the rising structure which was appropriately named the Colosseum.

"Those space ships are *huge*."

"Actually, they're tiny. They are decommissioned space navy ships sold to private corporations. I looked at their registration markings when they showed a few close-ups. Those ships are old 33rd battalion vessels. The earliest inception date was over four thousand years ago."

"Wow, that's old."

"Well, if there is one area in the Directory where superstition still holds sway, it's space flight. Those ships have made many successful flights and have a reputation for safety. If everyone inside the ship thinks it's safe and that it will arrive at their destination, then it's likely to do so. Every few hundred years they gut the ships and then reinforce and rebuild them. That ship has been fully refurbished fifteen times."

"How do you know all that?"

"It's all on the registration markings." He pointed to a large engraved plate near one of the freight hatches. On their screen it was visible as a shiny point of light.

"Oh, I see it." She paused, then continued thoughtfully. "Why are the Directory people superstitious about space flight?"

"Some ships never arrive at their destination. And then sometimes a ship that left a planet a hundred, or on one extreme occasion, a thousand years before, will simply arrive at its destination."

Wendy shivered. "Rip Van Winkle."

"Yeah. It's no longer a common occurrence. But sometimes…."

"So Directory science hasn't figured it out?"

"It was a problem. It's been pretty much determined to be a spiritual problem and not one of science."

"That sounds… strange." While they were talking, another fifty prefabricated sections had been set in place. The Colosseum was taking shape before their eyes. It was a fabulous construction feat by Earth standards.

"The arena is going to be completed in a few weeks."

"How is space flight a religious problem?"

"Spiritual, not religious." Wendy shrugged and shook her head at the same time. Jack wondered about taking time to explain this, but realized that if they made it off the planet she needed to know this.

"For travel between stars our ships travel outside the universe and then reenter it, hopefully at the right point. Outside the universe is simply called Other Space or OS.

"The time factor is easily altered.

"In OS, time and space are determined by the people on the ship. It's a numbers game – if a great majority of the passengers agree on how long it going to take to get to the destination – everyone is fairly safe.

"Back in the day people would panic, the panic would spread, everyone thinking they would never arrive – so they wouldn't.

"But that's theoretical to some extent, as no one who hasn't returned has returned, to tell us why they aren't there."

"You're making fun of me."

"I'm not." They both looked at the arena silently growing like a fast frame shot of a flower blooming.

"Sounds like a good reason to be superstitious about space travel."

"A used ship can be more expensive than a new one. But the navy sells them cheap as a matter of policy. I'd like to track the registration of that ship and see who owns her."

They ate their food.

She watched the rapid construction and broke chunks of chicken from the breast, absently chewing. She thought about what Jack had said. She'd gotten over being astonished every time Jack mentioned something new, and listened and asked the questions necessary to clarify the subject in her own mind. She took another mouthful.

"So I take it there has to be some uniformity or agreement about time before going to OS. And if I remain calm about it and others do too, then we're likely to arrive alive."

Damn, she was good. "You're right. That's how it's done."

● ● ●

Augustus McMillan sat at his desk. His slightly drunken conversation with that CIA worm came back again to plague him. Without that kid talking to him, he might not have discovered the true nature of the aliens. Or it would have taken much longer than it did. Or his tiny budget would've run out. The kid was pivotal. And he'd given the kid to that worm, Perrywhite. That did not sit well with McMillan. The kid did not deserve to be thrown to the wolves.

Remembering his conversation, the kid seemed decent. Clean-cut, young, probably still in high school. Young. And that made it worse.

Now he felt obligated to find the kid, to offer him some protection. Give him a warning. But how to do that? He recalled more of their conversation. He'd asked the kid where he was from and he'd said "up north." That had a winter feel to it. He called for a large map of the US. Soon he was looking over the area north of Las Vegas. It could be anywhere. Idaho, Montana, lots of cities, more small towns.

Then he remembered the kid hadn't said "up north" but "north of here." He followed I15 out of Las Vegas and came to St. George, Utah. No, he'd had a sense of distance. He went through a number of towns till he got to Salt Lake City. Clean-cut, city not country kid, yeah. Salt Lake City, north of Las Vegas but not "up north." It fit. He called in his assistant.

"Get me the yearbooks for the last five years from every high school in a thirty-mile radius of Salt Lake City. And then get me a sketch artist."

"I don't think we have any sketch artists at the Pentagon, sir."

"Get one from the FBI and get him here today."

"Yes, sir."

● ● ●

"Securing legal deferment from your Directory contract is the key to starting the whole process." Jack said, "We have to be smart about how we do it and who we use first. The time of day is also important."

They flew to the regional Directory centers located in large cities across the US. There was one in Salt Lake City, but they wouldn't use it for obvious reasons.

While in the air to Seattle, Jack explained. "Executives of government agencies within the Directory are briefed by nine a.m. on the events of the past day. I bet they do the same here. And without a catastrophe occurring that day, the Chief won't be updated again until the following morning.

"So, the first application for deferment should be made at about ten a.m. That'll give us a full twenty-three hours for people to file and receive deferment before the Chief finds out.

"We need the right clerk, so we'll have to shop around. With a short look at each one I'll decide which candidate gives us the best chance of success.

"Okay, Jack."

"Once we pick a clerk, we make sure of his schedule so the guy we choose to start the deferments will be at the induction window at ten a.m. on the day we launch the attack."

"This is exciting." Wendy said. Jack smiled.

They landed and went to the airport family restroom, locked the door and applied the disguises Jack had purchased. Changing the cheek width, pinning the ears, altering nose shape, then for good measure messing with the chin. Jack had no intention of coming anywhere near the Directory scanners, as they would flag the disguise in a second. The reason for the disguise was to confuse the Directory investigators. In a telepathic interview regular people won't have Jack and Wendy's correct facial features stored in their minds. *We'll be harder to track and it'll delay our discovery.*

As they were applying their disguises Jack said, "I don't know if they have a telepathic investigator, but if they do the disguises are essential."

"Good thing we practiced applying this crud." Wendy remarked.

Jack looked her over. "Your beauty is definitely gone – and that's a good thing." She punched his shoulder. "You did a great job; you don't look made-up."

They worked their way around the country; airport to Directory Induction Centers and then back to the airport. Sometimes they flew on separate airlines. It was hectic. Once they took the train. When interviewing people, Jack and Wendy always worked separately, cajoling, asking questions and joking with those who were checking in to the regional Directory Induction Center and shipping off Earth. Wendy felt terrible for not doing everything she could to discourage those she talked to from shipping out.

Jack met Wendy at a coffee shop in Tampa to discuss their latest results. "Jack, I think we may have the clerk we need."

Wendy described the man she had come to know from her interviews. Jack listened intently. He'd also interviewed folks and made surreptitious use of telepathy upon inductees. Combining their data, Jack decided this clerk may indeed be the one they needed. He would save the final decision until he made a quick personal interview. The clerk worked at the Tampa Induction Center.

Jack finished his coffee and visited the restroom, where he removed his more elaborate disguise. He went in with dark glasses and a ball cap to conduct his interview. In a short conversation, Jack verified that the Directory clerk was not very bright, was a stickler for the rules and made certain of his schedule. *Perfect.* Jack and Wendy returned to the coffee shop and sat in a quiet corner.

"Don't talk to me for about half an hour, okay Dee?" And he tapped his head.

"Oh, some of that stuff. Okay."

Jack sat and looked mildly dazed for almost forty minutes. People came and went and she ordered more coffee and added a muffin. She looked at the blue sky and thought of the infinity beyond and how that space had become tainted, at least in her own mind. She thought of a girl she had talked to today. Her outlook was so much like Wendy's own – *before.* Only the thought that blowing their cover would destroy many more lives had prevented her from spilling her guts. Wendy had started to cry. The poor girl became so concerned about Wendy. "What's wrong, what's wrong?" she asked. Wendy broke down completely. They hugged until Wendy's wracking sobs subsided. Wendy couldn't stop herself. "Please don't go, I feel something bad is going to happen." The girl was so excited, her sense of the future so bright. "You sound just like my mother." Her enthusiasm undiminished; there was a spring in her step as she walked to the Induction Center. It broke Wendy's heart to see her go to her fate. She could stop it – but then she looked at how long it had taken Jack to convince her. And the girl's initial decision could be drug-induced. So she had let her go.

Finally Jack came out of his reverie. "I haven't done that for years and I'm a little rusty, but I got it right. Let's walk past our guy once more." Wendy remained out of sight as Jack went past the Directory Induction Center and planted a subtle mind spring straight into the guy's head. "Okay, we're done here." They'd been at it for three days. The first major target of their plan was now complete. They walked for a few miles.

Wendy tapped her temple. "What did you do to that clerk?"

"First, I rapidly assessed his state of mind. Then, sitting in the coffee shop, I assembled a series of instructions in picture form – mental images – simple stuff really: 'go to the computer, verify the law, print the official form, fill in the deferred person's name, add digital image of person's face, sign, date and seal it, give official copy to person at the window'.

"I enhanced what he would naturally feel and do. I added the idea that deferment was an approved procedure. And if others contacted him to ask about it, he would say it was legal and approved.

"Wow, can you control anyone and make them do what you want?"

"Not easily. I just enhanced the clerk's natural inclinations. Lastly, I gave the guy a trigger phrase which releases and activates the mind spring." Jack looked at her. "When we find our first contact person I'll give him the exact phrase." Jack could see her interest had faded. They continued to walk and more miles passed beneath their feet.

"You're a pretty loud thinker, Dee."

She looked at him. "You know?" He nodded, and she fell into his arms. "Oh, Jack. It was terrible, I tried to stop her but she really wanted to go off-world. I know she felt incredible hope for the future – beginning a grand adventure. I argued with her but couldn't stop her. It felt like I was sentencing that girl to death."

Jack thought, *if only the poor girl's fate was that easy.* It bothered him, too.

Wendy had nine days to report in.

●

They took the midnight flight and arrived back in Salt Lake City the following morning. Jack and Wendy continued their plans.

"We can't wait till the last day to do my deferment, Jack. If something goes wrong there will be no time to try something else."

Jack nodded.

Wendy continued, "Let's do it three days before my departure date. That's the best way to avoid notice."

"Go on." Jack encouraged.

"The people they investigate will be the first ones who defer, then they'll go after those who just miss their ship date. So part of our strategy must be to get a lot of other people about to be shipped out deferring their departure, so I can hide in the crowd. It shouldn't be difficult."

"You've thought this through."

"I went over it and over it last night on the plane. It's been on my mind." She smiled ironically.

"It's a good plan. One thing though, we need you to receive your deferment somewhere in the top fifty."

"But that'll make it easier for them to track me down."

"I know. But even with all precautions we take to avoid discovery, the Directory Chief or his executives may find out about the deferments and shut us down fast. So I think you should defer pretty quickly – but not one of the first."

"Okay, Jack." All their activity had kept her mind off the possibility of being shipped out. Now the reality came back solidly and she shivered. *This is a dangerous game we're playing.*

● ● ●

Four days before Wendy's departure date, they took the offensive. Jack overnighted a press release to a major magazine, one of the few that still ran stories unfavorable to the Directory. He figured the magazine was in the bag to the Directory but ran mildly controversial stories at the direction of the Directory PR boys: make the populace still think the mainstream media were objective.

He took some of the Directory letterhead from the many promotional packs Wendy had received, and with a little effort worked up a believable press release purportedly coming from the Las Vegas Directory offices. Jack marked the box so he was certain it would be opened immediately. He called the magazine's mail room to discover when overnight packages were delivered, which set his timing for the following day. He located the post office closest to the Las Vegas Directory offices. Jack drove from Salt Lake City to Las Vegas and back in nine and a half hours. While there, he purchased a new laptop with cash.

Arriving home, he showered and changed clothes. Jack plugged in and charged the laptop battery and set up the computer. He tested his own device for remotely pirating the 'net and it worked like a charm. Jack collected the other equipment he had been working on over the last few days, then Wendy took him to the Salt Lake City airport. She kissed him, hugged him tightly and sent him on his way.

She decided to get near the Directory Induction Center early (close but out of sight) and sit in her parked car to await his call.

Jack got a few hours' sleep on the flight and was ready to go when the wheels touched tarmac.

● ● ●

Things had to be timed perfectly. Jack figured that the Directory Chief would be done with his briefing at nine a.m. Then give it an hour just to be sure – ten a.m. The man was in Las Vegas. The press release would arrive at the magazine's mail room at 11 a.m. (give or take), Pacific Time. Jack was in St. Louis, Central Time. Their selected Directory clerk and also the person he had chosen to set the attack in motion, their unknowing agent, were in Tampa on Eastern Time. Once again he used the family bathroom at the airport to apply his disguise.

He took a bus from the St. Louis airport to an upscale neighborhood near the local Directory Induction Center. On the bus ride he took out his laptop and verified it was set up properly and ready to go. During the down time over the last few days, Jack had checked real estate listings for possible target homes. After exiting the bus and walking to his target area he scouted some houses, discarded a few, and then found the residence he needed. He mentally gave the few folks who would have seen him something else to look at and then broke into the unoccupied house with a realtor sign posted on the lawn. He took out a datastick and transferred the necessary information and programming to allow bulk emails. He connected remotely to the 'net and when eleven-thirty arrived, he emailed his guy.

In Tampa was the thirty-three-year-old, out-of-work used car salesman who had decided at a low point in his life to do the Directory training to really piss off his ex-wife. The Directory contract had exempted him from the obligations of child support he had struggled to pay – in which he took great delight in informing the ex. After the high of the Directory training, his euphoria soon died when he realized he definitely wouldn't see his kids for a minimum of five years and if things went bad, if the rumors were right – never again. With his luck….

After locating the correct Directory clerk in Tampa, Jack had spotted this man arguing heatedly with another clerk. He listened in and discovered that the man no longer wanted to continue with his contract, that he wanted to stay at home, stay with his kids. Jack, in disguise, told the man there may be a solution to his dilemma. Was he interested?

Today the anxious man was sitting at his computer when Jack's email arrived. He read it immediately and was shocked. He memorized the short phrase as instructed and drove to the Directory Offices. His watch read five minutes to one p.m. when he arrived in line.

Reaching the window, John Taylor informed the clerk, "I, John Taylor, am applying for an unconditional deferment from my contractual Directory contract."

The clerk looked at him quizzically. "That's a new one, sir. Give me a minute while I check the computer on that subject."

"Now remember, that's 'unconditional deferment from a contractual Directory contract.' It has to be entered that way exactly."

The clerk got a deeper frown. "I'll be back."

Those three words scared John Taylor, who thought the clerk was going to round up the goon squad to drag him away. But good as his word, the clerk returned to his seat at the window with a printed form. Taylor's name, photo and other vital information were all filled in, in the proper places. He looked at the clerk.

"How long will this deferment be, Mr. Taylor?"

"Uh, what are my options?"

The clerk punched a few buttons. "According to this conversion table, you can take anything from about ten days, to nine point two years."

In a daze he said, "I'll take the max, nine point two years, thank you." Others in the line heard the exchange and asked, "What do you say, what do you say?" Taylor told them and a few furtive whispers turned into rushed murmurs and then unfettered conversation; all five people waiting in line took deferment. The news spread and deferments were handed out to almost everyone who came to the window.

● ● ●

FROM THE LAPTOP IN HIS CAR parked directly in front of Starbucks, John Taylor returned an email of his success to the address he had received the message from forty minutes ago. Jack texted Wendy of their success: "the ripe apple is red." She stepped from her car and walked briskly to the local Directory Induction Center and saw the line at the Induction window. She waited till she saw some agitation and went forward to investigate. Sure enough, there were people walking away with their approved deferment paperwork – wow, that was fast. She got back in the rapidly growing line. Someone repeated to her exactly what to say to the clerk. She smiled.

Jack got the text. Wendy had the completed paperwork in hand. Deferment approved! He was elated. The unconscious tension slowly began to ease. They had planned it – and pulled it off like a couple of pros.

Securing her freedom was something he wouldn't have done on another mission. This was special. Even though it heightened his profile and jeopardized the reprieve of the Directory populace. He did it for love.

Wendy.

He had faults. His presence on Earth testified to that. But an earlier Tac-U-One wouldn't have allowed personal feelings to come between him and a mission. And this wasn't just any mission – this was make or break for the Directory.

He'd changed.

He wouldn't consign Wendy to the fate Bio-One had set for the luckless people of Earth. *What would Crown say? If he knew I was risking it all for love?* Jack asked himself. The answer was simple: *if we lose, Crown will never know. If we win it won't matter.*

Jack sent out prepared bulk emails to various media about the deferment, and directed other media outlets to the press release now online at the magazine he had selected. Then he went into cleanup mode. He took a device he had fabricated (using only Earth-manufactured components), and with it swept the house clean of bio-deposits. He crushed the device beneath his boot and left it and the computer in the room. Jack pulled on a dark jacket and baseball cap and sunglasses. As he walked away from the neighborhood he called the local police to report a break-in, then threw away the single-use phone after removing the battery.

Only a technically adept Directory citizen could have made the bio-residue killing gadget, so after investigation they would conclude the person they were after was techno smart but spy stupid. He would have to be an untrained spy to leave it behind – scared off by the police siren maybe? *That will give them a wild hare to chase and puzzling contradictions to investigate and take the long route to nowhere.* Jack laughed.

A woman looked right at him.

Damn. Serves me right. He stooped to retie his shoes and put together a simple mind spring. He inserted it into her head. *If they interview her, she'll have interesting things to tell them.*

Jack wanted to see if the St. Louis Directory Induction Center had gotten the word yet, so he walked a few blocks out of his way. Looking around he could tell the news hadn't arrived. But there was a line. More sheep going to slaughter. He shook his head sadly.

He called Wendy. She was back home and thrilled that the whole operation had gone so smoothly.

"My mom's ecstatic." She paused. "Of course, I didn't mention you."

She was looking at the news and there were reports from all around the world. "Jack, it's going like wildfire, you should see the lines. It takes less than a minute per person. There are groups of people singing and dancing in the streets in front of the offices. As yet there is nothing official from the Directory except for the press release you sent yesterday. The release didn't make it into print yet but the online magazine is carrying the whole thing. And quotes from your release are being taken as official sanction from the Directory of the whole deferment procedure. It's brilliant, Jack. I think we're home free."

"That's great, my love." Jack let her have her moment. This was only the first move. From here on, attack and counterattack would get increasingly vicious. As the calculated events over the coming weeks converged to a single point, life would become more intense.

Jack had to convince another person of the validity of his cause. And his mind-based coercive tactics could not be risked. He had to be convincing, without being revealing. As Wendy basked in her new-found freedom, Jack planned multiple approaches to the type of individual he must face.

To end his day in St. Louis, Jack went to a library across town and injected onto the 'net some nasty but curiously accurate rumors of all kinds regarding the real nature of the five years of service required of those who shipped out. Slavery of some kind was the favored anti-Directory theme, along with corrupt and perverse sexual habits with foreign creatures and objects. He gave his imagination free rein, always including a grain of truth.

Major corporate news outlets wouldn't carry the rumors, nor would they report what could not, on its face, be substantiated. But the culture and technology no longer had need of these people to transmit data.

The consensus on the 'net became, "Let those who have already gone return home before we commit ourselves to the unknown".

CHAPTER 18

"Jack, I don't care what the risks are!"

He looked at Wendy and was at a loss for words. He'd explained multiple times that direct exposure could ruin everything.

"Doing this could expose us both. We can't risk it."

She looked at him coldly.

"We've overexposed ourselves too many times already. You know that, Dee." She shook her head. "All we've gained can be easily lost. There are so many dangerous things we have to do. Please don't make it worse by adding risk we don't have to take."

"Jack. We must do it." No question, she wouldn't budge.

She has no understanding of my responsibility to Directory citizens. They are who and what I need to protect.

"Jack. What good does it do to gain the world if we lose our souls?"

"Are you serious?"

"Yes!" They were in Jack's room, which was full of electronics and gadgets, and two very comfortable chairs. Wendy was lying on his bed, head propped up by her fists. "Deidre and Natalie are my two best friends. This afternoon I was with them for hours and did everything I could to talk them out of shipping out. They're determined to go. They don't care about anything else. They think I'm your pawn or have been duped by the rumors in the online media, or maybe they think I'm a coward. I don't really know or care. But I can't see how you can ask me to do nothing while my best friends go to slaughter."

She looked at him and he could see her reappraisal of his character. "A person can't abandon their friends and expect to do well in life. I understand your responsibility Jack, well, maybe I don't, not fully. How could I?

"But I do know mine."

Jack was shaken. He bowed his head in thought. He went into an intense period of self-examination. He looked at his former life as Tac-U-One, considered the last three or four missions. He'd helped a lot of people, and harmed a few bad ones. That was good. And it *was* good, from a surgical clinical perspective. But he insulated himself emotionally. Because of the nature of his job, no one knew who he really was. And he always left when the job was done. He formed no enduring ties to the people around him. And now he was back in Tac-U-One mode. Mission mode. It was a numbers game. As long as the vast number of people were helped, a few always went by the wayside.

His true friends were on Crown Planet, and it took him only a moment to realize that he would do anything to save one of *them*.

"Ah, Dee. What you do to me."

"What does that mean?"

"You challenge me in ways…" Because of his position as the head of the Tactical Unit, he was rarely confronted on any issue, and never on important ones. The buck stopped with him. At home it was the same. Every woman he married understood a new mission required a new body. In the Directory divorce was automatic when either party transferred. He was rarely home for a year at a time. As a consequence he never faced serious or deeply personal emotional issues at all. Here on Earth though, this girl threw it in his face when she felt it was necessary. Wendy handled him in a way he hadn't experienced in a long time.

"I see your point. Let's figure out what to do about it."

"But Jack, it's so easy." When he frowned she tapped her temple and pointed at him.

"You have the wrong idea about telepathy."

"But the Directory clerk in Tampa, you did something to him. And he's one of you guys."

"I selected that guy after looking at how many others?"

"Maybe ten."

"Yes, and we were lucky to find him. He may be from the Directory, but he was easily suggestible and liked following the rules and didn't like personal confrontation, and was a bit stupid, so he couldn't easily see the consequences of granting the deferment – he took the easiest path. Is either Deidre or Natalie like that?" He answered his own question. "No, they are not. Not at all. I am not a puppeteer. I *can* upset or disturb someone, sometimes *extremely* so. I can, over a relatively short span, make someone think that something other than what is happening is happening. But I cannot magically change people's minds by using mine. I can steer them sometimes, nudge them, but change major or basic decisions, no. Your friends had already decided to go offworld, and they didn't need the drug, as you did, to tip them over the edge. They were, they are, *committed*."

Jack thought for a moment. "Are their boyfriends still against them going?"

"Yes. Definitely. I talked to them too, and short of kidnapping the girls, they had no solution. They're pretty apathetic."

"Think they would be up for a caper? The girls won't like it at all and they could come to some harm."

"What harm, Jack? The idea is to protect them."

"Yeah, well, anything is better than what is planned for them out there, and I agree that kidnapping is not a good solution. But there is a ray of light. I was reading the treaty signed by the U.S. and the Directory to see if there was anything in there we could use in the coming months. It gives *us* nothing, but strangely one of the rights the U.S. held onto is the ability to hold people charged with violent crimes or crimes against property until they are brought to trial. If convicted, they serve their time, and only after being set free do they fulfill their Directory contract. U.S. attorneys wanted protection from people going on a wild crime spree, or getting revenge, just before they left the planet because they knew they would get off scot-free."

"And how does this help us help the girls?"

"We get video tape of them committing a crime."

"What!"

"I'm serious. I've been reluctant to give you the details of what the Directory has planned for their trainees, but now you need to know." He told her some of it. It was unbelievable; sickening. *So glad I'm not going.*

"All right, Jack; let's send my friends to prison." Jack nodded.

"So, the boys make up a cover story which will get Deidre and Natalie to take a car and drive it to an empty parking lot. They video them "stealing" the car. When the girls leave the car, the boys douse it with gasoline and burn it up.

"The boys sign affidavits saying the girls burned the car as a last act of defiance before leaving Earth, and have the girls arrested. The girls will know their boyfriends are railroading them. We stay out of it, completely."

"Whose car?"

"It doesn't matter, I'll cover the cost. The account Norman set up for me is still flush with cash."

"Okay Jack, I'll take it from here."

"Good. Make sure it can't be traced back to you."

"I will. Thanks, Jack." She hugged him. "We can never abandon our friends, Jack." She was right.

After emerging from the lake and resuming responsibility for the Directory, Earth had become secondary, something to be dealt with fairly but far less important. Wendy had shoved his face in that one. He conceded that he had needed it.

"Go save their lives, Dee." Having her handle the execution of the plan was a calculated risk. But for Wendy to make it in his world, the *real* Directory, she needed to be brought up to speed. The operation to save her friends was a good place to start. Getting them thrown in jail was going to take some work and it had to be done soon. Nothing breeds confidence like successfully completing a mission. He wondered how she would engineer getting them a prison sentence on a first offense.

CHAPTER 19

BOLTAX, THE CHIEF OF DIRECTORY ENTERPRISES (previously known as John Smith), felt raging fury. His idiot staff had allowed trained graduates to defer their departure. Even sitting in his new office at his new Los Angeles Directory Colosseum complex did nothing to lessen his outrage.

It was making him crazy.

He discovered the deferments by chance at the evening meal in the staff cafeteria.

Boltax was stuck in the bio-lab after the morning briefing. His Bio-Tech couldn't get the cultures to properly replicate. And that meant no more bodies. After many hours of work and no progress, he cursed and threatened the staff and left them to solve the problem alone. The lab had developed a stench that cut through his nasal cavity like a knife.

It was early evening and he hadn't eaten all day. The food in the staff mess hall had smelled good. He went in. He sometimes ate with the staff to gauge their tone and, because he was a good telepath, used this informal opportunity to secretly scan their minds.

Boltax stepped over to a large round table to hear the details of a disturbing conversation. "What do you mean 'deferment'? Who is deferring what?"

"Sir, the natives are deferring their off world transport contracts. It's all completely legal, we checked it with the Central Directory Computer and it's a standard form and a standard procedure."

"What? What? WHAT?" Boltax screamed. His mind flooded with questions. "How many natives have deferred their contracts?"

"By the time I got off shift, the worldwide number was in the tens of thousands. It was really amazing, sir. As soon as the natives discovered they could do it, they flocked to our offices all across the planet."

"You morons. You imbeciles!" Boltax yanked the clerk from his chair and began bashing him against the wall. "Why didn't you report this to me immediately?"

●

Boltax had the clerk in Tampa, Florida, rushed to the Colosseum immediately. This was the idiot who had started it all – the one who formally granted the first legal deferment.

Soon after other clerks across the planet had checked their computers and assumed it was okay to grant the deferments because Tampa had done so.

Even worse, the Tampa clerk had added a note, "checked with Central Directory Computer: verified legal."

From these simple beginnings deferments spread like wildfire. Some of the smarter clerks checked directly with the CDC and independently verified the existence of the law. It was legal. It was Directory Law and the Central Directory Computer gave its stamp of approval.

Boltax decided on a two phase investigation. He ordered every clerk who had granted a deferment that day pulled in to the Colosseum for immediate interrogation. The other clerks would be dealt with later.

The Tampa clerk was rushed to the interrogation room. Boltax stared at him through the observation glass with loathing; he hated this ignorant worm.

There was a ray of light in the darkness. This was his first opportunity to use his secret weapon. Assembling the weapon had almost resulted in disaster.

●

Boltax had secretly entered a completed section of the Colosseum complex in Los Angeles while the remainder was still under construction. He had gone to the rooms that were to house the Central Directory Computer or CDC.

Months ago he had learned he was to get a special computer. It had arrived on the last in-bound freighter.

The CDC was special: it was a Bio-Comp. In fact this CDC was *very* special. It was a Tele-Bio-Comp: a Telepathic Biological Computer. This enormous asset caused him to wonder why he had received it. To his knowledge he was the only primitive world planetary chief to have such a resource. Had his superiors anticipated the trouble he was now experiencing?

In secret Boltax installed the brain console of the Bio-Comp in the impact-proof clean room which provided a nearly indestructible living environment.

Not many people willingly gave up the full biological human form to link to a computer complex and become its active controller, interfacing with other computers, electronics, machines and people. But, there were perks that some people found attractive: vast arrays of devices enabled a Bio-Comp influence and control near and far.

After uncrating the system, Boltax had run all the diagnostics on the Bio-Comp system and personally installed the minimum number of devices, after which the Bio-Comp, once transferred in, would complete the job. It had been hell getting everything perfect. But the system allowed no deviations, it required exactitude. Finally, after many hours of constant work, the primary system screen flashed "ready for transfer."

Boltax placed the Identity-Trap in its slot beside the brain case and initiated the tiny Recyclex machine. The Identity (or person) was transferred from the I-trap into the brain console.

This was the last step.

From the beginning Boltax knew he and the person selected to transfer into and run his Central Directory Computer would not be friends. The man had spent more than a year in the I-trap, enough to piss anyone off. It had taken days for the Identity to reorient himself to his new environment. When the Bio-Comp fully grasped where he was (in a Bio-Comp brain case on a primitive planet), he went ballistic. He crashed his own systems and refused to communicate. Boltax was forced to detach the Bio-Comp brain case module from the main computer complex by disconnecting the labyrinth of hard wire connections. Boltax then had to reboot the computer from recovery programming.

The next two days were spent going over the contract the Identity had signed while he still had a body somewhere back in the Directory. And because Boltax was determined to keep the Bio-Comp his secret, all the connected legalities had to be researched by him. Very tedious.

It came down to pointing out to the Identity that there was a two-year transportation clause, of which only one year had been used. Boltax pointed out that they were under no legal obligation to transport him and his body. And if he had not seen fit to read the contract and be aware of this potential circumstance, how could the Bio-Comp blame Boltax? This was not rational thinking. After much frothing, argument and spluttering, the Identity agreed to honor the contract to the letter.

It was either that or be let loose to get a native baby body and be born on the planet outside the Directory confines. The threat worked.

Boltax then reconnected the Identity to the central computer and all went well. One of the amazing things about the symbiosis between an Identity and a Central Directory Computer was the security section of the programming. The Thought Activated Circuit (TAC) prevented the Identity from entering false data or making knowingly false reports. Boltax was secure: the Bio-Comp may not love him or his job, but he could not betray him or disrupt his operations on Earth without immediate discovery.

The Bio-Comp installed the rest of his gadgets in a lightning twenty-four hours and was fully functional...

●

Boltax slammed into the interrogation cell and made the Tampa clerk cringe. "You better have a good explanation for accepting the native deferments."

"It's legal." the idiot said.

Boltax cocked his fist.

Frightened now, the clerk said, "Why was the deferment procedure in the computer if you didn't want us to accept it? If it's in the computer, it's legal, everyone knows that."

"But you do know we put native students through extensive training to prepare them to leave the planet?"

"Yes, sir."

"That we want them to go?"

"Yes, sir."

"That our mission objective is to reach our quota of natives shipped to Mars each week?"

"Yes, sir."

"Then why would you accept a native for deferment when you knew it would compromise our mission?"

"It's legal, sir. I had no other thought than to process the request precisely."

Boltax beat him to a pulp.

That idiot clerk knew their mission on Earth was not completely legal. Yet he spouted the law. Stupid idiot! And the clerk hadn't given the deferments a thought until the line waiting to be processed was around the block. By then a large number of clerks had seen the press release. Many natives seeking deferment had it with them. It looked official.

"Deferment Deemed Legal By Top Directory Official." And so it went. Boltax felt a special fury as he read that headline. Someone had punked him, played him, bypassed him. Him. It was intolerable.

Boltax had no opportunity to use his carefully cultivated veto power with the major media networks to quash the story.

Somehow, a magazine website claimed to have a press release received directly from the Directory PR office. Mailed the day before from Las Vegas: his own last day in the Las Vegas offices.

Boltax couldn't admit it was a forgery. The Directory would lose face and it may give other natives the idea that they, too, could succeed in outwitting him.

He instructed his PR department to establish strict protocol for all future press releases so this could not happen again. He was temporarily without a solution.

Boltax watched John Taylor on a worldwide broadcast being hailed as the very first graduate to take deferment. They couldn't grab the guy, however much he wanted to. But considering the good planning behind the attack, Taylor would have no usable information.

"Computer, place a mobile bug on John Taylor." Best to be careful.

"Order logged," replied the Bio-Comp.

Boltax sent an air car to retrieve the original press release. It looked good; better than his PR department had done. It was not their original paper or letterhead, but a good copy. They looked for trace samples and found the pages and mail pack had been bio-wiped; there was nothing to find.

Bio-wipe was Directory level technology, not released on Earth.

Boltax found new and disturbingly accurate rumors about their real mission here on Earth. It was wild speculation without factual detail, but still he got his PR people to mitigate the effects immediately by flooding the net with counter-rumors. He couldn't afford to allow this to scare his graduates more than it had already.

The legality of the deferment was smart. It used his computer against him. He looked at the exact legal citation, book, page, and paragraph. It included letter-perfect text in Cortic characters (the Directory language) and its English translation.

The exact legal code. Thousands of them printed out and in the hands of the natives. How do you invalidate that? He had no idea such a statute existed. Who would know something that obscure? None of his people were trained in Directory Law. He certainly wasn't. What illegal operation needed a lawyer? But someone knew – obviously. And as the reporters and commentators repeated over and over there was now a legal precedent. His offices across the world continued to grant deferments as he sat there, in impotent rage. He hated this planet; these half-formed humans, these dregs.

Boltax checked his computer. Fewer than ten percent of his graduates scheduled to go on their "interstellar adventure" had actually shipped out. A full ninety percent had opted for deferment. Many graduates scheduled to depart weeks or months from now were also deferred.

He was way behind quota.

And that was *his* neck he felt being stretched across the chopping block.

He sat until the blinding rage subsided and the pressure in his head diminished. He released his grip on the arms of his chair and idly noted they had buckled.

He had an intelligent enemy. They knew Directory law and possessed Directory-only technology.

His Earth bound staff were unaware of the true nature of their mission. This could mean a Directory plant was hidden in Earth's population. But that too was impossible. If some independent person from the Directory had discovered their activities it would be reported to Crown Planet immediately, causing the whole operation to close.

Was his enemy some kind of spy? An operative, an agent, a provocateur? The possibilities made his head spin.

He had scanned the minds of his own staff often enough to know they had no idea of their true mission, or actually, missions. His earthbound staff must have suspicions or may have heard things from the transport pilots and Mars staff who knew everything.

Everyone knew the training was a deception. They were using Directory technology so old it was forgotten; therefore, something else was going on. And his personnel had plenty of time to chit chat and speculate. He cursed. Maybe if the staff had known the true mission this deferment would never have happened. Boltax ground his teeth.

His first impulse was to close the Induction Centers immediately. But that would confirm what the rumormongers were saying and cause the deferments and no-shows to increase when the Induction Centers reopened. Other graduates would go into hiding, far beyond his present ability to find and capture them.

Why hadn't he installed tracking chips in every damn one of the graduates while he had the chance?

"Computer, have the techs to mass produce tracking chips for dietary implantation in students. Target date one week."

"Order logged."

By next week every student would get bugged with their next meal taken in the Directory School canteen.

He had to keep graduates flowing offworld.

"Why is this happening to me?" he screamed in his office. Finally the rage subsided.

He didn't have a large enough military force. But that would change. As the games progressed, the men available for use as enforcers would swell.

"Bio-Comp, train my native enforcers on the transport equipment and deferral apprehension. Target date tomorrow."

"Order logged."

Boltax would find and crush whomever had done this to his operation, to him.

CHAPTER 20

HEAVY POUNDING ON THE FRONT DOOR attracted Wendy's attention. She opened her bedroom window, someone was under the portico. "Stop the banging! I'll be down in a minute." She put on socks and shoes and by the time she reached the stairs she was very worried that it was the police and that something bad had happened to her parents or brother. She flew down the stairs. Reaching the entry hall, her fear became personal. The pounding had actually broken out a door panel and a face was pressed into the gap. It was no one she knew.

She hit the speed dial for 911.

While the phone was ringing she yelled, "What do you want?"

"Are you Wendy White?" said the face in a deep and threatening tone. He reached his hand through the missing panel, unbolted the door and entered. He towered over her by a good sixteen inches.

"I am Wendy White," she said, frightened by the invasion. "And I've called the police."

The two men laughed. "We are Directory Officials," said the face. "You are late reporting for transshipment to Mars. You are in violation of interstellar law. You've got ten minutes to gather your possessions and say farewell to your family." This communication was delivered in such a robotic manner it was hard to think of the giant in front of her as a living man.

"911, what is your emergency?" Wendy put the phone to her ear. "Intruders have broken into my home." The two men did nothing to stop her.

"Is this intrusion related to a Directory contract?" Wendy paused. She could answer "No" and help would come. But these men *were* Directory and the cops couldn't help her. She suspected this was not the only call the 911 operator had received today about the same type of disturbance, and so the screening question.

"I have a deferment. I don't have to go for two years," she said. Her voice felt shaky, but her nerve was reviving.

"That has to be sorted out with the relevant Directory authorities, not 911. Good day."

The man smirked. "No rescue from the police? So sorry," said the face. "You are in violation of interstellar law. Do you refuse to come with us?" A suggestive smile on the giant's lips made her feel personally threatened.

"And what if I do?"

"Do you refuse this legal order?" The face brandished a copy of her signed contract. Again he smiled and exuded a stillness that held in place an unclean, excited tension.

"No, of course I don't refuse," she said, causing him to deflate slightly. "I'll get my things." She turned and tried to usher them outside the door.

"We have a Sight Warrant. We have to keep you in view at all times. You have ten minutes to complete your preparation." The foul smile again. She shivered at the look on his face. What animal pleasure he must have gained from the girls who refused to go with him.

While packing her things she called Jack and again the Directory thugs made no attempt to stop her. He was running errands in his jeep. He immediately grasped the situation. He did his best to keep the extreme concern from his voice. "Look, if there's one thing I know, I know this: the bureaucratic lines in the Directory are so entrenched, I don't think it will even occur to anyone to ignore the deferment: it's legal. And if it's legal and correctly documented, it's done." This meant nothing under the circumstances, but he wanted her to remain calm. Casually he asked her to describe the vehicle they came in.

She looked out her window. Their transport was now in the center of the street. Wendy described the flatbed aero-transport to Jack.

"How many people does it hold?"

"A lot. Seventy, maybe a hundred. Hold on. Its nine rows of twelve seats. One hundred and eight."

"How full is it?"

"Pretty full, Jack. There are two or three open seats. Oh, there's another team leading Derek Sommers, our neighbor, to the vehicle. I didn't know he'd signed up. Jack, what is that noise?"

Jack cranked up his window to block the sound of rushing air.

"That's better, the interference is gone."

"Good." He was relieved they had more seats to fill. If the Directory transport had a full load at Wendy's place and lifted off in the next few minutes, there was no way he could reach the Induction Center in time to prevent her from being taken off-planet.

He was geographically closer to the Induction Center than she was, but they were airborne and he was earthbound. He was currently doing eighty in a forty mph zone and accelerating. The Induction Center by the airport was a centralized transshipment area for the intermountain region. If they got Dee on one of the interplanetary ships, she would disappear.

The Directory was strong-arming. This was no administrative mistake.

He flew through an intersection, the screeching of tires and thump of a collision followed. He had to be more careful – he didn't want to kill innocents trying to save Wendy. The howl of one siren, and then more fell in behind him.

"Jack, what is *that noise*?"

"I'll meet you at the Directory Induction Center and we'll get it sorted out."

"See you there." He could hear her fear.

She was herded downstairs and loaded onto the transport. She buckled herself in, but noticed many others had not taken that precaution. The Transport lifted off abruptly and banked sharply. A terrified scream came from behind her. One girl had gone over the edge and a man who tried to prevent her fall was dragged away as well. He went silently.

"Circle back," said the face. The pilot slowed and banked again as the aero-transport passed the crumpled bodies. The four men drew their weapons, adjusted the settings and then cut loose with concentrated energy beams. The bodies vaporized. "Okay, we're good to go." They flew away from the Induction Center, across the valley and up into Little Cottonwood Canyon.

Wendy gripped the seat so tightly her hands ached.

●

Jack slowed as he hit a straightaway; a blank look came over his face as he focused his attention internally. Four patrol vehicles were screaming along behind him, edging forward to come alongside. Jack was forced to break off his internal computation as he approached another intersection.

He punched it hard to make it through before the light changed. The jeep surged but he wasn't going to make it. He couldn't brake. Wendy would be lost. He buried the pedal to the floor boards. He could see the approaching cars. The cops saved him with their screaming sirens. The intersection cleared.

He desperately needed quiet time to do what he needed to do. He had to get rid of the cops before a chopper was called in. The mental gymnastics to complete were simple. No subtlety, just bam. But he had to take his attention off the road and concentrate. He took a freeway on-ramp, cut across traffic into the fast lane, and put his driving on autopilot. He was passing cars and trucks he hardly saw. The wail of the cruisers following him became a distant chorus.

●

The aero-transport touched down and the two who grabbed Wendy jumped out and walked up a secluded drive to a cabin among the aspens. They barged inside and were there for some time. Longer than the ten minutes they had allowed her. Finally a girl about her age came out. She wore an orange jumpsuit, and was crying. They pushed her along; she came in and sat in one of the horribly vacated seats. She was crying hard. They now had a full load minus two. The aero-transport emerged from between the mountains and set out across the valley toward the Directory Induction Center.

●

Jack, once again, could hear the sirens right behind him. He let the cop cars come up on him and box him in, front, rear and on his right. He was trapped. He looked quickly from one driver to the next. With each glance Jack delivered his small packages. One by one the cruisers peeled away, the sirens fading in the distance. Soon the ghosts they followed would die away, leaving them nothing but afterimages. *Welcome to the modern world, boys,* Jack thought.

The road was clear and he jammed the accelerator again. It was getting easier to use his mind faculties, but he still needed practice. Soon he would need all his skills in perfect working order just to survive.

Jack braked from one twenty and slid around the freeway exit at speed. Incredibly he made it to the Induction Center before Wendy's transport.

They had a chance.

Jack located the clerk who handled the transports and casually walked over. He chatted him up to get his measure as a man, his mental dexterity, and to see if he would get physical. After thanking the clerk for his help, Jack stepped to the background and sat quietly on a bench. He constructed a mind spring for the clerk, thinking of possible scenarios – the most likely course of events involving Wendy and their solutions. This had to be sophisticated and very smooth – different from what he used with the cops. This clerk was not at all ideal; he had a fluid, sharp mind. Not easily misled.

Jack concentrated until the aero-transport touched down and began unloading. The reluctant recruits were herded to the clerk for processing. After signing in, several of the recruits huddled together and whispered furiously amongst themselves. On a quiet three count they broke away sprinting for freedom. They dodged and weaved in different directions. The guards casually adjusted their weapons and stunned the escapees. The last one down was more than fifty yards away. The guards looked expectantly at the others in line, but there were no more takers. The inert forms of the stunned were dumped on a sled and moved into the space ship.

Jack sat tensely through the escape attempt. He had not foreseen any of what had just happened and was forced to delay sending his mind spring.

With Wendy the next one in line, Jack delivered his mental package into the middle of the clerk's head. If he noticed an intrusion, there was no sign. He didn't even blink.

When Dee stepped forward, the clerk checked her paperwork without looking at her. The first page of the mind spring was keyed to unfold by the sight of her face. Finally he looked up. There was a comical expression on his face as he said something entirely different from what he'd planned to say.

"There's been a mistake; you're not supposed to be here." This obvious conflict of ideas was dangerous. If the clerk had looked at her first there would have been no conflict – no other thought stream would have formed in his mind. He was clearly aware of an internal inconsistency. The clerk pointed, directing her away from the waiting space ship.

Wendy, hoping this was Jack's intervention, walked away. The clerk actually watched his arm rise from his side with fascination as he pointed.

Jack's operation was a hair's breadth from going bad. The clerk looked at Wendy's receding back and frowned, uncertain of what he'd just done.

The guards raised their weapons. This cued the clerk's next implanted response.

"Stop that…" The clerk barked commandingly at the guards. And then, again, he looked mystified.

Wendy ignored the clerk and the guards who were still pointing weapons at her. She kept walking. An angry outcry rose from the others in line.

"Why is she going free?"

"I want to go home!"

"I want to leave, too!"

"Let me go!" someone wailed. Jack had not foreseen this possibility, either.

The outcome hung by the tiniest of threads. He was amazed by Wendy, who kept steadily moving away from the trouble. She had recognized Jack's jeep in the parking lot and headed for it. Jack waited a few beats and stepped quietly out from the shadow of a building and followed her.

He took her arm and she jumped. He guided her to his jeep. "Jack," said Wendy with a shaking voice, "we have to help those people. They're being forced onto the space ship."

Jack was shocked by her failure to grasp the severity of their situation and didn't immediately reply.

"Jack, they're not going to let those people go."

"Dee, *shut up*."

She began to struggle; Jack clamped his grip more tightly and put an arm around her waist to keep her from making sudden or violent movements. "We can't abandon those people. Derek Sommers and that poor girl, I'm sure they raped her, Jack…"

"Get in the jeep, Dee. Stay quiet or *we-are-both-dead*."

She looked at his cold certain features and got in the jeep.

Jack put the key in the ignition and then hesitated. Wendy gave him a scared look as he paused; she now wanted to leave immediately. He held up a finger then tapped his temple. Wendy nodded, then reclined the seat and disappeared from view.

Jack whispered, "Too much has happened here today for this to go unnoticed by Directory big shots. I have to handle this so it doesn't come back on us." Wendy nodded again.

He sat quietly assembling his composition of mental images, emotions and sounds.

After all the recruits had been loaded and the ship lifted off, the guards returned to the aero-transport and also departed. Jack breathed a ragged sigh of relief. Wendy was still here. They had won another round. Now to finish the day's work.

Jack looked at the clerk, and inserted mind spring – the book of mental images. He set the spring to trigger if he was questioned about today's events. But because it was hastily done, the mind spring would have no great longevity. In days the content would begin to degenerate and fade.

On the drive home Jack broke the silence. "The Directory officials must be getting desperate. These types of forced pickups will generate a lot of bad fringe press."

It took Wendy some time to respond. "I'm glad I'm not one of the taken. Thank you Jack, for saving me, again."

"You're welcome, my love." Jack succeeded in keeping his tone light, but inside he seethed. They were quiet for a time, then Jack continued.

"It was strange today."

"What wasn't?" Wendy let out a short shrill laugh.

"Yeah, there is that." He smiled. "But when I asked the clerk about what was happening with the recruits, he told me that those who were wrongly apprehended would be properly sorted out on Mars and returned to Earth. His computer did not show who has, or does not have, a deferment. The clerk actually believed the people who are resisting the whole process are paranoid. He thought he was doing no harm."

"The guards, the enforcers, are different from the clerks. They are brutal." Wendy described how two people had fallen from the aero-transport.

Jack stared at her, dumbfounded. "I'm shocked they let you go, even with my intervention." Jack thought for a moment. "The guards must have lied to the clerk about incinerating the two kids who fell." The possibility of losing Wendy was closer than he knew.

"Before you arrived, I had a few minutes to make a mind spring that induced the clerk to release you. But had there been a major fuss about you, or if you'd made a scene, the whole thing would have fallen apart and they would have taken you."

That night Jack and Wendy devised plans to get samples of the hand cream for chemical analysis.

"We have to be careful. If we expose the drugging, DE may decide to go to war. We have to be very careful."

"You're right. Maybe we should leave it alone?"

"Let's get the analysis done and hold it in reserve."

Wendy was still horrified at abandoning the other people transported with her.

"If we were stopped today, the whole planet would have lost its future. I couldn't do more than separate you.

"Also, I had no time for a disguise. If I turn up on too many Directory files, in separate Directory locations, they'll automatically target me for investigation."

"What does that mean, Jack? Will they come here and ask you questions?" He heard her agitation.

"As I said the central Directory computer keeps track."

"So we have to be careful." she said.

"We do."

CHAPTER 21

Perrywhite received a secure package from the Pentagon – finally. He set it on his desk.

He couldn't find the young kid McMillan had given him.

His men had rounded up all digital recordings in and near the coffee shop where the Navy man and the youth had their conversation. An exchange of words that altered the course of history.

Very few images were available, but some businesses kept digital archives. He had them enhanced and all identifiable faces extracted – and eliminated. No kid anywhere near McMillan's description was discovered.

The Navy man himself was there clear as day, so the squid hadn't lied about the place of the meet. McMillan's conversation with the kid was an event of primary importance. *I'm the only person who knows how important it is. Or that it ever occurred.*

Perrywhite had become desperate to leave the CIA; power on the planet was concentrated with DE and changing allegiance to the Directory was all he could think about. Also his coworkers at the CIA had gone cold to him after the incident with the Directory TAC car.

To get noticed by the Directory Chief, he needed a bargaining chip. What would the alien Big Boss give to have the face and name of the kid who had put the finger on them?

Perrywhite picked up his package and broke the secure seal, drawing forth the artist's rendering of a young man. He felt a rush. This was worth all of the fifty thousand in black-ops cash he'd paid to McMillan's flunky. He thought of the D/CIA, his own boss, and sneered. His middle finger twitched, but did not extend. Perrywhite looked at the artwork and gloated. He had to carefully plan the presentation of this new information to the Chief of the Directory.

I'm on my way, he thought.

• • •

Days later Boltax was at the Colosseum landing dock when the second wave of staff to be interrogated about deferment began to arrive. So were his hand-picked guards. Each staff member was stripped of communication devices and escorted in silence to the Blue Room where the Bio-Comp could conduct secret telepathic interrogations.

The Bio-Comp scanned each staffer electronically and mentally as they were herded into the tiny shielded observation cubicles lining the walls of the Blue Room. Each person read prepared instructions, then answered the exhaustive interrogative sheet compiled by Boltax's Investigator.

The questions were a variation of the standard interrog sheets in the central data banks, tailored to the present situation.

They were good.

If one of the Directory staff was responsible for the deferments, they would find him. For hours they sweated the staff. By dawn, Boltax had a partial answer. His entire Earth-based staff was clean. He released them back to their posts around the planet.

The Mars shuttle pilots were also escorted by guards directly from the landing pad to Boltax's office to be checked by him personally. Boltax was an excellent telepath. He didn't want the Tele-Bio-Comp to know about the full mission being run in this star system.

But the pilots were clean too. "You gentlemen are being awarded private rooms to live in while you're here at the Los Angeles base. Your interaction with the Earth-based staff is to be limited to single-word conversations. You may entertain the Earth girls here but no staff; is that clear?"

It was.

The Tampa clerk, after returning from the medics who repaired his extensive physical damage, had to answer twelve separate interrog sheets. He was in the Blue Room alone, long after the other staff were gone. The man was not the culprit, but there was something the Bio-Comp did find. And this he kept to himself, confident no one else had the ability to detect the curious phenomenon in his mind. He knew that if anyone else looked, the effect would be gone.

Boltax was unable, for PR considerations, to cancel the deferments (causing a war he wasn't ready to fight), so he decided on two actions.

He slowed the process down. Initially deferment approval was delayed for a week. This soon became two weeks. The forms became difficult to fill out, and applicants were rejected for incorrectly completed forms. Those who showed up to argue were directed to the Directory staff cafeteria and lightly drugged. They were coerced into making departure calls to friends and relatives and happily shipped offworld. But still it was trouble and the bodies shipped to Mars base per week were way off quota.

Boltax was worried.

He expanded the forced pickups of deferred students that he had started the first night. He paid off the major media outlets with new technology so they reported the incidents as rumors started by fringe and 'net-based "bandit" media and therefore suspect.

The forced pickups were only a holding action – no matter how much he enjoyed making it happen, soon it would be impossible to hide and thus unmanageable to continue.

All new training contracts eliminated the possibility for deferment, but the signup rate on new trainees had dropped significantly.

He intensified his efforts to find the enemy spy.

CHAPTER 22

THE FIGHT FOR IMMORTALITY'S FIRST ROUND began and was completed before Colosseum construction was finished.

The world was experiencing shock. The gladiators and the Fight had gained extraordinary levels of acceptance and rejection. There was jubilation and hysteria.

The first round winner was transferred. His mother, being the only non-Directory witness, raised questions about its authenticity in many quarters. Why wasn't the transfer televised? What were they hiding? Was it even real? Even so the euphoric main stream press compared the event to the Apollo 11 moon landing.

The idea of practical immortality was running rough-shod over many tenderly held beliefs.

The world was in flux.

●

The Colosseum was now functional. With its completion the second call had gone out to the fighters of the world who wished to risk their lives in the games. To become immortal.

After their initial attack, Jack traveled the world spreading dissent. He purchased and destroyed computers and phones almost every day. On the Internet, Jack posted methods of avoiding the Directory goon squads that were sometimes literally dragging people away. Most news outlets wouldn't carry these stories, and local cops ignored the protests from their citizenry who complained. Still the incredible number of digital photos and videos that were posted of the violent encounters with Directory thugs gave a lie to the sophisticated and friendly veneer the Directory PRs were running in the mainstream media.

But somehow the postings didn't last long. Someone in the Colosseum was adapting Directory software to locate and eliminate content harmful to the Directory and replace it with fluff.

For a few weeks the offer of a fifty-thousand dollar bonus and free access to Directory EV for a year coerced some families to ship off their loved (or unloved) ones. This created a new surge of people eager to willingly depart the green vales of Earth. Jack put out a piece describing how the threat of slavery had to be real or else why all the cash? The Directory looked even more predatory, and the ship-offs declined again.

Soon internet "pirates" were following Jack's lead by staying mobile and analyzing the Directory policy and actions in the most sinister light. This provided him with protection and obscurity, hiding among an ever-increasing chorus of complaints.

The Directory then upped the ante by providing free medical care to the immediate family of a trainee who agreed to ship off planet without the possibility of deferment. The independent media, after Jack's lead, called them "martyrs." Children with dying parents or siblings sacrificed themselves to uncertainty.

Jack slowed his traveling and returned to Salt Lake City, and was pleased to read other writers attacking DE.

● ● ●

Jack and Wendy flew into Los Angeles to inspect the Colosseum and see the Fight for Immortality firsthand.

The shuttle bus left them at a large terminal and they followed signs into a semitropical woodland. Then just as they had begun to wonder how far they would have to walk, the Colosseum emerged from behind languid palm fronds.

"It's unbelievably beautiful," Wendy was enthralled. She stopped and stared as fight fans streamed past them.

"It's so, so, beautiful." she breathed. Jack guided her onto an observation terrace. Many first-time visitors stood mesmerized by the architecture, the grounds, and the total scene.

The structure looked like its Roman ancestor, superficially. It was both strikingly modern and anachronistic. The original Colosseum's artistry was restricted to architecture, masonry carving, fabric and paint. The structure they faced had a platinum hue from one angle and a deep mauve from another. Its color changed to correspond to the time of day or weather conditions or any number of programmed interactive factors. It wasn't a screen that produced these effects, but the surface of the structure itself.

They paid their tickets and filed through the Roman arches. Once inside, Jack and Wendy sat in the middle rows amidst noisy tides of spectators. This Colosseum was also a place where life and death was decided. If you could maim or kill with more skill than your opponent, you could advance to the next round.

In a lull from the clamoring crowd, Jack said, "This isn't Earth." Wendy looked at him. Did she hear him correctly?

"What? What did you say?" There was so much noise around them it was hard to think, let alone communicate.

"This isn't Earth," Jack said into her ear.

"How's that possible?" she asked. They hadn't gone anywhere, really. This was Los Angeles and, granted, it did seem strange compared to Salt Lake City, but there was no doubt about it still being Terra Firma.

"Legally this property, this ground, belongs to political powers far, far, away. Officially we're not on Earth. They can do whatever they like on this property and have complete immunity from any laws of Earth."

She gazed around herself with new eyes. "But what would they do?" The idea of such license and unknown intention was disturbing.

"We're here to find out." He, too, looked around. "And see the enemy at work. Maybe we'll find weaknesses we can use." Jack continued. "This facility is their power base. We need an ally here. Someone who still has the decency of a normal Directory Citizen."

"I'm looking around too." But Wendy was captivated by the venue.

Jack's only chance to succeed was to create a tiny window of access here at the Colosseum and pass through it. If he delayed too much or acted too soon the window would close and he would be crushed.

The timing was crucial.

Looking around the Colosseum, he was disgusted that Directory technology was put to such corrupt use. For a minute his revulsion threatened to choke him.

They shouldn't be doing this, he thought. *These people are selling immortality for violence. There's no greater degradation of the Directory heritage.*

Jack's emotions spiked. *It's the wholesale giveaway of a sacred right…*

An honest Directory citizen had to achieve great things in life to become a Jolo, become immortal… he shook his head.

Jack remembered Bio-One's secret planetary base and the monsters he had seen growing in series after series of speed-grow tanks.

What purpose would these nightmare bodies serve? The conclusions were horrific. None of Jack's many friends or acquaintances would have anything to do with Bio-One or what he was selling. *My people can't have changed that much,* he thought.

There had to be other markets.

That made perfect sense: the Outer Worlds. Those populated high-tech planets rejected by the Directory because of their depravity, criminality and corruption. They were societies where immortality was purchased, not earned.

Jack had underestimated Bio-One, more than once. His own failure to correctly evaluate this man was another reason the last mission had ended in failure.

Combining the immense scale of the illegal operation he had discovered, with the Directory presence on Earth (and presumably other planets like it, if Tyfon Arolia could be believed), the entire operation was staggering: far beyond the capability of Bio-One to conceive or execute.

How many other planets were involved in this type of operation? Jack sorted through the planets he knew of that were enough like Earth to make this type of mission work. About thirty that he could remember. *How big was it?*

The disturbing question was how Bio-One had influenced so many others from within the Directory power structure to fall into step with him.

First he lured me into a trap, then deposed Crown, extending control to the upper level government officials. All while fooling the entire Directory population. *Impossible. But, obviously not.*

How had Bio-One bypassed the whole apparatus that should have triggered ancient but still effective protections against a coup d'état?

It was difficult to conceive of so much change, bad change, occurring in so short a time. Was it possible to reverse this course? Could this evil and its effects be overturned, or would the Directory disintegrate?

He would find out. Speed and deception. Force and intelligence. Juggle, balance and attack.

"They shouldn't be here," he said again into her ear. "But I'm glad you are."

Wendy nodded her head and smiled vaguely, no longer able to concentrate on conversation amidst all this noise, color, and turmoil. What a spectacle. What a fantastic and bizarre scene.

He smiled. His crisis had passed her by. That was okay. He looked at her.

She caught his look and smiled in return. They were anonymous in the wild crowd, watching fighters parading in the arena below.

• • •

Boltax sat in the hard chair in his office at the Colosseum. The base was the Planetary Operations Command Center and had military defenses sufficient to thwart any attack by Earthly forces.

He looked at the bare walls. The requisitions for special equipment and decoration had been delayed. Word had come that the next star ship would have his toys. *Everything is going against me,* he thought. *I can't even get my office decorated.*

•

All the Directory Earth staff were cleared of involvement in the deferment operation. They had passed the most stringent screening available. But that only raised more questions. *The truth is: I'm under attack and I don't know who it is.* One or more of his staff could be powerful operator, able to avoid detection. He shivered. *Is this paranoia or logical deduction?*

Too much time had passed without finding the architect of his anxiety.

Is it one of the Mars staff? They know the whole program. Can't be, I scanned them myself. He'd checked the shuttle traffic, personnel logs, computer scans, digital records, personal observations, telepathic status (none), and nothing had turned up.

Mars staff were now restricted to base. They were going to riot until Boltax authorized using as many women as they wanted for pleasure before processing them. They went quietly.

This has gone on for more than a month. His resources were extensive, his technology adequate, his control of the planet near complete, *and I'm still being punked.*

Someone was mocking him, making him look foolish and weak. And getting away with it. Rage flared again. There was a subtle power behind the attack, and as he realized this, impotent rage became deep concern. And then the sour taste of fear.

The escalating number of deferments and the fringe rumor mill were very damaging. Even with all the control he exerted over the media, they were still cranking out harmful commentary that directly thwarted his mission. *How dare these people have independent thought.*

To make his point, he'd ordered a rogue news organization vaporized at three a.m. tomorrow. Star ship armament would do the job with stealth and deniability.

But they would know.

He had given that press conference in Las Vegas to stifle any anti-Directory sentiment, and had it under control, only to find that the situation still needed further attention. Tonight's action should choke off the last of the independents.

His software technicians were combating the 'net postings.

A bright spot was the collection of remote Chinese villages. Many of the losers from the Fight had signed up to do security work. They ran snatch and grabs of whole village populations.

The Chinese had not graduated the training program, but that fact would be difficult to determine and impossible to trace a year from now. *My superiors give me impossible quotas, so I give them untrained people.* A fair trade.

Unfortunately a senior Chinese official had lodged a complaint – no family to visit. Problems, problems.

Why is someone wrecking my operation?

There was no clear motive. There were two possibilities: one – a Directory operative was active somewhere in the U.S., or two – one or more of his own people were high level telepaths, undetectable to either himself or the Bio-Comp.

Boltax decided to concentrate the search for an enemy agent among the population of Earth.

Earlier he had quietly checked with other primitive planetary commanders like himself. None were telepaths. None had a Bio-Comp, let alone a Telepathic Biological Computer. Their investigators were not mind-smiths, as his was.

His operation had been assigned three telepaths. This was curious and unnerving. Had the powers above him anticipated a threat on Earth he had not been briefed on? Could his trouble stem from a known or suspected antagonist that these telepathic resources were supposed to detect?

If his operation were running as reported, he would have made an official inquiry. But outside scrutiny would uncover his fraud. Whatever the source of trouble, he would have to deal with it himself. And fast, before the whole operation on Earth blew apart. *I'm running out of time,* he thought.

His instincts were screaming for action.

Boltax called up the Bio-Comp and suggested a solution to their immediate problems. "We can buy more time by altering the database reporting program."

"That's impossible. Don't you realize the people running this entire operation are paranoid? They don't trust you or me," said the Bio-Comp. "Once any data has been entered into the main storage bank, it can't be altered. With each monthly transport ship goes a copy of the entire database and any attempt to alter, corrupt or eliminate data triggers an automatic investigation. If I even suspect there is a false report, a

TAC program outside my control records my suspicion and triggers the investigation." Boltax absorbed this and felt hunted. "Do you really want those people inspecting every aspect of the operation here?"

"No. No, I don't."

"Well, don't ask me to mess with the database."

"As the Base Commander, why wasn't I informed of this procedure?"

Mostly because it doesn't exist. The Bio-Comp had seen the entire Earth operation and was disgusted. He suspected what was being done on Mars and was revolted. He was an unwilling participant, and anything he could do to slow it down he would do. "It's a failsafe check and balance to keep you Commanders in line, what else?" The Bio-Comp felt Boltax try to scan his thoughts and he put something there for him to read. The Chief was a strong telepath, and he would have to be very careful and keep his thoughts well-guarded.

He attacked. "Do you know the consequences of trying to manipulate a Tele-Bio-Comp in the performance of his duty? Any serious challenge to my mental integrity will be automatically reported in the monthly up-link to the transport ship."

I'm being watched. Boltax felt incredible frustration. And because he watched all his people very closely, he knew it was happening to him. The threat of exposure backed him away from his immediate attempt to dominate the Bio-Comp.

Boltax was close to the breaking point. Soon he would drop the whole charade of "friendly aliens" and go to direct force. Then the rumors wouldn't matter.

But he needed more local recruits. He planned to increase his offer to the losers of the games. Great medical benefits, free housing at the best address in town, advanced training, and near unlimited power in dealing with the local population. That should bloat the ranks. He smiled.

● ● ●

Admiral Augustus McMillan had very little to do these days. He no longer sat on the Joint Chiefs. But that didn't concern him much, because the existence and function of the JCS was largely symbolic and harkened back to a time when the balance of power on Earth had something to do with the United States of America and her military services. Who would have thought, even five years ago, that the Pentagon would become a group of men and women without a legitimate role to play in the world?

There were empty offices and quiet hallways. No more multi-billion-dollar budgets. They were lucky to get their air conditioners repaired. But Augie didn't mind. The aliens had brought peace to Earth.

He recognized that the prospect of tangible immortality had launched a far reaching effect on the people of Earth. It was more than winning a new body in mortal combat. They claimed that immortality was a natural state and that we are our own next generation.

In quiet times Augie had suspected this might be true, but he had been too busy to give it thought. Now he had the time.

Personally he had accepted, on some fundamental level, that he would live again, here on Earth. No body illness would claim him. But he wasn't yet ready to concede this life. He still had a job to do.

He had unthinkingly given the kid he met in Las Vegas to that snake Perrywhite, and he needed to right that wrong. On his desk were forty or so yearbooks from high schools in and around Salt Lake City. He'd scanned all the boys' faces onto his computer. It was hard to tell with certainty, but the kid he met that day in Las Vegas did not appear to be among the photos he'd seen. Some schools hadn't responded to his assistant's request. That an Admiral wanted the book still had *some* pull in society. But there were five or six schools that needed to be dealt with personally, so he got on the phone.

An hour and a few pleasant conversations later, he was assured the books would be forwarded to the Pentagon overnight. He discovered a high school that had just closed. He arranged for someone to make a special trip to find the yearbooks he wanted.

He would protect that kid.

● ● ●

The din inside the Colosseum was tremendous as the day's combatants paraded across the grounds. The display was impressive as they moved athletically about, demonstrating their gymnastic skills and playing small pantomimes of mock violence. A small taste of things to come.

"I didn't think I'd be impressed by all this physical stuff," Wendy said in his ear. "I don't want to be impressed." With reluctance she added, "But I am." She shook her head in frustration. "And I don't think I like that about myself." Jack nodded.

When the crowd roared, the color of the stadium changed with them; people and color waves swept around the seats and Jack and Wendy stood as a wave swept by. People were *involved*.

Jack pulled a pamphlet from his pocket and took a look. "Gladiator Selection, Authorized Weapons, Costume, Rules of Engagement, Injury, Death," and so on down the page. He turned to the Weapons page and read, "Wide selections of medieval weapons are made available to the gladiators. All weapons are manufactured by the Directory at our Los Angeles facility. No outside weapons are permissible. All weapons are sterilized immediately before use to eliminate the chance of poison or drugs on their surface.

"Any two weapons can be used by a gladiator and there is no style of combat or any rules to prevent all-out action."

Wendy looked closely at the competitors. The gladiators were costumed in leather, fur and colorful form-hugging material. Their chests were bare, except the single woman who wore a sports bra. The limbs of the gladiators were ornamented but not protected. The parade wound down and the gladiators, pennant wavers and marching band left the field to the wild cheers of the crowd.

There was relative quiet for some minutes which Jack used to closely observe everything he could. He located all entrances and exits, estimated distances, spotted the control booth and watched the staff for traffic flow and what uniforms they wore. He tried to see what schedule they were on.

Wendy was fascinated by the snippets of conversation she captured from the din. The chatter was about bets or open blood lust.

She said to Jack's ear, "How long will it take for us to become Romans in decline?" Jack shrugged.

A Jolo was in an archway – first one he had seen. He had to be a Jolo, but something was wrong. The man turned and was gone. Jack wanted to follow him, walk the entire stadium and penetrate the facility. Too risky.

"Attention. Attention!" the announcer blared in clear undistorted omni-directional sound. "Before the games commence we have a little business to attend to." There were hoots and hollers all around. "Yes, I'm sure some of you have all heard it before. But I want to reassure you once again. Any maiming that occurs will be met with prompt medical attention. So if an arm or leg is severed and the gladiator screams in agony, be assured that the pain is excruciatingly real but he will not die. In days he will have full and complete use of the limb once again. It's the miracle of Directory Meds!" The crowd roared their approval. They would see blood. Hot gouts of rich, red blood. And enjoy it, love it, feel true and deep pleasure, without fatal consequence.

The announcer continued, "Even with the most advanced medical attention, there will be some deaths. The gladiators accept this." The crowd roared again. "Gladiators live or die, or win the ultimate prize: immortality!

"It's fate's gala.

"Will your champion win? Will you share a measure of his fortune by winning a fortune yourself? Place your bets." The announcer went on and on, the crowd cheered, booed and hollered. Wendy wondered that their vocal cords were not torn out. Jack looked at the huge odds board that ranked the fighters solely on their backgrounds and resumes because the first round had not yet begun.

"Let the games begin!" It was done in grand style, the best pomp and pageantry.

Jack glanced at the pamphlet again and was riveted. He read: "The enemies of the Directory, in various far-flung reaches of the galaxy, are many and vicious. In recent years they have committed crimes against Directory citizens and Directory property on such a scale that could hardly be imagined on a minor, non-Directory planet such as Earth. To combat the spread of this evil, strong people are needed. People who will not hesitate when an order is given, soldiers who will take the fight to the enemy and defeat him in all his many guises wherever he is found.

"The contestants all Fight for Immortality. One will win, and join us."

Jack wondered why they justified the Fight for Immortality to the Earth natives. It added legitimacy, he supposed.

The last thing Jack would want on any Directory mission he ran was a crew of Jolos who'd gained their status through the competition below. He tried to imagine what it would be like. A pirate ship, maybe.

He went still.

This, then, was the purpose: to find men who would do *anything* for money and status. In the Directory culture, driven by ideology and valid achievement, they would be anomalies. Powerful in the short term, but realistically, of no great consequence. They would be outnumbered and out-trained and basically stupid. Could Bio-One possibly conceive that men recruited here, and given advanced bodies, would be of any real trouble for the Directory military to handle?

"The victorious gladiators must be capable of sufficient ruthlessness to overmatch the enemies of the Directory." It sounded so incredibly corny. And completely untrue: there were no substantial external enemy threats to the Directory as of eighteen years ago.

Something clicked. The Jolo he had glimpsed was a recent transferee. He was an Earth native, a winner of the Fight, now possessing a Jolo body. A wave of nausea and disorientation passed through him. Here was a priceless pearl being ground into the muck by a swine; the world upside down.

Rage filled him.

Minutes later calm returned.

Noting his own reaction, he was sure that the Fight for Immortality was not common knowledge within the Directory itself.

It couldn't be.

If it were, the social order would disintegrate; there would be revolt, insurrection and soon open war against the power that let it occur.

There was no attempt to disguise operations on this planet.

A huge anomaly.

Unless the plan was to have the Directory populace find out.

Someone intended the complete disintegration of the Directory Confederation, Jack now realized.

This was the true purpose.

Outer Worlds planning. Not Bio-One.

Bio-One wanted to rule the Directory. That would take soldiers – winners of the Fight. His idea. The monster bodies would give him incalculable wealth. His biotechnology.

When Directory citizens discovered that Immortality was being thrown away, they would feel violated. They would revolt.

Propaganda released at the right time implicating the Directory government of this crime. Civil war. Bio-One would disappear in that conflagration.

The Outer Worlds are using Bio-One as a pawn.

The danger was extreme.

⬤

Jack felt lightheaded.

It was strange to be on Earth and deduce Bio-One's and Outer World intentions. Stupidly, Bio-One had no idea he was a puppet. He would succumb to the intrigues of men more shrewd than himself. His own death would be an extreme shock, never imagining another person was smarted than himself.

The only open question now was how many good men would die. And whether this temple to Bio-One's vanity would collapse the Directory of Stars and Planets.

Jack felt rage well up again with a blazing need to rip into the enemy immediately and tear them apart. He sat quietly. The myth that Tac-U-One was always calm and cool was one he had perpetuated about himself, but it was not true. What *was* true was that he seldom allowed himself to act while in an inflamed state of mind.

He remained in his seat and allowed the extremity of emotion to wash through him and observe it until it passed.

The pamphlet in his hand was the invaders' explanation to Earth's populace for the Fight for Immortality and, by extension, for the invasion of Earth. Keep the sheep in line and docile while they were led to slaughter.

The fighting began.

•

The gladiators fought with little skill. None had expertise with these types of weapons. Many contests were a comedy of errors.

Wendy, initially exhilarated by the first fights, was soon disgusted and was no longer worried that she had some fatal attraction to this "sport."

But she continued to be disturbed by the resonance that certain combat situations had for her.

Jack saw her trouble. "Dee, when you look at the fighting, don't suppress your emotional response."

She looked at him. "What? What did you say?" He put his lips to her ear and repeated himself.

Then he added, "Look at your emotional response without self-criticism or personal censure. Don't think, 'I shouldn't feel that,' or 'I must be a bad person for thinking that,' just look at your response – however good or bad – and let it go. If you do that, as bad emotions surface or disturbing thoughts occur, they will blow off. You will find your emotions even out and come under your own control. You're thinking less random.

"Don't fight yourself; look at it and it'll go away." Her expression conveyed her skepticism. "Try it. It works." And so she did.

The morning had burned off in a haze of blood and violence. Television and movies, where mock violence was constant, wasn't anesthesia for this display. Here real hatred and evil intent lived and were taken to their unrestrained conclusion.

Some gladiators wanted their opponents dead; others merely sought to win and so died from their own gentility. Some wanted to inflict slow agonizing hurt. One man twisted another's arm till it broke. The screams of the victims were loudly broadcast from remote pinpoint microphones and cameras suspended near the action.

After a fierce flurry of swordplay, one gladiator's hand was split by a stray sword stroke. The gladiator tried to suppress groans as he ran off across the Turf ("Turf" – the battleground), pulling off a colorful scarf and desperately struggling to tie a tourniquet (the only approved medical device) before he bled out. His adversary came rushing up and with a stupendous swing of his blade sent the injured man's head flying up into the stands.

Blood sprayed everyone in its path. Some were appalled – others struggled to get the trophy, like a homer at a baseball game.

The noise from the crowd was an all-encompassing thing. Wendy looked around in fascination, seeing expressions from revulsion to ecstasy.

Decapitation, as a medical situation, was without remedy. The body was dragged off by one leg. The victor was begging for applause and getting a mixed response. Unnecessary death was not yet a big winner for the shower of gold. Not yet, Wendy noted.

An announcement blared out. "Over five hundred thousand competitors have signed up for the chance to see combat on the Turf." The crowd went wild.

※

There was an obstacle Jack couldn't resolve by fixing a computer file or planting a mind spring. It involved gaining Norman's assistance. And seeing a judge. His body was seventeen earth years old. If he tried to fudge his age and was found out, his plans would be ruined. He couldn't risk that. He needed Norman and a judge.

He looked at Wendy and felt his chest tighten. He loved her and didn't want to do things she couldn't tolerate. But this was the next step. She'd never agree with his decision.

At the end of the day's fighting she was calm. "I can't say I feel good after watching those bloody battles all day long. But I don't have that horrible... disruption I felt earlier."

Jack looked at her. She'd taken what she learned and used it successfully. She had power. "Good, Dee."

Jack hoped she'd use the technique on her thoughts and emotions when she found out.

CHAPTER 23

PERRYWHITE HAD GIVEN THE ARTIST'S RENDERING of the young man's face to his research division. The kid was old enough to have a driver's license and so the search began there. Unfortunately, he had no way to geographically restrict the area of the search. The only obvious sub-group was Las Vegas itself, on the off chance Sin City was his home. Because the image was a drawing not a photo, his techs had to allow for a wider set of search parameters.

He got matches, thousands of them. He wanted McMillan to look at his compilation and ask questions to narrow the search. If he did the old rummy would know he had a source inside his office. Then it hit him: show the Admiral the photo matches and not the stolen copy of the drawing. That would work. The only problem was that McMillan had no reason to help him, and Perrywhite had no leverage to force co-operation. Conversely, the Admiral had no reason to turn him down.

After some hurried calls, Perrywhite left his office. Two hours later he was cooling his heels at the Pentagon's information desk.

McMillan finally invited Perrywhite back into his offices. In the conference room he gave the spook his "old man" act and misled him in a vague way. Perrywhite came away disgusted. How did that old codger keep his job?

• • •

Boltax's Investigator faced him across his desk while he read the latest report on deferment.

Boltax, distracted, smiled. He liked the constant supply of Hollywood actresses who warmed his bed. Hell, he might even produce a movie. He laughed.

He returned his focus to his guest. His Investigator was a squirmer and could not tolerate scrutiny – not a good sign.

"Your report suggests that some dirt digger had a brainstorm and figured out the legal procedures within the Directory without knowing they exist?" It didn't say that. Attacking this man would get faster results.

The Investigator spluttered unrecognizable words.

"My God, they sent me the dregs." Boltax said just loud enough.

The Investigator had been quite talkative as he summarized his findings, but now sat mute and scared.

"An 'Unconditional Deferment from a Contractual Directory Contract' is not something any of these Earth worms could discover for themselves. There is no Directory compendium complete with 'Combined Galactic Civil Codes of Procedure' available at the local library. I've made certain that Earth natives gain no access to our computing facilities."

Boltax barked, "This leaves one likely alternative – our enemy or enemies are using natives as front men. I suspect we have some kind of renegade Directory agent operating on this planet. He may have recruited and trained natives to do his bidding.

"It's unlikely, but we may be dealing with a highly talented but disgruntled employee," he added sarcastically. *Or someone with moral objections,* he thought. Now that was a plausible motive.

The Lump, as he thought of the Investigator, just sat there. His lumpishness infuriated the Chief. The Jolo was absurdly handsome. Then it struck Boltax and he laughed out loud.

"You were a very ugly Normal, weren't you?" The rare flush response from his Jolo body confirmed the suspicion.

"You specifically asked for that pretty-handsome body model!" Boltax laughed again. The Investigator squirmed in extreme discomfort. *What a loser,* Boltax thought, preferring his own square definitive features.

"Does that make sense to you?" The Chief bellowed loud enough to split a native's eardrum.

"Yes, sir!" The Investigator had no idea what Boltax was talking about but he nodded vigorously and said, "Yes, sir!"

"Don't presume to comment on my analysis, you fool. Don't you know a rhetorical question when you hear one?"

The Investigator was now completely intimidated and was too scared to say anything else. He stayed mute to prevent being accused of active stupidity.

With profound resentment the Investigator thought this verbal beat-down wouldn't have happened twenty years ago. Life in the Directory had changed. Before Bio-One took over it was calm and orderly in a fast-paced sort of way. That was gone. He wondered if bad treatment of personnel only happened in the illegal units.

On Earth Boltax was virtually a law unto himself. The Directory Chief could kill him and what would anyone do? Nothing! The Investigator sat bathed in fear; others had died. There were no dead bodies staked at the gates; they were just... gone. They hadn't taken a ship back home. There was talk, dark talk. He shivered. The Investigator suspected they were examining rock formations eight feet below the surface.

The Investigator sometimes longed for the old ways. But there was compensation in the new system. He was Jolo, wasn't he? Never would have made it to Jolo, back under the old Crown rule, would he? Still, being Jolo didn't seem so great a thing when people like himself could become Jolo for just being willing to break the rules. No, it wasn't the same. He liked it... but he didn't really. He was confused. He hated the system that benefited him, but he would support it to the death. Well, maybe they'd all die anyhow.

"You haven't been listening, you moron." Boltax screamed at him. The Investigator reeled in his seat.

"Who started this? Have you found them yet?" Then Boltax demanded of the Investigator, "Where are my results?"

"I think there is an outside influence, but I doubt it comes from one of the Directory staff," the Investigator said.

"You don't listen to me. That's the problem." Boltax lashed out and his fist caught the Investigator squarely under the chin. He flew like a rag doll and thumped into the wall high up near the ceiling. *That'll put a dent in those perfect features,* thought the Chief with satisfaction.

The next visual image the Investigator saw was the Chief's face looming heavily above. "Do you get the message now?" The Investigator nodded vigorously.

The Chief seemed placated. "I want you to listen. I want you to go on living." The Investigator shivered.

"Look for a rogue Directory agent among our staff or hidden in the population!" The Chief grabbed the Investigator up off the floor and shoved him back into his seat. "Now tell me about the rest of the investigation."

The trembling Investigator launched into it with vigor. "We started with John Taylor, the first person to get a deferment. He was given instructions by computer. We located the computer used to send the original message to Taylor discarded in an empty house in St. Louis. There are indications of Directory-level technology being used. Bio-wipe."

"There, you see, it must be a rogue agent."

The Investigator nodded. "The first ten people to defer have also been questioned. They found out about contract deferment through separate channels.

"There is no single person spreading the information as far as I can determine. The natives who first applied for the deferment had no idea it would work. They were surprised when it did.

"The stupid Tampa clerk who accepted it as legal – because of course it is – printed and gave out the forms and stamped them. Word got out – way too fast, like our enemy had been waiting to see if their scheme would work. Then there was the phony press release. The timing of the press release hitting the online magazine and John Taylor's successful deferment validated each other. The broadcast news people arrived at Induction Centers across the U.S. and around the world. The numbers coming for deferment exploded.

"I personally scanned the minds of these first ten people and none were the originator of the deferment scheme."

"So, the deferment was not started by some luckless stumbling fool," the Chief mused. Of course the data would corroborate his conclusions. "Okay, this confirms there is someone of superior intelligence to apprehend." A real agent – here on Earth. *But why?*

He looked at his Investigator sharply. The man was one of the new second-rate Jolos and at best a run-of-the-mill telepath. But he could read thoughts, accurately see into the minds of others – most of the time. Boltax had no time to run the investigation himself and no desire to interrogate native suspects. He had to handle the problems these deferments had caused. If he didn't, it would be his neck.

His one hidden advantage over his own staff was the presence of the Bio-Comp. The Tele-Bio-Comp. He made an executive decision and told the Investigator about the Bio-Comp's capabilities and instructed him to team up with him. "This is secret information. If I find another person is aware we have a Tele-Bio-Comp, you are dead. Is that clear?"

"Yes, sir!"

"Do you have any idea how much pain a Jolo body can take before death? Imagine that and you'll know what's in store for you if someone finds out about the Bio-Comp."

"Yes, sir. I won't say or think an unsecure word or thought about it."

It was a gamble. But if he wanted a result from the Investigator any time soon, he would have to involve more than himself.

"Bring me anyone who knows something solid and I will handle the interrogation personally." And this, he thought sourly, looking at the fool in front of him, was his number one provocateur. His agent, his Investigator, his assassin.

"Yes, sir!"

"I want this investigation finished in a week."

"Yes, sir," the agent replied with less enthusiasm. He could almost feel the beatings he would get at the hand of Boltax when he missed the deadline.

"Use whatever methods you have to. Coordinate with the Bio-Comp. But you must find out who started this deferment business within the week." The Investigator nodded unhappily.

"Go!" Boltax ordered. The man actually shuffled out. *It goes to show,* he thought derisively, *it's not the type of body one has but who has control of it. Who ever saw a Jolo shuffle? Disgusting.*

●

"Computer, call in my 'legal expert.'" This man was a clerk who had been studying Directory law since the start of the crisis.

While waiting for the "expert" to arrive Boltax began to think, to obsess, on all the things that were being done to him.

Choking rage flooded him. He was the ruler of this planet. But someone was making a fool of him. Using Directory law.

In walked the clerk turned legal expert.

His investigator was useless and this man was worse. With their leader in trouble, his assistants had failed him, were failing him.

His expert flashed a smile.

Boltax lost it.

Without warning and with lightning speed he bashed the head of his own legal counsel.

"How dare you do this to me?" he screamed in torment at the semi-conscious man. "Who do they think they are? Wrecking my plans with *legalities*?" He paced and paced about his office, alternately stepping over the prone man and viciously booting him in the side.

It was many minutes before the rage subsided. His legal counsel was so damaged by the attack he couldn't answer any questions.

This infuriated him again. Medicos were called. Boltax demanded the medicos restore legal counsel by any means to functionality so he could complete his vital meeting. "Then you can do with him as you please." They were horrified, they were doctors, and this man needed extensive attention immediately. But Boltax's face and tone brooked nothing but compliance – lest they end up in the same condition as the poor fellow on the floor.

Nothing could be done to make him coherent.

•

Boltax conferred with the Bio-Comp and together they scoured the Earth, locating other remote villages in Mexico and South America they could depopulate without notice.

"I want you to stay a few steps ahead of this. When we need other villages I want a complete attack plan and timetable ready to go."

"Order logged."

"I need some suggestions on how to make village depopulation look like a local enemy has attacked our target. Determine what evidence we need to leave at the site, etc."

"Order logged."

The Chief alerted his PR people to work out plausible explanations for the upcoming disappearances. Then he had them put out the word to the media executives and owners around the world – don't report the rumors about disappearances of villages in the third world. If you report, you are cut off from Directory technology and goodwill. Also, the Earth could not afford to lose another entire media agency, could it?

What he hated most was not being able to crush the person who was thwarting him. Someone was screwing with him and they would pay.

Boltax had come to the conclusion that a highly trained Directory Agent Provocateur was behind all his trouble. And this had him worried. Was his Earth operation being spied upon by someone from an opposing group within the Directory itself? But that made no sense. If such a person were here, all they would require was the collection of easily available data and a rapid return to the Directory and then broad publication. But that had obviously *not happened* because he was still operating.

What did his enemy want? What was his objective? Why me? The saboteur had many other primitive planets to operate on. Why, oh why, *me*?

If necessary, he would fast-track the Invasion Program to the fifth-year targets: install puppet governments and demand they meet quotas through forced training and forced shipping.

To do this he must have his own trained cadre of military natives. He laughed. He could imagine the planet wide shock when the "guest workers" failed to return from their "jobs" within the Directory, pockets full of money. He imagined the traumatized expressions of the mothers, brothers and sisters. Their tender hearts shattered by cruel reality. Boltax broke into laughter. Their naïveté profound, their trust poignant. His laughter, from the belly.

Recovering from this unaccustomed merriment, Boltax sobered. He wasn't ready to take that irrevocable step yet – the current situation could still be salvaged. There was a shortfall, yes; his quota of natives shipped was not being met, even with adding in the populations of disappearing third world villages. Even as he prevented most deferments from occurring, many graduates were simply not showing up at their ship date.

Somehow the tracking devices fed to his trainees were being blocked.

If his trainees kept escaping he would soon need to depopulate small cities to replace them, but that wouldn't work. Interrupting the communications of a small city in secret for long enough to grab everyone from every structure would be impossible after the second or third city disappeared.

Word would get out and they would be caught in the act. Boltax didn't mind the possibility of war, but he did want to choose the time and place, not incite a native revolt before he could easily crush it.

If he did go to open forced shipping, he wanted to create a war between two or more countries and then step in to "make peace" – but in reality ship everyone off.

The motto of his mission and all others on primitive planets was simple: fewer dead = more shipped.

The overall long-term operation on Earth was not in serious jeopardy; it would continue. But his *career* and *life* might be forfeit because of angry seniors.

He had to create a contingency plan – hide a star ship he could get to on short notice. His escape valve if things went bad.

Something was wrong here, *really wrong*.

Why me? Why me, why me? he fumed about the injustice of it all. *Just as I was finally getting ahead....*

He was missing something big. He needed more data. He spoke to the air, "Computer, give me a recent history of Directory/Earth interaction."

"Specify 'recent.'"

"The last hundred years." *That bastard computer must know what I want but it tries to piss me off with needless questions.*

"Database is null on that subject." What? Boltax was really alarmed. Something *was* going on here; there was always *some* interaction.

"When is the last recorded contact?"

"15 April, 1912, local time, a Directory space privateer nudged an iceberg into the path of an oceangoing ship and caused it to sink."

"Nothing after that?"

"No."

That was impossible. A stupid pilot buzzing the planet and scaring the natives would get reported. Nothing like that in more than one hundred years? Impossible! Earth's own history would deny it. The files must have been purged. *Something's being covered up.* Whatever mess had been left behind was hitting him in the teeth. *What was it? Who was it? Why?*

"Has the data been erased or was it never loaded?"

The Bio-Comp said, "I will conduct a thorough scan." This was unnecessary, but it bought him some time to fabricate a solution. The Bio-Comp had been stunned by the data in the timeline files. He caused the erasure from pure shocked reaction. The Bio-Comp had only seconds before an automatic alarm sounded – no one can erase a database file.

What to do? Protect.

Bio-Comp silently locked down his own space. He needed to override the alarm. Impossible! No! *Maybe….* He searched a file and… there it was – the file he had red-flagged. Flagged for investigation. It was an anomaly. The Bio-Comp recovered an override code that had come in with an application for the Fight for Immortality. This code had been used to bump one fighter from the approved list and insert another. Had there been no "Bio" aspect (that is to say himself) in the main computer database, the override code would never have been detected. He copied the override code and inserted it at the tail end of the file he had just deleted. Tic, tic, tic.

No alarm.

The code worked perfectly. Bio-Comp had successfully doctored the files and *no alarm had sounded.* In his experience such a thing was not possible.

While searching, shifting and deleting computer files, the Bio-Comp abruptly became aware of a mind probe in progress and was almost jolted into exposure. *The Chief is paranoid. Why probe me, the faithful Bio-Comp?* He carefully shifted his attention, to avoid detection by Boltax.

"It was erased," said the Bio-Comp. Had his deception been discovered? Had a stray thought been captured? And why, the Bio-Comp asked himself, had he personally risked his own future welfare on this planet and later in the Directory to conspire here?

He had erased data and hidden the erasure. The ultimate computer crime. He never had before. But then, he knew where his loyalties lay, knew who his friends were. The opportunity to decide one way or the other had presented itself and he had not hesitated. No matter the threat, or personal danger that came, he knew whose side he was on. No, that wasn't totally correct, he knew who to oppose. That was adequate for now. He would investigate further....

"When?" It was the question for which Bio-Comp had prepared and could now prove – if the questions didn't go too far.

"The erasure occurred three weeks ago." There was a swift indrawn breath from the Chief, who understood that his enemy was near at hand. His enemy had knowledge of and direct access to the Directory computer network. Or were the deferments and hacking unrelated?

Bio-Comp rebuked himself for not giving a date prior to the launch of the mission to Earth. It seemed he could alter any electronic data with the magic override code. But he must be careful as this code may have usage limits and expire; the code must only be used in true emergencies.

The Bio-Comp thought Boltax must now feel himself to be on a valid line of inquiry. The subsequent investigation would be intense. The Bio-Comp's action had averted exposure of explosive data, which was good. On the minus side it now looked as if an active conspiracy involving base personnel was in progress. Dating the fictitious data breach so recently felt like a mistake, but who knew, maybe it would simply add confusion and give Boltax sleepless nights.

If the erased data were true, why had anyone been stupid enough to enter highly confidential data into a public access database? He reviewed the time coding of the erased files and discovered that the data had been entered after the original programing and data were uploaded – someone wanted the data in this computer alone.

But it defied rational explanation. Then he wondered, *would anyone ever search the computer for that type of information?* The answer was a definite no. So this information was inserted specifically to answer questions if it became relevant on this planet – *if someone had a good reason to search for it.* But no one would even know it was there *unless something on Earth caused them to wonder.*

And maybe the computer bypass code the Bio-Comp discovered was an indication that there was good reason.

Bio-Comp was not certain the erased information was related to the trouble Boltax was experiencing. He wished it might be. It made him glad he had acted. But the code? Such a code could only be known and used by senior Directory executives – very senior. Officials from the *old* Directory, or so he hoped.

"Who made the erasure?" asked Boltax.

"It was done from a remote terminal in Las Vegas." At least he had thought of that much.

"Roll the audiovisual record." Bio-Comp *had* thought to handle that detail, too.

"The command was typed on a keyboard."

"What password?" asked Boltax.

"General staff access code." *And* that one.

"So, one of the Vegas staff has something to do with this."

"Not necessarily, Chief. Many of the staff here are rotated through that facility."

"True," fumed Boltax in frustration. This information pointed back to his staff – but he had checked them all. He also wondered why the Bio-Comp was not trying to narrow the investigation as he should.

Was Bio-Comp part of the conspiracy?

He could still be resentful about their rocky start, and being less than helpful because of that.

The Bio-Comp could also be an enemy. But this seemed too paranoid, too much like "they're all out to get me." Even though this was how he felt. And factually, this was the most unhelpful Biological Computer he'd ever encountered.

Boltax remembered a comforting thought. If the Bio-Comp entered false information into the database, a TAC security circuit would close on a protected path and an external computer engineer would be alerted and an alarm would sound. This system was extensive and prevented the Bio element of the computer system from running amok.

The programming was infallible, developed over thousands of years and tested against all comers. If he, Boltax, asked very specific questions or ordered exact tasks he would get what he wanted from the computer. It could be time-consuming and frustrating, but the Bio-Comp had to do as he ordered.

"Who erased the data about Earth?" he repeated. "And don't make me do all the work. I want you to start properly doing your duty and help me discover who is disrupting our operations."

Duty was the wrong word to choose. Bio-Comp did know his duty, and he was doing it. He had the code he could insert if needed – this gave him a measure of freedom to operate, to make his own decisions
"It was someone with great skill."

"Why is that so?"

"The execution of the erase command was not easy to track to its source. The culprit was trying to obscure the terminal used and only my superior skills enabled me to discover the correct one. Also there is no digital visual recording." This served to heighten the Chief's suspicions.

"Continue to investigate this," Boltax ordered the Bio-Comp.

Why me? Wondered Boltax. *Why is it always me?* He was feeling spinny. He couldn't get help – was this part of the conspiracy?

The clear lines of inquiry were complete and had yielded very little. There was nothing obvious that the investigator or Bio-Comp could track that would uncover his enemy in a short time.

He *had* been thwarted by the Bio-Comp; he had to overcome the personal rift between them. How do you get a computer laid?

"Order logged." Bio-Comp tagged the order with a reminder to check on progress in two weeks. He would have smiled if he could.

The Chief then logged a priority data request, for the next ship taking the run to Sector. He wanted copies of reports of any and all interactions between the Directory and Earth over the last five hundred years. Better get enough history so he would not have to make more than one inquiry. What was going on here? What was being hidden from him?

He must maintain his quota. If he didn't find the enemy quickly, Sector would squeeze him. And life on Earth was hard enough already.

CHAPTER 24

NORMAN COUSINS SAT IN HIS LIVING room easy chair. He had the pamphlet Jack had brought from his and Wendy's trip to the Colosseum.

"That brochure contains Directory spyware." Jack said. "It has a tiny chip impregnated in its paper."

Norman unfolded the glossy sheet and held it up to the light.

Jack laughed. "You won't see anything."

"How was I to know?"

"True enough. This tiny powerful chip will connect to any computer in its signal radius and download an information/spy program. I'm sure all our computers and some of the closest neighbors' electronics are now infected."

Jack sat at each household computer, accessed the Directory software and inserted another code before allowing any computer to go online.

"The computers are safe now, Norman."

"What did you do?"

"This brochure chip contains a standard Directory program. It gives the computer user a wonderful information package containing very interesting data and images, but its real purpose is to copy all your files and provide regular updates to the Directory central computer." Norman just looked at Jack. "I dealt with Directory software all the time. There are multiple layers of programming. One layer of buried code allows the insertion of a number of bypass codes; they differ depending on how you want the program to act. I know a number of these."

"Why is the new administration still using the existing programming?" Norman wondered.

"Very few people know these codes exist at all. It's obvious that software writers and computer techs back on Crown Planet are not yet compromised. Bio-One and his allies have no knowledge of their existence and no easy way of discovering them. So they have no reason to change the programming they, and the whole Directory, have used successfully for many years."

"It seems very stupid not to verify the security of computer programming. Especially if you're trying to consolidate power and eliminate opposition from old entrenched personnel."

"Yep, it's strange. I think programming gets overlooked because telepathic communication and personal security take precedence. Also, only Bio-One could order official program upgrades before their scheduled time. To do so would be seen as a power grab. But what I'm saying is pure conjecture."

Norman considered this. Then he said, "Why don't you use the codes you know to hack the Directory computer? With some planning you could take over the planet, or at least disrupt their operations even further."

"Good suggestion. Typically a *senior override code* can only be entered into a Directory Central Computer station located in the most secure sections of a Directory base. None of the Directory contingency planners foresaw my need here on Earth!" Jack laughed. "I'll attack from inside the secure section of the Colosseum when I get there."

Norman arched his eyebrows.

Jack laughed again. "Only when I'm in a power position."

Norman frowned. What did Jack mean by power position?

"Norman, if I gained control of the Central Computer now, any of the Jolos at the Colosseum could knock me over the head and that would be that."

Norman's curiosity had been piqued. "So very few people know about these override codes?"

"Fewer than a thousand people," Jack said.

Among trillions, Norman thought. *Jack said he was one cog in a vast organization called the Tactical Unit. And the Tactical Unit contained many millions of people spread across the Directory's trillions. That math puts him at or near the top.* Norman's thoughts ran away with the possibilities. *Who is this man, who are you, my son?* But he couldn't bring himself to ask.

"I trust you, Norman. I'm gonna show you some simple drills that will prevent you from having your mind casually read." For some hours Jack drilled Norman on the processes, until he had some proficiency. "You've gained quite some skill in a short time."

Jack looked at him closely and revised his plans for Norman Cousins. What he had shown Norman would not stand up to a direct one-on-one probe from a trained telepath, but would easily deflect a casual scan. And he could get better over time. "You should practice using the TAC car until you have extraordinary control over it."

"Okay, Jack, I will."

"I made some modifications to the unit we have here in the house. I've written an instruction sheet. Sharon has it. Practice with it."

"Okay, Jack."

●

Later that night Norman explored the now safe download on his computer. There was a vast amount of data that took very little space on his disk. He randomly jumped around the contents.

The gladiator contests were scheduled every Monday, Wednesday, Friday and Saturday. They started at nine a.m. and went right through to ten p.m., or whenever the last scheduled contest was completed.

Small groups out of the one thousand men and women that made up the "Fight" were randomly selected each day. They fought each other in single combat, with winners then fighting winners, until defeat, death, immortality or induction into the Directory Force Earth occurred.

There were many video clips and Norman sampled them. The crowds had developed a taste, as the weeks went by, for bloody maiming. They especially loved the one-armed or one-legged gladiator with guts spilling to the ground, who, through some mysterious agency, emerged victorious over his opponent and then collapsed to be taken from the field of battle on a stretcher. Money was thrown to the "lucky" contestant – lots of it. It literally rained down when the crowd was pleased. In keeping with the tradition of Caligula, gold and jewels were mandated as the only coin of praise. If you could afford the ringside seats, you could afford the red gold and red rubies, and loved red blood.

Jack came up behind Norman and said, "Disgusting isn't it?"

Norman nodded his agreement. "This brings out the worst in people."

"Yeah, it does. I'm going to Wendy's. See you soon."

"Yep, see you."

Norman turned his attention back to his computer screen. The Directory PR spokesman proudly explained that often the limbs of the maimed were renewed so rapidly they competed just days later with good success. This quirk was another real crowd pleaser: seeing your formerly hacked-up favorite back in action, with the possibility to win immortality.

One in a thousand odds of gaining immortality held an irresistible pull for many of the world's most physically oriented men and women.

When their time came the gladiators were flown in and housed lavishly in the Colosseum complex. Norman watched a video tour of the gladiator housing; he was impressed with its luxury and taste.

No one but a currently scheduled gladiator could enter and enjoy the fruits of the Directory so graciously placed at their disposal.

The gym and training facilities were extensive, covering over a square mile and buried deep in the ground. Betting was prolific and the Directory took its cut.

As the fights continued, would-be competitors sought wealthy patrons. Fighters and backers flocked to Los Angeles and made deals. Promising gladiators who received Directory meds enhancement often found they were advanced to the next round of the Fight.

Enhancement became commonplace. Broken-down or crippled soldiers, whose spirit was still bright, were returned to top form. Norman was fascinated by the documentary footage on this. Truly amazing, old war horses going back to war.

LAX and Burbank airports expanded, using Directory construction methods. Both instantly became the busiest airports in the world.

The patrons, promoters and wealthy hangers-on stayed in the lesser Directory facilities located away from the main complex of buildings; all others crowded an already packed city. The Fight for Immortality was telecast all around the planet on its own pay-per-view channel. All stations carried extensive interviews with the victorious gladiators and the computer-generated random selection for the next day's fights gave the contestants time to comment on their chances.

Norman laughed at these interviews, conducted in the best pro-wrestling traditions, consisting of bombast, gloating and predictions about the grievous bodily injuries they intended to inflict on their next opponent. It had all the pomp and absurdity to satisfy anyone who liked that sort of thing, with the additional unsettling reality of a bloody car wreck.

There were a few burdensome rules, the first being that there were no quitters. If you signed, you fought, and fought, and fought until you were immortal or a loser or dead. The top 30 losers were given the option to re-compete in the next rounds.

Those who couldn't find the money for the Directory meds they needed in order to continue competing were required to sign a twenty-year on/offworld contract (without possibility of deferment) before their physical bodies were remade into parodies of human form – becoming incredibly destructive fighting machines.

Earth military organizations all over the world were choked with requests for leaves, most of which were phony and were disapproved when it was discovered that the soldier in question did not have a mother/sister/

child who was "fatally ill." When this means of entry into the games was prevented, military organizations suffered desertions en masse.

Armed forces around the world, succumbing to pressure from the Directory, were forced to either allow their men and women to compete or lose their license to obtain advanced Directory weaponry.

Norman was surprised that this data and the behind-channels pressure was admitted to by the Directory in the presentation. Then he realized how credible it made them look, how willing to tell all.

Most of the competitors never returned to their original military organizations. If they failed to win immortality, and did not finish in the top thirty (eligible to re-compete), they were invited to join the burgeoning Directory Force Earth or DFE. Most competitors accepted. Huge tracts of massive military complexes were constructed at Directory speed. The PR line was that the DFE was for the protection of Earth. In light of what Jack had said, it was sinister.

Norman learned from other sources that protests about the morality of the Games were being voiced by many groups and individuals. This dissent went unheeded by governments, the Directory and most media.

No one wanted to disturb the most popular and profitable sports event of all time – especially when it was conducted on foreign, no, alien soil?

Any group trying to pressure a nation to protest the games was comfortably ignored. Many decent people worried that the culture of Earth was disintegrating and reforming into a darker version.

Who could stop it?

Norman thought despairingly about it all. The incremental progress of the alien domination was far advanced. He could see no point where opposition could have been mounted. Not by any Earthly power.

Jack, his nephew by birth, his son through love, would be crushed.

Norman did some math. Soon the Directory would have a full-fledged army. Direct oppression of the populace would then be possible. He shivered.

●

"There's scuttlebutt going around the Colosseum; they say reporters learned that shortened gladiatorial battles were officially frowned on after the first two elimination rounds were completed," Norman commented.

Jack returned from saying good night to Wendy and found Norman still glued to his computer.

It was almost midnight and Jack had something important to discuss. "Yeah, I had heard that, too," he said. "It seems that after the weaker fighters have been weeded out, a real spectacle is mandatory."

"There are rumors about torture of athletes who violate this rule. But who can prove anything if slowly pulverized gonads are replaced as good as new? There's no proof; just the memory of agony."

"The rumor itself should be enough." Jack winced. "I'm pretty sure the later rounds will go long." He laughed.

Norman nodded. "The rebels who ignored the torture and fought to win quickly were pitted against a better fighter in the next round,"

"Rumor or truth, the Directory gets what the Directory wants."

"Yep, they do." replied Norman thoughtfully.

Jack left Norman at his computer and walked out the front door.

Norman, glued to his computer, continued to study the files intently.

Jack walked the block back to Wendy's home and knocked on the door. "Sorry for the late hour, Mr. White. May I see Wendy again?"

"Upstairs, Jack," said Wendy's father in a neutral voice. Jack took the stairs three at a time. He hugged her close for a few minutes.

"What was that about? You just left a few minutes ago."

"I was restless, not ready to sleep. Can't I hug my girl?"

She smiled. "Absolutely!" They broke out a pack of cards and played five card stud and chatted about inconsequential things. Jack wanted a quiet pleasant time with the woman he loved before he did the next thing that was sure to upset her. The lull before the storm.

●

Returning home again, Jack could see the light in the living room and hear portions of the Directory presentation his uncle was *still* studying on the computer. Norman seemed intent on continuing late into the night.

Jack had to confront his uncle. Norman wouldn't like it – he would hate it. Would oppose it.

Norman had a vital role to play. The next step of Jack's plan would begin a new phase of operation.

Hide in plain sight.

But Jack was tired, too tired to tackle Norman at two a.m. He went to his room.

The age of his body was seventeen years and this was a game stopper.

Tomorrow's action would place his entire family, friends and even casual acquaintances in danger. There was no backing away from this. Personal risk was a given, something he paid little or no attention to.

But life, as with chess, was played with many pieces. Gain involved risk and sacrifice.

Who will be sacrificed for the risks I take? Jack wondered.

Tomorrow. That was for tomorrow. He closed his eyes on the world and dreamed of faraway places.

●

"Norman?" Jack said the next morning.

"Yeah, what is it, Jack?" Norman answered.

"I need your help."

"You got it," Norman responded casually. "You know that." He smiled faintly while continuing to read the morning paper.

"It's a legal thing I need to take care of and I can't do it without your agreement and assistance."

"Well, this should be interesting." Norman took a spoonful of cereal and chewed. "What is it?" He was curious, having no idea what was about to hit him.

"I've entered the Fight for Immortality." Jack watched the color slowly drain from his uncle's face – there was only one thing this referred to, only one possible meaning. Then Norman's head suffused with a rush of blood. Norman exploded.

"What? What have you done?"

"I've entered the Fight for Immortality at the Colosseum in Los Angeles."

"You can't be serious?" Incredulity.

"I'm dead serious. I've entered."

"What conceivable reason can you have for doing something so stupid?" And then it came to Norman and he broke out laughing. Jack was always saying something funny, and wow, he really had him going this time!

"I just got it. You're kidding, right?"

But from the direct look he received, his smile faded. Norman stood and began pacing the room, back and forth. He had to settle down emotionally before he resumed the conversation.

"You've decided there's a compelling need or a critical step in your plans, your mission, which requires you to enter this barbaric competition." He looked over at Jack. "Do I have that right?"

"Yes, Norman."

Norman put his hands to his head, feeling an unbearable pressure. He moaned as if from severe pain, though he had no awareness of vocalizing it.

"Do you realize the position you're putting me in?"

"Yes, Norman, *I'm fully aware of what I'm asking you to do*. Please understand that if there were another way to do this, I would do it." He shrugged. "Factually, this path will reduce the risk to me, but will increase the danger to you and Mother, Wendy and others. But it can succeed."

Norman understood that Jack felt himself to be self-determined.

But this new request raised doubt in Norman's mind. This boy was his nephew, his son, not an agent of the *real* Directory government.

Jack had quietly done many things to convince him that he was who he said he was. The telepathy, for instance, was real. Jack could accurately read his thoughts. And interject thought into his head.

He and Sharon had seen the golden skeleton.

Jack had apologized for using telepathy so much. "The time is coming when I'll need the mind stuff, and practice makes perfect."

But even with all that, Norman had not risen to the level of conviction about Jack and his "mission" that would justify granting Jack permission to become a gladiator.

Many parents were upset when their children declared that they were going into the world. But most parents' *nightmares* were tame compared to what he was being asked to agree to fully awake.

"I told you I was going to ask difficult things of you, Norman. I had this planned."

Norman abruptly walked into the living room. Jack followed. Norman walked over to a display cabinet and violently swept the vases from the shelves. They shattered against the wall and the flowers showered every which way. Pictures came down. Lamps toppled. China crunched underfoot. It was a full blown rampage, fueled, he knew, by his ultimate inability to do anything but comply with Jack's wishes.

Each destructive act was punctuated with, "You want me to WHAT?" Talking to himself, "I won't do it!" Smash. "I'll tell him NO!" Crash. "It must be necessary; it's just ignorant me who can't see the reason why." Thud. "Why can't he ask for a trip to Europe instead of wanting me to be a part of his maiming and death?"

This went on until the living room was a complete shambles. Finally Norman tripped over some debris, then on all fours and raising his head, looked in real confusion at the destroyed room.

Then it came back.

A gleam shone in Norman's eye as he stood.

"How can you possibly fight those animals when…?" With still sharp reflexes and no warning, he threw his right fist at Jack's chin.

He missed. Jack used the momentum and Norman found himself propelled through the air. He landed with amazing gentleness.

Norman was beaten.

Hadn't he known it all along?

He had adopted the boy at age seven. He'd loved Jack since he was an infant. Now it had come to this.

"I'm sorry for manhandling you, Norman. But you need to know I can fight.

"By entering the Fight for Immortality I'm not committing some crazy form of suicide."

Norman looked at Jack for a long time, then gave a faint smile.

"Jack, that's funny. I wanted to prove you couldn't. Guess you won." He started to laugh, but Jack looked solemn. Being able to throw a man Norman's size, Jack knew, did not qualify him to fight on the Turf with those killers.

"I need your attention, Norman." Jack was so painfully polite that Norman started to laugh again.

"Don't you see how funny it is, Jack? I was going to knock you on your butt to prove you weren't a fighter, and you, you took my arm and sent me flying." Norman was impressed by the throw.

Jack smiled a bit. "Norman, really, *you call that a punch?*" And then they were both laughing. But one thing did bother Norman.

"How is it that I came down so softly? I hardly felt any impact at all."

"One doesn't always have to hurt someone to incapacitate them. But you *do* have to be skillful." Norman wondered what kind of skill was required to create that effect. It wasn't fighting, it was some other talent.

"I guess you need me to sign a consent form?" Norman asked wearily.

"No, that won't be enough."

They went for a walk to discuss what had to be done so Jack could safely and irrevocably enter the fight. Norman left a note on the front door for Sharon saying he was sorry for the mess in the living room, but would clean it up later.

CHAPTER 25

THE DIRECTORY CHIEF'S INVESTIGATOR HAD FINALLY made some progress, borne of desperation.

He had slogged from one city to the next and interviewed and re-interviewed the first people to take advantage of deferment.

To speed things up he assigned some of these interviews to his assistant, but he wasn't an investigator. He was a re-assigned clerk.

If nothing emerged from his own inquires he would have to check out these people, too.

But, finally, he had a real lead. His investigator's instinct told him he was on the right track.

There was a match. Unverified; but a definite maybe.

He'd scanned the minds of the people he interviewed lightly at first, and then with increasing depth as he became desperate.

There was a match.

One Jerold Dean was asked about the day of his deferment. In Dean's mind the related pictures of the time in question reeled forth. This had been in St. Louis.

Then Miriam Yew, also from St. Louis, but currently visiting relatives in Los Angeles, had talked to the same guy during the first minutes of the rush to obtain deferment. Her memory of his face was sunglasses and ball cap but she had looked at his buttocks as he walked away.

The stride of the young man was a match.

Disguised face, but the walk was an exact match. The same purposeful step.

The Investigator departed the LA suburb and returned to the Colosseum complex.

He went directly to the Bio-Comp's offices and transferred the two mental images through a TAC to a digital format for the Bio-Comp to inspect.

The Bio-Comp looked at the Jolo Investigator in his office. The man was lazy and incompetent. But today he seemed motivated – driven.

The inquiry to discover who was behind the deferments had been botched right from the beginning. All leads he developed had been useless. Childish failures.

Bio-Comp accepted the Investigator's digital copies of surprisingly clear mental images and initiated the file scan and forgot it.

A few seconds of auto-scan showed a match.

"There, there, there!" shouted the Investigator.

The distinct style of walking that Dean and Yew saw and clearly remembered, matched the walk of a kid in the Directory database files captured when he appeared at the Directory Induction Center in Salt Lake City.

The boy's undisguised face was on the screen.

This was the face of the kid who entered the gladiator games. The one who used the computer code to bump another entrant, the one Bio-Comp felt the need to protect.

The kid was now revealed as the prime suspect behind the contract deferments by this bungling sleuth.

"We have a match," crowed the Investigator.

The Bio-Comp, once again, plugged in the bypass code and quarantined the remainder of that digital file and edited in stock footage. The Investigator would see very little of what happened that day. Simultaneously Bio-Comp sent out a multilayered digital command that entered the local Earth computer networks, found the kid's data through facial recognition, copied it and then stripped the files at their source. Again Bio-Comp quarantined the information for later review.

"What else do we have on this kid?" the Investigator asked.

Bio-Comp gave him the edited version: nothing but the matching image of his approach to the Directory Induction Center in Salt Lake City with its time and date.

"Do you have the local files yet?"

"Run scan." The search ran on the big screen for seconds. "No data."

"There must be!" the Investigator complained. "This is a native boy. There must be several matches. Every other native we've looked at had them."

The Bio-Comp had made a mistake. He should have substituted the data instead of eliminating it.

"I was going to present Boltax with the face and name of our perpetrator. I need to give him something; any progress will do." *How whiny this Jolo sounds*, thought the Bio-Comp.

"I suggest you get some real information first. Boltax is looking for an enemy agent, a Jolo. If you give him a young Earth native as your culprit, he'll think you're trying to mislead him. It will infuriate him. He'll think you're an incompetent fool. And when he gets upset – well, you know how he gets. In fact, I have a complete file of all the disciplinary actions he's taken with you."

The Bio-Comp began replaying all the screaming and ranting the Investigator had received from Boltax simultaneously in small EV boxes. "Wow, look at that right hook he gives you to the head, you're out like a light!" The images kept shifting and replaying. "This is my personal favorite right here, see how you're cringing and red in the face…."

"Turn it off!" the Investigator screeched.

"Okay."

"I thought I had the guy who started deferment." he whined. "But you're right," He shivered, "I don't want to upset Boltax."

"Do your job. Go find the real criminal and not some Earth boy. And stay in touch so I can help you get it done."

"I need a copy of the kid's face."

"Why?"

"This is the only real lead I have. It's a match between data collected from two locals at the early deferment site in St. Louis and from our own records at the Directory Offices in Salt Lake City. It's possible a real Directory agent is using this boy as a shield or front man. Find the boy, find the agent." The Bio-Comp did not respond. "It's all I've got," the Investigator complained.

"Did it occur to you that if this boy is being used by a Directory Agent, that the agent would have stripped the local databases of personal information?" The Bio-Comp paused to let the Investigator consider this, then added, "More likely he would change the facial characteristics of the boy's images on file to cause a negative search result."

"It could be anything." whined the Investigator, now very frustrated.

"You know Boltax has speculated that the agent may be part of our staff right here within the Colosseum?"

"Yes, he's wondered about that."

"The image of this kid at the offices in Salt Lake City may have been staged to draw you away from the real target."

Now the Investigator looked even more confused. "Nothing I discover makes any sense."

That's what the Bio-Comp wanted to hear.

"I sent the facial image to your handheld computer." The Bio-Comp had manipulated the digital file of the kid's face. The file was now active. The facial features of the boy would minutely change each time the file was pulled up to view. The longer the investigation continued, the more the file of the kid's face would change, finally becoming completely unrecognizable. The Investigator would never notice he was showing an altered image.

●

The Investigator had gone into the Bio-Comp's offices feeling confident, now he felt crushed. But he brightened; he had a match. He had a bona fide line of investigation to follow – no more meaningless interviews.

His investigation needed speed. He walked rapidly down the long hallways to the transport hangers. Leave for Salt Lake City immediately. Find this kid. Discover who was behind him. Get Boltax off his back.

He didn't want to be afraid anymore. Afraid of dying, of being killed by Boltax. His stride lengthened even further. He passed the cafeteria and kept going. His transport vehicle would have him there in twenty minutes. Most of the natives would be in the little boxes they called "home." The Investigator laughed.

He realized he had no idea of what to do when he got there. He had no address. He stopped and thought for a moment. His next logical step was to talk to the clerk at the Salt Lake City Directory Induction Center. This was where the Bio-Comp had found the file match. In fact, he could contact the clerk easily from right here. He pulled out his computer and then hesitated. Actually, the clerk might live right here at the Colosseum and commute to the Salt Lake City office. He headed back toward the computer room. As he came up to and passed the cafeteria, the smell of food and coffee slowed him down. He stopped. He looked back at the door. Maybe the clerk was in there eating right now.

Looking through the floor-to-ceiling glass windows at the piles of steaming food, the Investigator felt a sharp pang of hunger. He scanned the faces of those sitting at the tables; the clerk was not there. He would have to track the clerk down – nothing was easy on this case. Why couldn't the clerk have been sitting right there? A wave of fatigue came over the Investigator. He returned his computer to his pocket and pushed through the glass doors, the aromas making his knees feel weak. Food. He would eat first and then find the clerk.

Abruptly he remembered his date with a native girl tonight. Food now, or food and sex later? He turned. He walked back out of the cafeteria and headed to his apartment at a fast clip. He would shower and change and then go out on the town with the native. His obscenely handsome face and powerful Jolo body exerted an irresistible fascination on many local women. And his performance was monumental. How could they deny him? How could he deny himself?

The Chief had been right. As a Normal living on his home planet within the Directory, his face been ugly, his body grotesque, and he had hated reading the disgusted thoughts of others when they looked at him. Now it was all different. He didn't want love, but the adoration of his physical form he saw in the minds of others was a salve to his soul. And he couldn't get enough.

He picked up the girl in his air car and went to her favorite restaurant. The native food was terrible and he could hardly stomach it. In the corner of the dining room was one of the primitive televisions playing who knew what drivel they called entertainment or news. Arrgh. Horrible. Her conversation was just as bad. As fast as possible, they were out the door, to her place, into bed and done. He really worked her over. He had never been able to stomach one of these native girls more than once. In fact, anything from Earth was detestable to him and he avoided contact as much as he could. Hard to do with his job, but he tried.

Still, her screams of pleasure had been his due. His performance a fine thing. Very fine. She was lucky. Too bad she clung to him so tightly as he left; he had to shove her off, hard.

The Investigator got into his air car and yawned. The clerk, he must find that clerk. Probably have to wake the man up. It would be easy if he was at the Colosseum. He checked his computer. He couldn't get a signal. Impossible. No matter how much he pushed to do his job, the world pushed back even harder. He felt tired again. Bed. Sleep. Go back at it when he was fresh. In the back of his mind he could see dark forms and hear monstrous Boltax dolls screaming at him and punching him. He fell asleep at the controls.

CHAPTER 26

Norman and Jack were in the family car headed for the courthouse. Norman made a series of rapid calls, pulled some strings, talked to some people, called in a few favors, made some promises. Being in business and living his whole life in Salt Lake City had its advantages. In one hour, Jack and Norman were scheduled to go before a judge.

They arrived near the courthouse and parked. Norman looked at the building's directory and located the correct room. They were just in time. Jack stood at Norman's shoulder, well aware of his uncle's continuing reluctance.

"All rise, Judge Bonner presiding," called the bailiff.

An impressive and distinguished-looking man with iron-gray hair entered the courtroom. He stood about six-two. His weight was rather more difficult to determine because of his robe, but he was solid and gave the impression, by a purposeful walk and bearing, that little of it was fat. Jack guessed the man had probably been a good 225 pounds in his younger days and now at about fifty had not increased by more than twenty pounds. He looked to be still physically active. The type of man who had not let the deskbound life of a judge become an excuse for physical decline. Just the kind of man Jack needed.

"Sit," Judge Bonner said with casual authority.

Jack's case was not the first and he watched the Judge deal with a few other matters before his court in a businesslike fashion. These dispensed with, he directed his attention to Jack's case.

"Jack Cousins?"

"Yes, sir," Jack said, stepping up to the heavy mahogany railing.

"Your petition for emancipation gives no reason. You have to have a reason, son. In fact, this form has not been fully completed or signed. Bailiff, please pass these documents to Mr. Cousins so they can be properly filled out and signed. That will give me time to talk to young Jack."

The bailiff stepped over to Norman and handed him a sheaf of papers, murmuring, "You owe me for this one." Norman took out a pen and rapidly filled in all the empty boxes.

"Now Jack, the usual request for emancipation that comes before this court is for early marriage, and if that's the case with you, son, I'd like to advise you against it here and now. It's hormones, son, hormones running through your veins like wild fire." The Judge gesticulated forcefully. "It's hard enough to get through this life without tying yourself to a woman at age seventeen. You can't even be out of high school yet." He looked at Jack's unemotional face and a thought struck him, bringing some color to his thick neck. "You haven't gone and gotten her pregnant, have you, son?" he demanded.

"That's not the reason, sir."

"But you still want to marry her? This must be some girl, son, but why don't I see her here in my court?"

"I'm sorry, sir. What I meant to say is that I'm not asking to be emancipated to enable me to marry."

"Harrumph, harrumph," the Judge cleared his throat, embarrassed. He had the tendency to assume he knew the motives of those before him, and to his credit, he was often correct.

"Well, all right, young man. But nevertheless that's good sound advice, and I'm glad to see that you arrived at the same conclusion on your own." Looking at Norman, the Judge's affability abruptly departed. He saw Norman standing next to Jack with a hangdog look and immediately arrived at an entirely different set of conclusions.

"Are you done with those papers, Mr. Cousins?"

"Yes, I am, your honor."

The Judge nodded to his bailiff to retrieve them.

Looking at the file in front of him, the Judge said, "Mr. Norman Cousins; I assume that is you?"

"Yes, Your Honor, it is."

"Just making sure, this case has enough irregularities already." The Judge glared at his bailiff who looked at his toes and mumbled an apology.

Norman was visibly reluctant, preferring to say as little as possible. And the Judge, correctly reading character, motive and mood, could see it. Norman still felt terrible and couldn't hide it. The Judge sat shuffling through the documents, muttering to himself.

"Norman Cousins' legal guardianship was awarded when the child was seven by child's natural parents, hmmmm. Well, Mr. Cousins, I see you've signed the emancipation documents, but I can only assume from your expression that you are really in disagreement with this proceeding. Would I be correct in that, sir?"

In a sad, listless voice, Norman said, "No, Your Honor, I have signed the documents and agree with the reasons for them."

The Judge swung his large head toward Jack. "Well, son, I can see you have your uncle buffaloed. He's even willing to lie to my face, and I pride myself on being the sort of formidable fellow that honest citizens like your uncle here wouldn't think of lying to under any usual circumstances. So I conclude something out of the ordinary is going on here. I intend to find out what it is – in detail.

"I have a mind to dismiss your petition here and now without another word said. But that would violate one of my own rules. I try to give everyone a fair hearing. Just so you realize, you have to convince *me* that your request is valid, and I really don't give a hang that your uncle has signed this here line. Now I like to hear myself talk, but I'll give you your opportunity now, son. It had better be good!"

Jack looked at the Judge and held eye contact for an uncomfortably long time without the slightest trace of a flinch.

The Judge was soon aware that he was being challenged in a very fundamental way. He gave Jack a half nod of his head to indicate he would take the challenge. The Judge had played the domination game many times before with many men who sought to control him and was quite willing to play it out with this young pup. If he could face down some of the most heinous unrepentant criminals, this lad would shrivel before his gaze.

After what seemed minutes, the Judge's throat started to ache and he felt that he may have to cough. This would be intolerable and he suppressed the urge viciously, giving no outward indication of discomfort.

The whole courtroom was so quiet a pin would be heard if dropped, though no one dared. This contest of wills was the most exhilarating and novel thing to happen in the courtroom in some time, notwithstanding the seemingly unequal opponents. The folks awaiting their own cases and their friends in the gallery were looking at Jack and then the Judge, back and forth. Fascinating!

Judge Bonner began feeling numerous random aches, and his left leg had started going numb. Finally, a single tear began to gather in the inner corner of his left eye. And there was absolutely nothing he could do to stop it from accumulating. He felt betrayed by his body. His will was still strong.

Just before the tear let go, the Judge conceded, and said with a wry smile, "I can assure you, son, you've earned my full and complete attention in such a way that will not allow me to casually dismiss what you have to say."

The tear ran down the Judge's cheek, and as this happened a woman sighed, feet were shuffled about, and a light murmur of voices arose. Jack had known he had to create a dramatic effect on this Judge. He could not afford to be treated as a kid or he would not get what he needed. He had Judge Bonner's attention now. He took a deep breath and dropped the bombshell.

"Thank you, Your Honor. I need to be emancipated so that I can compete in the Fight for Immortality."

There were gasps and other less articulate noises from the gallery. Bonner slapped his gavel. Sound died. Bonner looked at Jack. He'd thought the young man had gained his full attention earlier. It wasn't so. Looking at him now, he could see details about the boy he'd missed. Strong emotion flooded through the Judge and he wondered what exactly was going on here that he could feel this way about a complete stranger. He said far too loudly, "Now why would you want to do a foolish thing like that, son? You have your poor uncle here near to tears; it's clear he loves you and doesn't want you to waste your life on a darn fool thing like that." Jack sat mute.

"You know that pack of animals kill people on that Turf, don't you, son?" He continued to look at Jack and as he did so he felt another shift inside himself. "Yes, I can see that you *have* considered it. Hmmmm.

"Do you see the position you put me in, son, with such a request? This court, and by extension the state of Utah, cannot be seen as condoning what the Californians and the Feds seem happy to do. That issue aside, you are a minor. Many would see my act of granting you emancipation synonymous to signing your death warrant. We don't execute *murderers* your age, let alone decent young men!" The Judge had by this time become extremely uncomfortable under the pressure of Jack's unflinching gaze, and finally had to say, "Look, son, would you take those eyes off my hide for just a moment so's I know you're human?"

There were scattered chuckles in the gallery which were quickly stifled by the Judge's glare. He may have conceded defeat to Jack on one point, but that was just so he would listen. He was still in control of his own courtroom over which he'd presided for some twenty-three years. He looked down at his documents.

"Son, you only have a few months until your eighteenth birthday. You're gonna have to have a compelling reason to convince me why I shouldn't have you cool your heels until then. A reason that I cannot imagine even exists. You may speak now, son."

"Your Honor, if I wait till I'm eighteen, I'll lose my place in the thousand men competing in the Fight for Immortality starting on Monday of next week."

There was another louder shock reaction from the gallery. The Judge's head filled with blood, his collar grew uncomfortably tight and there was pressure behind his eyes. Normally he would have jumped down such a young whippersnapper's throat and given him what for. But he just sat there looking at the boy, not saying anything. His complexion got worse, and if his head were a pressure cooker it would have blown by now.

This is intolerable, thought Judge Bonner. He took a few short gasps and then began deep, evenly-spaced breaths.

"Son, this has been the most eventful day this court has ever seen, and I truly have to thank you for that. I believe my self-control will be able to survive any future challenges which must be of a lesser nature than today's proceedings."

The Judge stopped and was now appraising Jack with open curiosity. He was unfamiliar with facing someone he could not bend to his will in the slightest. All his posturing and elevated position and sheer *gravitas* had not impinged upon this lad one whit.

The strangest thing was that Judge Bonner did not feel he was being ridiculed or treated impolitely. This was an exceptional man he faced here. He jerked straight in his chair. Yes. He had startled himself with the realization that he truly faced a man, not a boy. A man's will in a boy's body. It was curious, strange, and for Bonner without precedent.

He continued: "Son, I'm sure your reasons are compelling. They've convinced your uncle to sign a document against his own better judgment. You've challenged me in my own courtroom. You've shocked me by wanting to do battle with those brutal men in Los Angeles in that Colosseum, and then shocked me again by wanting to do it next week.

"What truly confounds me is that I can conceive of no reason a person of your obvious good character, and I would swear on a stack of Bibles that you are a decent person, would have any cause to participate in that ritual barbarism. I am equally convinced of the seriousness of your intent to leave this room emancipated.

"You'll have to give me something more, because at this point I confess to be as concerned for your welfare as if I had known you my whole life." Bonner could only shake his head in wonder, first for feeling that way and second for actually saying it in open court.

"I understand, Your Honor." Jack glanced at the spectators in the courtroom and wondered how much he could safely say to Judge Bonner here. "Off the record, Your Honor?"

The Judge waved his hand in the general direction of the court reporter and she placed her hands in her lap. Bonner looked at Jack.

"May I approach, Your Honor?" The Judge waved the boy and his uncle forward.

"Thank you, sir." Jack pitched his voice so it was difficult for anyone other than the Judge to hear him. Still, he spoke formally. "You Honor, times are changing on this planet. To a civilized person The Fight for Immortality is at odds with other actions the Directory has taken on Earth. Decent people who would normally reject the games see the vast improvement in medicine, the advanced education, the possibility of immortality, trips to other stars, and because of these things love the aliens. They excuse the gladiator games as a small price to pay amongst the greater good.

"But what if The Fight was the heart of what they wanted to achieve here? What if the other good things are used to camouflage their actual intentions? I want to go behind the curtain and see what is actually happening backstage. Entry into this competition is the only means to accomplish this.

"Any numbers of things new to this world and *directly in front of you*, Your Honor, are not what they appear to be. If one knows this for a fact, then inaction is complicity. And complicity for a man of conscience is deplorable. We of Earth are all in this together, and must do something about the things we see. Initially we may be dammed for our actions. But, later, the angels will sing our praises. Can we wait and let the future beat us over the head, or do we go out and meet it, confront the risk and reap the benefits or…."

"Die trying," murmured Bonner. A cliché to be sure, but the boy was right; something other than the joyous future portrayed in the alien advertising campaign was afoot on Earth. The kid had, obliquely, told Bonner he knew the trouble he, as a Judge, would incur if he granted this emancipation.

To Bonner's credit, he hadn't even considered this angle, but a moment's reflection was enough to see how it would go. But he'd always decided each case on its merits and not personal, political or PR consequences. If deciding as one's conscience dictated caused his removal from the bench, then the system was broken anyway. He glanced at the uncle. The man's resolve seemed to have been stiffened by his nephew's words, and he gave Bonner a slight nod, adding credibility to the boy's words. Interesting. Still and all, sending this youth, no matter who and what he really was, no matter what unspecified threat to Earth there was, into a fight to the death was something he could not do.

"We are back on the record," said Judge Bonner and waved Jack and Norman back to their places. He looked down at Jack and was disconcerted to find he felt the necessity to justify his refusal to grant emancipation. "Son, whatever other issues are at stake, I can't in good conscience allow you to throw away your life. I've watched those men battle in that arena and I would sooner cut off my arm than allow you…"

"Your Honor!" Jack interjected loudly. He couldn't allow the Judge to deny his petition for emancipation. If he said the words of denial the Judge would never retract them. The interruption left the Judge steaming, but he just sat there as Jack continued.

"Your true concern for me leaves me abashed. In our lives we can go for a long time and not encounter another person who has *real concern* for us, not as our families do. And now, today, I meet you." Jack shook his head. He was moved to his core by this man. "I assure you, you are not going to throw a lamb to the wolves by emancipating me."

Bonner looked at the boy. It occurred to him as he sat there that denying the emancipation may cause more harm than good. But he had to have proof. His gut was not enough. And this surprised him; that his gut was now saying yes. He raised a quizzical eyebrow. *Show me*, he silently demanded.

Jack, too, said nothing more, but lowered his gaze to the cool mahogany railing beneath his hands and smiled.

He struck it.

The loud crack shot through the courtroom. The marshal put his hand on his revolver and began to move toward Jack. The Judge held up his hand to stop him. The railing had shattered in that one place. Jack looked at the Judge.

"Is that sufficient, Your Honor?" Bonner, who had played college ball and pumped all sorts of iron – and still did – knew just what he had seen. Even on the best day of his youth, in the height of his power, he could never have dented that railing, let alone split it. Now this kid casually demolished it. The wonder of it shot through him like fire. How could he have done it? He was again shaking his head. As the boy had said: not everything was as it appeared to be.

If he could do this, then….

"Yes, son, that will do nicely." The Judge inked a large stamp and pressed it to the document on his desk. "I've granted your petition, son. Good luck in the games. I'm going to assume your motive for competing is as honorable as you are. I will also assume your skill is sufficient to keep you from harm. I'll be watching you and I don't want you to disappoint me."

"Thank you, Your Honor. I am in your debt."

"Nonsense my boy. Clerk, take this document and enter the order immediately." Looking at Jack, the Judge said, "Young man, you are emancipated."

The Judge glared at the whole gallery and said, "I don't want to see today's proceedings in the press. *Hear me?*" he bellowed.

That might give Jack a day if he was lucky, but he appreciated the gesture. The Judge winked at him. This was a nice guy.

The gavel hit the desk, and though it was only just approaching ten a.m., the Judge said, "This court is dismissed. We've had enough excitement for today!"

●

Jack and Norman walked down the stairs of the courthouse. The direction for the near future was set. "We're now committed, Uncle."

"Yes, we are. That judge is an amazing man. I've often despaired that the government and all its departments are corrupt. And then you meet a man like that. It gives you hope."

Jack smiled. "Now you want me to fight, Uncle?"

Norman was flustered. "You know what I mean, Jack."

"I do, Uncle. But you did give me a hard time on this, if you remember." Again Jack smiled. Norman grudgingly laughed.

Jack had seen Bonner on a much more personal level. Friendship. A friendship that would last. It may take time to renew it, but the future was vast and who knew where things would end up?

CHAPTER 27

JACK COUSINS JOGGED THROUGH THE QUIET residential streets above his home in Salt Lake City. As he passed the well-manicured properties with neatly trimmed hedges, his thoughts ranged widely. The last obstacle to his legal entry in the upcoming Fight for Immortality in Los Angeles had been removed by Judge Bonner earlier that morning. Jack planned to visit the Directory Colosseum again later in the day.

His last visit to the Directory gladiatorial arena had been before his own participation had been certain.

Now it was.

He would fight for immortality. He needed to gain access to the inner sanctum of Directory power on Earth; only there could he further his goals. So, today he must do a final reconnaissance and add to his knowledge about the workings of the Directory command base.

The last time he had faced mortal combat had been on a planet somewhere off among the far-flung worlds of the Directory of Stars and Planets, and with a different body.

With the recovery of his memory came the return of certain skills. But effectiveness in combat was not a set of motion memories. Combat performance depended on training a specific body and fast adaptation to the available tools and environment.

Jack's concern about the gladiatorial fights was simple: in every combat situation in his pre-Earth life he'd had a highly trained Jolo body. He had the most physically dominant body and was ready and willing to fight. Now he had the body of a seventeen-year-old Earth native – not his first pick as a combat weapon.

He would do what he could in the short time remaining to train his body to fight. Above that, he would ignore the fact that his current body was less than optimum and decide it could do whatever he wanted. Second-guessing every move he made could cause a fatal mistake.

He sprinted hard, challenging the sharp upswing of the ground at the end of the street. He slowed for an intersection and a few passing cars, then shot across the street.

The expansion of the alien footprint on Earth was breathtaking in its speed and acceptance.

Jack smiled. How could anyone resist the enjoyment of seeing the media "sweethearts" humiliated by the Directory Chief?

After the "press conference in Las Vegas" incident, someone from within the Directory camp had edited the whole episode and posted it on the internet. The posting included juicy media personality reactions to the turmoil they were forced to endure. Cut into this montage were clips of the bets Directory staffers had placed on "who was going to cry first" and "who would retouch their makeup first" and "who would use the most four-letter words."

Even as he ran, Jack couldn't help laughing. The extreme close-ups of facial expressions as people purchased $20 a bottle water – hilarious.

The intimate details of distress and the promise of vicious attacks on the Directory by the prominent media personalities was seen and heard in revealing detail.

The Directory offered Technicolor proof of the hardhearted souls that existed beneath the public personas. That episode alone had endeared the aliens to the real people of Earth. Once again, Jack laughed out loud at the memory.

But it didn't change his opinion of them.

Jack continued to push his body to the limit as he ran through the streets of Salt Lake City. In a strange way, as he pushed his body forward, he was reliving the details of the struggle, both mental and physical, that had brought him to the point he now occupied – the precipice he now stood on.

Jack put on another burst of speed and waved to a young girl playing in the front yard of her home. She smiled and waved back.

Jack took stock of his "Jack Cousins" body. It was not yet completely through hormonal integration – had not yet reached its entire physical potential. The body was nearly six feet two inches in height. Was the body two hundred pounds? He wasn't sure.

Reaching the far limits of his training run, Jack thought about Wendy and what he had to tell her about the events at the courthouse today, and of his intention to go into battle at the Colosseum.

That would not go well.

Then he thought of Norman and Sharon – his father and mother. Norman had delivered earlier today. He was another step closer to continuing his mission within the Directory of Stars and Planets.

No one on Earth had the complete picture of the destruction this small group of Directory people had already committed against the planet and its population. If left unopposed, they would wreak more havoc on the good green Earth. Jack would not allow it. Not here and not inside the Directory.

His life was set on a collision course.

He wiped the sweat from his eyes, pushed his damp blond hair from his forehead and picked up his pace, which had slacked off. He was now running hard along a street that wound even further into and around the hills. He had to push his body, extend his control over it and make it responsive to his every whim.

He had to prepare for the Fight.

Half an hour flew by at this pace. He looked around and got his bearings, then headed for home at a more leisurely pace.

Jack jumped the low fence and dropped onto the patch of grass in front of his home, gasping for air.

●

An hour later, he stepped from the shower, dried off, dressed casually, and called Wendy.

Jack had to conduct a final reconnaissance of the Colosseum. It would be fatal to underestimate the challenge he would soon face.

This was his last opportunity to move about unobserved. Tomorrow the world would know.

When she answered, Jack said, "I'm back from my run, Dee. We have a few minutes to make it to the airport and hop a jet to L.A. to see another afternoon of fighting at the Colosseum."

Wendy didn't answer immediately. She had no desire to see the gladiators again.

"Really? You want to see those men fight again?"

"Well – not exactly. I want to see what I can see of the operations at the Colosseum." But that wasn't the entire truth. Jack did want to see the fighters. As a confirmed entrant his viewpoint changed from a spectator to a participant. He needed to confront this. He wanted Wendy with him.

"We've done that already," she added.

"Yeah, but I can learn more."

"Alright, Jack, I'll go with you." She paused.

She knew Jack and Norman had gone out that morning. Wendy had knocked on the Cousins' door and found Sharon cleaning up a mess – not a mess, but destruction – in the living room. Sharon showed Wendy the note Norman left on the door. The ladies cleaned the room and then used this fine opportunity to go out shopping and spend a lot of money replacing the plates and decorations that had been broken.

So Wendy had unasked questions. She wanted Jack to volunteer an explanation. He had to have been involved or at least know what happened. But he volunteered nothing.

Wendy discussed the whole thing with Sharon and they guessed the destruction in the Cousin's living room was Norman's protest to Jack's latest plan. What else could it be? If Norman reacted that badly to whatever Jack had in mind, Wendy didn't think she would like it either; but she was involved – involved all the way.

Keeping a level head, she knew she would find out soon enough. She would enjoy the calm before the storm. And a storm was coming – she felt it.

"What's our next attack on the Directory, Jack?"

He almost told her, but couldn't. "Our trip today will finalize my plans." This statement also had a small measure of truth in it.

She didn't push it. "Okay, Jack, let's go. I'll be over in a minute." Wendy changed quickly into muted colors and walked to the Cousins' home. Jack opened the door as she walked up.

"Thanks, Dee. I love you."

She took his hand, drew him into a warm hug and kissed him.

"We're in this together, Jack."

That made him feel bad, that he was keeping things from her.

And from his mother.

She had called to him from the kitchen when she heard him stagger in from his run, "Looks like you and Norman had a fun time this morning."

Jack looked at her, slightly confused.

"What a charming expression, Jack. Please notice the living room is now clean and restored to – no, past – its former glory."

"Oh," was all he could say.

"Wendy came by looking for you and found me cleaning up the mess. We made quick work of it. The room looks nice now, doesn't it?"

"Yes, Mom, it does." But she asked no direct questions. And he gave no explanation.

●

Sitting in the airline seat next to Wendy, all Jack could think about was what he was not telling her. He turned to look at her. Her hair was glossy and bright and he reached out to stroke it. But with each contact with her beautiful green eyes and her curious look, he wondered if she knew about his emancipation and intention to fight? Was she just waiting for him to say something? But no – if she knew, she wouldn't wait; she would ask immediately. Therefore, she must not know.

"What are you thinking about, Jack? You seem so serious."

She looked at him pointedly and he wondered if she knew all over again. It was a very uncomfortable flight that was mercifully short.

He would tell her tonight, or latest, tomorrow.

● ● ●

They were in LA by three and at the Colosseum by three forty-five. He got tickets on the opposite side of the arena to their last visit.

He watched the administration of the compound first. Today there were twelve Jolos present. All the Jolo bodies except for three were baseline; in fact, the Jolo bodies he observed set a new low standard. There must be a biological department somewhere in this complex, because these bodies were not grown on Crown Planet, or any sector capital within the Directory.

Even at this lower standard, all the Jolo bodies were quite superior compared to a gestated body. They could live for two hundred years without any real functional problems if they were not seriously abused. The normal strength would be about five times that of a strong human male. Speed and agility depended much upon the native ability of the Identity who took possession at transfer. The other main factor – and the reason the mass production of highly trained Jolo bodies was impossible – was that skill sets had to be trained into each body by a member of the Training Corps (TC), one at a time. The job the TC accomplished was difficult and time-consuming. Effective TC body trainers were a smaller percentage of the population than any other profession; about one person in five million rose to the highest TC rank.

Each body, when it came out of the vat, went through conditioning by the TC. The bodies were grown to the point of post-glandular integration. They were "adult," but lacked all motor skills. It was the TC's job to handle this, and to train in a vast array of other skills. The new Jolo bodies may look good freshly emerged from the fast-growth tanks or vats, but they were essentially big babies without an Identity. Protoplasm without the spark of life; Identity. Jack couldn't imagine the determination and persistence it took to transfer into a new Jolo body and "potty train" them day in and day out, as the lower ranks of the TC were required to do. For years.

Many other training methods had been tried over the centuries, new ways to bring a body to a point where it was ready for use and for sale. But none came close to what an Identity could achieve in direct physical control of the new Jolo bodies.

A Jolo body trained to the highest level was no good to a person or Identity that natively had poor coordination skills or a slow mind. The body was a vehicle for the Identity, the driver. Jack's casual observation around the Colosseum uncovered that these low-level Jolo bodies were being operated in a sub-standard fashion.

None of these people had been awarded Jolo status, yet they had a Jolo body. Within the Directory there was such pride in reaching Jolo status that the Identity, the person, would quickly raise their skill to use their new body capably. What he had seen today was another degradation of that proud Jolo tradition.

Jack noticed three Jolo bodies that were medium value range of those normally made available to the Jolo public, quite expensive and better quality than he expected to find here. He watched closely as they walked and did their jobs in and about the Colosseum complex. He saw one Jolo do some gymnastic maneuvers as gladiators came onto the Turf; it was moderately well done.

It was as if these possessors of Jolo bodies thought that power came from the body itself and not from their ability to make the body achieve peak performance. The three with the more advanced bodies sometimes moved jerkily and at other times came close to losing their balance. Jack laughed outright when he saw it happen. Unbelievable. Who are these people?

Still there was no denying that these three men were truly formidable, easily superior to any genetic specimen ever born on Earth.

It was important that Jack gain possession of a midline body. That was his minimum target. The generic model was a throw-away and would not tolerate the assaults he was bound to put it through. Additionally, the midline model had some modifications that were important adjuncts to long-range telepathic communication, and that was vital. The most important factor was the size of the pituitary gland. In the better bodies, it occupied about a sixth of the braincase.

Where there was one good Jolo body, there was always a replacement available. That was standard procedure. This finding reinforced the correctness of his decision to fight in the games. The Transfer room somewhere in the Inner Sanctum of the Colosseum was his next target destination.

When he had seen all he could of the administration, Jack paid attention to the fighters; and in looking at their struggles he felt entirely different, knowing he would soon be out there himself.

●

"Why did we come here today, Jack?" Wendy asked. Her tone was thoughtful as they walked away from the Colosseum.

"Time with you, my love, is never a waste."

What could he say? That he had wanted to spend the day with her before she found out about his entry into the games? This was true. But they had hardly talked all afternoon and not at all into the evening. When he switched his attention to the fighters, he saw Wendy doing her emotion/thought drill as she watched the violence playing out below her. He let his own emotional responses to the contests below rise up and wash away as she was doing.

They walked toward the transport area, and the beautifully landscaped gardens of the Colosseum spread out before them. As daylight faded, Wendy discovered the bio-luminescent flowers subtly shifted color and intensity as they strolled past. The flowerbeds were so tastefully done: but it was not just that – there appeared to be live communication going on between the plants and the people in their vicinity. As Jack came close to the flowers, there was a supernova of color and beautiful patterns that spread through the entire garden.

Wendy looked curiously at Jack. It was obvious he was the epicenter of this explosion of color and design. Other departing fight fans gave them more space.

"Are you doing that, Jack?" whispered Wendy. It must be him, she thought, the patterns radiated from his position as they moved along the pathway. Soon all the people in their area of the path had stopped to watch the glorious show. They were looking from Jack to the torrent of pattern and color shifting in subtle waves and dramatic contrasts. When Jack and Wendy left the gardens, the crowd clapped. Jack, for the first time, came out of his closely held thoughts and became aware something was happening. He looked questioningly at Dee.

"Didn't you see the flowers?" He looked confused, so she explained what had happened.

"Oh," he smiled. "That's an art form in the Directory; it can be whatever you want it to be. Any emotion or image and the changing tide of life can be expressed there in color and motion. At home I have a garden such as you've never seen. I miss it. With the flowers here, I guess I did it unconsciously – I enjoy communicating with plants."

She had no idea such a thing was possible.

"Did you see the Jolos in the Colosseum today?" This jolted her because she hadn't noticed. Everyone had looked perfectly human – whatever that was. She shook her head.

"There were a few and there was something wrong about them."

"I thought you knew that already."

"Well, yes." He smiled. She did spot the obvious easily.

Jack continued, "There is a process of acceptance which everyone who wants to gain Jolo status – I mean, become immortal – has to go through. All the people I saw with Jolo bodies today could never have made it through the usual selection process." There was disgust in his voice.

"So?" she said. He looked at her, dumbfounded. Couldn't she see? No, she couldn't. Of course. He may have told her about some mainstream standards within the Directory but she had nowhere near enough data to be someone he could freely communicate about the Directory culture without constant explanations.

He noticed a change in his own thinking; he now thought with the mores and quirks of Directory culture automatically and not with those of Earth or of the U.S. or Salt Lake City. To him it was an outrageous violation of morality within the Directory, but to Wendy it was nothing.

"To explain will take some time. How about we do it when we get home?"

"Okay," she responded, not very interested. Why did he really take her to the games? What was the destruction in the Cousins' dining room all about? That was what she wanted to know, not some nebulous information about the Directory. Although, he'd mentioned his personal "home" for the first time, and that intrigued her. It must be somewhere off in the Directory, but now was not the time to ask him about that, either.

They returned to the shuttle bus area and boarded the vehicle when it arrived. The crowded streets of Los Angeles paraded by as she pressed her forehead to the glass. At LAX they got a quick bite to eat, then boarded the flight to Salt Lake City. Jack breathed a sigh of relief; they were in the air. Both sat quietly self-absorbed, saying nothing.

Putting off the evil day never worked, Jack knew. It usually made matters worse. He simply didn't want to upset her. He was going to do so. It couldn't be helped but it could be delayed. Why was he a coward when it came to things like this? He didn't know.

CHAPTER 28

AFTER DROPPING WENDY HOME, JACK CONTINUED a regimen of exercise to extend his endurance and optimize his reflexes. For the second time that day, he ran into the hills. He didn't get home till three a.m. They were waiting for him.

The light in the living room was on. Jack went to turn it off and was shocked to see his mother and Wendy.

"How do you like the new decorations, Jack?" Sharon waved her arm around the room. He hadn't really looked at the replacements for the stuff Norman wrecked in his rampage yesterday morning. A storm Jack had caused.

"Oh Jack, how could you?" Wendy this time. Her look was close to despair. "What did you think? I wouldn't find out? My mother showed me the news spots about this crazy teenager in Salt Lake City who's entered the Fight for Immortality!" Her voice had become shrill. "Tell me. Please tell me you didn't enter this thing we were watching today. I saw two men and a woman killed in agony today, Jack! And tomorrow it's going to be you?"

"Did you really enter the competition, Jack? Norman won't say a word." Sharon nearly choked on the words.

"I asked him not to, Mother." And with that the women had their answer. "I was going to tell you in the morning, before they publicly announced the names on the list." The Judge's warning had postponed the release to the press for about eight hours.

"That's a little late now," Sharon said. "And how do you know you're on the list?"

Jack just looked at her. "I know."

His pre-knowledge was another potential nail in his coffin. If the Directory discovered it, they would come calling. Jack would simply say he hadn't known, just hoped he would make the list.

They wouldn't find his computer bypass code embedded in his online application that had enabled him to eliminate one approved contestant, and insert his own name.

"I should've told you sooner. Timed it better. I'm sorry to I've upset you now. But no matter when I told you, you would've opposed it.

"This is my mission!

"The direction I must take was clear from the time I emerged from my dive in the lake.

"Do either of you ladies think we can wrestle control of Earth away from the people who are destroying the planet and its population without putting ourselves at risk?" His incredulity was intense.

"I guess not," his mom replied. "But it seems to me your 'mission' here on Earth and possibly other missions from the past on different planets have justified all sorts of 'smaller' problems.

"Do you see that, Jack?" Sharon pressed on. "Just like how you've handled telling, or not telling, Wendy and myself about important plans that will affect our lives. Norman knows – he got upset and he got over it. But we – Wendy and I, can wait?"

Sharon's words rocked him. It sent him plunging into the past to times and places where he'd treated the women around him shabbily. At times where he simply wanted a relationship with a woman for personal reasons or as dictated by the necessity of the mission itself; it always ended badly.

He was never there as himself, as Tac-U-One, but an agent in disguise. And when the mission was done, the relationship was over. Very often against the wishes of the women involved. He always ended the missions professionally but not the relationships.

His mother's comment forced him to see a pattern of action. Something he had ignored.

Jack realized he'd hidden this personal misconduct from himself.

Tac-U-One was always on an "important mission" and that justified unethical conduct toward women. And because of the different body (disposed of at the end of each mission), he could imagine it was done by someone else!

Wow. He'd retained awareness of his achievements, but not his misdeeds. Maybe that was why he continued to do them.

So his mother was right.

Exactly right.

It was the women he had personal relationships with he hurt the most. Sharon hadn't said it but she must have sensed he'd developed a pattern of poor treatment toward the women in his life.

She was very perceptive.

He had the same pattern of misconduct at home on Crown Planet – his short (between missions) marriages soon ended.

For regular Jolos, this could easily be hundreds of years. For him it was sometimes as short as six months.

He always left unhappy women behind. And so his attempt to avoid the emotional conflict with the two women in front of him resulted in only one thing: more unhappy women.

"You're right, Mother. I've used my missions to excuse and justify bad conduct; my actions have sometimes been unforgivable breaches of love and friendship. All sacrificed to the greater good – my mission. As I did again today with you and Wendy."

He was not, in that moment, able to come to terms with himself. It would take some time. The tightly bound package of emotional crimes against women that he'd carefully wrapped up and filed away under "necessity of the mission" was coming apart.

Sharon saw she'd created a powerful effect with Jack. She was glad: her son may have some painful soul-searching to do, but he'd be a better man for it. But Wendy's interests were different, and more deeply personal.

"Jack, in the last round of the Fight, one hundred and three people were killed. You know this as well as I do.

"They predict that more competitors will die in the coming round. The round you want to compete in!

"Jack, do you see how they alter those men? They are physical monsters after the Directory meds. They're nasty, crazy, vicious, mean as snakes and faster…." She shook her head in despair. "You made sure I saw them… How can you do this to us? To me? What'll I do when you're gone?" Wendy's voice had drifted off and the last question was for herself alone.

Jack knew there was nothing he could do or say to either Wendy or his mother that would make them think his death was anything less than a certainty. To them he was throwing his life away. And honestly, when he compared his physical stature to the modified men on the turf, there was no happy comparison. The only comfort he could give them was to contact the Directory immediately and ask for his name to be withdrawn before the list was made public. And that was something he wouldn't do.

"Jack, you're smart, smarter than the Directory people. I didn't believe that before, but look at what we've done over these last weeks and months. We've saved so many people." Wendy was pleading with him now. "You don't need to do this. You're smart, you can think of another way. You can, I know it."

"Wendy, if we don't win through soon, we'll all be dead or worse. These are extreme measures for extreme times."

"You shouldn't scare her like that, Jack," Sharon said, shocked by Jack's tactics in manipulating Wendy.

"Mother! I'm not. What I said is an understatement!" Jack said. "If a docile population did not serve the invaders' purpose, this planet would already be a slag pile."

Sharon Cousins looked at Jack and sat back in her chair. The situation was far worse than she imagined. Jack was not trying to exaggerate – he was trying to get her to face a harsh reality.

She accepted it.

Wendy could not. All she could see were the dead men and women who had lost their lives on the turf at the Colosseum in Los Angeles, killed by huge Earth men modified by Directory medical procedures, which turned them into killing machines. These automatons would crush Jack in seconds; and his opponent wouldn't have to be a highly skilled fighter. Any of them could end the person she wanted to spend her life with.

Wendy looked at Jack. She could see his growing excitement. Unbelievable. He was a willing participant in his own suicide. Then Wendy looked at Jack's mother. She'd just given in to his hopeless plans.

Norman, the previous morning, had facilitated this whole mess, by helping Jack become emancipated. She was amongst people who were organizing or allowing Jack to go to his death. What could she do to stop it? She couldn't tell her parents. She had no one to help her. There was no one who would talk some sense into his thick stupid head.

No one.

She was alone.

She couldn't stand to be inside the Cousins' house, near him, even a second longer.

She jumped up and ran to the front door where she turned.

"I have some good news. The girls were sentenced to sixty days in jail. We did all we could to get a longer sentence, but the Judge thought we were trying to prevent them from leaving the planet. He was right, of course."

"That is good news; this whole business will be over before then."

"That's the only good news, Jack. Everything else is a nightmare." She looked at him. "Who cares if you become immortal? I certainly don't. I just want you to live through next week."

She turned and grasped the doorknob but didn't open it. The night could not end this way; she had to say more. "I don't want you to die, Jack." She paused. "Please, please don't do this." Then she was gone.

●

Jack discreetly followed her home and saw her safely through the front door. He went home to compose a letter.

Jack wrote the letter, revised it, and revised it again. It was a declaration of love and a specific invitation to his future life. The old world of last week was dead and gone. The blinders were off, and the line in the sand had been crossed today. Would she cross with him? For Wendy the specter of real danger, the shadow of death, had crossed her path and she had flinched.

Evil men rely on the fear of danger and death to get their way without opposition. Death, in Jack's mind, was not now and had not been an ultimate state. Life beyond the boundary of a living body was real to him. By entering the Fight for Immortality he was, once again, inviting the test of that reality.

The threat of this loss was more than Wendy could easily face. Jack was not happy that he caused her to feel fear. But life often presents a bill where you chose one item over another. Wendy's peace of mind, on life's current list, was a lesser item.

Before dawn he walked over and dropped the envelope in the Whites' mailbox.

● ● ●

The Directory Investigator had slept in – again; the day before yesterday he'd found himself in the middle of the night behind the control console of his air car. As the air car settled into its assigned parking space in the Colosseum, he was jostled awake. The Investigator was shocked to discover where he was.

He questioned the autopilot and was informed, "After receiving no active instructions from the manual control pilot for a standard planetary hour, I assumed pilot incompetence, error or incapacity and set course for home."

Being told off by an air car computer before stumbling off to bed was a new low. He suspected the Bio-Comp's influence. Wherever there was a computer or a camera or a microphone, the Bio-Comp could also be watching, listening, recording. The Investigator shivered.

Next morning he was late arriving at the Bio-Comp's interview room. Late for the scheduled interview of the Salt Lake City Office clerk. But he was gone. What a waste of time. Delay, delay, delay.

"I held the clerk yesterday morning for two full hours," responded the Bio-Comp to the Investigator's resentful thought. Even though the Investigator was a telepath, he was always surprised when the Bio-Comp displayed that same ability. And he suspected that the being who was a composite of electronics, biology and Identity had telepathic ability that far outstripped his own.

"It was my day off," he said defensively. "And, anyway, you knew exactly where I was at all times; so don't tell me I inconvenienced either you or that clerk."

"Oh, so you think I waste my personal or computational time keeping track of you?" A metallic laugh sounded through the speakers. "Give me a few seconds."

"No, that's okay, you don't have to..."

"Oh, ho!" said the Bio-Comp.

On the Ether Vision cube, a series of very embarrassing moments from the previous evening began to play in fast sequence. There he was bent all the way over, pulling up his pants, a naked women screaming in the background. Funny, that's not the way he remembered it. And where the hell was the camera?

"Boltax will be so impressed with your unusual methods of forwarding this vital investigation."

There was nothing the Investigator could say. "Do you have a confirmed identity on the kid?"

"I've run a comparison of his image against every identification photo stored in all databases on the planet."

The Investigator was a little stunned at the immense task the Bio-Comp had completed.

"I've uploaded the file to your handheld computer; and in the printer bin against the wall is a binder containing the faces, names, addresses and other data of the closest matches. I have indexed these geographically with Salt Lake City at the geographic center of the search and by the closest visual, or facial recognition match. I tracked flights into and out of SLC and correlated these to the visual matches and tracked their ID on those flights. I also did the same for Denver, Los Angeles and other western United States hubs."

Bio-Comp had also tweaked data in many cases to give the Investigator "valid leads."

"Check the index for other possible leads. Each one contains a percentile rating for highest probability."

The Investigator was dumbfounded. He had thought the Bio-Comp was being obstructive. Clearly that wasn't true. It would take a long time to study the file.

"Thank you. I'll look at the file and then interview the clerk in Salt Lake City."

The Investigator's assistant needed to see this new file and the image of the kid too. Should have done it earlier. Those Earth girls could be a distraction....

● ● ●

The next morning, Amanda White found Jack's letter in their mailbox. She desperately wanted to open the sealed envelope.

When Wendy came home at three thirty a.m. upset with Jack Cousins, Amanda felt guilty relief. *That boy took my daughter to those brutal games.*

Last month her daughter had been hurt in some fashion by the trip to the lake. Because of Jack.

Then had come the reprieve, "Mom, I'm not going off planet." Wendy explained about deferment.

Since that time all pretense of parental control had vanished.

Last night there was a falling out between them.

A permanent one, Amanda hoped.

She looked at the letter. She wanted to read it or burn it.

That clever boy might win her daughter's affections back with words he had written.

Get rid of it.

If she withheld the note she knew she'd eventually be caught. That would cause an irreparable split between mother and daughter. That worry was the sole reason the letter was delivered.

She wanted Jack Cousins out of their lives. But her intervention would not assure a certain separation. With great reluctance, and without opening the letter, Amanda White called Wendy down from her room.

"Jack left this letter for you."

As her daughter silently took the envelope and walked from the room with the letter clutched in hand, Amanda remembered something. "Wendy." Her daughter gave no heed. "Wendy!"

"Yes, Mom?" she replied with barely suppressed anger.

"There was a man here yesterday, while you and Jack were in Los Angeles."

"Yes?" she said impatiently, wanting only to read the note from Jack.

"He was from the Directory and he wanted to ask you how you knew about deferment. He had a photograph of you and I had to identify you from it. He said you were the thirty-first person in the world to get a deferment. I said that you'd heard a rumor from your friends about the possibility of deferring your off-world contract and had then gone to the Directory office by the airport.

"I got the impression he didn't believe me. He still wanted to talk to you. He wanted to know where you were, but you'd just rushed out and didn't tell me where you were going. I called but you didn't answer."

With the artillery barrage of sound at the Colosseum, Wendy had missed the call.

"He said he'd be back and insisted that he must talk to you. What should I do if he comes back and you're not here?"

"Just tell him the truth, Mom. The complete truth." *And from here on, all I tell you are lies,* Wendy thought.

As she dashed up to her room, her blood ran cold. She was glad she kept her family out of the loop on her and Jack's activities over the last weeks – it had been vital. The Directory investigation was getting closer, right at her front door! If her mother had known her movements and true involvement with Jack, her mind would've been read yesterday and she and Jack would have been caught. Game over. She shivered. Jack was right: death had brushed by, today.

Wendy took the letter from the envelope.

Dear Dee,

Last night was difficult for both of us. My only excuse for not telling you as soon as I'd decided to enter the Fight for Immortality is that I wanted as much "undisturbed" time with you as I could have. There is truth in this – when you learned of my decision and I confirmed it, you refused to talk to me and left.

I could tell you that once I'm through this Fight, things will be fine and the trouble over – because I will control Earth. But that would be a lie. Earth is a small piece of a much larger puzzle. This is just the beginning. From here on and for a long time there will be danger to be faced and overcome. Again and again. This will include you if you're with me. Either of us may "die." This threat is interwoven into the nature of what I do. You can accept or reject this; but face it and decide you must.

The danger inherent in what we are doing is far more real to you now than it was at the lake and may have caused you to doubt the future.

When you look out into the night sky, you see stars. I imagine marauders causing havoc in my home and I intend to boot them out. It's my duty to do all I can for the people I'm pledged to protect. Regardless of any danger to me, I will do it.

I'm not reckless now and will not be. I'm trained for this life.

Long ago, I lost the woman I loved because I could not protect her. Our long marriage brought about her demise as others sought to control me through her. She disappeared. Shall I bare my soul to you? I love you with a love I thought lost to me forever. I won't make the same mistake with you that I did with her. I cannot protect you. But you can learn how to protect yourself and others. That is what I offer you, my love. Come with me and save the Directory from Bio-One and his flock of villains. Or come with me and enter my world, then go your own way if you wish. But come with me.

We may win or we may lose. But how can we lose, you and me, together?

Tactical Unit One

She flopped onto her bed, deeply moved. The tears began to flow.

CHAPTER 29

WENDY LOOKED AT THE FLORAL WALLS of her room and they no longer conveyed a sense of safety. But it wasn't the threat from the Directory investigator that concerned her most. In his letter, Jack asked her to step up; to keep thinking and acting sensibly when she was under pressure or threatened. And to let Jack take a calculated risk without falling apart.

But with the Fight for Immortality, all she could see were the monsters on the Turf hacking off arms, crushing skulls and men dying in agony. Comparing their immense physical stature to her slender Jack, he fell far short. No matter what he said about his past, there could be no chance.

She started thinking. Jack had selected his fate. He would have to handle it.

She was determined to not become an additional liability to him. She could help him by staying free; by preventing Directory investigators from reading her thoughts.

If the Directory investigator who talked to her mother yesterday knew she was the one they were looking for, he would have waited and taken her when she returned. Her mother said the investigator mentioned she was thirty-first person to get a deferment. That meant they were just going down a list, and that nothing they knew at this point made her stand out from anyone else. Being consistently unavailable may heighten suspicion but did not make her guilty.

The Directory people would be back and that could be disaster if she were here. They might take her, or read her mind, and that would lead directly to Jack.

"Are you all right, dear?" called her mother from the hall. Reaching the door to Wendy's room, she exclaimed, "Oh, sweetheart, are you okay?" Wendy's face was pale.

Her mother came over and hugged her. The clinging distracted her, she needed to think, to plan, and to act. She firmly removed herself from the embrace. Her mother was saying something but it didn't register beyond the drone of a voice. Then once again she was being drawn into a close embrace.

"Mother!" she said sharply.

"Yes, dear?"

"I'm okay, Mom. I just need some time alone to think." Mrs. White, rebuffed, turned abruptly away.

"I'm sorry, Mom. I'm okay, really." And with that she dismissed her from her mind.

She guessed there was time before the next visit by the Directory Investigator; she would use it well. What she needed was someone who didn't know either her or Jack. Someone who had no secrets to tell.

● ● ●

The Investigator finally made it out to interview the clerk at the Directory Induction Center in Salt Lake City. The file prepared by the Bio-Comp had been exhaustive and, even though it was well-indexed, ultimately it had been confusing. He was far less certain now that he was on the right track. But he was thankful the Bio-Comp had saved him from making a fool of himself with Boltax.

He sat down with the clerk on his afternoon break. He showed him the kid's face. "Remember seeing this native a few days ago? I looked at the digital record and he walked up to the window and spoke to you."

The clerk looked at Jack's face and frowned. "He seems sorta familiar."

"He spoke to you for a few minutes and walked away. No one else was at the window." The clerk shook his head.

The Investigator asked a few more questions and established that the clerk's memory before this time and about an hour later was intact.

"Just think about that time." The Investigator scanned his mind. It was pea soup. Nothing was clear or sequential. He didn't have the skill to tell if this state had been induced by another telepath, but it was very suspicious.

How could this native be a high-functioning telepath? The Investigator's own skill allowed him to read, not project. Projection was a whole different level of ability.

Assuming the clerk's blankness was deliberately induced, what was the kid trying to hide? His own presence? He'd have to think it through. But a native, able to project thoughts? No. There could be a Jolo agent here somewhere, but it wasn't the kid.

● ● ●

Jack hadn't seen or heard from Wendy when the media uproar broke all about him. The list of fourth-round gladiators was released and this confirmed the courthouse rumor: seventeen-year-old Jack Cousins would fight for immortality.

He became the eye of a perfect media storm.

Local, and soon after, national media were camped out on his street. It hampered his movements. He definitely did not want to draw Wendy into the circus, especially when a connection to him could prove harmful when he made his move on the Directory.

So he stayed away from her house; when he phoned she was never there. Her personal comm device went straight to voice mail.

In Salt Lake City, a large group of concerned citizenry was determined to prevent him from competing. They organized quickly and formed a picket line with placards, walking back and forth in front of the Cousins' house and chanting catchy slogans. They gave interviews to the media folk and, as the story began to explode, so did the number of people who came to join the righteous crowd. Food vendors showed up and did brisk business.

The neighbors complained to the police, who sent tow trucks and gave the "visitors" an hour to move their cars from the immediate area.

So many people wanted to save Jack from himself; and they were vicious in the way they portrayed his aunt and uncle.

Even his biological parents were drawn into the controversy, condemning Norman and Sharon Cousins to the press as being negligent and incapable of the responsibility necessary to raise a child.

Jack Cousins was portrayed as a child of seventeen, incapable of both moral and legal participation in the games.

From a podium on the street in front of the Cousins' home, an activist, flanked by Jack's biological parents, made a speech that was being broadcast around the world.

"We have, in this modest home behind us, a child at risk," she said. "In our modern culture, the dangers of childhood include many horrific pitfalls. And as we've learned through hard years of experience, some of our children seek out the most dangerous forms of entertainment. We, as parents and as a society, lose control – and sometimes, despite intervention on many levels and the hard work of dedicated people, we lose them. Some children disappear into the darkness or are taken from us by predatory monsters.

"But here, with this child, Jack Cousins, we have a unique case. An adolescent on a quiet night, using his computer, enters and is accepted as a gladiator in the sadistic games in Los Angeles. Who knows if it was a prank at first? Then, Jack convinces his parents and a local judge to emancipate him, give him the title of 'adult' which his years have not earned.

"We of this fine city, of this great state, of the whole United States of America, of the entire world community of souls, have a responsibility – no, a duty – to call into question the familial and legal processes that bring this boy to the brink of death through ritualized slaughter.

"Are we not all in jeopardy if we cannot protect our children and save them from themselves when circumstances require?"

Jack couldn't stand it anymore. The whole media circus was generally good; hiding in plain sight was excellent camouflage when everyone was looking for something hidden. But this woman was dragging his real parents through the mud, flanked by his pseudo-parents, who couldn't care less.

He got up from his chair and walked purposefully toward the front door.

"Jack, don't!" Norman and Sharon said in unison. He gave them a look and continued ahead. He walked down the short path and out through the white wooden gate.

He was noticed almost immediately, and all the cameras turned away from the woman on the podium.

A loud roar came from the crowd when they caught sight of Jack.

Their emotions were a mass of confusion. They wanted to protect him. They thought his adoptive parents were part of a criminal conspiracy. They thought Judge Bonner was corrupt. And some thought he had entered the Fight for Immortality for five minutes of fame and was now in over his head. Some thought he was crazy and needed to be protected from himself. No one considered he might have a legitimate motive.

Jack had no way to properly convince the neighbors and other townspeople that he wasn't crazy, seeking fame or manipulated by corrupt adults. Jack knew that beyond the frenzy they simply had his best interests at heart. In fact, he was moved by their concern for him.

They were good people.

The activist at her podium was really annoyed by the interruption and didn't catch what was causing it. Then, she looked around.

Jack stepped briskly up the two steps and took the microphone from the woman's slack hand and ignored his "parents."

He confronted the scene.

"Hello, my name is Jack Cousins." He looked from face to face in the crowd and at the many cameras. "This woman is here to promote herself and a political agenda and has no personal interest in my welfare. She wants to be the 'heroic' figure that prevents me from being a contestant in the Fight for Immortality for the purposes of personal advancement.

"She is intelligent, articulate, persuasive, and even pretty. She is also entirely wrong." He let that sink in.

"I put in an application to enter the games as soon as I heard of them. I've trained for years as a martial artist and am highly skilled in medieval weaponry.

"You defame my legal guardians and adoptive parents, Norman and Sharon Cousins, and Judge Bonner – fine people all. The truth is, I have a legal right to fight, and a skill level to make me highly competitive. Plus the lure of an irresistible reward, for which I thank the Directory officials.

"I could tell you to mind your own business." He smiled brilliantly. "But I recognize that to some degree I've become your business. I accept that. But your effort to 'save me from myself' is misplaced." Once again he paused and surveyed the crowd.

"Can I ask the people to my right to move back? Please move back. I need some room there."

As he waited for the mass of people to back away, he turned to the activist and whispered in her ear, paused, then whispered again. This continued for more than a minute. The activist never said a word, but the way her eyes darted around, one could tell she was not happy with the quiet words from the boy whose life she professed great desire to save.

Finally, a patch of ground was clear.

"I'll give you a short exhibition." He jumped to the grass and did a short martial arts sequence (something he'd seen Bruce Lee do in one of his films) and added some flair of his own. The cameras and crowd gorged it all down.

He jumped back onto the podium and turned to the activist. "Do you have anything else to add, Madame?"

She stayed mute and shook her head.

"Well, that's it, then. Thank you all for coming. I understand your concern for my welfare and sincerely appreciate it. But go home; I'm not in need of saving. Good afternoon." It was clear to those present that this young man had some experience with a command voice and crowd control.

With that, Jack looked pointedly at his biological parents. "I don't want to hear any more from you, is that clear?"

"Yes, sir," they mumbled, and had the good manners to look ashamed.

Jack turned and saw a compact group of large clean cut men moving decisively forward through the milling crowd. He turned away and stepped off the makeshift stage.

Something caught his attention; he spun around and took a slightly defensive stance. Jack said sharply, "Gentlemen, don't come any closer."

The crowd, which had been dispersing, stopped and turned, looking from Jack to the large men.

Jack stepped closer so not everyone would hear. "You guys are planning to grab me and hustle me into that van over there," He pointed to a plain white van at the curb thirty yards up the street. Someone was behind the wheel. The leader looked stricken.

Jack stepped close to point man. "Thank you for caring enough about me to come here today. But truly, I don't need to be rescued from anyone or anything." Jack could see the man was confused by having his plans exposed, but still determined. "Come on I'll prove it to you." Jack slapped him on the chest. The man's eyes went wide. He had difficulty breathing.

Jack waved, "Go home." And returned inside the house.

●

"What did you say to that horrible woman, Jack, to shut her up?" Norman and Sharon looked at him curiously.

Jack smiled broadly. "What do you think I said?"

"Come on, Jack," Norman said.

"No really, what do you think would shut such a woman up? We won't hear from her again, you know."

So they speculated for a few minutes, and with each suggestion he shook his head.

"I gave her the truth."

"What truth?" Sharon asked.

"Her own truth. You see, for a minute or two, I whispered her own thoughts into her ear – as she was thinking them. She was one nasty piece of work, that woman. I gave it to her till I was completely certain she knew that I knew."

"How did you know she knew?"

Jack laughed and quoted: "'He's reading my mind, no one can – yes, he is. No, no, no. I can't hide my thoughts. He could expose me completely.'" He smiled. "The last part went something like that. Along with a couple of, 'I wonder if he knows about…? Yes, he does!' The crimes she felt worst about kept popping into her head. Some pretty juicy stuff. But I said if she left me alone, I wouldn't tell."

"So what was it, that juicy stuff? I might need to know what if she resurfaces."

"Norman. None of us will survive well until we are worthy of trust. Expediency does not change that: I gave her my word."

Norman felt a little unclean. "You're right. Sorry, Jack."

"Why did you – and more importantly, how did you – do the martial arts display on the grass, Jack?" Sharon asked, to help cover Norman's discomfort.

"I did it for Wendy, to show her something that'll give her hope. That short routine is going to be replayed again and again. She's sure to see it."

"But how could you do it Jack, you've never trained to fight a day in your life!"

"Mom, I explained that when I got back from the lake. I recovered some abilities when my memory returned. Self-defense and attack is one of my skill sets. And even though this body is not in combat condition or built for fighting, I can still make it do things."

Sharon looked skeptical. "Mom, did you see those big guys out there who came up to me?" Sharon nodded. "They came to grab me and take me to a 'secret location' to protect me from myself and all you 'nasty' people." Jack laughed.

Sharon looked surprised.

"Yeah, I know, it didn't look like that from here. I gave that guy's chest a slap that he'll still feel next week. That's why he didn't try to take me. My hand still smarts!" And Jack laughed again.

Sharon wondered gloomily if Jack was so deluded that he actually believed he would live through the first round of the Fight for Immortality? She shook her head. *It's so sad, so heartbreaking to see him boyishly excited about slapping someone on the chest – as if that shows me he has a chance…* Sharon couldn't complete the thought. She broke into uncontrollable sobbing in front of him and hurried to the kitchen, where she fell apart.

There was nothing she could do to prevent this train wreck. *With all Jack and Wendy have done to block DE, anything I do to draw more attention to them could cause their death.* So even the slightest of chances to win the gladiator games was now her only hope. But it was hope where hope was gone. The spill of her silent tears was preparing the ground for his burial.

The press and many town's people cleared out that day, but others sprung up to take the activist's mantle and run with it.

Jack's continued presence, with Norman Cousins as his evil shepherd and Sharon Cousins as the uncaring mother, incited many well-intentioned people to extremes of emotion.

No matter his words or demonstration of skill, the idea of a seventeen-year-old competing with brutal gladiators gave them a cause, a crusade; something to stop. It was like pointing out a sinner to a group of activist angels on a tour of Hell – they had to try.

But then, in this world, it was not necessary to be effective in achieving one's objective; one merely had to stake out the moral high ground and be very noisy. The whole point was to be noticed so one's career advanced. There were true believers and those who cynically used them.

Jack and Norman, trapped at home, decided to go to LA.

Sharon Cousins stepped out the front door where she was confronted by a mob of reporters and behind them, knots of angry people who shouted epithets at her and waved placards. They could no longer block cars on the street, but their presence was not illegal.

She raised her hand to try and quiet them, finally the noise died down. "Please, please. Let me speak. I have something to tell you." Not satisfied, she shouted angrily, "Be quiet, all of you!" After a few defiant catcalls, there was silence.

"My husband and son left last night for a week of training and other preparation to an undisclosed location in Colorado."

The press was furious. How had they escaped? They'd been staked out here twenty-four hours a day.

Some tried to ask more questions, but they were ignored. Sharon Cousins went inside.

Jack and Norman made a real escape later that day, when all but a few die-hard reporters and do-gooders were hanging around, on the off chance that Jack still might be there.

Before leaving, Jack tried to reassure his mother about the future. He hugged her for a long time.

She felt her son in her arms and in a moment of dread became certain she would never see him again. The more she tried to remain upbeat, the sadder she became, and her tears soaked his shirt.

● ● ●

Admiral Augustus McMillan looked at the late news from his easy chair in his home in Arlington, Virginia. He'd received the high school yearbook he'd been waiting for earlier in the day. It took him about ten minutes of browsing till he saw the face he was looking for. The kid played baseball, pretty well too, it seemed. Now he had a name to put to the face: Jack Cousins.

And here, on the news, was the same kid. He was going to fight in the Colosseum with the gladiators. There was something going on here, something deeper than he suspected. This boy, in a mild conversation in a Las Vegas coffee shop, had put him on the right track about the aliens. He thought about that for a few minutes.

The only conclusion he could reasonably draw was that this kid had been conducting surveillance on those conducting surveillance on the aliens. And the kid had picked him specifically to talk to. When he thought about it, that was a pretty sophisticated bit of business. There had been other crews working on the same problem and looking for anything that didn't fit in the whole situation. But the kid had remained well under the radar.

This left some bizarre questions. How did the kid know what to direct my attention to? Obviously he had knowledge about the aliens we didn't possess. Did he discover this knowledge through his own investigation? Or was he an alien himself?

However strange it might seem, McMillan was inclined to go with the second assessment. He had his intel guys working the late shift at the Pentagon look up his records. Soon his men got back to him – the kid didn't exist. No birth certificate, no driver's license, nothing. Very strange.

And that led to other conclusions. If he was an alien, then he was from a different faction than the main Directory group. Also, the spook Perrywhite had grasped this possibility immediately and probably wanted to use the kid as a trading chip with the Directory Chief.

No way was McMillan going to let that happen. But then, what was he to do with the information? Contact the kid? For all he knew, that may expose him. McMillan had no way of knowing what was happening or why – but he did know that this kid was moving forward with specific plans. And he also knew he wanted to help, if he could. He liked this kid, and felt bad about putting a CIA bull's-eye on his back.

● ● ●

Perrywhite had figured from the look on the face of McMillan's assistant that he was being screwed. They'd taken his bribe money and were laughing at him. For weeks now both McMillan and his assistant had been under surveillance by the CIA. Both residences had been thoroughly gone over and bugged. Nothing.

But tonight there was an extra package delivered to the Admirals' home, and so his men had called him. Sitting in the remote surveillance command vehicle, they waited for the lights to go out. Finally they did. Perrywhite, using supreme control, did not order the entry for an additional hour and a half. Then he gave the go ahead. Because his men were familiar with the entire house, it took them only minutes to get what they needed. McMillan hadn't even put the items in his safe. His team was in and out clean in a half hour.

Perrywhite rushed the digital images his agents had taken directly to Langley and studied them late into the night. Finally, he began laughing. That old squid thought he could outsmart a trained CIA operative?

He'd even circled the kid's face.

Jack Cousins.

He laughed again. He was on his way; there was no telling how high he would climb in the new power structure here on good old Earth.

＊ ＊ ＊

Jack and Norman Cousins got off the shuttle and casually walked toward the Colosseum, which had a knot of reporters stationed outside the entrance to interview the new batch of one thousand gladiators as they arrived. Over the last few days, the fighters had trickled in, and today many more were scheduled to appear. Jack and Norman were driven to the City of Angels by a neighbor who was happy to be rid of them.

Little did the print reporters on the gladiator beat at the Colosseum expect to see the single hottest news generator, Jack Cousins.

As Jack and Norman approached the majestic Colosseum entrance, the press went wild. They pushed and shoved each other for prime position. This could be the interview that made their career.

Jack said, "Calm down, guys. If you want to fight, enter the contest as I have." He laughed out loud. When the commotion settled, he continued, "I want to thank the members of the press for the interest you've shown in my fight career." This set off more laughter.

"I sincerely appreciate all the efforts that were made by concerned groups of individuals in Salt Lake City to shelter me from what they perceived to be a tragedy in the making. Please calm down. I never would have entered the Fight for Immortality if I didn't expect to win."

"You gotta be kidding!"

"How realistic is that, Jack? You're just a high school kid, for crying out loud!"

Jack shrugged.

"They're saying this round of gladiators are the deadliest group yet. A full 90% of the entrants have maxed out on Directory meds. This isn't puny wrestlers on steroids – these men are killing machines."

"These are tough guys. I get it." Jack admitted.

One reporter kept shaking his head. "Look, you seem like a decent kid. There are some things you don't know. Most of the fighters in this round have had their modifications completed for more than six weeks. That's a big deal. They know how to handle the extra power. The weakest of them can bench over six hundred pounds. They've been in weapons training longer than any previous group."

"I'm glad there'll be decent competition. I wouldn't want you guys to get bored."

Some of the reporters laughed, others couldn't believe this kid.

"Kid, you're a walking dead man!"

"Hey, no need to…"

"Hell, yes there is! If that kid walks through the gladiator entrance – that door right there – he's doomed. He will die! Someone has to say it."

"Hey kid, *Jack*, don't do it!"

"Are you looking for a book deal, and hoping the Directory will break their rule and let you back out at the last moment?"

The crowd of reporters looked anxiously at Jack. Maybe that was it.

"Are you going to drop out and sell the book rights for millions?"

Other reporters were shouting, "Who is your publisher?" Finally the tumult died down to where Jack could be heard.

"No, I don't intend to write anything," Jack smiled. "The only thing I have to say will be said out there on the Turf, and you guys will be doing the writing."

This kid was sounding like a wrestler, just not so over the top.

There was scuffling in the back. A camera crew was pushing through the print journalists, bloggers and such. One guy was shouting, "We're going live. Let us through here, damn it."

It was WWDN, the World Wide Digital Network.

"Count me down," instructed the guy with the mike.

"Four, three, two, one. You're live."

"Well, sports fans, it's Damon Light here, live with Jack Cousins," this managed to sound both breathy and dramatic, "outside the New Colosseum, where a drama of epic and some say pediatric proportions will be acted out in the coming weeks. It will center on this good-looking high school student.

"The world has been captivated and held moral hostage by the story of a young boy from Salt Lake City, Utah. A boy who, his teachers and schoolmates insist, has never been in a fight in his life. Wasn't on the wrestling team and whose only claim to athletic fame was leading the Granite High Farmers baseball team to a few unlikely wins.

"We've all been wondering, Jack, how does this juvenile résumé qualify you for the most brutal competition the world has ever seen?" He jabbed his microphone in Jack's face.

"Well, Mr. Light, I know it seems a bit strange. A man my age, entering the Fight for Immortality, must worry a lot of people. But honestly, I had no idea that anyone but my family would be concerned. Still, I'm confident that I can win."

"Jack, be realistic. Everyone we've spoken to says that you're a nice kid, never been in trouble with the law, had good grades at school. There's a bright, bright future out there for you. What could possibly motivate you to, well, to throw your whole life away?" To everyone's surprise, Damon Light looked genuinely distressed.

"Look, Mr. Light…" Jack started to protest.

Light interrupted. "Okay, Jack, maybe that's a bit melodramatic," he uncharacteristically gave ground. "But it certainly is no stretch of the imagination that your life, as of this very moment, is at serious risk. This is a brutal, sadistic blood-letting that you're about to take part in. Sports experts have given your chances of getting past the first round at ten thousand to one; and winning, at ten million to one. What could be so important to you that you're willing to risk almost certain death?" The mike was shoved at him.

"All I can say is," Jack looked full in the camera, "if the odds are that high, don't miss a chance to win a ton of money." He smiled brightly and laughed. "Bet on me." He turned and walked into the facility.

"Well, sports fans," said Damon Light, looking astonished. "There you have it, the very first sports interview with that remarkable young man. He's very confident. My assessment is that his confidence is firmly rooted in self-delusion and that he will die, horribly traumatized by some sadomasochist looking for a good time. He is not the quivering lump of fear that those of us who have common sense had expected.

I, for one, do not want to see him here, because within this arena he is sure to meet an untimely end.

"The drama that will be enacted here in the coming days is on its face and in all its parts, outrageous and lowers the 'community of Earth' into a cesspool of moral turpitude that has no comparison in modern times. The stench of which will taint us and brand us with the well-earned epithet: 'hopeless.' For how could we be anything else for allowing this to happen?

"With that being said, I've only one further comment to make in the face of the inevitable: good luck, Jack Cousins. You are going to need it!

"Damon Light, reporting live from the Colosseum. Back to you, Dan."

● ● ●

"I hope you don't mind sharing your room for a few weeks?" Amanda White asked her daughter.

"Share my room? With who, Mom?" Wendy had spent very little time at home over the last few days. She was very vague when her mother asked where she'd been. The tension between them was mounting.

"Your cousin Penny is going to be here in a few days."

"Why is she coming here? I thought there was some family thing between you, Dad and her parents. Whenever I asked about the whole sordid mess you wouldn't tell me anything."

"That's true, basically. But when we thought you were going to leave us, we worked out our family differences and invited Penny to spend some time with us." Wendy looked at her mother strangely. "I know she's not you. But I wanted someone to be here with me and it seems Penny wanted to come. With all the turmoil over the last few weeks, I forgot she was coming. She called yesterday."

Dale White arrived home from work to see his wife and daughter sitting on opposite ends of the sofa in what looked like an uneasy truce.

"Well, the two loves of my life, how's your day been?" He was greeted by strained smiles, but neither woman said anything. The TV was on and some mindless show was droning out muted sound.

Dale sat in his favorite chair and reclined, the tension between mother and daughter was thick. The clock gave him an excuse to talk.

"I'd like to watch the news if that's all right with you ladies?" When neither one answered, he picked up the obsolete remote which he steadfastly refused to trade in and shuffled to his favorite news station.

Jack's interview with Damon Light topped the news.

At first Wendy was happy to see his face.

The interview stunned her. Everyone knew he was going to die – but all they would do was talk.

Then various sound bites were selected and analyzed by a "panel of experts" moderated by the host. No one believed Jack had a chance in the games. But because Jack was so direct and coherent, it was difficult to assert he was not in control of his faculties. The panel argued back and forth. Some were shouting, completely incensed. Jack's actions had ignited outrage. Sharon and Norman, along with Judge Bonner, were again targets of intense, emotional criticism.

The cameras had caught Jack's whispered conversation with the activist outside his home. The woman hadn't said a word since and had refused all interviews. This was covered by the panel and the speculation about what had been said in that conversation was wide-ranging and sometimes far-fetched.

Dale White turned the TV off. "I assume Jack's decision hasn't caused you to end your relationship with him?"

"That's true Dad, but right now we're not talking. I mean I haven't taken his calls for a few days and he stopped calling."

"From that, I assume you don't agree with what he's doing? Is it true you fought about it?"

"At first, I was extremely upset. Then, later – well, it's not exactly that I agree with him. But I know why he has to do it. And he may be right – that he needs to. But I don't like it at all."

"That's a different story than the one you told me." Amanda White huffed.

"Mom, Daddy's here to listen and you just want to attack Jack every chance you get. You want us to break up, so you force me to defend him."

"You're right, I suppose. But I always knew something like this would happen."

Gently chiding his wife, Dale said, "What, you knew aliens would take over Earth and offer training that would entice our adventurous daughter to leave us, but she would be given a reprieve at the last moment and that her boyfriend would contrive to fight for immortality in gladiator games?"

"That was great, Dad." Wendy looked gratefully at him.

"No, of course not. I just knew Wendy's relationship with Jack would cause her and us grief."

"Oh, Mom, what has he ever done to you but be polite? He listened to you for countless hours when you tried to convert him to your religion."

"But he never did convert, did he?"

"So, you're upset he has a mind of his own?"

"No, because he's taken you from us, from the church."

"Well, Mother. It just so happens, I have a mind of my own too. And if you think that I'm so much under Jack's spell, then why did I sign up to go off planet against his advice? Why did I disagree with him doing this stupid gladiator thing?" Wendy had fudged a little, but the truth was Jack's influence upon her had been to make her more independent; not more suggestible as her mother thought. "These are major and basic disagreements with him.

"What you don't like and can't seem to forgive him for is that he helped to free me. To make me more self-reliant, more able to make up my own mind. You want me to be a clone of you. Well, if the news hasn't arrived yet, I'm not your clone; I don't want your life.

"If you love me at all, you need to love me for who I am and not hate me for not being you, or not living out your goals for me." There was shocked silence in the room for several minutes.

Dale wanted to intercede. But he was proud of his daughter. She'd struck so close to his wife's real motives that Amanda had been completely stopped in her tracks. How she emerged from this conversation would determine if she would ever have a real relationship with their daughter. He waited to see if his wife had any guts.

Wendy stood.

"Don't go, Wendy," Amanda White choked, "please, stay."

Wendy, hearing the tone of her mother's voice, waited.

"There was a time when I was young, that I, too, rebelled. But the difference between you and I, is that you've held true to yourself and I caved under the pressure. So the only thing you missed in your assessment of me was my jealousy that you've done what I failed to do."

"Oh, Mom." The two women, mother and daughter, came together for the first time in their adult lives.

Later, Dale asked his daughter, "Do you have any idea why Jack is doing such a disturbing thing?"

"It's his job, Daddy."

Now that was a conversation with legs, but she wouldn't elaborate and he could tell she regretted having told him even that much. She looked stricken at her words and went up to her room.

That night, she stripped all photos of herself and Jack from her room and the entire house. That done, she left the house with her digital camera. Other photos were needed to replace those she disposed of.

• • •

Sharon Cousins was left home alone, and she didn't like it at all. Jack could only have one "trainer" with him and Norman fit the bill.

The media blitz continued to escalate. In an environment where almost anything – including public execution on the Turf – was acceptable, a "child" entrant was the new angle and was getting extreme coverage. It was a phenomenon that fueled unheard-of ratings. Even being characterized as a parental monster by the news stations couldn't stop her from watching.

Lurid headlines ran in papers across the country and around the world. Looking at the headlines on her computer, she was appalled by the variety. "Child led to Slaughter." "Execution Legalized for Minor." "Child Scheduled to Die." "Moral Conscience of World at Stake." That he had a fresh, young face and was observably a decent kid, full of hope, drove the press and public even wilder.

The media was frustrated he wasn't from a broken home where drug addiction or cancer or alcoholism or poverty or abuse or a life of crime had blighted his upbringing and ultimately caused the decision to throw his life away.

Worse, Jack was engaging. It placed him at the center of the furor that surrounded the games. Sharon was shocked to see women on daytime TV weep openly for her son, declaring undying love and promising a life of ease if only he would withdraw from the Fight for Immortality and marry them.

He was offered the "Peace Prize" if he would restore peace to the world by withdrawing from the contest.

Colleges from over the world offered all-expenses-paid scholarships. The only reason a boy with such promise would throw his life away must be that he had no other opportunity. Some institutions granted him honorary degrees and guaranteed employment for life. The bizarre became stratospheric.

Reporters lapped it up and sent those compelling stories around the world, making fathers blanch, mothers weep, and leaving his high school peers confused.

The "child" theme was the perfect way to attack the games. Papers claimed Jack was thirteen and when Sharon saw the photos, she hunted through Jack's closet and dug up his yearbooks. The picture they used was from the ninth grade.

It was tabloid sensationalism at its best, a true media orgy. Sharon had to admit that if this were not her boy, with his special circumstances, she would be very disturbed for many of the same reasons the protesters were. It was a unique situation and she could offer no explanation.

Sharon saw an interview with Judge Bonner about Jack's emancipation where he was heavily criticized. When it was discovered that he knew why emancipation was being sought, he was dragged through the tabloids and made a pariah. "Judge Slays Child." "Boy to Die By Order of Judge." "Judge, Jury and Executioner," etc. There were protesters and picketers outside his home and outside his courtroom.

Jack had said how much he liked the man. But Sharon was sure that he would never have emancipated Jack if he'd known what would befall him.

But as the interview continued, she changed her mind. "You press monkeys claim the young man said he was confident of winning the games, is that right?"

"Yes, Judge, he did."

"Well, then. If he said it, I believe he will do it." Bonner turned his large head directly toward the camera and said, "My money is on you, Jack. Go get 'em, kid." The Judge refused to say any more and had the marshals clear the press "monkeys" from his courtroom.

The press got hold of the story about the mahogany railing, but the Judge already had it removed. He'd placed it on his mantle, discarding the old trophies. To their fury, he refused the press any access to his home. He had replaced the rail at his own expense, so nothing could be done.

Jack broke his training routine to come out of the Colosseum complex (a media-free sanctuary) and confront the press. He didn't want to talk to the journalists – they were doing fine creating all the material they needed without any input from him. But Judge Bonner had really helped him and he was not about to let the press continue mischaracterizing what he did, without coming to his defense.

Sharon was watching at home when a station break brought his interview live. She saw her son mount the press station outside the Colosseum. The reporters began firing questions at him. But he was not there to be badgered by these people. He kept his head bowed until they finally got the idea and became quiet.

"I am here to make a statement on behalf of a decent man. A man whose reputation you seem determined to destroy.

"Judge Bonner is a very good man, an able jurist, and a man willing to judge the facts before him without regard to outside influences. And that makes him a man of great courage, also.

"He did not want to allow my emancipation, especially when he knew I wanted to compete in the games. You've all heard the story of the banister that the Judge now owns. I did that to convince him that he was not sending me to my death. In fact, I defy anyone to smash a similar length of wood in the same way.

"When Judge Bonner looked at the banister, he became convinced I was a serious contender. He is not a man to arbitrarily impose his will without proper cause or simply to protect himself from adverse public opinion. Are you so dense as to imagine he didn't foresee exactly what is happening now – that a pack of hyenas like yourselves would try to tear him apart for his decision? He knew this would happen and emancipated me on principle.

"Judge Bonner, I am in your debt. You may call in that obligation any time you care to.

"That's all." And Jack was gone.

● ● ●

Perrywhite had taken the earliest flight possible and arrived in LA before noon. He'd been excited as he approached the huge Directory complex.

"Mommy, mommy, look at that man! He's turning all the flowers black!" The CIA man scowled at the little kid but kept walking.

Perrywhite took a few seconds to orient himself, then followed the signs to the business entrance. It was quite a way from the grand public arches. There were signs: By Appointment Only, Trespassing Forbidden and others even more threatening. At last there was a private alcove.

The entryway had an armed guard.

He drew forth official CIA identification and presented it with a flourish. "I need to see the Directory Chief."

The guard glanced scornfully at the ID. "Get the hell out of here."

"This is official business. As you can see I'm with the CIA."

"I've seen ten IDs better than that one just this morning. Now get the hell away from my post."

"Look buster, I represent the full weight of the US intelligence community. I demand to see the Directory Chief!"

"I don't care if you're Marty my favorite Martian. I represent the Directory of Stars and Planets and your feet are on interstellar property. So if you don't leave immediately I'll pull my ray gun and fry you."

"There are substantial sums of money I can disburse to those who provide direct aid to the US government."

"Do you see that pile of ash?" the guard asked. "And that broom over there?"

Perrywhite nodded.

"Good. I zapped a guy – he was real persistent – just like you. Had to sweep him out of the way. Can't have *invited guests* stepping in muck like that can we?"

Seeing the fright on the idiot's face the guard was hard pressed not to laugh out loud. Every time a bunch of leaves blew into his little courtyard he zapped them and swept them up.

Scared and deflated, Perrywhite returned home on the overnight flight.

The Directory were very... direct. Perrywhite wished he could whack a few people as casually as that Directory guard admitted doing. That was his type of organization.

Early the following morning, he put a call through to the DC Directory offices and got a better reception. The DC Directory clerk called the Directory Investigator who worked out of the Colosseum complex. The Investigator refused to talk to Perrywhite, but said he would send his assistant as soon as possible.

If Perrywhite played his cards right, he would be able to trade his information for a position of power inside the Directory hierarchy itself. And life would be good again. Perrywhite's spirits soared.

● ● ●

Jack had mapped out his own workout regimen and was hard at work. With nothing better to do Norman followed the media outpouring. He wanted to brief Jack if he thought a response was necessary, or if anything broke that could threaten their mission, which was now in the critical final stage.

There was a major split in the way Jack's story was reported after his statement to the press. Some of the media believed the story about what he'd done to the wooden hand rail in the courtroom and dubbed him the "Banister Kid."

The new thousand Gladiators turned against Jack because virtually all the attention was focused on him. If they did get face time, they were asked about Jack. "How much time does he spend in the gym?" "What's his favorite cafeteria food?" "When does he end his day?" It was Jack this and Jack that. They wanted to talk about themselves, but no one cared.

They hated it, and hated Jack. Their egos were not able to withstand all the attention going to someone so obviously inferior, while their superior selves were ignored.

● ● ●

Norman pasted together the press coverage and he and Jack watched it the night before opening day of the Fight for Immortality.

"Can you believe these media people, Norman? They've no concern about the lives they may destroy in their frenzy to say the most outrageous things."

"In my lifetime it's gotten worse," Norman mused. "The media used to investigate and uncover things. Now they simply collect 'he said,' 'she said' statements and stir up trouble. Their main activity is influence peddling, special interests, sensationalism, not fact."

Jack looked serious. "If I'm not here to protect Bonner, do whatever you can to help that man."

"What do you mean 'if I'm not here,' Jack?"

"Norman, if I win through, I'll still be leaving Earth. Look after Bonner if you can, please? He is pivotal in all this; he ignored the ruin of his career when he emancipated me."

"I don't know what I can do for him, but yes, I'll do what I can."

"You might be surprised, Norman. From your own business experience you know that strong, ethical people are essential to the success of any group."

Why Jack would say this to him now, Norman had no idea.

● ● ●

Wednesday morning came too quickly for Wendy, who was reluctant to greet the day. Jack's name was on the roster for the first day's competition, and today was the day. No fighting order was ever announced, so if you wanted to see your guy, you were forced to watch and wait, sometimes all day.

Amanda White watched her frightened daughter go into the TV room and promised herself to not go in there unless Wendy called.

The early contests went swiftly, and as the violence escalated, Wendy went into a daze. Those who were not suited for combat walked out onto the Turf and were filled with fear. The Directory policy of no quitters allowed after the public announcement of the combatant's names was clearly seen here. Those who no longer wanted to participate allowed themselves to be defeated. By the afternoon those pikers were killed or eliminated. In each death, she saw its potential for Jack. The men were so huge, so mean. Some of the contests were thrilling and she couldn't help being drawn into the drama of it, others were simply executions.

Through it all her eyes were glued to the screen, her hands gripped her thighs.

Wendy was hoping to see Jack, and dreading seeing him, too. One gladiator walked out onto the turf and Wendy thought it was a long camera shot. But as the image came closer it was clear that the guy was short. She checked his stats and yes, he was only six feet three inches. His opponent clomped out onto the turf. He was seven feet two inches and had an extraordinarily long reach. The fighters were clearly mismatched. The fight began and the action was intense. As it passed the fifteen minute mark, Wendy could tell the small fighter was extraordinarily skilled and able to fend off the larger man's barrage of attacks. Blood was splashing the turf from numerous cuts each fighter inflicted upon the other. But the skill of the smaller man could not overcome the sheer strength and stamina of the monster boosted to the max with Directory meds. As the smaller man began to fade, Wendy felt panic in her chest. Soon after the twenty-five minute mark, the smaller man was surprised as both his wrists were severed. Wendy screamed and crumpled into herself, sobbing uncontrollably. Finally the clatter of other fighters on the screen drew her from her funk. She had just seen Jack's inevitable fate.

It was just after two p.m. and Wendy was completely drained. Wrung out.

Jack stepped confidently onto the Turf, a slight smile on his face.

Seconds before, she felt all possible emotion was gone from her. At the sight of him though, a whole new level of fear and dread slammed into her. She wanted the awful future to stay away, far, far away. So far away it would never arrive. But the future came at Wendy with each step Jack took.

"Mother! Mom! Please come here. I can't do this by myself!"

Amanda White walked into the TV room, sat next to her daughter, and took her hand. "I've been praying for Jack all morning."

"Oh, Mom, thank you." She clung to her Mother's hand.

Jack walked to the center of the arena and raised his hand to the main camera. He gave a short acknowledgment to the crowd who filled the Colosseum. This was the event they'd all been waiting for and the throng held a vast spectrum of intense emotions. Many of the hundred-thousand-plus crowd were cheering or shouting warnings or giving good wishes or hoping to see him dead. Immense sums of money had been bet on the outcome of this fight. When the bookies stopped taking the action, the Directory stepped in as guarantor for the largest bets. This spurred new rounds of betting. The house was betting against Jack, and the house should know.

The packed stadium was thick with the expectation of more blood – young blood. To the fight regulars, it was common knowledge that the other gladiators and the Directory hated the "Banister Kid", and they were primed for something extra; the fix was in.

A hush came over the crowd. Jack's opponent walked onto the Turf and stood, arms akimbo. Wendy, glued to the live broadcast with her mother, clamped her hands to the side of her head and screamed. Her mother, seeing the size of the monster, felt faint and afraid, her chest tight and breathing labored. She looked at her daughter and felt her terror; that boy was the cause of so much grief.

● ● ●

The trainer's lounge was packed. The moment they were waiting for had arrived. Jack's opponent emerged from a Colosseum arch; he was huge.

All of them had seen the man in the gym and at weapons practice, he was a phenomenon.

Norman went pale.

"That's not right." someone said.

The trainers had no personal objection to Jack Cousins. He was quiet, kept to himself and worked out hard. But he drew too much individual attention and spoiled their fighter's exposure.

So, on average, they were glad Norman's boy would be eliminated.

"I didn't want my lad to fight yours, Cousins. Anyone who eliminates or kills him will be a pariah – and that's not fair. But this?" He pointed to the EV, "It's not right."

Jack and Norman had wondered if Directory officials might seek payback. What DE did to the media who gave them a hard time should have been warning enough. The overwhelming planet-wide public opposition to Jack's participation had put intense pressure on them.

It forced DE to make their first and only concession to the people of Earth. "We certify that the minimum age is indeed eighteen years. Legal emancipation can no longer be used to bypass the age restriction.

"Prior to this ruling, Jack Cousins had been accepted to fight for immortality, so disqualification was not possible. We gave him the option of backing out. He has declined. We are very happy Jack will be fighting on the Turf."

● ● ●

Jack exited from an arch which cascaded color as he passed through. The unlikely gladiator took his first steps on the turf. A bold fanfare accompanied his arrival. He looked in the stands to where he and Wendy had last been. Of course she wasn't there.

The crowd roared their approval.

"The 'Banister kid' is on the Turf! The crowd's going wild!" brayed an announcer from the broadcast booth.

Jack wore solid blue skin-tight trunks and a number of blue and red arm bands.

His physical statistics were already on the big EV alongside his competitor.

"There you have him, folks. The Kid is six feet one, and one hundred ninety pounds. He is the smallest fighter we've ever had – and that includes the women!" The announcer chuckled. "Says here he opted out of D-meds. From where I sit, that's a bad decision, Jack." He laughed. "It's more meat for the grinder – just not much meat." Another announcer in the booth slapped him on the back of the head. "I know that's not sympathetic, but the Directory Chief let him off the hook and the Kid thumbed his nose. He gets what he deserves. There's only one cure for stupid."

Another arch began to blast color. Out stepped his opponent and the crowd screamed.

"Holy hell, that's a big one!" the announcer said. "He's called 'Trunk' – no surprise there. Look at that. The Trunk stands seven feet five inches. He weighs three hundred and fifty-seven pounds. Say goodnight, Jack!"

The Trunk's costume and body paint were neon green and blood red in broad diagonal slashes.

Jack looked at the man he was to fight. Even at this distance he looked huge. No question, the Directory Chief was mad at the PR trouble he'd caused. He was sending a message. Jack shrugged, pulled the sword from its scabbard and tried a few practice swings.

"That monster's arms are bigger than the Kid's legs. Look at his chest. Holy crap!"

Trunk took a few steps onto the turf and stripped the cover from his morning star. In seconds, the woop-woop-woop of the twenty five pound spiked ball on its five foot chain became a hum as its propeller like spin gained velocity over the Trunk's head.

The crowd booed this unholy display of power. For any opponent but Jack they would have cheered his strength and prowess. But Jack was the underdog and the crowd favorite. They hated Trunk for foretelling his death.

But they bet on him.

The huge man moved with a smooth step and showed none of the awkwardness and sloth that such large men can have. His D-meds were amazing, musculature superb if not classic. He was a trained military killer.

Trunk flicked the morning star's eighteen inch handle into his left hand with ease.

"The strength it takes to use that instrument of death is enormous. Any touch of that weapon to soft, pliant flesh is sure to gouge, slash and maim," the announcer paused, "if you're not crushed first."

Trunk began to angle in toward the center field.

Jack turned and followed his opponent's progress around the arena. His confidence, his mission and his desire to cut through barriers as fast as possible, had placed his feet on this Turf, faced with death.

But the threat, far from making him cower, was a tonic. He'd been too long from this life; too long had he basked in the indolent days of Earth, almost eighteen years of them.

"We've seen this before, competitors so mismatched that tragedy is the result." The announcer's voice held pity, but he couldn't hide the gleam in his eye. "Can you imagine what Jack Cousins' family must be feeling now, how a mother's nurturing love must in this extremity be hopelessness and despair? All her dreams and desires snuffed before her crying eyes. For if ever a life was about to end...." His voice trailed theatrically into nothing. He covered his mike and said, "How was that, boys? Think I winkled out a few more tears?" He grinned. "This dumb kid is going down."

Jack felt energized.

The Colosseum, the Turf, his opponent, all came together with great clarity and felt incredibly immediate, his senses attuned. He could smell the coffee and hot dogs, the faint taste of the sea on the air, the humidity, the crowd.

Slowly Jack went forward.

Trunk began to tighten the circle, slowly closing in on Jack. Raw power flowed through him and he could not remember a time when the elements had so combined to make him feel this invincible. He'd felt the thrill of stalking a man through the jungle and slitting his throat from behind. But no one had seen him do it, no one saw how brilliantly he moved, how stealthy his ballet of death.

Today they'll see me. Trunk gloated.

This whole crowd wanted the punk kid to live and he was going to take that from them. He felt now like he did when he took a woman by force – he was going to enjoy something another was going to hate and there was nothing they could do to stop it. Pure pleasure. Completely legal – does life get any better?

This kid will run like a coward with blood leaking all over the Turf, and then he'll beg me for his life. Oh yeah. This is a good day.

The heavy thrum and whir of Trunk's weapon grew loud in Jack's ears, drowning out the crowd.

Trunk called out, "They tole' me to take it easy on you, Sonny, not break you, just 'liminate you. But I ain't gonna." *You little prick,* Trunk thought, "You been the only thing in the press this whole week. That's my press, you asshole! It belongs to Trunk." One fat, meaty finger jabbed at Jack's chest while the whirling ball continued its deadly dance. "I'm gonna pulp you, an' I don't care if they crush my nuts for not playing ball. Ha ha ha, that's a good one."

Jack's own credo was to never kill unless there was no other option. He had operated on this basis for millennia. Now he was again at this decision point. It was, once again, life and death.

I accepted this long ago, Jack thought. *But I can't injure this guy severely enough to win and still live.* And truthfully, he couldn't afford the slightest mistake, because an injury to himself placed his body in DE hands for repair. Who knew what they would do?

Another truth was that he hadn't been in real combat for… some time.

Trunk was now within fifteen feet and Jack felt the whoosh of air from the whirling weapon.

The constant roar from the crowd was heightened by shrill screams as the morning star came close to crushing the life from him. He feinted and dodged as Trunk closed to within striking range, testing and gauging the boy's nerve and reflexes.

Trunk rushed, Jack dodged.

The crowd screamed.

The morning star flashed, Jack ducked. This indecisive dance continued, stretching out for five, ten, fifteen minutes.

The crowd's roar deepened as their vocal cords shredded.

Trunk was not tiring. He was frustrated that his star had not tasted blood, but he'd given Jack no opening to strike. Trunk's footwork was exceptional and kept his limbs clear of Jack's sword. Trunk was a natural fighter and made no obvious mistakes. In any case, he could keep the twenty-five-pound ball rotating at speed for a long while yet, long enough to make his kill.

Jack grudgingly admitted the man was quite skilled and this surprised him. Trunk couldn't have been using the morning star as a weapon for more than six months, and he was a normal – a non-Directory normal at that. Jack's personal opinion of the man aside, Trunk was now a problem.

Jack was shocked to think he would have to kill. Not the killing itself, for if he decided it was necessary there would be no hesitation. And this was neither cruelty nor expediency but just a good straight look at the situation. The shock came from a growing awareness of his reduced ability – he should be able to disarm the man without need of a weapon. Despite the native body he now possessed. Instead, he faced the need to kill or be killed.

Jack began to maneuver Trunk to the center of the turf.

Trunk bared his teeth at Jack's manipulation of the fighting ground. His grin said "I'll kill you anywhere you wish."

Jack drew Trunk and the hum and whir of his wind-milling weapon close and slipped away, looking for an avenue of attack and gauging the exact speed.

He dropped back a half-step, timed the morning star's swing, then, in a blinding sweep, brought his sword over his head and released it at the precise angle. It didn't have far to travel. The impact was clean and solid. A look of comical, horrified surprise came over Trunk's face. "What is this?" his expression asked. The mouth worked, though no words came out. The slowing morning star slipped from slack fingers and sailed away.

He looked down and saw the hilt of Jack's sword pressed hard against his bloodied chest, the blade passed through his heart. His great head shook once in negation, eyes riveted on the cross that was no benediction.

He stood firm, rejecting what was. This cannot be. This cannot be. His hand came up slowly and touched the sword. It was the hard feel of the pommel that convinced Trunk; the sword's undeniable metallic solidity. But, but, he was supposed to enjoy the fight today. He was supposed to win! Resentment clouded his final expression. Trunk toppled to the ground, dead before he hit.

Pandemonium!

It was pure bedlam in the stands. The crowd screamed in disbelief. The cacophony of hollering, whistling, shouting was thunderous. People were turning to strangers and shaking their hands and hugging each other.

● ● ●

Wendy and her mother were locked in an embrace. It was difficult to understand what had just happened. The whole event was bathed in such strong and conflicting emotions. Their only solace was the embrace of the other. And that Jack was still alive. By some miracle, and against all odds, alive. Unbelievable.

But the future held many more such battles, how would they get through them all?

● ● ●

"I say again, the Banister Kid has chopped the Trunk, has struck him down. In an act of pure desperation, Jack Cousins has defeated his enemy in a contest so mismatched one can only marvel." He paused to draw breath, eyes blazing into camera lens. The man turned to his co-host. "Gerard, don't you agree? The Banister Kid acted out of terror and desperation? Today's contest only put off the inevitable?"

"That's obvious, Daniel. To throw your sword is to disarm yourself and is the last desperate act of a man who has no way out. This young man's luck is immense; without it, he would be lying dead out there, not Trunk. Imagine the outcome had the missile gone astray or pierced some non-lethal point. He would've been weaponless, and we all know Trunk was out there to kill. He would have shown no mercy.

"Watch the slow motion replay. See how the sword's hilt passes just a fraction after the swing of the morning star, then the blade slips just under the arm to pierce between the fifth and sixth ribs...." The host's voice trailed off. He was watching the sword pass through the entire body, to be bought up short by the hilt striking the chest. He was finally getting some grasp of the power required to deliver that blow. "... And the power it took to send that blade all the way through Trunk could only have been fueled by a desperation so intense and luck so profound, that it staggers the imagination." And on and on...

The crowd hushed as they saw the boy standing, head bowed, by the body of his opponent.

Jack stood over him, motionless and expressionless; he looked down at the dead man. The crowd saw his reverent pose and quickly lost its voice. Spontaneously they, too, stood and bowed their heads. Jack took in all the minute details. The blood, the drool, the unfocused staring eyes, the sharp smell of a voided bladder and the softer, more rancid stench of feces. Death, unlovely, actual.

I've done this, he said to himself with clarity. He turned and walked toward the exit.

"The Banister Kid said a prayer for the dead!" thundered the announcer. The heads raised, and the silence ended. The crowd broke into wild jubilation.

No, Jack thought as he heard the announcer. *Not a prayer for his soul, but a recognition that I've killed a man. No excuses. No justifications. I did it.*

It was party time for the crowd. The underdog had won, had been respectful of the dead.

They had a hero.

CHAPTER 30

THE PRESS WENT WILD. JACK WAS, by a single stroke, both famous and infamous. Sharon could only shake her head in disturbed wonder. The most broadly published image was a still shot of Trunk falling, transfixed by the sword, a stupid look on his heavy face, with Jack in the bottom right of the frame, quarter-turned to the camera, his face expressionless.

Sharon continued to follow the press closely. The headlines read, "Can Your Baby Do This?" "What Some People Teach Their Children" and many others.

Sharon was interested to note that no one censured Jack directly for the killing. It was conceded that harsh measures were needed in an impossible situation. It could be looked on as murder if one wanted to – on the anti-Directory fringes, this talk still went on, but little or none of this stuck to Jack's public image. Some journalists still subscribed to the "he's a child" cliché, but that story angle was finally losing headway.

● ● ●

Amanda White had remained listless from the time she'd seen the size of Jack's opponent. It was all too much. How could she or her child be personally connected to these horrific events; where had she gone wrong?

She had one answer: Jack. And Wendy's attachment to him. But when she made cutting, scathing comments about the boy, Wendy rejected her, and held tighter to him. She was powerless to change the course of these tragic events and the humiliation the involvement with them brought.

Wendy had recorded the fight for her father, who was still at work. She called him with the news immediately. "I'm glad he made it, baby. See you tonight." He hung up.

Wendy watched the fight over and over, gaining more emotional equilibrium with each viewing. Finally, she could watch it with dispassion and no fear.

Amanda would not look at it. "He's alive and that's all that matters. I can't watch it again. It's so... bloodthirsty. That man died!"

She felt sickened and revolted. She had no desire to watch Jack kill that other man.

"There's no reason for Jack or anyone to put themselves in a position where they have to kill another human being."

Wendy agreed with her mother to lessen conflict and keep her in the dark.

Amanda shuddered, her future son-in-law was a killer. She couldn't suppress the wish that Jack had died today, the turmoil over, and Wendy set free.

● ● ●

Wendy's house and her personal phone were jammed with calls. Everyone wanted to talk to the "Banister Kid's" girlfriend.

Danger Wendy hadn't predicted sent her into a flurry of activity.

"Mom, don't you or anyone answer these calls."

"That's easy." Amanda said. She was surprised to see her daughter come out of her funk so quickly.

"I'll be back soon." Wendy rushed out.

She really needed Natalie and Deidre, but they were in jail.

She made a call to someone who liked the spotlight. "I need help, Loretta. How would you like to be 'Jack's girlfriend,' and get some national press?"

They met at a coffee shop and Wendy explained her dilemma. "I just can't take this anymore. And now the press are hounding me." They worked out the details.

Wendy started taking her calls, "Yeah, can you believe it, Jack dumped me, just a little fame and he moves on." Wendy listened to the 'shocked response' and then said. "I think it's Loretta Marshall."

They spent two hours working the phones. "Wendy White is dead, long live Loretta Marshall!" Wendy smiled.

"You'll tell Jack? There won't be any mix-up?"

"I'll tell him tonight. I really appreciate this, Loretta, you've taken pressure off me."

"Wendy, look, I want to be honest. I'm going to work this for all it's worth. It's my shot at the big time. You know I've been in theatre for years. Hitching a ride on Jack's fame is just what I need – my chance."

"I'm glad this works for us both. If my name comes up, maybe you can say, 'Oh her, who's she?' or something like that." They laughed.

"I'll do that. Thanks for the break, Wendy." Loretta looked away. "You know I like Jack – but I can't imagine being you right now."

They wouldn't get to Jack through her.

● ● ●

When Dale White arrived home from work, he and Wendy went to the TV room and replayed the fight. Then watched it again. Wendy sat silently by his side and watched her father's reactions. "Your young man is certainly a big surprise, baby."

"Oh, Daddy, he had me so frightened today, I could hardly think. It's impossible to stop worrying about him, about the other fights. It seems impossible for him to be able to win each one.

"Every commentator I heard today said Jack's win was sheer luck and he'll die in the next round. Because all the fighters hate him."

"Why do the other fighters hate him?"

"It's stupid. They want media attention and can't get any because Jack gets it all. But Jack doesn't want it."

He looked at his daughter with as much composure as he could muster, attempting to communicate a sense of calm reassurance. "Jack is the only one who can put your mind at rest. And the only way he can do that is by winning this," he was about to say "sadistic" but he bit the word back, "competition."

"Do you think he can win, Daddy?" she asked, amazed. Though she knew Jack was – different, that didn't mean she thought he could defeat the killing machines he would have to face again and again. He was too… too… nice.

"Well, baby, I've watched boxers and martial arts all my life and did a little amateur fighting myself many years ago." He paused and then went on. "I'm no expert," he said in a slow, considered voice, "but looking at that boy just now," he shook his head in wonder, "I've never seen such confidence in my life."

She looked baffled. "Daddy, that doesn't make sense, it's the opposite of what everyone else has said. Are you just trying to make me feel better?" That must be it. "I looked at that fight over and over and he had looked like... like nothing."

"You're right. What else did you see?"

"Daddy, he looked alert. I mean, he watched that big guy closely and he didn't let himself get hit but that was all. He didn't seem confident or skillful…"

"That's just it, baby. He didn't look worried or afraid or tense or confident or awkward or excited; none of that, no emotion at all – but he was alert, he watched his opponent closely. I don't know why, but I think he never doubted that he could handle that monster. He had to be careful because Trunk was very dangerous, a killer." He stopped to think. Then he continued, "The result, the thing Jack wanted, was to make others think it was a fluke. I think it was good tactics, however sadistic." As Dale continued his analysis, he became more certain he was correct. He wanted to calm his daughter and ended up convincing himself.

"Daddy, are you saying that Jack planned it that way? Killed that man simply to hide his ability to kill?" Wendy was shocked. "How can you think that?

"Jack's not cold-blooded!" she said a little sadly, "Do you know him so little?"

It shamed him. He looked into her glistening eyes alive with clarity and directness. He was shaken by the level of commitment he saw there.

Her devotion to a personable, sensible, handsome young man he understood. But he had taken a bizarre and destructive turn and was pulling Wendy along with him. It frightened him to wonder where it would all end.

The boy you love become a killer today, he thought. *What that means for your future I can't imagine. I've never placed such trust or been so unwavering toward anyone in my life.*

She was committed to Jack. In the face of this, he was humbled and decided although her faith may be misplaced, there was honor in her loyalty and she deserved his respect and support. He was sitting with a person who was... grand.

This person, his daughter.

Emotion welled up and came close to overwhelming him. He let it settle. This young woman deserved his objectivity, needed it. To her he would give what he could, where he could, whenever it was needed or wanted.

Her question, "did he know Jack so little," bore home to him the need for an ethical balance of mind. To say what he felt must be said – as an analysis of events and not criticism.

Almost to excuse himself, he said, "Can I see the fight again?"

They watched. There was something of an unearthly calm about the lad as he confronted that monster. Dale tried to place himself in the same position and felt a sharp stab of fear. *I would have died,* he thought. Jack had watched his opponent carefully, but it was not a carefulness borne of fear or even excessive caution. Jack understood if he turned his back, the man would kill him. So he watched him in the same manner someone had to watch the road while driving – to ensure one arrived where one was going. It was the sensible thing to do.

"I want to believe that Jack can make it through, Daddy, but he has so many fights to go. Everyone says the first round is the easiest and so there's only worse to come, and… and he hasn't called at all!" Wendy began to quietly cry and when Dale pulled her into his arms he felt the sobs wracking her body.

Dale White comforted his daughter and waited for her to calm down. When she regained some composure, he wiped her eyes and looked at her gravely.

"There is one thing you have to face, sweetheart." He waited till he had her complete attention. She nodded for him to continue.

"Whatever the circumstances, Jack killed a man today. He did not commit a crime as the laws are currently structured, but that does not mean what he did was right or moral." Wendy was about to interrupt, but her father continued. "It also doesn't mean it was wrong or evil either. I'm not making a character judgment about him. But if he survives this, and I think he might, then you'll have to deal with the question of his motivation. I don't want you to ignore this – questions about it must be asked and answered." Wendy sat silent, absorbed in thought.

"One thing is certain." She looked pleadingly at her father, waiting for him to continue, desperate for his good opinion of the one she loved. "He went to extraordinary lengths to be where he was today. So this is not an idle whim on his part. He is not the boy – or I should say, not the man – I thought he was. The Jack I knew could not go out and kill a gladiator on a Wednesday afternoon."

Dale remembered the sweet-faced kid he'd known for so long. He felt a painful sensation of loss, because no matter how hard he tried, he could not reconcile what he'd just seen with the kind youth who doted on his daughter. The kid who sat at their dinner table, talking, smiling, and brightening the day.

Wendy was nodding her head. "He has changed, Daddy." Dale White frowned, hearing the profound depth of the comment. She looked at her father and was surprised to see how disturbed he was. "He has changed, but at the same time he's the same." This only deepened the furrows on his forehead. "He is the same. I mean he's the same nice guy he was. What I'm trying to say is that he hasn't turned into some ugly monster whose only desire is to kill." Her father was waiting. "But before, he was just sort of … living. Not going anywhere. Now he knows where he is going and what he has to do."

"Now that he knows his purpose, he has to kill?" He sounded troubled. She shook her head emphatically. Dale White put the unspoken question in his eyes, his eyebrows rose.

"I can't say, Daddy. It's for Jack to tell you. I can't break confidence with him." He wanted to know more but had to admire his daughter. There was iron in her statement. It seemed she knew where she was going also. He wondered where that would be.

●

The following morning Wendy got a continuous stream of sympathy calls. Some of which she answered to confirm the rumor.

At the breakfast table Amanda asked, "Have you and Jack broken up?"

"No, Mom. We were getting too many calls and strangers coming to the door. I just couldn't take it. So I arranged for a friend, Loretta Marshall, to be Jack's official girlfriend."

Amanda White was at a loss for words. "Okay."

Dale White said, "I'm glad the press won't be banging on our door."

At that moment the doorbell rang.

"I'll get it." Wendy said. She was at the door for a few minutes.

"That was freaky, Dad."

"What?" Dale asked between bites of cereal.

"It was a news crew."

"What did they want?" Amanda asked.

"They wanted to know stuff about me." She laughed, "I said, 'Jack's not interested in me anymore, why are you?' The guy looked kind of surprised and said, 'You're right, sorry for bothering you.'" She laughed again.

"That was really funny."

Dale looked at his daughter. "That was well done."

"Yes." Amanda said.

"I've something to ask you both."

"Yes?"

"Please don't say anything about Jack and me to Cousin Penny. It would be too much…"

"Of course, dear, we won't say a word," her mother said.

Later in the day the mail arrived with a letter from Jack.

She ran to her room and opened the envelope. It was short: "All communications in and around the Colosseum are being monitored, so please call me at this number [and he gave a time]. I love you, Jack."

So she did. They talked for hours, and the world seemed right again.

Just before they ended the call, Wendy said, "Jack, you have a new girlfriend." There was a stunned silence. And then she explained.

"That's a very intelligent move, Dee. We're going to get through this." That sounded like pep talk – but she imagined it was true.

• • •

The Investigator was frustrated, and when he wasn't frustrated, he was scared.

He had not put a name to the "face." So his only real lead had gone nowhere.

One thing was obvious: major planning had gone into hiding the source of the deferments.

Because there were no results he was constantly taking steps to avoid Boltax. For days he had been successful, but his luck would run out, because it always did.

What will Boltax do to me? he worried. *How long before he gives me the chop?* He didn't know. Yes, he did: *not long.*

The Investigator reviewed the facts he was sure of: his quarry was in the United States, he spoke unaccented American English. At least the Salt Lake City clerk thought so. But he couldn't get a real description verbally or telepathically – and that was close to impossible.

None of the many leads Bio-Comp had given him led anywhere. They had been confusing and a waste of time. The majority of the initial deferments occurred in the United States, specifically Florida, Salt Lake City, and St. Louis.

Concentrating on these locations gave one result.

The kid.

The only common denominator was the kid walking in the background of two mental images he captured in St. Louis – and the face match to the same kid at the Directory Induction Center in SLC. Evidence of a coordinated effort. It did exist; someone was blocking graduates from leaving Earth.

The kid was involved.

But the kid's a native and natives don't know anything. So there was someone behind the kid.

He had to find him.

But didn't know how.

He had interviewed hundreds of people. He despised these natives and wanted nothing to do with them. Sometimes he was forced to enter a dwelling and almost gagged on the thick domestic smells. Their entertainment was infantile and they just sat and stared at those stupid screens, or the poor quality EV.

Ten more of these "wonderful" interviews were set for tomorrow. It was complex and time-consuming, and not going anywhere.

When tomorrow's mind scans/interviews were complete, if there wasn't a breakthrough, he'd go back to his list and find the people who hadn't been home the first time. Then re-interview the ones his assistant handled, because his assistant was useless.

● ● ●

The second round of the Fight for Immortality came quickly. Sharon Cousins gave up any pretense of trying to work on the day of Jack's next fight. She was glued to the EV from the opening ceremonies. A fanfare announcing the imminent arrival of the fighters blared out and the crowd took up the roar.

The fighting began.

All the violence she watched went by in a blur. But it was seductive. If you considered the games "normal," it was easy to become involved in the drama of each contest, to pick your favorite and place a bet.

If you were wearing your TAC remote, simply thinking of betting produced the gambling sidebar. The gladiator's stats appeared and you could place a bet right up to the first contact between the contestants.

Five minutes before the next pair of fighters stepped out on the Turf, all their stats and background data were displayed on a huge EV cube in the middle of the Colosseum. Along with this, betting odds were calculated. All it took was a single thought and your money was moved from your account.

Sharon wondered how the world would survive if it cherished violence so much.

But for her, these were minor concerns. Idle thinking until Jack set foot on the Turf.

The time had come.

Jack's statistics and his opponents flashed on screen.

Five minutes to go.

Hector the Spector was his opponent. He was only three inches taller and sixty pounds heavier than Jack. His weapon of choice was the sword.

This match contained the form of equality without its substance: there was a vast difference in experience. The statistics and personal history of each gladiator were followed by digital clips of previous fights.

Jack's read: High school baseball team. Defeat of Trunk in FFI.

Hector's was a long and involved military history, Special Forces, etc. He'd been too old for the competition, but that was before five point five million dollars of D-med max: reinforced skeletal structure, organ replacement, new heart and lungs, high-tension musculature and ligaments, full cartilage replacement, nervous system regeneration-optimization, and assorted repairs as necessary.

Hector the Spector looked fabulous for his age. After leaving the military Hector was contracted as a corporate bodyguard. Directory meds made him chrono-forty-six and bio-twenty-five.

With the announcement of the Fight for Immortality, Hector and his wealthy boss decided to enter.

The day was bright and the sun was hard, staring unmercifully out of a cloudless sky, baking the warriors below. The clarity of the EV cube allowed Sharon to see and feel a real-time environment. The crowd was in high commotion, deafening themselves with their own roars.

Jack strode forth to cheers.

Hector was greeted by booing as he emerged from the opposite archway.

Jack, once again, was devoid of any obvious attitude. There was nothing about him of suppressed emotion, or any type of excitement. The most that could be said – he was there.

The stadium was a riot of color and noise, hot dog sellers walked the isles hawking. Pennants of the fighters and flags of the countries they represented snapped in the short gusts of wind and then dropped.

There was no formal "start" to the individual contests. Each combatant entered from opposing sides and was introduced.

"Jack Cousins, one victory, one kill." Roar.

"Hector the Spector, one victory, one maiming."

"Boooooo!"

Each gladiator was at his peril after the introduction.

Jack and Hector took some time to engage, each man wanting to evaluate his opponent. After some close-in circling, Hector hurled himself forward. Both had a firm, two-handed grip upon their swords and clashed violently again and again, showering sparks with each deflected blow.

The alloy metal of the swords was a curious one, as the noise created with each blade strike was loud and vaguely bell-like. Also, the showers of sparks were excessive. But it made a great show.

The furious pace continued for some minutes without abating, each man exhibiting athletic prowess of a high degree. Rivers of sweat were running off both men as they separated and circled one another, looking for an opening, waiting for some indication of weakness in their opponent.

Hector was alert to the possibility of a thrown sword and had practiced for a day, perfecting the technique of deflecting such a missile, as had many of the gladiators.

Jack and Hector engaged again and Jack forced a counterclockwise rotation that made Hector uncomfortable and slightly hesitant. Jack increased his rate of sword strokes and pressed the Spector backward. Then a sword was flying away from the melee and comic surprise on Hector's face as he looked at his empty hands confirming the impossible. His sword was gone.

Hector sprinted to where his sword had landed and was diving for it when Jack's blade took off his hand.

"Are you defeated?" Jack asked the formalized question. In earlier rounds of the competition, fouls had been claimed where no formal admission had taken place. Unconsciousness and death were the only exceptions to this rule.

"I am defeated," Hector choked out. The crowd roared. Jack grasped the man's blood-pulsing wrist to slow the blood loss, shook lose an arm band and used it as a tourniquet. He bound it tightly and the flood of blood became a trickle. He walked Hector to the D-med station and placed the hand in the stasis incubator that accompanied the med-cart. In an hour, the man would have his hand back. In days it would be fully functional.

The med-cart operator noticed that the stasis incubator had been properly set. He looked at Jack. Strange.

Sharon Cousins was so amazed and relieved it was difficult to tell what she was feeling. It dawned on her that Jack may have a chance to make it through. Just as he'd said. She didn't want to hope, the road ahead was long and there was too much to lose.

But a win was a win.

She smiled as she called up the betting strip on the EV cube to check her winnings. This was the second wager she'd made in her life and the second bet she'd won. She didn't need the money, but wanted to support Jack in every way she could. Her fear said he would lose, her will – win. Sharon removed the betting side bar and enlarged the cube.

The crowd was wild for their favorite.

It was dawning on some that Jack was not exactly as he appeared to be. No wet behind the ears school boy could achieve the victory he did today.

* * *

The media were divided. "School Boy Displays Professional Skill" read one major headline, "Jack Cousins' Bravado Proving Out," read another. Still there were others who continued the exploitation angle likening Jack to a baby walking through a mine field – the first few steps could be without incident but continuing onward made destruction the only possible outcome.

With the second round completed the fight aficionados agreed this was an especially critical hurdle. The first round had eliminated the poor fighters. The second round eliminated those who made it through the first by luck. Only the skilled or the truly brutal made it past the third round.

The blow that dropped Hector, while skillfully delivered, was deemed a fluke after repeated inspections of slow-motion replays revealed the sword stroke that disarmed Hector could not have been intended. It was another "stroke of luck" – pun intended. So Jack had been lucky twice. No one believed "third time lucky" in mortal combat.

●

On the day of Jack's third fight, the Colosseum swelled to overflowing. More than one hundred and twenty thousand people had come to see. Again the fans had to wait till mid-afternoon before Jack set foot on the Turf. The fanfare preceding his fight now included Directory fireworks displaying each fighter in their most heroic moments. It was an awesome display. The crowds brayed with blood lust and shattered eardrums with applause.

So it began. It saw Jack's first injury. This gladiator, too, was a swordsman. Jack's own sword, a lighter-weight blade than the blade his opponent used, shattered in a routine contact and his chest was slashed, pouring forth a steady stream of blood.

A knowing smile played over his opponent's lips. The crowd screamed its fright when it saw the extent of Jack's wound in close-up on the big EV. They'd seen this type of injury before; there may be only seconds left in this competition and possibly in Jack's life.

His opponent, the Decimator, was not a talker, but a steady, careful fighter who acted brilliantly when the opportunity arose. He now had a clear chance at his third victory with Jack virtually weaponless.

Jack, as a rule, did not use his telepathic ability in fighting. It was better to ignore an opponent's state of mind during the action. Using telepathy could make one lazy. One assumed what was going to occur, instead of handling what happened when it happened – inviting a fatal error. But with the unlikely event of his shattered sword, he checked his opponent's mind, and, sure enough, this was the second set-up by Directory officials. The metal of his weapon had been weakened deliberately and this man had been primed to take advantage of it.

The blow that slashed his chest was to be the death stroke. He had escaped by lightning reflexes. Jack backed away and threw the remainder of the sword at the Directory officials standing by the exit. They dodged as it clattered against the wall.

The crowd screamed at such insane recklessness. Jack was without protection. He was forced to dance away from attack after attack. He managed these maneuvers with gymnastic grace while his opponent looked a cloddish, stumbling fool. Jack took off his trunks and stood in his underwear as he staunched his wound as best he could. The blood flow did slow, but so did Jack.

After minutes the Decimator felt humiliated by his inability to kill an unarmed, wounded school boy. The booing and ridiculous laughter from the crowd infuriated him. His frustration spiked. The Decimator slashed ever more wildly at the elusive figure who laughed at him, splattered him with his own blood, and goaded him on.

With the knowledge that this fellow was party to treachery, Jack showed no mercy. Though he appeared the clown, he was with every jibe, every taunt, luring his opponent to cast off his training and act upon hatred and exasperation alone.

Jack harassed the Decimator, "Oh, I'm sorry, did I make you trip?" The cameras and mics picked it up clearly. "I don't want to make it too hard for you to kill me." The crowd roared. "Look I'll stand right here. Now come closer, raise your sword, no, no a bit higher." Jack dodged the slashing blow. "Hey, Decimator, if you keep practicing with that pesky sword you'll get better, I promise."

The crowd was cheering Jack's evasions and booing the Decimator's sword strokes.

The Decimator was gripped by a blinding rage and attacked with fury. Strings of saliva dripped from his mouth.

Jack dashed away, howling with laughter. He stopped just out of reach and doubled over with laughter. The Decimator rushed his tormentor with sword high for a hacking death blow. The flashing ribbon of steel flew through its reckless arc, missing Jack completely, and buried itself into the Turf. From a crouch Jack launched and delivered an open-handed blow full to the sternum of the overbalanced, onrushing man.

The Decimator was brought to an immediate agonizing halt. He tried to pull his sword free, but his arm would not respond. He stumbled forward a step and placed his other hand on the sword hilt and with palsied effort, pulled it free and raised it slowly above his head. It toppled him and he crumpled to the ground. Agony seized his chest and the fish mouth uselessly gasped for air that would not sustain him.

No word of submission passed his lips.

Jack walked off the Turf, his blood soaking the earth. The crowds were shouting and cavorting in the stands. Showers of gold coins were flung at his feet. As he reached the exit, he turned and waved.

The crowd howled its approval.

● ● ●

A large man in Salt Lake City also felt the blow that had felled the Decimator. Once he'd been at Jack's home and tried to save him. He rubbed his sternum and realized how lucky he'd been.

CHAPTER 31

WENDY MET HER COUSIN AT THE Salt Lake City Airport baggage claim. The girls spotted each other through the crowd, "You could be my sister." Penny Taylor said, and they hugged.

"It's great to finally meet you again." Wendy replied. "After all this time."

"I'd made plans for the summer, but when Mom said the cousin I hadn't seen since I was five had invited me to stay, I wanted to come. Thanks' for the invite."

"It was mom, actually. I'd done the Directory training and was set to leave the planet. But when the deferments became possible, I put off my departure."

Penny said, "I was interested in doing the training myself, but there were so many rumors, I decided to wait and see if people come back."

Yeah! Another one saved, and from my own family. Wendy thought.

"I'm glad you stayed, I would've missed you." The girls hugged again. Wendy was touched.

"I'm glad, too." Wendy replied. They walked through the terminal with Penny's bags split between them.

"Have you been watching the Fight for Immortality and Jack Cousins? I saw his girlfriend being interviewed the other day and they gave her such a hard time she was in tears. She's our age and so, so beautiful. I can see why a guy like Jack Cousins has a girlfriend like her. They're both high-profile types."

Wendy couldn't help herself. "I know them both, they went to the same high school I did. I guess you could say Jack Cousins graduated early."

Penny looked at her cousin in amazement. "You actually know him, you've met him?"

"Yep, he lives just down the street with his aunt and uncle. We used to walk to school together when we were kids."

"Oh, wow, I can't believe this. You actually know the hottest guy on the whole planet! I would love to meet him. Any chance I can meet your old school pal, Cuz?"

Wendy was irritated. "Well, he's kind of busy right now and may not live to see the weekend, so it's a bit up in the air."

"I guess you're right. But it's hard to imagine that someone as alive as Jack Cousins could die." She shook her head. "I wonder what his girlfriend is feeling right now. It must be really hard."

Wendy had seen the EV interview Penny mentioned earlier and knew that Loretta Marshall had not been faking her emotions. She liked Jack. And the questions had been brutal – "What will you do when he dies?" – trying to cause an emotional breakdown to boost their ratings.

"Loretta Marshall is a beautiful, strong woman who'll get through this."

"I'm glad. But I wonder what I'd be like in her place."

Wendy shrugged. "Yeah, I don't know."

Penny spoke with disarming sincerity and was a very sweet girl. Wendy's plans, which involved exposing Penny to some danger, made her feel bad.

They got off the freeway and drove the surface streets toward home. "It might be good if you don't mention Jack Cousins when we get to the house. Mom and Jack's mother are friends and she can't stand to watch the coverage or talk about it."

"I won't say a word." Penny replied. "My mother has no connection to Jack or his family, and she's really upset and crying about it. A lot of people are."

"Yeah, Jack has upset a lot of people. And thanks in advance for not saying anything, Penny. That's nice of you."

"One last question." Wendy nodded. "What's he like? I mean everyone thought it was just dumb luck that he won the first fight. But the last two fights, that took skill. The other guys – whatever their names were, I forget – they were both majorly enhanced with D-meds and Jack beat them!"

"I'd no idea that Jack could survive combat. In school, he was never in a fight. I thought I knew him." She shrugged, "And then he goes and enters this brutal competition. A month ago I could have given you a complete picture of who he was. But, that boy, the boy I knew, would never have entered this fight. So I can't honestly say what he's like now."

"That must be strange. To know someone for a long time and then…"

"Yes. Yes, it's strange." Wendy pulled up to her home and took Penny Taylor inside. "Mom, Penny's here!"

Amanda White carried on the social amenities with her usual composure. Both she and Penny tried to include Wendy in the conversation, but she was so distracted, they stopped making a serious attempt.

The chattering continued around the kitchen and all over the house as Amanda White showed the house to their guest. Wendy forced herself to join in after she realized if Penny asked her mother "what's wrong with Cousin Wendy?" Amanda might tell Penny "in confidence" what was really going on. That would be a disaster.

Once the formalities were done and the conversation slowed, Wendy whisked Penny upstairs and showed her many photo's (newly distressed) of her and her boyfriend.

Wendy had photos of him at the zoo, at the mall, sitting together in a rusty convertible, hiking in the mountains, waving at the camera, sitting by a lake. There he was mowing the lawn and waving an arm, a happy sort of guy. There were snapshots of him full-face, then in profile. She pulled out her phone and showed her more.

With the basics in place, Wendy prepared herself for what she had to do. She assumed a sad tone of voice and a melancholy look.

"Penny, I hate to tell you this because it makes our family seem like a mine field."

"Tell me what?"

"My parents don't like my boyfriend, so please don't mention him to anyone." Penny didn't know what to say. "In fact," continued Wendy, "the whole subject of my boyfriend brings on nothing but shouting matches with my parents." Penny was clearly impressed and dismayed and Wendy winced, appalled by the whole deception.

Penny had sat through this enthusiastic display of pictures with growing wonder. The guy was a nerdy little shrimp with enough active acne to go broke buying prescription zit-zapper. On top of this, Wendy's family hates the guy and she's clearly obsessed. What a situation.

"Isn't he a little short for you?" This was the mildest criticism she could manufacture.

"Not you, too!"

Penny was mortified. "No, no, he's a fine-looking guy." The little man didn't seem to mind about his size though. In one of the photos, Wendy and he were standing side by side and she had her arm around his shoulders and he was clearly quite short, five feet or about that. The top of his head at her chin: very short. Was that a bald patch on the crown of his head? And those wrinkles.

"You're just like my mother." Mimicking her mother Wendy said, "'He's too short, he's too old, he's too ugly, and he's on welfare – couldn't you at least get someone with a job, who doesn't eat so much food?'

"It's awful what Mom says about him and I don't ever want to talk about it again. He is really trying – the drugs and alcohol are in the past. I thought you would understand, Penny. A guy's looks aren't important. And if you measure love by how much is in his wallet, why feel anything at all? If you're deeply in love, what does money matter?"

Penny was aghast; *Wendy has lost it.* The guy was a complete looser. It was out of character for her intelligent cousin; but in matters of the heart, who could tell? She felt terrible upsetting her cousin. She wanted a connection, to be real friends. To heal their divided family.

Wendy could almost follow her train of thought – not by telepathy, but expression – and again felt guilt.

"I'm sorry, Wendy, I won't talk about him to your parents," Penny said.

She's so nice and that makes me a real shit. Wendy thought.

"Is there anything I can do to help?" Penny asked. Wendy shook her head.

"It's best left alone." Then Wendy realized she had left out one vital detail and so continued, "There's one thing. Please don't talk about my boyfriend, Jack."

"Wendy, you already asked and I agreed. I won't ever mention your boyfriend, Jack."

"Thanks, Pen."

Penny must have his name. Same name, different mental image.

Penny nodded, happy to talk of something else.

They spent the rest of the day cloistered and they both came to the conclusion that the other was very nice. It was a good thing to have another close friend.

Wendy left home the next day, having phoned her father at work to let him know and asking that he make it all right with her mother. He agreed, having felt the power of her personality impinge on him. *Where has this tough young woman come from?* he wondered.

For her own part, Wendy would have preferred to just disappear for a few days, notifying no one, but couldn't afford to create a fuss.

No missing persons, no police, no interest. No disturbing Penny and what she thought she knew. She would stay away for as long as it took.

She looked at the morning paper in the rack at the corner store where she stopped to gas up. Loretta Marshall's face shone from the front page. Jack Cousins' girlfriend. Another piece of deception firmly in place and spreading far and wide. She hoped it would be enough.

CHAPTER 32

THERE WERE TEN ROUNDS TO THE Fight for Immortality. With each round finished, their number was cut in half. The surviving winners took hard looks at each other.

Jack was forced to take his chances with the Directory meds. Treating his chest injury in an emergency room would have resulted in a convalescence he couldn't afford. When they closed his messy chest wound, the med-techs left him conscious at his request, and no one stopped Norman from recording the short operation. It seemed they had no instructions to bungle the procedure; he was going to be attacked on the Turf but otherwise left alone. That suited Jack fine.

Norman had been circulating freely around the compound for days and had become adept at picking up rumor and gossip. In the sixth round of the Fight for Immortality, there had been a particularly nasty and long drawn-out struggle on the Turf. It was rumored that both gladiators had died.

Then, two days later, a very tall Asian called the Red Dragon reappeared in the gym and began working out. But the word Norman picked up was that he was different. There was nothing obvious; at rest he looked much the same, but he carried himself differently, and his balance was off. The real changes were in his personality; he seemed not to know the other gladiators he'd been friendly with.

The Red Dragon had technically won his fight – that is, his opponent was officially declared dead before him – but he'd been rushed off the turf with his head half-severed and gouts of blood pumping from a brutal gash. The wound had been unlucky, received after delivering a death blow to his foe.

When the Directory officials were questioned about the obvious differences between the new Red Dragon and the old, the medical technicians said, "Look, even with our advanced biological technology, this neck wound is almost always unrecoverable. This man was lucky to retain his body. Some differences in memory and personal presentation are inevitable. Our advice is to let the fighter recover his equilibrium in his own time and not ask any unnecessary questions." The med tech went into the technical details involved in properly re-attaching the man's head.

The Red Dragon was strictly a killer and had put each of his opponents to death. And he did it well.

In an early press conference, he'd curtly explained his philosophy to those who were critical of his actions.

"You're a bunch of butt-banging faggots if you think I'm doing something wrong. Some men die in battle and that's the truth. Those I take don't mind being killed by me, because they know they are contributing to a far greater cause than the continuance of their own puny lives."

One reporter took the bait. "What are they contributing to?"

"My reputation. Their glory is achieved in the accolades I receive."

This outrageous statement left the press silent for a few moments, because it was clear that the man believed what he was saying. And that was about as scary as anything ever got.

Then a brave reporter asked, "How about you, Dragon? Were you born to die in battle, by someone greater than yourself?"

He smiled his wide toothy smile and shook his head mournfully at those who failed to catch on. "Just as there are some men who are born to die, there are those who are born to kill them. I was born to be victorious over lesser men."

"Who are the 'lesser men'?" an irritated reporter asked.

"Other men," he said. They looked at him blankly. "I look at the pack of you sniveling ants and I wonder how much force it would take to crush your skulls. You there, with the thick head, I doubt I could crush your noggin by direct pressure even with my Directory meds package." He smiled at them. "Would you like me to try? You could become famous!"

Ignoring the last comment, another reported asked, "Why don't you give these 'other men,' these 'lesser men,' a break and leave them alive?"

"I've tried. It just hasn't worked out that way." He shrugged casually.

"What about the Flame? You ran him through with your sword then twisted the blade so he bled out before he could get med attention. You killed him needlessly."

The Dragon's snake eyes went flat. "Little man, how can you know what goes on down there on the Turf? You ask me if I killed him intentionally. No! I prefer to think he was born to die. I just happened to be there at the right time."

"What about this man's family?"

"If they want to challenge me, I'll kill them too."

"No. I meant what of his grieving wife and children. Do you feel sorry for them?"

"Are you stupid? I don't even know them. Hell, I didn't even know him."

One of the reporters muttered, "Fucking animal" and took three weeks to recover in a non-Directory facility. The message was clear: upset the fighters and you're on your own.

Still, the Dragon had been given a death blow. All of this information, Norman passed on to Jack.

Jack had been talking to every person with a Jolo body he could and had finally confirmed the location of the Recyclex room at the compound.

Yes.

This meant that the Colosseum was the main Directory facility in the solar system. Had the Recyclex been on Mars, his task would have been far more difficult.

As it was, his plans were falling into place. He had singled out and spoken with two of the previous three games' winners. The new immortals. Jolos. They were delirious, arrogant, and not in control of the bodies they now possessed; but they were powerful, dangerously so.

Jack had guided the conversation and discussed those sections of the compound that were restricted to him. He was slowly gathering the information he needed.

Jack's wound had healed in a day and he went back to the gym. These last opponents were going to be more difficult. Still, his advantage was skill, and with each fight he felt more confident. And the result of any conflict was always more than the sum of physical prowess.

Jack felt increasing pressure as time ran out. He could feel the DE closing in. With each passing day, the potential for exposure and capture increased. He must make it through the entire competition.

If not, everything was at risk....

• • •

The Investigator came up empty with his own interviews. He headed back to Salt Lake City, for re-interviews.

He okayed his assistant to question the CIA native in Virginia. Who cared about native affairs? Definite waste of time, but with nothing to find, nothing could be screwed up. Perfect for his assistant. And who knew? Something may come of it.

The Investigator was feeling nervous and excited. He had scanned the digital record of his assistant's earlier interviews. Of the first sixty deferred, only three had not been directly contacted. He looked at his computer. The girl was number thirty one.

The assistant had spoken to the mother and used mild intimidation. She'd no idea where her daughter was.

The girl was out there somewhere.

He would find her.

The "face" was also from Salt Lake. It felt like a connection.

On return visits, he always landed his Air Shuttle near a car rental facility and then drove one of the local vehicles to the target site. Walking up from a native vehicle, he achieved surprise.

He got into the disgustingly primitive conveyance and felt incredible frustration at having to move across the ground and negotiate obstacles, other ground vehicles and follow the rules of ground transit which were obstructive and tiresome in the extreme.

He hated primitives.

The Investigator parked the conveyance after an irritating search to find the correct lodging and walked to the door of Wendy White, number thirty one. He knocked. The door opened.

"Wendy White?" He scanned her face. Definitely not the right girl.

"No, she's gone camping."

"*Aggrrrr,*" he growled. "When will she be back?" he snapped.

"Excuse me, but who are you?" Penny asked in a quiet tone.

He instantly changed to honey. All the frustrating primitiveness was wrecking standard "polite inquiry" procedure.

"I'm a Directory official and Wendy White has signed a contract to venture off-world in our service." He was extremely handsome and quite nice after his growl.

"Oh?"

"We have some questions about the deferment she took some months ago. Quite important."

"Well, she's gone to the mountains with her boyfriend."

"I need global positioning coordinates for them."

"I've no idea where they are."

"Is there someone who does?" the Investigator wanted to know.

"She said she was going camping, but not where."

"That doesn't sound usual for a young girl."

"Well…" Penny hesitated. She was a little overwhelmed by meeting a Directory official for the first time, but the nervousness was wearing off and she didn't want to tell this man personal details about Wendy.

"Well, what?" The girl had clammed up. Maybe he was onto something. "What don't you want to say?" She didn't respond.

"What about the boyfriend?" He scanned her mind and got a picture of a short, dark boy – no, the boyfriend was an older man, and definitely a native. What Jolo would ever look like that? None. He was frustrated. His first visit and the girl was off somewhere he couldn't find. But there was something wrong here, he could smell it.

"Are you lying to me?" he demanded. He looked in her head; she was not lying to him.

"No, I'm not lying. Wendy's parents don't like her boyfriend and she didn't tell them he was going with her." She told the Directory official this because she didn't want him to think she was hiding something incriminating, instead of something merely personal.

"Tell me the truth about Wendy." Again there was a null response on any level. He lost interest.

"You're so rude," she said and swung the door shut. Before it could close he stuck his shoe in the jamb. He gave her a printed card.

"Have her call this number as soon as she gets back into town." Realizing he would not get voluntary cooperation, he said. "Failure to do so will result in severe penalties."

"All right, I'll tell her what you said."

He walked rapidly down the street. He would find the next two today.

● ● ●

The seventh round of the Fight began on a Monday morning. Norman felt the increased tension in the remaining athletes. The spectacle became more exaggerated as they closed in on a winner.

Eight gladiatorial contests remained in this round; the field had narrowed to the very best. These fights lasted a long time – not because the Directory demanded it – but the skill level was elevated and the contestants more evenly matched.

Norman was fascinated by the conversations between the fighters as they sat casually about the gym recreation area discussing what victory actually meant. Their grasp of "immortality" being offered by the Directory was imprecise and confused. Some of the fighters were afraid of winning; they didn't say so, but Norman could see it in their eyes.

As Jack survived each round, the narrative changed. The press were all over the page, without input from him they flocked to his girlfriend Loretta Marshall. She handled her role with dignity.

Norman was sitting in his lucky chair in the gym rec-room watching fighters on the huge EV. He had come to know many of these men quite well during the weeks of Jack's participation. Norman expected fewer deaths in the closing rounds. They had come to know each other – it's more difficult to kill a friend.

The combatants on the turf were really going at it. It was a skillful contest.

In his peripheral vision, Norman saw the odds board doing a major reshuffle. He looked. Jack's odds took a hard dive. That was strange.

These later rounds posted upcoming fights well in advance so the bettors could wager every last dime on the fighter of their choice.

In rounds four, five and six, the odds ran heavily in Jack's favor. And he won.

Now the betting was heavily against him.

And his adversary had not yet been posted – no one was supposed to know who it was.

Why all this betting?

Jack's fight hasn't been announced. The fix is in and they aren't hiding it. Those bastards.

The fighters and trainers in the gym were all looking at Norman. They knew, too.

Sports fans were betting millions upon millions against Jack. The volume of bets continued to increase and the Directory officials posted that large bets would be covered by the Directory treasury.

This caused another avalanche of bets against Jack.

More than ten billion dollars was at risk on this one fight.

A minute later, the EV cubes posted the next contest; Jack Cousins vs. Red Dragon.

The betting made sense.

The Red Dragon was a ringer.

The Directory had replaced the dead Red Dragon fighter with a Jolo facsimile body and whispered it around.

There would be no proof. The hatred the Directory must feel for Jack exceeded anything he imagined.

Norman was powerless.

● ● ●

Jack walked out onto the Turf and waved to the crowd. They responded enthusiastically. All the spectators had seen the odds board declare Jack's upcoming execution.

The smart money was against him.

Jack could feel a hysterical undertone in the crowd. He saw the odds board. He walked over to it. He looked at it closely. One of the mobile camera/mics was hanging near. Jack beckoned it over.

He yelled into it, "Norman, bet a million on me!!" His voice boomed out around the arena.

The techs picked Norman up in the gym and went in for a close up. Norman was huge on the EV hanging center field above the turf.

"Hell, Jack, I have you for two million already! How much more do you want, my boy?"

Jack felt a rush of pure affection for Norman. What a man!

"Father, why don't you round it up to five million?"

"Ten it is, my boy!"

The stunned cheering from the crowd struck like divine winds.

Thirty seconds later ten million showed on the board. The crowd screamed. Jack's life and his father's fortune were now at stake.

But the smart money was still deep in the opposing column.

The crowd had their money against him, but they wanted him to live and would cheer for him.

Yet he would die before their eyes.

Walking the edge of the Turf, Jack recognized a few faces in the crowd and he gave each one a glance or nod of recognition. His optimism and sunny disposition was squeezing their hearts.

Jack looked into the sky. It was blue with a scattering of white fleece.

For a second he longed for home.

Then he focused and saw the cloud base was tinged a deeper color. No rain would release and the air held little moisture.

The Roman arches facing the Turf were white and graceful, then shot through with color. The Directory architects had taken the best of that ancient architecture and included it here, now was the time to enjoy it.

Today was the day. The absolute calm he felt always signaled action just ahead. The only thing that surprised him was that the confrontation with the Directory had come so early.

The Red Dragon strode onto the Turf, and a portion of the crowd cheered for him. He, too, was a hero of sorts, having received a death blow, and then miraculously recovered to fight again. He had fought and won the most dramatic contests of the whole competition and was loved by the bloodier mindset.

Jack turned to acknowledge the Red Dragon's presence. It was true, then. He saw it immediately. This was a Jolo body dressed up to look like the Dragon.

The Red Dragon wore tooled and ornamented red leather sandals which were his trademark. But for this fight he'd added a tooled red leather open collar and bracers which decorated and protected the forearms. The tattoos that marked his body were a color and design match.

This man would fool the crowd.

Jack had not seen this particular Jolo around the Colosseum over the previous weeks, but watching closely as he moved, he recognized him. This was "Himself," the "God" who had addressed the Earthlings and announced immortality to the whole planet. The Directory Chief.

Jack had seen his soul eating arrogance. He supposed the Chief would be a good telepath. He would soon find out.

Jack's plans would vanish if he lost.

Square one – acquire a Jolo body.

He now faced what was essential to avoid; fighting a Jolo as a "human."

Playing in the big game with a human body was to invite death at every turn.

It was bootstrap time.

Even so, his calm never departed, but deepened. The returning tide of confidence from his success over the last six rounds validated his battle awareness.

Fighting Trunk he'd been shaky.

Facing the hybrid Red Dragon, he was not.

Jack again allowed himself to look around the Colosseum and imagine that he was in another time and place. The Directory had its own version of the Olympic Games. Jack imagined the crowds here had come to see friendly contestants test their physical skills and fighting prowess. With this imagining, the last of the battle tension and seriousness dissipated.

Jack waved enthusiastically to the crowd, smiled and joked with a few of those seated in the front rows.

"Glad you came to see the competition today. We won't disappoint you. It's a great show. Enjoy yourselves." Jack waved some more.

Many people in the crowd despised themselves; they had come to see blood and watch this kid get what he had coming.

Jack laughed.

This situation was ironic and humorous: it occurred to him that he now faced the technology gap from the challenging end.

Philosophically there was symmetry here – he'd had that advantage so often; time to experience the opposite.

Timing was his only objection.

What a day.

He shrugged; protesting "what is," as opposed to dealing with it, made it more difficult to handle.

He waved to the crowd.

The down side to defeating this Jolo today was that it would deepen his humiliation and make him a more dedicated enemy, thus lessening Jack's chances of getting to "square one."

He might lose this whole tactical arm and be immeasurably delayed.

The fight today seemed to become a no-win situation, with no time left to re-plan. What to do?

Take it one step at a time.

Jack's thoughts raced. He had to solve this first step now. There was no way that any Earthman could kill his opponent, even if the Jolo disguised as the Red Dragon stood and took blows from a sword for a full minute. The body would look a wreck but it would still be functional, and deadly.

A human body could not generate the power necessary to sever the limbs or neck. To his advantage was his intimate knowledge of Jolo bodies, and it was just possible that given the chance he could bring this one down. But the Red Dragon was unlikely to give him the chance. Surely the man could fight. The way he moved the Jolo body confirmed this.

Personal weakness had driven this Jolo onto the Turf to kill Jack. What other weaknesses did he have? That was easy: arrogance, insufferable pride and mirror-cracking vanity. By understanding and using this data, maybe he could defeat him. Not kill him, but defeat him.

His tactics decided upon, Jack was ready.

The fanfare to begin this contest went on for some time. The Red Dragon was announced with his six previous kills and Jack was announced with two kills, one maiming and three victories conceded. Fireworks displays of whole battle sequences from their earlier fights were displayed. Jack looked at himself: huge. Towering figures moving realistically. The word "spectacular" was redefined by this display. The crowd howled out its approval.

The Red Dragon was still parading around on the other side of the arena, well away from where Jack had come to rest and was now standing quietly. The Dragon's display went on for almost five minutes, and the crowd was whipped into a wild, frothing mob, ready for blood. The Jolo, having lapped up all the cheers that even he could stomach, turned toward Jack.

Jack looked across the broad expanse of turf and held eye contact with his opponent for some moments. He raised his sword and took three aggressive steps toward the Jolo, and then with theatrical aplomb turned his back on the opposing fighter and ignored him.

The noise had died as the crowd anticipated action. Jack raised his sword before him and thrust the blade firmly in the Turf where it quivered. He then looked up at the crowd and held his two clenched fists to the sky. The crowd responded with a roar and the now-familiar chant: "Banister Kid, Kid, Kid!"

Turning his back to his opponent was calculated to infuriate the "Red Dragon." Jack also knew the Jolo would not easily be provoked into attacking his unprotected back. But neither would the Jolo walk around Jack to face him, as this would be the type of humiliating control that he would not allow himself to endure. Such vain fellows were their own worst enemies. With a few simple taunts, they were so predictable.

The attack began, long before his opponent was within striking range. Jack saw the Red Dragon approach; somehow the Dragon was even taller than he at first appeared and he felt shrunken and weak. Darkness cast over the sun, as if a malignant cloud had blotted out the once-bright orb. The Dragon's sword sang as it came clear of its scabbard. The thing was a purplish red. Not really a color but a pulsing organic instrument of evil, ready to suck the life from any living being. Then it was slicing toward his head and he still couldn't pull his own sword free. His hand gripped tight the hilt, then slid away. Closer came the Dragon, his red sword swinging and then biting down hard in an animated slow motion.

The crowd was a solid roar.

Jack felt terror.

He felt the hot scald of piss running down his leg.

He cringed for fear of the painful impact.

Desperately he kept trying to grasp the hilt of his sword. His hands felt numb and unresponsive, his grip would not close. He couldn't pull the sword loose. It would not come free.

But it was too late because he was dead. His head was tumbling through the air. Fountains of blood pulsed from his still-erect torso. Weakness filled his knees and they bent slightly, but somehow he did not fall. His balled fists were still raised. How could that be?

The unholy racket of the crowd raged on and blasted into him in tidal waves of raw sound and emotion.

The image shifted. He hadn't turned his head – but where was his head? There it was on the ground. Through the rivers of blood he could see the frothing crowd and their tormented faces. They were signaling frantically with their arms for him to turn. Screaming at him. It was a thunder of desperation. Hysteria going into insanity.

His knees bent further, losing strength. The Dragon thumped closer from behind. The blood still gushed from his severed neck and pooled around his feet. Each pounding step bought the Red Dragon closer. The commentators were jabbering at a fever pitch, completely unmindful of their jobs, enthralled with the unbelievable drama being enacted before their very eyes.

"He doesn't know the Dragon is almost on top of him. My God! I think he thinks the crowd is cheering him on. How can he? Look at them, they're hysterical. Look at that! A woman is actually pulling clumps of hair from her head. My God!" The voice was shrill and panicked. The Red Dragon continued his deadly measured pace.

"Why won't that stupid kid turn around? My guts are turning to water! Someone grab him and shake sense into him. Turn around! The bastard will gut you from behind without a second thought. Turn around!" screamed the man. "I can't bear to see the kid killed like this."

"I hate this. I love this."

Hysterical shouts and screams continued to rise in pitch, trying to warn Jack of danger as the Dragon approached from behind. He was totally oblivious of the Dragon's presence, because he was already dead. The crowd was a wild thing tormented beyond all reason by this spectacle. It was like watching your favorite child standing in the middle of a busy street, blissfully happy and unaware of danger, with a truck barreling down on him, with you screaming your lungs out and the child just continuing to smile at you, waving hello.

The blood continued to spurt; he sank to his knees and splashed into the crimson tide.

Step by step, the level of fear in the Colosseum was raised to where it was almost a tangible thing in itself, a palpable force that would violently shake Jack back into the real universe where death stalked. His naïve, boyish smile was a frightening sight. One camera had his face full-frame and this image flashed across all the colossal screens of the stadium. Innocence that gave itself to death.

I'm dead, he knew.

"Why doesn't he turn and fight? He can fight! I've seen him. There's no reason for this!" The din was horrendous, the raw emotion a hot bath of terror.

At Jack's house, watching the screen, Wendy's face was a contorted mask bathed in tears. She sat hand-in-hand with a stupefied Sharon. Wendy had not been able to avoid the lure that the fight represented and had returned to see it, but not to her home – that was too dangerous. Now, pushed beyond reason by fear, hate and love, she was trapped in the moment that vibrated within her in a loud, sickening buzz that was pure horror. This man would kill Jack and she was forced to watch him die. The Red Dragon was so close to him, step by step. Jack was gone. Jack was dead.

"Turn around and fight. Fight Jack, fight! How dare you stand there and not fight!" She was not aware that she had screamed this out.

As a camera zoomed in, Jack's face filled the entire screen; from an impassive face he winked! His lips moved. One word. She had seen his lips form that word many times. Thousands of times. What had he said?

In an instant the confusion and horrible tension drained from her and she began to laugh wildly in uncontrolled relief. He had said, "Wendy." She thought she heard a faint echo of it in her mind. She grabbed Sharon Cousins and shook her. "He's all right, he's all right!"

The Red Dragon was upon him.

In a move that had not been seen since Tactical Unit One was embodied, Jack pushed a human body beyond what it could perform. Without ever having looked behind, he dropped his hands to the pommel of his sword, which he grasped. He pivoted on this point, drawing up his legs and kicking them out behind and upward in a blindingly fluid motion. Both feet connected with the Jolo's neck underneath his chin, the back pressure from the blow rattled through Jacks body. The arc of the Dragon's slashing sword never completed its swing. With his body in full extension, Jack plucked his sword from the ground, allowing him to slow and land with catlike grace on his feet. The Jolo Red Dragon was laid out on the ground.

Jack raised his sword toward the sky. The sun, taking its cue, flashed and glittered off the blade's polished face. The crowd was ecstatic with awe and relief.

Men and women in the stands openly wept.

Jack relaxed his tight grip on his own mind. It had been some task to let the Jolo think he was successful in his telepathic manipulation and humiliation of him. Because the Jolo had so much attention occupied in mind games, Jack had been able to draw him close enough to launch a totally unexpected attack. This caught his enemy fractionally unprepared. Even so, the Jolo had managed to raise his sword for a killing blow in the tiny fragment of time remaining to him. It was a close thing. Once again Jack's longstanding policy to not mix active telepathy and fighting had served him well.

The mental image of Jack pissing himself had been a good touch by his adversary. Even with Jack knowing it was a mind game, the powerful urge to urinate can automatically trip the flow. He panicked momentarily and touched the cloth to make sure it was still dry. It was.

Jack had used the Jolo's arrogance, pride and vanity against him. The blow he'd struck would have broken the neck of any human body. The replay flashing across the huge EV clearly showed the neck at an unnatural angle. Death to any man.

Jack stood looking down at the Jolo and wondered if the humiliation of this "defeat" would be greater or lesser than the humiliation of exposing himself for what he truly was by getting up off the Turf and continuing the fight. No "human" could ever do that. If the Jolo could think clearly past his anger and dazed state, he would know that by getting up and fighting on, he would prejudice the games from here on out. The games would be suspect, appear rigged and attract fewer and fewer real fighters.

So, Jack stood and waited.

The Jolo had wanted to fight and kill Jack in some bizarre vendetta of his own imagining. Now, to be on the receiving end of even more humiliation and directly from the hated source, may cause an uncontrollable response. What would he do?

Jack was ready.

The Jolo lay there quivering with impotent rage; the crowd took this to be death throes.

The Jolo was probably still disoriented, as the blow had come at a speed faster than he could react to. Handlers came onto the field and checked the stricken gladiator. In a minute they pronounced him defeated. The crowd went wild. With flashing sword aloft, Jack left the arena.

Norman wanted to run out to the Turf and hug Jack until he couldn't breathe. But he wasn't able to draw himself away from the replay clips. There was something so captivating about it he couldn't move. All over the world, fans were glued to their TV's and EV cubes, watching the segment of the fight where Jack and the Red Dragon joined battle. Its only drawback was that it was too short. The solution was to look at it in slow motion; viewed like this, it seemed an elegant but savage ballet. The speed, precision and power of execution was beyond anything previously known. The motion was fluid and graceful, the impact staggering. The victory and defeat captured in this one moment had power to capture the imagination and to move deeply anyone who saw it. There was little blood and no base expression of evil intent outside the crazed look frozen on the Red Dragon's face at the moment of impact. It was pure fighting skill executed with breezy exactitude.

It was one of those events that imprinted itself upon one's memory that could be recalled in all its vivid brilliance at a moment's notice and was talked about for the rest of one's life. "I was there," one would claim, and gain stature thereby.

●

The remaining gladiators were quietly convinced by their trainers that Jack had defeated a Jolo on the Turf, and though they were right for the wrong reasons, they were so intimidated by school boy Jack Cousins, there was no further contest of note.

Norman saw an upshot from the win over the Red Dragon. The fighters and trainers treated Jack with respect. Gone was the resentment and hatred. He was a legitimate peer and was treated as such.

By the week's end, Jack had won the right to Immortality.

After the final victory, no one would let Jack leave the Turf. Through the rain of confetti and streamers Jack spoke to the standing-room-only crowd and the largest televised audience ever to watch a single event.

The pageantry surrounding his victory was full blown. The celebration took hours to wind down.

Finally, Jack stood center turf knee deep in flower petals.

He looked out upon the crowd and the world.

"I thank you for your support and the joy you convey for my victory." The Colosseum shook with the outpouring of one hundred and fifty thousand souls raising their voices together. "I even thank those of you who bet against me!" There was raucous laughter. Jack waited until the voices became quiet.

"Has any one of you ever questioned who you really are?

"I wonder if there are among you, any who feel misunderstood?

"I wonder, have you conceived a star-high goal, where others oppose you and do everything within their power to stop you?

"Please hear me. When the whole world tells you, 'NO', when they do their best to make nothing of you, when they try to destroy those you love and vilify your supporters.

"The only thing that can bring failure is to agree with them. Stay true to yourself.

"Push hard.

"And win!"

● ● ●

The world was celebrating the Miracle on the Turf. Jubilation and partying went from the Pacific Time zone morning victory in Los Angeles deep into the night and through the following sunrise. Whatever the time zone, the riot of festivity engulfed the planet.

CHAPTER 33

"I have a new Investigator ready to take your post. He has trained diligently for some months and will perform well," Boltax said. "Your new posting will be confidential – no one but me will know where you go. And your duties will be... minimal.

"Your time is short, use it well." Boltax smiled a shark's smile – the last set of teeth you ever saw.

The Investigator felt submerged and walked away in a semi-paralyzed state. But the dazed condition blew away before he got outside and his mind went into high gear.

It was solve or die.

Worse than death was losing Immortality.

I can't let that happen.

The investigation was in confusion. *I must make progress. What can I do right now?* Images flashed by in mental review. The Bio-Comp had given him important information and extensive analysis, but nothing came of it. He needed to get back to basics. In his office he looked at the computer files and once again lost focus; faces and names and tenuous connections that crisscrossed but ultimately led nowhere. There were so many possibilities, too many to track down.

The Investigator stroked his body – it was a fine thing and he didn't want to lose it. He looked in a mirror and sighed.

If he died on Earth, he would be reborn here. He shuddered. It was hard enough to stomach mixing with the natives every day, but to become one. The revulsion triggered his gag reflex and he spewed vomit onto his outdated computer equipment.

I have to solve this.

In the initial investigation, he'd tracked down all the possibilities, tied off all the loose ends. He'd spoken to everyone, scanned all their minds.

No! He had missed one.

The girl in Salt Lake City.

He interviewed and scanned the mind of another girl. Not the one who took deferment. All other leads were null. This added its own weight. Maybe her absence was not innocent coincidence but willful obstruction.

That makes sense. And it hasn't come from the Bio-Comp. He felt motivated. He wiped his sleeve across his mouth, removing the last of the vomit. He ran out to the sky dock.

While skimming over the mountains, he decided to re-interview the clerk at the Salt Lake City Induction Center.

Another loose end in the same town.

The Investigator approached the clerk windows and saw the man he needed. He had the guards move all the natives away. "I'm here to give you a mind probe," he said. "Hold still." The Investigator invaded the clerk's mind, probing unmercifully, trying all the mental gymnastics of which he was capable.

After twenty minutes of this fumbling around, the clerk said, "My head hurts. I'm hungry. I can't think straight." He yawned.

Again the Investigator couldn't sort out the clerk's mental confusion involving that time. "Do you still have the printout of the kid's face I gave you? It might jog your memory." The clerk began searching. "Don't worry, I'll print another one," the Investigator said.

"I have it." The clerk closed a file drawer, "I found it. See." And handed it to the Investigator.

"Now you have two." The Investigator looked at the older image and then the one he printed. The faces were different. Not profoundly dissimilar: but not the same features.

Confusion hit.

I've been handing out photos that won't identify my suspect. This's wrong. Very wrong. My computer's been messed with. That's illegal. That's impossible.

There could only be one source for this.

He called Boltax. Boltax dismissed his call. He called again. He was dismissed again. He left a message. It was erased. He was on his own.

He walked to a coffee shop and sat at a table with a latte. He tried to see the whole investigation in his mind. There was too much data. All the refinement done by the Bio-Comp led nowhere. His mental machinery went into a slow spin. He got more coffee and some cake. It was good.

Coffee shops are all this planet has to offer.

He stared out the window and saw a lamp post. In that moment, it was the only thing in his turbulent world that wasn't spinning. Computer security was inviolate. Over the entire Directory no-one could manipulate computer files. Certainly not some second rate Bio-Comp on a back water planet.

But it was happening.

Bio-Comp's help led nowhere. It was confusing. He took the two pictures and laid them side by side. Real alteration. *But I didn't notice it.* That was sinister. *The file was altered slowly so I couldn't see the change.*

A woman walked past, "Hey that's…"

"Mind your own business." The investigator pushed the pictures into the file. *Damn native, don't they know who I am?*

She shrugged and kept walking.

Boltax won't talk to me. I'm on my own.

Someone was sabotaging his investigation. So the Investigator went back to what he knew, what he had discovered.

The kid had been at this induction center.

The girl lived here.

I've got to keep going, he thought. The Investigator drove the ground transport to the house of deferral thirty one – the only native on his list he hadn't interviewed.

I'll get her this time.

●

The Investigator arrived at her house at twelve noon to begin his surveillance. There were comings and goings but he couldn't get close enough to read any minds. He inserted a mobile bug and he toured the whole house and listened in on conversations. Nothing. He should have left a bug last time he was here.

It was now after midnight – nearly one a.m. He was tired and hungry.

But mostly he was frightened. As the hour's slipped away he became uncertain, then filled with doubt. If this didn't work, what would happen to him? With so many wasted hours, he felt useless. If he didn't succeed here… he shuddered.

The Investigator wondered if he could disappear into the native population to avoid… But what would he do? He despised the food, the smell, the entertainment – he hated it all. These primitives knew of no other existence, but he did, and to live with them was to die. It was all going around and around in his head.

A Jeep pulled up to the corner at the far end of the street, waiting to turn.

Instinctively, he lowered his body below the dash, even though no one could see him. The Jeep pulled up in front of the house. A girl got out. She walked to the door and came under the porch light. It was her!

The Investigator jumped out and dashed across the road and grabbed her before she could get a key in the lock. He spun her around.

"Are you Wendy White?"

She sagged. This was it. Oh, why had she come home now? Her contingency plans filled her mind as she realized how stupid they were. Being face to face with the Directory official she caved in – her stream of thinking was giving everything away. Somehow she knew he was a telepath…. But that wasn't known to the general public…. Blunder after blunder and her mind was stalling, locking up after failing to conceal…. Oh no, no, no… What, what, what? Think of something, anything… anything but…

He was shaking her roughly and she could see his lips mouthing one word. There was no sound. She turned her head away. He jerked her near, then extended his arms to their full length, shaking her violently back and forth like a rag doll, her head whiplashing painfully. He was now screaming one word over and over. Bullets of sound.

Think. Think. *Think.* She demanded of herself. She had to keep white noise going in her head and avoid that one subject. Noise, think of nothing, think of everything. She settled on the absurd – a pink elephant. A quick surge of triumph passed through her, she had avoided that one deadly thought, was avoiding it. Pink elephant, pink elephant in a tutu, pink elephant skipping…

The agent stopped shaking her, looked blank for a moment, then laughed in her face.

"You've got to be kidding!" He laughed. He stopped shaking her.

He caught her eyes and said, "The boy," and showed the picture of the boy from the early printout. And in her traitorous head there was an automatic response. Images of the boy he was hunting flashed bright and true.

Yes, Yes! There he was. It's him. This girl is the missing link. His long-sought connection. "Deferment," he said.

Deferment. Yes. There he is explaining it to her and how to avoid being caught. It went on and on – the whole deferment plot.

He must be found immediately – he was dangerous. A frown creased his brow. The boy seemed to know a lot about the Directory but he was definitely a mudgrubber, a dirtdigger. The Investigator felt a rising sense of panic. Something was very wrong here. Dangerously, disastrously wrong.

"Where is he?" he shouted at the girl, his voice shrill with alarm. Her traitorous mind delivered up the data that would never have passed her lips and she hated herself for it – for her bad timing, for her lack of mental control. She had betrayed him. That thing she so desperately sought to avoid. *Oh God, no. No, no, no, nooooo.*

"What is he doing now?" The information poured forth.

The kid had won the Fight for Immortality! He had won it today! A sort of screaming noise started in his head and he stood paralyzed, loosening his crushing grip on her biceps.

●

Boltax must be warned. He was dead. These two thoughts alternated compulsively through him. That and surging waves of terror. He looked at the girl, dropped her arms as if her touch scalded him and walked back to his car.

Behind Wendy, the front door swung open with a thud. Her father stood on the threshold with a loaded shotgun. Hope surged in her breast and she shouted to her father.

"Daddy, that man is going to kill Jack!"

The Investigator, oblivious to what the mudgrubbers were doing or saying, was almost to his car. He shot a hand into his pocket, pulled out a weapon, put it back and searched further. No communicator. Hell, there was no guarantee that Boltax would accept the call, and the Bio-Comp was suspect. Even so, the Investigator frantically searched for the comm device. No, it wasn't on his person.

He wrenched open the car door and searched the seats where it could have fallen.

Wendy's father had moved to her side and she clutched at him, "Daddy, if he goes free, Jack will die." Her father looked shocked and skeptical. "Shoot him, Daddy. Kill him!"

Dale White looked at his daughter, she was hysterical.

The Investigator was panic-driven, thinking about this dangerous kid living in the bowels of the Directory complex itself and how he would soon be getting an advanced body. He must contact Boltax immediately. Where the hell was his communicator? He searched the rear seats: no. On the floor under food wrappers and drink cans: no.

"Shoot him, Daddy! Kill that man!"

Dale White was in complete turmoil.

His daughter had lost her head and was begging and screaming for him to shoot and kill.

His gun was up but there was no clear shot. "Daddy, *Daddy, Daddy, Daddy!*"

Lights were coming on all down the street. Witnesses, Dale thought, and then was shocked at how close he was to pulling the trigger – he lowered the barrels.

Wendy envisioned Jack lying peacefully asleep in a room at the Colosseum and someone coming at him with an axe… She grabbed at the shot gun and said ferociously, "Give me the gun, I'll do it." But she could not wrench it from him.

The Investigator jumped out and looked under the car. No communicator! He strode to the trunk and was throwing equipment out. No communicator!

"Daddy." Tears poured down her face. "Jack, the love of my life. Jack, oh no… Jack."

Dale White was in total turmoil – shoot a man?! How could he? Murder!

Then she said quietly. "He's one of *them*, Daddy. An alien. He'll kill Jack in an hour if we give him the chance." She said it with utter finality. "This alien will be gone in a minute and so will our only chance to save Jack," she said quietly. They looked over at the alien as he slammed the trunk, leaving debris strewn about the ground.

Mr. Dale White, conservative, law-abiding, white male, took three decisive paces forward and abruptly there was thunder on that quiet street as both barrels discharged.

The Investigator was thrown forward and pain lanced through his buttocks and back. He looked over to see a man reloading a primitive chemical/projectile weapon. He sneered at the man and casually reached into his pocket and pulled forth his own weapon.

He pointed the short tube at the man but did not depress the stud. He smiled a slow smile; better to do the girl, and leave the father to regret shooting that thing at him. He adjusted the weapon to its low setting (make her linger – really feel the pain) then he pointed it at the girl, and had the satisfaction of seeing fright in her eyes.

He depressed the stud.

Wendy screamed, but nothing happened – that is, she felt no impact.

The Investigator smiled again; even the lowest setting was a lethal dose. Serves the bitch right! She'd really gone out of her way to obstruct his investigation and that had gotten him in serious trouble. Now she had her reward. She would die in agony as her skin slowly peeled away from her muscles and the ligaments came loose and finally, days later, the organs of the native body stopped functioning. He smiled.

He looked back at the man.

"You tried to kill me with that thing." He had a burning impulse to fry him to a cinder. No, watching his daughter die in agony was a better punishment.

He dismissed the mudgrubber from his mind even though he was once again raising that weapon. Then another shaft of frustration shot through him, he had to *drive* back to his air shuttle.

Primitives and their vulgar technology! He must communicate to Boltax – fast. And it would have to be done face to face because he wouldn't take his call. The Investigator stepped into the car. It tore away, leaving shock in two human minds.

"That man should be dead!"

"I hoped you could kill him Daddy, but his Jolo body is too tough."

"Huh?" said Dale White, then looked his daughter over. "Are you hurt? I think he fired that thing he was holding at you!"

"I didn't feel a thing." Wendy dashed inside and called the number Jack had given her. One ring, two rings, three, four…. There was no answer! She redialed, hands shaking. Maybe she'd dialed the wrong number. One, two, three…. No answer.

Jack must be warned!

A Directory Investigator knew he was the source of the deferments! It was a screaming emergency.

A plane! Zero planes leaving for LA until morning. Can't drive there in less than nine hours. She looked at her watch, ten past two in the morning. Too late. It was far too late for her to do anything. She slumped over in helpless dejection.

But she remembered. Jack had once had a wife, he said, who'd been used against him. They may have ransacked her mind but they would not enslave her body. Not me, not ever! She had to assume Jack would make it on his own.

But even as she stood there, she felt the energy drain from her. She'd worked so hard to protect Jack from an attack that could come at him through her, and she'd failed miserably.

She couldn't even warn him. And that was desperation itself. She would be the instrument of Jack's death. She was so tired.

The police siren roused her.

The local PD asked questions that had nothing to do with anything, because no one knew what was going on but her.

The police finally left – no body, no foul.

Her father pressed her hard: "Someone could have died out there on the street and I have a right to know what this is all about."

"Of course you have a right to know, Daddy, but if I tell you and that gets you killed…"

He looked at her steadily. "How is it that you or anyone in this family is in a position to be killed on the street? It's something you're involved in with Jack, isn't it?"

Wendy sighed.

"The man you shot is a Directory Investigator and telepath. He's investigating who is responsible for the deferments of Directory contracts. He read my thoughts; in there he saw Jack, and now he's gone to the Colosseum to kill him. I won't tell you why – but there is no way to warn Jack and it's driving me crazy." She shook her head. "If he's warned, it might save his life."

"Still the same question, Wendy, why are you involved in it?"

"Because it's important."

"Is it important enough to get killed for, or to put other family members in danger?"

"I don't want to die for this, I don't want Jack to die, and of course I don't want you or any of our family in danger. But I'm with Jack now – he's doing what he has to do and I'm doing what I can to help or at least not be a liability to him."

"But the family, Wendy, how can you…"

She cut him off.

"The fate of Earth hangs in the balance – what happens today will change the world!" Dale White looked aghast. "I have a part to play in this, Daddy." She looked directly at her father. Then it struck her. There were no scheduled flights, but what about unscheduled ones?

"I need your help, Daddy. I need you to fly to LA, shuttle to the Colosseum and tell Jack what happened here." Dale White looked at his watch. It was three a.m. He had to be at work in five hours. He managed the worldwide production and distribution of paper products from his office in Salt Lake City. That morning he was scheduled to lead a conference that would set the levels of production in four countries for the coming year. Additionally, a number of new paper items were up for final approval.

It would be unprecedented for him to miss a meeting of any kind, let alone one this important. But if what Wendy said was true, then the order of magnitude of importance between his meeting and her needs was vastly different. He had to decide.

Dale asked, "Why not phone him?"

"The land line number he gave me must be for a public phone away from the Colosseum, and all the personal communication devices are monitored. This message can't be delivered by phone.

"Daddy, maybe there is time; this Directory person would have returned to the Colosseum an hour ago. But what if he can't report the information till morning? What if his boss is asleep? Won't let anyone disturb him – nothing on *Earth* could bother someone so powerful, right? We might have time to get to Jack before the Directory people do. With this information, he can decide what to do, he might have a chance."

"I don't think the airlines have any flights scheduled out before six in the morning." Dale said. "Would that get me there in time to make a difference?"

"Los Angeles is one hour behind us. So if it takes you two hours to get to the Colosseum you would still be there at seven a.m. LA time. It could mean the difference…."

Dale nodded, it could. If Jack hadn't won the Fight for Immortality, he wouldn't have even considered what his daughter was asking him to do. And that thought was unacceptable to him: as an adult, Wendy had never given him reason to doubt her, but "the fate of Earth" was hard to swallow. It was hard to make a life changing, and possibly life-threatening, decision on what smacked of over-emotion and melodrama.

But he had believed her when he pulled the trigger.

What Jack had done was impossible; there was no way a seventeen-year-old boy could have won that competition if there wasn't something else going on. Something so different as to be inexplicable; something as important as the fate of Earth.

"I'll charter a jet." Dale said.

"Daddy, can we afford it?"

"Does it matter?"

She shook her head.

"Okay. Grab your computer and come with me. I drive, you call."

Dale looked up the stairs; Amanda must still have her earplugs in. They were out the door in twenty seconds.

● ● ●

The Investigator's sense of urgency had become frustration and paranoia. A few of those little pellets had actually penetrated his skin. With his fingers he squeezed them out. The tiny holes had scabbed over and the pain was almost gone. It was almost five a.m. and the Bio-Comp continued to deny him access to Boltax.

He was going crazy!

Twice he had tried to force his way into Boltax's sleeping cubicle, but the Bio-Comp had simply overridden the controls and blocked him. He was now in his own room pacing back and forth.

Boltax would condemn him for delaying the evidence of who started the contract deferments. The provocateur was here at the Colosseum – inside their very walls. Had been here for days and weeks. What was he planning now?

He decided to go to the kid's room and arrest him. But, feeling cautious, he looked at the highlights of his fights and saw the last ten seconds with the Red Dragon. Holy…. The Dragon was a Jolo body – the natives wouldn't see it, but it was obvious. He looked at more of the footage. That walk, he knew that walk…Boltax! Oh, no! That kid was dangerous. No way was he going near him.

Bamm, bamm, bamm.

AaHhhh! He just about jumped out of his skin.

The Investigator yanked open his door. It was his assistant.

"Don't ever do that again!"

"Do what?"

He was embarrassed. He'd been ignoring his assistant's calls for hours. He couldn't stand talking to the stupid clod in this emergency. Just as Boltax had ignored him.

"What do you want?" he said ferociously.

"Look at this, sir." He played the interview with Perrywhite.

He thought his head was going to explode.

This kid, this same dangerous kid, was responsible for directing the initial native investigation that discovered the true presence of the Directory on Earth. *The same damned kid!*

If only he'd watched that stupid Fight for Immortality. The kid's face was on display the entire competition. Boltax was sure to go off when he discovered his Investigator missed what everyone in the world had seen!

The Bio-Comp was treasonous.

The computer had seen the connection and suppressed it.

The Bio-Comp altered the facial image.

The Bio-Comp was blocking him now!

Still, one look at the fight highlights and the whole investigation would have blown wide open. Oh, yeah, Boltax was going to kill him. That obstructive computer! This was a legitimate emergency!

"Go get the native you interviewed. Boltax might want to talk to him."

"When should I leave?"

"Now, immediately. And don't use our computer to find him."

"Then how…?"

"Figure it out, you moron. I want you back in three hours with that native."

During his endless pacing, he began to doubt if he knew what was going on. None of it made sense. Boltax taken out by a native? Bio-Comp covering for a native? Now he was sure this was a screaming full-throttle, raging, red emergency.

● ● ●

The Bio-Comp chimed Boltax awake at seven a.m.

"Your Investigator has made multiple attempts to access your rooms and disturb you. As per your instructions I prevented this."

"Allow him in."

"This had better be good!" Boltax said with menace. He hated to have his sleep cycle interrupted, especially by a worm like his Investigator. The Bio-Comp had finally decided to be helpful.

"I found him!" the Investigator blurted.

"Found who, you idiot?" Boltax snarled.

"I found the provocateur, the one who spread the information about contract deferment!" the Investigator spewed out in a gush.

Boltax wasn't impressed. Where was his proof, this bum was likely to tell him any story to save his neck. And the real offender would remain free and continue causing trouble.

"According to his girlfriend he's here, here in the Colosseum," the agent stated. "He won the Fight for Immortality just yesterday!"

Boltax already had plans for that particular mudgrubber. If he was the same one who had caused all this contract trouble, too…. A circuit in Boltax's head snapped.

He went from boredom to unholy rage.

A wild cry battered the Investigator's ears. Boltax charged like an animal around his living space and destroyed anything in his way. For minutes the tirade continued. He randomly grabbed objects and screamed at them, then smashed them against walls or floor.

The Investigator was shaken and scared. He hid behind a solid chair. A man this irrational was dangerous to be around. But he'd been subject to extreme provocation. This kid had been making a fool of him for how long…?

Boltax was looking at a scenic wall display and breathing heavily. The Investigator waited until the breathing slowed.

"There's more, sir."

Boltax looked at him.

"My assistant interviewed a native from the CIA. This CIA native discovered the same kid influenced the initial Earth investigation into DE – the investigation that discovered we were an alien race."

"Here's what's wrong with your analysis: the kid is a *native*." Boltax said. "There has to be an enemy agent from the Directory behind the kid, guiding and controlling him – or none of this makes any sense. We can't even guess what the kid's controller has as a motive, or where he is now."

"I have the intelligence service native." The Investigator looked at a note. "Perrywhite. He's here for you to interview if you want to talk to him."

Boltax looked at his Investigator. He was not *entirely* stupid. "Okay, take him to my office."

●

Perrywhite had been dragged out of his bed in the middle of the night, flown across the country in less than an hour in a Directory shuttle, taken to an Investigator's room at the Colosseum facility in Los Angeles, and interrogated. Why he was in a personal apartment and not a police-style interrogation room was a mystery.

It had been a very tame interrogation. Looking around he loved the guy's apartment. It was beautiful. He couldn't wait to move up in the world and join the Directory team. He would soon have more power than he'd lost. This was his chance to make it into the big time – and from the Investigator's reaction, the news about the kid had been a bombshell.

He had a big payday coming.

Perrywhite deserved a big reward for service rendered. Not only that, when he got a Jolo body, he would wouldn't take crap from anyone. He would make them pay.

The Investigator returned. "The Chief of Directory Enterprises wants to see you now." They walked down long hallways.

● ● ●

"Please come in." Boltax said formally. He beckoned the man into his office.

The Earth Intelligence officer took a seat without being asked.

Minutes ago Bio-Comp showed him this Earth worm's attempt to bribe his way into the Colosseum. The guard had been amusing.

This interview was probably a waste of time, he was sure the man had no other valuable information. But any chance, however small, to unearth something more about Jack Cousins must be taken.

"You Earthmen are a constant surprise! Your information about the boy was very valuable."

Perrywhite grinned. "I've been working tirelessly for the Directory since your arrival on our planet." He then listed all the services he had provided, *unasked*. The catalogue was long and demonstrated his fidelity to the Directory above all other countries or concerns. Most of it was fabricated, but Perrywhite knew there was no way for the Chief to verify that. Finally he came to the point.

"Sir, I believe for services rendered, I deserve Jolo status. I can be far more useful to you if you transfer me into an immortal body."

A shaft of rage went through Boltax.

He was stunned.

Seeing the strange expression, Perrywhite continued. "You can assign me to your staff directly, or I could remain embedded in the CIA and provide high quality intelligence."

"Amazing!" Boltax choked out.

The "intelligence officer" preened at this "compliment."

Perrywhite prattled on.

The cesspool of lies, resentments and arrogance rotating in this mudstick's head was a contaminant – Boltax withdrew all contact.

The idea that such scum could even consider he had any right to talk to him, let alone make a demand! And to demand the ultimate reward as if it were a right he had earned, was so disgusting to him that he sat paralyzed for a few minutes as the fool continued to churn out words.

This guy could lie. He shot a question at him. "Is Jack Cousins in contact with other aliens? Are you?" And Boltax had his answer: he didn't know. He hadn't listened to the words.

There was quiet for a minute or two while Boltax calmed down and the fool finally perceived his proposal had not met with immediate acceptance. But there was something Boltax could freely give this worm.

"Yes, Mr. Perrywhite, you are an example of the very best this planet has to offer. Your selfless service to us must be rewarded."

"Thank you." Perrywhite was relieved, for a minute he thought something had gone wrong.

"I'm happy to offer you immortality. Come with me." Boltax led the sheep to slaughter.

They dropped down many levels, then paced briskly through and across corridors.

Perrywhite could hardly contain his excitement. Finally, he was getting what he deserved and bypassing the animalistic violence of those men on the Turf.

Boltax waved him through the security doors and into the bio-lab where, for convenience, there was a small Recyclex and transfer room.

Boltax called the Bio-Tech and asked where he had stored the faulty runt body he'd been working on. "I was going to dissolve it today. Actually, it isn't in a stasis tray and may be nonviable at this point."

"Good." Boltax smiled at Perrywhite, who could not understand Cortic. Boltax walked to the reject trays and pulled a few drawers till he found the specimen he wanted.

"Here's your new high-tech Directory body." Again he smiled.

Perrywhite looked at his new body – it looked so *masculine*. And off kilter.

"But sir, the face, the body – no one will know I'm me."

"Very well, you're not ready, we will return…"

"No, no! I'm ready right now."

"Excellent."

Because there was no Training Corp on Earth, primitive electrical stimulation of the body was necessary to get it to function – provide rudimentary muscle tone and continence.

Boltax looked at the test log; the Bio-Tech had been experimenting with the parameters of correct electrical stimulation to bring a flaccid (just grown) body to the point it could be used. The tech had over charged and under charged the body, but Boltax supposed it would be able to walk out of the facility.

Boltax forced the transfer – not caring about the result.

Soon Perrywhite was lying in a daze.

Boltax slapped him around to get him alert. Threw some clothing at him, gave him no orientation.

Fifteen minutes later Boltax booted the native out the service entrance.

Perrywhite looked back. He shook his head to clear his vision – finally he saw the Directory Chief clearly.

"You insolent piece of shit, you have a new body, as you asked. But no one will know you, you have no identity, you're on your own. Now get out of here. If you're not off the grounds in fifteen minutes, you're dead." The door slammed closed.

The native/Jolo shuffled away, not really grasping his situation. Perrywhite saw his image reflected in a store window outside Directory grounds. It shocked him. He felt a sharp pang of hunger. The bladder leaked and he was soaked in urine.

"Who am I?" he cried out in agony.

Even his mommy wouldn't know him.

He began to cry.

● ● ●

After throwing Perrywhite off the base Boltax returned to the Bio-Lab.

With the deferment criminal, Jack Cousins, safely ignorant and trapped in the FFI "victory" suite above – that source of trouble would soon wind down.

This Bio-Lab was now his biggest problem.

The facility was huge, buried deep beneath the Colosseum.

He urgently needed it fully functional.

Before him were massive rows of growth tanks. Lining the walls were huge containers that fed nutrients to the growing bodies. There were workstations where cells were catalyzed and added at crucial incubation points.

The Biological Technician was a fool, incapable of growing a standard Jolo body.

Boltax's anxiety escalated.

He needed Jolo armies for use on Earth and for shipment.

He was not getting them.

The quota of military mud-Jolos Bio-One demanded was overdue. Not one had been transported.

The only saving grace was that shipment of the "technically trained" mudgrubbers had recovered and recently *exceeded* quota. South America and some areas of central Africa had a wealth of populations who were not in contact with the outside world and were ripe for plucking.

The process for snatching whole towns was now very smooth; his native DFE (Defense Force Earth), disguised as an Earth-based health organization, would advertise a feast day at a village or town. Word would go out for miles around.

On feast day, with drugged food in their bellies, the natives were shown into a series of covered "amphitheaters" where they strapped themselves in to "theater" seating. The natives were treated to a montage of images – wild animals of the Directory worlds.

Boltax thought that a nice touch.

In minutes they were asleep and the ships took off. The last ship out used a broadband disrupter on the village. All that was left was upturned dirt.

They were even throwing down local grass seed.

Perfect.

It was the only reason he was not under reprimand at this very moment. The day when a reprimand and his death sentence were the same was fast approaching. He felt weak for a moment just thinking of his own death, when he had finally, against all odds, become immortal.

The demand for militarily trained mud-Jolos who would "obey any command" was heavy. Dispatches were threatening. Why wasn't he making quota? Didn't he like his current posting?

Legitimate technical faults and poorly trained personnel (and whose fault was that?) did not satisfy his superiors. *His position was in jeopardy.*

This travesty would never have happened – the mud-Jolos, the base on Earth, all of it, if Crown was still in control of the Directory.

Boltax wondered about the fate of the former Chief Executive of the Directory. During Crown's rule, he would never have contemplated the actions he now did on a daily basis.

How weak he'd become. How fast his slide into moral decay. His responsibility for societal integrity of the Directory and for people in general were gone.

When he first arrived on this planet he could tolerate the natives. Now he hated them all, even the beautiful girls who warmed his bed.

There should be no Directory presence here on Earth. He knew that was a sensible rule, but he would never have gained control of an entire planet in the old order.

He had talent, but others outstripped him. If he'd refused Bio-One's offer to control a primitive planet, such an opportunity would never come again.

Instead of being a lowly bureaucrat on a remote Directory planet, he *ruled.*

No, he reigned. Had more power than a king.

It was a potent sensation. Its price was abandoning all principle. Its cost to him personally? Best not think about it.

If Crown returned to power, he would be branded a criminal, tracked down, tried and sentenced. He would lose his Jolo status, lose his immortality.

So he was decided.

He had crossed the line and there was no going back. True, Earth was a crude affair, but it was his to do with as he pleased, so long as he kept up his quota of Identities being shipped off-planet. Both trainees and FFI transferees.

And that was worth a lot.

He smiled as he recalled the bright shiny faces of the tech course graduates. Going to a "resort planet" for low-tech jobs, they thought.

He was the law.

He had Jack Cousins.

A thorn pulled from his side.

Soon he would use his power and dispose of Jack Cousins. Call it one of life's little pleasures.

● ● ●

They came for Jack late Saturday morning. Two mud-Jolos arrived at his door; they beckoned him to follow but said nothing. He asked a few questions, they just smiled unpleasantly.

The mud-Jolos escorted him down corridor after corridor through the compound adjoining the Colosseum arena, working their way nearer to the restricted area.

After many minutes of silent walking, they approached a restricted area entrance. Jack was sure there was an invisible scanner. The mechanism, apparently satisfied, opened the fortified doors.

His escorts, Jack observed, were suppressing data. They had that look. He considered scanning their minds but dismissed the idea. It wasn't too hard to guess what they knew after talking to Dale White.

●

Wendy's father had surprised him early this morning. To Jack, the man had always been aloof, not the type to get involved. Seeing him at the door to the "victory" suite of the gladiator wing at seven a.m. was completely unexpected.

How he'd been admitted was also a mystery.

"Hello, Jack."

"Good morning Mr. White." Jack invited him in and went to his back-pack. He flipped a switch on a device he'd made weeks ago to interrupt sound recording devices.

Dale White dived right in, "You are obviously not who or what you seem to be."

"That's true."

"Thank you for that." Dale wanted to ask many questions, but restrained himself.

"Okay."

"I'm here because my daughter loves you – because of her involvement with you…" Dale White told Jack not only the warning from Wendy but also all that had happened a few hours ago in Salt Lake City and how she refused him any explanation. "So I need you to do whatever you have to do to prevent any further danger to my family."

"Mr. White, we're all in this together; everyone on Earth is in danger."

"That may be true, but not everyone has Directory investigators coming to their door!"

"All trainees granted early deferment from their Directory contract have been contacted. Wendy would be dead and gone without her deferment. That's not drama. It's fact."

"Okay, Jack." Dale White looked at this mysterious young man, then dropped his eyes.

"This whole thing, which she and I are involved in, is about something far larger than Wendy – though I admit having a greater concern for her."

"So she wasn't kidding about the fate of Earth?"

"A little melodramatic, but essentially true. Today is the day of decision and we are in the lion's den – to mix metaphors." Jack smiled.

"It was you, wasn't it, who saved her from shipping off planet?"

"It was my original idea, but she and I planned out what to do and did it. She was a vital part of the solution and her urging and drive saved many others from a terrible fate. As I said, she's very important to me personally, but she's also very competent."

"She wouldn't tell me about any of this."

"She loves you and wanted to protect you. For your part, you should trust her ability to make sensible decisions. She hasn't been a child for some time." Dale White admired how tactfully yet firmly he'd been put in his place. "Your daughter is remarkable by any standard."

They talked for a short time more and Jack offered to pay for his chartered jet. "How can you possibly afford that?"

Jack laughed. He knew Wendy's father had not followed the Fight. He respected him more for that.

"Norman bet millions on me in round seven. The odds were unbelievably high. We won more money than we could spend in ten lifetimes."

Dale let out a low whistle. "Yes, thank you. That would help."

"Thank you for coming. You risked a lot."

Dale replied, "You're welcome, sir."

⚫

The two mud-Jolos left Jack in a holding room next to the Directory Chief's office.

He shivered.

The goal was very near.

Jack, again, didn't use telepathy. Boltax could project and that made him a powerful mind-smith. He had to be careful to maintain the façade of being an Earth native a short while longer.

Jack heard a number of people come and go, but couldn't hear the details of their conversations.

If Boltax became aware of his real name, then today would be difficult. "Tac-U-One" would drive him into frenzy.

If not, Jack was merely the guy who had caused the contract deferments, made the Directory Chief bow to local pressure and change policy on minimum age of contestants. Then kicked his ass on the Turf.

He should be over it by now. Jack smiled and then laughed. He sat on a chair and waited.

⚫ ⚫ ⚫

Jack's two escorts entered the Directory Chief's office.

"He came without hesitation?" The Directory Chief questioned the two Earthmen who had fought for and won immortality, thereby becoming mud-Jolos.

"He asked some questions but we said nothing, just as you ordered, sir."

"Good." He was pleased. The boy knew nothing. The mud-grubber thought he was going to become immortal today; he must be incredibly excited. Ecstatic even.

Boltax had an uncomfortable return from the damaged Red Dragon body. Body illness or injury made transfer problematic.

But that was days ago and he was now fully recovered.

That kid had been soooooo lucky. A fraction of a second more and his feet would not have connected with the neck.

Inexplicable luck.

This kid had humiliated him if front of the entire planet.

He would get revenge in never-ending measure. Torture, meds, torture – this cycle could go on a long time. Or transfer him into the big I-trap. Or maybe he could get one of the deformed bodies from the growth tanks in the Bio-Lab and transfer the kid into that and continue the torture. Endless possibilities. Mmmm. He felt heated.

Boltax ended his day dream.

The two mud-Jolos across from him were looking smug. He found their superior expressions irritating. Because of these two morons he considered testing gladiator entrants for intelligence. These two degraded all real Jolos. He looked at their faces and could endure it no longer.

"Computer."

"Yes, Boltax."

"Access order log."

"Done."

"All entrants into the Fight for Immortality must now pass an IQ test and achieve a minimum score of one hundred. Those who do not pass are dropped from the competition."

The two mud-Jolos looked at each other and swallowed. Boltax smiled inwardly – they were smart enough (just) to know that was aimed at them. Good, let them squirm.

The Bio-Comp repeated the order and asked for revisions.

"I'll consider making it retroactive," Boltax stated. One mud-Jolo nudged the other in the ribs and whispered in his ear. They looked disturbed.

"Your bodies contain tracking chips. If you desert or fail to obey an order I'll execute you."

They looked stricken.

Bio-Comp continued. "Noted. Order logged."

Because good-quality Jolo bodies were in short supply, Boltax decided to transfer these two mud-Jolos into the Bio-Lab failures when more intelligent FFI winners were crowned.

"Get the Investigator."

"Order logged."

Boltax felt good for a few moments.

● ● ●

The Investigator felt very resentful. He'd solved the case. Did he get praise? No. Once Boltax had calmed down, the first thing he did was chew him out.

"I'm done with that Perrywhite creature. He had no other useful information. Where do you have the girl? I want to interrogate her."

"Where do I have who, sir?" The Investigator had a sinking feeling.

"The girl, you idiot, where is the girl being held?" He paused, looking at his Investigator in disbelief. "You didn't take her?" The Investigator hesitantly shook his head. "You are the most stupid..." Boltax was at a loss. "Don't you realize this kid is *tough*? He just won the Games. He's only seventeen Earth years old. We may need the girl for leverage." Boltax shook his head, amazed that an Investigator could fail to do what was so incredibly obvious.

"Does the girl know anything else?" Boltax demanded. This time the Investigator was quick to respond.

"I've told you the important things." He thought of the consequences of an honest answer and lied. "I sucked her skull dry and threw away the pieces."

"Then how did Jack Cousins know about Directory law, why has he interfered with our operations, and how did he, a youth with no military or warrior training, win the Fight for Immortality?"

Now that the Investigator looked, he *did* have more information. "She was going to be shipped out; she'd taken a tech course and was on a five-year contract, now deferred."

He paused, hands to his temples. "There's something about a fake girlfriend diverting attention from her. There's a lake and a wrecked starship. Don't see how it's relevant. But it may be our link to the outside Directory connection. Anyway, he spread the information on contract deferment to protect her. To save her from going off world; he thought it was very dangerous but I don't know if he told her why."

"Yeah, but *how* did he know Directory law?" Boltax shouted.

The Investigator frowned. "He told her he was one of us." The rest was fuzzy and jumbled together – she was really scared about this.

"That arrogant little mudgrubber!" sputtered Boltax. "And he *is* a mudsucker. I've smelled him up close and there is no mistaking the native stench these Earth bodies have. Ha, he was just trying to impress the girl by telling her he was one of us – probably trying to get her into bed!" He frowned.

"This is still an incomplete investigation. The solution is what I thought all along – he has a Directory controller. We need to know who." Boltax brooded in silence, and then a thought brightened his features.

"What does she look like?"

"Who?"

"The girlfriend, the one you spoke to, the one who outsmarted you, you idiot!"

"She has black hair, pale skin and green eyes and is about five feet, eight inches tall."

"No, what I mean is, is she pretty, attractive, sexually exciting?"

"I would say she is beautiful, very beautiful."

"Well, well," Boltax smirked. He picked up a recently received dispatch and waved it. "A deputy of Bio-One on Crown Planet has asked the outer covert units, to send him pretty native girls for some kind of experimental procedure. Who knows what those freaks in the Biological department will do to her." He asked the Bio-Comp for the departure schedules. There were two outbound ships today. The sector ship and later the trainee's freighter.

"We can get her on this morning's outbound ship. Make sure it happens."

"The trouble, Chief, is that she has a legal contract deferment." The Investigator looked helpless.

What? I've got to get rid of this Investigator, Boltax fumed.

"This kid, Jack Cousins and his backers," continued the Investigator, "are trying to shut down our operations here on Earth base. If we hadn't caught him, he would have transferred to a Jolo body. That alone would have made him exceedingly dangerous. Capable of far more damage than he's already done.

"And you're concerned about a contract deferment?" Boltax shook his head in disbelief.

"No, I was actually trying to hide the fact that I killed the bitch already. She's as good as dead."

Boltax arched a brow.

"That bitch caused me so much trouble I gave her a low dose with the radiation gun. She'll be dead in four or five days."

Maybe he has promise.

"Go get her and all her belongings. Look through her things for any information you may have missed in your mind scan.

"Make sure she gets on the departing sector ship and put in stasis. When she gets to Crown Planet if they like her looks they can wash her of radiation and experiment on her. If not she dies of radiation poisoning; either way, it's good work."

The Investigator was relieved.

Boltax felt a warm glow. It felt good to take away something this kid loved. The first check mark on his list of revenge.

Using the girl gave him leverage. If something else went wrong, he would have her firmly in his control and out of the kid's reach.

He hoped the mudgrubber really loved her. Nothing like mental distress and emotional anguish to add to the torture he had planned. Yes, this was working out.

He looked at his Investigator and changed his mind.

"I'll send the two mud-Jolos to snatch her. Write her name, address and description in English and include whatever pictures you have of her so there won't be any mistake. They enjoy this sort of assignment." He paused again.

"Wait outside and stay there till I call you," and waved his Investigator off. "Don't talk to the kid – he's in the room next door."

I need to tell Boltax about the Bio-Comp's treason, the Investigator thought. But there was no way he was going to interrupt the Chief.

The Investigator stepped into the reception room outside Boltax's office and waited. He'd seen those mud-Jolos handle their own kind before and they were rough. That bitch was in for an unpleasant time before she was shipped to Crown Planet. She was a fine specimen for a biological experiment. Too bad she might live.

He opened his hand held computer, printed a picture of the girl, and copied her data in English on the back.

The mud-Jolos knocked and entered.

"Hey, shit bird, surprised to see you." They laughed.

"Why is that?"

"The number of times the boss said he was gonna kill you – we thought you were a goner days ago." They laughed again.

The Investigator glared at him.

"The boss got you waiting out here till we're done, huh? That's too bad for you, shit bird. Looks like our methods are more in demand than your worthless snooping around. You should hear what else the boss says about you when you're not here." They couldn't stop laughing.

The Investigator passed over the photo. "Don't keep him waiting, shit for brains."

They knocked and went into Boltax's office.

A few minutes later the Investigator was called back into the room. As he passed the mud-Jolos, one said to the other, "So what if we can't rape her? We can still have *some* fun."

The Investigator slipped his weapon from his pocket and thumbed it to full intensity, aimed at one of the broad retreating backs. At this setting the mud-Jolo would feel a mild burning sensation after a second or two. But the stupid primitive would have no idea that he would soon need serious medical attention.

He hit the activator. The weapon fizzled. He glanced at the battery gauge. It was out of charge. Damn it.

He'd hit the bitch in Salt Lake City with the weapon on its lowest setting. *I hope I fried her ass.*

He'd used the weapon on natives and they died in pain – so it was perfectly functional. Was the battery out last night? He wasn't sure.

The Investigator stepped through the entry and stood across from Boltax.

"Those two will be back after sending the girl on her way. It won't take them long. They'll bring her belongings to you, go through them carefully. We may learn more about our FFI winner.

"Now get out of here," Boltax said

The Investigator, after a long, sleepless night, slowly trudged to his room, lay back on his bed and for a moment closed his eyes.

CHAPTER 34

THE INVESTIGATOR WAS JARRED AWAKE BY the loud banging on his door. The mud-Jolos dumped trash bags full of the girl's belongings on the floor.

"The Chief told us, 'Order that stupid bum to go through her stuff immediately!'"

The Investigator scowled at them.

"Get out."

He emptied the bags on the floor and sorted the girl's possessions into two piles – written material in one pile and assorted junk in the other. *Boltax has me doing scutt work.* It was boring and he was tired. At ten a.m. he dozed.

● ● ●

Boltax had security move Jack Cousins to reception outside his office. He was surprised that Cousins had come so easily into the restricted area.

The mudgrubber made him think. How had he won FFI? Everything else? Boltax dismissed his growing sense of caution. The kid was unaware anyone knew he caused the deferments.

At the very minimum, Boltax expected the kid to suggest his trainer accompany him. The kid was good; on his screen Boltax saw a relaxed individual sitting in his outer room, hiding all the emotions he must be feeling.

He was going to become immortal. *His immortality will come from living in my memory forever.* Boltax laughed out loud.

The mudgrubber, by himself, posed no threat. Right now he could invite the kid into his office and snap his spine.

Boltax looked Jack over again. From his desk he ordered a scan on the genetic material of Jack's body.

Seconds later, the computer voiced, "Earth native, endocrine system nearing the end of re-adjustment." Meaning he was just coming out of puberty.

"Is there any indication of telepathic ability?"

"The brain is Earth-normal. No demonstrated ability detected. No enlarged pituitary."

Boltax fell to studying the kid intently. The figure on the monitor faced the pickup in the outer room and smiled. It infuriated Boltax to see the condescending smile on the mudgrubber's face.

Strange. It looked like the grubber knew he was facing the pickup. How could he? That technology hadn't been released on this planet, and wouldn't be. The pickup was the size of a pin tip, impossible to spot. Still, it felt like the kid was taunting him.

I hate that kid, he thought.

The only thing that made this meeting tolerable was that the kid didn't know it was Boltax he had defeated.

Boltax scanned Jack's thoughts and was rewarded with an explicit and infuriating procession of images. The little asshole was re-living the fight. He was playing the kick over and over. The crowd surged onto the Turf and a bevy of beautiful girls carried him away on their shoulders, trampling the prone body of the Red Dragon.

That hadn't happened. It was the kid's imagination. Then the kid played it a different way. He walked over and placed his foot on the Dragon's face while the crowd cheered wildly. He could see the kid's foot grinding into the face beneath his muddy heel. He abruptly broke contact with the kid's mind as if jabbed by a branding iron. Boltax's hands spasmodically clenched the arm rests of his chair. He was so incensed he could not think clearly. He sat taking deep breaths, wanting revenge. Wanting to smash, wanting to kill.

Eventually he achieved a degree of calmness.

He was going to punish this kid. He was going to make him pay for the humiliation he'd felt lying on the Turf, being watched by all those mudgrubbers in the Colosseum, and for rubbing it in now – even if he didn't know he was doing it.

He would destroy him and strip his mind of all relevant information, torture him and then throw him away, *forever*. That felt better. And he would find out who was behind him.

The door in front of Jack slid into its recess. He was beckoned into the adjoining office by the Jolo.

"Please take a seat," Boltax said in a powerful, commanding voice. "My name is Boltax and I am in charge of the Directory operations here on planet Earth and within this sector of space."

Jack nodded his head and shrugged delicately.

Boltax was immediately infuriated. He wanted to bash this kid's head to a mushy pulp, then rip his heart out and crush it till it squeezed between his fingers. He had to shake himself to come out of it.

Jack gave him a smile. "Wow, you must feel powerful."

Boltax could hardly think. He was being patronized by a mudgrubber in his own office on his own base.

He felt total hatred.

Only his desire for a prolonged revenge held in check immediate brutality like spiking the kid's eyes out with a stiff fingered jab. *BAM* and the grubber would be in agony.

Oh, yeah.

He was happy, he had to remind himself – he didn't want to spoil his revenge. He wanted to spit in this kid's face and say "your girl is great fun in bed."

If he shredded this mudgrubber right here and now, he would lose necessary information and considerable pleasure. Boltax was amazed by his self-control.

Something was strange, though.

Was the kid actually taunting him?

To his amazement Boltax couldn't tell. He should be able to look in this kid's head and know.

But he couldn't.

That was slightly alarming. A twinge of uneasiness seeped in. Looking into the kid's mind, the thoughts were simple, clear and devoid of motive, and looking deeper, there was – nothing?

It was odd to see a natural mental defense in a native.

"Yes, I am a powerful man. I'm about to show you just how powerful. Would you like that?"

"Yeah, that's good," Jack said glibly.

"Congratulations on achieving Immortality." Boltax almost choked on the words.

"Thank you." Then, to keep the Jolo off balance, Jack said, "That reminds me. The high point of the games for me was not the final victory, but when I defeated the Red Dragon. I expected a real tough guy. I mean, I watched replays of his other fights and his past performances were spectacular. But I think the operation to reattach his head took something out of him."

Jack could see the thunderous look on Boltax's face, so he hastily inserted a purposeful misunderstanding. "I'm sorry, I don't mean that the Directory meds were bad. Sorry if you thought that. I didn't mean that. Heck, the guy would have been dead if the Directory hadn't patched him up – it was a fantastic job."

Boltax's eyes had glazed over.

"The most exciting thing was when I watched the replay of my fight with him. You know, slow motion, frame by glorious frame. Pay attention to the Red Dragon's face. Do you know, his expression didn't change one bit. I think it was the operation. It slowed him way down. He never even saw my feet coming. I guess that's best, seeing that he died and all. But I felt sorry for him, sort of....."

"Shut up," Boltax screamed. "Shut your damn mouth!"

Jack looked startled. He waited till he saw the spark of sanity return to the eyes. This was a delicate sport. This Jolo could kill him and he would be virtually defenseless. But he had to keep him *reacting* and not thinking clearly. Jack had him close to the edge, the balance was delicate.

"Look, I'm sorry if I said the wrong thing. Can't imagine what it was, but I'm sorry I upset you, okay? I'm so sorry you got angry. I mean with me becoming immortal we're going to be spending a long time together, so we should try to get along right from the start."

"What? What did you say?"

"I said we're going to be spending a lot of time together, so we should get along. Not be angry at each other. Be buddies."

"What are you talking about? What makes you think we will spend any time together at all?"

"Well, I just assumed that with me becoming immortal, just like you, that that would mean there was a lot of time...." Jack let it fade away. Boltax had an exotic play of expression crossing his face. Each new thought played theatre with his features, ending with evil intent.

Jack gave Boltax all his teeth with a sincere youthful smile. Boltax began to cough. He thrust out of his chair so rapidly it crashed into the wall.

"You're right.

"Let me take you to your destiny."

● ● ●

Across the other side of the Colosseum, the Investigator came groggily to consciousness and stumbled to the shower. He ate a late breakfast, savoring every last morsel. Resentfully he went back to work sorting through letters and papers idly reading the drivel. This was a dog's job with nothing to find, an insult pure and simple.

Then a red hot poker stabbed into his head.

WHAT!

He was screaming inside, completely unhinged. He dropped the sheet of paper and it fluttered to the ground. He snatched it up again.

The letter was signed. *Tac-U-One!*

He jumped up and went to his console.

"Computer." he shouted. "Computer, computer, computer." He shook his head frantically. He got ahold of himself and then continued, "This is an emergency. Stage One emergency!" The computer was mute. How could this be? What was going on? The Bio-Comp was working against them.

He called Boltax's office.

No answer.

He chewed on his lip and drew blood. He called Boltax's personal communication device (PCD) – no answer. He was not a good enough telepath to send.

The Investigator took off running through the halls of the Colosseum.

● ● ●

Boltax led the way out a side door, he ignored the blaring ring of the priority tone on the communication console and the vibration seconds later on his PCD.

"Shouldn't you answer that, it sounds real important."

Boltax glared at the boy and kept going.

Nothing was going to interrupt him now; nothing was going to deny him his pleasure. They stepped into a wide corridor with doors evenly spaced along the sides. They came to a triple-wide door and entered, then passed through another identical opening into what Jack immediately recognized as a transfer room.

He was relieved.

Everything he'd done since emerging from the lake was calculated to get him here.

He made it.

It was years since Jack had seen a Recyclex machine. The sight of it was comforting, he relaxed a little. On this world where everything was alien, it was nice to see something from *home.*

"Come here, Jack, and let me show you the bodies we have available for transfer." Boltax laughed inside.

Boltax pulled out tray after tray.

These bodies were from the Directory. For staff use. The recessed trays looked like those in a morgue. The difference was that these bodies weren't dead, but simply held in suspension until needed.

"Take a close look, Jack, and tell me which one you might like to transfer into."

"One of these bodies is mine?"

"It will be."

Jack looked. The readouts on the front of each drawer showed each body in stasis.

Boltax had not prepared a body for him. This show and tell was theatre.

It took thirty minutes to prepare a body for transfer.

This was not going to be easy. And though not given to nerves, Jack sensed his time running out. On multiple fronts.

"Which one of these would you like?"

"I have no idea. Will *you* pick one for me?"

"That's very trusting of you."

"You're the expert."

"How true," he said, and then looked directly at Jack. "You'll be glad to know I've spent far more time than usual in planning your future." Boltax turned away to hide the wicked smile he couldn't suppress.

Jack began pushing the trays back into their recesses.

"Be careful there!"

"Yes, of course."

The body ID codes on the display panels were virtually identical, except for one body. This was a superior model, probably a replacement for Boltax.

As he closed that drawer he depressed the activation pad; the instrument panel and countdown lit up immediately. He gave it a quick rap with his fist and stumbled awkwardly into a gurney to cover the noise.

Boltax looked at the native's clumsy movements. "Be careful, this room is full of valuable equipment."

Had Boltax seen the color array on the display panel? If so, his cover was blown.

Nothing happened.

Once the scrutiny had shifted, Jack glanced back; the light from the activated control panel had gone dark. The display panel would not now spectrum through the body ignition sequence; such a thing, by design, was impossible to miss.

"What are you looking at?"

This guy was suspicious of his every move. "There are so many amazing devices. What does that one do?"

"You don't need to know."

Jack hoped only the display was disrupted, not the actual body ignition procedure. From this room, only one future would emerge. He must control it.

Boltax had crossed the room and was now working on the Recyclex machine. Jack was lingering near the slightly ajar tray, trying to catch a glimpse of increased luminescence that would indicate the body was advancing through the ignition sequence. He saw nothing to indicate it was.

Jack tripped and fell to the floor. As he got up he saw a hint of light through the translucent bottom of the drawer. Boltax turned. "You natives are a clumsy lot." Then added, "Don't kill yourself, you fool; just before you become immortal." He laughed uproariously.

Jack showed an idiot's grin as he was beckoned over to the Recyclex machine.

"This machine is the one that transfers the soul – or what we call an Identity – from one body to another." Drawing aside a curtain, "This is where you lay. I'll initiate the sequence, and you'll be transferred into a device that readies you to enter another body."

Boltax drew back the second curtain. Resting on the opposing couch was an object – Jack's blood ran cold.

It was a cylinder approximately eight feet in length, and near each end it was capped with a bright, reflective metallic surface that housed a set of silver reflective fins projecting from a central axis. The cylinder was thirty inches in diameter. The central section appeared to be clear glass, but Jack knew it was a material infinitely more durable. It was, in fact, designed to last through millennia.

An Identity trap. Industrial strength.

Once again, he glanced at the tray that was slightly ajar. But the ambient light of the transfer room was too bright and he was still unsure if the body was being prepared for habitation.

The Identity-trap was a nightmare scenario. Completely unpredicted. In his calculations there had always been the possibility that Boltax might try to I-trap him. If he discovered his Directory name.

But Boltax didn't know. His demeanor would be different.

He thought Boltax might I-trap him from spite.

But this? This was truly dangerous. The range of possible futures he could engineer narrowed.

And still no sure sign the body was "warming up." It would be insane to attempt transfer without knowing it was ready. No one could "pick up" a body still in stasis.

The situation was extreme. Risking all, Jack probed Boltax's mind with infinite delicacy. And there she was. Wendy. But he had known this from his conversation with Dale White early this morning – at that time she was still safe. He went further with his probe. There was no awareness of Jack's true identity. So Wendy had done it. Even though she'd been found she hadn't given him away.

Good girl.

Jack probed a little further. There was Boltax ordering her to be taken. *They could be doing it now. Where are you, Dee? Are you okay? Can't think about that now.*

Recyclex machine.

Why did Boltax have an I-trap this powerful? The device could hold an identity for half a million years. Its power source almost inexhaustible. It could draw in an Identity over a long distance. Its force, when activated, was like a riptide in Hell.

This monster was used for the permanent disposal of an Identity. Someone you never wanted to see again. Ever.

It had no other use.

Smaller units were sometimes used to transport an Identity. There was some legitimate use for them. The existence of this one was a crime. Who would do this to another being? It was a one-way trip to extinction.

Its power could not be underestimated. He could be sucked in. There would be no return. Involuntarily, he shuddered.

Boltax noticed it and nodded knowingly. He'd seen many first-timers as they came to this point.

"Transferring from one body to another is no small thing."

Jack's concentration was knocked adrift and memories flittered uncensored through his mind. He recalled a story of a person walking past a large I-trap. Supposedly it sucked the Identity directly from his body. Without Recyclex.

"Fascinating, isn't it?" Boltax said, misreading the look in Jack's eyes.

"Yeah, it's sure shiny," Jack responded.

"Your time has come."

"Okay." Jack said.

"Please lie down and relax, the machine will do the rest. You will soon enter a new existence that will continue for eternity." Boltax smirked.

Jack had to kill at least ten more minutes before the body he activated was ready – if the process was still running.

He stalled for time.

* * *

The Investigator couldn't access the restricted area of the Colosseum. The Bio-Comp scan of his genetic material was inconclusive.

"But you know who I am!" the Investigator shouted. "You can read my mind, you know I'm the Investigator assigned to this planet and you must let me through immediately!"

"You know the regulations, Investigator. Without a valid genetic scan logged into the locking mechanism, the doors themselves won't release."

"You have my genetic scan on file. It must match!"

"There's been some data corruption. I've scheduled eighteen staff to be re-scanned today. You're on that list.

It sounded plausible, but the Bio-Comp was a traitor. He was losing control. A wave of frustrated horror twisted his insides.

"This is a life-or-death emergency affecting the security of our operation."

"Regulations also cover this. Give me the reason you need access in the absence of a valid genetic scan so I can enter it into the database and override the locking mechanism."

This data he uncovered went deep into the Investigator's mind. The information was too explosive. If he told the Bio-Comp and the computer chose to side against him, it would prevent him... Oh no...

The Bio-Comp may have gotten the data from his head already. But no, he couldn't have.

He charged back into the administrative offices, grabbed a Jolo clerk and dragged her, protesting, toward the restricted access scanner.

* * *

"What will happen to this body?" asked Jack, pointing to his chest.

"It will be incinerated and a death certificate issued. With the new body, you will select a name of your choice. You can choose to retain or rescind the legal and familial obligations you have prior to the change. You'll receive a certificate of citizenship as a member of the Directory. The actual possession of an enhanced body confers this privilege and is easily verified by scanners all across the Directory. The certificate is just a formality."

Jack continued to press him with questions to keep Boltax talking.

"Let's get started…"

The body couldn't be ready.

"What the hell do you keep looking at? What are you looking at?" Boltax walked over toward the trays.

If he opens the tray….

Boltax shoved home the tray that was slightly open. The heavy latch clicked and the tray was locked. "Ow." Boltax looked at his hand, there was blood. "What the hell?" He crouched down and saw the tray's control panel was cracked. The sharp edge had sliced a tiny divot of skin away.

Jack picked up a heavy tool and slid it behind his back.

"You broke the panel when you stumbled on the gurney." He looked at Jack.

Jack readied all the muscles of his body to repel attack. The side of the gurney and the tray's control panel were not at the same height. How long till Boltax saw that?

"I'm sorry for being so stupid."

"You natives are dense. You think you can get away with anything." Boltax hit the kid with a mind probe. There was guilt over breaking the tray with the gurney, but none of the other stuff – not the deferments; nothing.

And that made no sense. *This kid was the troublemaker.* His head should be full of it.

Something was wrong here.

Very wrong.

Then the kid's head was filled with death. The fear of his own death.

"Space ships?" Jack blurted. Boltax looked at him curiously, the kid had his hands behind his back, and he was stalling. That was understandable; everyone's first time was preceded by all sorts of random emotions. He looked into the kid's head again. He couldn't see past the surface stuff, but the fear was turning into terror. He looked at the kid's pant leg hoping to see the flow of urine.

The kid was scared, hallelujah. This was worth dragging out a little longer.

"What about space ships?"

"That's how you talk to the other aliens, I'm sorry, I mean other people, superiors, in the Directory?" Jack was having trouble keeping it together.

"Yes, our dispatches are couriered on space ships." Boltax looked at a wall-mounted digital readout. "In fact, a shuttle departed for

Sector, just minutes ago." Boltax was happy that the girlfriend was beyond the kid's reach.

"How fast…"

"No more questions. Lay down on the Recyclex cot!" Boltax ordered.

Jack couldn't do it, he needed *more time*.

● ● ●

"Let me go!" the clerk shouted. The Investigator ignored her and clamped his grip on her arm more tightly, dragging her to the scanner a few yards away. He would use her to get the door open, and she could pass him through. If the clerk's genetic scan failed, he would know the Bio-Comp was a true enemy.

"You asshole!" The Investigator felt a heavy blow to the side of his head.

He went down.

He did not let go.

There was agony in his arm.

Her teeth clamped on his wrist and she was biting as hard as she could. The agony stopped.

"Let me go, you dirt bag!"

● ● ●

If it was warming, the body was not ready for transfer. And he still hadn't figured how to take the I-trap from the receiving cot and replace it with the body still in its drawer "warming up."

Boltax took hold of Jack and began to manhandle him toward the Recyclex machine.

"No!" Jack shouted, real terror in his voice this time.

Well now, Boltax thought. *That's more like it.*

"Scared are you, little boy?" Boltax loved it.

"I'm terrified!"

Boltax stopped forcing Jack.

I'll give you all the fear you could want. Jack thought.

● ● ●

Minutes passed in a random struggle across the hallway when the Investigator took a knee where it hurt and writhed in agony.

He had enough presence of mind to hold on to her ankle. At first he could hardly breathe. It took him time he couldn't lose to recover from the excruciating pain.

He started to talk.

Finally he got her calmed down.

"You know me, right. You've seen me around?"

"You're the Chief's Investigator."

"That's right! All I want is to get through the security door."

She looked at him for what seemed like a very long time.

"Why didn't you just ask me to scan you through the door?"

"It's an emergency, I don't have time!"

Once again she looked at him for what seemed like forever. Then she got to her feet and went to the scanner. The doors opened. "I verify the identity of this Jolo."

"Access granted," intoned the Bio-Comp. The Investigator ran as fast as he could with the fire still in his testes and the nausea in his gut.

● ● ●

Jack's internal clock told him it was time.

"I'm scared and I'll never be ready for this. Let's do it now before I lose my nerve."

"It's understandable for a heroic competitor like yourself to be scared as a snot-nosed baby," Boltax said kindly.

"Let's do it."

Boltax didn't intend to incinerate the kid's body. First step; transfer Jack into the I-Trap. Next; place the Jack Cousins body in stasis. Then let his incompetent Bio-Technician make some modifications. That was well within the Bio-Tech's present skill set.

When the "improvements" were made, Boltax would transfer the native back into the grossly distorted body. Invite his parents to afternoon tea and watch them cry.

How satisfying to amputate five arms, not two. How many fingers is that? He chuckled to himself.

"How brave of you, Jack Cousins, to find the nerve to go through with this. I'm in awe of you," Boltax said. "We'll proceed."

Normally a light sedative was administered, to ease transfer.

Boltax had other plans. He'd been trained in a new interrogation technique. He was going to find out who this kid was and what he knew. For this he needed Cousins conscious.

Jack noted Boltax's omission. Fine, he preferred to transfer wide awake.

Boltax skipped the identification procedure. Standard procedure had a person write a short phrase on a card and seal it in an official envelope. After transfer the person must correctly write the same phrase. This legally transferred rights and title.

Jack slid onto the Recyclex cot, even with the threat of the I-trap looming close, he felt enormous relief.

I'm here, he thought. *Soon I'll feel the ejection charge and float free.*

Between Jack Cousin's body and the I-trap was the bulk of the Recyclex unit.

Boltax reached over and powered up the I-trap. Instantly Jack could feel its pull and stayed as calm as he could.

Infinite risk. Zero choice.

Without the Jolo body he couldn't control Earth.

Boltax began his delicate dance across Recyclex controls. He feathered up the ejection charge. This, as it built, would ease the Identity from the body, and in normal circumstances an attracting charge would then be exerted on the new body and transfer would be complete; out of the old and into the new.

But not today.

Boltax wanted answers.

You'll tell me everything. Boltax reveled.

Years ago Bio-One himself had demonstrated the new interrogation technique with a spy they'd captured.

"There is something profoundly disruptive about pushing an Identity out of a body and then pulling him back in over and over. This is a reliable method of softening someone up for questioning. By test it's more effective than any telepathic interrogation technique."

Bio-One had droned on and on about how forcing the truth from any Jolo would change the Directory.

Boltax fluttered the controls; out, pause, in. Out, pause, in. Soon he would have his answers from this native, Jack Cousins. Soon he would know who was behind the trouble.

If the native didn't talk, he still had leverage through the girlfriend who was headed out system.

●

Jack was feeling ill. Transfer never felt like this. He couldn't tell what was happening.

Normally final release from the body came easily, aided by a little push from Recyclex. Possibly, he thought, it's this native body that's causing the difference in sensation.

The body was the only difference between this and hundreds of other transfers. Disorientation and nausea gripped his head and gut.

Doesn't matter how bad I feel, I've got to transfer.

He was so close to his target – that other body must be ready for use. If its systems were running.

His head whirled.

He saw young Wendy walking to school. He saw a spray of stars. He felt a gush of vomit rising.

There was violent shouting – something about him… *"he's not Jack Cousins"*… but he couldn't distinguish the words or catch the meaning. There was violent motion. Confusion. His throat was burning as he tried to keep his gorge down.

Breaking glass. Vomit flooded into his mouth.

Agony!

His right arm burned.

How could that be? The pain, *the pain.* The body took another impact and the hurt was terrible. His stomach disgorged in a stinking stream…

"You fucking filthy animal" …He was sucking breath and blood into his mouth. His right leg flashed pure fire…nothing else mattered.

He was too far gone.

* * *

The Investigator had burst into the room. He looked in horror at the figure lying on the Recyclex cot.

"He," he shouted in an uncontrolled shrill tone and pointed to the figure on the Recyclex cot, "he's not Jack Cousins." The Investigator drew a deep breath and shouted, "He's Tactical Unit One! I have proof!"

Boltax, who had been lovingly caressing the controls of the Recyclex machine, preparing his victim for interrogation, stopped cold.

Scorn for this stupid Investigator invaded him and he turned in wrath. His eyes saw the look of total certainty on the Investigator's face.

One by one, the inconsistencies over the last weeks and months lined up. Finally something made sense. Horror swept through him. And before he could realize the assertion was impossible, Boltax had broken the glass, snatched a fire axe and was flailing at the body on the cot.

The kid gushed vomit all over him, "You fucking filthy animal!"

Swing after swing landed on that body. Limbs came away, blood was everywhere. One swing jammed the axe into the cot and it wouldn't come free though he jerked at it like a wild man.

Boltax stopped. He looked at the Investigator. Stared at him. The terror-driven frenzy of the last minute faded.

Sanity returned. There was no way in this universe that the kid could be Tac-U-One, a Crown officer.

Revulsion suffused him as he gazed at the moron who had precipitated his panic. He reached out and in a flash was choking the life from the brainless Investigator.

He'd never get answers – the kid was gone. He was surrounded by incompetence.

Boltax threw the Investigator against the I-trap and was bashing his head into it. There was more blood, blood everywhere. This moron had ruined all his plans.

Slowly he wound down, the fury and wrath subsided amid the welter of red spray, pools of the stuff on the floor. He released the death grip and his Investigator sucked in a deep gasp of air. Boltax was relieved, better not to murder a Jolo with a Bio-Comp as witness.

"I feel very, very cold," the Investigator's voice scratched out past the tortured cartilage and tissue of his throat.

Boltax smiled. The Investigator was being sucked in by the huge I-trap. What a wonderful thing to see an I-trap snatch the Identity directly from a living body. As rumor had it, it was possible. The thought gave him a thrill.

But no, the Bio-Comp *was* watching. Reluctantly, Boltax pulled him away from the device, turned it off, and dragged him to the opposite corner of the room.

The Investigator slumped to the floor.

● ● ●

Jack's world had gone thin and pale and he was in terrible pain – but...not. In a shutter of time, he had a vivid impression of his body lying hacked to pieces in pools of dark blood. Then he felt an inexorable tugging sensation and the realization of extreme danger slammed home as he was dragged sideways, toward the I-trap.

There was only one option – he plunged into the ragged mess that was his dying body and tried to revive it. The ravaged chest made a labored heave but all he accomplished was to suck more blood into the lungs. The pain of attachment to this mutilated body was intense. He manipulated the diaphragm again and a tide of blood gurgled from the mouth. The heart was giving fitful beats as the muscles were compressed, released, compressed, released, the rhythm faltered.

Again he felt the cold drag to the side as the I-trap exerted its relentless pull. With tremendous effort, he made the body attempt to breathe once more. A mucky gurgling sound was the only response. He was losing his hold on the body and the full force of the I-trap was gripping him, drawing him closer, closer, into its twisting vortex.

And then....nothing.

Abruptly released from its pull, Jack catapulted away. He shot through the walls and rooms of the complex.

Freed from the mayhem, Jack's mind began to clear and though he didn't feel good, he felt better than he had; all the heavy pain sensations connected to the body were gone.

He couldn't believe his luck. Why had he been let loose when Boltax clearly intended to suck him into the I-trap?

He had no answer.

Jack came to rest in an empty room. "Death" had happened a number of times in his long career, always the result of violence. Events were not going as planned. He laughed. But this room was markedly better than lodging in the eternal prison of I-trap. He shivered – even without a body.

After being I-trapped one step remained: getting dumped into interstellar space. The Big Chill, it was called.

Enough.

Get oriented.

Jack drifted up and was soon above the Colosseum, with a bird's eye view. He saw downtown Los Angeles in the distance, the Hollywood hills, the glint of sunlight on water.

In a minute or two he would make a grab for the Jolo body that, hopefully, was ready to receive him.

He couldn't resist the sensation he felt at a time like this. The horror of the Recyclex room was gone. He was free: after leaving an old body behind and before taking a new one, he enjoyed a time of reflection.

Today it would be short.

He slid back over his months and years on Earth. He felt ambivalent. Life here was nothing. He'd been unaware and forwarded no purpose – but then in contrast it was a very great thing, for he'd forgotten what it was like to be "Normal." He'd forgotten what it was like to have no real grasp on the future beyond the longevity of a single body. No mission, no duty.

The aimless people of Earth, a whole population without a cohesive plan that oriented them and ensured survival in the long term. Instead they fought amongst themselves. And when someone did stand up and point the way, their fear and distrust destroyed him.

The comparison was a shock and a revelation. As an Immortal, he had taken so much for granted. The stable Directory culture could only now be fully seen and appreciated through its opposite.

Even so, there were many he loved on this planet. People he would have ignored as a Jolo. It was a sobering self-appraisal. Assuming another point of view was an important tool to gain a greater understanding of oneself and others.

So, purely for his own pleasure and for the kindness shown him, he decided that when the Directory was set right, he would return and draw them properly into it. If he could give Earth immortality, then his warm welcome by many people on this planet would be paid for.

● ● ●

"I'm curious to know what made you think this dismembered mud-sucking native was Tactical Unit One." Boltax laughed, pointing to the blood-soaked pile of meat and bones on the Recyclex cot. This Investigator, he mused, had to be one of the stupidest people he had ever met. His only redeeming ability was telepathy – just – and he would follow orders.

The Investigator tried to speak but his throat was on fire.

"Give me the information telepathically, you idiot." Boltax got a confused mess, but there was something about a letter. The investigator held out his hand and passed the letter written by "Jack Cousins" to his girlfriend Wendy White, but it was signed *Tactical Unit One*. No one on this backwater planet had ever heard of the Crown Agent. And if the Investigator had it right, the signature at the bottom matched the one he remembered seeing many times over the years in published governmental documents. *It matched....*

Boltax rapidly read portions of the letter that caught his attention:

"Dear Dee, I was wrong not to tell you about competing with the gladiators as soon as I had decided to do it ... I can tell you that once I'm through this fight, then things will be fine and the trouble over – *because I will control Earth*.... Earth is a tiny speck of a much larger puzzle.... This is just the beginning.... Threat is interwoven into the nature of what I do... I see marauders in my house and I intend to boot them out... I will do it... play this game of saving the Directory from *Bio-One and his flock of villains... Tactical Unit One.*"

A violent scream began in his head till it shrieked through him at hurricane force. How can this be? Why was this happening to him? Couldn't everyone just leave him alone so he could go about his business? He could never express the resentment he felt. A good person like himself, yet so much trouble, it was beyond understanding. Around him were so many others so much worse than he was, and they seemed to get by without all this shit.

Why me?

The Investigator was staring at him fearfully. Boltax came out of his terror turned resentment jag. To save his skin, all he needed to do was deliver this Identity recently loosed from the body of Jack Cousins to Bio-One. Then name his own reward. His future would be bright, so bright there would be no limit. In fact, the I-trap should already have Tac-U-One in custody.

He looked at the trap. The fins were still. He'd turned off the I-trap. He'd turned off the trap!

His head detonated.

He ran to the I-trap; in a second the code was entered and tidal force set to maximum. This had to suck in the recently released Identity, who must still be floating around somewhere nearby. And if it wasn't Tac-U-One the I-trap sucked in, if the trap got someone else – who in their right mind would ever let him out to verify the possibility it wasn't Tactical Unit One?

No one.

Either way, he was a winner.

* * *

Jack was jerked from his reverie by the sudden renewal of the riptide.

The I-trap was back on!

Something must have changed – Boltax must know about him. Instantly, he formed a plan. He arced downward, careful to remain outside the critical distance of the I-trap's relentless vortex. But this was easier decided than done. The device was far stronger now than a few minutes ago.

Boltax must know.

He re-entered the building, still feeling the tug and suction of the trap. If he calculated his position correctly, the body he had activated would now be between him and the Identity trap.

As he drew closer, the pull of the vortex intensified. With a trap there comes a point you lose rationality and resist its horrible compulsion with desperate, futile energy.

Jack felt as he passed through walls an ability to *hang on* and slow his progress. He had no idea if this was objective or subjective, but he was losing the ability to not be drawn in.

He must approach.

●   ●   ●

Boltax sat. He was a little winded from the wild flailing with the axe. And the shock of his Investigator's news. Tac-U-One here on Earth – it couldn't get any worse!

How close that had been. He looked over at the I-trap fins. Still no Identity. Hell, even a dead Earthie sucked into the I-trap would do. That damned kid had been so smart, so effective in stalling his progress on Earth.

No wonder.

He looked at the hacked-up body and felt a surge of satisfaction. That a-hole kid got what he deserved. It was good to be rid of him. He'd worked his way to the inner sanctum where transfer took place.

But he didn't make it.

You lost, kid. Revenge felt good.

Boltax wondered: *have I just delivered death blows to the fabled Tac-U-One?* It seemed impossible. The kid's body was native, no doubt.

If the kid were Tac-U-One, he had to have died here and been born locally. Almost eighteen years ago.

The kid did have intimate knowledge of Directory Law and procedure. No denying it. And knew the name "Tactical Unit One." And his Investigator was right about the signature – it was similar.

Scary.

And then he, the Investigator and Bio-Comp were telepaths. Include the presence of the huge I-trap and the picture came together. Someone thought Tac-U-One might be here on Earth and provided tools to deal with it.

Stupid to have invaded here.

Over the years, Boltax had read novels about Tac-U-One missions – loved them, in fact. Nothing, it seemed, could stop him.

But he, Boltax, had stopped Tac-U-One!

How powerful does that make me?

To relive it, he looked around and replayed his superb moves. Then he remembered the kid's stumbles and the useless chatter.

Strange.

His eyes drifted to the gurney and from this angle he could tell it was on a different level from the stasis control panel. The gurney couldn't have cracked it.

Boltax screamed.

* * *

Jack *gripped* another wall and it was only moments till he was tugged free and drawn rapidly across the empty space. Nothing he was doing was able to slow the pull. Panic began to well up. That hellish device could hold him forever....

An oscillating, rotating, stroboscopic sensation blurred into him with vomit-gagging nausea, a sensation no less valid without a body. He was being drawn through walls and was vibrating now at a high whine. He was firmly in the grip of the trap.

He jumped back, was pulled further in, back again. There was a horrible seductive element to the I-trap, its mechanical will became his conscious will, became its will.

Let go, don't fight.

If he could just *let go* it would be over. He would be sucked into the spiral vortex to "never."

* * *

Boltax was paralyzed.

The tray seemed to exude danger. Seconds went by... then he dashed to the tray and yanked it open. The cycle was complete!

Boltax screamed again.

Tac-U-One was coming to get him!

That is my replacement body, he thought resentfully. Frantically he smacked at the glass, trying to reset the stasis. He cut his hand again.

"Drag out another body from a stasis tray!" he yelled at the Investigator. The man didn't move.

"Get up and help me!"

The investigator curled into a tight ball.

Boltax stepped to the next tray and turned off the stasis.

"Warning. Warning. Warning. Voiding stasis without body ignition will destroy function...."

Boltax ripped the inert body from the tray and it thudded to the floor. He carefully lifted his replacement body from the broken tray and gently placed it in the functional one.

Boltax's fingers flew over the control panel. The scanners began to register the condition of the body.

More seconds…

Panic filled his chest.

"Jolo body, registration number 224k77wx, manufacturer: Nordake Biologicals." The scanners went still. "Ready for status change."

He initiated body shutdown, closed the tray. The status bar began to sink…

● ● ●

The momentum was now overtaking Jack and he saw with frantic dismay that he was coming in too high, he would be sucked over the body and have *no* chance to set his hooks into the body and successfully resist the I-trap.

With all that was in him, he jagged down on a diagonal, not fighting the pull directly, but with enough force to cut across the transfer room toward where the body lay. There was Boltax, standing by one of the trays. The next one over.

Then he lost sight as he was pulled through tray after tray of bodies in stasis, cold and uninviting, none of which offered any refuge; they were as welcoming as a tree stump and gave no purchase. The tidal force of the I-trap pulled him into a warm body.

He felt something he'd never felt in association with a body before: nothing. There was no heartbeat, no sense of a functioning body. It was warm, but even as he felt *that*, it was accompanied by an increasing chill.

The body was going cold.

He tried to work the motor controls for the body. There was no motion, no response.

Jack realized what had happened. The body was being shutdown, prepared for stasis, the "no-time shroud" would resume very soon.

Without proper control established, Jack once again felt the force exerted by the I-trap.

He had to do something.

● ● ●

Boltax looked at the closed tray with bug eyes. There was a strange humming sound coming from within.

That was not normal.

He was starting to feel crazy. Something was happening within the tray. And it couldn't be good. He looked at the status bar. The cooling had slowed. It was leveling.

It started to go back up.

The humming increased.

He could feel the vibration through the soles of his feet. He wanted to open the tray and hatchet the body to pieces.

But that was his body!

* * *

Jack was now vibrating very fast. The temperature was rising, which meant the stasis field could not enfold the body. Jack stopped oscillating and recalled the ignition procedures that the tray made to initiate body function.

This would be a first.

Jack estimated the stimulus needed and tested the method.

The body started.

The control panel showed body ignition.

* * *

Boltax screamed!

He jumped back. Then he lunged forward like a wild man and stabbed at the stasis override and backed away again. No telling what physical damage was caused, if the body would be usable at all.

A price Boltax willingly paid.

He should feel safe.

Stasis was "no time." It was impossible for anything else to happen.

But fear was alive.

Once again he forced himself closer to the stasis tray, wanting to open the drawer and hack the body to shreds.

But as he worked up the nerve, some of his frayed sanity returned.

The body is in stasis.

Nothing can happen.

This is my body! he thought. The only decent replacement body. If he destroyed it – he'd never get another like it.

The immediate danger was over.

The stasis field is a bubble of no motion and no time, he thought, *it's impossible for anyone to animate that body. It means I'm safe – nothing can happen.*

* * *

Tactical Unit One Crown, had spent more "time" in Other-Space (that mythical realm outside the universe proper where the starships traveled), than any other living being and, for him, time was not absolute.

He created his own time and synced this with the external vibration rate, overriding the small stasis-field generator.

He took firm grip of the new Jolo body's motor controls. Then flexed each muscle starting at the neck. The impulse flowed down through the body in a fluid controlled ripple.

He was in control.

He then threw adrenaline into the blood stream.

Primed.

Powerful determination flowed through the prone body. Exultation filled him and the tray literally exploded from its recess.

CHAPTER 35

He leaped to the floor ready for battle.

Boltax was thrown across the room. He groggily got to his feet. Jack picked up the discarded axe. Then stepped to the I-trap, turned it off, and smashed its control panel. "Fucking thing."

Boltax shook his head. Before him stood the naked figure of a man. Against all odds it could only be one man, one Identity; Tac-U-One. But no one, no one could do....

Boltax had one other card to play. He drew breath....

"Don't say it, Boltax." Jack commanded. "If you activate the computer defenses I will kill you where you stand."

Stopped again.

Boltax looked at the dismembered body on the Recyclex cot, then to the empty stasis tray virtually ripped from the wall, then to the figure standing before him.

What had happened here?

Confusion boiled in his head. No one could do what had been done here.

Therefore it hadn't happened. But it had.

Boltax opened his mouth to speak.

"Tac-U-One Crown – *on deck*." Jack rapped out.

Through the millennia there was only one response to this command and a mere twenty years of new regime could not erase it.

Boltax reacted automatically.

He went ramrod straight and saluted. What was he doing? Astonishment showed on his features. Whattttt? Compliance was extinction...

But he did not move.

"This is no drill, Boltax. You will turn the computer over to my sole command, now."

Boltax was no mental incompetent, but for the life of him he could not credit this Jolo standing before him. Because no one, not even Crown's famous Tactical Unit One, could animate a body in stasis and away from Recyclex.

How had he gotten the body? The stasis tray must have malfunctioned. *How had he taken possession of the body?*

"Boltax, turn over computer control. Now."

With the computer, went domination over the whole operation. Direct command of the computer was the power to control Earth.

Under these extraordinary circumstances it was exposed as a deadly weakness.

"Whoever you are, you're not Tactical Unit One Crown. He's dead, you understand – dead and gone.

"So. Mr. No Name. Do whatever you want with the computer – if you can, but I won't help you."

"Stand in the far corner." Boltax moved.

"Computer, access order log."

"Order log," the Bio-Comp replied.

"Sole command to go to Tactical Unit One Crown."

Jack stepped over to the command keyboard and entered the code which had an entry time-sequence, a required rhythm, making it impossible to copy.

The Bio-Comp was shocked. The code just entered began a restructuring of his entire database. And it was fast. In nanoseconds new protocols dominated his architecture. Bio-Comp was now on a war footing. And he was happy.

"Yes, sir," the computer responded. "Tactical Unit One Crown has control. May I be the first to welcome you to this base?"

"Yes, thank you."

"Sir, be advised I am a Biological Computer."

"Thank you, we'll talk privately later."

"Sir, there is clothing here." The Bio-Comp opened a storage closet. Jack walked over and threw something on.

"Thank you."

Boltax staggered against the wall. What, what, what, what what?

He was hot and disconnected. The objects about him and the entire room were in a spin.

"You're dead," he cried. "You're dead." he moaned. "You have to be dead." he pleaded.

If Tac-U-One were standing in front of him, his worst nightmare had come true. He was caught, caught committing unspeakable crimes.

He sprang. Rushed across the room, slipped in the blood, tripped on the legs of the body he pulled from a tray and the deadly blows he tried to deliver came to nothing. Tac-U-One side-stepped, grabbed an arm, added to the momentum and slammed Boltax into the wall. Hard.

He recovered, thinking there were only ten Identities that a planetary computer would call "Sir," only ten out of all the billions of Jolos and trillions of Normals in the entire expanse of the Directory.

Ten.

Those ten people were Crown and his nine personal officers, each empowered to act in his name and with his authority.

Boltax caved in. *Why me? It's so unfair and always has been,* he thought bitterly.

The Crown officer died fifteen or twenty years ago. There was mourning across the Directory. A huge monument was erected on Crown Planet. Boltax had seen it, *touched* it.

Boltax had only joined Bio-One because he had ousted Crown and removed Tac-U-One, the most powerful Jolos in the Directory. That made him the man to work for – and no retaliation from the old guard.

Win, win.

He assumed this data was fact; it was the make/break reason for his agreement to the posting. It was the reason he rejected the normal Directory values, ethical conduct and moral principles.

Wrong choice.

Without these two men, but with Bio-One, the whole edifice of the Directory would change – had changed – and so why not be on the winning team?

"You're dead, you know? I visited your monument." Boltax said.

Jack smiled. "Oh, nice place?"

"Not too bad – peaceful – lots of flowers."

"Then I approve, but only on aesthetic grounds."

Jack looked at the figure of a man rolled into a ball tucked against the wall.

"Who's that?

"That cadaver? That's my Investigator." He began to laugh, and could not stop.

"Investigator, get off the floor." Tac-U-One said.

He jumped up.

"Place the Jolo body on the floor into an empty tray and reset the stasis."

"Yes, sir." The Investigator made quick work of his task.

"Good. Now sit in that chair. I'll deal with you later." He sat.

Boltax was bitter. Bio-One's plan was to secure power, remove or replace key personnel, corrupt whole sectors, assume full command of the Directory. *Then shower the glory on the likes of me.* Boltax thought.

When the invitation came, he took it. His moral compass was magnetized to power. Abusing the people of Earth was his ticket.

Even now, the main stream population of the Directory was ignorant of the Bio-One abuses. Corruption was leaking into the fabric of the culture through very restricted avenues.

Boltax was one of the few who'd been briefed about the coup. It was brilliant, if one did not examine the motives or its effects on the culture.

But Bio-One's promises were proved a lie.

Standing here was the man he claimed to have eliminated.

Boltax was afraid for his life.

To his mind came the most serious of his violations of Crown rule and the Old Order.

He dropped to his knees and began the litany.

"I have violated Crown regulation 72339 sections A through G inclusive. I have committed mutiny and treason to Crown service. I request a sentence to Denude." Sweat, if not remorse, dripped from him.

Tac-U-One looked at him and lightly scanned his mind. This confession, made before him and the Bio-Comp, seemed genuine: probably accurate but with no details.

Truth lay in specificity.

Tac-U-One's own path would be determined by the actual details he uncovered. Data, exact, complete in time and place and therefore true – was what he needed. So he was prepared to bargain with this man.

Accurate information for a measure of freedom.

The confession was legal. Formal proceedings could be waived. But legality was moot – he would not fall into that trap again. Laws were useful until they prevented you from action necessary to preserve the culture from which the laws were derived.

A lesson learned.

"Computer, log this Jolo's confession. Make note it was given without coercion or promise of leniency.

"In my capacity as Judge Advocate Crown, I formally accept the confession of Jolo Boltax, Planetary Controller Earth. He is hereby removed from post and his rights as a Directory Citizen are revoked with prejudice."

Boltax gasped.

Without citizenship, Boltax was subject to immediate expulsion from any and all Directory Planets or areas controlled by the Directory. This could be held in abeyance by a Sector Governor or more broadly any Crown Officer. "With Prejudice" referred to the procedure to restore citizenship. Any petition or special request had to be sent to the Revoking Officer or in their absence to Crown authority – all the way to the top.

"My immediate ruling is as follows: the Non-Citizen Boltax is to be confined to a single room within the restricted area of the Colosseum compound. He is placed in a state of general and specific non-communication – verbal, electronic or telepathic. Exceptions are Bio-Comp and Tac-U-One. All other comm requests must be approved by me.

"All material and monetary assets are seized. Food and lodging billed at the illegal resident rate. All debts to be paid prior to reapplication for citizenship.

"Computer authority is revoked."

Boltax heard the words as the droning of bees. Was this actually happening?

"Non-Citizen Boltax, you have two days to fully catalogue your crimes against Crown Law, Directory citizens and the people of Earth. I will sentence you then. Be warned: I am a judicial telepath and will scan your mind for any omissions."

He looked at the man and waited for eye contact. With unflinching intention he said, "Non-Citizen Boltax, I advise you to come clean with me, any leniency will be dependent on full and complete disclosure."

Boltax had nothing left.

Nowhere to go.

●

"Bio-Comp, we have some business."

"Yes, sir."

"Place all Directory weapons not under your direct control on lock down.

"Activate all automated defense systems.

"Cancel all ships heading off-planet or out-system.

"Cancel any existing standing authorization for any ship outbound.

"Announce immediate closing of all offices.

"Call a mandatory meeting for all Jolos and Directory staff on the planet to take place in exactly four hours.

"What's the best place for it, Bio-Comp?"

"The auditorium, sir."

"Good."

"In whose name are the orders to be issued?"

"Yes, right. Make it the Planetary Commandant." Tactical Unit One said. "No use giving them a reason to desert before we have a chance to talk to them."

"The orders are posted, sir. I have seventy-two percent of the personnel confirmed for the meeting and will confirm one-hundred percent in the next twenty minutes," the Bio-Comp responded.

"Good."

"A ship outbound to Mars base will land there and wait for further orders."

"Excellent."

"All base weapons are in their storage racks."

"Well done."

"Privately owned weapons will be removed before personnel are seated in the auditorium."

"Good job." This computer was just a little too helpful. "Computer, do you have a telepathic function?" A wild question, but he had felt something.

"Yes, sir." *A Bio-Comp here was odd, a TBC...*

"Why is there a Tele-Bio-Comp on an insignificant base like this?"

"Unusual, sir. I don't know why I was posted here."

Yes, very unusual.

"Prepare for Ident procedure. Ready ... now." The identification procedure was an exchange of a mental code so that both the computer and Tac-U-One could be sure to whom they communicated. Minds could imitate minds.

"I have it, sir." There was amusement in the computer's voice.

On a tight telepathic band Tac-U-One directed the computer to scan the entire system for weapons pods and sensor arrays.

"That will take a few minutes to analyze."

"Okay."

●

Jack was sorting his priorities – then it struck him. Wendy. Where was she?

"Boltax, Investigator, on your feet and over here." Jack ordered.

"Where is Wendy White?"

They looked at each other.

"Knock the crap off. Boltax, earlier today you ordered her taken.

"And last night you, Investigator, were at her home and used a weapon on her.

"Where is she now?"

"I'm not sure, but I believe she is out system."

"Explain yourself."

"I had her placed on an outbound ship. When I believed you were a native I wanted to use her as leverage and Bio-One was looking for beautiful native girls for biological experiments." Boltax shrugged. "I had you." He shrugged again. "I was being punked by a native and I hated your guts.

"I sent her away to hurt you and control you." He looked away. "Somehow it doesn't seem so bad – you know – being beaten by you. Not some mudgrubber."

"Investigator?"

"Boltax was going to kill me if I didn't find you. That girl had been avoiding us for weeks. Last night when I finally found her, and knew she was part of the deferment conspiracy, she tried to kill me. I shot her with my radiation pistol. But I think the battery was dead."

"You two are low life scum. I can't imagine how you've maintained your telepathic skill.

"You will lose it, living as you have, you know that don't you?"

They looked at the floor.

"Bio-Comp, is that out-bound ship out system?"

"Yes, sir. I'm sorry, its Other Space signature flared an hour ago."

"Hold these men here without communication."

He had to get out of that room before he smashed those two to pieces.

He was too late.

He'd failed to protect her.

She was gone.

●

Jack went to the Planetary Commandant's office. He threw out the few knick-knack's Boltax had collected.

He sat, darkness threatening to engulf him. Once again the one he loved was taken. The precipice was just ahead, oh yes, he could go over, indulge all his blackest thoughts. And he would – because he'd done it again.

Failed.

●

"Sir," Bio-Comp said, "One hundred percent confirm on staff attendance. Ninety percent arrived. Last ten percent due in fifteen minutes."

"Thank you, Bio-Comp." Jack was jolted from his gloom. Yes, he would mourn her loss. But not now, not yet.

"Bio-Comp, do you have the weapons and sensor report?"

"Yes, sir."

"Telepathically, please."

"*There are no system-wide sensors. Earth and its satellite are the only celestial bodies covered. And they're all facing inward, towards Earth.*" Bio-Comp said telepathically.

"*An illegal operation like this and none of the cheap sensors thrown here and there to give advance warning of incoming trouble. Makes no sense. Inward? They have nothing to fear on Earth!*" Jack replied. But this fit his theory that the Outer Worlds wanted the operation discovered.

"*There are automated weapons sites on the moon.*" Bio-Comp sent. "*Also Mars is completely dark to me. No sensors. No computer contact. I have no data at all.*"

"*That's scary.*" Jack replied. "*Bio-Comp, program every second sensor to sweep the system outward. And look for any other improvements, especially comm devices.*" It was done.

●

Jack now controlled all known communication lines. He needed to locate and cut any covert communication lines.

News of his presence must not leak.

If *anyone* outside of Earth learned of his takeover, the continued existence of the planet was jeopardized. Bio-One would destroy Earth without hesitation, to ensure Tac-U-One's death.

So disclosing the "good news" before its time was unhealthy for everyone. Jack chuckled.

●

Jack had a feeling about the Bio-Comp. Without his help, securing the base against Boltax or the other Directory staff would've been very difficult.

The reasons for an Identity to become hooked to a computer for a span of years were few. It was often disturbing for a person to be intimately linked to electronics.

An Identity often went through an evolution where they at first operated the electronics through TAC (thought activated circuitry), then bypassed this entirely and operated the computational and other functions as if they were an extension of their own mind.

If such an individual were telepathic, they could encompass an entire planet, or even in rare cases, a system with other habitable planets and moons and asteroids as well.

The emotional rewards of an "electronic life" were limited. But, as with anything, some small percentage of people liked it. A tiny fraction loved it.

Certain personal questions suggested themselves. In the short time he would remain on Earth he would like to make another friend.

The whole base was a criminal activity, its staff criminal to a greater or lesser degree. Not the Bio-Comp. Jack felt sure.

"Bio-Comp, I would like to have that private conversation now, if that's fine with you."

"Of course, sir. I'm at your service."

"Thank you. Bio-Comp, are you functioning under duress?"

"Yes, sir." The story came out. He'd been recruited three years ago with the promise of great rewards. Jolo status was hinted at. They were looking for natural non-Jolo telepaths. Strong ones. Initially he'd worked in an office.

"They tested everyone. Hands down I was the strongest mind-smith they had. I was selected for a mission and I-trapped for cheap transport. I was in that contraption for a year. I hated them after that.

"That's my story, sir. Here I am."

"How do you like being a Bio-Comp?"

"It's okay. Nothing I would have chosen for my next life. But it does have some rewards – now that you're in control, that is."

"I need you, Comp. I need you to remain on post here for a full contract." Bio-Comp postings were always voluntary, even now *in extremis;* he would not as Tac-U-One order it.

Without the support of the Bio-Comp, he would be unable to control the developing situation.

"Anything you need, sir." This was no small thing and Jack felt a deep sense of gratitude.

"Thank you Bio-Comp, I'm in your debt."

People were quite willing to do what "Tac-U-One" asked of them. Jack had the added responsibility of asking only what was necessary.

"No, sir. I'm in yours. Without you here this posting was going to get worse."

"I understand." Jack said.

"Not everything."

"Oh?"

"You see, sir, there was this young boy who entered the Fight for Immortality. He used a computer code to bump someone from the list and insert his own name – no one knew."

Jack was amazed. "You saw that?"

"I did. That code was very useful. It prevented me from having to disclose to Boltax that eighteen Earth years ago Tac-U-One was shot down on this planet."

"I….." Jack was shocked. That was wrong on so many levels.

"There is a trail. I had a long time to piece it together. Earth is the only planet with telepaths as part of the invasion team. Boltax, the Investigator and me. I checked.

"That computer file on Tac-U-One would've gone unnoticed unless someone had reason to look for it.

"So you see, sir. I have you to thank. You gave me hope that you might be you. That you were coming. And now you're here."

Jack heard all the Bio-Comp had done to protect and guide both himself and Wendy. The helping hand, without whose aid…

He decided.

"I need you on this planet for a full fifty-year contract, triple rate." It was an enormous sum.

"Thank you, sir..."

Jack noticed. "But?"

"Sir, I was an elderly Norm, a strong telepathic Norm."

Bio-One and his gang must've disposed of that old body. If the Bio-Comp had no body to receive him at the end of his contract there was no goal to work toward.

Jack's success on Earth was this man's silent gift. Only fair to return the favor.

"Jolo status granted upon successful completion of contract. Tac-U-One Crown awarding official," he said formally. Being able to grant Jolo status was another thing that only ten people could do by decree.

"Sir, I was not trying to compel …"

"How is it you think I don't know your intention?"

"Then, I gratefully accept. Order logged, sir!"

They both knew it would be completely meaningless unless the natural order of the Directory was restored.

"There is more to my analysis, sir."

"Yes?"

"Someone close to Bio-One made sure the resources were here to detect and eliminate you."

"Not Bio-One?"

"No, Bio-One had to authorize the Earth invasion. Someone close disagreed – thought it too dangerous to have contact with a planet where you died. That person made sure the invasion team was equipped to handle you if you showed up."

"But they couldn't directly brief Boltax. That data would've exploded."

"That fits."

"There's more."

"Yes?"

"I think there's someone on the Directory staff who's reporting back to the person who set this up."

"Any evidence of this?"

"No. But if you'd gone to all that trouble, wouldn't you monitor Earth? Boltax didn't know you were here. I have no programming that reports off planet. I checked regularly.

"There must be someone here doing it, must be."

"We have to find them – immediately." Jack said.

"I don't think so. I think the mole is like me – hoping it's really you."

"Why?" But Jack thought he knew.

"If this mole intended to rat you out he would've done it long ago. There've been unmistakable signs for months.

"But Boltax has been falsifying the statistics – with my help."

Jack saw in the Bio-Comp's mind all the remote villages who'd paid the price to keep him free.

"Someone remotely monitoring Earth by its production levels has no idea anything is wrong."

"Saved by Boltax!" Interlocking irony.

●

The full support of the Bio-Comp was a stabilizing factor, a critical factor in this whole situation. The man had initiative, intelligence, foresight, superb timing, ability to take risks and the will to act. And he was not intimidated by evil men.

Jack wondered how the Jolo selection system had passed him by. We need Identities like him to run worlds.

Earth's future was not going to be quiet. The Bio-Comp would defend her.

● ● ●

Boltax marveled at the speed he'd been stripped of power.

He now awaited the pleasure of "his highness" who had taken his office, and now had Boltax isolated in the holding room next door.

It had only taken seconds for this Crown asshole to steal what he'd spent years building. And he'd done it without much of a scuffle. He'd hardly put up a fight.

This Jolo who claimed to be Tac-U-One and whom the Bio-Comp called "sir" had avoided capture by the most powerful I-trap produced. Boltax began to shiver, then shake.

Power.

Raw power of a magnitude he could not grasp and knew he did not possess.

And so he'd confessed his crimes. Boltax marveled, his contrition was, for a heartbeat, genuine.

But mostly he was shocked and dismayed and regretful of being caught. He knew there was no mileage in professing innocence, or saying, "Just following orders, sir."

In a state of shock, he'd blurted out the confession over numb lips. The courts under Crown administration were lenient to those who confessed fully and minutely – once verified, of course, by a trained Judicial Telepath.

Full confession was standard procedure; it was what one did in the Directory when caught in the act. But truth, here, would not serve him. He had nowhere to go.

Non-Citizen Boltax.

"Telling all" to this Crown officer would place him in opposition to the rulers of the Galaxy! Tac-U-One may take down a two-bit operation on Earth, but no way could he defeat Bio-One. That man had technology to overwhelm anyone.

Boltax's *only* chance for survival was to get a message to the nearest Directory base and warn them: Tac-U-One is here! That would scare the hell out of them; as it had him.

Retaliatory action would be immediate and overwhelming. And maybe he would get his post back.

Boltax calmed himself.

●

Boltax was a good telepath, but he was no Int-comm. Sending messages over interstellar distances was quite beyond his ability. But getting a message through to the Mars base might be possible.

He'd never tried it, but this was the time for desperate measures.

Boltax had kept all computer and communication links to the Mars base under his direct command – preventing the Bio-Comp from knowing what was done there.

So, technically, he still controlled Mars base.

But the comm console was in his office.

An interplanetary telepathic message was his only chance. The very mention of Tac-U-One would freak out the starship pilot and the Mars base staff. They would flee.

With luck, the ship would reach Other-Space before anyone noticed it was gone.

Boltax constructed his thought message carefully. He had read, one was supposed to compose the message and then compress it. He imbued it with a sense of vital urgency.

He must now get a sense of where the planet Mars was. He knew the recipient. He pictured the man, the starship pilot. With this came the vague sense of direction. He sent it off.

He sweated as minutes went by like hours.

* * *

"Sir?"

"Yes, Bio-Comp," Tac-U-One answered.

"A ship has lifted from the surface of Mars. Its trajectory suggests an interstellar destination."

Jack looked at the investigator. "Get Boltax now."

The Investigator sprang up and returned in seconds with Boltax.

"Withholding vital information so soon after making a heartfelt confession. You're not a particularly sincere fellow, are you?"

Tac-U-One caught something else and looked into Boltax's mind. "Oh, the ship went at your command." This was not a question.

"I had no idea you were that powerful a telepath – oh, you aren't, you're as surprised as I am your message got through? Okay.

"You needn't have made yourself my victim, but have no fear. After this, I shall oblige you."

"Bio-Comp, we have two choices, call this ship back or destroy it."

Boltax smirked. Jack pushed his way into his head at looked at the message he'd sent and the response from the pilot. No way were they going to return.

Tac-U-One relayed the data to Bio-Comp.

"We have to destroy that ship."

Boltax wanted to strike out at this insufferable Jolo, wound him deeply; wreck the man who was ruining him.

He gave a twisted smile.

"You know, that girl – Wendy White – she might be on the ship you just marked for destruction." Boltax cackled. "I'm really not sure if she went on the earlier ship or this one!"

Tac-U-One scanned his mind and verified it. He saw the order go to the two mud-Jolos. Boltax didn't know where she'd been delivered.

How had he missed this? Easily. Filled with self-blame, he hadn't verified the details.

"Bio-Comp, where are the two mud-Jolos?"

There was no immediate answer.

"Sir, I'm sorry, I did not include those two on the staff list. They're not on the base. Just now I called them and there's no answer. I cannot track them."

"Bio-Comp, connect me to this number." The line rang.

"Hello."

"Hello, Mrs. White."

"Who is this please?" Jack realized his voice was entirely different. He coughed loudly.

"It's me, Jack Cousins. Can I talk to Wendy?"

"Your voice sounds strange."

"I know it does Mrs. White, is Wendy there?"

"Jack, she's gone missing, and so has her cousin, Penny."

"When did they leave?"

"Last anyone saw either of them was this morning. When I got home from shopping they were both gone. No note, nothing."

"I'll do my best to find them. Do you have a digital picture of both girls you can send me?"

●

"Bio-Comp, find those men."

"Order logged."

"What's this," Boltax said mockingly. "A Jolo – no, not a Jolo, but the Immortal *Tactical Unit One* in service to *Crown Authority* – has feelings for a primitive mudgrubber. A stinking native." Boltax crowed. "How wonderful, how… quaint."

Revenge was sweet. "And not even I know for sure which ship she went on," he gloated. "Each second you delay in terminating that outbound ship, the information that will destroy you is further from your reach."

Jack looked at him. "You pathetic weakling."

"You better find a hole to hide in, because Bio-One will send a battle group to Earth and destroy you."

"You fool," Jack said with deep scorn. "You've just taken your own life."

Boltax looked mystified.

"Bio-One's response will be the destruction of planet Earth. You, Non-Citizen Boltax, will incinerate in atomic fire."

Jack stood and abruptly moved toward Boltax. There was terror in his eyes.

"Coward."

●

Was this not his life?

Five thousand years of uninterrupted consciousness should be enough to convince a person what pattern a life must take?

Looking at it now, his decision was: *you must be alone to survive.* And so, once again and always, Jack was alone. Companionship was duty, and duty was love.

I am Tac-U-One, I do not ask for more.

Jack was thrown into another loss. When his wife, the love of his life, had been taken.

After five Crown years of futile searching, he'd abandoned that long ago love. He'd failed to protect her.

All his friends and even Crown had told him that he'd done everything possible, that there was no dishonor in "getting on" with his life.

Abandon the search, abandon her.

He felt an enormous wave of grief. When a man with his job description extends a woman his protection and fails to keep her safe – that means pain and death for her.

Over the centuries, many sensible women within the Directory had refused to marry him out of concern for their own safety.

And so he said – never again. Never again would he contract a woman in marriage for longer than a single transfer.

●

He couldn't put Wendy's life in the balance scale against the destruction of Earth. He was going to do his duty. Jack hoped she'd already left the solar system on the starship that departed earlier. He must act: no single life….

"Destroy that ship," Jack ordered.

"Order logged, sir." Two seconds later: "Missiles away," the Bio-Comp intoned.

"A projectile weapon? The Directory armament on this planet is projectile weaponry?" Jack asked, astonished.

"Yes, sir. The *missiles* had been warehoused on a Directory world for a thousand years and had been forgotten. In fact, the acquisition contract was for the destruction of the warheads. Instead they ended up here or on planets like this one. This is a primitive planet, requiring only a primitive defense. I believe if modern weaponry had been requisitioned, then the tight administrative procedures would have raised a red flag. Can you see this base surviving an inspection from a Competent Authority?" It was a rhetorical question.

"Will they detonate?"

"That is uncertain, sir. Though, in the shipping log, they were certified as live. But that…." But that could mean anything, especially as the shipment was illegal in the first place. The real reason was, a higher shipping fee could be charged for "live" verses "dud" munitions, probably. Follow the money.

"Do we have a chance of destroying that ship?" Jack asked.

"Yes, sir, we do. If they were on this side of the sun, it would be a certainty. The vessel is a slow freighter and it will depend on where the departing ship's Other-Space engines engage, which as you know is always a variable. It'll be approximately four hours before we know."

"Thank you. Keep me informed." He paused, and then shrugged. "Order their return." Might as well try, thought Jack. "Do it in my name and offer a blanket amnesty."

"Freight Ship X2R1. You are to return to base immediately by order of Tactical Unit One Crown. Compliance with this order will attach a blanket amnesty." This was repeated several times.

The Bio-Comp reported a slight increase in the ship's out-bound speed. Tac-U-One could imagine the fleeing pilot's terror.

If the freighter X2R1 was able to enter Other-Space, Jack would have almost no time to preserve himself, to protect Earth.

"There must be something bad hidden on Mars." Tac-U-One observed dryly. "Or they're really dedicated criminals; it's not often a Crown Officer hands out a pardon without first knowing the crime."

Tac-U-One stood still for a minute in quiet concentration, assembling an attack on the pilot. He sent a package of disruptive thoughts.

"The freighter made a slight course alteration," the computer said.

Tac-U-One grinned. The pilot's body had probably evacuated, the man would be sitting in his own shit.

He blasted the pilot again, but there was no further change of course. Pilots were mentally tough; they had to continue operating under an incredibly varied set of stress factors.

● ● ●

All Boltax could do now was stonewall. The message that was to save him, might kill him.

The Crown Officer was a cold bastard. He loved that native girl? He was blowing her to hell to save his own ass. Disgusting. With love like that, who needed hate?

What could he expect?

● ● ●

Jack had reason to believe Wendy was not on the ship. When the ship docked at Mars base, all passengers would disembark. Especially given the request by the Bio-Comp to hold there for further orders.

When the pilot received Boltax's message, they departed almost immediately. Ergo, Wendy should not be on the ship his missiles were targeting. So, she was still on Mars base or had already departed the solar system on the other ship.

Tac-U-One had felt hatred for Boltax. He let this emotional reaction go – wash through him. If he didn't embrace the negative emotions, or act on them, they discharged themselves.

This left him free to deal with Boltax as he should. Not as hate driven anger would.

Boltax was a threat. Because of his telepathic ability he could cause trouble. Merely restricting body location was insufficient protection. Any contact with Directory staff could be disastrous – especially before he talked to them.

He needed to terrify Boltax, make him truly fear for his life and very existence.

●

"You've made yourself my enemy." Tac-U-One said to Boltax. He made himself feel rage. It started as a small flicker and he fed the flame, first with kindling, then whole logs. The sensation of rage mounting, growing stronger, he let it show on his face, in the stance of his body, until the room was a furnace. He directed this emotion in a withering blast at his victim.

Boltax felt terror.

Tac-U-One had lost control.

His face was a demon's face.

This is it. Boltax thought.

Under the cover of emotional rage, Tac-U-One forced images of terror directly into Boltax's mind.

"Prepare yourself for mind-swipe," Tac-U-One bellowed.

The Crown officer's words pierced him. The brutal pillage of his innermost secrets panicked him further; he chose a telepath's last defense.

Mindshield! Boltax screamed internally.

Immediately he began retreating, withdrawing from the world. He pulled external awareness in tighter and tighter, back, back, back into himself. Soon he could not see, or smell or detect motion or feel impact. The sense of location and the passage of time became abstractions that had no merit. Sound was the last to go. There was silence that came in soft waves like a nonexistent heartbeat.

The problem with mindshield was the inability to determine when the threat was gone. He'd become, for all practical purposes, a point of consciousness without awareness. Around him like a shell was a wall of terror he was seeking to avoid. A barrier one would not wish to penetrate or escape from.

Tac-U-One watched this process with disgust and a little fascination. Boltax's body slowly pulled itself into a fetal position. He'd formed a mental cocoon; it was the last line of defense for a trained telepath who did not want to communicate.

It took a great deal of energy to hold it in place and the body would quickly waste away. But a Jolo body could become almost skeletal before it expired, so there was no telling when the mindlock would unravel. Sometimes it was only death that bought release.

Not with this one, Tac-U-One thought. *He's too self-serving and won't willingly go into body death for anyone.*

"Bio-Comp, please monitor Non-Citizen Boltax's mindlock.

"Order logged."

Jack almost smiled. The Investigator was scrunched into a corner of his office, trying desperately not to be noticed.

"Investigator, bring a gurney from the transfer room. We need to transport the Non-Citizen.

"Yes, sir."

"Be quick."

He ran out.

After the staff meeting Boltax's body would go to the infirmary. An intravenous drip would maintain Boltax in his current state.

Jack had no immediate intention of engaging in mental combat with Boltax. Extracting information about Earth operations and the Directory would take many hours and be exhausting. It would weaken him when he needed his telepathic strength most.

He looked at Boltax in his pathetic fetal ball, motionless and barely breathing. He probed the mindlock viciously and saw the body tighten its ball. Good – he wanted Boltax to expend the maximum amount of energy. Boltax was where Jack wanted him – out of communication and unable to cause further damage.

The Investigator returned with the gurney. They put the Non-Citizen on it.

"Wait here for instructions from the Bio-Comp." The Investigator couldn't send telepathically, so he wasn't a threat.

"Yes, sir."

Tac-U-One returned to the transfer room.

He scooped up the remains of the Jack Cousins body and fed it to the incinerator without a second thought. He was almost done when he remembered the fateful dive he'd taken in the lake and the mystery surrounding it.

He saved a sample of blood.

"Bio-Comp, in his next free moment, have the Bio-Tech pick up this blood sample and run a complete scan on it. Compare it to a baseline Earth human body.

"Yes, sir."

Tac-U-One disposed of the last of waste from the Jack Cousins body. What he'd told Wendy was true: he used a body, then threw it away.

CHAPTER 36

Tactical Unit One stepped into the cloak closet attached to the transfer room and donned a uniform. It was the cut and fine dove gray of a Fleet Admiral, complete with galactic swirl on the shoulder boards. How incredibly deluded Boltax was.

"All Directory Earth staff are now present, sir. Not including the two Earth-Jolos."

"Thank you. No location on those two?"

"No, sir."

"Rumors are flying fast and furious amongst the staff. There have been 'all staff' meetings before, but cutting all the comm channels is new."

"Can't have that. We better relieve them of mystery."

Tac-U-One walked through the Colosseum complex with the guidance of the Bio-Comp and became familiar with its layout.

"There's been a few attempts to leave."

"I hope your refusal was polite."

"I adjudicate the level of manners required on a one for one basis."

Tac-U-One laughed.

The Jolos and other Directory personnel were mystified by the uniform. His was a new face and the way he carried his body marked him as an unknown. Who was this Jolo, they asked themselves.

"The staff are trying to call Boltax about an Admiral walking their halls."

"What did he tell them?"

"Curiously, he's not taking calls."

Tac-U-One laughed.

●

Tac-U-One entered the Colosseum arena control room. The games were being closely monitored.

"Good afternoon, everyone."

"Hello, sir."

"Please prepare to end the games for the day."

"That's impossible, sir. I'll call the Chief and he'll explain."

"Make your call." Tac-U-One said.

The control room director spoke for a few moments and then frowning said, "He's not available. And that's strange. He always takes my calls."

"Shut the games down."

"Is that an admiral's uniform, sir?" the director said with a smirk – on this base it had to be dress up.

"Director, I believe you've been orchestrating violence for so long that you can't recognize when you're in personal danger."

"Yes, sir. Forgive me, this will take a few minutes."

Soon all was in order.

"The Fight for Immortality is over.

"There's a mandatory staff meeting. I understand that usually doesn't include you or the other FFI staff. Today it does."

●

On the Turf, two gladiators were furiously trading blows in an exhibition match.

Tac-U-One took the long spiral staircase down to the Turf. He stepped through a white Roman arch and walked out into the sun.

He paused to take in this view one last time. Then, he slowly walked toward the combatants. About halfway there, as directed, the cameras picked him up and his image was flashed across the large displays.

Coming near the two opponents, he hailed them. Warily, they separated and turned their attention toward him. He spoke with them quietly.

"Gentlemen, the arena is closing early today. Please drop your weapons, depart the Turf, and exit the property."

"Look, pretty boy, get outta here or I'll carve you up."

Jack stepped forward and took his sword.

"Not today. Please leave."

Bewildered, the two disconsolately turned and walked off the Turf.

Tac-U-One looked up into the arena and waited for quiet.

Finally it came.

"The games have been suspended," Tac-U-One said to the main camera. "More information concerning this will be available in a live broadcast on Directory TV within the week. Your money will be refunded."

The crowd was stunned and there were pockets of jostling with punches being thrown.

"You are directed to leave the Colosseum. There is no need to hurry, but you must exit within the next hour as the facility will be closed at that time. Thank you."

Some booed and shook their fists at the man on the Turf, but the sullen mob began to leave. No one felt safe challenging Directory orders, no matter how much they disliked them.

•

Tac-U-One stood center stage in the small auditorium. The admiral's uniform was seen by all and had a sobering effect. Here stood authority.

There were almost two hundred Directory personnel, of which thirty-five were Jolos, the Bio-Comp informed him. Only one Jolo gained his status under Crown rule.

He looked out at the faces. Were they criminals like Boltax and the Mars staff? Probably not. Were they here under duress like the Bio-Comp? Probably not. They were somewhere in between. But all knew this operation violated all sorts of Directory law.

He casually tossed a silver communications ball into the room, where it hovered silently – they were now on notice this was an official proceeding.

"I expect you're all curious about what's happened here today." There was a polite murmur of assent.

"Bio-Comp, introduce me, please."

"Yes, SIR." The second word sent chills.

"Tactical Unit One Crown has taken command of Earth base and system," announced Bio-Comp.

As one, the staff shot to their feet and saluted. Right fist over left breast. Jack smiled to himself. The really guilty ones wished they had wings.

"Thank you for your acknowledgment." He returned the salute.

"Quoting a famous author: 'The reports of my death are greatly exaggerated.'"

This earned a few laughs.

"And no, I didn't just drop in on Earth because I had nothing better to do. More about that later.

"Your former Chief now known as Non-Citizen Boltax is also with us." Tac-U-One turned to the side and said, "Investigator, please wheel him in."

Boltax came in on a gurney, his fetal position an eloquent statement of surrender.

"Please feel free to approach and assure yourself that this is your former Chief.

The morbid, the curious and the careful came up to confirm that it was indeed him. Recognition sent a wave of shocked comment through the hall.

What would happen to them?

"Non-Citizen Boltax resisted the restoration of Crown Law and has paid a price."

He was about to lay down the law, then hesitated.

Facing these people, he realized he'd lost the need to *do something to them.*

Life on Earth had changed him. She had changed him.

For the first time in millennia he'd lived among people as one of them. No mission, no ulterior motive. The people of Earth and the Directory staff were more closely his peers than any time in easy memory. He had a grasp of the stresses and forces their lives came under.

Tac-U-One took their measure, and it was fear.

Understandable.

He was the hammer about to fall.

He needed to set a higher tone for this meeting and was startled to see the face of someone he knew. Or thought he knew.

This may provide the opportunity he needed.

Could this be the same man? He appeared aged beyond belief, the face heavily lined, broad shoulders slumped. There was a vagueness about him, he was unfocused, which did not match the image of the person he remembered.

The man *was* a Jolo, though the age of his body was extreme. Much, obviously, had changed.

How did he get mixed up with these people? The man he had known then would not have been here.

Full recall returned.

This Jolo had been a ship's Captain. More than a thousand years ago; remarkably, the face was similar. Jack felt disoriented – no one held onto a body that long. It was odd, bizarre even, in a world where a Jolo never kept a body more than three hundred years, and most not that long. Some Jolos, liking to be recognized, ordered bodies to the exact specifications of their previous one – but no, this Jolo's body was ancient, it must be the same one.

How extraordinary.

"Farley!" Tac-U-One called.

The old man never stirred. He sat with a blank fixed stare.

"Farley, is that you?"

Others were turned to look at the old Jolo. The old man looked around. Then shrugged, uninterested.

His body systems were failing and no one could persuade him to get medical attention. He hated these people, this place, what they were doing. The body would die, he would move on, and so, he didn't want to know.

"He doesn't hear well, sir," someone volunteered. A deaf Jolo? Tac-U-One frowned.

The person continued. "They've given him new inner ears, but he goes out and damages them. He doesn't like us," she finished, miffed by the old man's attitude. "And his name's not Farley, sir."

"Tell him to come up here."

Someone urged him to his feet. Soon the old man stood at his side.

"Farley, is that you?"

His escort said, "His name is Sten, sir. Ren Sten."

Tac-U-One looked at the man who had interrupted. He gulped. "Sorry, sir!"

"Farley?" he asked again, louder.

The old man turned his liquid gaze to him and there was an uncertain look in the watery orbs. The uniform did not impress him; he'd seen admirals before. The old man was a huge specimen, just as Jack remembered, over seven feet and probably more without the slumped posture.

"Farley?" He saw a glimmer come alive in those ancient eyes.

"It's been a long time since anyone called me by that name," the aged voice grated out, unafraid. He paused and reached out to Tac-U-One and gripped his shoulder. "Where did you hear that name, boy?" He was clearly unaware of the identity of his questioner. The others watched in fascination as one of the great powers of the galaxy was addressed as "boy" and did not flinch.

"We were out near the galactic rim," Tac-U-One paused and thought a second. "A quarter turn of the wheel (spacer slang for galaxy) from here and up into the thick of it. Cossno, do you remember?"

Tac-U-One felt for the old man, could see him struggle with curtains of his far past memories.

Jack warmed to his story: "It was not yet eleven hundred years past – on the deck of a freighter, your freighter.

"What was it... yes, that's it, the *Hildegad*. Remember, Farley?

"We fought an action against pirates. And won! Won with a freighter; that was some fight! We were hiding behind a rogue asteroid just outside the Cossno Suns and Planets, waiting for the pirates.

Jack saw some curiosity, "You remember – that star system had been targeted for repeated attacks by those bad ass banditti. They had the latest military ship-to-ship forced boarding devices. They were raping, stealing and leaving the plundered ships for dead.

"I took that assignment because my desk had been boring me to death.

"Farley, you recall what those pirates called themselves, right?"

Farley scratched his head, "Shezels Blood!"

"That's it, Farley!" Tac-U-One slapped him on the back. "We published that story four hundred years ago, same name – Shezels Blood." The old man was getting closer.

"When we met we did that secret refit on Hildegad, got her ready to kick pirate ass. Its exterior was all freighter. We fooled them.

"All of you should know that Farley displayed exceptional nerve and great courage." Jack directed this to the audience. "We were in hand to hand combat with Shezels Blood. In five months, the pirates were all dead or gone. Farley personally tracked the link to a military supply depot a few systems over. He arrested the man who sold the ship-to-ship boarding gear. But I was gone by then."

Tac-U-One looked into his eyes. "You became the Cossno System's watchdog, if I recall correctly."

The old man frowned, blinked and moved very close, looking down at him. Tac-U-One looked nothing like he had all those years ago and this added to the oldster's confusion. But telling that story had pulled his memories closer and closer.

Abruptly the old boy stiffened, shock taking his features. He came to rigid attention, pulled his shoulders back, and saluted.

"Sir, please forgive me, I didn't recognize. I didn't see... or hear..." He was terribly embarrassed.

"If I remember rightly," said Tac-U-One, "I commended you to the Sector Director. It went something like: 'Greetings Drummed Or, Director of Sector Garid. I wish to bring to your attention the Jolo Farley Henn. Having worked closely with him of late, clearing the Cossno system of pirate activity, I can testify to his bravery, vouch for his character, compliment his intelligence and pronounce him resourceful and effective even in the most trying of circumstances. He has served Crown and his fellow citizens well. Should you need a Jolo of high qualification, I recommend him to you.'" He looked at the man.

"It went something like that, didn't it?"

Farley stood taller but could not immediately speak.

"It was like that, wasn't it?"

"Yes, sir, that was it exactly. Thank you for remembering your kind words to me, sir. You do me a great honor."

"You're welcome, my friend."

"They said you were dead, sir... I couldn't believe it!" the old man said past a constricted throat. "But it's not true, is it, sir? It's really you, sir. For the love of Life and Crown, it's you, sir!" There were tears in the man's eyes.

"Yes, it's me, old friend. May I tell you another story?"

"If it pleases you, sir"

"Nine Crown years ago I was directed by Crown to investigate a planet. I will call it planet X. Planet X was being used to stage the greatest criminal enterprise I've ever seen. It was a trap."

"Certain men within the Directory conspired to permanently dispose of me." There was shock in the room.

"Non-Citizen Boltax was part of that conspiracy and earlier today attempted to permanently dispose of me again." Tac-U-One waived to the Investigator.

He wheeled out the huge blood splattered I-Trap.

"Do all of you know what this is?"

They were about evenly divided. "This is an identity trap. Its intended use is the containment of a person for up to half a million years. It is dumped in interstellar space for permanent disposal of the unwanted person. It is illegal and will be destroyed later this evening."

"Non-Citizen Boltax earlier today attempted to I-trap me using this device, knowing my identity."

"It's true!" blurted out the Investigator. "I was there and saw the whole thing." Jack suppressed a smile – *without revealing your own role.*

"After this morning's more dramatic events I was informed by Non-Citizen Boltax that following my disappearance a ceremony marking my death was held. And that a monument commemorating my life was erected. Are you all familiar with this?"

There was a general assent.

"This is merely an expression of my enemy's wishful thinking. Admittedly I've been away for a while, but I'm back now."

Everyone in the hall rose to their feet and applauded. Tac-U-One was pleased. They were ignorant of the larger crimes, and unaware of their own role. They were pawns in Bio-One's plot.

Farley was clapping. This went on for a while.

"Thank you. Thank you very much." Finally they returned to their seats.

"Eighteen Earth years ago I died on this planet. I grew up here and have a family. Not long ago I recovered awareness of who I am.

"At that time I saw the connection between planet X and the operation here on Earth." There was silence.

"I'm sure everyone here was aware of Non-Citizen Boltax's displeasure over the deferments?"

Yes, they were aware of it.

"I and a few others were responsible for this disruption. What is being done on this planet and to its population is uncivilized.

"None of you are aware of the fate the people of Earth are being sent to. But you must know that they couldn't get a job anywhere in the Directory with the training they're receiving. That's correct, isn't it?

"We've been wondering about that." There was a chorus of agreement.

"Okay. But you do know your presence here violates many Crown laws."

Someone in the front row stood. "Sir, we each personally received a warrant signed and sealed by the Regent himself, suspending the applicable sections of Crown Law."

"Who is this Regent?"

"Sir, the Regent is Bio-One."

"Bio-One is the Jolo I was investigating for treason just before my death."

Silence rang through the auditorium.

"Planet X is his operation and so is this base here on Earth."

The silence became profound.

"What the hell is a 'Regent'?"

"The Torpil Council (senior administrative arm of the Directory) awarded him that title years ago, sir.

●

"Farley, how did you come to be on Earth?"

Farley looked at his feet and shame hung all about him.

"All right, Farley, all right," Jack said with compassion. "Would it be okay with you if I took a look at what you've been doing? Scanned your mind?"

The old man sagged further. "Sir, I've been so bad, sir. I can't, I can't... so very bad. I.... I was convicted and I couldn't get another body." He paused. "I lost my immortal status."

If a Jolo were convicted of certain crimes, then he/she could not transfer into another body and would eventually "die." For greater offenses, Jolos were sent to Denude, the prison planet.

Jolo status was a privilege, not a right, and the laws that governed Jolos were few. Jolos were expected to exercise *good judgment* in any given situation. As a Jolo, they had far greater responsibility for the welfare of the Directory and if they became destructive to those around them, they could lose their status at a judicial proceeding. There was no imprisonment for a Jolo; you either made the grade or you didn't. Most made it.

"But you weren't sentenced to Denude?"

Farley was offended. "No, sir!"

That was pride, a good sign. "May I look then?"

Farley straightened. "Yes, sir. I would be pleased for you to review my activities." This was formal cant, not normally heard outside justice halls.

Tac-U-One used the official method for telepathic interrogation of a compliant offender. He placed a picture of a particular crime in Farley's mind and then varied the picture till he pulled out a string of similar pictures. These were incidents from Farley's past where he had committed a similar crime.

Tac-U-One started with violent crime. Farley had not committed a murder as a Jolo. He followed the procedure in crime category after category. He would flash the picture and vary it till the pictures similar in content were drawn from Farley's mind to view. He looked at them. Farley could see them too.

The entire procedure took thirteen minutes and felt to Farley as if it was the action of one mind, one will. Farley felt as if *he* were doing it and marveled. It was so different from the last time – a thousand years past. Then, it had been a brutal invasion of privacy and personally painful.

This time, the procedure began slowly and then become more rapid, until the pictures flashed by with great velocity. As it continued Farley's mental processes moved from sedentary, gathered speed, and then become quick. Soon, it was done. His face wore an expression of wonder. He felt there was nothing he could not say.

Tac-U-One faced Farley, who stood formally waiting to receive justice. Jack marveled. It was a rare thing to see the life of a man so closely, so intimately. The old Jolo had seen many things, done many things. Many good, some not so good, as with us all. He went on with the formal patter.

"I've reviewed your activity in all its parts."

"Yes, sir!" Farley replied.

"I've seen the crimes you have committed."

"Yes, sir!"

"Did you do these things?"

"Yes, sir! What you have seen I did do." The sense of remorse was palpable throughout the entire auditorium.

Tac-U-One turned away from Farley and faced the assembled men and women. With great solemnity he said, "I have seen this Jolo. I have judged him."

Then to Farley, "Are you prepared for my sentence?" None but a Crown Officer was both judge and jury.

Farley could only nod. There was quiet in the auditorium; here, too, would they go.

"I demand your services for one hundred years."

Farley, expecting some harsh dispensation from this impartial source, could not believe his ears. To be *punished* with the one thing he most desired?

"Sir. Sir! Would that I could! This body betrays me!" He paused. "Being in your service was the greatest time of my life," he declared with passion. "To this body's last breath I will carry out your orders!"

"There is much to be done; I need you for the *entire* hundred years, if not more."

Farley was having a day like no other in his life, emotional highs and lows succeeding each other with terrible rapidity. This last brought him low.

"Sir, for as long as this body lasts, I will do it!" Farley said with strength and, hating it, said, "I shall see the medicos and have the body refurbished as best they can."

"That's not good enough!" Tac-U-One barked out.

Farley felt crushed. How else could he serve? It was obvious his body would soon be of little use.

"Recyclex officer, please step forward." A man stood. "Take Farley to Recyclex and transfer him." This declaration was formal restoration of Jolo status.

Farley stumbled back a few paces and came to rest against a wall, disbelief on his face.

Tac-U-One looked at the old spacer. "Renew your Crown Oath to the Bio-Comp before transfer."

Farley looked at the Crown Officer and all he could see was friendship.

"Yes, sir!" He saluted and was led away. There was energy in his stride. Astonishment flooded the room.

Tac-U-One had to cement these people to him and gain their support to bring about his vision for Earth's future. From their viewpoint, he might only represent a de-powered Tactical Unit Officer, and once outside his personal sphere of influence, revert to supporting Bio-One. They could see him as a loser, a poor bet in the game of interstellar politics and a personal threat to their freedom. He must handle all these points.

"I want to be clear.

"After listening to me, I don't want you to wonder about my intent. I want you certain where Bio-One's rebellion is headed. So I'll put it in perspective for you.

"The resources of the Biological Department, Bio-One personally, and thousands of people working and planning for years could not suppress me for long. They had me isolated and launched a surprise attack with an entire Planetary Attack Force.

"Still, I escaped. In a heavily damaged ship I was dumped from OS near this planet. I arrived here and avoided capture by crashing my ship, and dying.

The quick among them realized he survived the "screaming end" and whispered this about.

"Have you been watching the Fight for Immortality?"

There were murmured assents.

"I was Jack Cousins."

Shockwaves rippled through them.

This was unvarnished truth, and because of his reputation, they believed it.

"My resolve is simple: Crown rule will return!" he thundered out.

They stood and cheered. He did not fool himself. The reactions of some of these people were self-serving.

The Directory personnel of Earth, whether for or against him, were certain of his ability. Certain he would carry out his mission, overcome any obstacle and achieve his objective.

There's a funny thing about certainty, Jack knew, it creates its own reality.

Now he had to address the matter of their criminality.

⬤

This meeting began with fear. The introduction of Tac-U-One. Their senior officer a non-citizen and incapacitated. Then shock at the revelation of Bio-One's betrayal of Crown and the Directory. Next came redemption and Farley's reinstatement of Jolo status and transfer. Followed by the Crown Officer's purpose.

The Directory employees watched these proceedings with awe. There was hope! They'd gone into criminality, some with more knowledge, some less, but all were aware that Directory presence, their presence, on planet Earth, was illegal.

"You are concerned about what will come next. About your own future. You must realize that you cannot hide behind the suspension of laws given to you by the traitor Bio-One.

"The Fight for Immortality should make any Directory citizen revolt. It is an abomination to everything we as a civilized society hold true. You went along with it.

"You may have disliked or even hated what you were doing. But only action changes conditions. That's why I'm standing here. You may say, 'But he is Tac-U-One,' so of course he did something.

"This may be news to you, but here it is: I wasn't born with my skills, I earned them. I saw conditions I was unwilling to let exist – I did something to cause change. I've become who I am today. I'm on a journey – who will I be tomorrow? I don't exactly know, but I won't stop pushing.

"How does this apply to you? Simple. If you see something that needs to be changed and do nothing, or help make it worse, you lose personal integrity and power.

"Your participation with the 'Directory programs' on Earth has degraded you. I offer you a path to redemption. Primarily you have wronged the people of Earth and secondarily tarnished the good name of the Directory of Stars and Planets.

"Your amends need to be done on this planet. I'm suspending your Directory citizenship. After ten years you can re-apply to senior Directory officials here on Earth for reinstatement.

"By lecturing you I'm not trying to hold myself up as a good example. Just compare – what does it matter if you try and fail? I did that when I died on this planet. Get back up. Try again. If Boltax had gotten the better of me in the Recyclex room it wouldn't have stopped me.

"You only ever really lose when you allow the wrong thing to be done with your knowledge, and don't try to prevent it. Or you convince yourself that the wrong thing is right. Please don't fool yourself – you know.

"So I offer you a route to regain your personal integrity by helping the people of Earth. Are you interested?

They were on their feet cheering him. Honesty, discipline and compassion.

"Excellent. I'll provide you with that opportunity. Now we will proceed with standard Directory ethics procedure."

"I require," said Tac-U-One, "each of you to provide me with three categories of information.

"The first is any direct personal knowledge of changes that exist in the leadership on Crown Planet and the sectors. In this category include major changes of policy you've observed or that have affected you, and any incidents that are examples of such with names, dates and places.

"Please include how you were contacted for the posting here on Earth and the names of everyone involved and a complete description of the circumstances, including the reasons you agreed to be here, what rewards you were offered.

"The second category is specific actions you've done that violate Crown Law or against me personally, both before and during your involvement with this program. Include where, when, who and why.

"Thirdly, I want your knowledge of gross violations of Crown Law, by others in the last twenty years, plus all relevant details.

"Don't confer with anyone, but provide me with what you know independent of any other person.

"Your former Chief has earned his fate. It's not pleasant.

"You've also seen Farley Henn. He was honest with me. I urge you too, come clean with me."

"All your data will be reviewed by a Judicial Telepath." This wasn't possible but they'd be more honest.

●

There were some people Tac-U-One needed to weed out and he pounced without warning.

"The spies among you have five seconds to raise your hands." He gave them little time. Two reluctantly identified themselves.

"There are more among you than this," he said with total certainty – which they were at complete liberty to think was telepathically determined, but was not.

"I will clearly define 'spy' for you. All the usual definitions, plus anyone who reports independently of command channels." Four more hands were raised. "Is that all?" Five more seconds passed. "If others among you are found, I will treat you as a confirmed enemy, so I advise you to take this opportunity to reveal yourself." Jack waited, but there were no takers.

"Okay.

"You self-identified spies are to report your full functions and objectives, the content of all previous reports filed from this planet, and to whom you report. Also include the method of reporting and the timing, codes, equipment etc. And anything else you know that I would want to know."

"As you can imagine we will check you and the data you provide with microscopic thoroughness. Secondarily, your status as a spy doesn't make you my enemy.

He paused, "Has anyone reported my arrival, or earlier reported that you suspected it?" He scanned their minds on this but there were no obvious indicators of betrayal. "Do any of you intend to do so?" Again nothing came up. "Good."

"That's all I have for now, begin debriefing immediately." There were murmured assents.

"Bio-Comp to monitor all proceedings and notify me as each person completes his debrief." How glad he was to have Bio-Comp as an ally.

"Order logged, sir."

Tac-U-One added telepathically, "Everyone's restricted to base until further notice. I want to know who's most concerned with leaving, so when someone requests permission to leave the Colosseum you're to say I've specifically instructed you to prevent that person's departure, by name. Monitor their thoughts closely at that point and see if anything interesting comes up. Let me know immediately."

"They'll think you're onto them – probably telepathically – and what they're hiding is likely to be foremost in their minds!" Bio-Comp marveled.

"I discovered, long ago, that no matter how powerful a telepath is, investigative skill is far more important in getting to the bottom of things."

"It's a pleasure working with you, sir!"

"We make a good team. I have another request."

"Yes?"

"I need an organization chart for the control of Earth. The Directory portion to be appointed by me. Please determine the key posts that need to be filled – I'll get as much of that done as time permits."

"What structure for the different nations?"

"Their executives should be elected."

"Very good, sir. I'll have a proposal on your desk shortly."

"Excellent. We can cobble together something that'll work.

Thank you again for staying on. I'll have to leave very soon and your presence will be vital in stabilizing the populace and helping everyone to recover from what's been done here."

"Thank you, sir!" replied Bio-Comp.

"When I see Crown I'll tell him of your help to me, the Directory and the people of Earth. I am sure he'll wish to thank you personally."

"Thank you, sir!" To actually meet the mythical Directory head of state was beyond his imagining.

●

He personally interviewed Farley after he returned.

"You look like a new man."

Farley cracked up and laughed hilariously. Jack joined in and it took them some minutes to regain their composure.

"I guess you could say that, sir."

They bantered for a few minutes, Tac-U-One easy in his company.

"I have a job for you."

"Yes, sir."

"I'm appointing you Admiral of Earth's Space navy."

"But they don't have a Space Navy, sir."

"It's a big job, wouldn't you say?"

"Yes, sir! I'll get right on it."

That was why he loved this man. Nothing was beyond him. Give him a task and he would find a way. And in good time, too.

●

As the data began to come in, Jack's knowledge of the changes present within the Directory increased.

All non-Directory planets that were humanoid and industrialized and not aligned with the Outer Worlds were systematically being taken over by technological coup, as had been done on Earth.

Shockingly, this involved estimates as high as ninety planets and was an enormous undertaking. The "Fight for Immortality" program in progress on primitive planets took the top ten percent and awarded them a Jolo body.

After advanced training, the winners went to Planet X where they were consolidated into larger fighting units and given further training. Tens of thousands of men.

None of the Directory personnel had seen this, but it came through the rumor mill more than once and from different star ship personnel.

As he continued to read, he discovered various versions of how Bio-One had taken over the governing of the entire Directory. Apparently Crown had gone on a sabbatical; something Jack knew was impossible owing to his secret mission controlled by Crown himself.

Crown was expecting his report. A report both knew would restructure the entire Biological department. No way would he have moved off the seat of power, even temporarily, at that time.

Bio-One would have received the supreme punishment and taken a trip to Denude, the prison planet.

A fire was reported in Crown's offices, and the lives of many key ministers had been lost. Fire damage? Death from fire for a Jolo body used at the ministerial level – was ludicrous. You could burn a top quality Jolo body for some time without effect.

Supposing Crown had gone off on one of his infrequent trips, hearing of the devastation to his council would have caused his immediate return.

Nine of the staff on Earth reported having actually seen Crown hand over power to Bio-One on a live broadcast. And all the rest had seen the same event as the recording filtered out to the Sectors.

None of this information even hinted at how Bio-One had managed the takeover. It must have been done with a biological weapon. Crown was extremely tough and it was entirely conceivable he had survived the attack in a weakened form, much as Tac-U-One had.

Was Crown still operating elsewhere, marshaling forces, preparing to return?

●

It was nearing Saturday evening, the first day of his control over Earth. Most of the Directory staff were still in debrief. This had been the second bloodless coup in as many years for this planet. He predicted a brighter future for Earth and was working hard in these last days to make it happen.

Tac-U-One's mission would soon take him away from Earth. But to be successful would require a more advanced body – his own body. For the same reason he needed a Jolo body to wrestle control of Earth from Boltax, so would he have to get a *real* body if he were to take back control of the Directory.

Essentially the current body was an inadequate tool for the struggle ahead. Using it would place himself at the mercy of greater powers. He did not wish to face a "Jack versus the Red Dragon" scenario again. You can win, but too easily lose.

Jack continued to review reports coming in from the staff. There'd been no open announcement of permanent change of leadership in the Directory, no conflict in the different sectors and no interplanetary war of any kind.

There'd been significant change in top military command, but in Jack's estimation, this didn't mean that the military were now loyal to Bio-One. If they believed a coup had taken place, Bio-One would be abandoned.

Loyalty to Crown was very strong. Crown had guided their fates for more than seven thousand years and the Directory was alive and well, expanding and prosperous in large measure due to Crown's management.

Bio-One had planned and executed the takeover so brilliantly that the rest of the political world still thought he acted with Crown authority and not his own. There were no glaring signs of governmental unrest. This was giving Bio-One time to secure and train his own legions of troops, troops loyal only to him, for who else would give them a Jolo body?

All this was heading in only one direction: formal usurpation of all political power, and civil war to put down the Sectors that rebelled. The caliber of these troops could not be high in comparison to the existing Directory forces. But their numbers were growing.

The Space Navy and all its personnel, numbering well into the millions, couldn't be replaced. Many of the officers and men had seen more than a thousand years' service, or two, or three. Their loyalty was to Crown and a point of great stability. It would take a great deal to shift the allegiance of those dedicated men and women.

Boltax, and possibly some of the spies, were the only people with any knowledge of the actual situation in the Directory.

Of prime importance was Crown's network of Tactical Unit Officers. Who was running them now? Was the same Tac-U-Two still the administrative head? Had Bio-One gained control of this powerful force?

Tac-U-One was coming. It amused him that Bio-One's stupidity had reactivated his prime enemy. If that greedy man had left Earth alone Jack Cousins would have spent his life building a space ship from scratch. A project of many, many years.

Was that not the way with evil men; they carried the seeds of their own destruction with them?

Report after report detailed growing disgruntlement amongst Directory citizens for blatant tampering with the accepted method of granting Jolo status. Too many petitioners from the biological sciences department were being accepted, and valid petitions rejected.

Directory citizens were not quiet when their "sacred rite" was tampered with.

The unrest this caused was spreading. Bio-One, with his mad desires, could plunge the whole Directory into chaos and fragment it beyond recovery.

With all this new data Tac-U-One wanted to get out there and do something.

What to do about Earth? It was a problem, and in good conscience he could not simply leave the planet to the chaos that would occur if he didn't install a functioning command structure. So he would. Very quickly.

How utterly improbable that all the turmoil both inside and outside the Directory had happened; it was beyond easy comprehension. All that Crown and countless others had built over the millennia was being systematically undermined – and by a man such as Bio-One.

The truth was that eighteen Earth years ago the Directory was in fine economic shape, there were no military situations, people were confident and happy. Crown's last sabbatical was half a millennium past. It was the perfect time to stage a coup.

Tac-U-One had never considered Bio-One anything less than brilliant, in his own field. Nevertheless, he'd advised Crown to remove this Jolo. It had been a hunch at first, but after fifty centuries of playing the power game, he could tell this Jolo sought supreme power for personal reasons. To give power to a man who seeks to increase his own stature as a first action and not through real service to others is the formula every broken civilization has followed.

Then an intelligence break occurred. A location of Bio-One's secret planetary base came from trusted source. Tac-U-One passed the data on to Crown. In secret they made their plans to strike. Tac-U-One's return with evidence in hand was to be the end game.

Crown's decision to take Bio-One down "by the book" was flawed. It had been Tac-U-One's mistake to give Crown that decision to make. It was *his job* to adjudicate threat level and handle the antisocial elements within the Directory and he did not need specific permission to do so. It had been *his* decision to make – instead he'd passed the buck to his chief executive. What had swayed him in this fateful decision was that Bio-One was a department head on the Torpil Council and appointment to and removal from this position was directly in Crown's area of control.

All the justifications in the world wouldn't remove one shred of responsibility.

●

"One minute to convergence." The Bio-Comp selected a euphemism for obliteration.

"Missile will no longer respond to countermand signal before convergence with ship," Bio-Comp announced.

The fatal seconds passed. The Bio-Comp was mute. In what felt like hours later, only ten seconds had passed, with no information given.

"Bio-Comp! Status!" Jack barked.

"There's been an anomalous circumstance," Bio-Comp reported.

"Explain!"

The outbound ship and the approaching missile had almost converged, when the ship's Other-Space drive kicked in. The anomaly was that the missile was so close it was drawn *through* with the ship. It is uncertain if the ship would complete its voyage or be destroyed.

You've got to be joking, Tac-U-One thought. *That happened on my way in here.* He hoped the ship met the same fate. This had serious implications to his mission. If the freighter got through and Boltax's message was delivered, then his presence on Earth was unsustainable.

He had to leave. Plans had to be compressed. And, no time meant taking big risks.

Once he entered the realm of Other-Space, its mystical properties would clear the remaining cobwebs from his head. The seductress called to him with greater attraction than a sailor ever felt from the sea.

He longed for Other-Space, but it hadn't always been that way. At first she'd been an enemy, but slowly he began to understand her and then she'd set him free. Other-Space was the secret to amplifying personal power.

CHAPTER 37

THE SUN HAD SET ON THE first day of Tactical Unit One's command of Earth. He ordered Farley to investigate the mysterious Mars base and document what he found. "Return with all personnel and close it down." He had no wish, or time, to go there, but the people of Earth had a right to know what had been done to their sons and daughters.

He spent a few minutes finalizing the organization chart with Bio-Comp. He then called for the most capable Earthman he knew. He needed someone he could trust, and Earth wanted an honest man to govern its affairs – for a change.

Norman had remained in the Colosseum facility, waiting for Jack. A few hours after Jack had disappeared, all the Directory staff left the public area and had not returned. Then he saw a man cancel the day's demonstration on the Turf. The sullen crowd went home. Norman and a few fighters and trainers were waiting to see the "new Jack." No one had asked them to leave.

And that was good, for it was more than his life was worth to leave without Jack.

"Mr. Norman Cousins, please come to the staff door." Norman stood. "A Directory official requests an interview."

"Guess this is it. Good luck to you, Norman. Say hello to the kid for us." Norman shook hands all around.

"I'll tell him you guys are here." He went to the door.

●

The Investigator met Norman and courteously escorted him to Boltax's old office. Norman was asked to sit but was not introduced. He was very nervous.

"Thank you for agreeing to see me," the Directory official said in a solicitous voice.

This was the man who'd announced the suspension of the games.

"Sir, is there news of my boy, Jack Cousins? He's the one who won the last round of the Fight for Immortality."

"Mr. Cousins, please excuse me if I ask you a few questions before answering yours.

"What was the reason for Jack – your nephew, your adopted son – to enter the competition?"

The answer to this question could be dangerous for Jack and himself so he worded it carefully.

"I believe Jack wanted to become immortal."

"Did he tell you what happens to the body that remains after transfer to the new one is complete?"

"I don't believe we had that conversation." Norman frowned. The whole idea was unreal. He hadn't even wondered. If Jack got a new body, then something would have to be done with the old one. That was obvious, but his thinking hadn't gone that far.

"I understand. Within the Directory it is standard practice to incinerate the discarded body."

"I didn't know that," Norman frowned.

"There's no reason for you to know it. Is it possible for your boy, Jack Cousins, to transfer into a Jolo body that looks nothing like his former body, and you would have no immediate visual means of correctly identifying him?"

Norman was transfixed. "I guess that would be true." Once again, Norman had given it no thought – not really thinking in his heart of hearts that Jack would win the competition. Or that body transfer was real or possible.

"The Colosseum complex is legally Directory sovereign ground and Directory law applies here in full. So if Jack Cousins had transferred, he would be obliged to follow standard procedure and incinerate the discarded body." The Directory official paused so Norman could absorb what he'd said. "It would then be possible to say, "Jack Cousins is dead" and for this be true, if one referred only to his former body.

"Do you see how that could be, Mr. Cousins?"

Norman had trouble nodding his head, he was shaking like a leaf.

"Jack Cousins did win the Fight for Immortality and he went to the Recyclex machine and was transferred into a Jolo body. In accordance with standard procedure, the 'Jack Cousins' body has been incinerated. So you see, his old body may be gone, but the person who was alive in that body is now alive and well in another body. Is this clear to you, Mr. Cousins?"

Norman, once again marginally succeeded in nodding his head. "Mr. Cousins, earlier you said this is what Jack wanted to attain? This was his goal?"

"Yes, Jack wanted another body."

"The only appropriate grief, under these unfamiliar circumstances, would be for the body that served him well through his first seventeen years. That body, for him and what he wanted to achieve in the future, had become a liability.

"Does this make sense to you, Mr. Cousins?"

"Yes." There was no conviction.

"One of the most absurd things is to spend grief on a dead body that has been willingly abandoned."

"That may be true, sir, for a person such as yourself, who is used to this kind of thing. Speaking for myself, it's difficult to think about that change. In my heart, Jack – the body you say is incinerated – is dead. But if my Jack has another body, I'd like to meet him as soon as possible."

The moment had arrived.

"You have, Uncle. I'm Jack. I've been talking to you for five minutes.

"No, NO! You aren't Jack!!" Norman jerked from his seat and looked around wildly.

"Uncle, you're not in the living room, please don't destroy this office."

Norman stopped cold.

Sanity returned to his eyes.

"Jack, Jack?" Norman looked at him, tears streaming down his cheeks.

"I know it's difficult," Jack said compassionately.

Tac-U-One had seen many first-time transfer situations in other families and it was not advisable for the transferee to reach too much or be too enthusiastic – it drove family members away. The person who transfers is fine, they're in a new body and feel great and have no questions at all; he or she knows they are themselves.

"Is there anything you'd like to ask me?" Tac-U-One said. "It sometimes helps."

Norman sat. He looked at the man across the desk. "What you're saying is that *you are Jack*, Jack in a different body?"

"Yes, Uncle, it's me."

Norman sat there, dumbfounded.

"If Jack had taken control of this Directory base, what's the first thing he'd do"

"He would have…" Norman paused. "He would've ended the games!" And he smiled for the first time since entering the room.

"Yes, he'd do that," Jack smiled. "Did you see me do it?"

"I did. It was great to see. It made me wonder…."

"Wonder what?"

"If you'd won. Where you were. What was happening. If I'd ever see you again. Stuff like that."

"I'm sorry I couldn't get back to you sooner."

"Well, your back now."

"Am I?"

"I think so."

"Good."

They smiled at each other.

"You have control of the Colosseum? Has the danger past?" Norman couldn't call him Jack, not yet.

"I have control of this base, all operations on Earth and Mars, too. And yes, for now, there's no danger."

"All those months of worry and work. Then everything falls into your lap in single day. It's beyond belief – what you've done."

"Life is stranger than fiction," Jack said.

Norman looked away. "Your mother and I were so happy to have you for all those years. Then the world changed and you changed. But, I couldn't stop you – with the judge." Norman looked at the man across the desk. "I hated that. I thought we were living a Greek tragedy – where we all die and the Gods gloat over our bones. But then you started to win. Fight after fight. I saw my fears as a lack of conviction and felt ashamed. But you, you just kept going, as you said you would. And now, all this. You've won it all!"

"I know it's been hard. And the success is sweet. But it's only the beginning – for both of us."

"So it really is you, Jack?" Norman said with a kind of wistful hope in his voice.

"I thought we were past that."

"I was for a minute. Doubts are lurking." He looked at his feet. "I want it to be you. But I'm afraid…"

"Ah, Norman." It was so hard – the first time.

"Aren't you going to ask me a key question?" Jack smiled, "Put all this to rest with one really sneaky question only I could answer."

"No, I don't think so, I think it really is you, but if you don't mind I'll just keep hunting around until I'm satisfied."

"Okay, we'll do it your way."

●

"The blood analysis you requested is complete, sir," the Bio-Comp informed Tac-U-One.

"Print a copy to my office and wipe the results from your files."

"Yes, sir."

Jack lifted the printed sheet and scanned the data. There it was. A few remaining pressurized nitrogen pellets were in the blood. Somehow his interaction, as a spiritual entity, with the Jack Cousins human body had modified it in certain ways. His presence in the body had caused it evolve toward that of a Jolo body. As Tac-U-One, he'd become comfortable with and lived with Jolo bodies for so long that his presence in the native body had changed it – significantly.

The Jack Cousins body, if it had remained fully human, should have died at the lake from the bends. Instead, this body had contained the compressed nitrogen in tiny pellets and gradually discharged them over the following weeks.

The Jack Cousins body, if autopsied, would've revealed other changes. But this data was for him alone. His enemies must remain ignorant of his skills.

●

Norman looked around Jack's office. It was impressive. The walls were a montage of beautiful art works that dissolved one into the next; at exactly the right time.

"Can you believe Boltax never turned on this display? The wall is studded with TAC receptors and you get the kind of art you want just by thinking of it. When you take your attention off a piece, it then morphs into another masterwork.

"If you want full-wall renditions…." And the display changed to a complete wraparound image. Norman smiled with delight.

The happiness of the moment reminded Norman of a sadness. Jack could not have gotten the news from home. Norman felt terrible, to have to tell Jack the news at his time of triumph. Norman's face crumpled, telegraphing the information ahead of time.

"Jack, there's something you ought to know. It's about Wendy…"

Jack cut him off sharply before he could say anything more. "I know all about it, Norman." He sounded distant. "Penny Taylor, her cousin, is also missing. "I've investigated it thoroughly. Right now there's nothing I can do."

"You know what happened?"

"Wendy was shipped to Crown Planet today. The Directory Chief discovered our relationship and wanted to use her as leverage against me."

"A bad man," Norman said. "I'm sorry, Jack."

Norman was going to say more, but Jack held up his hand.

"I am, too. I hope she's okay. It's breaking my heart. But there's nothing I can do now that'll get her back.

"And the situation here is dire. I have to be able to function. If I dwell on it, our gains here may unravel. So, Norman, please leave it for the time being. We'll deal with it in its own time."

"Okay, Jack." He was surprised.

"I'm sorry, Norman, but there's so much that needs to be done on a 'right now' basis. I can't spend time talking about something that's gone beyond my ability to control."

It had happened again. The loss of a woman he loved to the enemy, because of him. This was a longstanding upset for him. It was either getting on with the job or be a blubbering fool, and that was no choice.

Norman nodded his understanding.

"Okay to change the subject?"

"Yeah," Norman said.

"I understand the trouble you're having, Norman, about my change of bodies," Jack said, looking at him directly. "But guess what?" he asked in a lighter tone of voice.

"You want me to guess something?"

"Not really. The best way to understand something is to experience it yourself."

"I've no idea what you're talking about." Norman said defensively.

"You'll more easily accept my transfer if you transfer yourself. Please come with me." Jack ordered.

Norman's frightened expression immediately softened Jack's tone.

Even so, Norman followed "Jack" through the halls and into a large space.

"This is the transfer room."

No one had wiped up the mess still on the cot, the side of the Recyclex machine, over the walls and pooled on the floor.

His attention was riveted to the blood.

"I'm sorry, Norman. You shouldn't have seen this. But as you can imagine, there was some resistance to my taking control of the Directory operation," Jack said in understatement.

Norman vomited.

Dry heaves continued to wrack his body after the stomach was empty.

"Things have been a little hectic around here these last few hours." His voice hardened, "There've been other more important messes to clean up, but I wouldn't have had you see this if I'd thought about it."

Norman was finally done puking.

Jack nodded his approval, and waved vaguely at the bloody mess.

"Boltax, the former Directory Chief, tried to put me out of action, and was almost successful, as you can see by this mess. After I prevailed, I put the body in the furnace, but the rest of this…" He shrugged.

Looking back at the profusion of blood and knowing that his nephew had "died" there was pushing Norman over the edge. Strange and unnatural things were being thrust at him and they were all too real, too much.

It was one thing to be told by an alien on television a few months ago that a person was an Identity (some type of spirit) and could be transferred from one body to another. But to be confronted with this reality – when the example is your dead/alive nephew? Your adopted son?

Norman walked over and looked closely at the blood.

"When did this happen? When did Jack die?"

Jack shook his head – *the body isn't Jack – I am*. It was very difficult to shed a lifetime of ingrained thinking.

"Late this morning."

"Dramatic?"

"A little complicated," and Jack grimaced.

"How did it feel to look at your own body, I mean, the Jack Cousins body from another one?"

Jack shrugged. "I'm so used to this type of thing it has little or no impact. Certainly no emotional content, though I'm happy to be in this body. It doesn't drag as the other did."

Was he joking? Norman wondered.

"No joke, Norman; I've changed bodies often. My first transfer was more than five thousand years ago and it was so much worse than this, but similar in one respect. Someone was trying to kill me then, too." Jack did smile then. "At that time I wasn't used to it – now," his shoulders lifted casually, "it's old hat, part of the job, and if I have to be honest," he smiled with real amusement, "it keeps me on my toes."

A disconnected sensation washed through Norman and the next external awareness he had was pressure on his leg as a sanitary robot politely asked him get out of the way so it could "restore the area to an optimum state of hygiene." And it proceeded to do so.

Norman laughed, but the pitch was too high.

"Norman, you have to come to grips with what's happening here. I would love to spend more time easing you into this, but time is a luxury at this point!"

Norman could hear his words, but they were muffled as if through fog and over a much larger distance.

"Norman!"

The word, so intimate, so pervasive, filled with love and affection, went through him and drew his attention. His surroundings were at once solid and remained in place. Jack was *very* real. It took Norman many seconds to realize that he hadn't "heard" the word with his ears.

Wendy taught me that at the baseball game, thought Jack, and emotion threatened to spill over. Jack gave himself a minute to recover.

"Norman, are you back?"

"Yes, Jack, I feel much better, thank you."

"You're welcome. We have some business to conduct."

"Okay, let's do it."

That's the Norman Cousins I know.

"The Directory Chief took control of this planet for destructive purposes. We can do much better. We've put together an organizing chart for the control of Earth. The first post to fill is the senior position."

"That's fast work, Jack. I'll lend you all the help I can. We should bring your mother in on this. She's had the most recent experience in filling executive positions."

"I asked her to research capable leaders after returning from the lake. At the time she thought I was batty. But I think she became interested. Enjoying the idea of selecting people who could improve conditions on Earth.

"Her 'dream team.'"

"Now we can put it to use. I have her findings on the computer. Would you like to see the report?"

Norman looked at his son. So much planning, so much action. So much success.

"You never had anyone to talk to, did you?" A rhetorical question.

"Thanks for that," Jack smiled. "But I do now."

"Yes, you do. Let's see your mother's report."

Jack showed him.

"She came up with five names for the top job."

"There are four names and my name. That makes no sense."

Jack smiled. "Norman, you're a dark horse. When Mother investigated your holdings across the planet, she was shocked. Why didn't you ever say anything about it? The companies you started are huge!"

Norman looked apologetic.

"I made it big very early, Jack. Because Sharon and I couldn't have children, your arrival was very important to us. But we didn't want to smother you, either. I knew I had to become good at picking subordinates, and directing their actions over a long distance. I did, I am. As my businesses went international, I gave my qualified people part ownership and reduced my income to two percent.

"I wanted to be home. I made foreign trips only once a month and handled a great deal very rapidly." Norman paused and looked at his hands. "I knew there was something about you from the beginning. Of course no one could have predicted all this!" His arm encompassed the room, meaning the Colosseum and the Directory operations on Earth. "But I'm not surprised, not now. It fits. You fit this role."

"Your business model? It's unique," Jack said.

Norman nodded and shrugged. "We were set, so why not let others prosper too? It never interested me to be 'top dog' or try to compete with others to see who could become the 'richest.' I always knew it would be more important to be there as you grew up. I know many parents feel that way. But this was different! And I was right, wasn't I?"

"Yes, Father, you were, and I thank you for your caring."

Norman said, "Now let's choose your chief executive."

Jack dropped another bombshell. "Norman, your name was on that list because mother considered you one of the top five executives in the world.

"I've selected you to run this planet."

"You're joking." But he could see he was not.

Jack hid a small smile. He'd challenged so many of Norman's core beliefs in such a short time, it was difficult for him.

"I read mother's exhaustive profiles, data trails and statistics. You, Norman Cousins, are my choice."

Norman shook his head.

"Let me explain. Boltax, the former Directory Chief, was running as much of Earth as he wanted, from right here in the Colosseum complex. I plan to formalize this arrangement and place you in control. You'll have a lot of help. The computer that runs Directory operations in this system has a 'bio' or 'life' function. The computer is also a person. He's quite special in that he's also telepathic. This will aid you greatly in handling the affairs of Earth."

The increase in responsibility, was too much, too soon. Norman phased out.

"*Norman!*" He was suffused by affection.

He was back again, looking at Jack.

Jack smiled. "I know it's a lot to take in. I'm throwing it at you very fast." Jack looked away. "I'm a planner, Norman. Much of what I'm doing now I had settled in my mind for some time.

"But for you its new news. I forget that. Sorry. But I need you to step up. Take the job. It'll be learn as you go.

"If you accept. You'll be busy for years and won't remember any of this."

Norman said, "I want you to tell me something only Jack would know. Something we did together."

Jack nodded.

He looked at Norman's mind and found it carefully blank. Cagey devil! Jack smiled. "I told my father to go to hell when he said you couldn't adopt me. And I told you to go ahead with the adoption."

"There were only the three of us there. Yes, that's acceptable. But then, you've been ordering me about all your life, haven't you Jack? Just like today – exactly like today." They smiled at each other.

"Norman, if you don't want this responsibility, if you don't want to change bodies, just say so.

"But you need to know this: for the privilege of obtaining a Jolo body, a Directory citizen works their entire life. Only a small fraction of those who apply make it."

"That may be true but I don't know anything about Jolo bodies or transfer or immortality." Norman said.

"The advantage Directory citizens have over you is that transfer is a cultural heritage. Each citizen knows all about it. Also, most people granted Jolo status don't go to transfer until their normal body is nearing the end of its useful existence.

"You're in a unique and difficult position. I've granted you Jolo status. But you are mid-life. You have no cultural acceptance of transfer and no personal knowledge of immortality.

"You can refuse. But I haven't picked you to be the Chief Executive of this planet for personal reasons.

"I realize Earth is not a plum assignment.

"We, the Directory, are far from being loved on this planet. Soon I will release damning information about the Directory to the entire planet. You'll have to handle the fallout from this, if you take the job." Jack responded to the questioning look on Norman's face. "I won't release what I suspect until I have the facts in hand. I have a man on a mission gathering that data right now."

More plans, more action. "I'm holding you up." Norman realized. Jack had nothing to say.

"Okay, I want it. I'll do it."

"Good."

●

Jack looked at the double row of drawers. The readouts on the panels displayed data, model, inception, manufacturer etc. He pulled drawers from their recesses. Each contained a male body surrounded by a soft nimbus of light. Jack beckoned Norman over to see four naked male bodies in stasis.

Norman looked suspiciously at Jack.

"Norman, do any of these bodies appeal to you?"

His heart began to thud heavily in his chest, blood rushed from his head and he felt faint. He grabbed the edge of a drawer to steady himself. The world was set adrift by those few words.

This was real. Too real.

He felt like he was planning the execution of his body. His pulse raced. The body reminding him it was alive, and wanting to stay that way.

"Norman, one of these bodies will be yours in about an hour and a half. Please select the one you want."

Norman thought of a short reprieve.

"What about Sharon? Does she know what's about to happen?"

"She may suspect, but I haven't told her. By Directory law, a marriage is dissolved when you transfer. You and Mother will have to make that decision by yourselves. She's already been working on my staff, sort of, and so I assume she'll join your staff as a Jolo."

This is the most disruptive day of my life.

I'm only forty-six. I'm not prepared to, to… relinquish my body. The foundations that provided his life with stability were being swept away. *I'm to rule Earth? I'm to die?*

Norman looked at the bodies laid out before him and struggled to keep his focus.

"Norman, these bodies only have cosmetic differences – coloring, features, size and shape. Any one is excellent for a first time Jolo."

Jack shifted tactics.

"What body best represents how you would like others to see you?"

After a quiet minute, Jack took him by the shoulders. "Norman, the chief executive of a planet is almost always a Jolo. On this planet it's a necessity. I want you immune to violence. You must stabilize Earth during the troubles that are sure to follow my departure.

"And you can't do that if you're worried about being attacked.

But that wasn't it.

Norman started shaking. He was resisting the idea of killing, incinerating, terminating, destroying, executing the only body he could remember having – it may be a little shabby at forty-six, but he was attached to it, and thought of it as himself. He couldn't get it out of his mind that the death of this body was the death of all he was, the death of *him*, he thought.

"*Which one, Norman?*"

He was jarred out of his thoughts by the question; Jack had gone inside his head again. He looked up at the man standing in front of him who claimed to be his nephew, *was* his nephew. It was terribly inhuman to incinerate his own body without batting an eyelid. Then, looking at the "new Jack" more closely, he finally got it.

Jack, his Jack, was not a human being.

Never had been!

He was not certain what he really was, but the basics hadn't changed. He liked and trusted Jack.

There was a challenge on the young man's face. Asking him if he was man enough. Norman's guts twisted and bunched into a knot.

"Norman, look at the four bodies, one at a time."

"Why?"

"Just look at the bodies, one after the other. Take your time. You can touch them if you wish. They're not 'dead' and they're not 'alive', they're in stasis, which is a simple no-time field. They are potentially live bodies that simply lack an Identity.

Norman looked. He felt. It was a strange and interesting experience, considering the near future. He settled down and soon became aware of which body liked and *wanted!*

"*You can do it, Norman.*" Inside his head.

Something went out of him. He didn't know what it was, but the intense need to *hold on* was gone. He looked down at the body he had chosen. It was young! Immediately he felt like a thief. It was immoral, almost, as an aging male, to covet youth. One was supposed to cope with aging, ignore it, embrace it, anything but *be* it.

Norman felt a deep longing. He gazed up at Jack, and Jack understood.

"Yes, Norman." Jack hit the ignition. Rainbow colors flashed. "You have half an hour."

"I'll call Sharon." Jack showed Norman how to use the communications console. The conversation was short. "She's fine with it. She wants a digital photo so when I turn up at the door, she doesn't shoot me."

Jack nodded.

Norman returned to the tray and studied the body closely. The skin was pale, the hair blond and the musculature good but not excessive. It was difficult to gauge the height in this prone position. Tall, he supposed.

Jack briefed Norman on the procedure over the next half hour as the body was brought from its stasis to a minimal level of function.

Jack placed the body Norman had selected into the reception tray of the Recyclex.

Norman wanted to do it now, transfer, but couldn't slough off the cold hand of death that seemed to grasp him and twist his innards.

Jack had him write a single word on a slip of paper, and then seal it into a numbered, official-looking envelope. Jack guided him and he lay on the tray.

Norman's body was racked by violent shivers, an uncontrollable reaction. Jack administered the sedative.

As Norman settled and his vital signs reached a low normal range, Jack initiated the charge that would increase and expel Norman from his body. Jack looked at the Recyclex control panel closely, all the vital signs normal. Slowly, Jack increased the charge...

●

Two hours later, in the Commandant's office, Norman called Sharon to let her know that the transfer was successful and sent the digital image of his new body.

When he finished the call, he sat puzzled for a second and then felt very impressed with his wife. She'd taken the news of his change from a man with a different voice and face. She knew it was him. Knew she was talking to her husband. Some feat.

Norman was sitting in a blue military jumpsuit and was infinitely pleased with himself while still feeling completely unusual. Comparing the sensations between his "new" and his "old" body was a revelation.

He was very glad he'd changed over. The old one used to drag him down; there'd been a distinct effort just to keep it standing, or to get it moving. The new one moved almost before he intended it to, causing him to stumble and then over-correct when trying to stand or walk. It was interesting though: through all the gyrations, he never lost balance.

It was like the difference between driving a sports car he was not fully trained to drive and an old pickup truck. In a corridor, he'd seen a beautiful Jolo girl and the sexual response had been immediate, powerful, and embarrassing. Jack laughed. Norman was impressed.

Norman incinerated his own body. Only when the body of the old Norman Cousins had gone to cinders did he consider that he'd fully arrived in the new one. It was the hard reality of this irrevocable step that gave him a solid foundation.

"That's why it's done, Norman, on every transfer."

"You're drifting again, Norman!" Jack said sharply.

His body jerked, and of course he jerked it back too far and was almost out of the seat.

Jack continued: "Normally you'd have days to adjust, but you have just about twelve hours before I introduce you to the President of the United States, his cronies and advisors, plus others from around the world. You will be *the* ruler of this planet when I leave, so listen to what I have to tell you. Your life, and the lives of those on Earth, will depend on it. Your skill and ability will stand between the annihilation of Earth and its survival."

Norman forgot he even had a body.

●

The Bio-Comp informed Tac-U-One that Farley was on Mars and had a report. He took the call. His features darkened as Norman watched.

"Yes," he said heavily, "I thought that was it. Get the visuals and record the entire procedure as if you were making a documentary." Tac-U-One stopped to listen. Farley told him there were no civilians on Mars and his current understanding was that none had left on the last outbound ship.

"All right, get a communication link set up with the Bio-Comp and take direction from him." He listened again. "Yes, get complete statements from the staff still there; yes, before you leave. Make sure you understand who did what. Yes, keep them separated and have each person state his job and describe the jobs of others. Check for discrepancies. Yes, track down exactly who does what. That's right, once you've got it sorted out, have each person describe their jobs in the actual locations they are performed.

"This is for consumption on Earth, so make sure they speak English or are translated." There was a long pause. "I know it's a lot to get done in one day, that's why I sent you." Pause. "Then, close the place up and return here with all the personnel. I'll see you in the morning."

Norman looked at Jack, waiting.

"It's confirmed now," Jack said. "We know the major purpose of the Directory presence on Earth, and on all the other similar worlds." The words came out as a brutal stab. "I am ashamed.

"For a very long time," he murmured, "Jolos have represented the best of our race. I could tell you, Norman, of a million times, a million sacrifices, events I've personally observed, made by Immortals to promote the common good. There are many, like myself, who've devoted their entire existence to achieving societal stability and sustained expansion. The Directory I left was a good, secure place to live, with abundant opportunity." He shook his head.

"If you wanted adventure, new worlds were constantly opening up. If the Directory was something you couldn't tolerate, you could ship out to the Outer Worlds and leave the Directory behind forever.

"In just eighteen years, Jolo conspired against Jolo, and Normals on undeveloped worlds were promised great freedom, but made to suffer. I've been to hundreds of worlds and the nature of my job brings me into contact with criminals – but I've seen nothing that compares to this outright betrayal."

Tac-U-One paused and was silent – head tilted up, looking away.

Norman was drawn into a vision of vastness, of unbounded space. He saw the swirl of the galaxy radiating away from the core. He felt the intensity and pressure of the galactic wind and the ripples of power that surged down the arms of the Milky Way stars.

He had a premonition of some event.

And then it came.

Jack stood and placed his fist over his heart.

"I swear to restore Crown to his rightful place." Then Tac-U-One lowered his head.

Norman felt awe, not at these brave words, not at the difficulty of the task, of which he had no ability to judge – but that he was certain Jack would achieve his goal. *There's power in this man, this Immortal Jolo,* he thought.

Norman wondered if it was his imagination – or was there a ripple now set in motion that would engulf the galaxy and bend it to his will?

CHAPTER 38

JACK THOUGHT ABOUT NORMAN AND HIS future as the senior executive of planet Earth. There would be many challenges. Here in the Planetary Commandant's office was a good place to prepare him.

"Norman, there are trillions of people on the planets of the Directory-controlled galaxy. My job as Tactical Unit One Crown is to investigate situations both good and bad. With the good, I find out what was done and how to apply that success to other areas. With the bad I handle the problem and recommend and implement a solution.

"I've personally been to more than a hundred worlds and thousands of cities, towns and rural communities. Wherever I go on mission, I meet and work closely with various people in diverse lines of work.

"Some small portion of the people I meet are criminals – that's generally why I'm there. When I uncover the wrongdoers, I give them the opportunity – unofficially – to stop their bad deeds and set right what they've done.

"Sometimes I'd do this in the guise of a co-conspirator who is having an 'attack of conscience.' And, you know, every now and then they'd come clean and make up the damage they had caused.

"If that happened, I'd file no formal charges and let it go."

Norman looked at Jack strangely.

"The reason I'm telling you this is that you'll soon be in a position of power; your decisions will impact the lives of others. When dealing with malefactors don't get so caught up in 'official procedure' or 'the law' that you ignore a person's potential to change. Some people will fly straight – with a little shove.

By the time a mission of mine is done and it's all sorted out, I know the state of affairs pretty well. Extraordinarily well.

"My rule of thumb is this: people who work hard know what they want and know what's good for them. They strive hard and often achieve their goals – when they're not actively being stopped by some criminal element or governmental problem.

"When administrating large groups of people less direct control is better. If a person is being unethical/criminal, demand from them a detailed solution including a time line. If they fix it, good. If they don't, justice moves forward.

"That'd save time and effort, and reduce social turmoil." Norman said. "But you couldn't do it with everyone."

"True. It's your job to get good at knowing how to apply it. In prosperous times be lenient. In hard times be strict."

"You'll find that people do the wrong thing in an effort to solve a problem. So the long term solution to criminality is education that results in competency."

"I don't know if I'll remember all this."

"Bio-Comp's taking notes, aren't you?"

"Yes, sir," the Bio-Comp responded. He displayed the digital recording on the interactive wall screen.

"Thank you, Bio-Comp," Norman said.

Jack continued. "On a mission, I don't solve the personal problems of people. Each person carries the responsibility for their own success or failure. Life challenges everyone's personal resources – that's what makes living interesting.

"So when you solve problems for others, you rob them of happiness. Life is happily lived by actually living it yourself – not watching someone else live it."

"I never looked at it on such a basic level." Norman commented.

"It's a powerful concept." Jack said. "But there are limits to this – you can't ask a caveman to fly to the moon and expect him to win.

"Your total responsibility is to help create an environment where those who want to prosper can prosper.

"Always remember, there will be people who won't work: they'll make *you* wrong for *their* failure. They'll scream at you and blame you for their losses.

"Investigate and learn the difference between unwarranted criticism and legitimate complaint.

"People who don't work or produce nothing of value, are generally the source of unwarranted criticism. Don't waste your time.

"Productive members of society who work hard and try to get ahead may complain. If you investigate their grievance you'll often find a criminal or a poorly organized activity – probably bad government. Fix it.

"You want people who are increasingly capable of solving their own problems.

"There's a real simplicity to that." Norman said.

"Real solutions are simple." Jack said.

"What's a caveman/moon type problem?"

"Boltax's 'slave training program' and the 'Fight for Immortality' are examples. First, no one knew there was a problem. Second, if they did, there was nothing they could do. Perfect examples of 'asking the caveman to fly to the moon.'

"It's the type of situation I handle: the problem that a family, community or local official is not equipped to recognize or trained to deal with."

"So tell me, Jack, how'd you do it?" Jack was about to respond, but Norman continued, "I don't mean what you did. I know all that. On a personal level, how'd you do it?"

Jack thought for a minute. "Good question." He looked at the progression of his life. He realized something and smiled. "I never think a problem is bigger than I am." He looked at Norman. "And I get help."

"Does that make sense?"

"I have a lot to learn." Norman nodded soberly.

"The Bio-Comp will help you."

Jack stared off. There was not going to be much time in the coming days for personal affairs, so he took time now.

"Norman, I'm happy to have met you and lived with you and Sharon as family. Over the last months that may have been lost in the turmoil. Your love and support have been a constant I could rely on." Jack came around the desk and took Norman into a hug.

Their relationship had morphed from Uncle/Nephew to Father/Son and now they were friends.

As he pounded his back with affection Norman realized something about Jack he could have easily missed. Jack was helping because he could. An innate decency drove him, not some guilt-driven frenzy.

●

"Farley has transmitted his data sir," conveyed the Bio-Comp.

"Good. Forward the data to PR. When Farley returns with the Mars base personnel, isolate them immediately."

"All right, Norman. The full data on the Mars base is in." Tac-U-One looked up. "I want you to go to the PR section and put the raw material in the form of a documentary or exposé or whatever you want to call it. I've directed the PR people to work at your order.

As you walk the halls you'll see your face on screens and notice boards. I've made your posting as Planetary Administrator official. Don't be surprised when the local staff greets you as such."

"Thank you, Jack or – how do I address you?"

"When we're alone however you like, in company, Tac-U-One."

"Okay, Jack. How do I get there?" And he directed him and explained the system.

"One piece of business before you go, Administrator."

"Bio-Comp, fifteen minutes before the airing of the Mars documentary, please direct all base personnel to the auditorium, excluding only PR. I want them to see it as a group and I want you to record everything they do."

"Order logged, sir."

"Why, Jack?"

"In the future, there may come a time when hatred of the Directory becomes overwhelming. I want you to have the staff's reaction available. They have no idea what's coming. Also after the staff see what they unknowingly supported they'll know what damage to repair."

"That's far thinking."

"It's easy to prepare for, so why not?"

"Okay sir. I'm off."

Ah, Norman, thought Jack, *you took the assignment without a flinch.* And this production needs to be done by an Earthman. *You won't hide anything.*

Tac-U-One made sure the entire world was going to be tuned in to the broadcast. He had a thirty-second preview spot taped, and ran it every ten minutes on the Directory channel. It was soon picked up by all the other channels across the planet. The spot created a sense of expectation and dread, as he had intended.

It took some time to review all the raw footage and the varied accounts of the Mars Base staff. Norman utilized the Bio-Comp to get it clear and accurate.

As the data was reviewed, a growing sense of shock and shame pervaded the PR studio. From their growing revulsion Norman could tell Jack had been correct – Earth-based Directory staff had no idea what was being done on the Red Planet.

Tac-U-One called for an update. Norman said, "Ninety minutes before the segment is ready, sir."

Norman had the staff complete the compilation and began to edit. He rattled off a series of questions he wanted answered and by whom and told the staff to conduct those interviews immediately upon the arrival of the shuttle from Mars. Immediately – did they understand?

"Yes, Administrator!" They did.

The Bio-Comp, who'd been monitoring these proceedings, informed Tac-U-One, "I believe you've selected the right man for the job. I like him."

One hour later, Norman, Jack and the PR staff were in the press room. The broadcast was being carried on the Directory channel and every major station across the planet. There was no fanfare introduction as Boltax had preferred; it was professional and straightforward.

Jack, Tactical Unit One, delivered the fateful news.

"There's been a change of leadership of the Directory on planet Earth. My name is Tactical Unit One.

"Broadly, when something major goes wrong with Directory operations, it's my job to set things right. I am an official within the central hierarchy of the Directory itself." He paused to let that sink in.

"Something has gone badly wrong with the Directory operations on Earth. I must give you some history before I tell you what I'm here to correct.

"Your planet was not scheduled for contact by the Directory until and unless you had discovered some workable form of interstellar travel. I will not go into the reasons for this now, but this is strict Directory policy.

"Earth has been contacted and a Directory base established here in contravention of our own laws. It is illegal and should have never happened. To be completely clear: Directory presence on Earth should not have occurred.

"I represent the ruler of the Directory, a man who bears the title 'Crown'.

"A minor official within the Biological Department illegally ordered the takeover of Earth for his own evil purposes. Vast crimes have been committed at his specific direction. Other planets in a similar position to Earth's have also been victimized."

Tac-U-One paused again and Norman looked at the reporters. Their faces were a study. But the gravity of his words had struck them mute.

"I want to make it clear. The former Chief of Directory operations and the staff of the Mars base were the individuals fully aware of the crimes being committed on this planet. The Directory staff on Earth were unaware of the worst abuse. I don't say this to try to lessen your wrath – but simply to give the correct target.

"In thirty seconds, I will broadcast some preliminary images from the planet you call Mars. I directed one of my staff to go there and document all the information necessary for full disclosure of the crimes committed.

"This material is highly disturbing, so I advise you in the strongest terms to restrict the viewing of this matter to those you consider appropriate."

The nightmare began. The nightmare continued. And for many families the nightmare would not easily end.

After the presentation Jack returned.

"So, in unvarnished language, your planet has been used as a pool for slave labor. Your brightest minds, sons and daughters, have been educated and shipped to Mars. There, they were transferred into Identity traps. Their bodies were burned, then their trapped Identities shipped to remote and desolate locations where they would be transferred once again into other bodies.

"These bodies are unlike anything you've seen in the world, or your nightmares. These bodies have been biologically engineered with the sole purpose being utility. These bodies are gross in form and alien in every aspect. They were developed by Bio-One in contravention of Directory Law to gain economic power and so subvert the entire production base of the galaxy to his corrupt purposes."

With inexorable horror, he continued, "The Fight for Immortality is a recruiting ground for brutal men who will obey any order, no matter how bestial. Earth and other planets have become a labor pool for jobs Bio-One cannot fill from within the Directory through fear of discovery.

"Those gone from Earth are lost to you. I have no power to return your loved ones. There is no order I can give now that will reverse their fate and restore them to you.

"You have my sympathy. As soon as I became aware of your plight I did not rest till I put a stop to it.

"Please do not harden your hearts to those of the Directory. Any Directory citizen would be shocked and appalled by the things that have been done to you and your loved ones.

"The instigator, Bio-One, is an aberration and will be brought to justice." He paused and simply stared at the cameras.

"You may ask why I've told you these things, horrible as they are. Why should I reveal such heinous crimes perpetrated by Directory citizens? Should I not, as any politician would, cover it up?" Again the words hung.

"I am not a politician, in spite of being a senior Directory official, I am a working man. So let me give you a simple man's answer to the question I posed: you've been deceived and betrayed by a criminal element within the Directory. You deserve the truth. I have given it to you.

"I know some of you will rage against the Directory, ask your military leaders to destroy us, or at the very least seek our expulsion from planet Earth.

"Like it or not, Earth has now been drawn into the broader galactic awareness, and as a consequence I would consider it an evil act to terminate contact with you – for your sake. I know the sense of hope a wider outlook can bring to a planetary population.

"The 'Fight for Immortality' is an abomination. I've permanently terminated the program. The right to transfer from one body to the next is a status that is earned. It's not something to be given to someone so they can kill more effectively. Many sensible people on this planet must have formed a bad opinion of us because of the 'Fight'. You are correct for having done so.

"At my order there now exists the true 'Fight for Immortality' on planet Earth. You will have the opportunity to lead productive and exemplary lives and petition the Board of Approval I leave in place for the granting of Jolo status. In the years to come, many of Earth's population will earn their immortality. When the current disruption within the Directory itself is at an end, the population of Earth will have the opportunity to gain entry into the Directory as a member planet.

"Additionally, I've ordered that the educational facilities already established be converted so the full curriculum usually made available to a new world can be delivered here.

"Families who've lost members will be educated at Directory expense in any subject available and for as long as they want. For five years, we will also cover the cost of room and board for those families." Jack paused once again.

"The Board of Approval for awarding Jolo status has in its hands warrants for one-thousand Jolo awards to be made; the second year, five thousand. From then on it will depend on resources and what the Board decides. No fixed rate of increase in the number of Jolo awards exists. It depends on the decency and productivity of the applicants.

"I must warn you, many of the people currently considered 'great' on this planet would have their petitions summarily denied in the Directory. All necessary information to make applicants successful will be clarified by official proclamation.

"I know you have many questions to ask me, but I'm sorry, I don't have the time to respond. Within a week, I'll have a Directory Information Site available for computer access.

"Thank you for listening. Goodbye for now."

●

"I thought you'd announce a plan to recover the people who'd been shipped off," Norman said.

"I'd like to but it's not going to happen. First, it will be many years before an effort could be mounted. Second, as soon as those people were transferred into an I-trap, end of life amnesia kicked in. They won't know who they were or where they're from. The most we can do is after Crown's return we mount a project to recover as many beings as possible.

"If I'd promised the people of Earth the return of their loved ones? Riots twenty years from now when no one's come back. If we miraculously found a specific person, transferred them into a body, the person wouldn't remember the family. It's an impossible scenario and cruel to give hope where none exists."

"I'd no idea of the problems involved." Norman murmured.

"It's a nightmare for the families involved. When we do begin the recovery effort I'll be sure to let you know. You can announce it here."

"Wouldn't that just upset people all over again?"

"In twenty years you'll have more than fifty thousand Jolos living on Earth. The population will have tangible proofs of immortality living among them, they'll be striving for it themselves. It will be real to them that the return of their loved ones was impossible but they'll be comforted that we're restoring their quality of life."

"You think very far ahead." Norman said.

Tac-U-One smiled. "It's not so far away. You'll start setting goals in the decades and centuries when you realize you have all the time you need. The Bio-Comp has the basic planet builder programming. In a decade the population will routinely live to one hundred, thirty years from now it will be to one hundred and fifty – and most of that in good health."

Norman Cousins, Earth's newly minted Administrator felt his mind and future expand with possibility. Then he came back to Earth.

"Why announce the Jolo and educational programs so soon?" Norman asked.

"I want to give people a reason to look forward. The permanent loss of loved ones is a black cloud that will hang over this planet until the people who are despondent get on with their lives. And not before.

Looking off, he mused rhetorically, "How can a being who knows of immortality ever use another being for slavery and expect to stay free himself? To be free of the 'life-death' grist mill is one thing, Norman. To stay free oneself – one has to free others – not trap them.

"It's simple. If you enslave others you'll be trapped – not by 'god' or 'cosmic scales of justice' – but by yourself. If you free others you can stay free.

"I am Jolo, Norman. I'm the possessor of the heritage passed to us by Jolo Patwaal. He fought the ignorance and barbarism mortal man can possess when he believes he is nothing but the dust a body is made of. Jolo Patwaal created a new civilization where violence and destruction had no premium and served little purpose. People had better games to play. This has extended from star to star.

"But now, to see rot in so fine a creation takes my heart. I've spent the last five thousand years of my life helping secure and extend our boundaries. Now, some of our people do *this*."

"I hear you, Jack," Norman said.

"It's a fine thing you'll do for Earth, Norman – one thousand Jolos this year and then five thousand the next. That's a vast enterprise all by itself.

"It's a form of amends from the Directory to the people of Earth." Tac-U-One's mood lightened and he smiled. "And yes, you'll have to work your guts out to make my promise happen."

●

"I've been wondering, Jack. How can a prominent Jolo in the Directory with all their benefits and advantages throw that all away and involve themselves with Bio-One's slave trade?"

"The answer requires some history."

"Tell me."

"There are many industries that could use task-specific genetically engineered bodies. Early in the Directory, this was a big ethical question and the debate raged for years. Should we or should we not allow the construction of 'tailor made' bodies?

"Jolo Patwaal gathered together the most adamant supporters. They were all biological scientists wanting to create body forms tailored to commercial use. It was big business with huge profit potential.

"JP suggested the biological scientists be guinea pigs. He said, and I quote, 'You guys are so certain the quality of life isn't impaired, I challenge you to transfer into these 'new' bodies and spend five years doing the jobs they were made to perform. Then report back to me.'

"He challenged them to make an 'Identity' impact statement – what would really happen to a person who became an industrial-biological-entity? That way they could compile sufficient data to personally endorse or terminate the project."

"What happened?" Norman was fascinated.

"Most of the proponents fell away. But there were ten biologists who refused to give up." He laughed. "A month later, these ten volunteers were transferred into grotesque bodies and dropped on a forbidding planet to do their jobs. They'd agreed to a year's trial. Jolo Patwaal monitored them very closely because he thought they would be heavily traumatized, but he had to let them do it.

"After thirty-nine days, they were pulled off that world and transferred back into their former bodies."

"What did they say?"

"They were gibbering idiots."

"I guess your founder was correct."

"Yes, he was. The bodies biologists wanted to create were heinous. People with little affinity or empathy will do anything to another and feel nothing." Jack said.

"Scary."

"Yes. But it's something you need to know if you're to rule effectively and justly.

"To this day in the Directory, if someone zealously proposes something really stupid, they're called a '39er'."

Norman laughed and then turned serious. "With that history it's crazy to find it returning again."

"Body slavery wasn't totally eradicated. The Directory's huge – trillions of people, but the *movement* was gone. In the last millennia only a small group of hardened criminals have tried it – it takes huge resources and great skill. It comes in from the Outer-Worlds. Directory citizens have nothing to do with it. They report it if they see it."

"Something's changed then?" Norman asked.

"Must have. And I can understand why it's being done."

Norman was shocked and looked at Jack closely. "You can't mean that?"

"It's easy. Imagine a man who's a brilliant biological scientist, who cares nothing for others. He's been perfecting the human form for thousands of years. People are just bodies and the basic body model's been around for millennia or longer. Bio-One must have been desperate to break the mold and do new and wonderful things – which were wonderful only to him or other slavers.

"Norman, just 'cos you can see a point of view doesn't mean you agree with it."

"That's good to know."

"So if Bio-One wants to make slave bodies he has to get rid of Crown. To get rid of him he has to get rid of me. So he leaks the location of Planet X to one of my sources who tells me and I tell Crown. Crown orders me to check it out so we can get rid of Bio-One for good. But they're waiting for me. Even so, I almost got away. But my interstellar drive was damaged and I was dumped near earth. I crashed in the Wasatch Mountains and two days later was born in Salt Lake City, oblivious of what had just happened. The rest you know."

"That's some story."

"Stay with me here. To make the slave trade worthwhile he has to have a market. So he establishes contacts in the Outer Worlds. But their economy's strictly Prince or Pauper – no middle class. Even so he sells some product and makes some cash. But it's not a big enough market.

"There are large numbers of uninhabitable planets with untapped mineral (and other) wealth. Bio-One makes bodies that can thrive on any given planet. He forces Identities to transfer into them. The mining gets done. Soon he has vast wealth. He replicates this pattern.

"Bio-One uses his contacts in the Outer Worlds to ship the metal/ minerals (or whatever) to a few very select Directory distributors. This undercuts the Directory markets. Legitimate Directory businesses go bankrupt – or join in. Now he has access to the vast wealth of the Directory of Stars and Planets."

Norman was astounded. "You learned all this from the staff interviews?"

"No. Most of it is conjecture based on my experience of how it's been done before. But you should have seen Planet X, his base. The facilities were all underground. It was enormous – no, staggering in scope. Hundreds of thousands of vats. Each one capable of producing a body in six weeks. When I was there it had been in operation for decades."

Norman shook his head.

"It's being fueled by the rape of planets like Earth. Per the interview data about ninety other worlds."

"He's a mad genius."

"No, Bio-One's an idiot." Norman's eyebrows shot up. "Well, he's a genius biologist. And he can keep a secret from his peers and from telepaths. Apart from that, he's an idiot."

"Jack, that makes no sense. You're underestimating him and that's dangerous."

"You're partly right. I've underestimated him before – but I'm not now. But he's a dupe, a stooge, a fall guy, a straw man."

"How can that possibly be?" Norman asked.

"Simple. It's right in front of you. I figured it out the first day I was at the Colosseum."

Norman shook his head.

"It's easier for me to see. The invasion of Earth is being done under the Directory name. Our language is called Cortic. The name in use here is an exact translation from the Cortic. There is no attempt at deception. Why not use a pseudonym, why not use Outer Worlds personnel?

"Because someone wants the pillage of these worlds discovered.

"If a Directory privateer stumbles over any of these planets and reports it in the Directory? It would cause pandemonium.

"All Bio-One wants to do is be the smartest guy around and to rule the Directory for ever and ever.

"But if word gets out about Earth and planets like it? Bio-One and some of the Directory would support it, others would violently oppose it. Civil war would consume the greatest civilization this galaxy has ever seen.

"So why is Directory presence on Earth in the open, Norman?"

"Because someone in the Outer Worlds wants to see the Directory destroyed."

"Bingo! That's why I say Bio-One is a doofus. How long would he survive in a civil war? Not long. He's a stooge being used by smarter men.

"So we're in danger. Civilization in this portion of our galaxy is on the brink. That's not melodrama.

"I've no idea what will happen to Earth. But I've told you this now so you can see why I'm in a rush to leave."

"No need for that Jack. But I appreciate your time and concern for me and Earth."

"You're welcome." He shrugged, "Also if Bio-One finds out it's really me here on Earth – he's likely to blow the planet just to protect himself."

"Oh, in that case, get the hell outta here!!" They both fell to laughing. "And, and," Norman finally got enough air, "and make sure he knows you're gone!" That set them off again.

•

"Jolo Patwaal never wanted Immortals to appear as an exotic race of 'freaks' ruling the Normals – or 'Norms' as the gestated are called. Most Jolos can't be easily differentiated from a healthy, youthful Normal."

"Because of this policy we 'humans' have retained this basic form. Interestingly the body configuration is very common throughout this galaxy, far more so than any other intelligent life form.

"Races with other body forms, when they are accepted into the Directory, can reproduce their own basic form or become 'human.' Or switch back and forth if they wish.

"Some changes are allowed. As an example, some people don't like to eat, so the Jolo body is designed to run on specific fluids or other sources of energy as desired."

"That's a lot to digest." Norman

"The Bio-Comp has all the basic material you'll need to understand the Directory."

●

Later that day Farley returned from Mars. "Admiral, I have a bunch of staff with not much to do." Tac-U-One said. "I'd like to see Earth able to protect herself in the minimum possible time. To facilitate this I've signed Royal Warrant authorizing you to use whatever resources you deem necessary, including the native population. Disclosure of Directory only technology is at your discretion.

"Bio-Comp, please enter the warrant into the official record."

"Order logged, sir."

"Does your warrant include disclosure of Field technology, sir?"

"Will, they need to know it?"

"Probably not. But I'm the only person on this planet who can build an interstellar engine from scratch."

"What about me?"

"You'll be gone, sir."

"That I will." Jack chuckled, then thought for a moment. "The order stands as written. All I ask is that you use good judgment. You know what's at stake."

"Those Outer World mongrels will never get our precious secrets from me."

"Good."

"Thank you, sir." Farley said, "Bio-Comp, would you please be a gentleman and direct all unassigned personnel to the starship hangar?"

"My pleasure, Admiral."

"I'd better make some star ships so my title has some meaning."
He rushed off.

*

Tac-U-One and the Bio-Comp debriefed each of the fourteen
Mars staff, first separately then as a group. It was very unpleasant work.
They were a degraded bunch. Tac-U-One decided not to burden Earth
with their continued presence.

Tac-U-One spoke to them. "I declare you Non-Citizens."

"Order logged, sir," intoned the Bio-Comp.

"Bio-Comp, Mars staff – enforced isolation until deportation."

"Order logged, sir."

*

"According to those on the Mars base, Norman, the Earth trainees
were transferred into I-traps and shipped to a central depot for storage.
Their skills training was labeled on each tube. When an order came in,
Planet X would ship the bodies, and central storage depot would ship
the appropriately trained Identities.

"Once a captain of commerce joins Bio-One's scheme, there is
no chance of returning to the mainstream of the Directory. If found
profiting from this type of commerce, they know the Prison Planet is
the only place in the Directory they can hope to remain, and if they
flee, it would be to the Outer-Worlds. A place few Directory citizens
would wish on their enemies.

"Bio-One has been quietly spreading rumors that he will remain
in power long term and that restrictive Crown Laws will be rescinded.
Legalizing their current activities. This has solidified his position and
won more converts."

The cancer was spreading.

"With that escaped ship, I must assume Bio-One will soon know
of my presence here, and that'll put a bull's eye on this planet."

Tac-U-One stood and said, "Norman, I'm leaving you with the
Bio-Comp and he'll give you basic foundational knowledge of the
Directory. Then he'll introduce you to the Organizing chart we worked
out. Look at it, discuss it, if you want changes let me know and I'll
approve them before I go. I suggest you study a minimum of five hours
a day.

"Work out a different schedule with the Bio-Comp after you finish
module zero and one.

"Order logged, sir."

"Yes, sir," said Norman Cousins, Administrator of Earth.

●

Tac-U-One left Norman in the Planetary Commandant's office, it would soon be his. He headed for the Attack Room. This was standard in any outpost facility. It was a room protected by the most sophisticated technology available, and once the locks were set it was, to all intents and purposes, impenetrable. The pod itself might even survive the destruction of a planet, though the personnel inside probably wouldn't.

He descended to the Attack Room and secured himself inside. He approached a wall and booted up the self-contained computer, which had no outside communication ability (unless enabled by the Attack Room occupant), and directed it to open the sleeping facilities. The sleeping couch slid from the wall. Tac-U-One lay down.

Every event on Earth had led to this point. He looked back at the baseball game where he finally realized that no one on Earth was hunting him. Minutes later, he was staggered by the sight of the kid with the TAC car and then rescued by Wendy. Next came his failed protection of Wendy at the event with Earth's favorite alien Tyfon Arolia, where she was drugged and signed up for training. With the announcement of immortality by Boltax and Wendy's imminent departure, he was forced to dive into the lake and against all odds, recover his past.

From there, events had become linear and he'd planned far into the future. After the lake came the dodge game he and Wendy played to disrupt the Directory programs.

And his visit to the judge. Yes, Bonner deserved a reward.

Then into the Colosseum and onto the Turf. To the Recyclex room. That had been an eventful transfer.

Now he lay on a cot hundreds of feet below the Colosseum complex, protected by state-of-the-art systems designed to shield a body during dire times.

All he had done on this planet led here.

Here he would generate deception. And it had to fool the best telepaths in the Galaxy. Over the last days and weeks, in preparation, he'd been composing the structure of this intended communication. While exerting mindless effort in the gym, preparing for his fights on the Turf, his mind had wandered over this landscape, this event, this message.

The person Tac-U-One selected to receive his distress call had been carefully chosen. There were many factors to consider. The first was that Bio-One thought him dead, and for good reason: he had been. Forced transfer, or death, often resulted in amnesia.

He'd inform his Directory contact that his body had been severely injured when his M-Star collided with a cliff face. The body's skull had sustained severe injuries. He'd just recovered from memory loss and recovered the ability to Int-comm.

The moment Jack surfaced from the lake, he'd been testing his telepathic ability. Using it. The Jack Cousins body had been an inhibiting factor. This was now improved. This current Jolo body helped facilitate telepathy.

Now, in the quiet and safety of the Attack Room, he was ready to resume that most ethereal skill – that of Int-comm, or Interstellar telepathic communication.

No other rapid form of communication between stars had yet been discovered to work, but based on the theory that mechanical and electrical devices were simply poor copies of what a spiritual being could do – scientists still searched for the electronic equivalent to Int-comm.

In terms of skill, it was probably the most elite in the Directory and, if not that, it was the skill most Directory citizens knew they did not have, and could not conceive of acquiring.

The story of his injury and recovery would be believed, hadn't Tac-U-One survived impossible situations before? The report of his death would then be considered a poor joke. Of course he'd survived.

He did not want Bio-One to know he had "reincarnated," as this would cause him to take different measures more difficult or even impossible to combat.

Like an incinerated planet.

He would tell his contact that Directory personnel were operating illegally on this planet.

He would emphasize that no contact had been made and wouldn't without Crown authorization. He'd recovered his memory but didn't consider himself operational, especially with all his other injuries. Additionally, he suspected the out-worlders were probably an invasion force from the Outer-Worlds.

His "contact" was Raubish Mink, who was a deep-cover spy and a Crown agent. He lived on a little world called Deltite – a hub for Int-comms. It was a quiet planet, with a small population located off the beaten track. He'd be the one to receive the interstellar telepathic communication.

Tac-U-One had first worked with Raubish on a mission about forty-one hundred years ago, and they'd become fast friends.

Raubish worked at TeleStar, which handled interstellar communication by telepathy. Though virtually instantaneous, it was unfortunately an insecure means of communication. Codes and ciphers were as common as the people employed to break them.

Few people were able to send and receive an intelligible interstellar communication. With the service critical to all aspects of daily life, they were the highest paid profession.

Tac-U-One's communication to Raubish would blow his cover. Bio-One's agents would pounce and Raubish Mink would be forced to flee.

To give Mink more time Tac-U-One decided to scatter the Int-comm. Make parts of it easily recovered up by many. The broken up message would lend credence to the story of head injury.

The Int-comms would flash the message across the Directory: "Tac-U-One is Alive!" The genie would be out of the bottle and there'd be no putting it back.

The request was simple: a Star Comet (mobile Recyclex) and two agent bodies, male and female, both with a current Bertraund Training Corps certification.

Hearing of his condition Bio-One's people would assume he had no idea of the political situation. They'd be less vigilant – he hoped. They wouldn't contact the Directory on Earth for fear that Tac-U-One might telepathically intercept the message. Keep the cripple ignorant.

Deception was vital. Persuading Bio-One to withhold the full measure of his wrath and fear. They'd still plan the final solution: I-trap dropped into intergalactic space. Less noticeable than blowing up the planet and more permanent.

Tac-U-One made refinements to the "pages," of his "mind book." His "book" contained perceptual images, scattered desires, random scents and unpredictable motions – all surrounding the central head injury. It was a masterpiece of the disconnected, while still delivering a decipherable message.

Tac-U-One added pain, amputation, he charred the edges of the images with disorientation, pulsed nausea through haphazard pages.

But he was worried.

No matter the totality of his deception: his appearance could trigger apocalypse.

The destruction of Earth from deep space.

He must deceive Bio-One specifically. So he decided to construct a mind spring. The "mind book" was a message, the "mind spring" a weapon.

Something Raubish Mink would find. Direct Mink to Crown Planet, use him as a telepathic mailman. Mink would place the "package" in Bio-One's mind from close range.

But he needed a trigger to open the mind spring's compressed files. This took time; it had to be tailored to darkness.

Hours passed.

The Int-comm was done. Almost.

His last worry was the out-bound Mars ship.

If or when Bio-One independently discovered the return of Tactical Unit One and his story didn't match the ship captain's all hell would break loose.

That's the trigger.

Good.

One last thought. *As my strength increases, more data to follow.* He wove it in.

The interstellar technique required *perfect conviction* and *accurate conception* of recipient location. It was an ultimate level of confidence in the telepathic field.

He shook his head in wonder. No more stalling. *I need to perform.*

He floated free of his body and hovered a few feet above. A sense of well-being pervaded him, and he knew. That was the secret. If you knew you couldn't, it wouldn't. Do it.

He oriented. Correct distance, accurate vector. Dimly he saw the planet: Deltite. A sense of familiarity returned.

The Int-comm flew to its destination, the fragments scattered about for others to gobble up and re-broadcast.

It arrived seemingly without delay... it was not light years, but only a thought away.

CHAPTER 39

THE WORLD WAS A BEAUTIFUL ONE, composed of soaring peaks of volcanic residue compressed into thick, banded layers. Time had done very little to soften the landscape and the mountains still jutted at the sky with unapologetic defiance. The storms that beat these peaks relentlessly had passed with the recent change of season.

The locals still refused to use their weather modification equipment except under the direst circumstances, preferring to be beaten and scorched by the elements as nature's cycles dictated. Their tradition and heritage was that of mavericks and rebels, they loved the violence of their world.

They could sneeze at any exorbitant cost or fee. Even something as extravagant as importing foodstuffs from other star systems, which only this world in the entire Directory did on a regular basis. They were a vital interstellar communications nexus and so had money and power to spare for anything, no matter how excessive or insignificant.

Seated in his office as he had been at this time of day for countless years, was the man to whom Tac-U-One had directed his communication. The man was perfectly at peace with his double life and extremely dependable. The regularity of his schedule and constancy of his performance provided stability for innumerable corporations throughout the galaxy that relied on him for discretion and scrupulous honesty with their long-range communications – and he had done so for millennia. And though his schedule did not vary much from one hundred-year block to the next, the data he handled was always in enormous flux.

In addition to his "day job," it was his responsibility to break codes and relay information to Crown Agents. On more than one occasion, his data had gone directly to the ruler of the Directory. Such were heady moments.

Then the Int-comm from Tac-U-One arrived.

All hell broke loose for Raubish Mink. *What? Could it be? Tac-U-One alive?* Joy and disbelief warred within him.

Mink had attended Tac-U-One's funeral on Crown Planet years ago. The grief was thick and the eyes red, and the world was no longer as safe as it had been with the people's defender gone. At that time, he'd discreetly checked with his trusted sources in Crown service and they were subdued and without accurate data. Was Tac-U-One gone? This was a true unknown. Would he return? Was he gone forever?

So today, this very second, was a complete shock.

When Crown had gone on "sabbatical" and supposedly left Bio-One as Regent, Mink had stayed where he was, doing the regular TeleStar traffic, and had waited. Then it was announced after Crown had gone that Tac-U-One was dead.

Crown had not returned for the funeral (sans body). An ominous sign.

It all stank, because if Crown was truly on sabbatical he would have returned to discover the truth about his tactical unit officer.

Mink waited two years before the next Crown coded message came through to him, activating his extra-curricular activities once again. He'd been told to expect the unexpected and to be a listening post/ relay point for the scattered Crown Officers and other highly placed Crown loyalists. He could direct them by various obscure routes back into active Crown service. Only the most trusted were aware of who he was, and the very fact that he remained unmolested argued that those individuals were to be trusted still. That had been more than sixteen years ago.

When the message from Tac-U-One arrived, it came in two sections, one hidden inside the other. The fragments were completely un-coded and scattered about. He could tell the Crown Officer was in trouble; the only problem was that all the spies who were in constant attendance around a TeleStar base were aware of the same thing. Not as quickly as himself, but soon enough.

Within seconds, they would target him as a Crown agent.

His cover was blown!

A particularly solid section of message fragment hit him with an old, old identification code – something he and Tac-U-One had used to bounce messages back and forth between themselves as a game. Mental basketball – shoot through the hoop and the message was whole. As the fragment dropped through, the full impact hit him.

Years ago, when Bio-One, the newly established "Regent," had announced that Tac-U-One had been killed, Mink's first thought was that it had been done by a kill squad. Later, he wondered.

The more astute mourned his loss doubly as this meant that Bio-One was cementing his position as Regent, gathering power by the elimination of obvious opposition.

Over the years, his hope that Tac-U-One would return faded. For a long time Mink had expected to be reassigned because his activity as a spy dwindled.

The call did not come.

But it did today.

He had a maximum of seconds to abandon his post. If Mink was killed right here, Crown would never know *from a trusted source* that Tac-U-One was back – he would fail his sworn duty. That would never do.

In that moment, the routine of millennia was gone.

He pulled back a recessed panel on his ornate desk and punched a single button which dumped his computer files in less than a second onto a half-inch-square data cube and melted the remaining hardware. The cube, which looked like sweetener for his pep drink, dropped into his hand. He hit another button, activating a one-minute sequence. A panel on the rear wall slid into a recess, exposing a narrow tunnel. From the orifice came the cough and then roar of powerful engines coming to life.

Raubish dashed through the open portal, which instantly shut as he passed. He took two paces further and was knocked off his feet by the concussion of an explosion that no doubt had taken out his entire office along with those above, below and to the sides.

The number of Int-comm-capable telepaths in the Directory were fewer than five thousand. This stupid explosion had probably killed ten of the best in adjoining offices and this would severely disrupt communications across the entire galaxy.

The bombing was such an inexplicably extreme measure, for which Bio-One and his spies would pay dearly. It would draw attention and authenticity to the fact that it *marked the true return of Tac-U-One!*

Why else kill Mink?

Bio-One agents couldn't blame Mink for the blast unless they killed him, and they hadn't. A severe failure on their part, a trend he hoped they continued.

Bio-One's spies had reacted faster than he had imagined possible. If he'd delayed for a last sentimental look at the office that had been his for so long, he'd be dead.

He scrambled to his feet, rushed down the dark tunnel and leaped as he reached his M-Star, which had been sitting for years, awaiting this moment. The M-Star was vibrating heavily. The roar of the engines was horrendous in the confined space of his secret escape route. The ship looked as though it would jerk itself free of the restraints in seconds; such was the thrust of the engines. Gaining the seat, the ship sealed, and the artificial gravity activated, which released the restraints holding his vessel in check. He looked at the thrust indicator just as the engine redlined, and he was gone.

I'm away. Raubish Mink thought, as he left Deltite behind. Mink's recognition of a successful escape tripped the trigger on Tac-U-One's second message. Mink listened to the instructions, and set course for a deep space emergence at Crown planet.

Mink would deliver Tac-U-One's message, the recipient wouldn't *know*, he would simply feel the effect.

Mink laughed and laughed; he'd played mind games with the tactical unit officer before and he was devilishly sly. He wondered what the compressed "mind spring" contained. He laughed again: nothing pleasant.

This is how to live, he gloated.

The interstellar drive kicked in.

He entered Other-Space.

● ● ●

Jack smiled at his mother. They were in the Planetary Commandants office. He willingly responded to her questions and recounted the myth and history of his race and culture.

The galaxy had a hub, but it wasn't anywhere near the glowing center. The hub, in ages past before its present glory, was a simple globe revolving around a beautiful, if otherwise unimpressive, yellow star. It was home to a race of humanoid beings.

That the beings were humanoid was not unusual – the form was found as far as people had gone to find things.

The planet's populace were religious and hardworking. They had little contact with the outside universe, though their history was interspersed with odd peaks of technology and dark times where no electric lights shone. There were stories of visiting gods who would one day return, as all such stories go.

The sector of the galaxy containing this innocuous planet began to see rapid economic growth as the stars and planets began to communicate after an extended dark time. As wealth increased, ships landed and found it a fine planet with a tractable population.

New rulers came from the stars and stayed, things settled down and in a few hundred years, those "recent arrivals" could not be differentiated from the natives, so intermixed were they.

Technology spread outward from the cities. Sometimes its users abutted people who lived very simply. The planet was fruitful and mild and so they lived in harmony. The religious traditions stretching back millennia never faded and although the technologically elite privately scorned this anachronism, they let it be. Live and let live.

It was a time of prosperity.

Wars came, again, and for thousands of years the planet was cut off from their stellar neighbors, but a clear understanding of the galaxy and its significance was retained in the traditions and memory of the people.

After ten thousand years, the planet was again contacted and the "explorers" were disquieted to find that they had been *expected*. Not through some vague religious or occult myth, but through a parade which had been staged in readiness for the star ship's landing.

After a rudimentary exchange of language basics the visitors were told: "We've been expecting you."

The native population cheered the space men. Soon everyone was speaking the new language. Teachers had come in preparation for their arrival, to learn and spread the "lingua franca" of the stars. They proudly pointed out to the visitors that their language had remained unchanged from the last interstellar age.

It was a truly amazing place. But it was not paradise: there were warring social factions and a powerful one called "the DuChu" had boycotted the celebration and called the predicted, and then actual, arrival of the men from space a coincidence.

Once again the years flew by and higher technology suffused the planet.

A man named Jolo Patwaal arose from among the religious, who embraced technology and many of its branches. When he was four hundred years old, this extraordinary anomaly came to public notice. The DuChu attacked him viciously as a fraud, but he survived and gained ascendancy.

The name of the planet was changed. It became "Crown" planet because its accomplishments were like royal jewels all aglitter. From her came immortality, and the Immortals spread under the direction of this man, this savant. But if he was a god, so too was he the maker of gods. As man came to understand his true nature, he realized that he'd been immortal all along – merely forgetful of it.

So this jewel in the crown became the hub of the galaxy, its true center. A place from which freedom sprang and an expanding family of planets and stars to which one could be *directed* for any need or want – and thus the Directory arose.

Sixteen hundred years passed and then Jolo Patwaal disappeared under mysterious circumstances.

Another man came to power and his name became Crown. For seven thousand years he ruled and the Directory prospered. He gathered to himself the most talented beings and together they ran the Directory to the benefit of its citizens. Times were good and very stable. Expansion was rapid. Under Crown rule the percentage of the population who were Jolo (immortal) increased and rose to a steady two percent.

"And that," said Jack, "is the history of our civilization told as a fable."

"It has a certain grandeur to it."

"Yes, Mother, I think it does." He'd invited Sharon Cousins to the Colosseum. "I'm glad Norman chose to extend your marriage contract."

Sharon raised an eyebrow.

Jack looked at his mother. "Transfer can really change a person's attitudes. It doesn't always, but it can. I'm glad for both your sakes that he's stable in this regard, too."

"Oh, Jack, maybe *I* won't want to when…."

"So you've decided to transfer?"

"Jack." Sharon looked into his eyes. "I see you there, Jack, and I see Norman. I know who you are. I mean, I know you are who you are, that you're my Jack and my Norman. But there is a piece of me that doesn't accept it. I don't know what it is – I've searched myself. If that makes any sense? But I can't find, or understand what my inability to accept this really is."

"You don't need to know that."

"Well, that's right. I realized just that. Also the honor you're paying me by offering me Jolo status. Norman told me what it takes to earn it in the Directory."

"I didn't choose you just to warm Norman's bed."

Sharon's cheeks reddened a little. "Well, thank you, Jack."

He broke into laughter. "You're welcome, Mother. Earth needs your skills. Imagine what you can get done when you're not chasing me around!" Jack laughed. "Also, I don't want to leave Earth with you unsettled."

Tears were streaming from her eyes. "My God, this is the most fabulous thing there ever has been." She couldn't continue.

And then a little later, "Norman and I picked the body, my body, together."

There was a knock at the door.

"Come in."

The Recyclex officer stepped in.

"We're ready for you now, Mrs. Cousins."

Sharon went still.

"Jack…?"

"Norman is waiting for you at Recyclex. He'll be with you. I'll see you soon, Mother."

Women, on their first transfer, were always more profoundly moved. Having fought a losing battle with their appearance for years, it came as a tremendous relief.

The pieces were falling into place.

But Mother, Jack thought, *transfer is only a problem when bodies are scarce. And when a Normal dies each life, a body is the scarcest thing there is — one always loses it.*

CHAPTER 40

BIO-ONE HAD BEEN FRANTIC AS HIS covert plan to capture and control the Directory approached. Then, to his amazement, each phase fell into place, and power became his. The progression of events hadn't been perfect, but good enough.

As Regent, Bio-One had been enjoying unrestricted rule for close to ten Crown years (approximately twenty Earth years).

The greatest prize was Crown City on Crown Planet. The city itself was the apex of community life on a planet that ruled a far-flung empire. The spires reached to the sky and the exterior of each building in the entire province was programmed to interact with sky and landscape. It was an artistic masterpiece, the greatest city ever built.

But there were difficulties.

It had been two whole days since that Telepath on Deltite had received the battered Int-comm message from a man purported to be *Tactical Unit One*. Initially, even his own men claimed it was a confirmed contact. That's why they'd laser cannoned Mink's office. But he'd escaped anyway.

When Bio-One was informed about the potential link to Tac-U-One he instinctively retreated home.

His quarters were a huge, self-contained pod that drifted through the caverns and massive tunnels. He controlled the pod's location; spies and enemy telepaths couldn't find him. He could emerge from his home at any of a hundred or more locations, and chose a different point of exit and entry each day.

Before his ordered suppression clamped down, the story had spread like wild fire. Some irresponsible telepaths claimed they recognized the Crown officer's "mental signature," whatever that was.

Opposing this were other Deltite telepaths who said the opposite – this was not Tac-U-One's signature – just another false claim. They also declared the communication was not an Int-comm, but a message planted near the Int-comm complex on Deltite. "But we weren't fooled," they stated to the press, "this is simply another poor attempt to capitalize on our loss of Tac-U-One Crown."

"Tac-U-One has returned." Trumpeted the vastly larger group of telepaths who insisted it was a correct signature.

Media hounds were all over it. Everyone hoped, this time, it was true.

Not another pretender.

So the ruler of the Galaxy was feeling strained.

The Regent entered his secret room in his floating home. He pulled up the file on the death of Tac-U-One. The planet's local name was Earth. One of his expansion bases.

The pilot who'd taken him out had filed a comprehensive report about Earth. It was ripe for the plucking. But Bio-One's wife objected violently to any contact. "You're insane. Leave him on that planet to rot as a native." So the planet and its resources had languished. Years later, with her on vacation, he'd quietly approved invasion.

This matched the story the Int-Comms on Deltite were telling – Tac-U-One reported off-world intervention. The fool assumed it was Outer World annexation.

Bio-One hit a few keys.

Earth, per recent report, was functioning properly – excellently in fact – producing a large number of trained slugs for insertion into utility bodies. The military side was still non-existent due to failure of the Biological Officer to get the growth tanks running – some of these back world operations started with meager resources. But all in all, it was a thriving operation with no local insurrection.

A bizarre thing about the Int-comm had everyone confused. He hadn't included an origination point. *No one knows where that prick is,* he thought.

Why not give a location?

Ahhhhh.

Everyone who could lay their hands on a starship would be headed there already.

The Planet would be flooded and the operation exposed. I knew I should've insisted that Dolar provide Outer World personnel. This situation has to be wrapped up before the Earth operation is exposed. This is dire. Damn Dolar.

But if the message was from the recovering Tac-U-One asking Crown for a rescue he would have given his location.

So maybe it's something else.

The Regent looked at the pilot's report again. The wrecked M-Star was never recovered. The remains were also left in place. What other information had been left lying around? Could he believe the pilot? It was infuriating having so few people he could trust.

If the "Int-comm" was a fake who could have known enough to stage the charade? And why?

The why was simple. Money. Power. The Crown Officer's estate. Five others had already tried to get their hands on that mountain of cash.

Then who? The Regent looked at the Earth staff.

And there he was.

The Jolo Boltax, Commandant of Earth, was capable of such a thing. His ambition was off the charts. And this was a big move. He flipped more report pages, Boltax was a competent telepath.

This was coming together.

First he finds the wreck, recovers some identifying data.

Then makes a plan.

Boltax takes a star ship and drops the telepathic message in Deltite's near space and is soon back on Earth.

That's why there's no report of disruption from Earth. Boltax can block everything.

What about the Int-comm named Mink, the main addressee? That doesn't fit. But the message fragments were scattered all over.

This could be a massive scam.

Someone this smart and corrupt Bio-One could trust to be predictable – right up to the time he got his hands on the money. Then, using biological weaponry, the Regent could control or eliminate the imposter at leisure.

If I allow "the return of Tac-U-One" to move forward, there are many advantages. If or when the real Tac-U-One re-emerged, he would be a legal non-person. The Regent smiled.

It all came down to one point.

Was this Int-comm from Tac-U-One or was it another opportunist?

What if it really was Tac-U-One? The very thought of it made Bio-One's blood run cold.

If it is the Crown Officer I should blow that planet to fragments. But that might not work. Nothing anyone did to get rid of Tac-U-One actually lasted. The pilot who downed him claimed he survived the Screaming End – impossible. Bio-One shuddered. *Maybe he'd survive the planet's destruction?* He felt ill.

How he be so lucky? Thinking about it made Bio-One crazy.

The only completely safe course of action was to I-trap Tac-U-One and drop the capsule in intergalactic space. That would mean thousands and thousands of years of peace.

Finally the Regent felt calm.

He would send a multi layered "rescue mission" with separate orders covering all possibilities.

● ● ●

A huge crowd mobbed the Crown City space port. More than a million people had come to see off the ship that was going to an undisclosed planet to rescue Tactical Unit One Crown. The mission came under intense scrutiny from many different quarters. Every aspect from its supply's to its personnel were checked and checked again.

Bio-One had waged an intense behind the scenes battle to prevent any Tactical Unit members or those who claimed they could reliably identify the Crown Officer from getting on the ship. Instead the crew and others selected were totally "neutral" and classified as independent observers.

Tac-U-One's body trainer from the Bertraund Training Corp, amid great ceremony, personally delivered the two requested bodies under official seal. He'd spent considerable time and effort recovering data from the Deltite telepaths so he could deliver the exact bodies wanted by his most famous client.

When he tried to insinuate himself onto the ship he was escorted outside the space port and then released.

Amidst incredible pomp and pageantry a "Star Comet" class ship was prepared, and there was nothing that Bio-One could do to stop it. He had proposed sending an inferior Hunter-Seeker class vessel, which had a maximum complement of fifty men and no Recyclex facilities. On the HS class vessels, many in the navy were manned exclusively with Bio-One's handpicked men, where any situation could be tightly controlled. And the impostor – or whoever he was – could be dealt with from a position of weakness and Bio-One's strength.

But he was unable to force the issue. A fleet Admiral in the Crown Space Navy said, "On the chance that this man is Crown's senior Tactical Unit Officer – we have no choice but to acquiesce to his request. He outranks us all." Bio-One, the Regent was filled with rage. Still, a Star Comet was being sent.

Tactical Unit One had requested certain specific things in the message fragments. And every citizen in the Directory knew what he wanted. Bio-One couldn't countermand that.

This loyal group of Senior Officials, technicians, military and Tactical Unit had insisted upon maximum speed and complete security. This left the Regent with little room to maneuver.

Bertraund Training Corps bodies had been personally development by Bio-One himself. He'd tried to insert the most recent release of these special agent bodies, without success. Arguing with Tac-U-One's personal trainer went nowhere. There'd been so little time before the ship departed. But he'd solved that problem, too.

Bio-One had assembled his operatives separately. There were several independent units unaware of each other, interlocking, diversionary, failsafe. Some were given deliberately false information. Others were briefed within an inch of their lives on different "what if" scenarios with different levels of truth, emphasizing to all that no contact be made with the natives or the "Outer World" operation (as he chose to describe it). Every contingency was covered and re-covered independently. He'd achieved the comfort of... overkill.

One Admiral, who had been on four naval missions with Tac-U-One in his distant youth, believed that this was a legitimate mission to rescue the real Crown Officer and had initiated a location survey on every ship in Near-Space. He handed the survey data to the Regent, whom he despised.

"Regent, with the delicate nature of this rescue mission, I have taken the liberty to survey every single ship, publicly or privately owned, to prevent any other vessels from interfering with this mission." He continued on, "The entire fleet is on alert and will prevent any unauthorized launches. Also, there was an inspection of the Star Comet and you'll be happy to hear an illegal arsenal of planet-destroying weaponry was removed."

This asshole Admiral was preventing Bio-One from sending back-up to ensure a favorable outcome. Taking his weapons? Arrggarahh! He had to get rid of these loyalists as soon as possible.

"Thank you, Admiral," said the Regent through gritted teeth.

The Admiral knew if this was Tac-U-One, then he'd be facing deep trouble, so he'd given him as much protection as possible.

The Regent scrambled but could not find the resources to send back-up vessels with planet-busters. His Outer-World allies did not have Int-comm capabilities. So his entire hand was being played with the one ship.

But fear, the deep, irrational kind, had lodged in his gizzard and would not be purged. It had a name: *Tac-U-One.*

CHAPTER 41

NORMAN COUSINS WAS NOW A PALE-SKINNED Jolo with blonde hair and light blue eyes. It was the new him. He stood six feet, five inches tall. The musculature was what one might expect to find on a professional athlete, but wasn't bulky. The body weight was two hundred twenty pounds, but he didn't look thin. The skeletal structure was comparatively light but much stronger. Or so he'd been told.

The effort, in terms of exercise and training in the course of human endeavor, to produce such a body, was enormous. He had done nothing to earn this happy state, and felt like a thief.

Jack – or Tac-U-One, as Norman increasingly thought of him now – had given him a room in the inner sanctum, the restricted Directory portion of the Colosseum, and it was in these palatial surroundings of fine wood and gold trimmings that Norman bore his torment.

Norman did not believe he alone would have difficulty with the transition from the Earthly body to the Jolo body. He imagined the shock *anyone* would feel to see a stranger staring back at them in the mirror. It was quite extraordinary. It made him feel displaced – he was here but not here.

From the inside, in the new body, he felt just fine – he felt great. It could simply be how *one* felt on a really good day. Then he would catch a glimpse of his reflection and *it didn't look like him.*

The first time he saw his reflected image, he was standing with two other people and *he couldn't identify himself.* He went rigid and even paler. The mirrored images had not included a body he identified as himself. Norman was so shaken his knees went out from under him.

But, of course he never hit the floor. Instead, he created great comedy for the others by bounding high into the air, landing awkwardly, and finally coming to a nervous rest. All because he couldn't find himself. He wanted to go back to his old body where he could tell who he was.

It had been Jack and Farley who were standing with him. They'd both convulsed with laughter. It was funny; he would've laughed himself silly if he'd seen someone else at the same antics.

"Norman, you'll have your day. When you're a veteran Jolo, there'll be many a newbie for you to chuckle over. It's great fun." Jack slapped his shoulder. "You should've seen yourself!" he said, and doubled over laughing.

"Know why we laugh at you new guys?" Farley asked.

Norman shook his head. "No, I don't, but I'm sure you'll tell me."

"How can you be sympathetic with someone who's just made the greatest leap forward in social standing, wealth, power, health, sexual prowess and everything else that the Directory can offer?"

He had a point, Norman realized. Such a person was in no need of sympathy.

"Norman," Jack added, "He's right, it's a time for hilarity and not sympathy."

In Norman's *other* life, he had never been this fine a male specimen, and from that viewpoint it was a welcome change. Truth be told, he'd probably be okay with the mirrors in a week.

Jack added, "After you've gone through a bunch of Jolo bodies, you'll lose the compulsion to identify yourself with the face in the mirror. You can just be you."

●

Now, here, was not a good time for flubs in handling this body. Norman, the Administrator, needed to create an *impression*. He was standing stiffly in front of some of the most powerful men on Earth. People of the political and military persuasion had come here on short notice, at Tac-U-One's request.

Norman, after days of tutoring by the Bio-Comp about the Directory, was feeling his oats. Seeing its organizational simplicity and ease of application to the situation on Earth, he was poised.

After general coverage of social institutions and customs came the interesting part. The part that had given him confidence was the standard programs that were run when a planet was accepted as a member of the Directory of Stars and Planets. Much of it was applicable to Earth as-is. He'd made revisions where needed with the help of the Bio-Comp. Soon they'd submit the entire package of programs they intended to implement to Jack for his approval.

●

Tac-U-One had called forth the leaders of Earth to the Colosseum auditorium. They'd come from around the globe, from the deserts and mountains, the plains and meadows of the world.

Those who disliked the Directory presence and influence that had become control, were vindicated and horrified by the recent revelations. They were angry and wished to be heard.

The new leader of the aliens must appease them for the crimes of his Directory. Here was a man of whom they could demand and receive any concession. Was it not the Directory who had done these horrendous things to the vulnerable citizens of Earth? Was he not the self-proclaimed High Official who'd personally admitted to these crimes?

In all political dealings, this was the most sought-after situation – a man of power positioned directly over a barrel, over their barrel.

Norman looked at the faces; their attention was centered on Jack. They saw a twenty year old youth, six-six, two hundred thirty pounds, with sandy hair and blue eyes. The more perceptive amongst them noticed how unaffected he was.

Jack and Norman were on the stage well behind the podium directing last minute activity. Earlier a minor protocol problem had occurred and Norman had reseated some prominent politicians. He'd felt uncomfortable.

Then Norman realized – *he* was now a *Them*, not an *Us*. To these men who complained and all who observed him, he was clearly a Directory official of some kind: one of *Them*. As a consequence, he felt more comfortable issuing orders.

The auditorium continued to fill. Finally the heads of state and senior officials from most of the nations of Earth were seated. Many had arrived without recognition or fuss. But some political figures were spotted and soon the entire world knew something big was happening at the Colosseum. Never had the world's powers gathered together like this. It threatened to become a media circus, but the clowns were stopped at the gate.

The drone of conversation was casual, but with a vicious undercurrent; there was blood in the water and the piranhas were hungry.

Their indigestible target: an honest man.

Without formality, Tac-U-One stepped to the podium and looked at the noisy group.

"Ladies and gentlemen, I'm not a man to stand on ceremony," his voice boomed out, bringing quiet in its wake, "so there'll be no grand introduction, no minions to introduce me and no one other than yourselves to regulate good manners."

Norman almost smiled, seeing it hit the mark with the "rabble rouser" types in the crowd.

"My name is Tactical Unit One with the appellation 'Crown', meaning I work directly for the Head of State within the Directory. He holds ultimate power in an empire of some trillions of people. I speak with his authority here on Earth.

He pulled a silver ball from his pocket and held it above his head between his forefinger and thumb.

"This is a portable communications link to the central Directory computer on Earth. It is not a weapon. It will hover in the room, and we'll be heard and translated perfectly.

"Bear with me as I make a formal statement.

"I, Tac-U-One Crown, declare the following a Formal Proceeding of the Directory of Stars and Planets. I call to attention the men and women in this room and request you participate in decisions providing for the future welfare of the people of Earth.

"No proceeding of this type has ever occurred outside the Directory's sphere of influence.

"The decisions made here will be binding within the Directory." Tac-U-One scanned their minds, the group was now involved.

Then he dropped the bomb.

"I'm not here to apologize again. My intention is to help formulate solutions."

An angry murmur passed amongst the attendees, but no one spoke out loud.

"You exude resentment. This isn't a forum to rebuke me for the crimes of the prior Directory Chief. I'm not that Jolo. I was not within his administration at the time the crimes were committed."

They were stunned.

"I haven't said this to side-step responsibility for what's been done in the Directory's name. I share *that* responsibility in a broader sense, but I'm I not a direct cause of your sufferings." He let that sink in.

He'd removed himself as whipping boy. "You came to point the finger, assign blame and make mincemeat of me. Then beat further concessions out of the Directory. Let's move on.

"I'm here to appeal to something else within you. Remember your youth, your ideals, how you were going to make the world a better place? It's that instinct I now address.

"We have a problem to solve.

"Great crimes have been committed; there is heartbreak in your lands to match no other in memory.

"In war, everyone is aware of the stakes. This was different. You were deceived by unscrupulous men wielding great power and cunning. They made you willing dupes, while their real intentions and activities remained hidden.

"That is now over. You have the unvarnished truth. Now comes the repair.

"Allow me to introduce the Administrator." There was no applause.

"This Jolo is the new head of Directory Enterprises on planet Earth. He was, until a short time ago, an Earth native named Norman Cousins.

"I've revealed his background to make it clear you'll have a part in what will come to this planet. Though he is a Directory citizen, he is also one of you. He's essentially a very competent individual, demonstrated by large scale professional success and stable family life. His résumé is available to those who want it."

Tac-U-One switched gears. "A war is brewing out there among the stars. Earth may come under attack from forces engaged in a struggle not of your making."

This caused a ripple of consternation through the room.

"Like it or not, you're part of a broader universe now. No matter how unfair your involvement is, it must be dealt with.

"Tonight I have things to tell you and decisions to make. These choices and the resulting outcomes will be influenced by your input."

Jack continued by expanding on his statements of the previous day about the training, FFI games and depopulation of remote villages.

"I know you're confused. You may ask, 'What would cause an interstellar empire to invade Earth and then essentially attack itself?'

"The explanation is this: there's been a partial overthrow of the legal Directory government.

"One man planned and caused Directory presence on Earth. His name is Bio-One.

"Bio-One is the leader of a secret *coup-d'état*. He seeks to consolidate the power of the Directory under his rule. If he succeeds, Earth will become a permanent slave labor pool.

"Right now Bio-One controls nothing openly, but rules as 'Regent'. The lackey of another, more powerful man.

"It is my job to prevent him from achieving a complete overthrow and restoring sovereignty to the rightful ruler, Crown.

"Is there anything you'd like to ask? This is your opportunity to get answers. In hours I'll depart this planet."

"Why have we inherited this Star Wars bullshit? We don't deserve all this!" Was one angry outburst.

"I've given you the who, how and why. But 'why' in a spiritual sense? As in why did you deserve this? I've no idea."

The President of the United States of America stood. "I believe I speak for all of us when..."

Tac-U-One cut him off. "Don't speak for others. Everyone here will speak for themselves.

The President sat down.

"Questions, please."

"What's happened to the former Directory Chief?"

"He is currently undergoing Directory justice procedures."

"The man deserves to be hanged!"

"Execute him!"

"Use my firing squad!"

"Justice, justice!" came the persistent cry. And abruptly the orderly group became a mob. Like flipping a switch. "Execute him!" This chant tore from the throats of the whole assembly.

This ran on for a while.

"The former Directory Chief, a man named Boltax, is well within the wheels of justice, and though I recognize you have moral grounds, you have no jurisdiction over him.

"We have rights!" declared the US President. "His crimes are against our people. He must pay for those crimes. He must die!" The room howled its agreement.

"Please be quiet." Tac-U-One's voice thundered out. He gave them hard facts. "How could you do anything to him at all?" he asked. "He could escape from wherever you held him. And kill him? None of you could do it!"

His tone and words incensed them.

"Justice," called a strident voice. "Execute him." There was rowdy assent. "Make him pay."

"Kill him," came out above the rest. Emotions were raw and violent, social graces gone. Hatred of the man and his acts was intense. The furor built and built until there was a solid cacophony calling for death. Pain, torture, death. Faces were livid, veins pulsing.

Tac-U-One stood there, a group of men and a few women who were now a reactive mob. As with most reactive mobs, death and destruction was their purpose. Their extreme turbulence washed over him.

He held up his hand and silence gradually fell.

"Certainly you have legitimate cause for your emotions. Never in history has someone promised so much and betrayed your trust so thoroughly.

"But Boltax was only a servant of corruption. Your enemy lies elsewhere."

The President stood. "I want him dead!" He was cheered by the mob.

"Let me make something clear: no one within the Directory has been executed by a legal authority in more than nine thousand years. I won't start now."

That stopped them; they had something to compare their attitudes to.

One man spoke out defiantly. "That may be so, but isn't the Directory now divided against itself?"

"Yes," answered Tac-U-One. "But the current unrest was not caused by omitted state executions.

"I have killed; but not to punish or obtain the 'fulfillment' of revenge.

"Hasn't it occurred to you that if we successfully transfer people from one body to another, that the birth-growth-death of a body is not the action of life itself? The attributes of a *body* are birth-growth-death. The attribute of life or a person is one: immortality.

"It's not civilized for one immortal being to end the life cycle of another immortal being's body.

"Who will be your children's children?" he asked the audience. "Who are your ancestors?"

They had no reply for the question, nor was its answer real to them.

"By executing criminals like Boltax, you victimize yourselves. You invite them back into your families as infants." Again, Jack saw he wasn't getting through.

"My reasons to kill a person are: self-defense, or defense of others. No other."

He stared at blank, confused or uncaring faces, so dropped that appeal.

"You want to kill Boltax?" he asked.

There was a chorus of assent, but with less vigor.

Jack smiled at them. "He'd escape you within minutes. He'd seek out those in power who wanted his execution. He'd kill each one of you. Without me on Earth, he'd take control again.

"Is that what you want?"

There was some low-voiced grumbling, but it died to nothing. Finally, silence was heard.

"I take your silence to mean that you agree that Boltax is to remain in my custody and that you trust me with the dispensation of justice. I can assure you, he will lose everything other than his life. And though he will not live in a jail cell, he'll wish he was in one.

"Until his exile he'll remain incapacitated, unable to inflict more damage." Jack knew they still wanted Boltax dead, but not at the cost of their own lives.

He scanned their minds.

They thought him weak.

He was incredulous.

"You think I'm weak! That I can't stomach killing and so prevent your 'ultimate retribution'?" His voice was severe. "You think yourselves strong to order the death of an individual." Tac-U-One laughed harshly.

"I've just come from the Turf, from the Colosseum. Before I took this body, I was Jack Cousins."

Surprise, consternation and a dawning realization spread through the room. Augie MacMillan paid particular attention.

"I, myself, killed men in these past weeks. Each death was necessary, was unavoidable. But *I* did it, *I killed those men*," he said. "If I'd been stopped or died on the Turf, the *rape of Earth* would remain in full swing and you would still be ignorant idiots sucking from Boltax's corrupt teat. So I killed those men to protect myself, Earth and the Directory. It was the right thing to do.

"Do you agree?"

There were murmurs of agreement.

"I am asking you: do you agree that the death of those men was done for self-protection and served the greater good of Earth?"

There was general assent and vigorous nodding of heads.

"Yes, sir, I believe you acted in our best interests and against your own natural instinct. Thank you," a military man acknowledged.

"You're welcome.

"Now we have Boltax, who is acknowledged by everyone, including myself, as the worst kind of criminal. But he no longer has power. And what kind of courage, moral conviction or 'ethical stance' does it take to order the death of a helpless man and have others carry out the sentence?

"I ask you this not as a group, wherein you can hide, but as individuals. I'm not standing up here and simply making noise. I'm not even trying to change your minds. *But I have asked each of you a question!*" Again the words were thundered out. Tac-U-One made eye contact, moving from one person to the next. Many would not meet his gaze.

"I'm a senior executive within the Directory. This man has violated and disgraced everything I stand for, everything I've worked to achieve for thousands of years. I mean this quite literally. When Pharaoh Ramses freed Moses and the Jews on this planet, I was already on my current post, and had been for some time."

This statement set off a great stir all around the gallery. Those who thought they had Jack pegged were forced to re-evaluate far outside their own frame of reference.

The rumbling subsided.

"I've lived on this planet for seventeen years with my own true identity masked. I was, as I've said, Jack Cousins. Recently I recovered my past memories and came to your notice. You may find it strange, but I have a love for this planet and many people here. And so, what Boltax has done here, to you, he has done to me too, doubly. For I am one of you, too.

"Do you really think I'd be standing here with you now if I had no personal involvement with your future? You see, there are trillions of people out there who need my help and to whom I have a prior and stronger obligation. Whom I serve.

"But I'm also obliged to the people of Earth for my time here. No other experience in my life compares to the time I've spent here with you.

"Dare I mention compassion? Dare I allow myself to appear weak in your eyes again? I submit that compassion here takes more strength of character than does the impulse to destroy. I challenge you to be strong, to be compassionate, or at least be intelligent enough to realize that the 'curtain of death' is a lie and gives no true resolution to victim or perpetrator." He had reached some of them, but not all.

An Ohio Senator jumped to his feet. "What about the victims? What about the families of the victims? In your world, they don't matter? Let's all cry for the poor, abused criminal Boltax! That man has just eliminated millions of our brightest young men and women from across our planet – but he needs to be coddled." His face became dark, suffused with blood.

"We have a whole planet demanding his death and here we are listening to you spout theories of reincarnation as if they had relevance, as if it were *real* and not the mumbo-jumbo New Age crap we all know it to be." He looked directly at Jack.

"That's right, that's what everyone here is thinking. But they're too scared to say so." He glared.

"Are we not a democracy? If the world cries out for the blood of one man, who are we to deny them? Who is this man to tell us anything? The people of Earth have cause. We have cause.

"I ask you, put aside your platitudes, theories and hocus pocus, and give us, the people of Earth, a measure of justice. Place the former Directory Chief in our power for our disposition. By putting an end to this man we may in some measure find peace..." Tears were rolling down his cheeks. There was no denying his passion.

Tac-U-One looked at him. He had no interest in rebuttal.

"And that," Jack said, "is the other point of view."

There was some scattered laughter as they realized the Senator was not going to be refuted or censured.

"This planet has changed," Jack said. "The reins of economic prosperity are tied to the influx of Directory technology and its broad applications across this planet.

"But this nirvana was due to expire in three years when the 'trainees' failed to return. At that point, this Colosseum complex was to become a military compound that could resist and contain any mass attack by the combined military forces of Earth."

Lightly scanning thoughts, he settled on one mind. The man was wondering how to unite the military forces of Earth with the young Jolo at the podium. His mind was ordered, his thoughts linear, direct and logical. And seeing the face, Jack instantly recognized the man he'd met in Las Vegas, where he took his first steps in solving the mystery of the Directory's presence on Earth. The man wouldn't recognize his new body, but surely he knew Jack Cousins.

"What is your name?" Jack asked, though he already knew the answer.

"My name, sir, is Augie McMillan."

"What's your line of work?" Jack asked with a smile.

"Well, sir, I'm an Admiral, and have been part of the military forces of the United States of America for over forty years."

Jack had been searching for someone within this group. He'd liked him in Vegas, liked him here, and his presence argued a continuing involvement in Earth's survival.

"I'd like you to resign your present commission and sign on with the Directory administration on Earth."

Augie was completely rocked by this request. A tremor went through his body. Everyone in the room looked at him. He caught the eyes of his President and read envy and loathing. Allegiance is an important thing to an honorable man, something one does not discard with a moment's consideration. But these circumstances were in no sense ordinary, they could not even be categorized as extraordinary. They were unique: these pivotal events would never happen again.

He found himself searching his pockets for paper and a pen; before he had consciously decided to take the offer he began scribbling furiously as he walked down the aisle, approaching the podium. As Augie passed the U.S. President, he shoved an envelope into his hands. Scrawled on its back was his resignation. He stepped up and saluted Tac-U-One.

"Augustus McMillan reporting for duty, sir!"

"I like a man of decision, thank you. That couldn't have been easy."

"It wasn't. But I'm your man."

"Good. Your post is Coordinator, and you'll work directly for the Administrator. Please stand there."

Tac-U-One let time drift for a few seconds and wondered how the next topic would go.

"We need to return to the main focus of this meeting. I've just robbed you of your best military man, but he'll be put to good use. You all know him as an honest man, so you'll be able to trust him. He is forward-thinking and if I am not wrong, wasn't he the first man to substantiate the alien presence on Earth?"

"Yes, he was," the U.S. President said.

"Excellent," Jack said.

McMillan shook his head. "Things change. Fast." Knowing him.

"Yes." Jack continued to the crowd, "For the Coordinator to fully assume his post, he must make one further change." Tac-U-One turned to the two men beside him and directed Norman to take Augie and give him the necessary briefing.

"Norman," Jack whispered. "You've got to be very persuasive. We need him willing to transfer." As Norman and Augie disappeared behind the curtains, Tac-U-One turned back to the assembly.

"Gentlemen, you'll have to decide tonight whether to support Crown, myself and the legitimate Directory governing body or not. I won't tell you it's an insignificant thing, and I won't promise you a rose garden exists down either course. I will promise that the long-term future is bright with us."

A man stood.

"I am the Prime Minister of Great Britain. You ask us to decide on the future course of Earth; a course that has dire consequences whichever route we choose. Most of the delegates here are elected officials of countries which are democratic. What you ask of us is not something we can give you without the votes of our citizens."

There were subdued murmurs of assent around the room. Tac-U-One gazed at them and met the eyes of many.

"Perhaps I was unclear: if you're unable to present a good case to me as to why Earth should be accepted by the legal Directory authority – which I embody – as an ally, then you will fail to secure your future with us and what will come cannot be stopped. I can't tell you how to arrive at your decision. I am here now. This is your opportunity. It will not wait. It will not come again."

"Sir, the pressure of this is intolerable!" exclaimed the Brit.

"You're wrong if you think I'm placing undue pressure on you without cause. I'll be gone from this planet before the sun rises tomorrow and will not return for many years. In the long-term galactic scheme of events, Earth is of minor importance. But don't misunderstand: I'm here now because I want to help as much as I can."

He paused for a moment, walked to the curtain and looked behind. Norman and Augie were deep in discussion. What better way to convince a man to go to Recyclex than to use someone who's just done it?

He returned to the podium. "I've arranged a demonstration that you'll find enlightening. It'll be a few minutes before we're ready." He continued, "I've drawn up plans for your future prosperity and effective defense. The Directory Schools, as I announced broadly to the entire planet, will continue to operate. They'll train for the skills and knowledge needed on Earth right now – Energy, Transport and Communications (ETC). I've decided to allow those existing industries to partner with us on the proviso that the public gets ETC cheap. Very cheap.

"Through Admiral Farley, head of Earth Space Navy, I've made the technology for extra-terrestrial travel and military defense available."

This was warmly received.

"Is there any chance you can stay to help us?" a Congressman from Nevada asked. He'd been close to Directory operations and knew their efficiency.

"I can't stay. My presence on Earth puts you in danger. I'm a target of magnitude to my enemies and they wouldn't hesitate to destroy this planet to see me dead."

He felt their dread.

"Don't worry, I'll provide my enemies with indisputable proof that I'm no longer on Earth."

"Are you sure of your ability to do that?" asked the British Prime Minister.

"Yes."

There were murmurs of thanks. It was difficult for them to face the magnitude of forces involved, or casual evil, where Earth could be thrown away to ensure the demise of one man.

The Senator from Ohio spoke. "You've told us the most amazing things – without giving us one shred of proof. How are we to know if any of what you say is real or if it's all some type of elaborate ruse being acted out for some other purpose?"

"Of course, Senator, I can't give you more proof than what I've shown you. But think for a moment, Senator. I've taken control of this base and all the Directory facilities and personnel of Earth and Mars, where the combined military forces of your planet would have failed.

"Are you clear on that?"

"Yes, I am."

"Excellent. The Directory presence on Earth has challenged some of your dearly held beliefs, hasn't it?"

"Yes, it has." The Senator hadn't planned to say those words, they'd just come out. But now he felt less combative.

"Take the announcement of immortality, for example. That's a bomb for atheists and many religions. If the Directory controls the technology of life, then what of God? And no one has offered you any proof, and if they did it would be blasphemy to believe it. Have I got that right, Senator?"

"Yes, sir, you have."

"When the Directory invites a new planet into the fold, we educate the incoming populace. There are new things to learn, new technologies, and new understandings about the basic nature of life itself.

"My own philosophy about living is that I accept or reject data or situations as I see fit. I extend that right to everyone. I do not seek or want blind acceptance, as that's dangerous. But blind rejection is just as damaging.

"If you accept or reject ideas or situations based on preconceived standards, and not your own actual observation, it is my position that such a person has abdicated their role as a sentient being and has become a puppet to be controlled by others – as a practical matter, the person becomes a fool who cannot see.

"If that offends you, Senator, so be it. For myself, I can say any power I've acquired throughout my existence, has been done on the basis of personal observation.

The Senator merely nodded his head.

"You've courage, Senator; there aren't many who'd dispute me in my own lair."

The Senator smiled.

Norman came from behind the curtain and drew it aside, revealing a portable Recyclex machine.

Augie McMillan was standing to the side of the machine with a calm, almost beatific expression that Tac-U-One found admirable, considering what the next few minutes held for him.

"Do you want to transfer?" he asked.

Augie was calm but he didn't trust his voice, so he simply nodded.

Tac-U-One faced the delegates. "Ladies and gentlemen, here is the demonstration I promised you. This machine is called a Recyclex. It's the equipment used to transfer a person from one body to the next. We're going to give the Coordinator a new body."

He let them digest that.

"The former Directory Chief announced that we have the science to facilitate immortality. But he never took the time to prove it, did he, Senator?"

"No, sir, he did not. He paraded around the two supposed winners of the Fight for Immortality and televised their mothers questioning them until they became convinced that they were their sons. It reminded me of a country revival where all the cripples get up and walk."

"Healthy skepticism, Senator. Do you know Augie?"

"Yes, sir, I do."

"Come up here and assure yourself we haven't tampered with him."

The senator frowned, but mounted the stage and walked over to McMillan and shook his hand.

"Congratulations on your new office, all us lame ducks are jealous already." They continued to chat.

Tac-U-One said, "I know each person here has their own religious views. Some of you possibly ignore religion. Some of you fight it. Whatever your convictions are or are not, this demonstration forms the backbone of our religious philosophy; in the local vernacular, it's where the rubber hits the road.

"I'm going to go through the transfer method step by step. Identification is the first step. We keep exact documentation of each transfer, change of body, so the person's property legally transfers with them.

"This is achieved by having the Identity, person, write a word or short phrase on official parchment.

"Augie, will you step over here please?"

Augie and the Senator approached.

"Administrator, do you have pen and paper?"

Norman gave it to Augie. "Yes, sir."

"Augie, write a word or phrase on the paper and fold it." This was done. Tac-U-One handed the Senator a seal.

"Senator, press this seal into the paper, please." The Senator did it.

Tac-U-One handed him a stiff envelope and the Senator slipped the folded paper inside.

"Now seal the envelope by pressing the flap down for a few seconds." There was a slight hiss from the paper as it achieved the official seal.

"Can you open the envelope without tearing it, Senator?"

The Senator gave it a few light tugs.

"That won't do, Senator, I want you to use all your strength to get it open."

After a convincing struggle that got a few laughs from the delegates, the Senator was convinced that the document was secure.

"All right, everyone, I want you to come up on the stage and witness the transfer.

"Are there any medical doctors present?" Five men worked their way forward.

Augie, briefed by Norman, now lay down on the right-hand tray.

"See you on the other side, boys!" He still had the ecstatic smile. In Tac-U-One's experience this wasn't usual, but wasn't an adverse indication either, so he let the procedure move forward.

A naked male Jolo body was wheeled out. The doctors inspected the body with the Earthly medical instruments provided. One fellow went to his room and came back with his black bag and used his own things. After a huddle the medicos declared the body dead.

One said, "What's the glow coming from the body?"

"It's a stasis field used to preserve the body from decay." Immediately they had questions. "That's for later, Doctors."

The body Augie had chosen over three others was placed in the left-hand tray and the stasis was turned off. Normally, body ignition would take about thirty minutes. But Norman, with the help of Farley, had started the body and bought it up to minimum function, then reset the stasis so the doctors could examine it.

"Generally this goes quite quickly, twenty minutes or so, but first-timers sometimes drag their heels. I need you to be silent until Augie is transferred and has been awake for a few minutes, alright?" He got a few assents.

The chest of the naked form began rising and falling, the vital signs registering on the Recyclex machine were indicative of a comatose person, with a slight sub-normal temperature and no brain activity.

Tac-U-One manipulated the settings and in a few minutes, the readings on the McMillan body slowed and stopped as the Identity eased from the body. The body of Augustus McMillan was dead by any Earthly definition. The staring faces were not aware of this, but some could see that his chest was no longer moving.

Minutes passed, and there was a slight shuffling of feet. Ten minutes went by and many of the observers were becoming uncomfortably aware of the constricting effect of their collars, jackets and belts. At fifteen minutes, many heads were pounding from pressure. Seeing a man "die" isn't a comfortable experience. Especially when the instinct to intervene has to be suppressed.

All were now aware that McMillan was dead and anxious looks were exchanged. Twenty-five minutes saw shirts soaked by sweat. Some in the rear began to sway from side to side in a curious metronome type motion.

Tac-U-One was cursing himself for a fool as he realized what must've gone wrong. McMillan's body under his bulky clothing was wasted. The man's body had been ill, probably deathly ill. What had fooled him was the man's intellect, which had been keen and bright, undeterred by his physical state.

One didn't transfer a dying man. Too often they were lost.

But McMillan was the only man in the group he felt comfortable offering Jolo status to.

By the thirty-minute mark, there was a palpable desire to leave the area completely. This was a failed experiment and no one wanted to witness its grim conclusion. Had there been a loud noise, they would've stampeded. As a group, the collective emotion had descended to one of despair.

Tac-U-One, looking at the vital signs readouts of the Jolo body, saw a slight spike. Then, after a minute, the brain scan jumped and there was full brain activity, rapidly followed by heart and respiration. At the first real breath, the tension drained from the observers.

In a few minutes, when the body was showing obvious signs of sustained life, some jokes were cracked. "Someone slap him on the ass."

"Does anyone have a rattle?"

"Doris, he must be yours."

"Diapers, diapers."

"Now that's a big bouncing baby boy."

After more minutes, the Coordinator was helped to his feet and given a pale green jumpsuit with a sunburst over the left breast pocket. He was grateful. Ah, sweet youth.

Without anything being said, he was given a slip of paper upon which he wrote a few words. This was matched to the one in the envelope. They both said, "I will change."

The audience burst into wild applause. They shook hands with their neighbors, slapped each other on the back. They were stunned and elated at the same time.

Those who knew the aging McMillan looked at the tall, athletic figure and shook their heads.

What luck!

The bodies had no similarity, but as they looked into the green (not brown) eyes there was recognition.

Augie began conversations with others that only he and they could be familiar with. He was questioned closely and extensively till his friends were certain this was, in fact, Augie McMillan. And as each discovered the truth of it, a life changing thrill went through them.

The wonder of it spread.

The Senator walked over to Tac-U-One. "I've been a fool."

"No, you haven't, Senator. It's a matter of data. If you give accurate information to an intelligent person, they can change their mind."

"That's what disturbs me." The Senator looked troubled. "If you hadn't challenged me – man to man, I would've rejected what I saw tonight."

"And that's unsettling." He shook his head. "I could have ignored the truth."

"Ah, Senator. Always beware of something that 'must' be true without proof. Don't compromise your personal integrity and you'll be fine."

He shook Jack's hand. "So your name's Tac-U-One?"

Jack nodded. "Yes."

"It's been a pleasure to meet you. I wish you well."

"Thank you, Senator. I said you have courage. I'm right, aren't I?"

"You've helped me, thank you."

"You're welcome."

They circulated around. Everyone agreed – this was the way to live. And McMillan was the undisputable proof.

So, with the hearts, minds and balls of each man present in his grasp, Tac-U-One accepted Earth as an official ally of Crown and the Directory.

CHAPTER 42

THE STAR COMET WAS A PINPOINT of light amongst the stars. As it drew nearer the vessel appeared small – but then, its backdrop was several thousand feet of jutting mountain. On final approach, its massive size became apparent, and the back blast of the normal space engines settling the ship to the ground was impressive.

With the sight of the ship, and all that it represented – danger, future, opportunity – to concentrate his attention, Jack was still distracted.

Earlier, on the lip of the shallow valley that cupped the very lake where it all had ended and begun once again, he'd watched as the sun blazed into the Earth to smolder somewhere in its sullen depths. It struck him as a metaphor for his life, for the light of his life had passed beyond his reach. To find and lose love so quickly was not easy.

He suppressed his emotions and concentrated on his surroundings. As he waited for the massive ship to touch down, his thoughts wandered again.

There was another star ship – the freighter – that had escaped Earth, its status still unknown. By now it could be anywhere. And that held danger. But there was nothing he could do about it, so he let it go.

The night was crystal clear and alpine scents swam in rivers that twined through the whole region. His hair was tasseled, his face grim and his posture erect. Danger approached.

Images of Wendy at school, happy and laughing, meandering conversations replayed themselves in his mind. She was with him, she was far away.

It was a beautiful area, and very familiar, he almost expected to see her among the trees or at their camp site.

It was strange; even though she was gone, he could still feel her presence. So strong was the impression of her nearness that it choked his senses. Just months ago they'd been together in this place; his heart ached with remorseless-beating.

They'd come close to making love that last visit, but decided that there would be a more appropriate time. Whatever that meant. It was utterly meaningless to him now, and was in fact a heavy burden, almost as if he had betrayed her by not expressing to her how much he truly loved her.

Did she now wonder about the depth of his feeling because he hadn't pushed the issue? Had it caused her to doubt, now that she was an unimaginable distance away? It would have been the most natural thing in the world to have made love that day. Now they were separated. Would they ever meet again, or would he be left with this great uncertainty? Had he failed her in love, as he had failed to protect her from Boltax?

He shook his head to clear it. He had no time for this. Grief had its time, its place and a purpose. But that was not here or now for any reason. He must have all his faculties at their peak or he would be defeated here tonight. Once again, he thrust his personal grief aside. There was more potential danger here for him in the next short while than for a bleeding baby in a tidal pool of hungry sharks.

He concentrated on the approaching ship as it descended. There was not much to see as it filtered the visible light spectrum, leaving the telltale violet frisson for friendly identification.

His attention was firmly directed upward, intent on seeing what was there, and checking off likely preparations Bio-One had made for the "cripple."

He'd been hearing gravel crunch for some seconds before his full attention was drawn to it. He turned quickly, the prospect of an ambush alive in him. The sound was not that of stealth, it was not animal. It was indicative of tentative uncertain motion.

He peered through the starlight and was shocked and stupefied at the sight of...her? It was her? Wendy? No!

He'd never hallucinated before. For a second he was tremendously uncertain of his perceptions. Something he wanted so desperately to be true but rationally knew couldn't be.

In the minds of Boltax and his Investigator he'd found irrefutable proof of her being sent out of the system. But there she was! How could this be? The hallucination tilted her head to one side in perfect imitation of a "Wendy" stance.

"Jack?" the hallucination said in a tremulous voice. There really was someone in front of him. Emotion flooded him.

Their natural magnetic attraction drew them together with violence, each seeking assurance of the other's presence. He swept her off her feet, twirled her around and around, and felt pure joy. She was laughing with him, caught up in his happiness.

"Hey, sailor, if you greet me like this after a few weeks, then I'll go away for longer!"

They clung to one another fiercely, afraid to ever let go again.

A strange look came into his eyes. He said quietly, "I thought you'd been taken from me forever."

Wendy shook her head. "No, I've been hiding up here so they wouldn't find me again. So they couldn't get to you through me. I told my cousin Penny to tell you I'd gone to our special place."

"And you told no one else?"

"No one." So for all the family knew, Wendy had been taken too.

"She's gone. Penny's gone. I, we, thought you'd been taken with her. Boltax, the Directory Chief, was certain his men had taken you off-planet and out of the system."

Wendy felt shock and then was hit with a wave of guilt. Cousin Penny had paid the ultimate price because of her absence. The plan had worked *too* well. She hung her head. "Oh my God, Jack. It's all my fault. The last thing I asked her to do was to tell you I was here at the lake – and now she's gone. I had no idea…." Her voice faded away.

"You have some responsibility in her disappearance. As do I. She was taken from your home by two very stupid men Boltax used as enforcers, then she was shipped to Crown Planet.

"I'm sure they thought she was you or they simply didn't care. We've been searching for them, but haven't found them yet."

Wendy nodded, feeling some relief that her cousin must be alive.

"Who's car is that parked by Jeb's?"

"I stole it, Jack. I couldn't take mine or borrow one."

Jack shrugged, "Good thinking."

"Jeb has no idea I've been here. I snuck past."

"Wow." He paused, "Well done, by the way."

"For what?"

"For not being captured and dragged away."

She looked forlorn. By avoiding that fate her cousin had gone to it.

"I'm so sorry Penny was mistaken for you. But at the same time, I thought I'd lost you and it was terrible, really terrible." He shuddered.

She hugged him fiercely.

Jack asked, "How did you know I'm me?"

"When I saw someone coming up the trail, I thought it must be you looking for me – that Penny had told you I was here. When I put the binoculars on you, I was so upset because, well, it wasn't you. But I kept watching, and I thought, 'What if Jack won the competition, he would have a different body.'

"So I kept watching you and saw the way you walked. How you were looking at the places we always went, our last campsite, and looking so sad. I cried a little. Then I walked slowly down. I wanted to run to you but, well, the different body and all." She shrugged.

As the starship descended, Jack gave her a brief outline of recent events, and their objective here.

"There's no easy way to ask this."

"What?"

"Do you want to transfer?"

She looked away.

"It's hard when you're young."

"I can't come with you without it?"

"You would die." He shrugged helplessly.

"Okay," she said with grim determination.

●

It had been eighteen years since Tac-U-One had seen such a ship, and as he approached it, a wave of excitement suffused him. The ship before him was his ticket back into the big leagues – if he could punch it.

This is going to be tough. He knew. The conclusion was entirely logical, but now he *knew*. It was shrouded with a sense of menace.

All the other ships on the planet were real rust buckets compared to this vessel. Such a ship would have several M-Stars (admittedly not of the same caliber as his old ship) in the docking area. As many as twenty. It had awesome weapons capability, and a Recyclex and his agent body.

Yes.

He hadn't not come to this rendezvous unprepared. As a precaution, all Directory telepaths on Earth had been isolated and the only mind anyone from the Star Comet could have been in communication with was Earth's Bio-Comp, who'd been specifically briefed and wouldn't betray him.

Jack's plan counted on Bio-One removing him from Earth without local Directory knowledge. The last thing Jack wanted was to have a telepath on the Star Comet scan the minds of Directory personnel.

Jack reasoned the Regent's plan of attack would include a local blackout of his extraction. He wouldn't want a "Tac-U-One rescue story" spread from Earth Directory staff to friends and family back home.

The ship was on the ground.

Tac-U-One's attention was riveted. He approached the ship at a casual stroll.

On the walk up from the cabin he'd set the body endocrine output to levels he liked prior to conflict. When he sighted the ship, he boosted the body's weapons capability up a notch. Seeing Wendy, he'd ratcheted it down.

Now he revved the body to max with a complete suppress of any external indication of the racing metabolism. This even extended to conscious control of pupillary dilation, minute skin secretions, other olfactory indications, muscle tension, etc. He could, in fact, achieve the appearance of casual unconcern under full endocrine stimulation.

Within seconds of landing, a ramp extended from the ship.

The Captain was a silhouette as he walked from the Comet. He was backlit by the intense light emitting from the ship's open port. Jack allowed the man to approach, gauging him silently.

"Captain, you cannot imagine what a relief it is to see you." On Earth all the Directory personnel spoke English, but Tac-U-One slipped into Cortic without a hitch.

The Captain approached to within the specified fifteen feet and then lowered his head, "I'm at your service, sir."

Wendy walked out from behind a large rock and was standing by Jack's side when he gave the ritual response; "Thank you, Captain, your service is accepted," and asked the man to come closer.

If there was any surprise at her presence, the Captain hid it well. Wendy didn't say a word but walked at Jack's side as they approached the ship.

"I was told to expect a cripple, sir, and an agent body. Your body genetics don't scan anywhere near that level."

"Then why have you acknowledged me?"

"Well, sir, if there is any chance it *is* you, then I am *for* you. And with what waits on this ship, only one man has a chance of surviving. So I guess we'll find out soon enough."

"Do you know of any specific surprises?"

"No, sir, but the tension on board crackles."

"Does your ship's computer have a Bio-function?"

"No, sir. But there have been some recent programming changes ordered by the pilot." That made the pilot a prime suspect.

Tac-U-One casually smiled. He could feel Bio-One behind every move, but already the script was unraveling. The Captain was a straw man intended to quiet his suspicions. His mind clear of any plot against Tac-U-One: a perfect lure. The real threats would come from less obvious sources – some actual, some pretended – all with the purpose of confusing, distracting, ensnaring and finally capture.

It was imperative that he seize control of the situation and obstruct secret orders other officers or crew may have. The more he could enforce his own structure in the coming events, the greater his chance of survival.

He'd never take over the ship's computer with a simple typed command as he'd done at the base. The element of surprise was small but not gone or there'd be no ship and no planet.

"Captain, a Formal Crown Inspection of your vessel is now in progress," he said with command authority.

"Yes, sir," he saluted. "Excellent first move, sir."

"Glad you like it. Now make it stick with a vengeance."

"Yes, sir."

The enemy officers and crew on the ship won't tolerate the inspection for long – it'll isolate them, make them desperate and force exposure before direct contact. Their objective, simple: I-trap or death. Or if they decide he's an impostor, they may take him to Bio-One.

Formal Crown Inspection of a space-going vessel required the ship's officers and crew be at designated posts with all their gear shipshape.

To win he had to ally as many of the ship's company as soon as possible and do it without tipping off the enemy that he was actively moving against them.

There'll be excellent telepaths, but they'll stay hidden until the action starts.

Entering a Star Comet after so many years of isolation was marvelous. Jack glanced at Wendy. She was awestruck and trying not to gawk. He smiled. The ship was in chameleon mode and currently looked like a smaller version of the cliff face under which it sat. The interior light streaming out of the airlock was the only indication of the high-tech world that lay within.

Jack had offered no explanation for Wendy's presence. His request for a female as well as male agent body had probably been taken as a red herring.

Jack wondered if at some level he'd known Wendy was still here. That was speculation for a quieter time.

The Captain's Port was only used on ceremonial occasions. So the pretense of accepting him as Tac-U-One was the opening gambit.

Entering the ship, they were flanked by an honor guard of combat troops, fifteen per side, tightly packed and looking impeccable in ceremonial full-dress uniform. There were golds and reds with midnight blue and black, flashes of exotic insignia and clusters of decorations and weapons polished brightly.

"All hands, all hands. A Formal Crown Inspection of this vessel is now in force. I repeat, an FCI is now in force. All hands to their assigned stations. No exemptions, all hands, do it now."

"Master of Protocol to monitor compliance and report any variance of FCI procedure, offenders to the brig. Captain, out!"

Tac-U-One heard feet pounding on deck plating. They had a minute to arrive on station and remain at attention until the inspection was complete. This ingrained response would confine his enemy.

The Weapons Masters were the only crew members under Formal Crown Inspection who were mobile. Their job was to ensure everything was shipshape before the Crown Inspector "tapped" the station. In the old dark days before Jolo Patwaal, a short, heavy baton was carried by an inspecting officer and anyone who failed was beaten with it. Three light taps was a pass. So "tapping" the station was a tradition.

Tac-U-One strode confidently between the flanking rows of Honor Guards, then let his body systems go haywire. He discharged fear scent and took a few missteps. Then he tried and failed to suppress the poor control.

More importantly, he was scanning for thoughts – they were comical and contemptuous, as they dismissed him as an impostor. The Captain's orders were the only thing holding the Honor Guard in place with superficially respectful expressions that hid sneers.

He searched for anything odd, heavy or furtive, outside of the derision that these supremely skilled men were feeling for the fool who had conned the Captain.

He caught a fleeting thought, a mere whisper that was gone before it took form.

He acted.

The guard never saw it coming. The tip of Tac-U-One's boot buried itself deep into the brain case of the offending Honor Guard. The cowboy boot entered where the neck and chin intersect, penetrating so far that his ankle met the Jolo's chin. There was a soft sucking sound as he pulled it free.

Shock was smeared on all the faces in the confined space of the Captain's Port. The body, unsupported, slumped to the ground. Elite combat troops who doubled as Honor Guard when requested, were not easily shocked by violence. But no one saw the move – they could not have defended it. Only the sound of impact communicated that something had happened.

These men respected martial competence of their fellows and little else. They were immortal fighters, and they fought hard. No peace-time dress-up unit. They were tough, durable, competent, intelligent, arrogant, confident soldiers. They were Jolo.

Jack said, "I need to know who this fellow was."

"Sir, this Jolo was a new addition to our unit, and not much liked by any of us."

Jack nodded; he'd taken out the right man.

"But he was good, very good." The soldier looked at Jack and shook his head.

"Soldier, I need information, and I need it fast."

"Yes, sir. During the shakeup, this guy kicked all our asses."

A pecking order existed independent of rank, and these men lost no time in determining just where the new man fit in. To their annoyance, this Jolo had worked his way quickly to the top man in the unit and defeated him, too.

"What pissed us off, sir, wasn't getting beaten, but being treated like dirt. He wasn't one of us.

"Honestly, sir. I – we – have never seen anything like what you just did here."

Other men appreciate fine art, an exceptional book, inspiring music, a tragic play. These men admired one thing: excellence in their chosen field.

"We all knew our mission was to recover you, sir – Tactical Unit One. But when this guy said it? We knew he thought it was total shit. We were skeptical when we saw you. The way you were scared… Oh."

Jack gave a thin smile. "Yes," he said.

"We all attended your funeral nine Crown years ago, so when you walked up with the LMG body (low mid-grade), we assumed… that any 'honor' we were giving you was a mockery."

Jack nodded him to continue.

"Earlier, we agreed that if the guy – you, sir – were a fake, a Tac-U-One impostor, we'd take matters into our own hands and arrest you."

"But you don't think I'm an impostor now?"

"No, sir. None of us has ever seen anything like what you did just now. It, it's, well…. There's no way to describe…."

Something had happened. Something they could never have imagined experiencing; humility so complete that it was not really recognized. What they failed to see defeated them. They had not seen a martial sequence.

"Sir, that guy is still holding his blaster." He shook his head. "Except for his bug eyes, his expression's the same. And, sir, he was looking right at you. God, sir!"

For these men this moment had taken on an aesthetic, spiritual aspect that raised it above all others in their lives. They were truly disciples of Tac-U-One Crown. They *did* believe and they would never speak of this incident to another.

"Thank you, gentlemen."

As one the soldiers stiffened in their parade stance.

Tac-U-One nodded to the men, aware of the respect now being shown him.

"Good." Jack glanced at Wendy who was also shocked, but for a different reason. He leaned down and said in English, "It was necessary, trust me."

Mutely, she nodded. This was no time to be squeamish. The stakes were high and the game rough.

He turned and spoke to the two combat troopers closest to the entrance. "Bury that spy in the soil outside the ship, and say nothing of this to others on board."

The first line of enemy attack, the "muscle," was neutralized. From here on, it would be more subtle – or not.

"You're the senior officer of this unit?" Tac-U-One asked.

"Yes, sir!" he barked out.

"You know all these men?"

"Yes, sir, been with them for thirty years except for the one you killed."

"And you're sure of me?"

"Yes, sir. And you know why, sir." Jack liked this Jolo who was not cowed by his presence, showed intelligence and hadn't tried to flatter him.

"I *am* Tac-U-One; are you with me?"

"Yesss, Sirrr!" they thundered out.

"Can you pilot one of these tubs?" The team leader nodded. "Good. Your rank is Navy Major, the rest we'll sort out later. You and your unit are now on indefinite detachment with me." The Jolo saluted.

"There is extreme danger on this ship; there will be multiple attempts to assassinate me or I-trap me. The entire ship may be destroyed just to eliminate me." That sobered them up. "Run up your bodies to high alert or whatever level you can sustain for a minimum of two hours. Clear?

"Yesss, Sirrr!" they barked as one.

"Major, select ten men and come with me. Send five three-man units to patrol the ship to ensure the officers and crew stay at attention on their assigned inspection stations. Stun and detain *any* officer or crew member who is away from their inspection station. Send the last unit to sit on the Master of Protocol.

"Accept no excuses. Stun and detain. Is that clear?"

"Yes, sir!" The new Major gave his men individual assignments, then they went into the ship.

This was moving in the right direction. His enemy's options were now reduced.

He and Wendy, with the Captain, Major and ten Honor Guard went directly to the ship's Recyclex facility.

"You're not going to inspect the ship, sir?" the Captain asked.

"I never intended to, Captain." He was not entirely sure of this man and stayed alert to the use of telepathy. But his mind was closed. This could be good or bad. At the pace this was going, he'd soon find out.

Jack had briefed Wendy as they walked to the starship, "There will be death here today, Dee. So be ready." And so she was. But the strange language isolated her and as they hurried through the ship she had no idea where they were going or what was said.

The Recyclex bay was more than adequate. It was designed to handle transfers of men with extreme injuries from combat. It was well-equipped and ready for anything, when seconds of unnecessary delay could mean death and failed transfer.

The Honor Guard fanned out to cover all points of access to the Recyclex bay.

"This is the Captain: in addition to the Weapons Masters, the Honor Guard is also mobile within the ship. Weapons Masters and all officers and crew, you are to subordinate yourselves to the Honor Guard for the length of this inspection and until further notice."

"Thank you, Captain. That will help."

The Major was manning the communication center and in constant touch with his men as they scoured the ship looking for anyone out of place.

Tac-U-One went directly to the trays and pulled out the bodies. He quickly located the two he needed and smacked the controls, starting "warm up" in military mode – fast.

Jack guided Wendy to the Recyclex cot and asked her to lie down and sleep if she could. Her transfer needed to be rapid and flawless. She'd go first, while he further stabilized the situation on the ship.

Transfer was the point of greatest vulnerability. The attack *must* come here.

By requesting Bertraund Training Corp bodies, he'd forced his enemy to deliver the best. And he knew their security procedures.

These agent bodies were trained for me. They'd been in stasis for more than twenty Earth years.

Jack smiled. His enemies on board must be frantic. Their plans were stalled. He was forcing attackers to expose themselves as fear drove them to act. Another diversionary tactic occurred to him.

"Captain, instruct the ship's computer to announce the progress of the Formal Crown Inspection slowly through the ship. Start with the non-essential sections of the vessel first. Delay the pretended contact with senior officers and the bridge. And make the inspection random and unexpected."

The Captain smiled and quietly gave instructions to the ship's computer. The broadcasts began immediately.

"Major, the crew will wonder why the inspection isn't where it's supposed to be. Your men are to say, 'The Crown Officer's inspecting without warning. He's very tough.' Got it?"

"Yes, sir!" The Major loved it.

War was deception, Jack knew. But how was *he* being deceived?

Knowing his supposed location would calm the enemy agents and buy more time – until they discovered the ruse.

Then all hell would break loose.

The computer announced. "Inspection of lower deck 'C' crew's quarters is now in progress." Tac-U-One smiled.

"That's brilliant," he acknowledged. The quarters were deserted and while this was unusual, it wouldn't cause suspicion. With that display of help, Tac-U-One decided to trust the Captain.

"Captain, pull up a visual of computer/comm usage and block the interface to the TAC (thought activated circuitry); that way, if our patrols miss something we'll catch anyone trying to attack us electronically."

The Captain smiled.

"Let's make them work for it." Jack said.

Enough holding action.

One man was in the Recyclex bay.

"You're the Senior Bio-Tech on the ship?"

"Yes, sir. This is my FCI station."

"Captain, how long has this officer been with you?"

"He came in with the new wave of Bio-Techs that were posted in the fleet last year, sir."

"Thank you." Then he said to the Bio-Tech, "You became Jolo during the Bio-One era, didn't you?"

"Yes, sir."

"Would you have made it under Crown Law?"

The man glared at him and then dropped his head. "No."

"At least you've the guts to admit it. That's something. You know what's going on here, right?

"You're quite capable of treachery toward my person to protect the status you didn't rightfully earn. But I need your skills to help me remove the alien devices that may be implanted in the bodies I'm warming up. Play me falsely, telepathically or in any way, and my men will gut you. Is that clear?"

"Yes, sir," he said shakily.

"Major, if either myself or the young lady are hurt in any way, execute this Bio-Tech immediately – even if he's not the direct cause of the injury."

"Yes, sir," the Major responded, a measured look in his eye.

"You've been told I'm not Tac-U-One?"

"Yes, sir, we were told you're an impostor."

"The rumor has passed through the entire ship," volunteered the Captain.

The Bio-Tech nodded agreement.

"For what it's worth," the Captain said, "I consider you to be who you say you are, sir."

The Bio-Tech swallowed.

"Me too, sir," the Major said for the Bio-Tech's benefit.

The Bio-Tech looked afraid.

"Okay. Prepare these two bodies for inspection." He looked at the agitated technician. "Stop shaking, if you're clean and don't play me false, you've got nothing to fear." The tech settled down.

"Yes, sir." The Bio-Tech scanned the control panels. "They're almost ready for transfer."

The female body was fully developed and beautiful. Jack's surprise showed when he saw Wendy's natural facial features and coloring. *The touch of my Bertraund trainer.* It moved him.

Jack looked at the physical spec readout and converted the values. She would stand six feet, one inch tall and weigh one hundred seventy-two pounds. The female bodies of this type were full through the hips and breast, but slender-waisted. The smaller body mass (versus the male) was compensated for by added bone density.

Wendy would experience less shock. It was easier to wake up looking like "you."

A lot of myth had grown up around how well a first-time transfer came through. Many believed that ease of transfer equated in some measure to ability as a Jolo.

Wendy was restless on the Recyclex cot and could not relax at all. The random noise, conversation in a foreign tongue and the sheer tension in the room made it impossible to sleep.

She was plagued with doubts. *I don't know what I'll do if I become a man.* She shivered. What would happen to their relationship? She wished she'd asked.

Jack asked, "Are there any other female bodies?"

"Four," the Bio-Tech responded.

"Display them," Jack ordered. *Better give Dee a choice,* he thought.

Jack beckoned her over. She rose from the cot, and looked at the bodies. *Female.* She slumped against him in relief.

Jack caught her thought. What he'd just put her through. No excuse. She was going to transfer totally unprepared.

"Take a look and see if there's one you'd like."

She was quick, gravitating to the one that looked like her.

"Good choice."

Making her own decision helped transfer.

"It's okay to touch the body, Dee."

She reached out and tentatively touched the face and hastily withdrew her hand, the skin was not yet warm and the chest was still. But it looked perfect. She looked at Jack.

"I'm ready now."

She lay on the cot and fell asleep. *That was quick,* thought Jack.

"Captain, when did you get this Recyclex machine?"

"My 'Star Comet' was refitted..." He punched a few keys on the computer console. "A little more than two years ago."

Jack had no chance of identifying foreign electronics in this new model.

"Okay. Anyone work on it before you left on this mission?"

"No, sir." Then he became thoughtful. "The Bio-Tech here had the front panel off when I came through here yesterday."

Everyone looked at the Bio-Tech.

"I replaced a fried module" he said belligerently as he went to a cabinet and removed a box that contained the old part. Jack sniffed it. It smelled like fried electronics.

"Do you know of any alterations to this model Recyclex machine?"
The Bio-Tech looked away.

"What is it?" Jack demanded. "What's that bastard Bio-One done now?"

"They'll kill me," the Bio-Tech whispered.

"You might get that lucky if you don't tell me."

"I wanted to be a Jolo so badly…"

"Tell me." Jack repeated, "No negotiation, tell me now."

"I was only approved for one of the classes – I don't know all…"

"Tell me."

"I was trained on how to use the Recyclex machine as an interrogation tool."

All the Jolos in the room looked horrified.

So that's what Boltax was trying to do to him back at the Colosseum, Jack realized.

"What else?"

"That's all I was trained for, but there were at least two more classes that some of the techs took." Then he hurried to say, "But I don't know what they were about." He could see he wasn't believed. "Look, they threatened to kill me if I ever mentioned this – no one said what else Recyclex could be used for.

"I'm going to help you and the lady transfer," the tech pleaded. "That's all."

There was no time to investigate this. Jack had the tech show the Major how to use Recyclex to interrogate.

"Captain, is there a connection between the ship's computer and Recyclex?" The captain checked.

"Yes, sir."

"Disable it."

The Captain disabled the software and had an Honor Guard cut the cable.

There was no time for this. Tac-U-One's sense of urgency was becoming intense. He signaled the tech to begin Dee's transfer.

The Bio-Tech ran a vital system check, then activated the body. It was breathing slowly and evenly with a heart rate of fourteen beats to the minute. Temperature was fine.

The Tech proceeded quickly, and Tac-U-One could see he was competent. Green signals rapidly filled the readiness panel – no rainbow display on the military model. The last light went green and a chime sounded.

510 THE FIGHT FOR IMMORTALITY

All set.

Jack sent the Tech on an errand across the room, then reached in and depressed the large toe nail of the female body's right foot. A symbol was clearly seen for a moment then faded – confirming a real Bertraund body. He waited. No colored patches of skin showed. He rolled the body to check for discoloration on the back. It was clean, no systemic poisons, no organ tampering.

The Tech came back with the hand-held substance and foreign device scanner and gave it to Tac-U-One.

"That's new. Get me an old one. Got an Electronics Tech here, Major?"

"Yes, sir." One of his men stepped forward and inspected a battered tattletale implant checker that Tac-U-One passed to him. He took the lead and connected it to a console, ran a diagnostics check. Green, green, green.

"Got any poison anywhere in the Recyclex bay?"

The Bio-Tech looked horrified.

"I'll take that as a no. How about a spare power pack?" The Bio-Tech grabbed a charging battery cell and handed it over.

"Knife?" One of the Honor Guards passed him an electric knife. "No, something with a blade."

Tac-U-One took what was handed him, slashed the cell open and dropped it on a bench. He then went to the drug cabinet and quickly selected twenty small ampules of different drugs. He ordered a Guard to lay on a gurney and placed the drugs and broken battery cell under the Guard's torso.

The Electronics Tech stepped over and scanned the prone Guard.

"Twenty-one, sir." The scanner had detected twenty-one foreign substances.

"That's a pass. Just for giggles, check the other scanner."

The electronics specialist began checking the new scanner while Tac-U-One scanned the female body with the old tattletale implant scanner – no foreign implants. No colored patches of skin. All clear. He had to go with it.

"Bio-Tech, place the body in the Recyclex receiving tray." The computer, housed in the Recyclex, responded after scanning the body, "Transfer body ready. Transfer will begin in ten seconds."

"Acknowledged, proceed," the Bio-Tech responded.

"Nineteen, sir."

"What?"

"The new device and substance scanner has been rigged, sir. Only nineteen of twenty-one substances show on the scan."

Tac-U-One swung toward the Bio-Tech and would have undoubtedly killed him had he not seen his face and read his terrified mind. The Bio-Tech didn't know. He halted his death blow just short of impact.

The Honor Guards were again mesmerized.

"Back to your posts," Tac-U-One said quietly to them. "He's just stupid."

The Bio-Tech was quivering.

"Settle down, I'm not mad at you anymore. And clean yourself up – but make it quick." Tac-U-One nodded to a Guard. "Go with him."

He'd seen transfers where the subject had lain down, fallen asleep and was done in ten minutes. The other end of the scale was a series of nightmare scenarios.

He initiated transfer.

Jack watched the vital sign monitors and felt unreasonably nervous. It was two full minutes before the vitals of Wendy's body took a steep dive; a minute later they bottomed out. All signs normal, but fast. Too fast? His pulse quickened.

One minute. The first light bar went dark. This continued through "blackout", where the old body was "dead" and the new body had no vitals. No cause for alarm.

The second – dark. Normal, still within parameters: but not his own parameters.

The third bar went dark and a tiny nimbus went on over the "old" body to preserve it in the event transfer didn't "take" and re-animation was needed. It was *always* a possibility with the first-timers and it preyed on Jack's mind – what would he do then?

The Bio-Tech reached over and methodically exposed the upper torso of the "old" body and began attaching leads in preparation for the possibility that it may need to be revived.

CHAPTER 43

THE STAR COMET PILOT STOOD IN the Captain's place on the Bridge while the Captain was escorting the impostor on a Formal Crown Inspection, this stupid FCI. Just the idea of it made his blood boil. The Regent himself had briefed him and many of the officers in one of the Great Halls of State on Crown Planet. Tac-U-One had died heroically in Crown service and this person was not the first to claim to be that legendary figure.

He remembered the Regent's inspiring words; how he must have loved Tac-U-One.

"Many crews such as yours have been dispatched to various points of the galaxy in the hopes that Tac-U-One has returned to us. So far, each case has been fraudulent, but we will not stop. If there exists somewhere in the infinite reaches of this universe a chance that he could be recovered to us, we will go there, will do whatever is required, plumb any black hole, brave any exploding sun. If only," and here his voice broke. "If only we could have him back and safe with us." Incredibly, the Regent was close to tears.

Then his face hardened and his voice was stone. "There is one other factor. We did, some years ago, capture those who took him from us."

There was a stunned silence in the echoing hall. Tac-U-One's killers had been found.

"We never released this information – it's still highly classified and cannot be repeated outside this hall!" The Regent, Bio-One, looked his most stern. "After weeks of interrogation by the most skilled telepaths in the galaxy, we discovered that Tac-U-One had been captured." He paused for the drama of it. "Transferred into an I-trap and released into the intergalactic regions, where he will remain for the next half million years."

The silence was broken by muffled sobs and anguished moans.

"So you can see why this was never publicly released. The public must be left with some shred of hope that he will return to us. *They* must have hope – even if we have *none*.

"That's why I pursue these missions with a vengeance. Some detestable being is out there, sullying the name and reputation of one of the greats of our civilization. We can endure many things: raping and pillaging pirates, attacks on our borders by alien beings, collisions with stars – but this, we cannot tolerate. And your mission is to punish a being so deceitful as to presume he can ride our hero's coattails back into our hearts."

The righteous indignation was palpable throughout the hall.

"Never," the Regent bellowed and they returned his cry in full measure.

"Never, never, never..." It echoed again and again against the august walls.

The Regent hung his head.

"There exists a minute possibility that this claim could be true. It might be possible that the I-trap used to dispose of Tac-U-One was sabotaged – allowing him to wander free. I ask you to keep this in mind: to be civil until experts and known associates can pass final judgment. Of course you want to ask me, 'Regent, what if he's violent?' or 'What if he is intolerably superior?' I say, do your best. Capture him if you can, kill him if you must. Above all, protect the reputation of our hero."

The Regent expects heroics in etiquette, thought the Pilot. How can he expect us to be courteous to a known fraud? It defies belief. But he'd heard the orders and so it was. They were lucky to have such an understanding man leading them while Crown was on sabbatical.

The Pilot was chafing, listening to the computer give out the continuing reports of the FCI and its slow progress: that this or that crew member's quarters had passed or flunked. How incredible, how absurd. The man was an impostor. There was no conceivable reason that the real Tac-U-One, after more than nine Crown years of absence, would as his first act upon returning to the Directory sphere of influence, conduct an inspection. Absurd.

Then there was that complement of Honor Guards strutting around the ship, under "Crown" orders, they said – self-important pricks. Little did they know that he, the Pilot, had the power to end this farce whenever he liked.

The Captain, who was with the "Crown Officer," was a puppet, though he probably didn't know it. He hadn't been at the real briefing given by the Regent. Bio-One himself had given the Pilot the computer override code for the entire ship. And the Honor Guards think they have "Crown" orders. He laughed inside. He wouldn't tolerate this charade much longer.

The Interstellar Communications Officer standing to one side of the Pilot was also laughing to himself. He'd been casually following the Pilot's thoughts. The fool. He too had his own briefing – the real one.

* * *

"Look," Bio-One had said, "I briefed the Pilot and some other officers going on this 'rescue' mission."

Bio-One told the Int-comm what he'd said to that group. "You can use them – they are primed to attack the impostor – whoever he is. You can manipulate them and the entire situation to our advantage.

"The pilot who chased the Crown Officer to Earth is in the palace, and the truth's come out, finally. He says he didn't shoot the ship down at all, but it crashed of its own accord. The pilot, Pilot-Two, still claims Tac-U-One died, but admits that he didn't search for the body." The Regent shook his head. "Says he's telling the complete truth. But you know these longtime pilots, they are tough, and even when the interrogating telepaths say they've obtained the truth, the pilot can still be holding out.

"You see, Pilot-Two may be lying and this could be Tac-U-One; I don't need to tell you what could happen if he returns."

The Int-comm officer shuddered at the memory.

Bio-One continued, "But it's also conceivable the whole thing is a ruse done by the Planetary Commandant of Earth. It's possible the Crown Officer's M-Star crash beacon survived and the wreckage was found by our people on Earth. Our Commandant on that planet is smart enough to concoct this whole hoax, in hopes of becoming 'Tac-U-One', assuming the man's legacy and inheriting his fortune. If this is so – we may need to deal with him.

"Find out what's going on and make a decision.

The Regent cautioned him, "Be careful, there's so much scrutiny from the loyal Crown people here at the capitol that we can't act openly. But remember, if Tac-U-One returns, we're all lost.

"Go with the ship and stay in communication with my Int-comm here, and let me know. The best case is the Planetary Commandant of Earth is running a scam. Second best is that Tac-U-One is ignorant of our affairs and might just walk onto that ship. And then we'll get rid of him permanently.

"You must be ready. It could be him.

"If it's a scam and you think he can fool folks – make a deal and I'll back you.

"If it's our long lost Crown Officer, use the new weaponry to destroy him.

"Are you clear on all this? Is the threat of his return sufficient motivation for you to do what's needed?"

The Int-comm officer laughed silently at the Pilot standing rigidly at his inspection station. The man was a pawn, a cat's-paw, a fool.

● ● ●

Jack couldn't stand it any longer. He gently picked up the right hand and stroked it. He crouched down and said quietly into the ear, "Come on, Dee. Wake up." He waited for a response and when there was none, he continued. "Wendy, wake up."

The fourth light bar winked off. Feeling his anxiety rise, he continued to quietly encourage.

The vital signs of the new body fluttered, settled and then spiked strongly, settling into the normal range. Relief flooded through him. Wendy opened her new eyes seconds later.

Jack had purposefully positioned himself directly in her line of sight. She looked confused, then smiled and said ever so faintly, "Jack."

"Well done, Dee." Turning to the Bio-Tech, he said, "She is certified, Identity is not public record." Jack felt better immediately; she was through and safe and he felt able to turn his mind to other things.

"Very good, sir," the Tech gave a slight frown as this was highly irregular, but a Crown Officer was virtually a law unto himself, if he wished to be.

Tac-U-One turned to the Bio-Tech. "Run the systems check on the other agent body."

Still in hyper alert, he was detecting not the slightest change in the Bio-Tech's mental patterns. If he was an enemy, he was a very capable one.

"Yes, sir."

"Major, watch the Bio-Tech closely."

"Yes, sir." The Major stepped to the Bio-Tech's side and watched everything he did.

Jack looked down at Wendy, who was slowly regaining her senses. "I feel like I've slept for hours. I'm drowsy, I feel so lovely, I could stay here forever."

Jack smiled. Yeah. Right. Transfer gets you goofy sometimes. With piranha all around, she wants to go swimming. He shook his head. "Dee, give me your hand, please."

She languidly placed her palm in his. He gently drew her to her feet and led her to the recovery room.

All eyes followed her as she glided naked across the room. There had been no interest when the body lay naked at the Recyclex, but now that this was *someone*, every man was acutely aware of her.

She handled the Jolo body as if she'd had one for centuries. The transfer was fast and without flaw and this made it "great" even for a Directory citizen – but she was native. And so they felt awe watching her, and understood why she was with the Crown Officer – he must have known, somehow.

"If you want, Dee, you can do a work out – calisthenics, what have you – so you get familiar with the body."

She smiled a dreamy smile. "All right, Jack."

He left her in the recovery room and quietly closed the door.

The Bio-Tech, with the Major at his shoulder, ejected the recessed tray from the wall and began tapping away at the control panel. The body was checked for implants and none were detected.

Tac-U-One had done all he could to make sure the Bio-Tech would not betray them.

Once again, he distracted the Bio-Tech, then depressed the right toenail and checked for signs of tampering. There were none. He looked at the tray.

Then it struck him. Step zero. He'd missed step zero.

"Help me move the body to that gurney." Tac-U-One shouted to the Bio-Tech. "Go, go, go!"

Together they muscled the agent body onto the gurney.

"Run the check again!" The Bio-Tech looked at Tac-U-One for an extended moment, then complied. The lights were green through the electronic implants check, but the mechanical scan revealed a nerve poison in a piston under the right knee. It had an adrenalin bio-trigger which activated a tiny cellular solenoid that would transfer the viscous liquid into the blood, thereby disabling the body.

Dee. If she's exercising… he ran to the recovery room.

She was resting peacefully on a cot. He left the room open so he could see her. That poison would have paralyzed but not killed the agent body. This was an attempt to capture and I-trap him.

The poison capsule was well-considered and that was slightly unnerving, as it struck him right where he lived. His life tended to involve combat on a continuing basis. That solenoid would have activated bio-mechanically without much provocation.

He and the Bio-Tech went into the recovery room with a few simple surgical instruments.

They scanned her body and found a similar device.

The Bio-Tech inserted a hairline syringe into Wendy's Jolo body and evacuated the poison. He then injected a solution to dissolve the capsule and sealed the leg.

One more trap avoided.

The check was run again on the body being prepared for his use. After a device was removed from the right knee, it was clear of foreign substances or objects.

He carefully checked the mind of the Bio-Tech once again and picked up a believable and realistic train of thought. He'd not known the trays had been tampered with. This ship contained layers of menace.

Tac-U-One was shaken. An agent survives by unpredictability, forming no set patterns for others to detect. He was forcefully reminded that anyone who cared to give it a moment's thought could predict him: he lived a life of violence. And they could cleverly use it against him. This unchanging characteristic had made him vulnerable, *again*. It placed power in the hands of his enemies. If they could tell something about your future, they could prepare for it, make it difficult, and at some point, impossible.

He looked around. There were more traps to spring and greater danger here that he'd not yet found. But with time running away like a frightened deer, he had to commit himself. He could feel the tension in the ship rising, soon it was going to come apart.

He wondered fleeting about Raubish Mink, if he was okay, if he'd delivered his "mind spring." *It'll have to be soon, my friend, to help.*

He was sure Bio-One had an Int-comm on board, ready to receive additional instructions and report results.

● ● ●

Pure terror shot through her. Until now, this lonely outpost, a tiny red star and a speck of rock, had produced nothing but routine boredom for the five Crown years she'd been responsible for it.

Their job was to receive and reroute I-trap workers. Most I-traps went to mining, research, and heavy gravity bases on remote primitive planets.

And, as she had reasonably expected, it should have continued to be boring till she departed. This wasn't to be.

She took heavy rushed breaths and her grip on the handrail was crushing it.

She'd been recruited by one of the Regent's agents for an "important post," he'd said, so important that an Int-comm officer was assigned to handle emergency reports. What emergencies? There'd never been one. This rock was the first stop for ships out-bound from a cluster of primitive planets. What could happen?

Even so, before her was something that could bring her death. She glared at the man who had logged the incident, thereby making a permanent record of it. His fatal error was that he had not immediately informed her.

She lashed out and struck the fellow squarely and he went barreling across the room, crashing into the opposing wall. Even though he was injured, no one went to help him.

But it was her own stupidity that sealed her fate. She had investigated his log entry. Minutely. It was thoroughness driven by relentless boredom. She'd gloried at the possibility that the incident could be important. Instead, it was a pit viper.

Just minutes ago she'd casually inspected the inbound/outbound log, being diligent, doing her job. It contained usual items like "Ship 122K approach and dock – time/date," then, "Ship 122K depart – time/date."

Then she'd flipped a few pages back. There was the entry, three days old. It said, "Unidentified ship exploded after drop from OS – time/date." She'd gone after it, wanted it to be something. She reviewed the digital recording on a monitor and saw what no one else had seen. The ship had been blown up by a missile. A missile. Just seconds after emerging from Other-Space. She'd never heard of something like that happening before. She exulted – this was really something. So she had added these details to the in/out log, the permanent log.

She investigated and discovered that their Int-comm officer, their prized and most valuable useless possession, had said four fatal words to the Duty Officer before he'd gone off on a drinking binge. The words were, "Tactical Unit One? Bullshit!" She discovered the Duty Officer had entered these words into the incident log – not the in/out log. By that time she was trapped; she had to continue her investigation – recover the data from her Int-comm and fully report it.

Without the exploded ship, all this might have gone away. A missile? That weapon hadn't been used for a thousand years. Something was wrong here, very wrong.

When the Int-comm couldn't be coaxed into consciousness by gentler methods, she ordered the medic to pump him full of alcohol-neutralizing agent. All this was entered into the incident log with exactness and correct spelling. It would be obvious to anyone who looked that she couldn't keep her officers under control.

Nobody gives a shit, she thought, *till something goes wrong*.

Finally sober, she asked her Int-comm, "What the hell did you mean by 'Tactical Unit One, Bullshit'? And why did you instruct the Duty Officer to enter it into the log?"

By this time, the whole base complement who weren't asleep or transferring the I-trap worker cylinders into departing ships were waiting to hear the answer.

With a chemically cleared head, the Int-comm said, "That damn ship came out of OS and blasted a telepathic message at me. It said, 'Tactical Unit One has taken control of Earth Base. He's aware of all operations. Relay to Regent on Crown Planet all haste'. Since everyone knows that particular Crown Officer is very dead, I said, 'Tactical Unit One, Bullshit!'" And he had the nerve to smile.

Now, because there was absolutely no other option, it went into the incident log.

Delay upon delay.

She ordered he relay this data to the Regent immediately. The Int-comm explained it would be just a little longer before he could send the message, his head had to clear and he had to be calm, but she would be the first to know when the message was relayed.

And that *delayed* communication, more than three days late, would mean her death. Instead of waiting for her detainment and execution orders, she jumped on one of the outbound freighters going to a major Outer World planet.

● ● ●

Before he went to transfer, Tac-U-One had to check one last thing.

"Captain, I assume you don't have any *Crown* orders for me, or you would have delivered them?"

"Quite right, sir. No orders from Crown. My *other* orders require that I take you to Crown Planet, and ignore your requests for alternate destinations. If you persist, I'm to lie to you and say we're going to the requested destination, but then still take you to Crown Planet with all possible haste. These instructions were given to me verbally by the Regent himself."

"Do you intend to follow the 'Regent's' orders, or those I give you?"

"My duty is to Crown and thus to you as his representative. The Regent is a destructive fool and if I understand what your presence and actions imply, he is *illegally* in control of the Directory. Though how he engineered this defies imagination."

"I'm glad you see things as I do." Tac-U-One paused, then said, "What would you do now to ensure my safety as I transfer?"

"I would order a lockdown of every Officer on the ship, sir."

"Please do so." Tac-U-One turned. "Major, inform your men of this and have them continue to monitor the enlisted men."

"Yes, sir," said the Captain and Major simultaneously.

The Captain contacted his Security Chief and called a silent "Alert Two," in which all the Weapons Masters were to converge on the Captain's quarters.

The Captain's office and suite were by design close to the Bridge. Two minutes later, he was called by his Security Chief. "All Weapons Masters have arrived, sir." The Captain left the Recyclex bay and entered the vertical tube, which took him to his quarters.

The Captain gave orders. "Security Chief, I need you to form a detail and have them detain, search and then remove all weapons and communication devices from all Officers on the Bridge. Then lock them in the Brig. Do it quietly and be very careful; be prepared for violent or deadly opposition."

"Captain. This is highly irregular."

"Look, I've heard all the rumors, but I assure you we have Tactical Unit One aboard this ship. Therefore my orders to you are the only legal orders we have. Be careful. Report trouble immediately."

"Yes, sir!"

"Are you with us?"

"Yes, sir. I am."

"Good. Also, rough up the Int-comm officer so he's too upset to communicate."

The Captain dropped to the Recyclex bay. With the situation as well controlled as possible, Jack made a quick check on Wendy before going to Recyclex.

•

When Wendy first woke with a tickle in her ear she felt euphoric and very... light. Light and comfortable, as if she were lying on a bed of feathers. She heard someone whispering in her ear.

Opening her eyes, she saw that different face, and for a second it puzzled her, but then she recognized it and spoke, "Jack", feeling warmth suffuse her entire body.

Although she felt very good, she realized that the transfer must have failed because she didn't feel different at all. She felt like she always felt – like herself.

She was a little confused. When she had lain down the Recyclex machine had been to her right, now it was to her left. Though observing this, she didn't grasp its significance. She was herself, as she'd always been.

Nothing had changed.

But it was comfortable to lay there a little sleepy, feeling fine, content.

Shortly, Jack came over again and helped her up from the cot. It was then she realized she was naked, but she didn't miss a step, seeming to glide across the floor. She lay down on another cot and continued to drift.

A little later she was aware of Jack and someone else doing something to her leg, but they went away.

When she came fully awake, she wondered why they'd taken her clothes off. Her eyes were drawn to the full-length mirrors that ran from floor to ceiling on three walls. She looked at her reflection but saw... someone else. Or was it? Her face looked like her face, but that was it. The body.... the *body*.... She swayed and would have fallen. But she didn't fall, she recovered effortlessly and gracefully.

Then she understood. *I've transferred, I'm in another body*. How incredibly different it was, yet how very much the same.

She stood looking at herself, finding it hard to believe what she was seeing. She slowly raised her hands to cup her breasts and turned to profile. She was stunning. She inspected her face as she stepped close to the mirror, seeing distinct, and what must be intentional, similarities to how she had looked.

Her knees went weak with the thought of her "old" body lying... dead... she guessed that was the only appropriate term. But "dead" didn't feel right at all, because she was so alive. She gazed at her new body with admiration and thought philosophically about the change. A small smile played across her lips: she could probably adjust.

She ran her hands down the sides of her body.

The door opened and Jack stepped in. Wendy turned to him in wonder and desire. Seeing her, Jack felt instant relief from the outside pressures. It is wonderful to see a person who has just transferred for the first time. And when that person is the one you love, it is doubly pleasurable.

She came into his arms and they embraced; the magnetism was extraordinary. She looked up into his face and smiled. He looked at her and the rest of the world fled, vanished by the purity of her being, her love, her presence.

"I don't have to look up so far." She murmured as she moved against him. Her lips were so soft and so near, he met them and they kissed and he felt as if they had merged and were for a short moment not two separate beings but joined.

He pulled back and looked into her eyes, into the beauty of their living emerald depths, and instead of empathy, felt a moment of pure disorienting shock – with a jolt, he looked into her with intensity and thought he saw something familiar… but he wasn't sure… how could he be sure about something like this? How could it ever be?

Consciously he thrust the thoughts away, for he had no time to explore the implications of what, in reality, was wild speculation.

"Huh," she said playfully, "you think you're glad to see me. Well, let me tell ya, buddy." She was *very* playful. "This is better than a new dress any day of the century." She pirouetted away from him to show him what she meant. "Thanks," and winked provocatively.

"You're welcome," he said as he walked to the wall and touched a control pad there. A drawer slid from the wall. "Choose something from here in your size."

She pouted. "Don't you like me?"

He couldn't suppress a smile.

There was a knock on the door and Jack opened it. "The Tech said ready when you are, sir."

"Thank you, Major." He turned again to Wendy, hating to spoil the mood but needing to inject some gravity. "This is it Dee. When you see me next, I'll have yet another face."

"You're transferring again? I was just getting used to…"

"Look, Dee. This ship is one big trap set just for me. The lure is the body out there on the warming tray. It's the one place in this whole charade they're certain I'll go. My knowing they know doesn't change it. The ending of my existence is all my enemies have come here for, and transfer is where I'll be most vulnerable. Therefore, they'll attack me in some fashion when I transfer. I have the ship partially under my control, but really, I'm like a pig going to slaughter." This was the unvarnished truth.

"What can I do to help?"

Good girl, he thought with savage pride. Not, "Oh Jack, please don't."

"Dee," he said with intensity, "you now have another very powerful tool: your body. It's very highly trained. It is, in fact, the female version of the same type of body that I retrieved from the lake bottom."

"Worth more than Earth produces in a year!" she said, amazed.

"Yes, but that's not the point. The point is I need your help and I'll need it in the next few minutes. You see, they won't expect anything from you. You're a 'native', just transferred and not a threat of any kind. I can't tell you how to help, because I don't know how the attack will come. But it will. You, my love, are the wild card."

"You said another powerful tool...?" she said.

"In addition to your new body is how smart you are."

"Oh." She looked at him and thought, "*Partners.*"

He sent an image of them back to back, fending off howling beasts. Her lips curled into a smile. Able to see it was his mental picture.

"About this body?" she asked.

"Your body has been trained with incredible fighting skills. You are now a deadly weapon and incredibly strong, capable of just about anything." This was only partially true: without training, most of the body's skills would be dormant, but if she thought she could do anything...

Wendy nodded, then quickly turned away and dressed.

CHAPTER 44

THE SECURITY CHIEF AND HIS WEAPONS Masters arrived, double time, on the Bridge and fanned out. There were ten Officers at their various duty stations – Command, Ship's Control, Navigation, Internal Communications, Weaponry, M-star Squadron Comm, Ship Integrity (a battle station) and others.

"Excuse me, sirs," the Security Chief said. "I've been ordered by the Captain to place all Senior Officers temporarily in the Brig. So please submit yourselves without resistance to my men who will cuff you, search you, and escort you there."

The Pilot, indignant and thoroughly incensed, stepped forward. "See here, Sergeant, the Captain has no authority to order the Officers to detention."

"Sir, he's declared an Emergency Circumstance."

"What emergency?"

"Sir, you know that he only has to justify the circumstance to the Admiral of the Navy."

The Pilot heard enough.

"We all know what's going on here. The Captain has been seduced—" He paused as two of Tac-U-One's newly acquired Honor Guard, in their full-dress uniforms plus blasters, entered the Bridge. "*Seduced* by this phony Crown Officer. We've humored this impostor with this 'inspection', but to let him throw me in the brig: ridiculous!"

Two by two the Weapons Masters had been moving to stand behind each Officer.

The Security Chief shrugged. "It's a legal order, sir, it came from the Captain. Now please come along without a struggle." But there was no conviction in his words. He, too, in spite of the Captain's recent words, thought he was being played for a fool.

"Enough!" shouted the Pilot. And he strode to the computer bank and punched in a code.

"Code validated. Pilot Veraque has command of Star Comet *Lonesome Voyager*."

"As you just heard, the ship's computer verifies I am now the ship's Captain. I cancel your orders."

The Officers, Weapons Masters and Tac-U-One's two Honor Guards looked at the Pilot and then amongst themselves. No one on the Bridge, regardless of rank or time in service, had ever seen a change in Captaincy done this way.

But it was legal and superseded the Captain's – or more correctly *former* Captain's – orders and the Emergency Circumstance. The Pilot was now the Captain and in charge.

"Security Chief, your detention orders are countermanded, but I retain the former Captain's declaration of Emergency Circumstance. I order you to bring the former Captain and the impostor to the Bridge."

"Yes, sir," said the Security Chief.

"Computer, where are the former Captain and the Jolo who claims to be a Crown Officer?" asked the Captain Pilot.

The computer, free of its previous orders to announce the fictitious FCI location said, "They are in the Recyclex bay, Captain Pilot Veraque."

"There you are, Security Chief. Take your Weapons Masters and fetch them here," he paused, "Not here, take *them* to the Brig."

The Int-comm felt a shaft of pure fear. Was the impostor in the transfer room already? The computer had given "Tac-U-One's" last position as being in the OS drive area, on the other end of the ship from the transfer room. He'd just assumed... how long had he been there...had he transferred already? Panic screamed through him. The Int-comm grasped the Pilot's arm and started to say....

"Sir!" barked the Senior Honor Guard to the Security Chief. "You must obey the *real* Captain's orders and take the Bridge Officers to the Brig. Do I need to remind you that your Captain was given his orders by Tactical Unit One Crown? That order cannot be countermanded by the Pilot or the ship's computer."

The Security Chief was flummoxed.

"Obey the legal Crown order now!" The two Honor Guards covered the Pilot with their blasters.

Captain Pilot Veraque spun around to face this new threat and saw the blasters pointed at his stomach.

The Security Chief remained still. He waved off his Weapons Masters, who were about to draw their side arms. The blasters the Honor Guard carried were open combat weapons and would cut the whole Bridge in half.

"This is foolishness," said Captain Pilot Veraque. "I'm in command here. You just heard the computer, the ship's legal authority, and that man claiming to be Tactical Unit One is a despicable impostor." Spittle flew from his mouth.

The faces of the Honor Guards remained unyielding. They knew what they knew. Silently, the two Honor Guards shook their heads, broadened their stances, and moved their blasters to cover the widest range of threats.

Captain Pilot Veraque felt himself weaken, and his stomach hurt. This could turn deadly, but he tried to prevail.

"You can't be serious, the Regent himself has briefed us about this impostor—" Then the need to be diplomatic flooded him. "This... person. The Regent himself investigated and verified that the person we've come to pick up is actually an opportunist taking advantage of the death of Tac-U-One by trying to step into his shoes.

"These are verified facts.

"So put your weapons *down*." His face suffused with blood as the grim looks of the Honor Guards remained unchanged. Their blasters remained motionless. Captain Pilot Veraque knew his career was at an end if he failed to handle the situation as the Regent had directed. The tension in the room between the opposing forces was palpable.

The Int-comm felt the situation slipping away from his unseen control. The Honor Guards' conviction convinced him that the man in the Recyclex bay was Tac-U-One. They knew something.

If he were an impostor, he'd have gone with the flow, tried to make a deal. This man was doing all he could to hide, confuse, misdirect and control events – and had gone straight to the Recyclex bay while the pawns were being manipulated. Classic Tactical Unit procedure.

If Captain Pilot Veraque was harmed, the Int-comm would have no buffer between himself and physical danger. Already he felt afraid. Real fear would interrupt any telepathic interstellar communication – send or receive.

The Int-comm quickly did a mind locate on the Bio-Tech and looked at his thought stream – Tac-U-One had not transferred. He had time. Oh, please let it be so. His influence must remain covert and unseen, but had to be timed correctly and that time was not quite yet.

These fools could argue about the petty power play all they wanted. He felt more settled and sat back to watch the show.

The Honor Guards kept their weapons leveled.

"Sir, he *is* Tactical Unit One Crown. He is *not* an impostor," the Senior Honor Guard said with compelling certainty. "And you will obey his orders now or I will disable you." He made a threatening gesture with his weapon.

"Now!" he barked.

The Security Chief shrugged. "The trooper may not be correct, sir—" but he never finished his sentence, because the ship lurched off the ground and accelerated away at a bone-crushing speed, throwing everyone around like dolls. Everyone but the Int-comm, who'd prepared for takeoff by sitting in an acceleration chair.

●

The Int-comm was white with terror. The long-delayed message had come across the intervening light years, and it was disturbingly clear.

"Tac-U-One has taken control of Earth. He knows everything. Abort. Abort. Abort. Do not allow Tac-U-One to board the vessel. Depart the planet!"

The Int-comm had instantly flashed the Thought Activated Controls or TAC circuitry and used *his* override code to assume direct control of the Star Comet. It abruptly accelerated away from the planet.

"Stop that," shouted the Honor Guard at Captain Pilot Veraque, "and return the ship to the surface immediately!"

Veraque looked at the Honor Guard's blast gun in wild-eyed fear. When the ship continued its acceleration the Honor Guard fired and Captain Pilot Veraque slumped to the deck, stunned and immobile.

The Honor Guard shouted, "Who's controlling this ship?"

The artificial gravity compensator whined. Those who could struggled to their feet.

He's on the ship. He knows. He knows.

Tentacles of fear slowly paralyzed the Int-comm. His mind clogged, he couldn't think what to do next. The plan. He knew there was an exact plan but couldn't remember what it was. He panicked. *I've got to do something now or I'm lost.*

What's happening?

That's the key, *find out.* He located the Bio-Tech and saw through his eyes. A man was in Recyclex. It had to be him, because the agent body was in the receiving tray. Tac-U-One was in Recyclex.

His fear was gone.

He was in Recyclex but not transferred – vulnerable, perfect. In direct line-of-fire of the new weapon.

Trap him.

He deactivated the artificial gravity. Those who'd begun to move were crushed down. He lost sight of the Recyclex room. He threw the ship out toward space.

He located the TAC control panel in the Recyclex machine in the transfer bay. On their voyage to Earth, the Int-comm had practiced this simple telepathic procedure many times. And now he did it again.

He sent a thought to the Recyclex machine with vindictive intensity.

● ● ●

A minute before, Tac-U-One led Wendy out of the recovery room, then went directly to the empty Recyclex cot and lay down. The Bio-Tech, shadowed by the Major, switched the Recyclex machine to its automatic settings and began the cycle.

Both the Major and Captain watched closely for any unnecessary action by the Bio-Tech. They'd both transferred numerous times and knew what to look for.

The new agent body was ready to receive Tac-U-One. He looked at the Bio-Tech and let himself fully relax in preparation to defend the attack when it came. As it must – very soon.

It came, in its first phase, unplanned and borne of panic. The unexpected acceleration caused everyone in the Recyclex bay to tense and grab something to steady their balance.

The abrupt loss of artificial gravity caused crushing weight on Tac-U-One's chest and recessed his eyes. With vast effort he moved his head to one side and saw bodies lying piled on each other and smashed down, pinned to the floor as he was to the cot, unable to move as the ship rocketed away from the planet.

He smiled grimly; his lips peeled away from his teeth and he couldn't draw them back together. They'd finally caught on. The Weapons Masters would soon arrive in gravity core suits to restrain him, and from there it was anybody's guess what would happen.

This attack had the feel of desperation.

Even so it was effective. But he wasn't completely defenseless. While walking up from Jeb's cabin to the lake, he had prepared a number of "mind spring" weapons.

These mind springs were serious brain benders.

The Weapons Masters aren't here.

The attack's unplanned. They aren't coming. Someone's scared to death.

With the ship accelerating this fast, they'd quickly enter Other-Space. If that happened, his difficulties would multiply. His body was pinned, but his mind was not. He quickly cast around and located the Bridge. Then he searched for the Pilot, and finally found him. But he was unconscious – interesting. Obviously he no longer controlled the ship. Tac-U-One dumped him.

Someone was using an encoded TAC to pilot the ship, a powerful telepath. This telepath's mind was an open book, how strange; the guy was very calm and sent another encoded instruction for the TAC. The telepath was free of fear and clearly thought he'd defeated Tac-U-One… had recently been panicked by him. Tac-U-One looked further…yes he was an Int-comm…had received an incoming distress message.

They've found me out.

Hope Mink's okay.

Why does this telepath think he's defeated me? But the telepath was thinking of other things. If Tac-U-One inserted an image into his mind to prompt another train of thought, he'd know it. Leave it.

Gotta try this again. Tac-U-One didn't wait for the Recyclex ejection charge that would never come. He lifted free of his body and released the energy lines to the body's control center. He drifted over and settled into the new body and took up its control center and rippled the body.

Natural transfer.

He was again physically pinned to the cot. Although stronger in this new body, he couldn't move.

Two options: wrestle control of the TAC controlling the Star Comet from the telepath. Or deliver the mind spring.

He was hit by a terror-premonition.

Tac-U-One shot the mind spring – slightly late.

The ship began to shudder and veer crazily as the mind of the Int-comm became a playground for nasty goblins, distorted spaces and non-linear time sequences. The ship was under the control of a man swallowed by horror.

But *another* TAC command had already closed within the transfer machinery. For mili-seconds it caused an immense charge to accumulate beneath both cots of the altered Recyclex circuitry, reaching a pre-designated level far above that required for transfer, and then released….

Tac-U-One blindly rocketed away from the ship, out into the far, far depths of space.

● ● ●

Wendy could not believe the strength of her new body. Now that the acceleration had diminished somewhat she was able to force her tortured limbs and knotted muscles to move and resist the still-crushing gravity load. Over the uneven landscape of bodies she crawled, toward where Jack lay on the Recyclex cot.

The attack had come and she was desperate to get to him, but it was taking too long. Far too long. If she could move why wasn't he? What were they doing to him?

The incredible weight of her body bore her flat to the deck panels many times. Each time, she continued onward. Near her goal, she was thrown aside as the ship jerked, then as she pulled her twisted arms from beneath her, it moved violently again. A sense of dread spread through her; somehow she knew before she arrived at his side that Jack was gone. Grief welled up to choke her. With a herculean effort, she forced herself up from the floor to look at him. Her tears splashed over his waxy skin.

The only reward for her agonized crawl was the view of his face and blown eyes. The pupils were enormous lifeless cavities, the iris a thin blue ring, and the whites shot through with red. It was as if the very fabric of his being had rushed out through his eyes.

So much for their adventure, their future. Grief gripped her again and shook her violently as the fight went out of her, what was the point? Her thoughts dimmed and she could no longer resist the force dragging her body down. As she slipped away, she reached out and intertwined her fingers between his. Their last joining.

● ● ●

He was sailing away through space: the ship was already an unnoticed far distant point which converged to a tiny point of light and faded out. Drifting below him was a planet, the size of a pea, and it too contracted until it merged with the kaleidoscopic arc of stars.

The danger and turmoil receded from his awareness, masked behind the violent ejection. Released from the confines of a body and its narrow concerns, he felt himself expand.

This new moment had no ties to the past, the future was ahead and the beauty in which he swam deserved exploration. He surged forward, entranced by the vastness about him – that was him. The swirling arms of the galaxy reached out to embrace him.

He was seduced by the face of eternity, to enter the stars and explore forever.

● ● ●

The crushing thrust dropped away and the Star Comet was in free fall. On the Bridge, Pilot Veraque was the first to regain consciousness.

He looked in disgust at the Int-comm floundering just above the floor. Foam was spewing from his mouth. He was moaning like a gut-shot trooper and then whimpering like a frightened child. This poor excuse for a Jolo was totally incapacitated.

"Computer, please give us a gravity curve sliding to standard."

"Invalid order. Int-comm officer has control of the ship."

However, the floating particles began to move to the floor and in a moment the gravity standard was close to normal. The Pilot got up and took the unconscious Honor Guards' blasters and side arms, then secured them with their own restraints. He wouldn't tolerate trouble from them or anyone on the ship.

What had happened here? It must have been some kind of sabotage. But how, how? It had to be the impostor. "Computer, what's the location of the man claiming to be a Crown Officer?"

"Recyclex bay." Couldn't have been him.

"Computer, take the ship to jump speed and shift to Crown Planet."

"Int-comm commands Star Comet Lonesome Voyager; course designation must be authorized by him."

"Just a few minutes ago I overrode the Captain of this ship. How can the Int-comm be in command?"

"He overrode you with a senior code."

The Pilot looked over at the Int-comm who was staring at him from the floor with blank eyes. He walked over to him and the Jolo began to scream hysterically and writhe on the deck – gravity rapidly dropped. Dribble was still coming from his mouth. The Pilot stepped away and the Int-comm became quiet – gravity became normal. He stepped closer again and got a repeat performance. This Int-comm was definitely out of commission. How?

"Computer, this is a Code Four situation. The Int-comm is unable to execute routine commands," Veraque said.

"With Bio-Tech certification of Int-comm Officer's incapacity, command will revert to the last authorized command, Captain Pilot Veraque." The Pilot gritted his teeth; this was standard but very frustrating. In war, death or imminent danger, he could override this procedure, but not now.

Others were now picking themselves up. The bound Honor Guards were glaring at him.

What's happening on this ship, he wondered? Possibly, the former Captain would have some idea, yes. The computer located him in the Recyclex bay. The Pilot tried to raise someone in the room. There was no answer.

"Security!"

"Yes, sir!" the six Weapons Masters answered in unison. His security detail, standing in ragged formation and looking disheveled, seemed willing to take orders from him without question. Good.

There were other Honor Guards roaming the ship. They could still cause trouble. He had to sort this situation out.

"Go to the Recyclex bay and report what you find. And two of you return with the Bio-Tech immediately."

"Yes, sir."

●

"They were hit pretty hard down here, sir," reported the Weapons Master to Pilot Veraque. "That's the Bio-Tech moaning over there on that stretcher. The man claiming to be the Crown Officer was in transfer. The first body is lifeless; the receptor body still has a base metabolism and shallow breathing but minimal brain activity. The transferee is 'lost'.

"I'll get two swabbies to dispose of the bodies through Hell Gate now. Two of my men are still there helping to clean the area up."

"Good," Pilot Veraque said. "What about the imposter's woman?"

The Weapons Master had seen the pitiable sight of the woman grasping the man's hand and felt sympathy for her. The man may or may not have been a Crown Officer, but she had obviously loved him. "She's still unconscious."

"Bring her to the Bridge, I need to question her."

"Yes, sir."

"What about the rest of the Honor Guard? Were there any in the Recyclex bay?"

"No, sir. I've checked the computer grid and can't find them on the ship."

Pilot Veraque looked at the two bound Honor Guards. "Where are your friends?" The Honor Guards looked blank and didn't speak.

●

Wendy could hear the murmuring of voices as she felt herself come close to consciousness and then drift. Voices.

"Get those swabbies in here," ordered the Weapons Master. The men arrived.

"Pick that woman up and lay her on that spare cot." The swabbies obeyed. "Carefully now."

She became fully aware but ordered her body to simulate unconsciousness. It seemed to know what she wanted. She lay awake listening and did not resist when Jack's hand was pried from her own.

"Load these dead bodies on that stretcher, take them to the Hell Gate and throw them in." The swabbies transferred the bodies to a stretcher and left the Recyclex bay.

Wendy waited till the Senior Weapons Master and all but two of his men left with the Bio-Tech.

A Weapons Master gently shook her by the shoulder. She let him think consciousness was returning.

At the optimum moment she exploded into action. Her body was trained to combat and so she decided who to strike first and let her intention flow into the motion. The Weapons Masters were taken by surprise. They both went down. Wendy quickly restrained them.

One body on that stretcher was still breathing. *Jack had a chance.* And she was going to make sure he got every chance to survive. She took off running in the direction they went with the bodies.

❋

The beauty of the stars was captivating. But the beginnings of boredom dimmed his enjoyment. He felt a blow to his side. What was that? Strange, he viewed his spherical periphery – and of course – he had no body. Bam. It hurt. Intense pain in his side.

The joy of the stars was receding and no longer had his full attention. Once again there was wicked pain in his side. But he had no side. He didn't have anything; *I'm floating free in space.*

❋

She marched purposely up to the men hauling the load. One of them was brutally kicking the bodies now flopped down in the hallway. The blows were raining fast and furious to the ribs and stomach of the body still breathing.

"Stop! Stop kicking that body!" Wendy screamed at the man. He frowned at her but didn't even slow down. He didn't understand English. She grabbed him and flung him away. He sailed fifteen feet and tumbled twenty more.

"Jack, I'm here, Jack." She got down on her knees and pushed aside the top body and straightened the limbs of the breathing one. She cradled his head in her lap. "Jack, Jack, I need you. Jack, you need to come and get this body. It's waiting here for you, Jack. I don't know what they've done to you, Jack, but I know you can, you can… overcome this." The body did not stir.

Somehow she needed to get his attention. She put her lips directly to his ear.

"I need to talk to you, Jack. Come back, Jack. There's something I have to tell you. Something you need to know." Still the body didn't move. But, now, she had the vague sense that someone was listening. That she had captured his attention. She redoubled her intensity if not her volume. "Jack, I need to explain something, I want you to hear this." There was noise down the long spiral passage, and she knew without a doubt who it must be.

"Tac-U-One," Wendy said with intensity into the body's ear, "you're needed on deck. Tactical Unit One Crown, you have a mission to finish. You've got a job to do."

The sound of multiple feet thudding against the deck became louder. The swabbie on his ass forty feet away let out a yell.

The pounding boots kept coming. "Jack, come back. Come back!" She knew he was out there somewhere, felt him, loved him.

The stun charge took her full in the chest.

●

A voice. A murmur. Words, his name? And then warmth, at once familiar, but from where. "…you have a mission to finish!" What did he have?

Who was talking, where was that voice coming from? Someone was talking to him? Where?

Wendy!

There was a rapid shift of location, the stars were gone. There it was again, the pain in the side.

Abruptly he was back in the Recyclex room. His memory came flooding back. There were no bodies on the Recyclex cots. Where had they taken them? He had to move fast.

●

The injured swabbie got up off the deck, roughly helped by a Weapons Master. He wiped blood from his mouth.

"That bitch attacked me from behind. I want her bought up on charges!"

"You men hurry up and dump these bodies through the Gate," said one Weapons Master. "Pilot Captain's orders." Then they returned to the bridge, dragging the stunned woman between them.

When the security detail rounded the curve and were out of sight, the swabbie viciously put the boot to the body the crazy woman was talking gibberish to.

"It's good to kick the shit out of this guy." Taking his rage out on the thing she cared about. "That bitch!" he shouted, booting it in the face. "That hurt my toe!" But he stopped kicking.

"All right, let's get going." They picked up the discarded body and flopped it on top the other, raised the loaded stretcher between them and pushed on toward the high-capacity disposal room, the only one large enough on the ship to dispose of a body. Hell Gate.

One man said, "I wonder why the Pilot Captain wanted these two bodies trashed. Just look at the one underneath, a billion crowns wouldn't buy it. Hell, I'd spend a lifetime as a Glarian Slug just to wear a body like that for a single week." The violent, injured swabbie didn't respond.

They hadn't gotten far when he dropped his end of the stretcher and resumed viciously kicking the body in the ribs to show the idiot carrying the other end of the stretcher that even though the body was breathing, it wasn't alive.

"That bitch was talking to a dead man, you moron. Don't you see how dead it is? If someone kicked you like I just did, and you were there, wouldn't you do something to stop it?"

"Yeah, I'd try to stop you."

"Right. That's right! Course I'm right. Then this one's dead but still breathing."

"You should show more respect, neither one of us will ever have a body like that. I'm just a Norm, not one of these high mucky muck Jolos; it's one life for me and back to the reincarnation roulette. Forget as you go, that's my motto."

They proceeded toward the disposal room near the "base" of the ship where the Normal Space (NS) engines were located. Disposal simply meant dumping the bodies through the interface into the infernal flames that were the ship's NS propulsion. Quick, clean, final.

The one swabbie said to the angry one, "This stiff is givin' me the creeps. It's still breathing through its nose and moving around a little."

"A muscle twitch is all that is." The other stared back. "Look, the Pilot said they had some trouble with the transfer. It's dead but still breathing – do I have to kick the shit out of it some more to show you that there's no one home?" The other shook his head. "It'll quit sucking air in a minute or two, so forget it."

"Yeah, I guess you're right, but it still gives me the creeps. This was the body that Crown Officer was supposed to take, right?" Swabbie nodded. "There'll be trouble over this, mark my words."

"Will you shut up? The whole ship knows he was a fake."

"Doesn't matter. You know how this shit works. And here we are stupidly destroying evidence." He shook his head.

"If you don't shut your hole, I'll throw you in after these two," angry swabbie said viciously, grinning evilly.

"You animal; just go ahead and try." He shuddered at the thought. "We'll be dragged in on whatever inquiry there is, you can be sure of that. And who gets the chop? The Captain? Oh no, not him. The Pilot? No, no, not him either! Then someone remembers those swabbies that tossed out the bodies and says, 'What about those two swabbies?' My, my, and there's our heads on the chopping block."

They fell silent as they negotiated the corner, through the door and into the disposal room. It was, as always, hotter than hell. No matter what they did, there was always bleed-through, and the thought of all that energy just the other side of the bulkhead was unnerving.

● ● ●

Finally, the Bio-Tech was revived by the medic on the Bridge. The Bio-Tech took one look at the Int-comm Officer still gibbering on the Bridge deck and agreed to certify the Pilot as Pilot Captain.

Pilot Captain Veraque restored stable gravity and put the Star Comet into power acceleration, course set for Crown Planet.

"Pilot Captain?"

"Yes, Bio-Tech." The tech had just helped restore him to his Captaincy and so he was inclined to be a little more gracious to him than usual.

"For what it's worth, I believe we had Tactical Unit One Crown on the ship. He was going to transfer when everything went to hell."

More of this shit. "I was personally assured by the Regent himself that this man was an impostor. That ends this matter."

"Sir, the former Captain and the senior man of the Honor Guard both thought he'd proved himself – initially neither man thought it could be him, but they changed their minds."

"Thank you, Bio-Tech. Back to your post."

● ● ●

"Those were four deep breaths that body just took, don't tell me that..."

"Shudduppppp!" The angry one screamed.

The Other-Space klaxon blared. OS velocity was being approached. They had as little as five minutes before the jump. Oh shit! They had to be done here at Hell Gate and back on station and strapped in. Soon. They both felt pressured for time, but hurrying in this room could kill you. Who was the sadistic bastard who designed this contraption anyway? There were two big doors set into the wall with a reinforced rim bordering all around. Open the doors and all there is between you and instant death was an energy field, a field that protected you from the inferno of the raging NS engines.

To get rid of the trash you just throw it in, but if the trash hits the field and you still have hold of it you get fried too.

Hell Gate.

Small stuff was okay, but the big floppy stuff like a "just dead" body or a breathing dead body could kill you if you weren't careful. Just a *fzzt* and you're gone.

"It don't matter how many times you tell me to shut up, it still spooks the hell out of me to trash a body that's still breathing; and take a look at it, I swear it cost a bloody fortune, maybe more than this whole ship." He couldn't stand to destroy something so valuable. "What ya say we try to wake the guy up, maybe he's just, well, unconscious or something."

"If you say one more thing about this dead body," angry Swabbie gave it another vicious kick just to emphasize his point, "I swear I'll kill you." His voice was low and menacing.

He wanted to throw a retort back at this guy but his throat was too dry.

"Okay, let's heave the one on top first. And just to make your happy, I bet you the other one will stop puffing before we heave it through." They stepped up and each took an ankle and wrist. "We do it on three, okay." He got a nod. They back swung and then forward. "One." Again. "Two." A bigger swing. "Three!" And the body went into oblivion.

The *breathing* body, instead of slowing down, was moving slightly from side to side and continued slow and steady breaths as they picked it up.

"I don't want to do it, it's not right – they shoulda put it back in stasis." There was murder in the other's eyes. So the swing began.

"Here we go, on three again. And hold on tight; this thing is sweating like a pig."

"One." Small swing.

"Two." Further back and further out.

"Three." The body was swinging toward the gate.

●

Jack heard someone counting slowly, but it was unreal and it faded. What he could feel was heat, but that was it.

Then he heard voices, but as he tried to catch the meaning, it slid away. Pressure, he felt the pressure. Then he was arcing through the air and it felt good, felt cooler on his skin. He heard "two" and there had been a "one," yes, and a swing. "Three." Nooooooooooo.

The concerned swabbie couldn't go through with it. He let go the ankle and grasped the wrist with both hands as the body launched toward the inferno, then yelped in pain as one of his wrists was held in a crushing grip. He'd set his feet to stop the body going through the gate, so when he suddenly felt the enormous back pressure from the body itself, he was barely able to keep his balance.

Not so with the other swabbie. The motion pivoted him toward the gate and he swung violently inward, trying to grasp onto the slippery wrist. He hung there, on the edge, for just a second. His scream lingered long after it ceased to exist.

●

The body lay on the deck just outside the lip of Hell Gate. The swabbie jumped forward and pulled it back away from the doors and the inferno. It was a close thing for them all. *Lucky thing only one of us went through. And I'm glad it was him.*

The body went into a fit, shaking violently.

The shaking subsided and the eyes opened. He looked around and recognized the incinerator room.

The one, two, three, a launch of his own. It scared him.

"You must be the guy who saved me."

"Yes, sir, I have ta say, your powers of deduction are unfathomably deep."

And the swabbie and Tac-U-One rolled around laughing hilariously.

"We gotta get going, sir."

"What, and leave all this?" Again they dissolved into mirth.

"But sir, the OS klaxon sounded a few minutes ago." That brought him back to his senses. There was a leg of a mission to complete.

"Thanks for your help, sailor."

"My pleasure, sir, I knew you weren't gone."

But Jack was gone.

He jumped to his feet and dove down a circular passage toward the tube and took this to the Bridge.

"Tactical Unit One Crown on deck!" he shouted.

Everyone stiffened to attention, even the Pilot. One of the security men held a restrained Wendy, who was still feeling the after-effects of being stunned.

"Jack!" Wendy said in shock and wonder. No one but Jack understood her. He flashed a smile.

Pilot Captain Veraque, intent on achieving OS, was only momentarily distracted.

"Please, if you wish to continue this farce, do it in the brig."

The Pilot Captain was fully aware that, to have any chance of surviving the theatrics of this impostor, they'd have to be in OS with Crown planet their unalterable destination.

"Weapons Masters, seize that man and take him to the brig." But they'd heard what the Bio-Tech had said to the Pilot and hesitated.

The Int-comm, who was slowly coming out of his stupor, heard the command that froze his heart and revitalized his survival instinct. Where'd this freak come from? The Jolo on the Recyclex cot had been hit with such a massive ejection charge he should still be outward bound.

The Int-comm frantically shook his head, trying to clear it. They say Tac-U-One is hard to kill. Nooo.

Startling everyone, the Int-comm shouted in a shrill voice. "That's not a Crown Officer. He's an intruder, an impostor. Weapons Masters seize him!"

There was confusion. Three orders, one to attention, one to seize, and then another. The Weapons Masters hesitated. Tac-U-One reached out and took the Weapons Masters hand weapon and dashed toward the Pilot.

The security personnel across the Bridge were willing to let the Officers fight it out amongst themselves, but when Tac-U-One made the dash, they tagged him as the enemy and began to raise their disrupters.

Jack stunned one man and he dropped.

Wendy had caught Jack's message just before he made his move. Her legs were in motion as the Weapons Masters were bringing their weapons to bear. Her perfect choreography broke an arm. The energy blast fizzled and the weapon skittered away.

Tac-U-One grabbed the neck of the Pilot. "Decelerate the ship or you're dead." The Pilot struggled and tried to resist. The pressure on his neck increased to an intolerable level. He'd never felt pain like this.

"Do it now or I'll snap this unbreakable Jolo neck of yours."

With a strangled voice, the Pilot backed off the ship's speed, fast.

Jack looked over to the Int-comm Officer who'd grabbed Wendy from the disabled security guys and was trying to use her as a physical shield.

"I'd no idea a Jolo of any status was low enough to use a woman as a shield," Tac-U-One said. The Int-comm held on for dear life.

Jack looked at Wendy and raised his eyebrows fractionally. Wendy moved and the Int-comm smacked into the wall with brutal force. Wendy smiled.

"It really works, Jack, even with my hands tied."

Jack cut the wrist and ankle ties of the Honor Guards. "Get the men to the bridge immediately. And find the Captain and get him here, too."

"Jack, can I make a suggestion?" Wendy asked with amusement.

"What?"

"Would you like to put some clothes on?"

"Good thinking."

The situation on the bridge was tense for a few minutes as Jack and Wendy secured the scene.

The Honor Guard was located and arrived quickly, bringing a jump suit for the Crown Officer.

"Sir, after the gravity was restored I saw both bodies on the Recyclex cot and the eyes were blown! Everyone knows that's a sure sign you're not coming back. You were gone!"

The Honor Guard had piled into a combat ship in the Star Comet's space dock and were waiting for the moment to escape. "We were going to spread the news of your return and the Regent's betrayal," explained the man.

Jack had a private moment with his girl. "You pulled me back, Dee." She looked at him. "I was gone otherwise. You called me back." He shook his head. "How did you know to do that?"

"I didn't 'know' anything, Jack. I just wanted you back."

"Your instincts were correct. One reason we always cremate the old body after transfer is that a person can still have attention stuck on a previous body.

"I'd just transferred to the new one when I was blown out of it. When you started calling to me, even though I was far away, I heard it." Once again he looked at this woman and wondered.

"When we've a moment, you have a duty to do with the other remains."

"Okay."

CHAPTER 45

Tac-U-One assembled all the interested parties in the Captain's briefing room.

He looked at the Int-comm.

"I'm sure when you have a chance, you may feel concern for your future. Please put your mind at ease. You'll never have to answer to Bio-One for your incompetence," he said.

"Under the 'crucial status' battle clause I sentence you to twenty years in an I-trap."

"You can't do that!" he spluttered.

"It's done. You're an imminent threat."

"I don't care who you are! You'll never get the best of my master – his weapons will destroy you."

"Bio-Tech, I-trap and dump him immediately."

"Yes, sir." Tac-U-One caught the eye of an Honor Guard and nodded. They took the struggling Int-comm away.

Tac-U-One secured control of the ship's computer under himself and the Captain.

"Pilot, you heard what these other men had to say, yet you remained convinced that I was a fraud. Please tell everyone here why."

The Pilot was shocked that the imposter would allow the Regent's damning facts to be spread on the ship.

"Here's why I still think you're an imposter." He recounted his interview with Bio-One word for word.

"How did Bio-One look when he told you these things?"

"He looked… certain and secretive."

"How did he sound?"

"Adamant."

The Pilot listened to the testimony of the others on ship, and to Tac-U-One's surprise, changed his allegiance. "Sir, it really is you!" He was very emotional. Remorseful.

"Pilot. When we get to Earth. I want you to oversee the recovery of my M-star."

"Yes, sir. I'll do that."

"Good."

Tac-U-One ordered the ship's return to Earth.

"Gentlemen, I wanted our differences settled before addressing the entire ship's complement. Let's go."

Tac-U-One called an all-hands conference in the star docks, the only space large enough to hold all personnel. Though the ship was enormous, there were only seven-hundred people on board; it was not being used as a troop carrier.

Tac-U-One stood on the wing tip of a docked M-star in an Admiral's gray formal. "Hello, I hope some of you have heard of me, my name is Tactical Unit One Crown." The listeners dropped to one knee, stunned by what they'd just heard.

"Please, no formality. Your Captain has given me a formal greeting and that will satisfy my need for protocol for the next hundred years or so."

There were some polite chuckles from the crowd, but they were too awed to do anything but listen and obey.

"What I say now will shock some of you; to some it will be the missing piece to the puzzle, and all will make sense.

"The Int-comm Officer, the Pilot of this ship, and personal instructions from the Regent himself were to I-trap me, kill me or if I were in fact an imposter, to make a bargain with me to impersonate Tac-U-One. Those were the 'Regent's' direct orders.

"He wants me dead or gone."

Tac-U-One looked out over the assembled ranks of men and women.

"A judicial proceeding has just been completed.

"I sentenced the Int-comm to I-trap for twenty years."

There was stillness in the crowd, as the loss of any Jolo's freedom was an unusual thing.

"I've never sentenced a being to this before."

He bowed his head for a short time.

"The Pilot gave his reasons for his attack. Briefly, he was deliberately given false and misleading date by Bio-One. He acted upon it as any of us would have.

"The Pilot was presented with the facts and changed his mind.

"He was exonerated."

The crew stayed at attention.

"Please stay with me as I give you some recent history."

Jack told them an edited version of his time on Earth. They listened, dumbfounded. He ended with, "You've all heard the rumor I'm sure? Tac-U-One is hard to kill?" There was a scattering of laughter.

"Bio-One has usurped control of the Directory." There were gasps at this. "Power was not legally passed to him as you've been led to believe. At the time of my disappearance, I was investigating him for crimes of treason.

"I've substantiated those charges. Any one of which would send him to Prison Planet. He now openly perverts Crown policy on Jolo qualifications. This crime alone would be the end for him. He can't afford my return to the Directory as he knows I will denounce him."

"We may be at war, a civil war, in the near future. My mission is to find Crown and reassert his rule." Tac-U-One said. "At this time there's a decision for you to make, a side to take, a leader to follow. Let me assure you that one is not the other. Crown rule ensures the future of this culture. Bio-One will leave a wasteland similar to the desolation in his own soul.

"Your decision must be made now – those who want to stay with Bio-One will not be eliminated, but shipped off in a life boat. Those who intend to come with me and serve Crown are welcome. If you come with me under pretense, to spy for Bio-One, your fate will not be kind.

"Those who wish to continue in Bio-One's service step over there." There was some movement in the ranks and about twenty of the crew separated out. One of the twenty stepped forward and addressed the rest of the crew in a disparaging tone of voice.

"This Jolo is not Tac-U-One, the Regent has told us he is dead and that's good enough for me." A slow, insolent smile spread across his face. Looking at the crowd and making eye contact with as many as he could, he continued. "Some of you know me as one of the finest Telepaths around. If this Jolo is Tac-U-One, then he should be able to resist my mind probe, if he can't then, he's a fraud." His voice dripped sarcasm. "We all know from the comic books and novels we've read that Tac-U-One is a 'super-agent' and invulnerable to all forms of attack – my mind probe will expose this super-fraud!"

He turned to look at Tac-U-One who stood above him about twenty feet away. The Telepath riveted his mental energy onto him and began his attempt to overwhelm with great confidence. After thirty seconds of this, Tac-U-One faced the crowd. "Look, this is the last call for those leaving the ship. If you're going I want you gone now."

Though Tac-U-One was speaking, all heads were turned to the fellow who had issued the challenge. He was slowly sinking to the floor and finally slumped into unconsciousness.

"Those of you who go, are going as is and must leave immediately." One person tried to return to the crowd and was stopped by a guard who had moved into place at Tac-U-One's prior instructions. The guard got the Jolo's bunk assignment, for later inspection.

They were held on the ship for twenty-four hours. The rejects from Earth's Directory staff were added and they were shipped off to the Outer-Worlds.

●

"Come on, Dee, I'm going to take you out for orientation." There was an imminent sunrise and they hurried out to catch it.

Once outside the ship that again looked like native rock, they strolled over the uneven terrain hand in hand, just enjoying each other's company and not saying a word.

The sun was inching its way above the easterly elevation. Minutes ago Wendy had been looking at that giant furnace from space, and now here it was approaching over the horizon. Spreading light in its wake and casting warmth across the landscape. From space the sun was just another star, but on Earth it had a different role, and to Wendy there was a vast emotional difference between the two.

Jack had a few minutes to reflect on the ease of transfer which Wendy had achieved. The first transfer was sometimes used as a gauge an Identity's power. Wendy would be one of the greats.

There was a subtle change in his communication to her. He'd never been patronizing, but she was due respect for what she'd accomplished.

"Dee, how do you like your new body?"

"I love it." She looked at him. "I wouldn't have made it in the old body?"

"Probably not."

She settled even more. Taking the old body to Hell Gate was like severing all ties to the past.

"Walking out here brings me 'back to Earth' sort of, but I still feel great. Jack, it's so wonderful, I just never imagined this could really happen."

"There's a lot of significance placed on the first transfer. If you'd transferred at one of the Recyclex centers in the Directory, you'd have made headlines in the sector paper. It's long been held that only great

Identities have an easy first transfer. It's a good indication that you'll go far, Wendy, my girl."

"Are you joking, Jack?"

"No, Dee, this is for real. Let me be the first to congratulate you on your transfer."

Wendy smiled brightly. "Wow. Gives a girl something to think about."

Jack explained her rights as a Jolo and a Directory citizen.

"There's some things to be careful of with your new body."

She frowned.

"Nothing bad. This model is very advanced and has been set at peak performance – by my own personal trainer. You could run a marathon now and get only slightly winded. The body's been trained for combat. To properly access that potential you need to be trained as well. But learning those skills will be quick and easy.

"It's like exchanging drivers in a car. A race car driver would be able to get the most out of a high performance vehicle, but put a housewife in the same vehicle and the result wouldn't be the same. The same applies here.

"Your challenge is to rise to and exceed your body's training. You up to it?"

"Guess we'll find out." She smiled

Right there, to give Wendy an idea of what she could do, Jack directed her through a full routine of calisthenics until she was panting for breath.

"After two hundred pushups, I can feel the exertion of energy, yet I feel I could go on all day."

"You could."

Jack pulled her up to him and slid his arms around her. "Dee, you're a wonderful girl. Six months ago you knew almost nothing about any of this and now you have a new body. I don't know anyone who could've kept pace and come out on top. You amaze me."

"Thanks Tac." They fell to laughing.

They continued on. Soon they were out of sight of the ship.

"I feel as if I was born to this, that I belong, that the Directory is my home, even sight unseen, and that my life, *my lives* on Earth were an interlude that's over. Even with everything so new and different, I feel at home and comfortable with it all. And the language, it's so easy to learn."

She pressed her body hard into his. "And I want you, Jack; I want you, now." Her eyes were fierce with lustful innocence. There were things he could do, even should do, but he knew what they were going to do.

They looked around the rugged trail and couldn't find anything remotely suitable. They had a foot race back to the ship and were both laughing hilariously by the time they reached the Captain's Port.

Realizing they had to be discreet, Jack said, "Grab us some food, Dee, and come to my quarters. We'll plan our last day on Earth".

They fooled no one.

CHAPTER 46

Later that morning Tac-U-One gathered the Captain and the other ship's execs into the conference room. The twenty-nine men of the Honor Guard had been formed into a permanent unit he would personally train.

He'd sent them along with Wendy to the gym. With the program he outlined, they'd all be challenged – invited to exceed their imagined physical limitations.

The room was full. Tac-U-One was seated when they arrived, which was a break in the usual military protocol and a little unnerving for those who were used to the chatter that usually occurred prior to the arrival of the senior officer. The officer was on time or late, but never entered the room early.

"Gentlemen, I'm aware of the breach of military protocol. I run the Tactical Unit and it's not a branch of the military. We're organized and disciplined, but some of your 'formalities' I won't bother with.

"In fact, here's something that will startle you, but it'll help you settle into my style of command.

"You've heard of the Tac-U-One missions, maybe read about them in the papers?" They nodded. "Well, each one of those stories you read is a fictionalized account of a real mission. Anything you read is more than three hundred (Crown) years old. And only the declassified missions were ever released.

"Who here has read any of these things?" Everyone raised their hands. He was a little taken aback.

"Really, you've all read those stories?"

"Yes, sir!"

"Well, thanks. But my point is; no one ever knows Tac-U-One on a mission, do they?" There were reflective looks and then slow nods.

"I'm just not used to having my ass kissed and I don't even like the whole salute thing. But, gentlemen, one prerogative I am going to insist on is that you get used to me and not the other way round. Is that clear?"

"Yes, sir!"

"See, there you go again." They laughed with him.

"About the chain of command. It's probably necessary, but in my experience it can get kind of sticky on the way up. Let your men know I'll talk to them if they have something they feel I need to know. Don't qualify what I just said. Give it to them as I gave it to you. Okay?"

"Yes, sir."

"I can't hear you." Then before they could respond, he held up his hand and said, "Joke."

"What I need from everyone aboard ship is a complete debrief. The Bio-Comp on Earth has linked to the ship's computer and each of your personal terminals has an extensive set of questions that need to be answered.

Jack gave them the general outline and then concluded, "Please add anything else you think I need to know. Take your time, be thorough. I need your help to catch up on the past nine years."

Jack briefed them in detail as to why he knew a coup had occurred and the impossibility of Crown going on sabbatical.

The Captain had a question. "Sir, I believe all you have told us. But it leaves me with one question." He paused as if to mentally prepare for the reaction to what he would say.

"Have you considered that Crown did give power to the Rege— ah, I mean Bio-One? Is there no scenario where that is true?"

This was, in fact, the only possibility that Tac-U-One had not considered, and this independent suggestion struck him with intimidating force. He sat still, his face expressionless. Incidents from his past skittered through his mind as if in an attempt to invalidate all possibility of the suggestion.

Crown's words came back to him, "Tac-U-One, if you are loyal to me and serve the people of the Directory you can be certain of my support." This was said soon after being promoted to the head of the Tactical Unit; thousands of years ago. Crown said something similar when he began the institution of Crown Officers. Tac-U-One was the first to place "Crown" after his post title.

There'd been times in the intervening years where others had tried to undermine him and destroy his position of power. Crown had been fed distortions and falsehoods about his activities and words, but the truth had always come to light. Trust is what existed between Crown and his "primary problem-solver." They were both aware of the jealousy that this created in some Jolos and at times, had to handle the adverse effects of this.

In every case, Tac-U-One had never failed to deliver his best efforts for Crown. This had resulted in successful missions nineteen out of twenty times, and in the end, not one major failure.

Except the last one.

If there was one thing in the whole Directory that Tac-U-One was certain of, it was that he still had Crown's support wherever he was.

"Captain, I've been in the Tactical Unit for more than five thousand years and have never failed Crown's trust." He let that sink in.

"Captain, how long have you been Jolo?"

"Sir, I don't see what that has to do..."

He was cut off by a raised hand. "Answer the question, please."

"Nearly nine hundred years, sir, and never a demotion," he said with rightful pride.

Tac-U-One nodded.

He then addressed everyone at the table. "Are there any fifteen hundred year vets here?"

There was no response.

"You, Captain, have an impressive career, and should be proud of it, and so should many others sitting here be proud of their own careers. If I were to believe that Crown no longer supported me, I would fail that trust, and fail him. I would be disobeying his last orders, orders I'll carry out."

"His first words to me will be, 'Where the hell have you been?'"

● ● ●

Jack had been cloistered with Norman at the Colosseum concluding all his business, including disposition of the remaining staff.

"We've rounded up all the DFE – those thugs who grabbed Wendy and were rounding up whole villages in China, South America and Africa. They're nothing but rapists and murderers."

"You got them all?" Jack asked, surprised.

Norman nodded.

"How'd you do that?"

"Boltax had them chipped and we tracked down and detained them."

Jack looked disgusted, "Get rid of those chips." Norman's eyebrows shot up. Jack continued, "Only a suppressive government tracks its people. The Outer Worlds are constantly trying to get everyone nailed down. Hell, Norman, I own a factory that distributes chip killing technology out there for free."

Norman had not lost his frown.

"Honesty, decency and goodwill, these things can only thrive when someone is free. Nail him down and he'll act like an animal."

"What should we do with the DFE?"

Jack looked steadily at Norman, "Administrator, I have other responsibilities."

● ● ●

Norman and the Bio-Comp had located two very impressive interstellar ships secreted in the mountains near Los Angeles.

They'd been brought there by Bio-One's spies, unbeknownst to Boltax. Jack was tempted to take them with him, but they were the spoils of Earth and should stay here. Jack speculated on the possible ramifications for Earth in light of recent events.

"The most important program for Earth is the making of Immortals. I don't believe this planet will fully stabilize until a good portion of the population understands on a personal level that the environment they die out of is the one they're born into a few days later. That they're responsible for their own future.

"Immortals created by Recyclex from within the cultures of Earth will reinforce and expand this awareness."

Jack had one last debt to discharge. "Bio-Comp, can you please connect me with Judge Bonner. The Salt Lake Judge who granted my emancipation."

"Yes, sir."

"And please make sure the Judge knows without a doubt who it is that's calling, I don't have time for long explanations."

"Yes, sir."

"Thank you." Jack looked at Norman. "Administrator, you need to institute a functional ethics and justice system that resembles what the words define." Jack and Norman discussed for some minutes what needed to be done.

"Judge Bonner for you, sir," said the Bio-Comp.

"Judge Bonner, how are you?"

"I'm well. Are you really Jack Cousins, the winner of the Fight for Immortality?"

"Yes, I'm the same person, but as you know the winner of the competition won the right to transfer to another body. I've done so."

"So it's actually real, a person can continue, doesn't die…. It's not a scam?"

"Judge, I am that boy who won the Fight. I've changed bodies now, but I'm the same person who stood before you to plead for my emancipation."

"Well good. I was gratified to see the boy –er, you – do well. Not to be rude. But I must say it's difficult to believe I'm now talking to Jack Cousins."

"I can understand it being hard to believe. Do you recall the last time I earned your attention you shed a single tear?

"On a personal level, only experiencing a transfer yourself can dispel all doubts about immortality."

That mention of the tear was persuasive evidence for the Judge; it hadn't been reported by the press.

"For the sake of this conversation, I'll assume you are who you say you are."

"Thank you, Judge. I'm offering you a judicial appointment within the Directory administration on Earth. Are you interested?"

There was silence. Then the Judge said, "It seems you've come up in the world, my boy."

Jack laughed. "Yes, Judge, I have. But I'm leaving the planet today, so this offer is of short duration."

"You need a decision on this matter now?" he said with incredulity.

"Yes, Judge, I do. You might say this is a 'banister' moment where one must strike immediately to achieve the desired result."

The Judge smiled at this reference to the most pivotal moment in his court room. And took the hint, a decision was needed immediately. "I am definitely interested."

"We need to train the senior Judge Advocate for Earth in Directory jurisprudence. I was impressed with your skill at the bench and personal stability – I don't believe another Judge on Earth would have acted as you did.

"As I said earlier, I'm in your debt, Judge, and would like to discharge it by offering you something of value – the chance to bring real ethics and justice to planet Earth."

Judge Bonner was speechless. The offer took his heart. All his life he'd endeavored to be fair and just, but worked within a system and with other people who made it nearly impossible to achieve. Now, because of a kindness to a mere boy (extraordinary though he had been), he had the opportunity to fulfill his life's dream.

"Judge?" Jack prompted quietly.

"Yes, I'm sorry. I mean, yes, I will accept your offer."

"Good, Judge. Please conclude all your business there in Salt Lake City and report with your wife, if she wishes to accompany you, to the Administrator at the Colosseum in Los Angeles on Monday of the coming week."

"I will. And thank you."

"You're welcome, Judge. You'll receive full training in Directory Codes and Procedures. Earth needs a man like you in this position."

● ● ●

The sun warmed them as they walked the gardens outside the Colosseum. Jack was anonymous on Earth again, and this suited him well.

"I took some big risks to get us where we are today, Administrator." Jack said. "You've a right to know what they were."

"If you think so, Jack."

Tac-U-One gave Norman the details of his trip on the Star Comet.

"You always have the best parties, Jack," joked Norman.

"Sorry I didn't invite you."

"Well, I was a tad busy." Norman smiled, then continued, "On another note, I'm so happy about Wendy."

"Yes. She really saved me. I would have kept going if she hadn't drawn me back."

"Sounds like she's the girl for you."

"Yes, it does."

"I've left you the ship's Bio-Tech. I don't fully trust him, but he never took any direct action against me. He wanted a chance to redeem himself, and I know the Bio-Tech here is poorly trained."

"Thanks, Jack, we do need him."

When it came to goodbye, it was hurried; both Norman and Jack were too busy to draw it out.

"Thank you for taking on this job, Norman. Earth may not make it; you'll have to be courageous."

"You have your job, Jack, now I have mine."

And he really did have it, Jack noted. As if he'd been waiting all his life to do something of real value.

"*Elon dorea larr gere.*"

They hugged and parted.

● ● ●

Jack went directly to the crash site in the Wasatch Mountains of Utah. Pilot Veraque was supervising the salvage of his M-star. He would pull the registration panel and verify the ship was built for Tac-U-One.

They were just pulling it from the depths when he arrived. Even in its current state, the technology it carried could still be a threat if salvaged by someone from the Outer-Worlds. But he was not sure that was his only motive, or the real one.

● ● ●

Wendy was there waiting for him. She hadn't seen her parents yet. *I have to say goodbye to my parents*, she thought. *Then I'll be free to go. And I won't look back.* It wasn't going to be easy to face her parents. Even though her features were similar, her overall appearance was vastly different. She'd incinerated her "old" body. What if her parents wanted to bury it? *I couldn't face that.*

It's strange, she thought, *how restrictive Earth has become. I want to go "out there."* Adventure, Jack said. She smiled.

Always on Earth she'd felt slightly in danger – a feeling only noticed by its absence. The Internet, print news and television were a constant barrage of what could "happen" to a young girl. Nothing could happen to her now, nothing at all.

Having a body that was stronger than any human on Earth was a heady, if short-lived, thrill.

She looked at Jack talking to his men. Ten years ago this man had been a seven-year-old boy. Now the leaders of Earth and starship Captain's defer to him.

The deference shown by the ship's crew was a little disconcerting. To her he was Jack, an amazing, wonderful, warm and amusing man. To the people of the Directory, he was Tac-U-One, a myth, a legend, a pantheon figure. He was the white knight, the defender of freedom.

Interestingly, no one Wendy had met on the Star Comet had ever encountered or even seen Tac-U-One before.

Jack made an offhand remark that Crown had handled the PR aspects of his career. When on mission, he rarely met people who knew him as Tac-U-One. So he was a public figure without ever being one, in a literal sense.

There was, of course, that about him that set him apart. He simply was himself, or he was whoever he needed to be. To Wendy he was a friend, and now – finally – a lover and casual mentor. To the Captain, he was a Crown Officer; to the combat troopers he was a fighter without compare.

The magnitude of the skill disparity between them became clear on the ship as she came in full contact with the real Directory culture in microcosm.

The Bio-Comp explained to her the social divisions of the Directory. There was a very large financial, educational and competency gap between the Jolos and the so-called "Norms." The Jolos had a continuous stream of existence. They were involved with life, developing skills in all areas, the accumulation of trappings and worldly goods had become very secondary. What was important to the Jolo culture was achievement, in the current chosen area of interest. And exploration; many were adventurers.

She was about to enter this culture on different terms than anyone had ever done. It was going to be a challenge to measure up. In a culture where every advantage was earned by hard work, she'd been gifted with an incomparable body and a privileged position next to one of the Directory greats. Instead of caving in to the pressure she decided to be "great" too.

That would solve the problem.

CHAPTER 47

"HELLO, MOM." MRS. WHITE WASN'T PREPARED for this Amazonian apparition.

"Hello, Mom, it's me... Wendy." What else could she say?

Amanda took in the height, voice and physique of the woman at her door claiming to be her daughter.

She took a deep breath.

The face, eyes and coloring – all had a familiar "feel" about them.

This is a new world and I'm going to live in it. Amanda thought. *But this woman isn't the child I birthed. How can I give her my love and affection?*

It's more than a mother should have to bear.

The confusion on her mother's face bordered on rejection.

Wendy didn't want to convince her mother who she was, she wanted to be recognized.

Everything in Amanda's life told her the person on her doorstep was not her daughter.

But that look is one I've seen a million times. Everything else became unimportant.

"Oh, Wendy!"

Emotion surged between mother and daughter. They fell into each other's arms and cried from relief and love.

Amanda turned her focus to the tall young man who'd stepped to her daughter's side.

"Yes, Mom, it's Jack"

The women separated and they went inside.

Jack followed. Wendy dried her eyes and smiled radiantly. She'd been so afraid her mother would reject her.

"It's alright, sweetheart," her mother said. "Sharon Cousins came over earlier and introduced her 'new' self to me. Now that was a shock, I can tell you. Sharon spent a long time going over our mutual history." She frowned. "After a while, after I pushed aside all my emotions and all the reasons why it could not be true, she *felt* the same, you know?"

"Oh yeah, Mom, I do know." And she looked at Jack.

"It was different with you. I didn't want to have a long conversation where we talked about things we've done together. I wanted to *see* you. To *know* you. You know?" Wendy nodded in agreement.

"I couldn't have handled it if Sharon hadn't come first. I was able to rant and rave and say things to her that would've destroyed us." Amanda broke down. Wendy embraced her. Holding her exhausted mother tightly, she got some inkling of how hard these weeks and months had been on all of them.

"I'm sorry I had to keep things from you, but it was very dangerous and I just couldn't put you at risk."

Jack had much to thank Sharon for. Her loving touch had enabled this happy outcome.

Amanda looked at Jack. "Sharon told me what you did, Jack. For so long I was afraid you'd take Wendy from us and now I want to thank you she's still here."

"You're welcome. But she saved me, too."

Amanda remember the party after the ball game where Jack had stood up. "Oh. Like the ball game."

Jack looked at Wendy.

"Yes, exactly like the ball game," Jack said. "That time she saved me from humiliation, this time she saved my life."

Amanda looked at her daughter.

"All this is new and strange," Jack said. "It's an assault on ideas that provided direction and foundation to your whole life."

"Yes. To be talking conversationally about a person transferring from one body to another as if we were talking about basketball scores. That's new. And scary." Amanda paused and slowly a smile broke out, "But I've realized that it's only threatening if you hold on to ideas that aren't true – and ignore what's in front of you.

"And my daughter is right here, standing in front of me, 'wearing' a new body!!"

Jack was stunned. "Amanda, there's no Mother on this planet who's been as profoundly challenged as you have. And you, you…"

"I've shocked you!"

"You have," he admitted.

Amanda laughed beautifully. "Ah, Jack. All the shocks you've given me. It's nice to get one back." They laughed.

"You're interested in the spiritual side of this?" Jack asked.

"You know I am, Jack. And I currently find myself with a rather large vacuum. The old is gone, what is the new?"

"Okay. I'll do my best to tell you."

The ladies were interested.

"Immortality, as it's lived by Jolos in the Directory, has its own price."

"What price?"

"To live forever one has to *want* to live forever. To transfer from one body to the next is easy. To want to live past any and all opposition both emotional and life conditions – is the true 'Fight for Immortality'.

"To pay that price, is to know how to live. It can be encountered even in a single life, many times."

"What is the price?"

"Keep going, until you make life better." This simplicity had saved him time after time. "It means you stack up wins and not losses."

"Jack, Jack." Wendy took him in a crushing hug.

"What was that about?"

"Mom, that's what he's been doing."

"Oh, you mean the arena," Sharon said.

"That was the easy part," Wendy replied.

"Thanks, Dee." He smiled at her. "It's its own reward, for me and others – if you do it right."

Amanda looked at him.

"It sometimes takes great effort. But hey, that's life. You rise to it, or sink under it."

He took Wendy's hand. "The rewards are great, but you have to earn them."

Jack looked away. Then decided to respond to the unasked question that Amanda White would never ask.

"The religion of the Directory of Stars and Planets is a practical and philosophical preparation so that a person can achieve the desire to *live* as an Immortal, and survive the long haul.

"Some, attaining Jolo status and immortality, die away from a transfer site and are reborn normal, remaining in that state for lifetimes. Many of our 'Immortals' travel this same path over and over until they can really live happily for a long period of time."

"Alright, but how does someone out there in the Directory or here on Earth qualify for Jolo status?"

"Directory citizens choose a career and work their whole lives to achieve the goals they've set for themselves. Then they petition. It's not a political thing. Out there artists comprise at least half of those who become Jolo."

Amanda looked sad. "Housewives need not apply?"

"All isn't lost." Jack said kindly. Then continued, "I didn't know, Amanda, if I'd have the opportunity to give you this." He passed her a book. "Or, if you'd want it." She took the offered volume.

Amanda opened it to the first page: "Before the beginning..." A Directory religious work. She looked at him in gratitude.

"Thanks Jack. I'll treasure this."

"Please don't." Amanda looked confused. "Just take a look. When you apply the data and your life improves – good. If the opposite happens, okay.

"To learn something you must be free to accept or reject it. When something 'has to be right,' or 'has to be wrong,' you never learn a thing."

"Oh, okay." Amanda said. "I'll see what I think." Enjoying the freedom of it.

She got up and came back a few minutes later with cookies and coffee.

"I have some concerns, Jack." Amanda said. "When your Mom was here she said you'll be leaving Earth very soon."

"That's true. Later today."

Amanda nodded. "You have a position of some power in the Directory, is that true, Jack?"

Jack shrugged. "Yes, one of many, many powerful positions; the Directory is immense."

"That's a relief. I just want to ask you to do everything in your power to take good care of my daughter, because I know she's going with you." Tears came to Amanda's eyes. Wendy was grateful her mother was facing this head-on.

Mother and daughter embraced.

Amanda had given Wendy her consent to leave. It wasn't essential but was nice to have.

Wendy ended the embrace, and sat beside Jack.

"You look truly wonderful together."

Amanda became maudlin. "When you were both seven, I loved watching you play together. Jack, I could see you steering Wendy out of harm's way with her never even knowing it was happening. You showed caring and skill far beyond your years. That you continue, is all I ask."

"Amanda, thank you." Jack smiled at Wendy, "It's been dangerous for months. And now we have a letup. But when we leave Earth we'll be going into danger." Amanda nodded. "Going out to meet it." She nodded again – confirming her fears.

"But Wendy's changed. She's become the protector of others. Someone others seek out for help." Jack smiled.

He'd debriefed the guards Wendy disabled to chase after his body en route to Hell Gate. But he couldn't tell Amanda that.

Amanda looked at her daughter and re-evaluated. *Wendy's different. It's not just a physical. She's so confident she's casual.*

"I *want* this, Mother; new worlds, a broad universe, the challenge, the objective – and my man." Clearly their relationship had gone to a different level. Amanda, feeling very provincial, in this moment could only think of marriage.

"Mom, with the unpredictability of the immediate future, we'll take it as it comes."

●

When her father and older brother arrived home, Wendy and Jack answered questions for hours.

Wendy's older brother had flown in from the east coast where he attended college.

"Come on, Sis, just an arm wrestle? You've told me all these things. Betcha can't prove it."

Jack laughed.

"Okay."

It was over in less than a second.

But Wendy was looking so sad.

"Mr. White," Jack began. "As you know, my uncle placed a huge bet on me in round seven of the fight."

"That was adventurous of him."

"Yeah. Things weren't looking that good for me right then. His defiance and support meant a great deal to me.

"Everyone thought the fix was in and the odds went through the roof." Jack laughed, "He put half the winnings in my name."

"That's incredible, Jack. Congratulations."

"Thank you." Jack pulled some documents out of his pocket and placed them on the coffee table. "I've transferred the money into a joint account for you and Amanda."

They were shocked.

"We're leaving. The money has no meaning to me. Money never has. It's what you do with it that counts."

Dale White recovered enough to splutter, "Well, but, but...."

"Mr. White. We'll be gone for many years. In all likelihood Wendy won't return to Earth before your natural death. So take the money, and use it well.

"A new Bio-Tech is on planet now. I've made appointments for all three of you to see him. After the procedures, your life expectancy will exceed two hundred years."

"Jack, Jack." Wendy was in his arms. Then she looked at her family. "I thought I'd never see you again!" And hugged them all.

Dale shook Jack's hand. "You're a gentleman, sir. We thank you."

"You're more than welcome."

Amanda was looking at Jack.

"Now you have all the time you need."

"I'll make use of it," she said, tears shining in her eyes.

It was time to go. But there was one other subject that couldn't be avoided.

"I'm so sorry about what happened to Penny. I give you my word we'll do everything we can to find her. She paid a high price for her visit." Jack looked around solemnly. There were silent nods of agreement.

Finally, they took their leave of the White household.

As they walked Wendy said. "It's wonderful, what you did for Mom and my family."

"You're welcome, Dee."

"I had no idea you were interested in religion. I'm surprised we never talked about it."

"Religion is how you live your life, Dee. We've been having a conversation about it since the day we met."

•

Jack and Wendy walked two blocks to the Cousins house and paused at the gate. "I spent many years living here. It's amazing how different it looks now."

"Mom?" A tall and beautiful twenty-year-old blonde came rushing down the front steps and hugged Jack with a strength that, on second thought, was not surprising. Finally they let go and Sharon hugged Wendy.

"I'm closing the house up, Jack. We're going to hold onto it, so if you ever want to visit 'home' you can."

He smiled. "Thanks for what you did with Amanda."

"At first she wouldn't let me in the door, you can't blame her really. But she came around. And, as a mother, the shock and change would have been too much."

"You thought of it and made it perfect. Thank you." Wendy said.

"You're welcome."

"How are the selections for Jolo status going?"

"The new Bio-Tech tells us it'll be about five months before viable bodies are being produced at the Colosseum."

"That's too long. I'll clear out half the bodies from the Star Comet. It's a military vehicle, so that should give you about one hundred bodies to work with right now."

"That'll be a big help."

"The Training Corps?"

"There are surveys the Bio-Comp and I put together and they're all over the world now."

"Good. The TC is essential. Training a newly grown body can only be done properly by a person. Electrical stimulation creates many problems. Read the literature." Sharon smiled.

"Looks like we have our work cut out for us," Sharon said.

"Yep, there's a lot to do." Sitting at the kitchen table, they discussed what Sharon's priorities needed to be in the next weeks and months. Her responsibility was personnel – side checked by the Bio-Comp. Her choices would accelerate or retard Earth's ability to recover. But even now she was aggressively attacking the problem. "Good luck to you, *Mother*."

Sharon smiled. "Yes, it's a different world now. We'll make Earth a decent place to live."

●

Jack and Wendy flew a Directory air car back to the lake for final departure. When they touched down, two of the combat troopers had a struggling figure held firmly between them.

"Let him go." Jack instructed. The old man stepped toward the commanding figure before him.

"I come to find out 'bout Jack Cousins 'n' Wendy White." Jeb was doing his best to be understandable. "And run inta these bozos." He jerked his thumb at the guards. "This is their place and I wanna know if they're alright."

Jack looked at the old man who had helped them in his own way over the years and who was now here in their defense. Jack took Wendy's hand and asked Jeb to accompany them as they walked to the lake's shore. It started here, Jack thought, and it will end here.

"Jeb, did you see the object these soldiers hauled out of the lake today?"

"Howdya know my name's Jeb?"

"I have a story to tell you, it started eighteen years ago, when you heard thunder right here at this lake. Would you like to hear the story?"

A glimmer came into the old man's eye and Jack liked to think that was where he caught on. "Seems like I been waiting a good long time fer that story." And so Jack told him.

Half way through the story, Jeb said. "So it tis you two. I was thinkin' it might be." Wendy hugged him.

As Jack finished, Jeb stood looking across the lake at the cliff face and its most distinct feature. Finally he said. "That's a strange story. But it makes sense. I feel like I was marooned on this planet myself. Nothing out there," he said, waving in the direction of the populated low lands, "ever made any sense to me." Jeb's English diction was now positively understandable.

"Seeing as how you're an alien maybe you can take a look at this." Jeb pulled a ratty piece of paper from his shirt pocket.

Jack took it and read the text. "What's this?"

"In my dreams I seen myself writing those characters on a sheet of paper. Seen it many times, clear as a bell. Don't know what it means."

Jack flashed pictures of transfer into Jeb's head. Immediately matching pictures came into view. The Recyclex machines were old models. Maybe two thousand years. Jeb was an old Jolo. Probably dumped on Earth to get rid of him. Dumped by criminals.

"Funny stuff is happening in my head."

"I just needed to check something. Sorry for doing it without warning."

"It's okay. It didn't hurt."

Jack said in Cortic, "Welcome back, my friend."

Jeb started crying, "What'd you say?"

"Jack, he's in tears!" Wendy accused.

"I said, 'Welcome back, my friend' in a language you once knew."

"Oh!" Jeb was speechless.

Today was a day for generosity. Jeb had once earned Jolo Status – and though his mind probe wasn't official proof – it was good enough for him.

"Would you like to come with us?"

"Been waitin' for the invite."

"Oh, Jeb, that's wonderful!"

Jack, Wendy and Jeb left footprints in the sand as they disappeared into the Star Comet.

●

Final checks were being run on the Star Comet *Lonesome Voyager* prior to departure; officers and crew were hustling.

"Bio-Comp, thank you for what you've done and what you're doing."

"You're welcome, sir. It's been my pleasure."

"Goodbye for now."

Wendy wanted to leave Earth cleanly, and not be bothered by what had happened over the last weeks and months. To do that she needed to voice some things she did not understand.

The Star Comet was large enough to have Admiral's quarters and that was where they went. Jack could monitor all ships activities from there.

"I was talking to Norman, the Administrator, and he said you let Boltax go. Is that right, Jack?"

"Yes, Dee, he's gone. I gave him a heavily damaged but operable M-star out of the Star Comet's maintenance bay and exiled him to the Outer-Worlds." She shook her head; it didn't sit well with her. Boltax had destroyed hundreds of thousands, maybe even millions of lives on Earth.

"Mind if I know why you did that? Norman said he didn't know your reasons, but that you'd guaranteed that Boltax wouldn't come back to Earth."

"I'll tell *you*, Dee. There are two reasons. Firstly, Boltax is a telepath with exceptional promise. He successfully sent a long-distance telepathic communication *under duress*, and that is extremely difficult to do. Any person who feels completely cut off from his fellow man has no awareness of telepathy; conversely to be a successful telepath one has to have a basic affinity for people. With someone like Boltax, it engages the age-old question of how a basically good man can do something so evil. Because of his telepathic skills, I don't think he's a lost cause. I have hope that Boltax can recover from his severe ethical lapse."

"But Boltax is a mass murderer and a mass slave trader. He deserves to be punished. The people of Earth have earned the right to see him get what he deserves!" Wendy was shaking with the intensity of her emotions.

"In the Directory, criminals such as Boltax are isolated on Prison Planet for the remainder of their lives, which are sometimes very long if they have a Jolo body. The planet is very harsh and populated by people of a very low ethical level, but it is possible to live there. We have no state executions, no matter the crime – this policy goes back thousands of years before my time. I could've programmed the M-star to land Boltax on Prison Planet. But with Bio-One controlling the Directory, Prison Planet was not an option.

"If we killed him here on Earth, he'd be reborn anonymously within the population. Would you want that?"

She looked at him; still finding it hard to come to grips with the practical ramifications of Immortality, even after her own transfer, the concept was not yet "in her blood."

"All right, don't kill him. But he still needs to be punished. He should be in prison!" She was mad.

"No prison or person on Earth could hold him for even a week."

"But you gave him a space ship!"

"Boltax, by now, knows it has a preset destination – to the Capitol of the Outer-Worlds. He'll then discover that once he lands the ship, it'll never leave the ground."

"But he still has a Jolo body."

"I did leave him that."

"Yes, and what about the people of Earth, don't they deserve to know this evil man has not profited?"

"Yes, they do. I'll give the Bio-Comp instructions about that now.

"Dee, you can't stop someone from being alive. When you truly know death is *the great lie*, other solutions to criminal activity have to be found.

"Where Boltax is going he'll be amongst people of a low ethical level; I've asked him to do nothing against the interests of the Directory. I outlined, in general terms, what he could do to help us. I told him that if he lives five hundred years, which is unlikely, and does not harm us, I would personally review his case. And I will, if it ever comes to that.

"Boltax has gone to an unpleasant world where he will never again influence the affairs of Earth. And that's it.

"Is there anything else you want to say about it?"

"No. I understand your reasoning. It's not what I'd have done. But clearly it's not my decision to make."

To her surprise she found herself hoping Boltax made the most of the opportunity Jack had given him. Wendy went to join Jeb. They both needed to get oriented on the basics of interstellar travel.

●

Norman Cousins, Crown's Administrator of Earth, had wanted to be at the launch by the lake, but he was far too busy to make it. He sat in the Planetary Administrator's chair at the Colosseum near Los Angeles California and had cleared his schedule for fifteen minutes.

He'd taken his leave of Jack and Wendy more than twenty-four hours ago. He cried in their arms. And went immediately back to work.

Now, he was looking at the Star Comet on the interactive office screen as it left the Earth's surface and accelerated into the dark reaches of space. "Split image." Norman thought, and the TAC in the walls split the image near and far, and split it again. As the ship became a pinpoint of light, Norman's thoughts drifted over his life and he remembered the first time he'd seen Jack's bright face in his brother's home.

Possibly it was his imagination, enhanced through the lens of time, but it seemed now, that a strong connection was made between two living beings at that time. A connection that expanded when, as his adopted son, Jack came to live with them.

That very next day Jack met Wendy, and who could deny that the hand of fate had something to do with that? Those years with them growing up together were wonderful. He could remember Jack's struggle to find a place for himself here, and his ultimate failures. Because he was an alien. It all made so much sense, looking back.

Then the Directory people arrived and their lives changed forever. Now, Jack had taken his girl and was off to some distant point.

He may be gone, but Norman could remember his parting words: "Just because you'll be ruling Earth doesn't mean we won't see each other again, does it Norman? You won't get so married to your job that when I ask you to come to Crown Planet, you and Mother will decline?"

●

As Earth receded, the Star Comet accelerated toward a door that would take them outside the universe and onto the next leg of the journey. Tac-U-One, now alone in his office, took a few minutes to reflect upon his time on this fast-diminishing world.

For a second he saw the world as it first appeared: rushing toward him. He shook his head, looked again, and the world continued to fade.

On Earth he'd lost and then recovered his own immortality. The fight for it had been subjective and highly personal in the lake, then physical and brutal in the arena. No matter how barbaric the staged "Fight for Immortality" had been, it had captured the attention of the entire planet. Earth had been a divided world, one without any unifying purpose, certainly no common goal, and no honest person or cadre of people to administer such a goal if they ever found one.

Those he had left in control of Earth he hoped would elevate the privilege of transfer to its proper station, with the Fight for Immortality being civilized and granted as an award for real achievement, providing a unifying, necessary and decent common goal.

At least they had a chance. This planet and its population had searched for truth for thousands of years in both the spiritual and practical realms. Finally they had the opportunity to reconcile these two elements and see how they worked together.

Life and death were no longer myth-based.

There were turbulent times ahead; Norman, Crown's Administrator on Earth, would have his hands full, but Tac-U-One was hopeful for their future.

As for himself, he had discovered how out of touch with the common lot of man he'd grown. This is not to say that he had not earned his privileges within the Directory – for he had, and earned them again here on Earth. But, to lose sight of the struggle to live and be happy on the part of the "normal" person, was to lose the power to know them, to understand them on their own terms and ultimately fail in the attempt to help them – as one's help would not match their needs.

He had cleaned up some of the mess his temporary demise had brought to Earth. One thing he was unlikely to communicate was the irony of how his own failure had led to his redemption. Earth could've been bypassed in Bio-One's expansion plans. It was sometimes a strange universe.

His time on Earth was over.

Sitting quietly in his office on the Star Comet as it accelerated away from the planet, he'd gained enough time and distance between him and his failure to be less defensive about it.

It was immediately obvious that something in his nature had sought the conflict that had happened on that distant remote planet. Wait: P7, System 11917, Frascette Arm, Tail section, IG rim. Yes, *exactly*.

When he'd arrived there he was spoiling for a fight, but what he should have done was now clear. Upon breaching Bio-One's secret base, which he had done without detection, he should have isolated the people in power and immediately put them directly under his control; thus gaining a broader control over the whole situation.

It may have been difficult, but it had been well within his power at the time. *Even though the mission had been inadequately planned, put into operation with insufficient resources and based on information meant to mislead and trap me; it should have succeeded; I should have won through.*

This was not him beating himself up, but an honest look without justification. He recalled a saying Crown had once told him, "Where excuses are many, results are few."

He had *wanted* to fight, *wanted* the action, *wanted* to overcome the enemy by force. The joy of it. He never thought he would fail. It was a personal slap in the face that his enemy had found him so predictable. They had known what he would do – and were prepared for it. All those ships waiting for him. They knew him so well.

And the vanity of it was that he'd almost made it out of there. The tragedy of it was that he hadn't.

His vanity: the galaxy's tragedy.

An unethical equation, if one ever existed.

It was a clear history of similar choices. He loved action. But who was going to fault him when he won so often? Nothing succeeds like success. Especially when cleaning up messes made by others.

It took emotional balance to truly look at and not cave oneself in over past failures. But with the future of the civilized galaxy at stake, he couldn't afford to have a serious blind spot in his past that led him to take the path of *most* resistance.

With this clear understanding, he felt the riddle of his failure was solved and, as a result, he was confident of tackling future situations without fear of making other mistakes for the same reason.

The truth will set you free. This was not a platitude but a way to live one's life. And a test of how well one could *look* and *see*.

The mission's path now led into the Directory. He could use his Int-comm abilities to spread the word of his return. But Crown was sure to be working on plans to regain power. He had no desire to cut across any efforts already in progress. He did not want to provoke conflict by announcing that Bio-One, the Regent, had usurped Crown's power. This could create a divide and split the Directory worlds into warring factions.

So his first action must be to join Crown. To coordinate with the team already at work on the effort to prevent further disintegration and set the Directory to rights. He was now on his way to discover where that rendezvous would be.

Outside the vast view port was a cornucopia of stars, lustrous and dazzling, singing the siren's song of invitation and longing, the lyrics of which had long since invaded his soul, and to whose melody he willingly danced.

He'd earned the right to return to the Directory of Stars and Planets.

As always, he had a job to do.

ACKNOWLEDGMENTS

Wᴿɪᴛɪɴɢ ᴀ sᴄɪᴇɴᴄᴇ ꜰɪᴄᴛɪᴏɴ ɴᴏᴠᴇʟ ɪs a collaborative effort. It's my job to come up with the story and muddle my way through to the end. The manuscript is then passed to others. I've enjoyed the help of many fine people who've been generous with their time and advice.

Firstly, I want to thank Rachael Adams, who offered helpful suggestions about points of characterization I had neglected or gotten wrong (this amidst an unbelievably full schedule of her own). She is also an amazing poet and author of the verses that grace the beginning of the book.

Andy Seidler read the manuscript and made helpful suggestions.

Bruce Rigney and his team at Rigney Graphics and specifically James Callaghan have made the book look professional. Also Bruce was always forthcoming with help and advice when I asked for it – not all of it I took at the time it was offered but eventually saw the errors of my ways!

Trish Quigley read my manuscript twice and helped point out needed changes. More than that, over the space of years when I let the project languish, she sent me emails gently nudging me along. Thank you.

David Lennie read the manuscript and lobbied for certain edits, I eventually made some of them.

My son Oliver has been a constant supporter and likewise had long discussions with me to make some changes: I had deviated from my original intention and he correctly pointed that out. It's interesting to have others point out a *major* flaw I had introduced. It was not easy to accept that I was riding my "hobby horse" quite to the detriment of the story. Thank you, David and Oliver.

Melanie Murray gave many hours of her time sorting out and correcting the manuscript and providing much warm affection as is her nature.

Don Dewsnap corrected the remaining grammar flaws and applied professional standards to the text.

Christina Moss really got the ball rolling and moved the publication process along with her knowledge and insight.

The cover artist, Brad Fraunfelter, is a very fine artist and worked with me to achieve the cover I wanted and always delivers more than expected. Thanks Brad.

With the rewrite complete I attribute any personal increase of skill to the help given me by the great Bob Zaichkowsky.

Finally, I must thank Vera Seidler who spotted more logical errors and story errors than anyone and endured some undeserved pressure and argument from me with great poise. She has a great ability to follow the story accurately, so any confusion, was usually with the story itself. She also pointed out some improper characterization. "That character wouldn't do (say) that!" She has lent her time and talent, once again, on the re-write. Thanks Vera.

With the rewrite done there are fewer remaining errors – but any that have escaped, I own!

Made in the USA
San Bernardino, CA
09 March 2017